Introductory Readings
in the
Philosophy of Science

Introductory Readings in the

Philosophy of Science

Revised Edition

edited by

E. D. Klemke

Robert Hollinger

A. David Kline

PROMETHEUS BOOKS
Buffalo, New York

Published 1988 by Prometheus Books
700 East Amherst Street, Buffalo, New York 14215

Copyright © 1988 by E. D. Klemke, Robert Hollinger,
and A. David Kline

All Rights Reserved

Library of Congress Catalog Card Number: 88-61285
ISBN 0-87975-423-0

Printed in the United States of America

Contents

94438

Preface
To the Revised Edition

This revised edition, like its predecessor, is a collection of informative, lively, and accessible readings, organized under six main issues, and designed to provide a solid introduction to the problems of the philosophy of science.

We have been gratified by the response of both instructors and students to the first edition of this text. For this new edition we have made a number of what we hope are improvements.

Probably the most often expressed concern with regard to the first edition was the need for a better selection expressing the views of Thomas Kuhn. We not only remedied this but included a paper by Carl Hempel that examines some of the important themes raised by Kuhn.

The first edition did not contain a version of the standard account of theories given that most presentations were far too technical. The now-included essay by Rudolf Carnap is a nice nontechnical representation of the view. For similar reasons we only included a very qualitative discussion of confirmation in the first edition. The selection on the logic of confirmation, now included, was especially written for introductory students by Ronald Giere. It may require some additional help from the instructor but we believe it will be well worth the effort.

The opening part, "Science and Nonscience," has been expanded by one essay. This topic is especially exciting to introductory students. Our earlier suggestion, that one may want to wait until other topics have been covered to take up this issue, still stands.

The final two parts, on science and values and science and culture, which also have proven to be quite interesting to a variety of undergraduates, have been significantly revised. We eliminated essays that were too difficult or repetitive. The new essays also relate more directly to issues in the previous sections.

We would like to express our deep gratitude to all those people who helped us, in various ways, to prepare this book. In addition to the many who aided us with the first edition (see the preface to that edition, reprinted in this volume), for this new edition we are grateful to Carl Matheson, Warren Asher, Bernice Power, Edna Wiser, Ray Amsler, and Steven L. Mitchell and the entire staff of Prometheus Books.

Finally, we hope that instructors and students who have comments or suggestions for improving the volume or who wish to convey their evaluation of it will contact the editors.

E. D. Klemke
Robert Hollinger
A. David Kline

Preface
To the First Edition

It is a truism that in our time science has become a highly respected and venerated enterprise. It is widely deemed to be a Good Thing. There are many who hold it to be the most successful pursuit of knowledge in the history of the world. Others consider it to be the noblest intellectual achievement of mankind. It is also true that (in recent years, especially) many have found science to be undeserving of such high praise. Not only has science been attacked by proponents of ESP, astrology, and other pseudosciences, and by critics of modern technology; it has even been found wanting by some scientists and ex-scientists and others who know and write about science. (See Paul Feyerabend's essay in Part 1 of this volume.) Who is right, or more nearly correct, in this controversy?

It is our hope that the reader of this volume will be able to arrive at his or her own answer to this question. However, in our view, one cannot attempt to answer such a question without a clear understanding of what science is and what it is not. One of our major goals has been to provide that understanding and to provide it in such a manner that it is accessible to the beginning student and the layman.

Hence we would like to stress that this is an *introductory* work in the philosophy of science. Our principles of selection for the readings included have been these: The selection should be intrinsically interesting. It should be comprehensible to a beginning student. It should serve to provoke discussion and criticism. We have also tried to stimulate a kind of dialogue among the authors by selecting works which present varying and even conflicting points of view.

We have presented the topics in the order we have found to be most desirable. However, there may be one exception. Part 1 could be used either first or last—or, perhaps best of all, both. Otherwise we believe that the order of presentation should be followed. (However, it is not necessary that every reading within each part be used.)

A few other comments are in order. First, although all three of us worked closely together on all of the material included, the general introduction and the introductions to the six parts were written individually, not collectively. (The initials at the end of each indicate primary authorship.) Second, the Study Questions at the end of each of the six parts were composed by the author of the introduction to that part. Third, the bibliographies — one is given at the end of each part (and at the end of the general introduction) — are not exhaustive. They are intended to provide further sources which deal with some of the major issues discussed in the volume. Fourth, although we have spent much time in revising our format and the selection of readings, we may have overlooked some items which ought to have been included. If so, we shall be grateful to hear from instructors who use the volume and to receive their suggestions with regard to this — or any other — issue.

We would like to express our gratitude to all those who helped in various ways with regard to the preparation of our initial proposal and the final manuscript. We are especially grateful to: Rowena Wright, Bernice Power, Annette Van Cleave, Richard Kniseley, David Hauser, and Steven Isaacson. We would also like to express our appreciation to the members of the Philosophy Department of Iowa State University for their constant help and encouragement.

Acknowledgments

The editors gratefully acknowledge the kind permission of the authors, editors, and publishers that has enabled us to print the essays included in this book.

PART 1

1. Sir Karl Popper, "Science: Conjectures and Refutations." From *Conjectures and Refutations,* pp. 33-41, 52-59. New York: Harper and Row, 1963. Also published by Basic Books, New York, and Routledge and Kegan Paul, London. Copyright 1963, by Karl Popper.

2. John Ziman, "What Is Science?" *Public Knowledge,* pp. 5-27. New York: Cambridge University Press, 1968. Copyright 1968 by Cambridge University Press.

3. Paul Feyerabend, "How to Defend Society Against Science." *Radical Philosophy,* No. 11 (1975), pp. 3-8. Copyright 1975 by Paul Feyerabend.

4. Paul R. Thagard. "Why Astrology Is a Pseudoscience." *Proceedings of Philosophy of Science Association,* 1978, Volume One, pp. 223-224. Edited by P. D. Asquith and I. Hacking. East Lansing: Philosophy of Science Association, 1978. Copyright 1978 by Philosophy of Science Association.

5. Philip Kitcher, "Believing Where We Cannot Prove." In Kitcher, *Abusing Science: The Case Against Creationism.* Cambridge: The MIT Press, 1982, pp. 30-54. Copyright 1982 by Philip Kitcher. Reprinted by permission of the publisher.

PART 2

6. Carl G. Hempel, "The Logic of Explanation" In Hempel, *Aspects of Scientific Explanation,* Baltimore, Md.: Williams and Wilkins Co., 1948, pp. 135-75. Copyright 1948, The Williams and Wilkins Company. Reproduced, in edited form, by permission.

7. Karel Lambert & Gordon Brittan, "Laws and Conditional Statements."

In Lambert and Britten, *An Introduction to the Philosophy of Science.* Englewood Cliffs: Prentice-Hall, 1970, pp. 37-45. Reprinted by permission of the authors.

8. Baruch Brody, "Towards an Aristotelian Theory of Scientific Explanation." *Philosophy of Science,* 39 (1972), pp. 20-31. Copyright 1972 by Philosophy of Science Association.

9. Nancy Cartwright, "The Truth Doesn't Explain Much." In Cartwright, *How The Laws of Physics Lie,* New York: Oxford University Press, 1983, pp. 44-53. Copyright 1983 by Nancy Cartwright. Reprinted by permission of Oxford University Press, Inc.

10. William Dray, "Historical Understanding as Re-thinking." *University of Toronto Quarterly* (1958), pp. 200-215. Copyright 1958 by University of Toronto Quarterly.

PART 3

11. Rudolf Carnap, "The Nature of Theories," *Philosophical Foundations of Physics: An Introduction to the Philosophy of Science,* by Rudolf Carnap, ed. Martin Gardner, pp. 225-246. New York: Basic Books, 1966. Copyright 1966 by Basic Books, Inc. Reprinted by permission of the publisher.

12. Hilary Putnam, "What Theories Are Not." *Logic, Methodology and Philosophy of Science,* edited by E. Nagel, P. Suppes and A. Tarski, pp. 240-244. Stanford: Stanford University Press, 1962. Reprinted with the permission of the publishers, Stanford University Press. Copyright 1982 by the Board of Trustees of the Leland Stanford Junior University.

13. N. R. Hanson, "Observation." From "Observation," *Patterns of Discovery,* New York: Cambridge University Press, pp. 4-11, 15-19. Copyright 1958 by Cambridge University Press.

14. W. T. Stace, "Science and the Physical World." Reprinted from *Man Against Darkness* by W. T. Stace by permission of the University of Pittsburgh Press. Copyright 1967 by the University of Pittsburgh Press.

15. Stephen Toulmin, "Do Sub-Microscopic Entities Exist?" *The Philosophy of Science,* pp. 134-139. London: The Hutchinson Publishing Group, Ltd. Copyright 1953, The Hutchinson Publishing Group, Ltd. Reprinted by permission of the publisher.

16. Grover Maxwell, "The Ontological Status of Theoretical Entities." *Minnesota Studies in the Philosophy of Science,* Vol. III, pp. 3-14. Edited by H. Feigl and G. Maxwell. Minneapolis: University of Minnesota Press, 1962. Copyright 1964 by University of Minnesota Press.

17. Carl Matheson and A. David Kline, "Is There a Significant Observational-Theoretical Distinction?" Original essay for this volume.

PART 4

18. W. V. Quine and J. S. Ullian, "Hypothesis." From *The Web of Belief,* Second Edition, by W. V. Quine and J. S. Ullian, pp. 64-82. Copyright 1970, 1978 by Random House, Inc. Reprinted by permission of Random House, Inc.

19. Ronald N. Giere, "Justifying Scientific Theories." *Understanding Scientific Reasoning,* second edition, pp. 96-110, 112-117. New York: Holt, Reinhardt and Winston, 1984. Copyright 1984, Henry Holt & C. Reprinted by permission of the publisher.

20. Thomas S. Kuhn, "Objectivity, Value Judgment, and Theory Choice," in *The Essential Tension,* pp. 320-339. Chicago: University of Chicago Press, 1977. Copyright 1977 by Thomas S. Kuhn. Reprinted by permission of the publisher and the author.

21. Carl G. Hempel, "Scientific Rationality: Analytic vs Pragmatic Perspectives." *Rationality To-Day* edited by Theodore F. Geraets, pp. 46-58. Ottawa: The University of Ottawa Press, 1979.

22. Philipp G. Frank, "The Variety of Reasons for the Acceptance of Scientific Theories." *Scientific Monthly,* 79 (September 1954): 139-145. Copyright 1954 by the American Association for the Advancement of Science.

PART 5

23. Richard Rudner, "The Scientist *Qua* Scientist Makes Value Judgments." *Philosophy of Science,* XX (1953), pp. 1-6. Copyright 1953 by Williams and Wilkins Co., Baltimore, Maryland

24. Carl G. Hempel, "Science and Human Values." *Social Control in a Free Society,* ed. by R. E. Spiller, pp. 39-64. Philadelphia: University of Pennsylvania Press, 1960. Copyright 1960 by University of Pennsylvania Press.

25. Ernan McMullin, "Values in Science." Copyright 1983 by the Philosophy of Science Association, East Lansing MI, 18 Morrill Hall, Dept. of Philosophy, Michigan State University, East Lansing, MI 48824. From: *PSA 1982, volume two,* ed. P. D. Asquith and T. Nickles, 1983, pp. 3-28.

PART 6

26. Kurt Baier, "The Meaning of Life." Inaugural Lecture delivered at the Canberra University College, 1957. Copyright 1957 by Kurt Baier.

27. Robert Hollinger, "From Weber to Habermas." Original essay for this volume.

28. Herbert Feigl, "Naturalism and Humanism" *American Quarterly* I (1949), 135-148. Copyright 1949 by American Studies Association.

Introduction

What Is Philosophy of Science?

Most readers of this volume probably have some familiarity with science—or with one or more of the sciences. But the following question may come to mind: Just what is philosophy of science? How does it differ from science? How is it related to other areas of philosophy? We shall here attempt to provide answers to these and related questions.[1]

I. What Philosophy of Science Is Not

Let us begin with a discussion of what philosophy of science is *not*.

(1) Philosophy of science is not the history of science. The history of science is a valuable pursuit for both scientists and nonscientists. But it must not be confused with the philosophy of science. This is not to deny that the two disciplines may often be interrelated. Indeed, some have held that certain problems within the philosophy of science cannot be adequately dealt with apart from the context of the history of science. Nevertheless, it is generally held that we must distinguish between the two.

(2) Philosophy of science is not cosmology or "philosophy of nature." The latter attempts to provide cosmological or ethical speculations about the origin, nature, and purpose of the universe, or generalizations about the universe as a whole. As examples we may cite the views of Hegel and Marx, that the universe is dialectical in character; or the view of Whitehead, that it is organismic. Such cosmologies are often imaginative, metaphorical, and anthropomorphic constructions. They frequently involve interpreted extrapolations from science. Again, certain problems within the philosophy of science may aid the construction of or involve a consideration of such

1

cosmological theories. But here, too, there is wide agreement that they must be distinguished.

(3) Philosophy of science is not the psychology or sociology of science. The latter disciplines constitute a study of science as an activity, as one social phenomenon among many. Some of the topics that fall within such an inquiry are: scientists' motives for doing what they do; the behavior and activity of scientists; how (in fact) they make discoveries; what the impact of such discoveries is on society; and the sorts of governmental structures under which science has flourished. Again, certain problems in the philosophy of science may on occasion be related to such issues. But once more, it is reasonable to hold that these inquiries must be distinguished.

For the purposes of our study, the philosophy of science will not primarily mean or apply to any of the above. We will not try to comprehend the history of science. We will not present any grand cosmological speculations. We will not try to understand the scientific enterprise in terms of human or social needs. However, with regard to the latter, it is desirable to make a distinction. It is one thing to present a psychological or sociological account of science. This we will not do. It is another thing to examine philosophically the relationship of science and culture and generally of science and values. The latter parts of this volume will be devoted to these issues.

II. What Philosophy of Science Is

Let us attempt now to see what the philosophy of science *is*. By one widely held conception, philosophy of science is the attempt to understand the meaning, method, and logical structure of science by means of a logical and methodological analysis of the aims, methods, criteria, concepts, laws, and theories of science. Let us accept this as a preliminary characterization.

In order to illustrate or apply this characterization, let us focus on the matter of the concepts of science.

(1) There are numerous concepts that are used in many sciences but not investigated by any particular science. For example, scientists often use such concepts as: causality, law, theory, and explanation. Several questions arise: What is meant by saying that one event is the cause of another? That is, what is the correct analysis of the concept of cause? What is a law of nature? How is it related to other laws? What is the nature of a scientific theory? How are laws related to theories? What are description and explanation in science? How is explanation related to prediction? To answer such questions is to engage in logical and methodological analysis. Such an analysis is what philosophy of science, in part, is (according to this conception).

(2) There are many concepts used in the sciences that differ from the ones mentioned above. Scientists often speak of ordinary things—such as beakers, scales, pointers, tables. Let us call these observables. But they also often speak of unobservables: electrons, ions, genes, psi-functions, and so on. Several

questions then arise: How are these entities (if they are entities) related to things in the everyday world? What does a word such as 'positron' mean in terms of things we can see, hear, and touch? What is the logical justification for introducing these words which (purport to) refer to unobservable entities? To answer such questions by means of logical and methodological analysis constitutes another part or aspect of what philosophy of science is (according to the conception we are considering).

Now, with regard to the kinds of concepts mentioned in (2), one might ask: Why analyze these concepts? Don't scientists know how to use them? Yes, they certainly know how to use terms such as 'electron,' 'friction coefficient,' and so on. And often they pretty much agree about whether statements employing such expressions are true or false. But a philosopher, on the other hand, might be puzzled by such terms. Why? Well no one has ever directly seen a certain sub-atomic particle, or a frictionless body, or an ideal gas. Now we generally agree that we see physical objects and some of their properties — spatial relations, and so on. The philosopher of science asks (among other things) whether it is possible that a term such as 'positron' can be "defined" so that all the terms occurring in the definition (except logical terms, such as 'not,' 'and,' 'all') refer to physical objects and their properties. He attempts to reduce or trace such "theoretical constructs" to a lower level in the realm of the observable. Why? Because unless this is done, the doors all open to arbitrarily postulating entities such as gremlins, vital forces, and whatnot.

As we can see, throughout such conceptual investigations as those mentioned above, the standpoint adopted by the philosopher of science is often a commonsense standpoint. Thus certain questions which may be asked by other divisions of philosophy (such as epistemology) are not asked here. For example, whether a table really exists. If one wants to say that this means that philosophy of science has certain limitations, then we must agree. But not much follows from admitting this, for those other questions can always be raised later when we turn to other kinds of philosophical problems. Hence for the philosophy of science, we do not need to raise them. We may use the standpoint of common sense.

III. Some Main Topics in Philosophy of Science

The characterization of philosophy of science we have given in the preceding section does not adequately cover all of the kinds of issues and problems generally recognized as falling within the scope of philosophy of science. Hence it is perhaps best to resist trying to find a single formula or "definition" of philosophy of science and to turn to a different task.

Let us now briefly consider some of the main specific topics and questions with which philosophy of science is concerned. (In this volume, we will be able to focus on only some of these issues.)

(1) The formal sciences: logic and mathematics. Logic and math are often referred to as sciences. In what sense, if any, are they sciences? How do we know logical and mathematical truths? What, if anything, are they true of? What is the relation of mathematics to empirical science?

(2) Scientific description. What constitutes an adequate scientific description? What is the "logic" of concept formation which enters into such description?

(3) Scientific explanation. What is meant by saying that science explains? What is a scientific explanation? Are there other kinds of explanations? If so, how are they related to those of science?

(4) Prediction. We say that science predicts. What makes this possible? What is the relation of prediction to explanation? What is the relation of testing to both?

(5) Causality and law. We sometimes hear it said that science explains by means of laws. What are scientific laws? How do they serve to explain? Further, we sometimes speak of explaining laws. How can that be? Many laws are known as causal laws. What does that mean? Are there noncausal laws? If so, what are they?

(6) Theories, models, and scientific systems. We also hear it said that science explains by means of theories. What are theories? How are they related to laws? How do they function in explanation? What is meant by a "model" in science? What role do models play in science?

(7) Determinism. Discussions of lawfulness lead to the question of determinism. What is meant by determinism in science? Is the deterministic thesis (if it is a thesis) true? Or what reason, if any, do we have for thinking it to be true?

(8) Philosophical problems of physical science. The physical sciences have, in recent years, provided a number of philosophical problems. For example, some have held that relativity theory introduces a subjective component into science. Is this true? Others have said that quantum physics denies or refutes determinism. Is this true or false?

(9) Philosophical problems of biology and psychology. First, are these sciences genuinely distinct? If so, why? If not, why not? Further, are these sciences ultimately reducible to physics, or perhaps to physics and chemistry? This gets us into the old "vitalism/mechanism" controversy.

(10) The social sciences. There are some who deny that the social sciences are genuine sciences. Why? Are they right or wrong? Is there any fundamental difference between the natural sciences and the social sciences?

(11) History. Is history a science? We often speak of historical laws. Are there really any such laws? Or are there only general trends? Or neither?

(12) Reduction and the unity of science. We have already briefly referred to this issue. The question here is whether it is possible to reduce one science to another and whether all of the sciences are ultimately reducible to a single science or a combination of fundamental sciences (such as physics and chemistry).

(13) Extensions of science. Sometimes scientists turn into metaphysicians. They make "radical" statements about the universe—e.g., about the ultimate

heat-death, or that it is imbued with moral progress. Is there any validity in these claims?

(14) Science and values. Does science have anything to say with regard to values? Or is it value-neutral?

(15) Science and religion. Do the findings and conclusions of science have any implications for traditional religious or theological commitments? If so, what are they?

(16) Science and culture. Both religion and the domain of values may be considered to be parts or aspects of culture. But surely the term *culture* also refers to other activities and practices. What is the relationship of science to these?

(17) The limits of science. Are there limits of science? If so, what are they? By what criteria, if any, can we establish that such limits are genuine?

IV. Philosophy of Science and Science

We hope that by now the reader has a fair grasp of what philosophy of science is. In order to provide further understanding, let us examine one way by which one might contrast science with the philosophy of science. We may best do this by focusing on the activities and concerns of scientists and of philosophers of science. There are many ways in which these differ. Let us look at just a couple of them. According to one widely held view:

(1) Scientists (among other things, and not necessarily in this order): (a) observe what happens in the world and note regularities; (b) experiment — i.e., manipulate (some) things so that they can be observed under special circumstances; (c) discover (or postulate) laws of nature which are intended to explain regularities; (d) combine laws of nature into theories or subsume those laws under theories. Philosophers of science do none of the above things. Rather, they ask questions such as: What is a law of nature? What is a scientific (vs. a nonscientific or unscientific) theory? What are the criteria (if any) by which to distinguish or demarcate those theories which are genuinely scientific from those which are not? Furthermore, according to this view:

(2) Scientists, like almost everyone else, make deductions. For example, they often construct a certain theory from various laws and observations and then from it deduce other theories or laws, or even certain specific occurrences which serve to test a theory. Philosophers of science do not do that. Rather they clarify the nature of deduction (and how it differs from other inferences or reasoning), and they describe the role deduction plays in science. For example, they ask how deduction is involved in the testing of theories.

From these examples of (some of) the activities of scientists and philosophers of science, we may see that (according to the view we are considering): Whereas science is largely empirical, synthetic, and experimental, philosophy of science is largely verbal, analytic, and reflective. To be sure, in the works of some scientists—especially those who are in the more "theoretical" sciences—verbal, analytic, and reflective features may be found.

But the converse is not generally true. The activities of philosophers of science are, for the most part, not empirical or experimental, and they do not add to our store of factual knowledge of the actual world. And even in those cases where the more "philosophical" activities are found in science, they are usually not pursued with the same rigor or toward the same ends as they are by philosophers of science.

We may roughly see the difference by examining the following table:

Philosophy of science	— — —	is comprised of	— — —	a meta-language
				↓ which refers to
Science	— — —	is comprised of	— — —	an object-language
				↓ which refers to
Reality (or the world)	— — —	is comprised of	— — —	objects, processes, etc.

Thus we may see that, whereas science uses (an object-) language to talk about the objects of the world, philosophy of science (or at least a large "part" of it) uses (a meta-) language to talk about the language of science. In short, as a slight oversimplification, we may say: Science is talk about the world (a certain *kind* of talk, of course). Philosophy is talk about language (again, a certain kind of talk, of course).

To summarize the view we have considered: (1) The sciences consist of such things as listings of data, generalizations from them, the formulation of laws or trends, theoretical interpretations of data or laws, and arguments and evidence in favor of them. (2) Philosophy of science, to a large extent, consists of remarks about the language of science: the analysis of concepts, methods, and arguments of the various sciences; and also the analysis of the principles underlying science.

It is hoped now that our earlier characterization of the philosophy of science may be more readily understood and appreciated. Once again, according to that characterization, philosophy of science is the attempt to understand the meaning, method, and logical structure of science by means of a logical and methodological analysis of the aims, methods, criteria, concepts, laws, and theories of science.

One might reasonably object: But this view of philosophy of science does not do justice or apply to the list of topics in the philosophy of science provided in the preceding section. We are sympathetic to such an objection. Whereas our initial characterization does apply to many of the problems and concerns found in that list, it does not apply to others—for example, the topics of science and religion, or science and culture. Hence we propose that our initial characterization be modified in order to take such matters into account. We propose the following as an amended characterization of the philosophy of science. Philosophy of science is the attempt (a) to understand the method, foundations, and logical structure of science and (b) to examine the relations and interfaces of science and other human concerns, institutions, and quests, by means of (c) a logical and methodological analysis both of the aims, methods, and criteria of science and of the aims, methods, and concerns of various cultural phenomena in their relations to science.

V. The Scope of This Book

As we have mentioned, we cannot within a single volume do justice to all of the topics which fall within the domain of philosophy of science. We have therefore chosen six topics which (a) are crucial ones in philosophy of science, (b) are intrinsically interesting to the layperson as well as to the scientist or philosopher, and (c) are accessible to the beginning student. Similarly, the readings we have selected reflect those features. The topics are:

1. Science and Nonscience
2. Explanation and Law
3. Theory and Observation
4. Confirmation and Acceptance
5. Science and Values
6. Science and Culture

Since we have provided discussions of these topics in the introductions to the parts of the book, we shall not make further comments about them at this point.

We truly hope that the readers of this volume will derive as much enjoyment from the book as we have had in our production of it. We urge that the Study Questions at the end of each part be utilized. For further reading we have provided selected bibliographies.

E.D.K.

NOTE

1. Many of the views regarding science and the philosophy of science presented in this introduction and in the introduction to Part 1 stem from the lectures and writings of Herbert Feigl, May Brodbeck, John Hospers, and Sir Karl Popper.

SELECTED BIBLIOGRAPHY*

[1] Brody, B. ed. *Readings in the Philosophy of Science.* Englewood Cliffs N.J.: Prentice-Hall, 1970.

[2] Carnap, R. *An Introduction to the Philosophy of Science.* New York: Basic Books, 1966. [Good for the beginner.]

[3] Danto, A. and Morgenbesser, S. eds. *Philosophy of Science.* New York: Meridian, 1960.

[4] Gale, G. *Theory of Science.* New York: McGraw-Hill, 1979.

[5] Hempel, C. *Philosophy of Natural Science.* Englewood Cliffs, N.J.: Prentice-Hall, 1966. [A short but excellent work.]

[6] Hocking, I. *Representing and Intervening.* Cambridge, Mass.: Cambridge University Press, 1983. [One of the few philosophical studies of experimentation.]

[7] Kuhn, T. *The Structure of Scientific Revolutions.* Chicago, Ill.: University of Chicago Press, 1962. [Classical critique of positivist and other notions of scientific progress.]

[8] Michalos, A., ed. *Philosophical Problems of Science and Technology.* Rockleigh, N.J.: Allyn & Bacon, 1974.

[9] Morgenbesser, S., ed. *Philosophy of Science Today.* New York: Basic Books, 1967.

[10] Niddith, P. H., ed. *Philosophy of Science.* New York: Oxford University Press, 1968.

[11] Quine, W. V., and Ullian, J. *The Web of Belief,* 2nd ed. New York: Random House, 1978. [Relates philosophy of science to more general issues in theory of knowledge.]

[12] Shapere, D. ed. *Philosophical Problems of Natural Science.* New York: Macmillan, 1964.

[13] Toulmin, S. *The Philosophy of Science.* New York: Harper & Row, 1960. [Still worth reading; author takes a novel approach to science.]

*[1], [3], [8], [9], [10], and [12] are anthologies that deal with various issues in the philosophy of science, including many discussed in this volume.

Part 1

Science and Nonscience

Part 1: Science and Nonscience

Introduction

The major topics we shall discuss in this essay are: the aims of science; the criteria of science, or the criteria for distinguishing that which is scientific from that which is nonscientific; the question 'What is science?'; and the central issues of the readings which follow. But, first, let us begin by making some distinctions.

I. Some Distinctions

Before turning to the topics above it will be helpful to consider some ways of classifying the various sciences. Among these, the following should be noted.

(1) Pure sciences versus applied sciences. It is widely held that we must distinguish: (A) science as a field of knowledge (or set of cognitive disciplines) from (B) the applications of science. It is common to refer to these as the pure and applied sciences. (A) Among the pure sciences we may distinguish: (a) the formal sciences, logic and mathematics; and (b) the factual or empirical sciences. Among the latter we may also distinguish: (b1) the natural sciences, which include the physical sciences, physics, chemistry, and so on, and the life and behavioral sciences, such as biology and psychology; and (b2) the social sciences, such as sociology and economics. (B) The applied sciences include the technological sciences—such as engineering and aeronautics, medicine, agriculture, and so on.

It should be noted that there are at least two levels of application among the various sciences. There is, first, the application of the formal sciences to the pure, factual sciences. Since the factual sciences must have logical form and usually utilize some mathematics, such application is often held to be essential for the development of the pure factual sciences. Different from this is, second, the application of the factual sciences to the applied sciences. Here the findings of the pure, empirical sciences are applied (in a different sense of 'applied') to disciplines which fulfill various social, human purposes, such as building houses or roads and health care.

(2) Law-finding sciences versus fact-finding sciences. We recognize that such sciences as chemistry and physics attempt to discover universal laws which are applicable everywhere at all times, whereas such sciences as geography, history (if it is a science), and perhaps economics are concerned with local events. It is often said that the subject matter of the latter consists of particular facts, not general laws. As a result, there are some who wish to limit the term 'science' to the law-finding sciences. Upon the basis of the criteria of science (such as those which will be presented later, or others), we believe that we may say that both the law-finding disciplines and the fact-finding disciplines are capable of being sciences if those (or other) criteria are met. Furthermore, one might argue that there are no purely fact-finding sciences. If so, to speak of law-finding *versus* fact-finding may, in many cases, indicate an artificial disjunction.

(3) Natural sciences versus social sciences. Related to (2), we find that some would limit the giving of scientific status to the natural sciences alone. Sometimes the reason given is the distinction referred to above—that the natural sciences are primarily law-finding, whereas the social sciences are predominantly fact-finding. But sometimes the distinction is based on subject matter. Hence it is held by some that natural phenomena constitute the field of science but cultural phenomena constitute the field of scholarship and require understanding, *verstehen,* and empathy. But there are points at which the classification does not hold up. First, there are some predominantly fact-finding natural sciences, such as geography, geology, and palaeontology. And there are some law-finding social sciences, such as sociology and linguistics. Second, the distinction according to subject matter is not a clear-cut one. Hence we shall take a "liberal" view of science and allow the use of the term 'science' to apply to both the natural and the social sciences—with the recognition that there are some differences.

It is widely held that distinctions (2) and (3) do not hold up but that (1) is an acceptable distinction. However, as we shall see in the readings which follow, some have even raised doubts about the significance of (1). Here, as always, we urge the reader to reflect upon these matters.

II. The Aims of Science

Let us now turn to the question 'What are the aims of science?' Using the above distinction between pure (empirical) and applied science, we may then cite the following as some of the aims of science.

(1) The aims of applied science include: control, planning, technological progress; the utilization of the forces of nature for practical purposes. Obvious examples are: flood control, the construction of sturdier bridges, and the improvement of agriculture. Since this is all fairly obvious, no further elaboration is needed.

(2) The aims of the pure, factual sciences may be considered from two standpoints. (a) Psychologically considered, the aims of the pure, empirical sciences are: the pursuit of knowledge; the attainment of truth (or the closest possible realization of truth); the satisfaction of using our intellectual powers to explain and predict accurately. Scientists, of course, derive enjoyment from rewards, prestige, and competing with others. But they often achieve a genuine inner gratification which goes with the search for truth. In some ways this is similar in quality to artistic satisfaction. It is seen, for example, in the enjoyment one derives from the solution of a difficult problem.

(b) Logically considered, the aims of the pure, factual sciences are often held to be: description, explanation, and prediction. (b1) Description includes giving an account of what we observe in certain contexts, the formulation of propositions which apply to (or correspond to) facts in the world. (b2) Explanation consists of accounting for the facts and regularities we observe. It involves asking and answering 'Why?' or 'How come?' This may be done by subsuming facts under laws and theories. (b3) Prediction is closely related to explanation. It consists in deriving propositions which refer to events which have not yet happened, the deducing of propositions from laws and theories and then seeing if they are true, and hence provide a testing of those laws and theories. (b4) We might also mention post- or retro-diction, the reconstruction of past events. This process is also inferential in character. Since these issues will be discussed in subsequent parts of this volume, we shall not elaborate upon them at this time. (See some of the readings in Part 1 and those in Parts 2, 3 and 4.) However, we might mention that, here again, there is not unanimity with regard to the aims characterized above. Once more we urge the reader to think about these (and other) issues.

III. The Criteria of Science

In this section we shall state and discuss one view with regard to what are the essential criteria of science, that is, those criteria which may be used for at least two purposes: first, to distinguish science from commonsense knowledge (without claiming that the two are radically disjunctive—in some cases they may differ only in degree, not in kind); second, to distinguish that which is scientific, on the one hand, from that which is either nonscientific or unscientific, on the other—for example, to distinguish between theories which are genuinely scientific and those which are not. It has been maintained that any enterprise, discipline, or theory is scientific if it is characterized by or meets those criteria.

Before turning to the view which we have selected for consideration, let us consider an example. It is quite likely that most scientists and others who reflect upon science would hold that (say) Newton's theory of gravitation is scientific (even if it had to be modified), whereas (say) astrology is not scientific. Perhaps the reader would agree. But just what is it that allows us to rule in Newton's theory and to rule out astrology? In order to stimulate the reader's reflection, we shall consider one view of what the criteria for making such distinctions are. These criteria have been stated by Professor Herbert Feigl in various lectures and in writing (see selection 28). Our discussion of them corresponds fairly closely to the discussion given by Professor Feigl.

The five criteria are:

(1) Intersubjective testability. This refers to the possibility of being, in principle, capable of corroboration or "check-up" by anyone. Hence: *inter*subjective. (Hence, private intuitions and so forth must be excluded.)

(2) Reliability. This refers to that which, when put to a test, turns out to be true, or at least to be that which we can most reasonably believe to be true. Testing is not enough. We want theories which, when tested, are found to be true.

(3) Definiteness and precision. This refers to the removal of vagueness and ambiguity. We seek, for example, concepts which are definite and delimited. We are often helped here by measurement techniques and so forth.

(4) Coherence or systematic character. This refers to the organizational aspect of a theory. A set of disconnected statements is not as fruitful as one which has systematic character. It also refers to the removal of, or being free from, contradictoriness.

(5) Comprehensiveness or scope. This refers to our effort to attain a continual increase in the completeness of our knowledge and also to our seeking theories which have maximum explanatory power—for example, to account for things which other theories do not account for.

Let us consider these criteria in greater detail.

(1) Intersubjective testability. (a) Testability. We have noted that in science we encounter various kinds of statements: descriptions, laws, theoretical explanations, and so on. These are put forth as knowledge-claims. We must (if possible) be able to tell whether evidence speaks for or against such knowledge-claims. If the propositions which express those claims are not capable of tests, we cannot call those propositions true or false or even know how to go about establishing their truth or falsity. It should be noted that the criterion is one of *testability,* not *tested.* For example, at a given point in time, 'There are mountains on the far side of the moon' was testable though not tested.

(b) Intersubjective. 'Intersubjectivity' is often employed as a synonym for 'objectivity.' And the latter term has various meanings. Some of these are: (i) A view or belief is said to be objective if it is not based on illusions, hallucinations, deceptions, and so on. (ii) Something is referred to as objective if it is not merely a state of mind but is really "out there" in the external world. (iii) We often use 'objective' to indicate the absence of bias and the presence of disinterestedness and dispassionateness. (iv) 'Objectivity' also refers to the possibility of verification by others, and hence excludes beliefs, which stem from private, unique, unrepeatable experiences. Science strives for objectivity in all of these senses. Hence Feigl takes 'intersubjective' to include all of them.

(c) Intersubjective testability. It is often held that (according to the view we are considering) in order for a proposition or theory to be judged scientific it must meet this first requirement. Indeed, many of the other criteria presuppose intersubjective testability. We cannot even begin to talk of reliability or precision unless this first criterion has been met.

(2) Reliability. Science is not merely interested in hypotheses which are intersubjectively testable. It is also interested in those which are true or at least have the greatest verisimilitude or likelihood of being true. Hence the need arises for the criterion of reliability. Whereas the first criterion stressed the possibility of finding assertions which are true *or* false, the second stresses the end result of that process. We judge a claim or body of knowlege to be reliable if it contains not merely propositions which are capable of being true *or* false but rather those which *are true* or which have the greatest verisimilitude. We find such propositions to be true (or false) by means of confirmation. Complete verification, and hence complete certainty, cannot be achieved in the factual sciences.

It should be noted that, first, the reliability of scientific assertions make them useful for prediction; second, although the assertions of many enterprises are testable (for example, those of astrology as much as those of astronomy), only some of them are reliable. And we reject some of them precisely because they are unreliable. The evidence is against them; we do not attain truth by means of them.

(3) Definiteness and precision. The terms 'definiteness' and 'precision' may be used in at least two related senses. First, they refer to the delimitation of our *concepts* and to the removal of ambiguity or vagueness. Second, they refer to a more rigid or exact formulation of *laws.* For example, 'It is more probable than not that X causes disease Y' is less desirable than 'The probability that X causes Y is 98%.'

(4) Coherence or systematic character. In the sciences, we seek not merely disorganized or loosely related facts but a well-connected account of the facts. It has been held by many that we achieve this via what has been called the hypothetico-deductive procedure of science. This procedure includes: (a) our beginning with a problem (which pertains to some realm of phenomena); (b) the formulation of hypotheses, laws, and theories by which to account for those phenomena or by which to resolve the problem; (c) the deriving (from (b)) of statements which refer to observable facts; (d) the testing of those deduced assertions to see if they hold up. Thus we seek an integrated, unified network, not merely a congeries of true statements.

But, of course, we also seek theories which are consistent, which are free from self-contradictions. The reason for insisting upon such coherence is obvious; hence there is no need for elaboration.

(5) Comprehensiveness or scope. The terms 'comprehensiveness' and 'scope' are also used in two senses, both of which are essential in science. First, a theory is said to be comprehensive if it possesses maximum explanatory power. Thus Newton's theory of gravitation was ranked high partly because it accounted not only for the laws of falling bodies but also for the revolution of the heavenly bodies and for the laws of tides. Second, by 'comprehesive' we often refer to the completeness of our knowledge. This of course does not mean finality. We do not think of the hypotheses of the empirical sciences as being certain for all time. Rather we must be ready to modify them or even, on occasion, to abandon them.

To summarize: According to the view we have presented, we judge a law, hypothesis, theory, or enterprise to be scientific if it meets all five of the above criteria. If it fails to meet all five, it is judged to be unscientific or at least non-scientific. To return to our earlier example, it seems clear that Newton's theory thus passes the test. Astrological theory or Greek mythology does not.

It should be noted that, in presenting Professor Feigl's criteria for the reader's consideration, we do not claim that they are correct or free from defects. Indeed, as we shall see in the readings which follow, many writers have rejected some (or all) or those criteria. The reader should once again attempt to seek an acceptable criterion or set of criteria, if such can be found.

IV. What is Science?

A common characterization of science (or sometimes of scientific method) runs as follows. Science is knowledge obtained by: (1) making observations as accurate and definite as possible; (2) recording these intelligibly; (3) classifying them according to the subject matter being studied; (4) extracting from them, by induction, general statements (laws) which assert regularities; (5) deducing other statements from these; (6) verifying those statements by further observation; and (7) propounding theories which connect and so account for the largest possible number of laws. It is further maintained that this process runs from (1) through (7) *in that order.*

The conception of science has been challenged in recent years. Its most severe critic is Sir Karl Popper. (See the selection in Part 1 of this volume.) We shall not repeat Popper's criticisms. Instead we offer a characterization of science which some believe to be more adequate than the one mentioned above and which they deem to be free from the defects it possesses.

According to this view, the following is at least a minimal characterization of (factual) science (or of a science).

Science is a body of knowledge which consists of the following, coherently organized in a systematic way:

(a) Statements which record and classify observations which are relevant for the solution of a problem in as accurate and definite a way as possible.

(b) General statements—laws or hypotheses—which assert regularities among certain classes of observed or observable phenomena.

(c) Theoretical statements which connect and account for the largest possible number of laws.

(d) Other general or specific statements which are deducible from the initial descriptions and from laws and theories and which are confirmed by further observation and testing.

At least two things should be noted about this characterization. First, it indicates the role of the formal sciences in the empirical sciences. Mathematics is important for (a); logic is important for (d). Second, nothing is said in this characterization about the *method* of obtaining knowledge or of obtaining laws. It may be induction, but it may also be a guess, intuition, hunch, or whatever.

Since a number of the readings in Part 1 deal with the question "What is science?" we shall not attempt to provide a "final" answer. Instead, we encourage the student to come up with the best answer possible, based on his or her reading and reflection.

VI. The Readings in Part 1

Since the essays contained in Part 1 are clearly written and since they are accessible to the beginning student or ordinary reader, no detailed summaries will be presented here. We urge the student to prepare his or her own summaries and to make use of the Study Questions at the end. However, a few brief remarks may be helpful.

Throughout many of his works, Sir Karl Popper has been concerned with the problem of how to distinguish between science and pseudoscience (or nonscience). He claims to have solved that problem by having provided a criterion of demarcation, a criterion by which to distinguish theories which are genuinely scientific from those which are not. By means of this criterion—of falsifiability or refutability—he attempts to show that Einstein's theory of gravitation satisfies the criterion (and hence is scientific) whereas astrology, the Marxist theory of history, and various psychoanalytic theories—for varying reasons—are not scientific. He also wishes to separate the problem of demarcation from the problem of meaning and maintains that the latter is a pseudoproblem. (The reader should reflect upon why he holds that it is a pseudoproblem and whether he has succeeded in showing that it is.)

In the middle sections of Popper's essay, he claims that the problem of demarcation has provided a key for solving a number of philosophical problems, especially the problem of induction. Since this issue does not pertain to the main topics of Part 1, most of those sections of the essay have been deleted here. The problem of induction is: How, if at all, can we justify our knowledge-claims concerning matters of fact which we have not yet experienced or are not now experiencing? In the eighteenth century, David Hume maintained that we cannot provide any rational justification. Popper agrees with Hume's logical refutation of induction but disagrees with his psychological explanation of induction (in terms of custom or habit).

The selection by John Ziman consists of extracts from his book on science. In the first part he discusses and rejects various definitions of science which have been held. And he attempts to formulate a more accurate and tenable characterization based on what he takes to be the goal or objective of science, namely, consensus of rational opinion "over the widest possible field." In the second part, he provides his answer to the question "What distinguishes science from nonscience?" The reader should attempt to decide whether his "criterion of demarcation" is an improvement over Popper's and, if so, why. Since this selection is unusually clear and readable, no further comments are required.

Feyerabend's essay is, no doubt, one of the most controversial ones in this volume. Feyerabend claims that he wishes to defend society and its inhabitants from *all* ideologies, including science. He likens them (again, including science) to fairytales "which have lots of interesting things to say but which also contain wicked lies." He goes on to consider an argument designed to defend the exceptional status which science has in society today. According to this argument "(1) science has finally found the correct *method* for achieving results and (2) . . . there are many *results* to prove the excellence of the method." In the next sections he argues against both (1) and (2). He concludes his essay with a provocative discussion of education and myth. We urge the reader to reflect seriously upon Feyerabend's somewhat unorthodox views and to ask whether Feyerabend has adequately defended them.

Paul R. Thagard's essay constitutes both a further discussion of some of the above-mentioned topics (such as the criterion of demarcation) and an example of the application of them. Most scientists and philosophers agree that astrology is a pseudoscience. Thagard attempts to show *why* it is. After presenting a brief description of astrology, he attempts to show that the major objections which have been provided do not show *that* it is a pseudoscience. Thagard then proposes his principle of demarcation and, upon the basis of it, claims to show that and why astrology is unscientific.

There is a kind of dialogue which runs through the essays in this part. We urge the reader to critically evaluate the various positions presented and attempt to come to his or her own conclusion with regard to the questions "What is science?," "By what criteria can we distinguish science from non-science or pseudoscience?" and so on. The Study Questions should provide assistance in gauging the reader's understanding of the selections and in grappling with these and related questions.

E.D.K.

1

Science: Conjectures and Refutations

Sir Karl Popper

> Mr. Turnbull had predicted evil consequences, . . .
> and was now doing the best in his power to bring
> about the verification of his own prophecies.
> ANTHONY TROLLOPE

I

When I received the list of participants in this course and realized that I had been asked to speak to philosophical colleagues I thought, after some hesitation and consultation, that you would probably prefer me to speak about those problems which interest me most, and about those developments with which I am most intimately acquainted. I therefore decided to do what I have never done before: to give you a report on my own work in the philosophy of science, since the autumn of 1919 when I first began to grapple with the problem, *"When should a theory be ranked as scientific?"* or *"Is there a criterion for the scientific character or status of a theory?"*

The problem which troubled me at the time was neither, "When is a theory true?" nor, "When is a theory acceptable?" My problem was different. I *wished to distinguish between science and pseudo-science;* knowing very well that science often errs, and that pseudo-science may happen to stumble on the truth.

I knew, of course, the most widely accepted answer to my problem: that science is distinguished from pseudo-science — or from "metaphysics" — by its *empirical method,* which is essentially *inductive,* proceeding from observation or experiment. But this did not satisfy me. On the contrary, I often formulated my problem as one of distinguishing between a genuinely empirical method

A lecture given at Peterhouse, Cambridge, in Summer 1953, as part of a course on developments and trends in contemporary British philosophy, organized by the British Council; originally published under the title "Philosophy of Science: a Personal Report" in British Philosophy in Mid-Century, *ed. C. A. Mace, 1957. [Portions have been deleted by the editors for this publication.]*

and a non-empirical or even a pseudo-empirical method—that is to say, a method which, although it appeals to observation and experiment, nevertheless does not come up to scientific standards. The latter method may be exemplified by astrology with its stupendous mass of empirical evidence based on observation—on horoscopes and on biographies.

But as it was not the example of astrology which led me to my problem I should perhaps briefly describe the atmosphere in which my problem arose and the examples by which it was stimulated. After the collapse of the Austrian Empire there had been a revolution in Austria: the air was full of revolutionary slogans and ideas, and new and often wild theories. Among the theories which interested me Einstein's theory of relativity was no doubt by far the most important. Three others were Marx's theory of history, Freud's psycho-analysis, and Alfred Adler's so-called "individual psychology."

There was a lot of popular nonsense talked about these theories, and especially about relativity (as still happens even today), but I was fortunate in those who introduced me to the study of this theory. We all—the small circle of students to which I belonged—were thrilled with the result of Eddington's eclipse observations which in 1919 brought the first important confirmation of Einstein's theory of gravitation. It was a great experience for us, and one which had a lasting influence on my intellectual development.

The three other theories I have mentioned were also widely discussed among students at that time. I myself happened to come into personal contact with Alfred Adler, and even to co-operate with him in his social work among the children and young people in the working-class districts of Vienna where he had established social guidance clinics.

It was during the summer of 1919 that I began to feel more and more dissatisfied with these three theories—the Marxist theory of history, psycho-analysis, and individual psychology; and I began to feel dubious about their claims to scientific status. My problem perhaps first took the simple form, "What is wrong with Marxism, psycho-analysis, and individual psychology? Why are they so different from physical theories, from Newton's theory, and especially from the theory of relativity?"

To make this contrast clear I should explain that few of us at the time would have said that we believed in the *truth* of Einstein's theory of gravitation. This shows that it was not my doubting the *truth* of those other three theories which bothered me, but something else. Yet neither was it that I merely felt mathematical physics to be more *exact* than the sociological or psychological type of theory. Thus what worried me was neither the problem of truth, at that stage at least, nor the problem of exactness or measurability. It was rather that I felt that these other three theories, though posing as sciences, had in fact more in common with primitive myths than with science; that they resembled astrology rather than astronomy.

I found that those of my friends who were admirers of Marx, Freud, and Adler, were impressed by a number of points common to these theories, and especially by their apparent *explanatory power*. These theories appeared to be able to explain practically everything that happened within the fields to which they referred. The study of any of them seemed to have the effect of an intellectual conversion or revelation, opening your eyes to a new truth hidden from those not yet initiated. Once your eyes were thus opened you saw confirming instances everywhere: the world was full of *verifications* of the theory. Whatever happened always confirmed it. Thus its truth appeared manifest; and unbelievers were clearly people who did not want to see the manifest truth; who refused to see it, either because it was against their class interest, or because of their repressions which were still "un-analysed" and crying aloud for treatment.

The most characteristic element in this situation seemed to me the incessant stream of confirmations, of observations which "verified" the theories in question; and this point was constantly emphasized by their adherents. A Marxist could not open a newspaper without finding on every page confirming evidence for his interpretation of history; not only in the news, but also in its presentation—which revealed the class bias of the paper—and especially of course in what the paper *did not* say. The Freudian analysts emphasized that their theories were constantly verified by their "clinical observations." As for Adler, I was much impressed by a personal experience. Once, in 1919, I reported to him a case which to me did not seem particularly Adlerian, but which he found no difficulty in analysing in terms of his theory of inferiority feelings, although he had not even seen the child. Slightly shocked, I asked him how he could be so sure. "Because of my thousandfold experience," he replied; whereupon I could not help saying: "And with this new case, I suppose, your experience has become thousand-and-one-fold."

What I had in mind was that his previous observations may not have been much sounder than this new one; that each in its turn had been interpreted in the light of "previous experience," and at the same time counted as additional confirmation. What, I asked myself, did it confirm? No more than that a case could be interpreted in the light of the theory. But this meant very little, I reflected, since every conceivable case could be interpreted in the light of Adler's theory, or equally of Freud's. I may illustrate this by two very different examples of human behaviour: that of a man who pushes a child into the water with the intention of drowning it; and that of a man who sacrifices his life in an attempt to save the child. Each of these two cases can be explained with equal ease in Freudian and in Adlerian terms. According to Freud the first man suffered from repression (say, of some component of his Oedipus complex), while the second man had achieved sublimation. According to Adler the first man suffered from feelings of inferiority (producing perhaps the need to prove to himself that he dared to commit some crime), and so did the second man (whose need was to prove to himself that he dared to rescue the child). I could not think of any human behaviour which could not be interpreted in terms of either theory. It was precisely this fact—that they always fitted, that they were always confirmed—which in the eyes of their admirers constituted the strongest argument in favour of these theories. It began to dawn on me that this apparent strength was in fact their weakness.

With Einstein's theory the situation was strikingly different. Take one typical instance—Einstein's prediction, just then confirmed by the findings of Eddington's expedition. Einstein's gravitational theory had led to the result that light must be attracted by heavy bodies (such as the sun), precisely as material bodies were attracted. As a consequence it could be calculated that light from a distant fixed star whose apparent position was close to the sun would reach the earth from such a direction that the star would seem to be slightly shifted away from the sun; or, in other words, that stars close to the sun would look as if they had moved a little away from the sun, and from one another. This is a thing which cannot normally be observed since such stars are rendered invisible in daytime by the sun's overwhelming brightness; but during an eclipse it is possible to take photographs of them. If the same constellation is photographed at night one can measure the distances on the two photographs, and check the predicted effect.

Now the impressive thing about this case is the *risk* involved in a prediction of this kind. If observation shows that the predicted effect is definitely absent, then the theory is simply refuted. The theory is *incompatible with certain possible results of observation*—in fact with results which everybody before Einstein would have expected.[1] This is quite different from the situation I have previously described, when it turned out that the theories in question were compatible with the most divergent human behaviour, so that it was practically impossible to describe any human behaviour that might not be claimed to be a verification of these theories.

These considerations led me in the winter of 1919–20 to conclusions which I may now reformulate as follows.

(1) It is easy to obtain confirmations, or verifications, for nearly every theory—if we look for confirmations.

(2) Confirmations should count only if they are the result of *risky predictions*; that is to say, if, unenlightened by the theory in question, we should have expected an event which was incompatible with the theory—an event which would have refuted the theory.

(3) Every "good" scientific theory is a prohibition: it forbids certain things to happen. The more a theory forbids, the better it is.

(4) A theory which is not refutable by any conceivable event is non-scientific. Irrefutability is not a virtue of theory (as people often think) but a vice.

(5) Every genuine *test* of a theory is an attempt to falsify it, or to refute it. Testability is falsifiability; but there are degrees of testability; some theories are more testable, more exposed to refutation, than others; they take, as it were, greater risks.

(6) Confirming evidence should not count *except when it is the result of a genuine test of the theory*; and this means that it can be presented as a serious but unsuccessful attempt to falsify the theory. (I now speak in such cases of "corroborating evidence.")

(7) Some genuinely testable theories, when found to be false, are still upheld by their admirers—for example by introducing *ad hoc* some auxiliary assumption,

or by re-interpreting the theory *ad hoc* in such a way that it escapes refutation. Such a procedure is always possible, but it rescues the theory from refutation only at the price of destroying, or at least lowering, its scientific status. (I later described such a rescuing operation as a *"conventionalist twist"* or a *"conventionalist stratagem."*)

One can sum up all this by saying that the *criterion of the scientific status of a theory is its falsifiability, or refutability, or testability.*

II

I may perhaps exemplify this with the help of the various theories so far mentioned. Einstein's theory of gravitation clearly satisfied the criterion of falsifiability. Even if our measuring instruments at the time did not allow us to pronounce on the results of the tests with complete assurance, there was clearly a possibility of refuting the theory.

Astrology did not pass the test. Astrologers were greatly impressed, and misled, by what they believed to be confirming evidence—so much so that they were quite unimpressed by any unfavourable evidence. Moreover, by making their interpretations and prophecies sufficiently vague they were able to explain away anything that might have been a refutation of the theory had the theory and the prophecies been more precise. In order to escape falsification they destroyed the testability of their theory. It is a typical soothsayer's trick to predict things so vaguely that the predictions can hardly fail: that they become irrefutable.

The Marxist theory of history, in spite of the serious efforts of some of its founders and followers, ultimately adopted this soothsaying practice. In some of its earlier formulations (for example in Marx's analysis of the character of the "coming social revolution") their predictions were testable, and in fact falsified.[2] Yet instead of accepting the refutations the followers of Marx reinterpreted both the theory and the evidence in order to make them agree. In this way they rescued the theory from refutation; but they did so at the price of adopting a device which made it irrefutable. They thus gave a "conventionalist twist" to the theory; and by this stratagem they destroyed its much advertised claim to scientific status.

The two psycho-analytic theories were in a different class. They were simply non-testable, irrefutable. There was no conceivable human behaviour which could contradict them. This does not mean that Freud and Adler were not seeing certain things correctly: I personally do not doubt that much of what they say is of considerable importance, and may well play its part one day in a psychological science which is testable. But it does mean that those "clinical observations" which analysts naively believe confirm their theory cannot do this any more than the daily confirmations which astrologers find in their practice.[3] And as for Freud's epic of the Ego, the Super-ego, and the Id, no substantially stronger claim to scientific status can be made for it than for Homer's collected stories from Olympus. These theories describe some facts, but in the manner of myths. They contain most interesting psychological suggestions, but not in a testable form.

At the same time I realized that such myths may be developed, and become testable; that historically speaking all—or very nearly all—scientific theories originate from myths, and that a myth may contain important anticipations of scientific theories. Examples are Empedocles' theory of evolution by trial and error, or Parmenides' myth of the unchanging block universe in which nothing ever happens and which, if we add another dimension, becomes Einstein's block universe (in which, too, nothing ever happens, since everything is, four-dimensionally speaking, determined and laid down from the beginning). I thus felt that if a theory is found to be non-scientific, or "metaphysical" (as we might say), it is not thereby found to be unimportant, or insignificant, or "meaningless," or "nonsensical."[4] But it cannot claim to be backed by empirical evidence in the scientific sense—although it may easily be, in some genetic sense, the "result of observation."

(There were a great many other theories of this pre-scientific or pseudo-scientific character, some of them, unfortunately, as influential as the Marxist interpretation of history; for example, the racialist interpretation of history—another of those impressive and all-explanatory theories which act upon weak minds like revelations.)

Thus the problem which I tried to solve by proposing the criterion of falsifiability was neither a problem of meaningfulness or significance, nor a problem of truth or acceptability. It was the problem of drawing a line (as well as this can be done) between the statements, or systems of statements, of the empirical sciences, and all other statements—whether they are of a religious or of a metaphysical character, or simply pseudo-scientific. Years later—it must have been in 1928 or 1929—I called this first problem of mine the *"problem of demarcation."* The criterion of falsifiability is a solution to this problem of demarcation, for it says that statements or systems of statements, in order to be ranked as scientific, must be capable of conflicting with possible, or conceivable, observations. . . .

III

Let us now turn from our logical criticism of the *psychology of experience* to our real problem—the problem of *the logic of science*. Although some of the things I have said may help us here, in so far as they may have eliminated certain psychological prejudices in favour of induction, my treatment of the *logical problem of induction* is completely independent of this criticism, and of all psychological considerations. Provided you do not dogmatically believe in the alleged psychological fact that we make inductions, you may now forget my whole story with the exception of two logical points: my logical remarks on testability or falsifiability as the criterion of demarcation; and Hume's logical criticism of induction.

From what I have said it is obvious that there was a close link between the two problems which interested me at that time: demarcation, and induction or scientific method. It was easy to see that the method of science is criticism, i.e. attempted falsifications. Yet it took me a few years to notice that the two problems – of demarcation and of induction – were in a sense one. . . .

I recently came across an interesting formulation of this belief in a remarkable philosophical book by a great physicist – Max Born's *Natural Philosophy of Cause and Chance.*[5] He writes: "Induction allows us to generalize a number of observations into a general rule: that night follows day and day follows night . . . But while everyday life has no definite criterion for the validity of an induction, . . . science has worked out a code, or rule of craft, for its application." Born nowhere reveals the contents of this inductive code (which, as his wording shows, contains a "definite criterion for the validity of an induction"); but he stresses that "there is no logical argument" for its acceptance: "it is a question of faith"; and he is therefore "willing to call induction a metaphysical principle." But why does he believe that such a code of valid inductive rules must exist? This becomes clear when he speaks of the "vast communities of people ignorant of, or rejecting, the rule of science, among them the members of anti-vaccination societies and believers in astrology. It is useless to argue with them; I cannot compel them to accept the same criteria of valid induction in which I believe: the code of scientific rules." This makes it quite clear that *"valid induction" was here meant to serve as a criterion of demarcation between science and pseudo-science.*

But it is obvious that this rule or craft of "valid induction" is not even metaphysical: it simply does not exist. No rule can ever guarantee that a generalization inferred from true observations, however often repeated, is true. (Born himself does not believe in the truth of Newtonian physics, in spite of its success, although he believes that it is based on induction.) And the success of science is not based upon rules of induction, but depends upon luck, ingenuity, and the purely deductive rules of critical argument.

I may summarize some of my conclusions as follows:

(1) Induction, i.e. inference based on many observations, is a myth. It is neither a psychological fact, nor a fact of ordinary life, nor one of scientific procedure.

(2) The actual procedure of science is to operate with conjectures: to jump to conclusions – often after one single observation (as noticed for example by Hume and Born).

(3) Repeated observations and experiments function in science as *tests* of our conjectures or hypotheses, i.e. as attempted refutations.

(4) The mistaken belief in induction is fortified by the need for a criterion of demarcation which, it is traditionally but wrongly believed, only the inductive method can provide.

(5) The conception of such an inductive method, like the criterion of verifiability, implies a faulty demarcation.

(6) None of this is altered in the least if we say that induction makes theories only probable rather than certain.

IV

If, as I have suggested, the problem of induction is only an instance or facet of the problem of demaration, then the solution to the problem of demarcation must provide us with a solution to the problem of induction. This is indeed the case, I believe, although it is perhaps not immediately obvious.

For a brief formulation of the problem of induction we can turn again to Born, who writes: ". . . no observation or experiment, however extended, can give more than a finite number of repetitions"; therefore, "the statement of a law—B depends on A—always transcends experience. Yet this kind of statement is made everywhere and all the time, and sometimes from scanty material."⁶

In other words, the logical problem of induction arises from *(a)* Hume's discovery (so well expressed by Born) that it is impossible to justify a law by observation or experiment, since it "transcends experience"; *(b)* the fact that science proposes and uses laws "everywhere and all the time." (Like Hume, Born is struck by the "scanty material," i.e. the few observed instances upon which the law may be based.) To this we have to add *(c) the principle of empiricism* which asserts that in science, only observation and experiment may decide upon the *acceptance or rejection* of scientific statements, including laws and theories.

These three principles, *(a)*, *(b)*, and *(c)*, appear at first sight to clash; and this apparent clash constitutes the *logical problem of induction.*

Faced with this clash, Born gives up *(c)*, the principle of empiricism (as Kant and may others, including Bertrand Russell, have done before him), in favour of what he calls a "metaphysical principle"; a metaphysical principle which he does not even attempt to formulate; which he vaguely describes as a "code or rule of craft"; and of which I have never seen any formulation which even looked promising and was not clearly untenable.

But in fact the principles *(a)* to *(c)* do not clash. We can see this the moment we realize that the acceptance by science of a law or of a theory is *tentative only;* which is to say that all laws and theories are conjectures, or tentative *hypotheses* (a position which I have sometimes called "hypotheticism"); and that we may reject a law or theory on the basis of new evidence, without necessarily discarding the old evidence which originally led us to accept it.⁷

The principles of empiricism *(c)* can be fully preserved, since the fate of a theory, its acceptance or rejection, is decided by observation and experiment— by the result of tests. So long as a theory stands up to the severest tests we can design, it is accepted; if it does not, it is rejected. But it is never inferred, in any sense, from the empirical evidence. There is neither a psychological nor a logical induction. *Only the falsity of the theory can be inferred from empirical evidence, and this inference is a purely deductive one.*

Hume showed that it is not possible to infer a theory from observation statements; but this does not affect the possibility of refuting a theory by observation statements. The full appreciation of the possibility makes the relation between theories and observations perfectly clear.

This solves the problem of the alleged clash between the principles *(a)*, *(b)*, and *(c)*, and with it Hume's problem of induction. . . .

NOTES

1. This is a slight oversimplification, for about half of the Einstein effect may be derived from the classical theory, provided we assume a ballistic theory of light.

2. See, for example, my *Open Society and Its Enemies*, ch. 15, section iii, and notes 13–14.

3. "Clinical observations," like all other observations, are *interpretations in the light of theories*; and for this reason alone they are apt to seem to support those theories in the light of which they were interpreted. But real support can be obtained only from observations undertaken as tests (by "attempted refutations"); and for this purpose *criteria of refutation* have to be laid down beforehand; it must be agreed which observable situations, if actually observed, mean that the theory is refuted. But what kind of clinical responses would refute to the satisfaction of the analyst not merely a particular analytic diagnosis but psycho-analysis itself? And have such criteria ever been discussed or agreed upon by analysts? Is there not, on the contrary, a whole family of analytic concepts, such as "ambivalence" (I do not suggest that there is no such thing as ambivalence), which would make it difficult, if not impossible, to agree upon such criteria? Moreover, how much headway has been made in investigating the question of the extent to which the (conscious or unconscious) expectations and theories held by the analyst influence the "clinical responses" of the patient? To say nothing about the conscious attempts to influence the patient by proposing interpretations to him, etc.) Years ago I introduced the term "*Oedipus effect*" to describe the influence of a theory or expectation or prediction *upon the event which it predicts* or describes: it will be remembered that the causal chain leading to Oedpus' parricide was started by the oracle's prediction of this event. This is a characteristic and recurrent theme of such myths, but one which seems to have failed to attract the interest of the analysts, perhaps not accidentally. (The problem of confirmatory dreams suggested by the analyst is discussed by Freud, for example in *Gesammelte Schriften*, III, 1925, where he says on p. 314: "If anybody asserts that most of the dreams which can be utilized in an analysis . . . owe their origin to [the analyst's] suggestion, then no objection can be made from the point of view of analytic theory. Yet there is nothing in this fact," he surprisingly adds, "which would detract from the reliability of our results.")

4. The case of astrology, nowadays a typical pseudo-science, may illustrate this point. It was attacked, by Aristotelians and other rationalists, down to Newton's day, for the wrong reason—for its now accepted assertion that the planets had an "influence" upon terrestrial ("sublunar") events. In fact Newton's theory of gravity, and especially the lunar theory of the tides, was historically speaking an offpsring of astrological lore. Newton, it seems, was most reluctant to adopt a theory which came from the same stable as for example the theory that "influenza" epidemics are due to an astral "influence." And Galileo, no doubt for the same reason, actually rejected the lunar theory of the tides; and his misgivings about Kepler may easily be explained by his misgivings about astrology.

5. Max Born, *Natural Philosophy of Cause and Chance*, Oxford, 1949, p. 7.

6. *Natural Philosophy of Cause and Chance*, p. 6.

7. I do not doubt that Born and many others would agree that theories are accepted only tentatively. But the widespread belief in induction shows that the far-reaching implications of this view are rarely seen.

2

What Is Science?

John Ziman

To answer the question "What is Science?" is almost as presumptuous as to try to state the meaning of Life itself. Science has become a major part of the stock of our minds; its products are the furniture of our surroundings. We must accept it, as the good lady of the fable is said to have agreed to accept the Universe.

Yet the question is puzzling rather than mysterious. Science is very clearly a conscious artifact of mankind, with well-documented historical origins, with a definable scope and content, and with recognizable professional practitioners and exponents. The task of defining Poetry, say, whose subject matter is by common consent ineffable, must be self-defeating. Poetry has no rules, no method, no graduate schools, no logic: the bards are self-anointed and their spirit bloweth where it listeth. Science, by contrast, is rigorous, methodical, academic, logical and practical. The very facility that it gives us, of clear understanding, of seeing things sharply in focus, makes us feel that the instrument itself is very real and hard and definite. Surely we can state, in a few words, its essential nature.

It is not difficult to state the order of being to which Science belongs. It is one of the categories of the intellectual commentary that Man makes on his World. Amongst its kith and kin we would put Religion, Art, Poetry, Law, Philosophy, Technology, etc.—the familiar divisions or "Faculties" of the Academy or the Multiversity.

At this stage I do not mean to analyse the precise relationship that exists between Science and each of these cognate modes of thought; I am merely asserting that they are on all fours with one another. It makes some sort of sense (though it may not always be stating a truth) to substitute these words for one another, in phrases like "Science teaches us . . ." or "The Spirit of *Law* is . . ." or "*Technology* benefits mankind by . . ." or "He is a student of

Philosophy." The famous "conflict between Science and Religion" was truly a battle between combatants of the same species—between David and Goliath if you will—and not, say, between the Philistine army and a Dryad, or between a point of order and a postage stamp.

Science is obviously like Religion, Law, Philosophy, etc. in being a more or less coherent set of ideas. In its own technical language, Science is information; it does not act directly on the body; it speaks to the mind. Religion and Poetry, we may concede, speak also to the emotions, and the statements of Art can seldom be written or expressed verbally—but they all belong in the non-material realm.

But in what ways are these forms of knowledge *unlike* one another? What are the special attributes of Science? What is the criterion for drawing lines of demarcation about it, to distinguish it from Philosophy, or from Technology, or from Poetry?

*   *   *

One can be zealous for science, and a splendidly successful research worker, without pretending to a clear and certain notion of what science really is. In practice it does not seem to matter.

Perhaps this is healthy. A deep interest in theology is not welcome in the average churchgoer, and the ordinary taxpayer should not really concern himself about the nature of sovereignty or the merits of bicameral legislatures. Even though Church and State depend, in the end, upon such abstract matters, we may reasonably leave them to the experts if all goes smoothly. The average scientist will say that he knows from experience and common sense what he is doing, and so long as he is not striking too deeply into the foundations of knowledge he is content to leave the highly technical discussion of the nature of Science to those self-appointed authorities the Philosophers of Science. A rough and ready conventional wisdom will see him through.

Yet in a way this neglect of—even scorn for—the Philosophy of Science by professional scientists is strange. They are, after all, engaged in a very difficult, rather abstract, highly intellectual activity and need all the guidance they can get from general theory. We may agree that the general principles may not in practice be very helpful, but we might have thought that at least they would be taught to young scientists in training, just as medical students are taught Physiology and budding administrators were once encouraged to acquaint themselves with Plato's *Republic.* When the student graduates and goes into a laboratory, how will he know what to do to make scientific discoveries if he has not been taught the distinction between a scientific theory and a non-scientific one? Making all allowances for the initial prejudice of scientists against speculative philosophy, and for the outmoded assumption that certain general ideas would communicate themselves to the educated and cultured man without specific instruction, I find this an odd and significant phenomenon.

The fact is that scientific investigation, as distinct from the theoretical *content* of any given branch of science, is a practical art. It is not learnt out of books, but by imitation and experience. Research workers are trained by apprenticeship, by working for their Ph.D.'s under the supervision of more experienced scholars, not by attending courses in the metaphysics of physics. The graduate student is given his "problem": "You might have a look at the effect of pressure on the band structure of the III–V compounds; I don't think it has been done yet, and it would be interesting to see whether it fits into the pseudopotential theory." Then, with considerable help, encouragement and criticism, he sets up his apparatus, makes his measurements, performs his calculations, etc. and in due course writes a thesis and is accounted a qualified professional. But notice that he will not at any time have been made to study formal logic, nor will he be expected to defend his thesis in a step by step deductive procedure. His examiners may ask him why he had made some particular assertion in the course of his argument, or they may enquire as to the reliability of some particular measurement. They may even ask him to assess the value of the "contribution" he has made to the subject as a whole. But they will not ask him to give any opinion as to whether Physics is ultimately *true*, or whether he is justified now in believing in an external world, or in what sense a theory is verified by the observation of favourable instances. The examiners will assume that the candidate shares with them the common language and principles of their discipline. No scientist really doubts that theories are verified by observation, any more than a Common Law judge hesitates to rule that hearsay evidence is inadmissible.

What one finds in practice is that scientific argument, written or spoken, is not very complex or logically precise. The terms and concepts that are used may be extremely subtle and technical, but they are put together in quite simple logical forms, with expressed or implied relations as the machinery of deduction. It is very seldom that one uses the more sophisticated types of proof used in Mathematics, such as asserting a proposition by proving that its negation implies a contradiction. Of course actual mathematical or numerical analysis of data may carry the deduction through many steps, but the symbolic machinery of algebra and the electronic circuits of the computer are then relied on to keep the argument straight.[1] In my own experience, one more often detects elementary *non sequiturs* in the verbal reasoning than actual mathematical mistakes in the calculations that accompany them. This is not said to disparage the intellectual powers of scientists; I mean simply that the reasoning used in scientific papers is not very different from what we should use in an everyday careful discussion of an everyday problem.

. . . [This point] is made to emphasize the inadequacy of the "logico-inductive" metaphysic of Science. How can this be correct, when few scientists are interested in or understand it, and none ever uses it explicitly in his work? But then if Science is distinguished from other intellectaual disciplines neither by a particular style or argument nor by a definable subject matter, what is it?

The answer proposed in this essay is suggested by its title: *Science Is Public Knowledge*. This is, of course, a very cryptic definition, with almost the suggestion of a play upon words. What I mean is something along the following lines. Science is not merely *published* knowledge or information. Anyone may make an observation, or conceive a hypothesis, and if he has the financial means, get it printed and distributed for other persons to read. Scientific knowledge is more than this. Its facts and theories must survive a period of critical study and testing by other competent and disinterested individuals, and must have been found so persuasive that they are almost universally accepted. The objective of Science is not just to acquire information nor to utter all non-contradictory notions; its goal is a *consensus* of rational opinion over the widest possible field.

In a sense, this is so obvious and well-known that it scarcely needs saying. Most educated and informed people agree that Science is true, and therefore impossible to gainsay. But I assert my definition much more positively; this is the basic principle upon which Science is founded. It is not a subsidiary consequence of the "Scientific Method"; it *is* the scientific method itself.

The defect of the conventional philosophical approach to Science is that it considers only two terms in the equation. The scientist is seen as an individual, pursuing a somewhat one-sided dialogue with taciturn Nature. *He* observes phenomena, notices regularities, arrives at generalizations, deduces consequences, etc. and eventually, Hey Presto! a law of Nature springs into being. But it is not like that at all. The scientific enterprise is corporate. It is not merely, in Newton's incomparable phrase, that one stands on the shoulders of giants, and hence can see a little farther. Every scientist sees through his own eyes—and also through the eyes of his predecessors and colleagues. It is never one individual that goes through all the steps in the logico-inductive chain; it is a group of individuals, dividing their labour but continuously and jealously checking each other's contributions. The cliché of scientific prose betrays itself "Hence we arrive at the conclusion that . . ." The audience to which scientific publications are addressed is not passive; by its cheering or booing, its bouquets or brickbats, it actively controls the substance of the communications that it receives.

In other words, scientific research is a social activity. Technology, Art and Religion are perhaps possible for Robinson Crusoe, but Law and Science are not. To understand the nature of Science, we must look at the way in which scientists behave towards one another, how they are organized and how information passes between them. The young scientist does not study formal logic, but he learns by imitation and experience a number of conventions that embody strong social relationships. In the language of Sociology, he learns to play his *role* in a system by which knowledge is acquired, sifted and eventually made public property.

It has, of course, long been recognized that Science is peculiar in its origins to the civilization of Western Europe. The question of the social basis of Science, and its relations to other organizations and institutions of our way of life, is much debated. Is it a consequence of the "Bourgeois Revolution," or of Protestantism—or what? Does it exist despite the Church and the Universities, or because of them? Why did China, with its immense technological and intellectual resources, not develop the same system? What should be the status of the scientific worker in an advanced society; should he be a paid employee, with a prescribed field of study, or an aristocratic dilettante? How should decisions be taken about expenditure on research? And so on.

These problems, profoundly sociological, historical and political though they may be, are not quite what I have in mind. Only too often the element in the argument that gets the least analysis is the actual institution about which the whole discussion hinges—scientific activity itself. To give a contemporary example, there is much talk nowadays about the importance of creating more effective systems for storing and indexing scientific literature, so that every scientist can very quickly become aware of the relevant work of every other scientist in his field. This recognizes that publication is important, but the discussion usually betrays an absence of careful thought about the part that conventional systems of scientific communication play in sifting and sorting the material that they handle. Or again, the problem of why Greek Science never finally took off from its brilliant taxying runs is discussed in terms of, say, the aristocratic citizen despising the servile labour of practical experiment, when it might have been due to the absence of just such a communications system between scholars as was provided in the Renaissance by alphabetic printing. The internal sociological analysis of Science itself is a necessary preliminary to the study of the Sociology of Knowledge in the secular world.

The present essay cannot pretend to deal with all such questions. The "Science of Science" is a vast topic, with many aspects. The very core of so many difficulties is suggested by my present argument—that Science stands in the region where the intellectual, the psychological and the sociological coordinate axes intersect. It is knowledge, therefore intellectual, conceptual and abstract. It is inevitably created by individual men and women, and therefore has a strong psychological aspect. It is public, and therefore moulded and determined by the social relations between individuals. To keep all these aspects in view simultaneously, and to appreciate their hidden connections, is not at all easy.

It has been put to me that one should in fact distinguish carefully between Science as a body of knowledge, Science as what scientists do, and Science as a social institution. This is precisely the sort of distinction that one must *not* make; in the language of geometry, a solid object cannot be reconstructed from its projections upon the separate cartesian planes. By assigning the intellectual aspects of Science to the professional philosophers we make of it an arid exercise in logic; by allowing the psychologists to take possession of the personal dimension we overemphasize the mysteries of "creativity" at the expense of rationality and the critical power of well-ordered argument; if the social aspects are handed over to the sociologists, we get a description of research as an N-person game, with prestige points for stakes and priority claims as trumps. The problem has been to discover a unifying principle for Science in all its aspects. The recognition that scientific knowledge must be public and *consensible* (to coin a necessary word) allows one to trace out the complex inner relationships between its various facets. Before one can distinguish and discuss separately the philosophical, psychological or sociological dimensions of Science, one must somehow have succeeded in characterizing it as a whole.[2]

In an ordinary work of Science one does well not to dwell too long on the hypothesis that is being tested, trying to define and describe it in advance of reporting the results of the experiments or calculations that are supposed to verify or negate it. The results themselves indicate the nature of the hypothesis, its scope and limitations. The present essay is organized in the same manner. Having sketched a point of view in this chapter, I propose to turn the discussion to a number of particular topics that I think can be better understood when seen from this new angle. To give a semblance of order to the argument, the various subjects have been arranged according to whether they are primarily *intellectual*—as, for example, some attempt to discriminate between scientific and non-scientific disciplines; *psychological*—e.g., the role of education, the significance of scientific creativity; *sociological*—the structure of the scientific community and the institutions by which it maintains scientific standards and procedures. Beyond this classification, the succession of topics is likely to be pretty haphazard; or, as the good lady said, "How to I know what I think until I have heard what I have to say?" . . .

NOTES

1. This point I owe to Professor Körner.
2. "Hence a true philosophy of science must be a philosophy of scientists and laboratories as well as one of waves, particles and symbols." Patrick Meredith in *Instruments of Communication,* p. 40.

3

How to Defend Society Against Science

Paul Feyerabend

Practitioners of a strange trade, friends, enemies, ladies and gentlemen: Before starting with my talk, let me explain to you, how it came into existence.

About a year ago I was short of funds. So I accepted an invitation to contribute to a book dealing with the relation between science and religion. To make the book sell I thought I should make my contribution a provocative one and the most provocative statement one can make about the relation between science and religion is that science is a religion. Having made the statement the core of my article I discovered that lots of reasons, lots of excellent reasons, could be found for it. I enumerated the reasons, finished my article, and got paid. That was stage one.

Next I was invited to a Conference for the Defence of Culture. I accepted the invitation because it paid for my flight to Europe. I also must admit that I was rather curious. When I arrived in Nice I had no idea what I would say. Then while the conference was taking its course I discovered that everyone thought very highly of science and that everyone was very serious. So I decided to explain how one could defend culture from science. All the reasons collected in my article would apply here as well and there was no need to invent new things. I gave my talk, was rewarded with an outcry about my "dangerous and ill considered ideas," collected by ticket and went on to Vienna. That was stage number two.

Now I am supposed to address you. I have a hunch that in some respect you are very different from my audience in Nice. For one, you look much younger. My audience in Nice was full of professors, businessmen, and television

[This] article is a revised version of a talk given to the Philosophy Society at Sussex University in November 1974.

executives, and the average age was about 58½. Then I am quite sure that most of you are considerably to the left of some of the people in Nice. As a matter of fact, speaking somewhat superficially I might say that you are a left-ist audience while my audience in Nice was a rightist audience. Yet despite all these differences you have some things in common. Both of you, I assume, respect science and knowledge. Science, of course, must be reformed and must be made less authoritarian. But once the reforms are carried out, it is a valuable source of knowledge that must not be contaminated by ideologies of a different kind. Secondly, both of you are serious people. Knowledge is a serious matter, for the Right as well as for the Left, and it must be pursued in a serious spirit. Frivolity is out, dedication and earnest application to the task at hand is in. These similarities are all I need for repeating my Nice talk to you with hardly any change. So, here it is.

Fairytales

I want to defend society and its inhabitants from all ideologies, science included. All ideologies must be seen in perspective. One must not take them too seriously. One must read them like fairytales which have lots of interesting things to say but which also contain wicked lies, or like ethical prescriptions which may be useful rules of thumb but which are deadly when followed to the letter.

Now, is this not a strange and ridiculous attitude? Science, surely, was always in the forefront of the fight against authoritarianism and superstition. It is to science that we owe our increased intellectual freedom vis-à-vis religious beliefs; it is to science that we owe the liberation of mankind from ancient and rigid forms of thought. Today these forms of thought are nothing but bad dreams—and this we learned from science. Science and enlightenment are one and the same thing—even the most radical critics of society believe this. Kropotkin wants to overthrow all traditional institutions and forms of belief, with the exception of science. Ibsen criticises the most intimate ramifications of nineteenth-century bourgeois ideology, but he leaves science untouched. Levi-Strauss has made us realise that Western Thought is not the lonely peak of human achievement it was once believed to be, but he excludes science from his relativization of ideologies. Marx and Engels were convinced that science would aid the workers in their quest for mental and social liberation. Are all these people deceived? Are they all mistaken about the role of science? Are they all the victims of a chimaera?

To these questions my answer is a firm *Yes and No.*

Now, let me explain my answer.

My explanation consists of two parts, one more general, one more specific.

The general explanation is simple. Any ideology that breaks the hold a comprehensive system of thought has on the minds of men contributes to the liberation of man. Any ideology that makes man question inherited beliefs is an aid to enlightenment. A truth that reigns without checks and balances is a tyrant who must be overthrown, and any falsehood that can aid us in the over-throw of this tyrant is to be welcomed. It follows that seventeenth- and eighteenth-century science indeed *was* an instrument of liberation and enlightenment. It does not follow that science is bound to *remain* such an instrument. There is nothing inherent in science or in any other ideology that makes it *essentially* liberating. Ideologies can deteriorate and become stupid religions. Look at Marxism. And that the science of today is very different from the science of 1650 is evident at the most superficial glance.

For example, consider the role science now plays in education. Scientific "facts" are taught at a very early age and in the very same manner in which religious "facts" were taught only a century ago. There is no attempt to waken the critical abilities of the pupil so that he may be able to see things in perspective. At the universities the situation is even worse, for indoctrination is here carried out in a much more systematic manner. Criticism is not entirely absent. Society, for example, and its institutions, are criticised most severely and often most unfairly and this already at the elementary school level. But science is excepted from the criticism. In society at large the judgement of the scientist is received with the same reverence as the judgement of bishops and cardinals was accepted not too long ago. The move towards "demythologization," for example, is largely motivated by the wish to avoid any clash between Christianity and scientific ideas. If such a clash occurs, then science is certainly right and Christianity wrong. Pursue this investigation further and you will see that science has now become as oppressive as the ideologies it had once to fight. Do not be misled by the fact that today hardly anyone gets killed for joining a scientific heresy. This has nothing to do with science. It has something to do with the general quality of our civilization. Heretics in science are still made to suffer from the *most severe* sanctions this relatively tolerant civilization has to offer.

But—is this description not utterly unfair? Have I not presented the matter in a very distorted light by using tendentious and distorting terminology? Must we not describe the situation in a very different way? I have said that science has become *rigid,* that it has ceased to be an instrument of *change* and *liberation,* without adding that it has found the *truth,* or a large part thereof. Considering this additional fact we realise, so the objection goes, that the rigidity of science is not due to human wilfulness. It lies in the nature of things. For once we have discovered the truth—what else can we do but follow it?

This trite reply is anything but original. It is used whenever an ideology wants to reinforce the faith of its followers. "Truth" is such a nicely neutral word. Nobody would deny that it is commendable to speak the truth and wicked to tell lies. Nobody would deny that—and yet nobody knows what such an attitude amounts to. So it is easy to twist matters and to change allegiance to truth in one's everyday affairs into allegiance to the Truth of an ideology which is nothing but the dogmatic defence of that ideology. And it is of course *not* true that we *have* to follow the truth. Human life is guided by many ideas. Truth is one of them. Freedom and mental independence are others. If Truth, as conceived by some ideologists, conflicts with freedom, then we have a *choice.* We may abandon freedom. But we may also abandon Truth. (Alternatively, we may adopt a more sophisticated idea of truth that no longer contradicts freedom; that was Hegel's solution.) My criticism of modern science is that it inhibits freedom of thought. If the reason is that it has found the truth and now follows it, then I would say that there are better things than first finding, and then following such a monster.

This finishes the general part of my explanation.

There exists a more specific argument to defend the exceptional position science has in society today. Put in a nutshell the argument says (1) that science has finally found the correct *method* for achieving results and (2) that there are many *results* to prove the excellence of the method. The argument is mistaken — but most attempts to show this lead into a dead end. Methodology has by now become so crowded with empty sophistication that it is extremely difficult to perceive the simple errors at the basis. It is like fighting the hydra — cut off one ugly head, and eight formalizations take its place. In this situation the only answer is superficiality: when sophistication loses content then the only way of keeping in touch with reality is to be crude and superficial. This is what I intend to be.

Against Method

There is a method, says part (1) of the argument. What is it? How does it work?

One answer which is no longer as popular as it used to be is that science works by collecting facts and inferring theories from them. The answer is unsatisfactory as theories never *follow from* facts in the strict logical sense. To say that they may yet be *supported* from facts assumes a notion of support that (a) does not show this defect and (b) is sufficiently sophisticated to permit us to say to what extent, say, the theory of relativity is supported by the facts. No such notion exists today, nor is it likely that it will ever be found (one of the problems is that we need a notion of support in which grey ravens can be said to support "all ravens are black"). This was realised by conventionalists and transcendental idealists who pointed out that theories *shape* and *order* facts and can therefore be retained come what may. They can be retained because the human mind either consciously or unconsciously carries out its ordering function. The trouble with these views is that they assume for the mind what they want to explain for the world, viz., that it works in a regular fashion. There is only one view which overcomes all these difficulties. It was invented twice in the nineteenth century, by Mill, in his immortal essay *On Liberty,* and by some Darwinists who extended Darwinism to the battle of ideas. This view takes the bull by the horns: theories cannot be justified and their excellence cannot be shown without reference to other theories. We may explain the *success* of a theory by reference to a more comprehensive theory (we may explain the success of Newton's theory by using the general theory of relativity); and we may explain our *preference* for it by comparing it with other theories.

Such a comparison does not establish the intrinsic excellence of the theory we have chosen. As a matter of fact, the theory we have chosen may be pretty lousy. It may contain contradictions, it may conflict with well-known facts, it may be cumbersome, unclear, ad hoc in decisive places, and so on. But it may still be better than any other theory that is available at the time. It may in fact be the best lousy theory there is. Nor are the standards of judgement chosen in an absolute manner. Our sophistication increases with every choice we make, and so do our standards. Standards compete just as theories compete and we choose the standards most appropriate to the historical situation in which the choice occurs. The rejected alternatives (theories; standards; "facts") are not eliminated. They serve as correctives (after all, we may have made the wrong choice) and they also explain the content of the preferred views (we understand relativity better when we understand the structure of its competitors; we know the full meaning of freedom only when we have an idea of life in a totalitarian state, of its advantages—and there are many advantages—as well as of its disadvantages). Knowledge so conceived is an ocean of alternatives channelled and subdivided by an ocean of standards. It forces our mind to make imaginative choices and thus makes it grow. It makes our mind capable of choosing, imagining, criticising.

Today this view is often connected with the name of Karl Popper. But there are some very decisive differences between Popper and Mill. To start with, Popper developed his view to solve a special problem of epistemology—he wanted to solve "Hume's problem." Mill, on the other hand, is interested in conditions favourable to human growth. His epistemology is the result of a certain theory of man, and not the other way around. Also Popper, being influenced by the Vienna Circle, improves on the logical form of a theory before discussing it, while Mill uses every theory in the form in which it occurs in science. Thirdly, Popper's standards of comparison are rigid and fixed, while Mill's standards are permitted to change with the historical situation. Finally, Popper's standards eliminate competitors once and for all: theories that are either not falsifiable or falsifiable and falsified have no place in science. Popper's criteria are clear, unambiguous, precisely formulated; Mill's criteria are not. This would be an advantage if science itself were clear, unambiguous, and precisely formulated. Fortunately, it is not.

To start with, no new and revolutionary scientific theory is ever formulated in a manner that permits us to say under what circumstances we must regard it as endangered: many revolutionary theories are unfalsifiable. Falsifiable versions do exist, but they are hardly ever in agreement with accepted basic statements: every moderately interesting theory is falsified. Moreover, theories have formal flaws, many of them contain contradictions, ad hoc adjustments, and so on and so forth. Applied resolutely, Popperian criteria would eliminate science without replacing it by anything comparable. They are useless as an aid to science. In the past decade this has been realised by various thinkers, Kuhn and Lakatos among them. Kuhn's ideas are interesting but, alas, they are much too vague to give rise to anything but lots of hot air. If you don't believe me, look at the literature. Never before has the literature on the philosophy of science been invaded by so many creeps and incompetents. Kuhn encourages people who have no idea why a stone falls to the ground to talk with assurance about scientific method. Now I have no objection to incompetence but I do object when incompetence is accompanied by boredom and self-righteousness And this is exactly what happens. We do not get interesting false ideas, we get boring ideas or words connected with no ideas at all. Secondly, wherever one tries to make Kuhn's ideas more definite one finds that they are *false*. Was there ever a period of normal science in the history of thought? No—and I challenge anyone to prove the contrary.

Lakatos is immeasurably more sophisticated than Kuhn. Instead of theories he considers research programmes which are sequences of theories connected by methods of modification, so-called heuristics. Each theory in the sequence may be full of faults. It may be beset by anomalies, contradictions, ambiguities. What counts is not the shape of the single theories, but the tendency exhibited by the sequence. We judge historical developments and achievements over a period of time, rather than the situation at a particular time. History and methodology are combined into a single enterprise. A research programme is said to progress if the sequence of theories leads to novel predictions. It is said to degenerate if it is reduced to absorbing facts that have been discovered without its help. A decisive feature of Lakatos' methodology is that such evaluations are no longer tied to methodological rules which tell the scientist either to retain or to abandon a research programme. Scientists may stick to a degenerating programme; they may even succeed in making the programme overtake its rivals and they therefore proceed rationally whatever they are doing (provided they continue calling degenerating programmes degenerating and progressive programmes progressive). This means that Lakatos offers *words* which *sound* like the elements of a methodology; he does not offer a methodology. There is no method according to the most advanced and sophisticated methodology in existence today. This finishes my reply to part (1) of the specific argument.

Against Results

According to part (2), science deserves a special position because it has produced *results*. This is an argument only if it can be taken for granted that nothing else has ever produced results. Now it may be admitted that almost everyone who discusses the matter makes such an assumption. It may also be admitted that it is not easy to show that the assumption is false. Forms of life different from science either have disappeared or have degenerated to an extent that makes a fair comparison impossible. Still, the situation is not as hopeless as it was only a decade ago. We have become acquainted with methods of medical diagnosis and therapy which are effective (and perhaps even more effective than the corresponding parts of Western medicine) and which are yet based on an ideology that is radically different from the ideology of Western science. We have learned that there are phenomena such as telepathy and telekinesis which are obliterated by a scientific approach and which could be used to do research in an entirely novel way (earlier thinkers such as Agrippa of Nettesheim, John Dee, and even Bacon were aware of these phenomena). And then—is it not the case that the Church saved souls while science often does the very opposite? Of course, nobody now believes in the ontology that underlies this judgement. Why? Because of ideological pressures identical with those which today make us listen to science to the exclusion of everything else. It is also true that phenomena such as telekinesis and acupuncture may eventually be absorbed into the body of science and may therefore be called "scientific." But note that this happens only after a long period of resistance during which a science *not yet* containing the phenomena wants to get the upper hand over forms of life that contain them. And this leads to a further objection against part (2) of the specific argument. The fact that science has results counts in its favour only if these results were achieved by science alone, and without any outside help. A look at history shows that science hardly ever gets its results in this way. When Copernicus introduced a new view of the universe, he did not consult *scientific* predecessors, he consulted a crazy Pythagorean such as Philolaos. He adopted his ideas and he maintained them in the face of all sound rules of scientific method. Mechanics and optics owe a lot to artisans, medicine to midwives and witches. And in our own day we have seen how the interference of the state can advance science: when the Chinese communists refused to be intimidated by the judgement of experts and ordered traditional medicine back into universities and hospitals there was an outcry all over the world that science would now be ruined in China. The very opposite occurred: Chinese science advanced and Western science learned from it. Wherever we look we see that great scientific advances are due to outside interference which is made to prevail in the face of the most basic and most "rational" methodological rules. The lesson is plain: there does not exist a single argument that could be used to support the exceptional role which science today plays in society. Science has done many things, but so have other ideologies. Science often proceeds systematically, but so do other ideologies (just consult the records of the many doctrinal debates that took place in the Church) and, besides, there are no overriding rules which are adhered to under any circumstances; there is no "scientific methodology" that can be used to separate science from the rest. *Science is just one of the many ideologies that propel society and it should be treated as such* (this statement applies even to the most progressive and most dialectical sections of science). What consequences can we draw from this result?

The most important consequence is that there must be a *formal separation between state and science* just as there is now a formal separation between state and church. Science may influence society but only to the extent to which any political or other pressure group is permitted to influence society. Scientists may be consulted on important projects but the final judgement must be left to the democratically elected consulting bodies. These bodies will consist mainly of laymen. Will the laymen be able to come to a correct judgement? Most certainly, for the competence, the complications and the successes of science are vastly exaggerated. One of the most exhilarating experiences is to see how a lawyer, who is a layman, can find holes in the testimony, the technical testimony, of the most advanced expert and thus prepare the jury for its verdict. Science is not a closed book that is understood only after years of training. It is an intellectual discipline that can be examined and criticised by anyone who is interested and that looks difficult and profound only because of a systematic campaign of obfuscation carried out by many scientists (though, I am happy to say, not by all). Organs of the state should never hesitate to reject the judgement of scientists when they have reason for doing so. Such rejection will educate the general public, will make it more confident, and it may even lead to improvement. Considering the sizeable chauvinism of the scientific establishment we can say: the more Lysenko affairs, the better (it is not the *interference* of the state that is objectionable in the case of Lysenko, but the *totalitarian* interference which kills the opponent rather than just neglecting his advice). Three cheers to the fundamentalists in California who succeeded in having a dogmatic formulation of the theory of evolution removed from the text books and an account of Genesis included. (But I know that they would become as chauvinistic and totalitarian as scientists are today when given the chance to run society all by themselves. Ideologies are marvellous when used in the companies of other ideologies. They become boring and doctrinaire as soon as their merits lead to the removal of their opponents.) The most important change, however, will have to occur in the field of *education*.

Education and Myth

The purpose of education, so one would think, is to introduce the young into life, and that means: into the *society* where they are born and into the *physical universe* that surrounds the society. The method of education often consists in the teaching of some *basic myth*. The myth is available in various versions. More advanced versions may be taught by initiation rites which firmly implant them into the mind. Knowing the myth, the grownup can explain almost everything (or else he can turn to experts for more detailed information). He is the master of Nature and of Society. He understands them both and he knows how to interact with them. However, *he is not the master of the myth that guides his understanding.*

Such further mastery was aimed at, and was partly achieved, by the Presocratics. The Presocratics not only tried to understand the *world*. They also tried to understand, and thus to become the masters of, the *means of understanding the world.* Instead of being content with a single myth they developed many and so diminished the power which a well-told story has over the minds of men. The sophists introduced still further methods for reducing the debilitating effect of interesting, coherent, "empirically adequate" etc. etc. tales. The achievement of these thinkers were not appreciated and they certainly are not understood today. When teaching a myth we want to increase the chance that it will be understood (i.e. no puzzlement about any feature of the myth), believed, *and accepted.* This does not do any harm when the myth is counterbalanced by other myths: even the most dedicated (i.e. totalitarian) instructor in a certain version of Christianity cannot prevent his pupils from getting in touch with Buddhists, Jews and other disreputable people. It is very different in the case of science, or of rationalism where the field is almost completely dominated by the believers. In this case it is of paramount importance to strengthen the minds of the young, and "strengthening the minds of the young" means strengthening them *against* any easy acceptance of comprehensive views. What we need here is an education that makes people *contrary, counter-suggestive,* without making them incapable of devoting themselves to the elaboration of any single view. How can this aim be achieved?

It can be achieved by protecting the tremendous imagination which children possess and by developing to the full the spirit of contradiction that exists in them. On the whole children are much more intelligent than their teachers. They succumb, and give up their intelligence because they are bullied, or because their teachers get the better of them by emotional means. Children can learn, understand, and keep separate two to three different languages ("children" and by this I mean three to five year olds, *not* eight year olds who were experimented upon quite recently and did not come out too well; why? because they were already loused up by incompetent teaching at an earlier age). Of course, the languages must be introduced in a more interesting way than is usually done. There are marvellous writers in all languages who have told marvellous stories—let us begin our language teaching with *them* and not with "der Hund hat einen Schwanz" and similar inanities. Using stories we may of course also introduce "scientific" accounts, say, of the origin of the world and thus make the children acquainted with science as well. But science must not be given any special position except for pointing out that there are lots of people who believe in it. Later on the stories which have been told will be supplemented with "reasons," where by reasons I mean further accounts of the kind found in the tradition to which the story belongs. And, of course, there will also be contrary reasons. Both reasons and contrary reasons will be told by the experts in the fields and so the young generation becomes acquainted with all kinds of sermons and all types of wayfarers. It becomes acquainted with them, it becomes acquainted with their stories, and every individual can make up his mind which way to go. By now everyone knows that you can earn a lot of money and respect and perhaps even a Nobel Prize by becoming a scientist, so many will become scientists. They will *become* scientists *without having been taken in by the ideology of science,* they will *be* scientists *because they have made a free choice.* But has not much time been wasted on unscientific subjects and will this not detract from their competence once they have become scientists? Not at all! The progress of science, of good science depends on novel ideas and on intellectual freedom: science has very often been advanced by outsiders (remember that Bohr and Einstein regarded themselves as outsiders). Will not many people make the wrong choice and end up in a dead end? Well, that depends on what you mean by a "dead end." Most scientists today are devoid of ideas, full of fear, intent on producing some paltry result so that they can add to the flood of inane papers that now constitutes "scientific progress" in many areas. And, besides, what is more important? To lead a life which one has chosen with open eyes, or to spend one's time in the nervous attempt of avoiding what some not so intelligent people call "dead ends"? Will not the number of scientists decrease so that in the end there is nobody to run our precious laboratories? I do not think so. Given a choice many people may choose science, for a science that is run by free agents looks much more attractive than the science of today which is run by slaves, slaves of institutions and slaves of "reason." And if there is a temporary shortage of scientists the situation may always be remedied by various kinds of incentives. Of course, scientists will not play any predominant role in the society I envisage. They will be more than balanced by magicians, or priests, or astrologers. Such a situation is unbearable for many people, old and young, right and left. Almost all of you have the firm belief that at least *some* kind of truth has been found, that it must be preserved, and that the method of teaching I advocate and the form of society I defend will dilute it and make it finally disappear. You have this firm belief; many of you may even have reasons. *But what you have to consider is that the absence of good contrary reasons is due to a historical accident*; it does *not* lie in the nature of things. Build up the kind of society I recommend and the views you now despise (without knowing them, to be sure) will return in such splendour that you will have to work hard to maintain your own position and will perhaps be entirely unable to do so. You do not believe me? Then look at history. Scientific astronomy was firmly founded on Ptolemy and Aristotle, two of the greatest minds in the history of Western Thought. Who upset their well-argued, empirically adequate and precisely formulated system? Philolaos the mad and antediluvian Pythagorean. How was it that Philolaos could stage such a comeback? Because he found an able defender: Copernicus. Of course, you may follow your intuitions as I am following mine. But remember that your intuitions are the result of your "scientific" training where by science I also mean the science of Karl Marx. My training, or, rather, my non-training, is that of a journalist who is interested in strange and bizarre events. Finally, is it not utterly irresponsible, in the present world situation, with millions of people starving, others enslaved, downtrodden, in abject misery of body and mind, to think luxurious thoughts such as these? Is not freedom of choice a luxury under such circumstances? Is not the flippancy and the humour I want to see combined with the freedom of choice a luxury under such circumstances? Must we not give up all self-indulgence and *act*? Join together, and *act*? This is the most important objection which today is raised against an approach such as the one recommended by me. It has tremendous appeal, it has the appeal of unselfish dedication. Unselfish dedication—to what? Let us see!

We are supposed to give up our selfish inclinations and dedicate ourselves to the liberation of the oppressed. And selfish inclinations are what? They are our wish for maximum liberty of thought in the society in which we live *now,* maximum liberty not only of an abstract kind, but expressed in appropriate institutions and methods of teaching. This wish for concrete intellectual and physical liberty in our own surroundings is to be put aside, for the time being. This assumes, first, that we do not need this liberty for our task. It assumes that we can carry out our task with a mind that is firmly closed to some alternatives. It assumes that the correct way of liberating others *has always been found* and that all that is needed is to carry it out. I am sorry, I cannot accept such doctrinaire self-assurance in such extremely important matters. Does this mean that we cannot act at all? It does not. But it means that *while acting we have to try to realise as much of the freedom I have recommended so that our actions may be corrected in the light of the ideas we get while increasing our freedom.* This will slow us down, no doubt, but are we supposed to charge ahead simply because some people tell us that they have found an explanation for all the misery and an excellent way out of it? Also we want to liberate people not to make them succumb to a new kind of slavery, *but to make them realise their own wishes,* however different these wishes may be from our own. Self-righteous and narrow-minded liberators cannot do this. As a rule they soon impose a slavery that is worse, because more systematic, than the very sloppy slavery they have removed. And as regards humour and flippancy the answer should be obvious. Why would anyone want to liberate anyone else? Surely not because of some *abstract* advantage of liberty but because liberty is the best way to free development *and thus to happiness.* We want to liberate people so that *they can smile.* Shall we be able to do this if we ourselves have forgotten how to smile and are frowning on those who still remember? Shall we then not spread another disease, comparable to the one we want to remove, the disease of puritanical self-righteousness? Do not object that dedication and humour do not go together—Socrates is an excellent example to the contrary. *The hardest task needs the lightest hand or else its completion will not lead to freedom but to a tyranny much worse than the one it replaces.*

4

Why Astrology Is a Pseudoscience
Paul R. Thagard

Most philosophers and historians of science agree that astrology is a pseudo-science, but there is little agreement on *why* it is a pseudoscience. Answers range from matters of verifiability and falsifiability, to questions of progress and Kuhnian normal science, to the different sort of objections raised by a large panel of scientists recently organized by *The Humanist* magazine. Of course there are also Feyerabendian anarchists and others who say that no demarcation of science from pseudoscience is possible. However, I shall pro-pose a complex criterion for distinguishing disciplines as pseudoscientific; this criterion is unlike verificationist and falsificationist attempts in that it intro-duces social and historical features as well as logical ones.

I begin with a brief description of astrology. It would be most unfair to evaluate astrology by reference to the daily horoscopes found in newspapers and popular magazines. These horoscopes deal only with sun signs, whereas a full horoscope makes reference to the "influences" also of the moon and the planets, while also discussing the ascendant sign and other matters.

Astrology divides the sky into twelve regions, represented by the familiar signs of the Zodiac: Aquarius, Libra and so on. The sun sign represents the part of the sky occupied by the sun at the time of birth. For example, anyone born between September 23 and October 22 is a Libran. The ascendant sign, often assumed to be at least as important as the sun sign, represents the part of the sky rising on the eastern horizon at the time of birth, and therefore changes every two hours. To determine this sign, accurate knowledge of the time and place of birth is essential. The moon and the planets (of which there are five or eight depending on whether Uranus, Neptune and Pluto are taken into account) are also located by means of charts on one of the parts of the Zodiac. Each planet is said to exercise an influence in a special sphere of human activity; for example, Mars governs drive, courage and daring, while Venus governs love and artistic endeavor. The immense number of combinations of sun, ascendant, moon and planetary influences allegedly determines human personality, behavior and fate.

Astrology is an ancient practice, and appears to have its origins in Chaldea, thousands of years B.C. By 700 B.C., the Zodiac was established, and a few centuries later the signs of the Zodiac were very similar to current ones. The conquests of Alexander the Great brought astrology to Greece, and the Romans were exposed in turn. Astrology was very popular during the fall of the Republic, with many notables such as Julius Caesar having their horoscopes cast. However, there was opposition from such men as Lucretius and Cicero.

Astrology underwent a gradual codification culminating in Ptolemy's *Tetrabiblos* [20], written in the second century A.D. This work describes in great detail the powers of the sun, moon and planets, and their significance in people's lives. It is still recognized as a fundamental textbook of astrology. Ptolemy took astrology as seriously as he took his famous work in geography and astronomy; this is evident from the introduction to the *Tetrabiblos,* where he discusses two available means of making predictions based on the heavens. The first and admittedly more effective of these concerns the relative movements of the sun, moon and planets, which Ptolemy had already treated in his celebrated *Almagest* [19]. The secondary but still legitimate means of prediction is that in which we use the "natural character" of the aspects of movement of heavenly bodies to "investigate the changes which they bring about in that which they surround" ([20], p. 3). He argues that this method of prediction is possible because of the manifest effects of the sun, moon and planets on the earth, for example on weather and the tides.

The European Renaissance is heralded for the rise of modern science, but occult arts such as astrology and alchemy flourished as well. Arthur Koestler has described Kepler's interest in astrology: not only did astrology provide Kepler with a livelihood, he also pursued it as a serious interest, although he was skeptical of the particular analyses of previous astrologers ([13], pp. 244–248). Astrology was popular both among intellectuals and the general public through the seventeenth century. However, astrology lost most of this popularity in the eighteenth century, when it was attacked by such figures of the Enlightenment as Swift [24] and Voltaire [29]. Only since the 1930's has astrology again gained a huge audience: most people today know at least their sun signs, and a great many believe that the stars and planets exercise an important influence on their lives.

In an attempt to reverse this trend, Bart Bok, Lawrence Jerome and Paul Kurtz drafted in 1975 a statement attacking astrology; the statement was signed by 192 leading scientists, including 19 Nobel prize winners. The statement raises three main issues: astrology originated as part of a magical world view, the planets are too distant for there to be any physical foundation for astrology, and people believe it merely out of longing for comfort ([2], pp. 9f.). None of these objections is ground for condemning astrology as pseudoscience. To show this, I shall briefly discuss articles written by Bok [1] and Jerome [12] in support of the statement.

According to Bok, to work on statistical tests of astrological predictions is a waste of time unless it is demonstrated that astrology has some sort of physical foundation ([1], p. 31). He uses the smallness of gravitational and radiative effects of the stars and planets to suggest that there is no such foundation. He also discusses the psychology of belief in astrology, which is the result of individuals' desperation in seeking solutions to their serious personal problems. Jerome devotes most of his article to the origins of astrology in the magical principle of correspondences. He claims that astrology is a system of magic rather than science, and that it fails "not because of any inherent inaccuracies due to precession or lack of exact knowledge concerning time of birth or conception, but rather because its interpretations and predictions are grounded in the ancients' magical world view" ([12], p. 46). He does however discuss some statistical tests of astrology, which I shall return to below.

These objections do not show that astrology is a pseudoscience. First, origins are irrelevant to scientific status. The alchemical origins of chemistry ([11], pp. 10–18) and the occult beginnings of medicine [8] are as magical as those of astrology, and historians have detected mystical influences in the work of many great scientists, including Newton and Einstein. Hence astrology cannot be condemned simply for the magical origins of its principles. Similarly, the psychology of popular belief is also in itself irrelevant to the status of astrology: people often believe even good theories for illegitimate reasons, and even if most people believe astrology for personal, irrational reasons, good reasons may be available.[1] Finally the lack of a physical foundation hardly marks a theory as unscientific ([22], p. 2). Examples: when Wegener [31] proposed continental drift, no mechanism was known, and a link between smoking and cancer has been established statistically [28] though the details of carcinogenesis remain to be discovered. Hence the objections of Bok, Jerome and Kurtz fail to mark astrology as pseudoscience.

Now we must consider the application of the criteria of verifiability and falsifiability to astrology. Roughly, a theory is said to be verifiable if it is possible to deduce observation statements from it. Then in principle, observations can be used to confirm or disconfirm the theory. A theory is scientific only if it is verifiable. The vicissitudes of the verification principle are too well known to recount here ([9], ch. 4). Attempts by A. J. Ayer to articulate the principle failed either by ruling out most of science as unscientific, or by ruling out nothing. Moreover, the theory/observation distinction has increasingly come into question. All that remains is a vague sense that testability somehow is a mark of scientific theories ([9], ch. 4; [10], pp. 30–32).

Well, astrology *is* vaguely testable. Because of the multitude of influences resting on tendencies rather than laws, astrology is incapable of making precise predictions. Nevertheless, attempts have been made to test the reality of these alleged tendencies, using large scale surveys and statistical evaluation. The pioneer in this area was Michel Gauquelin, who examined the careers and times of birth of 25,000 Frenchmen. Astrology suggests that people born under certain signs or planets are likely to adopt certain occupations: for example, the influence of the warlike planet Mars tends to produce soldiers or athletes, while Venus has an artistic influence. Notably, Gauquelin found *no significant correlation* between careers and either sun sign, moon sign, or ascendant sign. However, he did find some statistically interesting correlations between certain occupations of people and the position of certain planets at the time of their birth ([5], ch. 11; [6]). For example, just as astrology would suggest, there is a greater than chance association of athletes and Mars, and a greater than chance association of scientists and Saturn, where the planet is rising or at its zenith at the moment of the individual's birth.

These findings and their interpretation are highly controversial, as are subsequent studies in a similar vein [7]. Even if correct, they hardly verify astrology, especially considering the negative results found for the most important astrological categories. I have mentioned Gauquelin in order to suggest that through the use of statistical techniques astrology is at least *verifiable*. Hence the verification principle does not mark astrology as pseudoscience.

Because the predictions of astrologers are generally vague, a Popperian would assert that the real problem with astrology is that it is not falsifiable: astrologers can not make predictions which if unfulfilled would lead them to give up their theory. Hence because it is unfalsifiable, astrology is unscientific.

But the doctrine of falsifiability faces serious problems as described by Duhem [4], Quine [21], and Lakatos [15]. Popper himself noticed early that no observation ever guarantees falsification: a theory can always be retained by introducing or modifying auxiliary hypotheses, and even observation statements are not incorrigible ([17], p. 50). Methodological decisions about what can be tampered with are required to block the escape from falsification. However, Lakatos has persuasively argued that making such decision in advance of tests is arbitrary and may often lead to overhasty rejection of a sound theory which *ought* to be saved by anti-falsificationist strategems ([15], pp. 112 ff.). Falsification only occurs when a better theory comes along. Then falsifiability is only a matter of replaceability by another theory, and since astrology is in principle replaceable by another theory, falsifiability provides no criterion for rejecting astrology as pseudoscientific. We saw in the discussion of Gauquelin that astrology can be used to make predictions about statistical regularities, but the nonexistence of these regularities does not falsify astrology; but here astrology does not appear worse than the best of scientific theories, which also resist falsification until alternative theories arise.[2]

Astrology cannot be condemned as pseudoscientific on the grounds proposed by verificationists, falsificationists, or Bok and Jerome. But undoubtedly astrology today faces a great many unsolved problems ([32], ch. 5). One is the negative result found by Gauquelin concerning careers and signs. Another is the problem of the precession of the equinoxes, which astrologers generally take into account when heralding the "Age of Aquarius" but totally neglect when figuring their charts. Astrologers do not always agree on the significance of the three planets, Neptune, Uranus and Pluto, that were discovered since Ptolemy. Studies of twins do not show similarities of personality and fate that astrology would suggest. Nor does astrology make sense of mass disasters, where numerous individuals with very different horoscopes come to similar ends.

But problems such as these do not in themselves show that astrology is either false or pseudoscientific. Even the best theories face unsolved problems throughout their history. To get a criterion demarcating astrology from science, we need to consider it in a wider historical and social context.

A demarcation criterion requires a matrix of three elements: [theory, community, historical context]. Under the first heading, "theory," fall familiar matters of structure, prediction, explanation and problem solving. We might also include the issue raised by Bok and Jerome about whether the theory has a physical foundation. Previous demarcationists have concentrated on this theoretical element, evident in the concern of the verification and falsification principles with prediction. But we have seen that this approach is not sufficient for characterizing astrology as pseudoscientific.

We must also consider the *community* of advocates of the theory, in this case the community of practitioners of astrology. Several questions are important here. First, are the practitioners in agreement on the principles of the theory and on how to go about solving problems which the theory faces? Second, do they care, that is, are they concerned about explaining anomalies and comparing the success of their theory to the record of other theories? Third, are the practitioners actively involved in attempts at confirming and disconfirming their theory?

The question about comparing the success of a theory with that of other theories introduces the third element of the matrix, historical context. The historical work of Kuhn and others has shown that in general a theory is rejected only when (1) it has faced anomalies over a long period of time and (2) it has been challenged by another theory. Hence under the heading of historical context we must consider two factors relevant to demarcation: the record of a theory over time in explaining new facts and dealing with anomalies, and the availability of alternative theories.

We can now propose the following principles of demarcation:

A theory or discipline which purports to be scientific is *pseudoscientific* if and only if:
(1) It has been less progressive than alternative theories over a long period of time, and faces many unsolved problems; but
(2) the community of practitioners makes little attempt to develop the theory towards solutions of the problems, shows no concern for attempts to evaluate the theory in relation to others, and is selective in considering confirmations and disconfirmations.

Progressiveness is a matter of the success of the theory in adding to its set of facts explained and problems solved ([15], p. 118; cf. [26], p. 83).

This principle captures, I believe, what is most importantly unscientific about astrology. First, astrology is dramatically unprogressive, in that it has changed little and has added nothing to its explanatory power since the time of Ptolemy. Second, problems such as the precession of equinoxes are outstanding. Third, there are alternative theories of personality and behavior available: one need not be an uncritical advocate of behaviorist, Freudian, *or* Gestalt theories to see that since the nineteenth century psychological theories have been expanding to deal with many of the phenomena which astrology explains in terms of heavenly influences. The important point is not that any of these psychological theories is established or true, only that they are growing alternatives to a long-static astrology. Fourth and finally, the community of astrologers is generally unconcerned with advancing astrology to deal with outstanding problems or with evaluating the theory in relation to others.[3] For these reasons, my criterion marks astrology as pseudoscientific.

This demarcation criterion differs from those implicit in Lakatos and Kuhn. Lakatos has said that what makes a series of theories constituting a research program scientific is that it is progressive: each theory in the series has greater corroborated content than its predecessor ([15], p. 118). While I agree with Lakatos that progressiveness is a central notion here, it is not sufficient to distinguish science from pseudoscience. We should not brand a nonprogressive discipline as pseudoscientific unless it is being maintained against more progressive alternatives. Kuhn's discussion of astrology focuses on a different aspect of my criterion. He says that what makes astrology unscientific is the absence of the paradigm-dominated puzzle solving activity characteristic of what he calls normal science ([14], p. 9). But as Watkins has suggested, astrologers are in some respects model normal scientists: they concern themselves with solving puzzles at the level of individual horoscopes, unconcerned with the foundations of their general theory or paradigm ([30], p. 32). Hence that feature of normal science does not distinguish science from pseudoscience. What makes astrology pseudoscientific is not that it lacks periods of Kuhnian normal science, but that its proponents adopt uncritical attitudes of "normal" scientists despite the existence of more progressive alternative theories. (Note that I am not agreeing with Popper [18] that Kuhn's normal scientists are unscientific; they can become unscientific only when an alternative paradigm has been developed.) However, if one looks not at the puzzle solving at the level of particular astrological predictions, but at the level of theoretical problems such as the precession of the equinoxes, there is some agreement between my criterion and Kuhn's; astrologers do not have a paradigm-induced confidence about solving theoretical problems.

Of course, the criterion is intended to have applications beyond astrology. I think that discussion would show that the criterion marks as pseudoscientific such practices as witchcraft and pyramidology, while leaving contemporary physics, chemistry and biology unthreatened. The current fad of biorhythms, implausibly based like astrology on date of birth, can not be branded as pseudoscientific because we lack alternative theories giving more detailed accounts of cyclical variations in human beings, although much research is in progress.[4]

One interesting consequence of the above criterion is that a theory can be scientific at one time but pseudoscientific at another. In the time of Ptolemy or even Kepler, astrology had few alternatives in the explanation of human personality and behavior. Existing alternatives were scarcely more sophisticated or corroborated than astrology. Hence astrology should be judged as not pseudoscientific in classical or Renaissance times, even though it is pseudoscientific today. Astrology was not simply a perverse sideline of Ptolemy and Kepler, but part of their scientific activity, even if a physicist involved with astrology today should be looked at askance. Only when the historical and social aspects of science are neglected does it become plausible that pseudoscience is an unchanging category. Rationality is not a property of ideas eternally: ideas, like actions, can be rational at one time but irrational at others. Hence relativizing the science/pseudoscience distinction to historical periods is a desirable result.

But there remains a challenging historical problem. According to my criterion, astrology only became pseudoscientific with the rise of modern psychology in the nineteenth century. But astrology was already virtually excised from scientific circles by the beginning of the eighteenth. How could this be? The simple answer is that a theory can take on the appearance of an unpromising project well before it deserves the label of pseudoscience. The Copernican revolution and the mechanism of Newton, Descartes and Hobbes undermined the plausibility of astrology.[5] Lynn Thorndike [27] has described how the Newtonian theory pushed aside what had been accepted as a universal natural law, that inferiors such as inhabitants of earth are ruled and governed by superiors such as the stars and the planets. William Stahlman [23] has described how the immense growth of science in the seventeenth century contrasted with stagnation of astrology. These developments provided good reason for discarding astrology as a promising pursuit, but they were not yet enough to brand it as pseudoscientific, or even to refute it.

Because of its social aspect, my criterion might suggest a kind of cultural relativism. Suppose there is an isolated group of astrologers in the jungles of South America, practicing their art with no awareness of alternatives. Are we to say that astrology is *for them* scientific? Or, going in the other direction, should we count as alternative theories ones which are available to extraterrestrial beings, or which someday will be conceived? This wide construal of "alternative" would have the result that our best current theories are probably pseudoscientific. These two questions employ, respectively, a too narrow and too broad view of alternatives. By an alternative theory I mean one generally available in the world. This assumes first that there is some kind of communication network to which a community has, or should have, access. Second, it assumes that the onus is on individuals and communities to find out about alternatives. I would argue (perhaps against Kuhn) that this second assumption is a general feature of rationality; it is at least sufficient to preclude ostrichism as a defense against being judged pseudoscientific.

In conclusion, I would like to say why I think the question of what constitutes a pseudoscience is important. Unlike the logical positivists, I am not grinding an anti-metaphysical ax, and unlike Popper, I am not grinding an anti-Freudian or anti-Marxian one.[6] My concern is social: society faces the twin problems of lack of public concern with the advancement of science, and lack of public concern with the important ethical issues now arising in science and technology, for example around the topic of genetic engineering. One reason for this dual lack of concern is the wide popularity of pseudoscience and the occult among the general public. Elucidation of how science differs from pseudoscience is the philosophical side of an attempt to overcome public neglect of genuine science.

NOTES

1. However, astrology would doubtlessly have many fewer supporters if horoscopes tended less toward compliments and pleasant predictions and more toward the kind of analysis included in the following satirical horoscope from the December, 1977, issue of *Mother Jones*: VIRGO (Aug. 23–Sept. 22). You are the logical type and hate disorder. This nit-picking is sickening to your friends. You are cold and unemotional and sometimes fall asleep while making love. Virgos make good bus drivers.

2. For an account of the comparative evaluation of theories, see [26].

3. There appear to be a few exceptions; see [32].

4. The fad of biorhythms, now assuming a place beside astrology in the popular press, must be distinguished from the very interesting work of Frank Brown and others on biological rhythms. For a survey, see [5].

5. Plausibility is in part a matter of a hypothesis being of an appropriate *kind,* and is relevant even to the acceptance of a theory. See [26], p. 90, and [25].

6. On psychoanalysis see [3]. I would argue that Cioffi neglects the question of alternatives to psychoanalysis and the question of its progressiveness.

The author is grateful to Dan Hausman and Elias Baumgarten for comments.

REFERENCES

[1] Bok, Bart J. "A Critical Look at Astrology." In [2]. Pages 21–33.

[2] _____, Jerome, Lawrence E., and Kurtz, Paul. *Objections to Astrology.* Buffalo: Prometheus Books, 1975.

[3] Cioffi, Frank. "Freud and the Idea of a Pseudoscience." In *Explanation in the Behavioral Sciences.* Edited by R. Borger and F. Cioffi. Cambridge: Cambridge University Press, 1970. Pages 471–499.

[4] Duhem, P. *The Aim and Structure of Physical Theory.* Translated by P. Wiener. New York: Atheneum, 1954. (Translated from 2nd edition of *La Théorie Physique: Son Object Sa Structure.* Paris: Marcel Rivière & Cie, 1914.)

[5] Gauquelin, Michel. *The Cosmic Clocks*. Chicago: Henry Regnery, 1967.

[6] _____. *The Scientific Basis of Astrology*. New York: Stein and Day, 1969.

[7] _____. "The Zelen Test of the Mars Effect." *The Humanist* 37 (1977): 30–35.

[8] Haggard, Howard W. *Mystery, Magic, and Medicine*. Garden City: Doubleday, Doran & Company, 1933.

[9] Hempel, Carl. *Aspects of Scientific Explanation*. New York: The Free Press, 1965.

[10] _____. *Philosophy of Natural Science*. Englewood Cliffs: Prentice-Hall, 1966.

[11] Ihde, Aaron, J. *The Development of Modern Chemistry*. New York: Harper and Row, 1964.

[12] Jerome, Lawrence E. "Astrology: Magic or Science?" In [2]. Pages 37–62.

[13] Koestler, Arthur. *The Sleepwalkers*. Harmondsworth: Penguin, 1964.

[14] Kuhn, T. S. "Logic of Discovery or Psychology of Research." In [16]. Pages 1–23.

[15] Lakatos, Imre. "Falsification and the Methodology of Scientific Research Programmes." In [16]. Pages 91–195.

[16] _____ and Musgrave, Alan, eds. *Criticism and the Growth of Knowledge*. Cambridge: Cambridge University Press, 1970.

[17] Popper, Karl. *The Logic of Scientific Discovery*. London: Hutchinson, 1959. (Originally published as *Logik der Forschung*. Vienna: J. Springer, 1935.)

[18] _____. "Normal Science and Its Dangers." In [16]. Pages 51–58.

[19] Ptolemy. *The Almagest (The Mathematical Composition)*. (As printed in Hutchins, Robert Maynard, ed. *Great Books of the Western World*, Volume 16. Chicago. Encyclopedia Britannica, Inc., 1952. Pages 1–478.)

[20] _____. *Tetrabiblos*. Edited and translated by F. E. Robbins. Cambridge: Harvard University Press, 1940.

[21] Quine, W. V. O. "Two Dogmas of Empiricism." In *From a Logical Point of View*. New York: Harper & Row, 1963. Pages 20–46. (Originally published in *The Philosophical Review* 60 (1951): 20–43.)

[22] Sagan, Carl. "Letter." *The Humanist* 36 (1976): 2.

[23] Stahlman, William D. "Astrology in Colonial America: An Extended Query." *William and Mary Quarterly* 13 (1956): 551–563.

[24] Swift, Jonathan. "The Partridge Papers." In *The Prose Works of Jonathan Swift*, Volume 2. Oxford: Basil Blackwell, 1940–1968. Pages 139–170.

[25] Thagard, Paul R. "The Autonomy of a Logic of Discovery." Forthcoming in the *Festschrift* for T. A. Goudge.

[26] _____. "The Best Explanation: Criteria for Theory Choice." *Journal of Philosophy* 75 (1978): 76–92.

[27] Thorndike, Lynn. "The True Place of Astrology in the History of Science." *Isis* 46 (1955): 273–278.

[28] U.S. Department of Health, Education and Welfare. *Smoking and Health: Report of the Advisory Committee to the Surgeon General of the Public Health Service.* Washington, D.C.: U.S. Government Printing Office, 1964.

[29] Voltaire. "Astrologie" and "Astronomie." *Dictionnaire Philosophique.* In *Oeuvres Complètes de Voltaire,* Volume XVII. Paris: Garnier Frères, 1878–1885. Pages 446–453.

[30] Watkins, J. W. N. "Against 'Normal Science.'" In [16]. Pages 25–37.

[31] Wegener, Alfred. "Die Entstehung der Kontinente." *Petermann's Geographische Mitteilung* 58 (1912): 185–195, 235–256, 305–309.

[32] West, J. A. and Toonder, J. G. *The Case for Astrology.* Harmondsworth: Penguin, 1973.

5

Believing Where We Cannot Prove

Philip Kitcher

I. Opening Moves

Simple distinctions come all too easily. Frequently we open the way for later puzzlement by restricting the options we take to be available. So, for example, in contrasting science and religion, we often operate with a simple pair of categories. On one side there is science, proof, and certainty; on the other, religion, conjecture, and faith.

The opening lines of Tennyson's *In Memoriam* offer an eloquent statement of the contrast:

> Strong Son of God, immortal love,
> Whom we, that have not seen Thy face,
> By faith, and faith alone, embrace,
> Believing where we cannot prove.

A principal theme of Tennyson's great poem is his struggle to maintain faith in the face of what seems to be powerful scientific evidence. Tennyson had read a popular work by Robert Chambers, *Vestiges of the Natural History of Creation,* and he was greatly troubled by the account of the course of life on earth that the book contains. *In Memoriam* reveals a man trying to believe where he cannot prove, a man haunted by the thought that the proofs may be against him.

Like Tennyson, contemporary Creationists accept the traditional contrast between science and religion. But where Tennyson agonized, they attack. While they are less eloquent, they are supremely confident of their own solution. They open their onslaught on evolutionary theory by denying that it is a science. In *The Troubled Waters of Evolution,* Henry Morris characterizes

55

evolutionary theory as maintaining that large amounts of time are required for evolution to produce "new kinds." As a result, we should not expect to see such "new kinds" emerging. Morris comments, "Creationists in turn insist that this belief is not scientific evidence but only a statement of faith. The evolutionist seems to be saying, Of course, we cannot really *prove* evolution, since this requires ages of time, and so, therefore, you should accept it as a proved fact of science! Creationists regard this as an odd type of logic, which would be entirely unacceptable in any other field of science" (Morris 1974b, 16). David Watson makes a similar point in comparing Darwin with Galileo: "So here is the difference between Darwin and Galileo: Galileo set a demonstrable *fact* against a few words of Bible poetry which the Church at that time had understood in an obviously naive way; Darwin set an unprovable *theory* against eleven chapters of straightforward history which cannot be reinterpreted in any satisfactory way" (Watson 1975, 46).

The idea that evolution is conjecture, faith, or "philosophy" pervades Creationist writings (Morris 1974a, 4–8; Morris 1974b, 22, 172; Wysong 1976, 43–45; Gish 1979, 11–13, 26, 186; Wilder-Smith 1981, 7–8). It is absolutely crucial to their case for equal time for "scientific" Creationism. This ploy has succeeded in winning important adherents to the Creationist cause. As he prepared to defend Arkansas law 590, Attorney General Steven Clark echoed the Creationist judgment. "Evolution," he said, "is just a theory." Similar words have been heard in Congress. William Dannemeyer, a congressman from California, introduced a bill to limit funding to the Smithsonian with the following words: "If the theory of evolution is just that—a theory— and if that theory can be regarded as a religion . . . then it occurs to this Member that other Members might prefer it not to be given exclusive or top billing in our Nation's most famous museum but equal billing or perhaps no billing at all."

In their attempt to show that evolution is not science, Creationists receive help from the least likely sources. Great scientists sometimes claim that certain facts about the past evolution of organisms are "demonstrated" or "indubitable" (Simpson 1953, 70, 371; also Mayr 1976, 9). But Creationists also can (and do) quote scientists who characterize evolution as "dogma" and contend that there is no conclusive proof of evolutionary theory (Matthews 1972, xi; Birch and Ehrlich 1967, 349; quoted in Gish 1979, 15–16; similar passages are quoted in Morris, 1974a, 6–8, and in Wysong 1976, 44). Evolution is not part of science because, as evolutionary biologists themselves concede, science demands proof, and, as other biologists point out, proof of evolution is not forthcoming.

The rest of the Creationist argument flows easily. We educate our children in evolutionary theory as if it were a proven fact. We subscribe officially, in our school system, to one faith—an atheistic, materialistic faith—ignoring rival beliefs. Antireligious educators deform the minds of children, warping them to accept as gospel a doctrine that has no more scientific support than the true Gospel. The very least that should be done is to allow for both alternatives to be presented.

We should reject the Creationists' gambit. Eminent scientists notwithstanding, science is not a body of demonstrated truths. Virtually all of science is an exercise in believing where we cannot prove. Yet, scientific conclusions are not embraced by faith alone. Tennyson's dichotomy was too simple.

II. Inconclusive Evidence

Sometimes we seem to have conclusive reasons for accepting a statement as true. It is hard to doubt that 2 + 2 = 4. If, unlike Lord Kelvin's ideal mathematician, we do not find it obvious that

$$\int_{-\infty}^{+\infty} e^{-x^2} \, dx = \sqrt{\pi}.$$

at least the elementary parts of mathematics appear to command our agreement. The direct evidence of our senses seems equally compelling. If I see the pen with which I am writing, holding it firmly in my unclouded view, how can I doubt that it exists? The talented mathematician who has proved a theorem and the keen-eyed witness of an episode furnish our ideals of certainty in knowledge. What they tell us can be engraved in stone, for there is no cause for worry that it will need to be modified.

Yet, in another mood, one that seems "deeper" or more "philosophical," skeptical doubts begin to creep in. Is there really anything of which we are so certain that later evidence could not give us reason to change our minds? Even when we think about mathematical proof, can we not imagine that new discoveries may cast doubt on the cogency of our reasoning? (The history of mathematics reveals that sometimes what seems for all the world like a proof may have a false conclusion.) Is it not possible that the most careful observer may have missed something? Or that the witness brought preconceptions to the observation that subtly biased what was reported? Are we not *always* fallible?

I am mildly sympathetic to the skeptic's worries. Complete certainty is best seen as an ideal toward which we strive and that is rarely, if ever, attained. Conclusive evidence always eludes us. Yet even if we ignore skeptical complaints and imagine that we are sometimes lucky enough to have conclusive reasons for accepting a claim as true, we should not include scientific reasoning among our paradigms of proof. Fallibility is the hallmark of science.

This point should not be so surprising. The trouble is that we frequently forget it in discussing contemporary science. When we turn to the history of science, however, our fallibility stares us in the face. The history of the natural sciences is strewn with the corpses of intricately organized theories, each of which had, in its day, considerable evidence in its favor. When we look at the confident defenders of those theories we should see anticipations of ourselves. The eighteenth-century scientists who believed that heat is a "subtle fluid," the atomic theorists who maintained that water molecules are compounded out of one atom of hydrogen and one of oxygen, the biochemists who identified protein as the genetic material, and the geologists who thought that continents cannot move were neither unintelligent nor ill informed. Given the evidence available to them, they were eminently reasonable in drawing their conclusions. History proved them wrong. It did not show that they were unjustified.

Why is science fallible? Scientific investigation aims to disclose the general principles that govern the workings of the universe. These principles are not intended merely to summarize what some select groups of humans have witnessed. Natural science is not just natural history. It is vastly more ambitious. Science offers us laws that are supposed to hold universally, and it advances claims about things that are beyond our power to observe. The nuclear physicist who sets down the law governing a particular type of radioactive decay is attempting to state a truth that holds throughout the entire cosmos and also to describe the behavior of things that we cannot even see. Yet, of necessity, the physicist's ultimate evidence is highly restricted. Like the rest of us, scientists are confined to a relatively small region of space and time and equipped with limited and imperfect senses.

How is science possible at all? How are we able to have any confidence about the distant regions of the cosmos and the invisible realm that lies behind the surfaces of ordinary things? The answer is complicated. Natural science follows intricate and ingenious procedures for fathoming the secrets of the universe. Scientists devise ways of obtaining especially revealing evidence. They single out some of the things we are able to see as crucial clues to the way that nature works. These clues are used to answer questions that cannot be addressed by direct observation. Scientific theories, even those that are most respected and most successful, rest on indirect arguments from the observational evidence. New discoveries can always call those arguments into question, showing scientists that the observed data should be understood in a different way, that they have misread their evidence.

But scientists often forget the fallibility of their enterprise. This is not just absentmindedness or wishful thinking. During the heyday of a scientific theory, so much evidence may support the theory, so many observational clues may seem to attest to its truth, that the idea that it could be overthrown appears ludicrous. In addition, the theory may provide ways of identifying quickly what is inaccessible to our unaided senses. Electron microscopes and cloud chambers are obvious examples of those extensions of our perceptual system that theories can inspire. Trained biochemists will talk quite naturally of seeing large molecules, and it is easy to overlook the fact that they are presupposing a massive body of theory in describing what they "see." If that theory were to be amended, even in subtle ways, then the descriptions of the "observed characteristics" of large molecules might have to be given up. Nor should we pride ourselves that the enormous successes of contemporary science secure us against future amendments. No theory in the history of science enjoyed a more spectacular career than Newton's mechanics. Yet Newton's ideas had to give way to Einstein's.

When practicing scientists are reminded of these straightforward points, they frequently adopt what the philosopher George Berkeley called a "forlorn skepticism." From the idea of science as certain and infallible, they jump to a cynical description of their endeavors. Science is sometimes held to be a game played with arbitrary rules, an irrational acceptance of dogma, an enterprise based ultimately on faith. Once we have appreciated the fallibility of natural science and recognized its sources, we can move beyond the simple opposition of proof and faith. Between these extremes lies the vast field of cases in which we believe something on the basis of good—even excellent—but inconclusive evidence.

If we want to emphasize the fact that what scientists believe today may have to be revised in the light of observations made tomorrow, then we can describe all our science as "theory." But the description should not confuse us. To concede that evolutionary biology is a theory is not to suppose that there are alternatives to it that are equally worthy of a place in our curriculum. All theories are revisable, but not all theories are equal. Even though our present evidence does not *prove* that evolutionary biology—or quantum physics, or plate tectonics, or any other theory—is true, evolutionary biologists will maintain that the present evidence is overwhelmingly in favor of their theory and overwhelmingly against its supposed rivals. Their enthusiastic assertions that evolution is a proven fact can be charitably understood as claims that the (admittedly inconclusive) evidence we have for evolutionary theory is as good as we ever obtain for any theory in any field of science.

Hence the Creationist cry for a quick Fools' Mate can easily be avoided. Creationists attempt to draw a line between evolutionary biology and the rest of science by remarking that large-scale evolution cannot be observed. This tactic fails. Large-scale evolution is no more inaccessible to observation than nuclear reactions or the molecular composition of water. For the Creationists to succeed in divorcing evolutionary biology from the rest of science, they need to argue that evolutionary theory is less well supported by the evidence than are theories in, for example, physics and chemistry. It will come as no surprise to learn that they try to do this. To assess the merits of their arguments we need a deeper understanding of the logic of inconclusive justification. We shall begin with a simple and popular idea: Scientific theories earn our acceptance by making successful predictions.

III. Predictive Success

Imagine that somebody puts forward a new theory about the origins of hay fever. The theory makes a number of startling predictions concerning connections that we would not have thought worth investigating. For example, it tells us that people who develop hay fever invariably secrete a particular substance in certain fatty tissues and that anyone who eats rhubarb as a child never develops hay fever. The theory predicts things that initially appear fantastic. Suppose that we check up on these predictions and find that they are borne out by clinical tests. Would we not begin to believe—and believe reasonably—that the theory was *at least* on the right track?

This example illustrates a pattern of reasoning that is familiar in the history of science. Theories win support by producing claims about what can be observed, claims that would not have seemed plausible prior to the advancement of the theory, but that are in fact found to be true when we make the appropriate observations. A classic (real) example is Pascal's confirmation of Torricelli's hypothesis that we live at the bottom of an ocean of air that presses down upon us. Pascal reasoned that if Torricelli's hypothesis were true, then air pressure should decrease at higher altitudes (because at higher altitudes we are closer to the "surface" of the atmosphere, so that the length of the column of air that presses down is shorter). Accordingly, he sent his brother-in-law to the top of a mountain to make some barometric measurements. Pascal's clever working out of the observational predictions of Torricelli's theory led to a dramatic predictive success for the theory.

The idea of predictive success has encouraged a popular picture of science. (We shall see later that this picture, while popular, is not terribly accurate.) Philosophers sometimes regard a theory as a collection of claims or statements. Some of these statements offer generalizations about the features of particular, recondite things (genes, atoms, gravitational force, quasars, and the like). These statements are used to infer statements whose truth or falsity can be decided by observation. (This appears to be just what Pascal did.) Statements belonging to this second group are called the *observational consequences* of the theory. Theories are supported when we find that their observational consequences (those that we have checked) are true. The credentials of a theory are damaged if we discover that some of its observational consequences are false.

We can make the idea more precise by being clearer about the inferences involved. Those who talk of inferring observational predictions from our theories think that we can *deduce* from the statements of the theory, and from those statements alone, some predictions whose accuracy we can check by direct observation. Deductive inference is well understood. The fundamental idea of deductive inference is this: We say that a statement S is a valid deductive consequence of a group of statements if and only if it is *impossible* that all the statements in the group should be true and that S should be false; alternatively, S is a valid deductive consequence (or, more simply, a valid consequence) of a group of statements if and only if it would be self-contradictory to assert all the statements in the group and to deny S.

It will be helpful to make the idea of valid consequence more familiar with some examples. Consider the statements "All lovers of baseball dislike George Steinbrenner" and "George Steinbrenner loves baseball." The statement "George Steinbrenner dislikes himself" is a deductively valid consequence of these two statements. For it is impossible that the first two should be true and the third false. However, in claiming that this is a case of deductively valid consequence, we do not commit ourselves to maintaining that *any* of the statements is true. (Perhaps there are some ardent baseball fans who admire Steinbrenner. Perhaps Steinbrenner himself has no time for the game.) What deductive validity means is that the truth of the first two statements would guarantee the truth of the third; that is, *if* the first two *were* true, then the third would have to be true.

Another example will help rule out other misunderstandings. Here are two statements: "Shortly after noon on January 1, 1982, in the Oval Office, a jelly bean was released from rest more than two feet above any surface"; "Shortly after noon on January 1, 1982, in the Oval Office, a jelly bean fell." Is the second statement a deductively valid consequence of the first? You might think that it is, on the grounds that it would have been impossible for the unfortunate object to have been released and not to have fallen. In one sense this is correct, but that is not the sense of impossibility that deductive logicians have in mind. Strictly speaking, it is not *impossible* for the jelly bean to have been released without falling; we can imagine, for example, that the law of gravity might suddenly cease to operate. We do not *contradict* ourselves when we assert that the jelly bean was released but deny that it fell; we simply refuse to accept the law of gravity (or some other relevant physical fact).

Thus, *S* is a deductively valid consequence of a group of statements if and only if there is *absolutely no possibility* that all the statements in the group should be true and *S* should be false. This conception allows us to state the popular view of theory and prediction more precisely. Theories are collections of statements. The observational consequences of a theory are statements that have to be true if the statements belonging to the theory are all true. These observational consequences also have to be statements whose truth or falsity can be ascertained by direct observation.

My initial discussion of predictive success presented the rough idea that, when we find the observational consequences of a theory to be true, our findings bring credit to the theory. Conversely discovery that some observational consequences of a theory are false was viewed as damaging. We can now make the second point much more precise. Any theory that has a false observational consequence must contain some false statement (or statements). For if all the statements in the theory were true, then, according to the standard definitions of *deductive validity* and *observational consequence,* any observational consequence would also have to be true. Hence, if a theory is found to have a false observational consequence, we must conclude that one or more statements of the theory is false.

This means that theories can be conclusively falsified, through the discovery that they have false observational consequences. Some philosophers, most notably Sir Karl Popper (Popper 1959; 1963), have taken this point to have enormous significance for our understanding of science. According to Popper, the essence of a scientific theory is that it should be *falsifiable.* That is, if the theory is false, then it must be possible to show that it is false. Now, if a theory has utterly no observational consequences, it would be extraordinarily difficult to unmask that theory as false. So, to be a genuine scientific theory, a group of statements must have observational consequences. It is important to realize that Popper is not suggesting that every good theory must be false. The difference between being falsifiable and being false is like the difference between being vulnerable and actually being hurt. A good scientific theory should not be false. Rather, it must have observational consequences that could reveal the theory as mistaken if the experiments give the wrong results.

While these ideas about theory testing may seem strange in their formal attire, they emerge quite frequently in discussions of science. They also find their way into the creation-evolution debate.

IV. Predictive Failure

From the beginning, evolutionary theory has been charged with just about every possible type of predictive failure. Critics of the theory have argued that (a) the theory makes no predictions (it is unfalsifiable and so fails Popper's criterion for science), (b) the theory makes false predictions (it is falsified), (c) the theory does not make the kinds of predictions it ought to make (the observations and experiments that evolutionary theorists undertake have no bearing on the theory). Many critics, including several Creationists (Morris 1974a; Gish 1979; Wysong 1976), manage to advance all these objections in the same work. This is somewhat surprising, since points (a) and (b) are, of course, mutually contradictory.

The first objection is vitally important to the Creationist cause. Their opponents frequently insist that Creationism fails the crucial test for a scientific theory. The hypothesis that all kinds of organisms were separately fashioned by some "originator" is unfalsifiable (Gould 1981b). Creationists retort that they can play the same game equally well. *Any* hypothesis about the origins of life, including that advanced by evolutionary theory, is not subject to falsification. Hence we cannot justify a decision to teach evolutionary theory and not to teach Creationism by appealing to the Popperian criterion for genuine science.

The allegation that evolutionary theory fails to make any predictions is a completely predictable episode in any Creationist discussion of evolution. Often the point is made by appeal to the authority of Popper. Here are two sample passages:

> The outstanding philosopher of science, Karl Popper, though himself an evolutionist, pointed out cogently that evolution, no less than creation, is untestable and thus unprovable. (Morris 1974b, 80)

> Thus, for a theory to qualify as a scientific theory, it must be supported by events, processes or properties which can be observed, and the theory must be useful in predicting the outcome of future

natural phenomena or laboratory experiments. An additional limitation usually imposed is that the theory must be capable of falsification. That is, it must be possible to conceive some experiment, the failure of which would disprove the theory.

It is on the basis of such criteria that most evolutionists insist that creation be refused consideration as a possible explanation for origins. Creation has not been witnessed by human observers, it cannot be tested experimentally, and as a theory it is nonfalsifiable.

The general theory of evolution also fails to meet all three of these criteria, however. (Gish 1979, 13)

These passages, and many others (for example, Morris 1974a, 150; Morris 1975, 9; Moore 1974, 9; Wilder-Smith 1981, 133), draw on the picture of science sketched above. It is not clear that the Creationists really understand the philosophical views that they attempt to apply. Gish presents the most articulate discussion of the falsifiability criterion. Yet he muddles the issue by describing falsifiability as an "additional limitation" beyond predictive power. (The previous section shows that theories that make predictions are automatically falsifiable.) Nevertheless, the Creationist challenge is a serious one, and, if it could not be met, evolutionary theory would be in trouble.

Creationists buttress their charge of unfalsifiability with further objections. They are aware that biologists frequently look as though they are engaged in observations and experiments. Creationists would allow that researchers in biology sometimes make discoveries. What they deny is that the discoveries support evolutionary theory. They claim that laboratory manipulations fail to teach us about evolution in nature: "Even if modern scientists should ever actually achieve the artificial creation of life from non-life, or of higher kinds from lower kinds, in the laboratory, this would not *prove* in any way that such changes did, or even could, take place in the past by random natural processes" (Morris 1974a, 6). The standards of evidence to be applied to evolutionary biology have suddenly been raised. In this area of inquiry, it is not sufficient that a theory yield observational consequences whose truth or falsity can be decided in the laboratory. Creationists demand special kinds of predictions, and will dismiss as irrelevant any laboratory evidence that evolutionary theorists produce. [In this way, they try to defend point (c).]

Oddly enough, however, the most popular supplement to the charge that evolutionary theory is unfalsifiable is a determined effort to falsify it [point (b)]. Creationists cannot resist arguing that the theory is actually falsified. Some of them, Morris and Gish, for example, recognize the tension between the two objections. They try to paper over the problem by claiming that evolutionary theory and the Creationist account are both "models." Each "model" would "naturally" incline us to expect certain observational results. A favorite Creationist ploy is to draw up tables in which these "predictions" are compared. When we look at the tables we find that the evolutionary expectations are confounded. By contrast, the Creationist "model" leads us to anticipate features of the world that are actually there. Faced with such adverse results, the benighted evolutionary biologist is portrayed as struggling to "explain away" the findings by whatever means he can invent.

Morris's own practice of this form of evolution baiting can serve as an example. Morris constructs a table (1974a, 12; see below and facing page) whose function is to indicate "The predictions that would probably be made in several important categories (1974a, 12). Morris admits magnanimously that "these primary models may be modified by secondary [additional] assumptions to fit certain conditions. For example, the basic evolution model may be extended to include harmful, as well as beneficial, mutations, but this is not a natural prediction of the basic concept of evolution" (1974a, 13). The idea that the "natural predictions" of the evolution "model" are at odds with the phenomena is used to suggest that evolutionary biologists are forced to desperate measures to protect their "faith." As Morris triumphantly concludes, "the data must be *explained* by the evolutionist, but they are *predicted* by the creationist" (1974a, 13).

The careful reader ought to be puzzled. If Morris really thinks that evolutionary theory has been falsified, why does he not say so? Of course, he would have to admit that the theory is falsifiable. Seemingly, however, a staunch Creationist should be delighted to abandon a relatively abstruse point about unfalsifiability in favor of a clear-cut refutation. The truth of the matter is that the alleged refutations fail. No evolutionary theorist will grant that (for example) the theory predicts that the fossil record should show "innumerable transitions." Instead, paleontologists will point out that we can deduce conclusions about what we should find in the rocks only if we make assumptions about the fossilization process. Morris makes highly dubious assumptions, hails them as "natural," and then announces that the "natural predictions" of the theory have been defeated.

(This example suggests a method for coping with Morris's "table of natural predictions." Each of these predictions can be deduced from evolutionary theory only if the theory is extended by adding extra assumptions. Morris saddles evolutionary theory with faulty additional claims. These are the source of the false predictions. Later, I shall show this in detail for some of Morris's "natural predictions" and the similar difficulties raised by other Creationists [Gish 1979, 53–54; Wysong 1975, 421–426].)

Category	Evolution Model	Creation Model
Structure of Natural Law	Constantly changing	Invariable
Galactic Universe	Galaxies changing	Galaxies constant
Structure of Stars	Stars changing into other types	Stars unchanged
Other Heavenly Bodies	Building up	Breaking down

Types of Rock Formations	Different in different "Ages"	Similar in all "Ages"
Appearance of Life	Life evolving from non-life	Life only from life
Array of Organisms	Continuum of Organisms	Distinct Kinds of Organisms
Appearance of Kinds of Life	New Kinds Appearing	No New Kinds Appearing
Mutations in Organisms	Beneficial	Harmful
Natural Selection	Creative Process	Conservative Process
Age of Earth	Extremely Old	Probably Young
Fossil Record	Innumerable Transitions	Systematic Gaps
Appearance of Man	Ape-Human Intermediates	No Ape-Human Intermediates
Nature of Man	Quantitatively Superior to Animals	Qualitatively Distinct from Animals
Origin of Civilization	Slow and Gradual	Contemporaneous with Man

To make a serious assessment of these broad Creationist charges, we must begin by asking some basic methodological questions. We cannot decide whether evolutionary biologists are guilty of trying to save their theory by using ad hoc assumptions (new and implausible claims dreamed up for the sole purpose of protecting some cherished ideas) unless we have some way of deciding when a proposal is ad hoc. Similarly, we cannot make a reasoned response to the charge that laboratory experiments are irrelevant, or to the fundamental objection that evolutionary theory is unfalsifiable, unless we have a firmer grasp on the relation between theory and evidence.

V. Naive Falsificationism

The time has come to tell a dreadful secret. While the picture of scientific testing sketched above continues to be influential among scientists, it has been shown to be seriously incorrect. (To give my profession its due, historians and philosophers of science have been trying to let this particular cat out of the bag for at least thirty years. See, for example, Hempel 1941; Quine 1952.) Important work in the history of science has made it increasingly clear that no major scientific theory has ever exemplified the relation between theory and evidence that the traditional model presents.

What is wrong with the old picture? Answer: Either it debars most of what we take to be science from counting as science or it allows virtually anything to count. On the traditional view of "theory," textbook cases of scientific theories turn out to be unfalsifiable. Suppose we identify Newtonian mechanics with Newton's three laws of motion plus the law of gravitation. What observational consequences can we deduce from these four statements? You might think that we could deduce that if, as the (undoubtedly apocryphal) story alleges, an apple became detached from a branch above where Newton was sitting, the apple would have fallen on his head. But this does not follow at all. To see why not, it is only necessary to recognize that the failure of this alleged prediction would not force us to deny any of the four statements of the theory. All we need do is assume that some other forces were at work that overcame the force of gravity and caused the apple to depart from its usual trajectory. So, given this simple way of applying Popper's criterion, Newtonian mechanics would be unfalsifiable. The same would go for any other scientific theory. Hence none of what we normally take to be science would count as science. (I might note that Popper is aware of this problem and has suggestions of his own as to how it should be overcome. However, what concerns me here are the *applications* of Popper's ideas, that are made by Creationists, as well as by scientists in their professional debates.)

The example of the last paragraph suggests an obvious remedy. Instead of thinking about theories in the simple way just illustrated, we might take them to be far more elaborate. Newton's laws (the three laws of motion and the law of gravitation) are *embedded* in Newtonian mechanics. They form the core of the theory, but do not constitute the whole of it. Newtonian mechanics also contains supplementary assumptions, telling us, for example, that for certain special systems the effects of forces other than gravity are negligible. This more elaborate collection of statements *does* have observational consequences and *is* falsifiable.

But the remedy fails. Imagine that we attempt to expose some self-styled spiritual teacher as an overpaid fraud. We try to point out that the teacher's central message—"Quietness is wholeness in the center of stillness"—is unfalsifiable. The teacher cheerfully admits that, taken by itself, this profound doctrine yields no observational consequences. He then points out that, by themselves, the central statements of scientific theories are also incapable of generating observational consequences. Alas, if all that is demanded is that a doctrine be embedded in a group of statements with observational consequences, our imagined guru will easily slither off the hook. He replies, "You have forgotten that my doctrine has many other claims. For example, I believe that if quietness is wholeness in the center of stillness, then flowers bloom in the spring, bees gather pollen, and blinkered defenders of so-called science raise futile objections to the world's spiritual benefactors. You will see that these three predictions are borne out by experience. Of course, there are countless others. Perhaps when you see how my central message yields so much evident truth, you will recognize the wealth of evidence behind my claim. Quietness is wholeness in the center of stillness."

More formally, the trouble is that *any* statement can be coupled with other statements to produce observational consequences. Given any doctrine *D*, and any statement *O* that records the results of an observation, we can enable *D* to "predict" *O* by adding the extra assumption, "If *D*, then *O*." (In the example, *D* is "Quietness is wholeness in the center of stillness"; examples of *O* would be statements describing the blooming of particular flowers in the spring, the pollen gathering of specific bees, and so forth.)

The falsifiability criterion adopted from Popper—which I shall call the *naive falsificationist* criterion—is hopelessly flawed. It runs aground on a fundamental fact about the relation between theory and prediction: On their own, individual scientific laws, or the small groups of laws that are often identified as theories, do not have observational consequences. This crucial point about theories was first understood by the great historian and philosopher of science Pierre Duhem. Duhem saw clearly that individual scientific claims do not, and cannot, confront the evidence one by one. Rather, in his picturesque phrase, "Hypotheses are tested in bundles." Besides ruling out the possibility of testing an individual scientific theory (read, small group of laws), Duhem's insight has another startling consequence. We can only test relatively large bundles of claims. What this means is that when our experiments go awry we are not logically compelled to select any particular claim as the culprit. We can always save a cherished hypothesis from refutation by rejecting (however implausibly) one of the other members of the bundle. Of course, this is exactly what I did in the illustration of Newton and the apple above. Faced with disappointing results, I suggested that we could abandon the (tacit) additional claim that no large forces besides gravity were operating on the apple.

Creationists wheel out the ancient warhorse of naive falsificationism so that they can bolster their charge that evolutionary theory is not a science. The (very) brief course in deductive logic plus the whirlwind tour through naive falsificationism and its pitfalls enable us to see what is at the bottom of this seemingly important criticism. Creationists can appeal to naive falsificationism to show evolution is not a science. But, given the traditional picture of theory evidence I have sketched, one can appeal to naive falsificationism to show that *any* science is not a science. So, as with the charge that evolutionary change is unobservable, Creationists have again failed to find some "fault" of evolution not shared with every other science. (And, as we shall see, Creationists like some sciences, especially thermodynamics.) Consistent application of naive falsificationism can show that anybody's favorite science (whether it be quantum physics, molecular biology, or whatever) is not science. Of course, what this shows is that the naive falsificationist criterion is a very poor test of genuine science. To be fair, this point can cut both ways. Scientists who charge that "scientific" Creationism is unfalsifiable are not insulting the theory as much as they think.

VI. Successful Science

Despite the inadequacies of naive falsificationism, there is surely something right in the idea that a science can succeed only if it can fail. An invulnerable "science" would not be science at all. To achieve a more adequate understanding of how a science can succeed and how it runs the risk of failure, let us look at one of the most successful sciences and at a famous episode in its development.

Newtonian celestial mechanics is one of the star turns in the history of science. Among its numerous achievements were convincing explanations of the orbits of most of the known planets. Newton and his successors viewed the solar system as a collection of bodies subject only to gravitational interactions; they used the law of gravitation and the laws of motion to compute the orbits. (Bodies whose effects were negligible in any particular case would be disregarded. For example, the gravitational attraction due to Mercury would not be considered in working out the orbit of Saturn.) The results tallied beautifully with astronomical observations. But one case proved difficult. The outermost known planet, Uranus, stubbornly followed an orbit that diverged from the best computations. By the early nineteenth century it was clear that something was wrong. Either astronomers erred in treating the solar system as a Newtonian gravitational system or there was some particular difficulty in applying the general method to Uranus.

Perhaps the most naive of falsificationists would have recommended that the central claim of Newtonian mechanics—the claim that the solar system is a Newtonian gravitational system—be abandoned. But there was obviously a more sensible strategy. Astronomers faced one problematical planet, and they asked themselves what made Uranus so difficult. Two of them, John Adams and Urbain Leverrier, came up with an answer. They proposed (independently) that there was a hitherto unobserved planet beyond Uranus. They computed the orbit of the postulated planet and demonstrated that the anomalies of the motion of Uranus could be explained if a planet followed this path. There was a straightforward way to test their proposal. Astronomers began to look for the new planet. Within a few years, the planet—Neptune—was found.

I will extract several morals from this success story. The first concerns an issue we originally encountered in Morris's "table of natural predictions:" What is the proper use of auxiliary hypotheses? Adams and Leverrier saved the central claim of Newtonian celestial mechanics by offering an auxiliary hypothesis. They maintained that there were more things in the heavens that had been dreamed of in previous natural philosophy. The anomalies in the orbit of Uranus could be explained on the assumption of an extra planet. Adams and Leverrier worked out the exact orbit of that planet so that they could provide a detailed account of the perturbations—and so that they could tell their fellow astronomers where to look for Neptune. Thus, their auxiliary hypothesis was *independently testable*. The evidence for Neptune's existence was not just the anomalous motion of Uranus. The hypothesis could be checked independently of any assumptions about Uranus or about the correctness of Newtonian celestial mechanics—by making telescopic observations.

Since hypotheses are always tested in bundles, this method of checking presupposed other assumptions, in particular, the optical principles that justify the use of telescopes. The crucial point is that, while hypotheses are always tested in bundles, they can be tested in *different* bundles. An auxiliary hypothesis ought to be testable independently of the particular problem it is introduced to solve, independently of the theory it is designed to save.

While it is obvious in retrospect—indeed it was obvious at the time— that the problem with Uranus should not be construed as "falsifying" celestial mechanics, it is worth asking explicitly why scientists should have clung to Newton's theory in the face of this difficulty. The answer is not just that nothing succeeds like success, and that Newton's theory had been strikingly successful in calculating the orbits of the other planets. The crucial point concerns the way in which Newton's successes had been achieved. Newton was no opportunist, using one batch of assumptions to cope with Mercury, and then moving on to new devices to handle Venus. Celestial mechanics was a remarkably *unified* theory. It solved problems by invoking the same pattern of reasoning, or *problem-solving strategy,* again and again: From a specification of the positions of the bodies under study, use the law of gravitation to calculate the forces acting; from a statement of the forces acting, use the laws of dynamics to compute the equations of motion; solve the equations of motion to obtain the motions of the bodies. This single pattern of reasoning was applied in case after case to yield conclusions that were independently found to be correct.

At a higher level, celestial mechanics was itself contained in a broader theory. Newtonian physics, as a whole, was remarkably unified. It offered a strategy for solving a diverse collection of problems. Faced with *any* question about motion, the Newtonian suggestion was the same: Find the forces acting, from the forces and the laws of dynamics work out the equations of motion, and solve the equations of motion. The method was employed in a broad range of cases. The revolutions of planets, the motions of projectiles, tidal cycles and pendulum oscillations—all fell to the same problem-solving strategy.

We can draw a second moral. A science should be *unified.* A thriving science is not a gerrymandered patchwork but a coherent whole. Good theories consist of just one problem-solving strategy, or a small family of problem-solving strategies, that can be applied to a wide range of problems. The theory succeeds as it is able to encompass more and more problem areas. Failure looms when the basic problem-solving strategy (or strategies) can resolve almost none of the problems in its intended domain without the "aid" of untestable auxiliary hypotheses.

Despite the vast successes of his theory, Newton hoped for more. He envisaged a time when scientists would recognize other force laws, akin to the law of gravitation, so that other branches of physics could model themselves after celestial mechanics. In addition, he suggested that many physical questions that are not ostensibly about motion—questions about heat and about chemical combination, for example—could be reduced to problems of motion. *Principia,* Newton's masterpiece, not only offered a theory; it also advertised a program:

> I wish we could derive the rest of the phenomena of Nature by the same kind of reasoning from mechanical principles, for I am induced by many reasons to suspect that they may all depend upon certain forces by which the particles of bodies, by some causes hitherto unknown, are either mutually impelled towards one another, and cohere in regular figures, or are repelled and recede from one another. These forces being unknown, philosophers have hitherto attempted the search of Nature in vain; but I hope the principles here laid down will afford some light either to this or some truer method of philosophy. (Newton 1687/Motte-Cajori 1960, xviii)

Newton's message was clear. His own work only began the task of applying an immensely fruitful, unifying idea.

Newton's successors were moved, quite justifiably, to extend the theory he had offered. They attempted to show how Newton's main problem-solving strategy could be applied to a broader range of physical phenomena. During the eighteenth and nineteenth centuries, the search for understanding of the forces of nature was carried into hydrodynamics, optics, chemistry, and the studies of heat, elasticity, electricity, and magnetism. Not all of these endeavors were equally successful. Nevertheless, Newton's directive fostered the rise of some important new sciences.

The final moral I want to draw from this brief look at Newtonian physics concerns *fecundity.* A great scientific theory, like Newton's, opens up new areas of research. Celestial mechanics led to the discovery of a previously unknown planet. Newtonian physics as a whole led to the development of previously unknown sciences. Because a theory presents a new way of looking at the world, it can lead us to ask new questions, and so to embark on new and fruitful lines of inquiry. Of the many flaws with the earlier picture of theories as sets of statements, none is more important than the misleading presentation of sciences as static and insular. Typically, a flourishing science is incomplete. At any time, it raises more questions than it can currently answer. But incompleteness is no vice. On the contrary, incompleteness is the mother of fecundity. Unresolved problems present challenges that enable a theory to flower in unanticipated ways. They also make the theory hostage to future developments. A good theory should be productive; it should raise new questions and presume that those questions can be answered without giving up its problem-solving strategies.

I have highlighted three characteristics of successful science. *Independent testability* is achieved when it is possible to test auxiliary hypotheses independently of the particular cases for which they are introduced. *Unification* is the result of applying a small family of problem-solving strategies to a broad class of cases. *Fecundity* grows out of incompleteness when a theory opens up new and profitable lines of investigation. Given these marks of successful science, it is easy to see how sciences can fall short, and how some doctrines can do so badly that they fail to count as science at all. A scientific theory begins to wither if some of its auxiliary assumptions can be saved from refutation only by rendering them untestable; or of its problem-solving strategies become a hodgepodge, a collection of unrelated methods, each designed for a separate recalcitrant case; or if the promise of the theory just fizzles, the few questions it raises leading only to dead ends.

When does a doctrine fail to be a science? If a doctrine fails sufficiently abjectly as a science, then it fails to be a science. Where bad science becomes egregious enough, pseudoscience begins. The example of Newtonian physics shows us how to replace the simple (and incorrect) naive falsificationist criterion with a battery of tests. Do the doctrine's problem-solving strategies encounter recurrent difficulties in a significant range of cases? Are the problem-solving strategies an opportunistic collection of unmotivated and unrelated methods? Does the doctrine have too cozy a relationship with auxiliary hypotheses, applying its strategies with claims that can be "tested" only in their applications? Does the doctrine refuse to follow up on unresolved problems, airily dismissing them as "exceptional cases"? Does the doctrine restrict the domain of its methods, forswearing excursions into new areas of investigation where embarrassing questions might arise? If all, or many, of these tests are positive, then the doctrine is not a poor scientific theory. It is not a scientific theory at all.

The account of successful science that I have given not only enables us to replace the naive falsificationist criterion with something better. It also provides a deeper understanding of how theories are justified. Predictive success is one important way in which a theory can win our acceptance. But it is not the only way. In general, theories earn their laurels by solving problems—providing answers that can be independently recognized as correct—and by their fruitfulness. Making a prediction is answering a special kind of question. The astronomers who used celestial mechanics to predict the motion of Mars were answering the question of where Mars would be found. Yet, very frequently, our questions do not concern *what* occurs, but *why* it occurs. We already know that something happens and we want an explanation. Science offers us explanations by setting the phenomena within a unified framework. Using a widely applicable problem-solving strategy, together with independently confirmed auxiliary hypotheses, scientists show that what happened was to be expected. It was known before Newton that the orbits of the planets are approximately elliptical. One of the great achievements of Newton's celestial mechanics was to apply its problem-solving strategy to deduce that the orbit of any planet will be approximately elliptical, thereby explaining the shape of the orbits. In general, science is at least as concerned with reducing the number of unexplained phenomena as it is with generating correct predictions.

The most global Creationist attack on evolutionary theory is the claim that evolution is not a science. If this claim were correct, then the dispute about what to teach in high school science classes would be over. In earlier parts of this chapter, we saw how Creationists were able to launch their broad criticisms. If one accepts the idea that science requires proof, or if one adopts the naive falsificationist criterion, then the theory of evolution—and every other scientific theory—will turn out not to be a part of science. So Creationist standards for science imply that there is no science to be taught.

However, we have seen that Creationist standards rest on a very poor understanding of science. In light of a clearer picture of the scientific enterprise, I have provided a more realistic group of tests for good science, bad science, and pseudoscience. Using this more sophisticated approach, I now want to address seriously the global Creationist questions about the theory of evolution. Is it a pseudoscience? Is it a poor science? Or is it a great science? These are very important questions, for the appropriateness of granting equal time to Creation "science" depends, in part, on whether it can be regarded as the equal of the theory of evolution.

VII. Darwin's Daring

The heart of Darwinian evolutionary theory is a family of problem-solving strategies, related by their common employment of a particular style of historical narrative. A *Darwinian history* is a piece of reasoning of the following general form. The first step consists in a description of an ancestral population of organisms. The reasoning proceeds by tracing the modification of the population through subsequent generations, showing how characteristics were selected, inherited, and became prevalent. (. . . Natural selection is taken to be the primary—but not the only—force of evolutionary change.)

Reasoning like this can be used to answer a host of biological questions. Suppose that we want to know why a contemporary species manifests a particular trait. We can answer that question by supplying a Darwinian history that describes the emergence of that trait. Equally, we can use Darwinian histories to answer questions about relationships among groups of organisms. One way to explain why two species share a common feature is to trace their descent from a common ancestor. Questions of biogeography can be addressed in a similar way. We can explain why we find contemporary organisms where we do by following the course of their historical modifications and migrations. Finally, we can tackle problems about extinction by showing how characteristics that had enabled organisms to thrive were no longer advantageous when the environment (or the competition) changed. In all these cases, we find related strategies for solving problems. The history of the development of populations, understood in terms of variation, competition, selection, and inheritance, is used to shed light on broad classes of biological phenomena.

The questions that evolutionary theory has addressed are so numerous that any sample is bound to omit important types. The following short selection undoubtedly reflects the idiosyncrasy of my interests: Why do orchids have such intricate internal structures? Why are male birds of paradise so brightly colored? Why do some reptilian precursors of mammals have enormous "sails" on their backs? Why do bats typically roost upside down? Why are the hemoglobins of humans and apes so similar? Why are there no marsupial analogues of seals and whales? Why is the mammalian fauna of Madagascar so distinctive? Why did the large, carnivorous ground birds of South America become extinct? Why is the sex ratio in most species one to one (although it is markedly different in some species of insects)? Answers to these questions, employing Darwinian histories, can be found in works written by contemporary Darwinian biologists. Those works contain answers to a myriad of questions of the same general types. Darwinian histories are constructed again and again to illuminate the characteristics of contemporary organisms, to account for the similarities and differences among species, to explain why the forms preserved in the fossil record emerged and became extinct, to cast light on the geographical distribution of animals and plants.

We can see the history in action by taking a brief look at one of these examples. The island of Madagascar, off the east coast of Africa, supports a peculiar group of mammals. Many of these mammals are endemic. Among them is a group of relatively small insectivorous mammals, the *tenrecs*. All tenrecs share certain features that mark them out as relatively primitive mammals. They have very poor vision, their excretory system is rudimentary, the testes in the male are carried within the body, their capacity for regulating their body temperature is poor compared with that of most mammals. Yet, on their simple and rudimentary body plan, specialized characteristics have often been imposed. Some tenrecs have the hedgehog's method of defense. Others have the forelimbs characteristic of moles. There are climbing tenrecs that resemble the shrews, and there are tenrecs that defend themselves by attempting to stick their quills into a would-be predator. Hedgehogs, moles, tree shrews, and porcupines do not inhabit Madagascar. But they seem to have their imitators. (These are examples of convergent evolution, cases in which unrelated organisms take on some of the same characteristics.) Why are these peculiar animals found on Madagascar, and nowhere else?

A straightforward evolutionary story makes sense of what we observe. In the late Mesozoic or early Cenozoic, small, primitive, insectivorous mammals rafted across the Mozambique channel and colonized Madagascar. Later the channel widened and Madagascar became inaccessible to the more advanced mammals that evolved on the mainland. Hence the early colonists developed without competition from advanced mainland forms and without pressure form many of the normal predators who make life difficult for small mammals. The tenrecs have been relatively protected. In the absence of rigorous competition, they have preserved their simple body plan, and they have exploited unoccupied niches, which are filled elsewhere by more advanced creatures. Tenrecs have gone up the trees and burrowed in the ground because those are good ways to make a living and because they have had nobody but one another to contend with.

The same kind of story can be told again and again to answer all sorts of questions about all sorts of living things. Evolutionary theory is unified because so many diverse questions—questions as various as those I listed—can be addressed by advancing Darwinian histories. Moreover, these narratives constantly make claims that are subject to independent check. Here are four examples from the case of the triumphant tenrecs. (1) The explanation presupposes that Madagascar has drifted away from the east coast of Africa. That is something that can be checked by using geological criteria for the movement of land-masses, criteria that are independent of biology. (2) The account claims that the tenrecs would have been able to raft across the Mozambique channel, but that the present channel constitutes a barrier to more advanced mammals (small rodents). These claims could be tested by looking to see whether the animals in question can disperse across channels of the appropriate sizes. (3) The narrative assumes that the specialized methods of defense offered advantages against the predators that were present in Madagascar. Studies of animal interactions can test whether the particular defenses are effective against local predators. (4) Central to the explanatory account is the thesis that the tenrecs are related. If this is so, then studies of the minute details of tenrec anatomy should reveal many common features, and the structures of proteins ought to be similar. In particular, the tenrecs ought to be much more like one another than they are like hedgehogs, shrews, or moles.

Looking at one example, or even at a small number of examples, does not really convey the strength of evolutionary theory. The same patterns of reasoning can be applied again and again, in book after book, monograph after monograph, article after article. Yet the particular successes in dealing with details of natural history, numerous though they are, do not exhaust the accomplishments of the theory. Darwin's original theory—the problem-solving strategies advanced in the *Origin,* which are, in essence, those just described—gave rise to important new areas of scientific investigation. Evolutionary theory has been remarkably fruitful.

Darwin not only provided a scheme for unifying the diversity of life. He also gave a structure to our ignorance. After Darwin, it was important to resolve general issues about the presuppositions of Darwinian histories. The way in which biology should proceed had been made admirably plain, and it was clear that biologists had to tackle questions for which they had, as yet, no answers. How do new characteristics arise in populations? What are the mechanisms of inheritance? How do characteristics become fixed in populations? What criteria decide when a characteristic confers some advantage on its possessor? What interactions among populations of organisms affect the adaptive value of characteristics? With respect to all of these questions, Darwin was forced to confess ignorance. By raising them, his theory pointed the way to its further articulation.

Since Darwin's day, biologists have contributed parts of evolutionary theory that help to answer these important questions. Geneticists have advanced our understanding of the transmission of characteristics between generations and have enabled us to see how new characteristics can arise. Population geneticists have analyzed the variation present in populations of organisms; they have suggested how that variation is maintained and have specified ways in which characteristics can be fixed or eliminated. Workers in morphology and physiology have helped us to see how variations of particular kinds might yield advantages in particular environments. Ecologists have studied the ways in which interactions among populations can affect survival and fecundity.

The moral is obvious. Darwin gambled. He trusted that the questions he left open would be answered by independent biological sciences and that the deliverances of these sciences would be consistent with the presuppositions of Darwinian histories. Because of the breadth of his vision, Darwin made his theory vulnerable from a number of different directions. To take just one example, it could have turned out the mechanisms of heredity would have made it impossible for advantageous variations to be preserved and to spread. Indeed, earlier in this century, many biologists felt that the emerging views about inheritance did not fit into Darwin's picture, and the fortunes of Darwinian evolutionary theory were on the wane.

When we look at the last 120 years of the history of biology, it is impossible to ignore the fecundity of Darwin's ideas. Not only have inquiries into the presuppositions of Darwinian histories yielded new theoretical disciplines (like population genetics), but the problem-solving strategies have been extended to cover phenomena that initially appeared troublesome. One recent triumph has been the development of explanations for social interactions among animals. Behavior involving one animal's promotion of the good of others seems initially to pose a problem for evolutionary theory. How can we construct Darwinian histories for the emergence of such behavior? W. D. Hamilton's concept of inclusive fitness, and the deployment of game-theoretic ideas by R. L. Trivers and John Maynard Smith, revealed how the difficulty could be resolved by a clever extension of traditional Darwinian concepts.

Yet puzzles remain. One problem is the existence of sex. When an organism forms gametes (sperm cells or egg cells) there is a meiotic division, so that in sexual reproduction only half of an organism's genes are transmitted to each of its progeny. Because of this "cost of meiosis," it is hard to see how genotypes for sexual reproduction might have become prevalent. (Apparently, they will spread only half as fast as their asexual rivals.) So why is there sex? We do not have a compelling answer to the question. Despite some ingenious suggestions by orthodox Darwinians (notably G. C. Williams 1975; John Maynard Smith 1978), there is no convincing Darwinian history for the emergence of sexual reproduction. However, evolutionary theorists believe that the problem will be solved without abandoning the main Darwinian insights—just as early nineteenth-century astronomers believed that the problem of the motion of Uranus could be overcome without major modification of Newton's celestial mechanics.

The comparison is apt. Like Newton's physics in 1800, evolutionary theory today rests on a huge record of successes. In both cases, we find a unified theory whose problem-solving strategies are applied to illuminate a host of diverse phenomena. Both theories offer problem solutions that can be subjected to rigorous independent checks. Both open up new lines of inquiry and have a history of surmounting apparent obstacles. The virtues of successful science are clearly displayed in both.

There is a simple way to put the point. Darwin is the Newton of biology. Evolutionary theory is not simply an area of science that has had some success at solving problems. It has unified biology and it has inspired important biological disciplines. Darwin himself appreciated the unification achieved by his theory and its promise of further development (Darwin 1859/Mayr 1964, 188, 253–254, 484–486). Over a century later, at the beginning of his authoritative account of current views of species and their origins, Ernst Mayr explained how that promise has been fulfilled: "The theory of evolution is quite rightly called the greatest unifying theory in biology. The diversity of organisms, similarities and differences between kinds of organisms, patterns of distribution and behavior, adaptation and interaction, all this was merely a bewildering chaos of facts until given meaning by the evolutionary theory" (Mayr 1970, 1). Dobzhansky put the point even more concisely: "Nothing in biology makes sense except in the light of evolution" (Dobzhansky, 1973).

REFERENCES

Birch, L. C., and Ehrlich, P. R. 1967. "Evolutionary History and Population Biology." *Nature* 214:349-352.

Darwin, C. 1859/Mayr, E. 1964. *The Origin of the Species.* Facimile of the first edition: Cambridge: Harvard University Press.

Dobzhansky, T. 1973. "Nothing in Biology Makes Sense Except in the Light of Evolution." *American Biology Teacher* 35:125-129.

Gish, D. T. 1979. *Evolution? The Fossils Say No!* San Diego: Creation Life Publishers.

Gould, S. J. 1981. *The Mismeasure of Man.* New York, Norton.

Hempel, C. G. 1951. "Problems and Changes in the Empiricist Criterion of Meaning." In *Aspects of Scientific Exploration.* Glencoe: The Free Press, 1965.

Matthews, L. H. 1971. Introduction to *The Origin of the Species.* London: Dent.

Maynard Smith, J. 1978. *The Evolution of Sex.* Cambridge: Cambridge University Press.

Mayr, E. 1970. *Population, Species, and Evolution.* Cambridge: Harvard University Press.

———. 1976. *Evolution and the Diversity of Life.* Cambridge: Harvard University Press.

Moore, J. 1974. *Should Evolution Be Taught?* San Diego: Creation Life Publishers.

Morris, H. M. 1974a. *Scientific Creationism* (general ed.). San Diego: Creation Life Publishers.

———. 1974b. *The Troubled Waters of Evolution.* San Diego: Creation Life Publishers.

———. 1975. *Introducing Creationism in the Public Schools.* San Diego: Creation Life Publishers.

Popper, K. R. 1959. *The Logic of Scientifc Discovery.* London: Hutchinson.

———. 1968. *Conjectures and Refutations.* New York: Harper and Row.

Quine, W. V. O. 1952. *Two Dogmas of Empiricism.* Reprinted from "A Logical Point of View," Cambridge: Harvard University Press.

Simpson, C. G. 1953. *The Major Features of Evolution.* New York: Columbia University Press.

Watson, D. C. C. 1976. *The Great Brain Robbery.* Chicago: Moody Press.

Wilder-Smith, A. E. 1981. *The Natural Sciences Know Nothing of Evolution.* San Diego: Creation Life Publishers.

Williams, G. C. 1975. *Sex and Evolution.* Princeton: Princeton University.

Wysong, R. L. 1976. *The Creation Evolution Controversy.* Midland, Mich.: Inquiry Press.

STUDY QUESTIONS FOR PART 1

1. According to Popper, what is the problem of demarcation? State Popper's solution of that problem.

2. Show why, in Popper's views, psychoanalytic theories do not meet his criterion of demarcation whereas Einstein's theory of graviation does.

3. In addition to the examples which he already gives, list several theories, statements, or enterprises which do *not* meet Popper's criterion of demarcation. Show *why* they do not do so.

4. Try to think of some theories or truths which (in your view) should be accorded scientific status but which do *not* meet Popper's criterion for being scientific. How would you revise—or replace—Popper's criterion in order to account for them?

5. Defend or attack Ziman's thesis that the distinction between pure science and technological knowledge is difficult to make.

6. According to Feyerabend, *how* should one defend society against science? *Why* should one do so? Do you agree with him? Why or why not?

7. Why does Feyerabend reject Popper's criterion of falsifiability? Has he provided *good reasons* for rejecting it? Why or why not?

8. What thesis, if any, in Feyerabend's essay do you disagree with or find fault with? Why?

9. What is Thagard's criterion for distinguishing science from pseudo-science? Compare and contrast with the views of Popper, Ziman, and Feyerabend. Which of the criteria formulated by these four authors do you find most acceptable? Why?

10. On the basis of Thagard's criterion, why does he claim that astrology is a pseudoscience? Has he (in your view) successfully shown that it is a pseudoscience? Why or why not?

11. How do (explicitly or implicitly) Popper, Ziman, Feyerabend, and Thagard answer the question "What is science?"? Which answer seems preferable to you? Why?

12. Write a detailed and critical reply to the following letter (from J. Somerville, "Umbrellaology," *Philosophy of Science,* 1941).

Dear Sir:

I am taking the liberty of calling upon you to be the judge in a dispute between me and an acquaintance who is no longer a friend. The question at issue is this: Is my creation, umbrellaology, a science? Allow me to explain. . . . For the past eighteen years assisted by a few faithful disciples, I have been collecting materials on a subject hitherto almost wholly neglected by scientists, the umbrella. The results of my investigations to date are embodied in the nine volumes which I am sending to you under a separate cover. Pending their receipt, let me describe to you briefly the nature of their contents and the method I pursued in compiling them. I began on the Island of Manhattan. Proceeding block by block, house by house, family by family, and individual by individual, I ascertained (1) the number of umbrellas possessed, (2) their size, (3) their weght, (4) their color. Having covered Manhattan after many years, I eventually extended the survey to the other boroughs of the City of New York, and at length completed the entire city. Thus I was ready to carry forward the work to the rest of the state and indeed the rest of the United States and the whole known world.

It was at this point that I approached my erstwhile friend. I am a modest man, but I felt I had the right to be recognized as the creator of a new science. He, on the other hand, claimed that umbrellaology was not a science at all. First, he said, it was silly to investigate umbrellas. Now this argument is false, because science scorns not to deal with any object, however humble and lowly, even to the "hind leg of a flea." Then why not umbrellas? Next, he said that umbrellaology could not be recognized as a science because it was of no use or benefit to mankind. But is not the truth the most precious thing in life? Are not my nine volumes filled with the truth about my subject? Every word in them is true. Every sentence contains a hard, cold fact. When he asked me what was the object of umbrellaology I was proud to say, "To seek and discover the truth is object enough for me." I am a pure scientist; I have no ulterior motives. Hence it follows that I am satisfied with truth alone. Next, he said my truths were dated and that any one of my finds might cease to be true tomorrow. But this, I pointed out, is not an argument against umbrellaology, but rather an argument for keeping it up to date, which exactly is what I propose. Let us have surveys monthly, weekly, or even daily, to keep our knowledge abreast of the changing facts. His next contention was that umbrellaology had entertained no hypotheses and had developed no theories or laws. This is a great error. In the course of my investigations, I employed innumerable hypotheses. Before entering each new block and each new section of the city, I entertained an hypothesis as regards the number and characteristics of the umbrellas that would be found there, which hypotheses were either verified or nullified by my subsequent observations, in accordance with proper scientific procedure, as explained in authoritative texts. (In fact, it is of interest to note that I can substantiate and document every one of my replies to these objections by numerous quotations from standard works, leading journals, public speeches of eminent scientists, and the like.) As for theories and laws, my work represents an abundance of them. I will here mention only a few, by way of illustration. There is the Law of Color Variation Relative to Ownership by Sex. (Umbrellas owned by women tend to great variety of color, whereas those owned by men are almost all black.) To this law I have given exact statistical formulation. (See vol. 6, Appendix 1, Table 3, p. 582.) There are the curiously interrelated Laws of Individual Ownership of Plurality of Umbrellas, and Plurality of Ownership of Individual Umbrellas. The interrelationship assumes the form, in the first law, of almost direct ratio to annual income, and in the second, in almost inverse ratio to annual income. (For an exact statement of the modifying circumstances, see vol. 8, p. 350.) There is also the Law of Tendency

Towards Acquisition of Umbrellas in Rainy Weather. To this law I have given experimental verification in chapter 3 of volume 3. In the same way I have performed numerous other experiments in connection with my generalizations.

Thus I feel that my creation is in all respects a genuine science, and I appeal to you for substantiation of my opinion. . . .

13. What are the central theses of Kitcher's view of scientific theories?

14. Show how, according to Kitcher, the Creationist account does not live upt to the requirements of being scientific.

15. Show how Darwinian evolutionary theory does live up to them.

SELECTED BIBLIOGRAPHY

A. What Is Science?

[1] Campbell, N. *What Is Science?* New York: Dover Publications, 1952. [Elementary but significant answer to the question.]
[2] Cohen, M. R. and E. Nagel. *An Introduction to Logic and Scientific Method,* Bk 2. New York: Harcourt, Brace, 1934. [Old but worthwhile.]
[3] Conant, J. B. *On Understanding Science.* New Haven, Conn.: Yale University Press, 1951. [Very readable; good introduction.]
[4] Feyerabend, P. *Against Method.* New York: Shoecken Books, 1977. [Very critical of all prevailing views of science.]
[5] Kemeny, J. G. *A Philosopher Looks at Science.* Princeton, N. J.: D. Van Nostrand, 1959. [One of many good introductions.]
[6] Kuhn, T. S. *The Structure of Scientific Revolutions.* 2d ed. Chicago, Ill.: University of Chicago Press, 1971. [A classic.]
[7] Nagel, E. *The Structure of Science.* New York: Harcourt, Brace & Worl.d, 1961. [Difficult in spots, but excellent.]
[8] Popper, K. *Conjectures and Refutations.* New York: Harper & Row, 1968. [A seminal and classic collection of essays.]
[9] ———. *The Logic of Scientific Discovery.* New York: Harper & Row, 1968. [A major and important work.]
[10] Toulmin, S. *Foresight and Understanding.* London: Hutchinson, 1961. [Contains interesting insights; very readable.]

B. Science and Nonscience

[1] Flew, A. "ESP." *The New York Review of Books,* October 8, 1964, pp. 15-16. [Short but worthwhile.]
[2] Gardner, M. *Fads and Fallacies in the Name of Science.* New York: Dover Publications, 1957. (See also the detailed appendix and notes to this volume.) [The best book of its kind.]
[3] ———. "Funny Coincidence." *The New York Review of Books,* May

26, 1966. [One of many essays by Gardner.]

[4] ———. "What Hath Hoova Wrought?" *The New York Review of Books,* May 16, 1974, pp. 18-19.

[5] ———. "Paranosense." *The New York Review of Books,* October 30, 1975 pp. 12-14. [See 3, above.]

[6] ———. "Supergull." *The New York Review of Books,* March 17, 1977, pp. 18-20. [See 3, above.]

[7] Hansel, C. E. M. *ESP: A Scientific Evaluation.* New York: Scribner's, 1966. [See 3, above.]

[8] Kline, A. D. "Theories, Facts, and Gods." In David Wilson, ed., *Did the Devil Make Darwin Do It?* Ames, Iowa: Iowa State University Press, 1983. [All of the essays in this volume are worth reading.]

[9] Popper, K. *Conjectures and Refutations.* New York: Harper & Row, 1968. [See A8.]

[10] ———. *The Logic of Scientific Discovery.* New York: Harper & Row, 1968. [See A8.]

[11] Toulmin, S. "Contemporary Scientific Mythology." In *Metaphysical Beliefs,* by S. Toulmin, et al. London: SCM Press, 1957 [Excellent exposure; a must.]

Part 2

Explanation and Law

Part 2: Explanation and Law

Introduction

It has been often held that one of the aims of science is explanation. What constitutes a scientific explanation? How (if at all) does a scientific explanation differ from an ordinary explanation in everyday life or an explanation in (say) history? In a scientific explanation, what is it that is being explained and what "does" the explaining? What is the role of the laws of science in explanation? What constitutes a scientific law? These are some of the questions to be pursued in Part 2. Before turning to these questions let us consider some examples of purported explanations.

I. Some Examples

Aristotle explains what appears to be the circular motion of the planets by appealing to the "fact" that they are members of the celestial region—a perfect and permanent region. Circular motion was regarded as the only motion appropriate or natural in that region. Kepler, at one point in his curious career, explained the distances of the various planets from the sun by drawing an analogy between these distances and the way the five Platonic solids will fit inside one another. (Platonic solids are solid figures that have faces of identical equilateral plane figures, e.g., a square and a tetrahedron. There are only five such objects.)

Scientific creationists claim that the biblical account in Genesis offers an alternative and more plausible explanation than Darwinian evolution of the origins and diversity of life. In several states Creationists are waging a serious political and legal effort to have creationism given a place alongside evolution in the schools' curricula.

B. F. Skinner thinks that to explain human behavior by appealing to what is inside the skin is pointless. In fact, it is claimed that inquiry along these lines will only lead to confusions and banalities, not real explanations.

Population geneticists have recently become quite self-conscious. What is it that population genetics explains? How must one understand fitness in order to have causal explanations of the fecundity of populations?

Over and above a desire to understand the quick of science, cases such as the above motivate an inquiry into the nature of explanation. The Aristotelian and Keplerian explanatory episodes strike us as bizarre. But there are important differences. The Aristotelian view achieved great prominence and endured for a considerable period of time. The Keplerian view was seen as quackery. The philosopher of science would like to know exactly why these explanations appear to us, not just false, but in a deeper sense misconceived. We also need an account of the perceived scientific respectability of Aristotle's effort and the lack of such respectability in Kepler's effort. This raises the further question whether the standards for explanation are in some sense historical. (Several essays in Part 1 bear on this issue.)

Regardless of one's religious views, it is clear that the creationist/evolutionist dispute has at its heart claims about the nature of explanation. Legislators and others cannot hope to think clearly about this issue without first forming a general and competent view about explanation.

The schools of psychology have long been at war. The present battle is between a brand of cognitive psychology called information-processing psychology and behaviorism, which Skinner prominently espouses. The literature on this clash is replete with claims about the "proper" way to explain human behavior.

A recent charge is that a central explanatory concept of population genetics, fitness, is tautological. In other words, fitness is used to explain changes in the gene frequency of a population but, as the charge goes, fitness is simply defined as some mathematical function of the change in gene frequency of a population. This issue has forced a rethinking of the explanatory adequacy of population genetics.

The above examples raise a number of specialized issues in explanation. The bibliography will help provide some access to the relevant literature. But one must begin somewhere. The appropriate place is with a general discussion of the fundamentals of explanation. The essays in this part are selected to initiate that general and fundamental discussion.

II. Explanation

A widely accepted view of explanation has come to be called the Hempelian or deductive-nomological view of explanation. The view has justly been named after Carl Hempel, who in a series of papers has lucidly and powerfully argued for the view.

It will be helpful to have a crisp statement of the Hempelian account before us. First a bit of terminology. Explanations are composed of a set of statements. The statement describing the event or law to be explained is called the explanandum. The statements that are put forward to account for he phenomena expressed in the explanandum are called the explanans. Now, for the account:

E, some purported explanation, is an explanation if and only if
(1) The explanandum of E is a deductive consequence of the explanans.
(2) The explanans of E contains at least one law of nature.
(3) The law(s) of nature in the explanans is required for the derivation of the explanandum.
(4) The sentences of the explanans are testable by observation.
(5) The sentences of the explanans are true.

In an early and readable essay titled "What Is Explanation?" John Hospers has provided a simple example of why this piece of copper conducts electricity illustrates these conditions.[1]

(a) All copper conducts electricity.
(b) This wire is made of copper.
(c) Therefore, this wire conducts electricity.

The explanandum, (c), is a deductive consequence of the explanans, (a) and (b). (A) is a law of nature that is required for the derivation of (c), and it is testable. Supposing that "this" refers to a piece of copper, the explanans are true.

The definition and example above rely on technical notions from logic. An argument as understood by logicians is a set of statements. One of those statements is the conclusion, that which is to be proved or established. The remaining statements are the premises, those statements which provide the reasons or evidence for the conclusion.

A special class of arguments are those which are deductively valid. An argument is deductively valid if, and only if, it is impossible for the premises to be true and its conclusion false.

Explanations, on the view being discussed, are arguments. Furthermore, according to condition (1) they must be deductively valid arguments.

Condition (3) with its technical term, 'derivation,' requires that if the law(s) of nature in an explanation were deleted from the argument, the argument would no longer be deductively valid. Crudely put, this requirement ensures that the laws are not just fluff, but rather are essential to the explanation. In the example given, (a) is required since, if it were deleted, (b) and (c) would not form a deductively valid argument.

Much of the history of philosophical reflection on explanation has been various attempts to provide the rationale for (1)-(5) or to show that one or more of (1)-(5) are not necessary conditions for explanation or to show that (1)-(5) are not jointly a sufficient conditon for explanation.

In your examination of the above account, it will be helpful to keep an important distinction in mind. Hempelians use this distinction to forestall certain criticisms of their view.

Consider two examples: When asked, "Why does this conduct electricity?" one might respond, "It's copper." When explaining to a group of fourth graders why the pressure on the walls of a closed pot increased, one might give the kinetic theory and the fact that the temperature increased.

One intuitions encourage us to believe that the former episode is an explanation although it does not meet Hempel's criteria. On the other hand, the latter episode, even if filled out in splendid Hempelian detail, fails to explain. After all, it is a rare fourth grader who has the slightest idea what the mean molecular speed squared is.

Hempelians have a response to these worries. We need to make a distinction between the logic of explanation and the pragmatics of explanation. An account of the logic of explanation explores the relation between two groups of sentences such that the former explains the latter. The pragmatics of explanation concerns the important considerations in explaining something to *someone*. Though the Hempelian account is not concerned with pragmatics, Hempelians do not deny the importance of such studies.

Using this distinction, we see that the last of the examples above is indeed an explanation, though not appropriate for young children. But appropriateness is an issue in the pragmatics, not logic, of explanation.

The conductor example can also be defused. Yes, we talk that way when we explain things to someone. But for it to really be an explanation, it must meet conditions (1)-(5). The reason one regards the episode as explanatory is that he is implicitly assuming certain rather obvious statements that enable the episode to meet Hempel's conditions.

The logic/pragmatics distinction has been drawn in a very rough way. It certainly deserves further clarification and perhaps criticism.

III. Laws of Nature

Law are at the heart of an explanation. They do the work in answering our why questions. What are laws? An initial account is that they are true universal generalizations. But this account, even if it gives some of the necessary conditions, does not give a set of sufficient conditions. Suppose a parent of Fred wants to know why his thirty-seven-year-old son is not married. Suppose further that we give the following "Hempelian" explanation: "Well, you see Fred is a bachelor and all bachelors are unmarried." A true universal generalization does play a central role in the deduction of the explanandum. But of course this is at best a bad joke, not a real explanation. The supposed law is a definition. We need to add the condition that laws be *empirical* statements.

Philosophers have argued that other more profound additions are also needed. Some of these issues are discussed in the essays of this part. In recent papers the necessity of our original conditions have been challenged—

in particular the truth condition. This, at least on the surface, is an extraordinary claim. You will have to see if it can be justified.

There is another issue, related to laws, that has received considerable attention. Consider an example. The general form of the law of conservation of momentum is as follows: The total momentum of an isolated system of bodies remains constant. Suppose we observe a car-truck crash and wish to explain why the combined velocity of the enmeshed car and truck is 6 meters/sec. We could do this by appealing to a specific form of the above law, $mv_c + mv_t = mv_{c+t}$, and the masses and velocities of the vehicles before the crash, car 600 kg. 20m/sec, truck 1400 kg. stationary. In Hempelian form the explanation would look like this:

(1) $mv_c + mv_t = mv_{c+t}$
(2) mass of t = 1400 kg.
(3) mass of c = 600 kg.
(4) velocity of t = 0
(5) velocity of c = 20 m/sec.
(6) therefore v_{c+t} = 6 m/sec.

But it should be clear that we could use this same form of argument not to explain the velocity of the joined car and truck but to predict it. If we did not know v_{c+t}, but knew that the crash would occur, we could use (1)-(5) to predict (6).

This example might lead one to suspect that the only important difference between explaining and predicting an event is when the event occurs relative to when the argument is constructed. If the event has already occurred, then one explains the event. If the event is yet to occur, one predicts the event. Perhaps from a structural or logical point of view there is no difference between explaining and predicting. This thesis deserves critical examination.

IV. Types of Explanation

Carl Hempel and many other philosophers of science appear to base their insights about explanation on examples from common sense and elementary physics. They have their critics even in this limited domain. But they also have critics of another sort. Some philosophers think that there are types of non-Hempelian explanation appropriate to certain subject matters. Put another way, is the form of explanation found in elementary physics also that found in chemistry, geology, etc.

The explanatory form found in historical work has received considerable attention from philosophers. An important philosopher and historian, R. G. Collingwood, has argued that history makes sense of human actions in a non-Hempelian way. Most crucially, historical explanations do not involved laws. They show, he claims, that actions are *rationally* necessary, not nomically necessary.

At present the debate over historical explanation is still open. Furthermore, additional non-Hempelian overtures have occurred, especially for the biological and psychological sciences.

V. The Readings in Part 2

Hempel's essay is *the* classical work in the philosophy of science. It must be taken account of by all subsequent work on the topic of explanation. The Hempelian view referred to in this introduction is elaborated in Hempel's essay and other works by him. The essay contains some technical concepts from logic but they are worth mastering, since they will occur in some of the subsequent articles.

Most writers hold that there is a genuine distinction between *accidental* generalizations and *nomic* or *law-like* generalizations—the latter being in some sense necessary. The issue is how to explicate this difference. Will the kinds of restriction Hempel and Oppenheim put on generalizations do the job? Lambert and Brittan do not think so. They introduce the role of counterfactual conditionals in understanding the concept of a law of nature.

Baruch Brody's essay should be understood as a critique of the sufficiency of the Hempelian view of explanation, by way of a critique of the account of law embedded therein. Furthermore, Brody has some exciting suggestions toward an alternative treatment of laws.

Nancy Cartwright argues against the covering-law model of explanation (held by Hempel, Hospers, and others), partly on the grounds that we do not have laws that cover the phenomena which they are assumed (by the adherents of the model) to cover. In fact, she maintains, we have no true laws, only "generalizations that hold under special conditions, usually ideal conditions." She still holds that scientific theories must provide explanations, but that they do not tell us what is true in nature.

The final article, "Historical Understanding as Re-thinking," by D. W. Dray is included as an illustration of an alternative account of explanation. Dray accepts the Hempelian view of explanation as adequate for the natural sciences. He does not think that it captures historical explanation. At a minimum, it is claimed, historical explanations make events intelligible without relying on laws.

A. D. K. and E. D. K.

NOTE

1. In A. Flew, ed., *Essays in Conceptual Analysis,* pp. 94-119. London: Macmillan Publishers Ltd., 1956.

6

Studies in the Logic of Explanation[1]
Carl G. Hempel

Introduction

To explain the phenomena in the world of our experience, to answer the question "why?" rather than only the question "what?" is one of the foremost objectives of empirical science. While there is rather general agreement on this point there exists considerable difference of opinion as to the function and the essential characteristics of scientific explanation. The present essay is an attempt to shed some light on these issues by means of an elementary survey of the basic pattern of scientific explanation and a subsequent more rigorous analysis of the concept of law and the logical structure of explanatory arguments. . . .

I. Elementary Survey of Scientific Explanation

1. *Some Illustrations.* A mercury thermometer is rapidly immersed in hot water; there occurs a temporary drop of the mercury column, which is then followed by a swift rise. How is this phenomenon to be explained? The increase in temperature affects at first only the glass tube of the thermometer; it expands and thus provides a larger space for the mercury inside, whose surface therefore drops. As soon as by heat conduction the rise in temperature reaches the mercury, however, the latter expands, and as its coefficient of expansion is considerably larger than that of glass, a rise of the mercury level results.— This account consists of statements of two kinds. Those of the first kind indicate certain conditions which are realized prior to, or at the same time as, the phenomenon to be explained; we shall refer to them briefly as antecedent conditions. In our illustration, the antecedent conditions include, among others,

the fact that the thermometer consists of a glass tube which is partly filled with mercury, and that it is immersed into hot water. The statements of the second kind express certain general laws; in our case, these include the laws of the thermic expansion of mercury and of glass, and a statement about the small thermic conductivity of glass. The two sets of statements, if adequately and completely formulated, explain the phenomenon under consideration: they entail the consequence that the mercury will first drop, then rise. Thus, the event under discussion is explained by subsuming it under general laws, i.e., by showing that it occurred in accordance with those laws, in virtue of the realization of certain specified antecedent conditions.

Consider another illustration. To an observer in a rowboat, that part of an oar which is under water appears to be bent upwards. The phenomenon is explained by means of general laws—mainly the law of refraction and the law that water is an optically denser medium than air—and by reference to certain antecedent conditions—especially the facts that part of the oar is in the water, part in the air, and that the oar is practically a straight piece of wood. Thus, here again, the question "*Why* does the phenomenon occur?" is construed as meaning "according to what general laws, and by virtue of what antecedent conditions does the phenomenon occur?"

So far, we have considered only the explanation of particular events occurring at a certain time and place. But the question "Why?" may be raised also in regard to general laws. Thus, in our last illustration, the question might be asked: Why does the propagation of light conform to the law of refraction? Classical physics answers in terms of the undulatory theory of light, i.e. by stating that the propagation of light is a wave phenomenon of a certain general type, and that all wave phenomena of that type satisfy the law of refraction. Thus, the explanation of a general regularity consists in subsuming it under another, more comprehensive regularity, under a more general law. Similarly, the validity of Galileo's law for the free fall of bodies near the earth's surface can be explained by deducing it from a more comprehensive set of laws, namely Newton's laws of motion and his law of gravitation, together with some statements about particular facts, namely, about the mass and the radius of the earth.

2. *The Basic Pattern of Scientific Explanation.* From the preceding sample cases let us now abstract some general characteristics of scientific explanation. We divide an explanation into two major constituents, the *explanandum* and the *explanans*.[2] By the explanandum, we understand the sentence describing the phenomenon to be explained (not that phenomenon itself); by the explanans, the class of those sentences which are adduced to account for the phenomenon. As was noted before, the explanans falls into two subclasses; one of these contains certain sentences $C_1, C_2, \ldots, C_k$ which state specific antecedent conditions; the other is a set of sentences $L_1, L_2, \ldots, L_r$ which represent general laws.

If a proposed explanation is to be sound, its constituents have to satisfy certain conditions of adequacy, which may be divided into logical and empirical conditions. For the following discussion, it will be sufficient to formulate these requirements in a slightly vague manner. . . .

Logical conditions of adequacy

(R1) The explanandum must be a logical consequence of the explanans; in other words, the explanandum must be logically deducible from the information contained in the explanans; for otherwise, the explanans would not constitute adequate grounds for the explanandum.

(R2) The explanans must contain general laws, and these must actually be required for the derivation of the explanandum. We shall not make it a necessary condition for a sound explanation, however, that the explanans must contain at least one statement which is not a law; for, to mention just one reason, we would surely want to consider as an explanation the derivation of the general regularities governing the motion of double stars from the laws of celestial mechanics, even though all the statements in the explanans are general laws.

(R3) The explanans must have empirical content; i.e., it must be capable, at least in principle, of test by experiment or observation. This condition is implicit in (R1); for since the explanandum is assumed to describe some empirical phenomenon, it follows from (R1) that the explanans entails at least one consequence of empirical character, and this fact confers upon it testability and empirical content. But the point deserves special mention because, as will be seen in §3, certain arguments which have been offered as explanations in the natural and in the social sciences violate this requirement.

Empirical condition of adequacy

(R4) The sentences constituting the explanans must be true. That in a sound explanation, the statements constituting the explanans have to satisfy some condition of factual correctness is obvious. But it might seem more appropriate to stipulate that the explanans has to be highly confirmed by all the relevant evidence available rather than that it should be true. This stipulation, however, leads to awkard consequences. Suppose that a certain phenomenon was explained at an earlier stage of science, by means of an explanans which was well supported by the evidence then at hand, but which has been highly disconfirmed by more recent empirical findings. In such a case, we would have to say that originally the explanatory account was a correct explanation, but that it ceased to be one later, when unfavorable evidence was discovered. This does not appear to accord with sound common usage, which directs us to say that on the basis of the limited initial evidence, the truth of the explanans, and thus the soundness of the explanation, had been quite probable, but that the ampler evidence now available makes it highly probable that the explanans is not true, and hence that the account in question is not—and never has been—a correct explanation.[3] (A similar point will be made and illustrated, with respect to the requirement of truth for laws, [elsewhere].)

Some of the characteristics of an explanation which have been indicated so far may be summarized in the following schema:

Let us note here that the same formal analysis, including the four necessary conditions, applies to scientific prediction as well as to explanation. The difference between the two is of a pragmatic character. If E is given, i.e., if we know that the phenomenon described by E has occurred, and a suitable set of statements $C_1, C_2, \ldots, C_k, L_1, L_2, \ldots, L$, is provided afterwards, we speak of an explanation of the phenomenon in question. If the latter statements are given and E is derived prior to the occurrence of the phenomenon it describes, we speak of a prediction. It may be said, therefore, that an explanation of a particular event is not fully adequate unless its explanans, if taken account of in time, could have served as a basis for predicting the event in question. Consequently, whatever will be said in this article concerning the logical characteristics of explanation or prediction will be applicable to either, even if only one of them should be mentioned.

Many explanations which are customarily offered, especially in pre-scientific discourse, lack this potential predictive force, however. Thus, we may be told that a car turned over on the road "because" one of its tires blew out while the car was traveling at high speed. Clearly, on the basis of just this information, the accident could not have been predicted, for the explanans provides no explicit general laws by means of which the prediction might be effected, nor does it state adequately the antecedent conditions which would be needed for the prediction. The same point may be illustrated by reference to W. S. Jevons's view that every explanation consists in pointing out a resemblance between facts, and that in some cases this process may require no reference to laws at all and "may involve nothing more than a single identity, as when we explain the appearance of shooting stars by shoowing that they are identical with portions of a comet."[4] But clearly, this identity does not provide an explanation of the phenomenon of shooting stars unless we presuppose the laws governing the development of heat and light as the effect of friction. The observation of similarities has explanatory value only if it involves at least tacit reference to general laws.

In some cases, incomplete explanatory arguments of the kind here illustrated suppress parts of the explanans simply as "obvious"; in other cases, they seem to involve the assumption that while the missing parts are not obvious, the incomplete explanans could at least, with appropriate effort, be so supplemented as to make a strict derivation of the explanandum possible. This assumption may be justifiable in some cases, as when we say that a lump of sugar disappeared "because" it was put into hot tea, but it surely is not satisfied in many other cases. Thus, when certain peculiarities in the work of an artist are explained as outgrowths of a specific type of neurosis, this observation may contain significant clues, but in general it does not afford a sufficient basis for a potential prediction of those peculiarities. In cases of this kind, an incomplete explanation may at best be considered as indicating some positive correlation between the antecedent conditions adduced and the type of phenomenon to be explained, and as pointing out a direction in which further research might be carried on in order to complete the explanatory account.

The type of explanation which has been considered here so far is often referred to as causal explanation.[5] If E describes a particular event, then the antecedent circumstances described in the sentences C_1, C_2, . . ., C_k may be said jointly to "cause" that event, in the sense that there are certain empirical regularities, expressed by the laws L_1, L_2, . . ., L_r, which imply that whenever conditions of the kind indicated by C_1, C_2, . . ., C_k occur, an event of the kind described in E will take place. Statements such as L_1, L_2, . . ., L_r, which assert general and unexceptional connections between specified characteristics of events, are customarily called causal, or deterministic, laws. They must be distinguished from the so-called statistical laws which assert that in the long run, an explicitly stated percentage of all cases satisfying a given set of conditions are accompanied by an event of a certain specified kind. Certain cases of scientific explanation involve "subsumption" of the explanandum under a set of laws of which at least some are statistical in character. Analysis of the peculiar logical structure of that type of subsumption involves difficult special problems. The present essay will be restricted to an examination of the deductive type of explanation, which has retained its significance in large segments of contemporary science, and even in some areas where a more adequate account calls for reference to statistical laws.[6]

3. *Explanation in the Nonphysical Sciences. Motivational and Teleological Approaches.* Our characterization of scientific explanation is so far based on a study of cases taken from the physical sciences. But the general principles thus obtained apply also outside this area.[7] Thus, various types of behavior in laboratory animals and in human subjects are explained in psychology by subsumption under laws or even general theories of learning or conditioning; and while frequently the regularities invoked cannot be stated with the same generality and precision as in physics or chemistry, it is clear at least that the general character of those explanations conforms to our earlier characterization.

Let us now consider an illustration involving sociological and economic factors. In the fall of 1946, there occurred at the cotton exchanges of the United States a price drop which was so severe that the exchanges in New York, New Orleans, and Chicago had to suspend their activities temporarily. In an attempt to explain this occurrence, newspapers traced it back to a large-scale speculator in New Orleans who had feared his holdings were too large and had therefore begun to liquidate his stocks; smaller speculators had then followed his example in a panic and had thus touched off the critical decline. Without attempting to assess the merits of the argument, let us note that the explanation here suggested again involves statements about antecedent conditions and the assumption of general regularities. The former include the facts that the first speculator had large stocks of cotton, that there were smaller speculators with considerable holdings, that there existed the institution of the cotton exchanges with their specific mode of operation, etc. The general regularities referred to are—as often in semi-popular explanations—not explicitly mentioned; but there is obviously implied some form of the law of supply and demand to account for the drop in cotton prices in terms of the greatly increased supply under conditions of practically unchanged demand; besides, reliance is necessary on certain regularities in the behavior of individuals who are trying to preserve or improve their economic position. Such laws cannot be formulated at present with satisfactory precision and generality, and therefore, the suggested explanation is surely incomplete, but its intention is unmistakably to account for the phenomenon by integrating it into a general pattern of economic and socio-psychological regularities.

We turn to an explanatory argument taken from the field of linguistics.[8] In Northern France, there are in use a large variety of words synonymous with the English 'bee', whereas in Southern France, essentially only one such word is in existence. For this discrepancy, the explanation has been suggested that in the Latin epoch, the South of France used the word 'apicula', the North the word 'apis'. The latter, because of a process of phonologic decay in Northern France, became the monosyllabic word 'ê'; and monosyllables tend to be eliminated, especially if they contain few consonantic elements, for they are apt to give rise to misunderstandings. Thus, to avoid confusion, other words were selected. But 'apicula', which was reduced to 'abelho', remained clear enough and was retained, and finally it even entered into the standard language, in the form 'abeille'. While the explanation here described is incomplete in the sense characterized in the previous section, it clearly exhibits reference to specific antecedent conditions as well as to general laws.[9]

While illustrations of this kind tend to support the view that explanation in biology, psychology, and the social sciences has the same structure as in the physical sciences, the opinion is rather widely held that in many instances, the causal type of explanation is essentially inadequate in fields other than physics and chemistry, and especially in the study of purposive behavior. Let us examine briefly some of the reasons which have been adduced in support of this view.

One of the most familiar among them is the idea that events involving the activities of humans singly or in groups have a peculiar uniqueness and irrepeatability which makes them inaccessible to causal explanation because the latter, with its reliance upon uniformities, presupposes repeatability of the phenomena under consideration. This argument which, incidentally, has also been used in support of the contention that the experimental method is inapplicable in psychology and the social sciences, involves a misunderstanding of the logical character of causal explanation. Every individual event, in the physical sciences no less than in psychology or the social sciences, is unique in the sense that it, with all its peculiar characteristics, does not repeat itself. Nevertheless, individual events may conform to, and thus be explainable by means of, general laws of the causal type. For all that a causal law asserts is that any event of a specified kind, i.e. any event having certain specified characteristics, is accompanied by another event which in turn has certain specified characteristics; for example, that in any event involving friction, heat is developed. And all that is needed for the testability and applicability of such laws is the recurrence of events with the antecedent characteristics, i.e. the repetition of those characteristics, but not of their individual instances. Thus, the argument is inconclusive. It gives occasion, however, to emphasize an important point concerning our earlier analysis: When we spoke of the explanation of a single event, the term "event" referred to the occurrence of some more or less complex characteristic in a specific spatio-temporal location or in a certain individual object, and not to *all* the characteristics of that object, or to all that goes on in that space-time region.

A second argument that should be mentioned here[10] contends that the establishment of scientific generalizations—and thus of explanatory principles—for human behavior is impossible because the reactions of an individual in a given situation depend not only upon that situation, but also upon the previous history of the individual. But surely, there is no *a priori* reason why generalizations should not be attainable which take into account this dependence of behavior on the past history of the agent. That indeed the given argument "proves" too much, and is therefore a *non sequitur*, is made evident by the existence of certain physical phenomena, such as magnetic hysteresis and elastic fatigue, in which the magnitude of a specific physical effect depends upon the past history of the system involved, and for which nevertheless certain general regularities have been established.

A third argument insists that the explanation of any phenomenon involving purposive behavior calls for reference to motivations and thus for teleological rather than causal analysis. For example, a fuller statement of the suggested explanation for the break in the cotton prices would have to indicate the large-scale speculator's motivations as one of the factors determining the event in question. Thus, we have to refer to goals sought; and this, so the argument runs, introduces a type of explanation alien to the physical sciences. Unquestionably, many of the—frequently incomplete—explanations which are offered for human actions involve reference to goals and motives; but does this make them essentially different from the causal explanations of physics and chemistry? One difference which suggests itself lies in the circumstance that in motivated behavior, the future appears to affect the present in a manner which is not found in the causal explanations of the physical sciences. But clearly, when the action of a person is motivated, say, by the desire to reach a certain objective, then it is not the as yet unrealized future event of attaining that goal which can be said to determine his present behavior, for indeed the goal may never be actually reached; rather—to put it in crude terms—it is (a) his desire, present before the action, to attain that particular objective, and (b) his belief, likewise present before the action, that such and such a course of action is most likely to have the desired effect. The determining motives and beliefs, therefore, have to be classified among the antecedent conditions of a motivational explanation, and there is no formal difference on this account between motivational and causal explanation.

Neither does the fact that motives are not accessible to direct observation by an outside observer constitute an essential difference between the two kinds of explanation; for the determining factors adduced in physical explanations also are very frequently inaccessible to direct observation. This is the case, for instance, when opposite electric charges are adduced in explanation of the mutual attraction of two metal spheres. The presence of those charges, while eluding direct observaton, can be ascertained by various kinds of indirect test, and that is sufficient to guarantee the empirical character of the explanatory statement. Similarly, the presence of certain motivations may be ascertainable only by indirect methods, which may include reference to linguistic utterances of the subject in question, slips of pen or tongue, etc.; but as long as these methods are "operationally determined" with reasonable clarity and precision, there is no essential difference in this respect between motivational explanation and causal explanation in physics.

A potential danger of explanation by motives lies in the fact that the method lends itself to the facile construction of *ex post facto* accounts without predictive force. An action is often explained by attributing it to motives conjectured only after the action has taken place. While this procedure is not in itself objectionable, its soundness, requires that (1) the motivational assumptions in question be capable of test, and (2) that suitable general laws be available to lend explanatory power to the assumed motives. Disregard of these requirements frequently deprives alleged motivational explanations of their cognitive significance.

The explanation of an action in terms of the agent's motives is sometimes considered as a special kind of teleological explanation. As was pointed out above, motivational explanation, if adequately formulated, conforms to the conditions for causal explanation, so that the term "teleological" is a misnomer if it is meant to imply either a non-causal character of the explanation or a peculiar determination of the present by the future. If this is borne in mind, however, the term "teleological" may be viewed, in this context, as referring to causal explanations in which some of the antecedent conditions are motives of the agent whose actions are to be explained.[11]

Teleological explanations of this kind have to be distinguished from a much more sweeping type, which has been claimed by certain schools of thought to be indispensable especially in biology. It consists in explaining characteristics of an organism by reference to certain ends or purposes which the characteristics are said to serve. In contradistinction to the cases examined before, the ends are not assumed here to be consciously or subconsciously pursued by the organism in question. Thus, for the phenomenon of mimicry, the explanation is sometimes offered that it serves the purpose of protecting the animals endowed with it from detection by its pursuers and thus tends to preserve the species. Before teleological hypotheses of this kind can be appraised as to their potential explanatory power, their meaning has to be clarified. If they are intended somehow to express the idea that the purposes they refer to are inherent in the design of the universe, then clearly they are not capable of empirical test and thus violate the requirement (R3) stated in §2. In certain cases, however, assertions about the purposes of biological characteristics may be translatable into statements in non-teleological terminology which assert that those characteristics function in a specific manner which is essential to keeping the organism alive or to preserving the species.[12] An attempt to state precisely what is meant by this latter assertion—or by the similar one that without those characteristics, and other things being equal, the organism or the species would not survive—encounters considerable difficulties. But these need not be discussed here. For even if we assume that biological statements in teleological form can be adequately translated into descriptive statements about the life-preserving function of certain biological characteristics, it is clear that (1) the use of the concept of purpose is not essential in these contexts, since the term "purpose" can be completely eliminated from the statements in question, and (2) teleological assumptions, while now endowed with empirical content, cannot serve as explanatory principles in the customary contexts. Thus, e.g., the fact that a given species of butterfly displays a particular kind of coloring cannot be inferred from—and therefore cannot be explained by means of—the statement that this type of coloring has the effect of protecting the butterflies from detection by pursuing birds, nor can the presence of red corpuscles in the human blood be inferred from the statement that those corpuscles have a specific function in assimilating oxygen and that this function is essential for the maintenance of life.

One of the reasons for the perseverance of teleological considerations in biology probably lies in the fruitfulness of the teleological approach as a heuristic device: Biological research which was psychologically motivated by a teleological orientation, by an interest in purposes in nature, has frequently led to important results which can be stated in non-teleological terminology and which increase our knowledge of the causal connections between biological phenomena.

Another aspect that lends appeal to teleological considerations is their anthropomorphic character. A teleological explanation tends to make us feel that we really "understand" the phenomenon in question, because it is accounted for in terms of purposes, with which we are familiar from our own experience of purposive behavior. But it is important to distinguish here understanding in the psychological sense of a feeling of empathic familiarity from understanding in the theoretical, or cognitive, sense of exhibiting the phenomenon to be explained as a special case of some general regularity. The frequent insistence that explanation means the reduction of something unfamiliar to ideas or experiences already familiar to us is indeed misleading. For while some scientific explanations do have this psychological effect, it is by no means universal: The free fall of a physical body may well be said to be a more familiar phenomenon than the law of gravitation, by means of which it can be explained; and surely the basic ideas of the theory of relativity will appear to many to be far less familiar than the phenomena for which the theory accounts.

"Familiarity" of the explanans is not only not necessary for a sound explanation, as has just been noted; it is not sufficient either. This is shown by the many cases in which a proposed explanans sounds suggestively familiar, but upon closer inspection proves to be a mere metaphor, or to lack testability, or to include no general laws and therefore to lack explanatory power. A case in point is the neovitalistic attempt to explain biological phenomena by reference to an entelechy or vital force. The crucial point here is not—as is sometimes said—that entelechies cannot be seen or otherwise directly observed; for that is true also of gravitational fields, and yet, reference to such fields is essential in the explanation of various physical phenomena. The decisive difference between the two cases is that the physical explanation provides (1) methods of testing, albeit indirectly, assertions about gravitational fields, and (2) general laws concerning the strength of gravitational fields, and the behavior of objects moving in them. Explanations by entelechies satisfy the analogue of neither of these two conditions. Failure to satisfy the first condition represents a violation of (R3); it renders all statements about entelechies inaccessible to empirical test and thus devoid of empirical meaning. Failure to comply with the second condition involves a violation of (R2). It deprives the concept of entelechy of all explanatory import; for explanatory power never resides in a concept, but always in the general laws in which it functions. Therefore, notwithstanding the feeling of familiarity it may evoke, the neovitalistic account cannot provide theoretical understanding.

The preceding observations about familiarity and understanding can be applied, in a similar manner, to the view held by some scholars that the explanation, or the understanding, of human actions requires an empathic understanding of the personalities of the agents.[13] This understanding of another person in terms of one's own psychological functioning may prove a useful heuristic device in the search for general psychological principles which might provide a theoretical explanation; but the existence of empathy on the part of the scientist is neither a necessary nor a sufficient condition for the explanation, or the scientific understanding, of any human action. It is not necessary, for the behavior of psychotics or of people belonging to a culture very different from that of the scientist may sometimes be explainable and predictable in terms of general principles even though the scientist who establishes or applies those principles may not be able to understand his subjects empathically. And empathy is not sufficient to guarantee a sound explanation, for a strong feeling of empathy may exist even in cases where we completely misjudge a given personality. Moroever, as Zilsel has pointed out, empathy leads with ease to incompatible results; thus, when the population of a town has long been subjected to heavy bombing attacks, we can understand, in the empathic sense, that its morale should have broken down completely, but we can understand with the same ease also that it should have developed a defiant spirit of resistance. Arguments of this kind often appear quite convincing; but they are of an *ex post facto* character and lack cognitive significance unless they are supplemented by testable explanatory principles in the form of laws or theories.

Familiarity of the explanans, therefore, no matter whether it is achieved through the use of teleological terminology, through neovitalistic metaphors, or through other means, is no indication of the cognitive import and the predictive force of a proposed explanation. Besides, the extent to which an idea will be considered as familiar varies from person to person and from time to time, and a psychological factor of this kind certainly cannot serve as a standard in assessing the worth of a proposed explanation. The decisive requirement for every sound explanation remains that it subsume the explanandum under general laws. . . .

II. Logical Analysis of Law and Explanation

4. *Problems of the Concept of General Law.* From our general survey of the characteristics of scientific explanation, we now turn to a closer examination of its logical structure. The explanation of a phenomenon, we noted, consists in its subsumption under laws or under a theory. But what is a law, what is a theory? While the meaning of these concepts seems intuitively clear, an attempt to construct adequate explicit definitions for them encounters considerable difficulties. In the present section, some basic problems of the concept of law will be described and analyzed; in the next section, we intend to propose, on the basis of the suggestions thus obtained, definitions of law and of explanation for a formalized model language of a simple logical structure [omitted here—Eds.].

The concept of law will be construed here so as to apply to true statements only. The apparently plausible alternative procedure of requiring high confirmation rather than truth of a law seems to be inadequate: It would lead to a relativized concept of law, which would be expressed by the phrase "sentence S is a law relative to the evidence E." This does not accord with the meaning customarily assigned to the concept of law in science and in methodological inquiry. Thus, for example, we would not say that Bode's general formula for the distance of the planets from the sun was a law relative to the astronomical evidence available in the 1770s, when Bode propounded it, and that it ceased to be a law after the discovery of Neptune and the determination of its distance from the sun; rather, we would say that the limited original evidence had given a high probability to the assumption that the formula was a law, whereas more recent additional information reduced that probability so much as to make it it practically certain that Bode's formula is not generally true, and hence not a law.[14]

Apart from being true, a law will have to satisfy a number of additional conditions. These can be studied independently of the factual requirement of truth, for they refer, as it were, to all logically possible laws, no matter whether factually true or false. Adopting a term proposed by Goodman,[15] we will say that a sentence is *lawlike* if it has all the characteristics of a general law, with the possible exception of truth. Hence, every law is a lawlike sentence, but not conversely.

Our problem of analyzing the notion of law thus reduces to that of explicating the concept of lawlike sentence. We shall construe the class of lawlike sentences as including analytic general statements, such as 'A rose is a rose', as well as the lawlike sentences of empirical science, which have empirical content.[16] It will not be necessary to require that each lawlike sentence permissible in explanatory contexts be of the second kind; rather, our definition of explanation will be so constructed as to guarantee the factual character of the totality of the laws—though not of every single one of them—which function in an explanation of an empirical fact.

What are the characteristics of lawlike sentences? First of all, lawlike sentences are statements of universal form, such as 'All robins' eggs are greenishblue', 'All metals are conductors of electricity', 'At constant pressure, any gas expands with increasing temperature'. As these examples illustrate, a lawlike sentence usually is not only of universal, but also of conditional form; it makes an assertion to the effect that universally, if a certain set of conditions, *C*, is realized, then another specified set of conditions, *E*, is realized as well. The standard form for the symbolic expression of a lawlike sentence is therefore the universal conditional. However, since any conditional statement can be transformed into a non-conditional one, conditional form will not be considered as essential for a lawlike sentence, while universal character will be held indispensable.

But the requirement of universal form is not sufficient to characterize lawlike sentences. Suppose, for example, that a given basket, *b*, contains at a certain time *t* a number of red apples and nothing else.[17] Then the statement

(S_1) Every apple in basket *b* at time *t* is red

is both true and of universal form. Yet the sentence does not qualify as a law; we would refuse, for example, to explain by subsumption under it the fact that a particular apple chosen at random from the basket is red. What distinguishes S_1 from a lawlike sentence? Two points suggest themselves, which will be considered in turn, namely, finite scope, and reference to a specified object.

First, the sentence S_1 makes in effect an assertion about a finite number of objects only, and this seems irreconcilable with the notion of law.[18] But are not Kepler's laws considered as lawlike although they refer to a finite set of planets only? And might we not even be willing to consider as lawlike a sentence such as the following?

(S_2) All the sixteen ice cubes in the freezing tray of this refrigerator have a temperature of less than 10 degrees centigrade.

This point might well be granted; but there is an essential difference between S_1, on the one hand, and Kepler's laws, as well as S_2, on the other: The latter, while finite in scope, are known to be consequences of more comprehensive laws whose scope is not limited, while for S_1 this is not the case.

Adopting a procedure recently suggested by Reichenbach,[19] we will therefore distinguish between fundamental and derivative laws. A statement will be called a derivative law if it is of universal character and follows from some fundamental laws. The concept of fundamental law requires further clarification; so far, we may say that fundamental laws, and similarly fundamental lawlike sentences, should satisfy a certain condition of nonlimitation of scope.

It would be excessive, however, to deny the status of fundamental lawlike sentence to all statements which, in effect, make an assertion about a finite class of objects only, for that would rule out also a sentence such as 'All robins' eggs are greenish-blue', since presumably the class of all robins' eggs—past, present, and future—is finite. But again, there is an essential difference between this sentence and, say, S_1. It requires empirical knowledge to establish the finiteness of the class of robins' eggs, whereas, when the sentence S_1 is construed in a manner which renders it intuitively unlawlike, the terms 'basket b' and 'apple' are understood so as to imply finiteness of the class of apples in the basket at time t. Thus, so to speak, the meaning of its constitutive terms alone—without additional factual information—entails that S_1 has a finite scope. Fundamental laws, then, will have to be construed so as to satisfy a condition of nonlimited scope; our formulation of that condition however, which refers to what is entailed by "the meaning" of certain expressions, is too vague and will have to be revised later. Let us note in passing that the stipulation here envisaged would bar from the class of fundamental lawlike sentences also such undesirable candidates as 'All uranic objects are spherical', where 'uranic' means the property of being the planet Uranus; indeed, while this sentence has universal form, it fails to satisfy the condition of nonlimited scope.

In our search for a general characterization of lawlike sentences, we now turn to a second clue which is provided by the sentence S_1. In addition to violating the condition of nonlimited scope, that sentence has the peculiarity of making reference to a particular object, the basket b; and this, too, seems to violate the universal character of a law.[20] The restriction which seems indicated here, should again be applied to fundamental lawlike sentences only; for a true general statement about the free fall of physical bodies on the moon, while referring to a particular object, would still constitute a law, albeit a derivative one.

It seems reasonable to stipulate, therefore, that a fundamental lawlike sentence must be of universal form and must contain no essential—i.e., uneliminable—occurrences of designations for particular objects. But this is not sufficient; indeed, just at this point, a particularly serious difficulty presents itself. Consider the sentence.

(S_3) Everything that is either an apple in basket b at time t or a sample of ferric oxide is red.

If we use a special expression, say 'x is ferple', as synonymous with 'x is either an apple in b at t or a sample of ferric oxide', then the content of S_3 can be expressed in the form.

(S_4) Everything that is ferple is red.

The statement thus obtained is of universal form and contains no designations of particular objects, and it also satisfies the condition of nonlimited scope; yet clearly, S_4 can qualify as a fundamental lawlike sentence no more than can S_3.

As long as 'ferple' is a defined term of our language, the difficulty can readily be met by stipulating that after elimination of defined terms, a fundamental lawlike sentence must not contain essential occurrences of designations for particular objects. But this way out is of no avail when 'ferple', or another term of its kind, is a primitive predicate of the language under consideration. This reflection indicates that certain restrictions have to be imposed upon those predicates—i.e., terms for properties or relations—which may occur in fundamental lawlike sentences.[21]

More specifically, the idea suggests itself of permitting a predicate in a fundamental lawlike sentence only if it is purely universal, or, as we shall say, purely qualitative, in character; in other words, if a statement of its meaning does not require reference to any one particular object or spatio-temporal location. Thus, the terms 'soft', 'green', 'warmer than', 'as long as', 'liquid', 'electrically charged', 'female', 'father of', are purely qualitative predicates, while 'taller than the Eiffel Tower', 'medieval', 'lunar', 'arctic', 'Ming' are not.[22]

Exclusion from fundamental lawlike sentences of predicates which are not purely qualitative would at the same time ensure satisfaction of the condition of nonlimited scope; for the meaning of a purely qualitative predicate does not require a finite extension; and indeed, all the sentences considered above which violate the condition of nonlimited scope make explicit or implicit reference to specific objects.

The stipulation just proposed suffers, however, from the vagueness of the concept of purely qualitative predicate. The question whether indication of the meaning of a given predicate in English does or does not require reference to some specific object does not always permit of an unequivocal answer since English as a natural language does not provide explicit definitions or other clear explications of meaning for its terms. It seems therefore reasonable to attempt definition of the concept of law not with respect to English or any other natural language, but rather with respect to a formalized language—let us call it a model language L—which is governed by a well-determined system of logical rules, and in which every term either is characterized as primitive or is introduced by an explicit definition in terms of the primitives.

This reference to a well-determined system is customary in logical research and is indeed quite natural in the context of any attempt to develop precise criteria for certain logical distinctions. But it does not by itself suffice to overcome the specific difficulty under discussion. For while it is now readily possible to characterize as not purely qualitative all those among the defined predicates in L whose definiens contains an essential occurrence of some individual name, our problem remains open for the primitives of the language, whose meanings are not determined by definitions with the language, but rather by semantical laws of interpretation. For we want to permit the interpretation of the primitives of *L* by means of such attributes as blue, hard, solid, warmer, but not by the properties of being a descendant of Napoleon, or an arctic animal, or a Greek statue; and the difficulty is precisely that of stating rigorous criteria for the distinction between the permissible and the nonpermissible interpretations. Thus the problem of finding an adequate definition for purely qualitative attributes now arises again; namely for the concepts of the meta-language in which the semantical interpretation of the primitives is formulated. We may postpone an encounter with the difficulty by presupposing formalization of the semantical meta-language, the meta-meta-language, and so forth, but somewhere, we will have to stop at a nonformalized meta-language; and for it, a characterization of purely qualitative predicates will be needed and will present much the same problems as nonformalized English, with which we began. The characterization of a purely qualitative predicate as one whose meaning can be made explicit without reference to any one particular object points to the intended meaning but does not explicate it precisely, and the problem of an adequate definition of purely qualitative predicates remains open.

There can be little doubt, however, that there exists a large number of predicates which would be rather generally recognized as purely qualitative in the sense here pointed out, and as permissible in the formulation of fundamental lawlike sentences; some examples have beeen given above, and the list could be readily enlarged. When we speak of purely qualitative predicates, we shall henceforth have in mind predicates of this kind. . . .

NOTES

1. This essay grew out of discussions with Dr. Paul Oppenheim; it was published in coauthorship with him and is here reprinted with his permission. Our individual contributions cannot be separated in detail; the present author is responsible . . . for the final formulation of the entire text.

Some of the ideas set forth in Part II originated with our common friend, Dr. Kurt Grelling, who suggested them to us in a discussion carried on by correspondence. Grelling and his wife subsequently became victims of the Nazi terror during the Second World War; by including in this essay at least some of Grelling's contributions, which are explicitly identified, we hope to realize his wish that his ideas on this subject might not entirely fall into oblivion.

Paul Oppenheim and I are much indebted to Professors Rudolf Carnap, Herbert Feigl, Nelson Goodman, and W. V. Quine for stimulating discussions and constructive criticism.

2. These two expressions, derived from the Latin *explanare*, were adopted in preference to the perhaps more customary terms "explicandum" and "explicans" in order to reserve the latter for use in the context of explication of meaning, or analysis. . . .

3. (Added in 1964.) Requirement (R4) characterizes what might be called a correct or *true explanation*. In analysis of the logical structure of explanatory arguments, therefore, that requirement may be disregarded. . . .

4. (1924) p. 533.

5. (Added in 1964.) Or rather, causal explanation is one variety fo the deductive type of explanation here under discussion.

6. The account given above of the general characteristics of explanation and prediction in science is by no means novel; it merely summarizes and states explicitly some fundamental points which have been recognized by many scientists and methodologists.

Thus, e.g., Mill says: "An individual fact is said to be explained, by pointing out its cause, that is, by stating the law or laws of causation, of which its production is an instance," and "a law or uniformity in nature is said to be explained, when another law or laws are pointed out, of which that law itself is but a case, and from which it could be deduced" (1858, Book III, Chapter XII, section 1). Similarly, Jevons, whose general characterization of explanation was critically discussed above, stresses that "the most important process of explanation consists in showing that an observed fact is one case of a general law or tendency" (1924, p. 533). Ducasse states the same point as follows: "Explanation essentially consists in the offering of a hypothesis of fact, standing to the fact to be explained as case of antecedent to case of consequent of some already known law of connection" (1925, pp. 150-51). A lucid analysis of the fundamental structure of explanation and prediction was given by Popper in (1935), section 12, and, in an improved version, in his work (1945), especially in Chapter 25 and in note 7 for that chapter.—For a recent characterization of explanation as subsumption under general theories, cf., for example, Hull's concise discussion in (1943a), chapter I. A clear elementary examination of certain aspects of explanation is given in Hospers (1946), and a concise survey of many of the essentials of scientific explanation which are considered in the first two aprts of the present study may be found in Feigl (1945), pp. 284 ff.

7. On the subject of explanation in the social sciences, especially in history, cf. also the following publications, which may serve to supplement and amplify the brief discussion to be presented here: Hempel (1942); Popper (1945); White (1943); and the articles *Cause* and *Understanding* in Beard and Hook (1946).

8. The illustration is taken from Bonfante (1946), section 3.

9. While in each of the last two illustrations, certain regularities are unquestionably relied upon in the explanatory argument, it is not possible to argue convincingly that the intended laws, which at present cannot all be stated explicitly, are of a causal rather than a statistical character. It is quite possible that most or all of the regularities which will be discovered as sociology develops will be of a statistical type. Cf., on this point, the suggestive observations in Zilsel (1941), section 3, and (1941a). This issue does not affect, however, the main point we wish to make here, namely that in the social no less than in the physical sciences, subsumption under general regularities is indispensable for the explanation and the theoretical understanding of any phenomenon.

10. Cf., for example, F. H. Knight's presentation of this argument in (1924), pp. 252-52.

11. For a detailed logical analysis of the concept of motivation in psychological theory, see Koch (1941). A stimulating discussion of teleological behavior form the standpoint of contemporary physics and biology is contained in the article (1943) by Rosenblueth, Wiener, and Bigelow. . . .

12. An analysis of teleological statements in biology along these lines may be found in Woodger (1929), especially pp. 432 ff; essentially the same interpretation is advocated by Kaufmann in (1944), Chapter 8.

13. For a more detailed discussion of this view on the basis of the general principles outlined above, cf. Zilsel (1941), sections 7 and 8, and Hempel (1942), section 6.

14. The requirement of truth for laws has the consequence that a given empirical statement S can never be definitely known to be a law; for the sentence affirming the truth of S is tantamount to S and is therefore capable only of acquiring a more or less high probability, or degree of confirmation, relative to the experimental evidence available at any given time. On this point, cf. Carnap (1946). For an excellent nontechnical exposition of the semantical concept of truth, which is here invoked, the reader is referred to Tarski (1944).

15. (1947), p. 125.

16. This procedure was suggested by Goodman's approach in (1947). Reichenbach, in a detailed examination of the concept of law, similarly construes his concept of nomological statement

as including both analytic and synthetic sentences: cf. (1947). Chapter VIII.

17. The difficulty illustrated by this example was stated concisely by Langford (1941), who referred to it as the problem of distinguishing between universals of fact and causal universals. For further discussion and illustration of this point, see also Chisholm (1946), especially pp. 301f. A systematic analysis of the problem was given by Goodman in (1947), especially part III. While not concerned with the specific point under discussion, the detailed examination of counterfactual conditionals and their relation to laws of nature, in Chapter VIII of Lewis (1946), contains important observations on several of the issues raised in the present section.

18. The view that laws should be construed as not being limited to a finite domain has been expressed, among others, by Popper (1935), section 13 and by Reichenbach (1947), p. 369.

19. (1947), p. 361. Our terminology as well as the definitions to be proposed later for the two types of law do not coincide with Reichenbach's, however.

20. In physics, the idea that a law should not refer to any particular object has found its expression in the maxim that the general laws of physics should contain no reference to specific space-time points, and that spatio-temporal coordinates should occur in them only in the form of differences or differentials.

21. The point illustrated by the sentences S_3 and S_4 above was made by Goodman, who has also emphasized the need to improve certain restrictions upon the predicates whose occurrence is to be permissible in lawlike sentences. These redicates are essentially the same as those which Goodman calls projectible. Goodman has suggested that the problems of establishing precise criteria for projectibility, of interpreting counterfactual conditionals, and of defining the concept of law are so intimately related as to be virtually aspects of a single problem. Cf. his articles (1946) and 1947). One suggestion for an analysis of projectibility has been made by Carnap in (1947). Goodman's note (1947a) contains critical observations on Carnap's proposals.

22. That laws, in addition to being of universal form, must contain only purely universal predicates was argued by Popper (1935, sections 14, 15). Our alternative expression 'purely qualitative predicate' was chosen in analogy to Carnap's term 'purely qualitative property' cf. (1947). The above characterization of purely universal predicates seems preferable to a simpler and perhaps more customary one, to the effect that a statement of the meaning of the predicate must require no reference to particular objects. That formulation might be too restrictive since it could be argued that stating the meaning of such purely qualitative terms as 'blue' or 'hot' requires illustrative reference to some particular object which has the quality in question. The essential point is that no one specific object has to be chosen; any one in the logically unlimited set of blue or of hot objects will do. In explicating the meaning of 'taller than the Eiffel Tower', 'being an apple in basket b at time t', 'medieval', etc., however, reference has to be made to one specific object or to some one in a limited set of objects.

7

Laws and Conditional Statements

Karel Lambert and Gordon Britten

We can begin with the concept of a law. The first thing to notice is that "law," like "cause" and "explanation," is used in a variety of ways, many of them only vaguely related.[1] In fact, we ourselves have used "law" (or "general law") interchangeably with "generalization," "regularity," and "statement of universal form." Before proceeding much further, these various expressions will have to be sorted out.

Following what is perhaps the most widespread custom, let us say that laws are *statements* that express *regularities*. The properties of laws in which we will be interested will be properties of statements. It is important to keep this in mind, for confusion results when one fails to distinguish between laws as statements and laws as what certain statements express. "Generalization" is ambiguous in exactly the same way: for reasons of clarity, we construe generalizations also as statements and not as what statements of a certain kind express. The question, then, is to decide whether there is a distinction to be made between laws and generalizations, as statements of different types.

One further preliminary. We are going to restrict our attention to the simplest case, where a law has the form of a nonstatistical *generalized conditional* statement. In other words: where a law has the form "For any (every, all) object(s) x, if x is such and such then x is so and so." Such nonstatistical generalized conditionals may also be said to be statements of *universal form*. For they assert that every object (or event or condition) that has certain properties also has certain other properties. One of the laws we have mentioned previously is a case in point: "For every piece of thread T, there is a threshold weight W, such that if an object is suspended from T and exceeds the threshold weight weight W, then the thread will break." It should be noticed that mathematically phrased laws merely appear to have form. *"G_s = W/V."* What is suppressed in the original mathematical statement is the reference to all objects, that is, its generality.

Let us assume that laws are statements of universal form.[2] At the same time, it does not seem to be the case that all statements of universal form are laws (for example, "All animals are men"). This claim can be defended by considering additional criteria that statements of universal form must satisfy to be counted as laws.

One criterion is that laws are universal statements that have empirical content. A use to which this criterion is frequently put is to rule out nonsense laws and spurious explanations based on them. For example, one might want to say that the universal statement "All glubbifiers are irascible" is patent nonsense, hence no law, and any "explanation" in which it figured would be unacceptable. It is not at all clear, however, that the line between "sensical" and nonsensical statements coincides with the (for the moment presumed) line between statements that have empirical content and those that do not. It is even to be wondered whether there is *any* effective way of separating sense from nonsense. For many of his sixteenth-century contemporaries, Copernicus' heliocentric hypothesis was the "Copernican Paradox." For one thing, it was virtually part of the meaning of the word "earth" that this planet be the center of the universe.

The criterion of empirical content is also intended to rule out, for example, "All bachelors are unmarried men," as a law, and the following as a genuine explanation of the fact that Jones is an unmarried man: "Jones is a bachelor and all bachelors are unmarried men; therefore, Jones is an unmarried man."

Indeed, we would undoubtedly be very hesitant to accept this as an *explanation* of the fact that Jones is an unmarried man. And it is tempting, as a result, to distinguish between laws and non-laws in terms of the empirical content of the former. . . . *Analytic* statements (that is, statements true by virtue of the meanings of the words they contain), even of universal form, are not *laws*. There is something circular about the "explanatory" arguments into which they enter. Thus, to consider another example:

1. All paranoids suffer delusions of grandeur.
2. Jones is a paranoid.

Therefore,

3. Jones suffers from delusions of grandeur.

If we assume that the definition of the word "paranoid" includes as part of its meaning the expression "suffers from delusions of grandeur" (that is, [1] is analytic), this "explanation" of Jones' suffering delusions of grandeur because he is paranoid does not appear to advance our understanding.

Despite the intuitive appeal of these remarks, however, we must be very careful. The notion of "empirical content" and the attendant analytic/synthetic distinction are unclear. Admittedly in the cases just considered, the intended analytic/synthetic, empirical/nonempirical contrasts are fairly easy to draw.[3] But cases of this kind are by and large trivial. In more complicated cases of the sort one typically encounters in science, a great many principles are involved in the explanation of particular events. Perhaps one can distinguish between these as having "more" or "less" empirical content; within the context of some specified theory, one can make the distinction sharper still. If the line of argument sketched in the final section of the previous chapter was sound, however, a general distinction between statements that have empirical content and those that do not, for example, between the laws of mathematics and the laws of physics, is at least problematic (once again excepting trivialities like "All bachelors are unmarried men," which are of negligible scientific and systematic importance). We do not have to abandon our earlier requirements that explanations have empirical content. But we should be alert to the possibility that it might need modification.

A second criterion laws might be expected to fulfill is that they be true. Thus, "All swans are white" does not count as a law (assuming provisionally that it satisfies the other criteria) because there are black swans; we cannot explain a particular swan's being white on the basis of it.

This criterion seems even more intuitive than the first. Surely we would not countenance false laws of nature. But there are difficulties with it as well.

The first is that many statements commonly regarded as laws, for example, those of classical mechanics, hold only approximately. They are not, in all strictness, true. If we insist that explanation essentially involve laws and that laws must be true, we are faced with the unpleasant choice of saying either that, for example, Galileo did not *really* explain certain facts about the behavior of objects on inclined planes, or that when he made them his statements were true but now no longer are. Perhaps a less painful move is to relax the requirement that laws be true. There are also reasons . . . for maintaining that at least some laws of nature are neither true nor false. Rather, they serve as general principles, somewhat on the order of moral rules,[4] whose function is to provide a theoretical framework with respect to which research can be carried out and empirical generalizations tested. To put it in a slightly different way, at least some laws of nature seem to have a primarily normative, not descriptive, function.

In any case, there are reasons for leaving it open for now whether laws must be true or not. We can do this by restricting our discussion to *lawlike* statements. Statements are lawlike if they satisfy all the other criteria for laws, independent of whether or not they have a truth value.

The third, and most important, of these criteria can best be taken up by way of example.[5] Consider the two statements:

1. All persons sitting on a certain bench in Boston are Irish.
2. Any body subject to no external forces maintains a constant velocity.

There are many (interrelated) differences between these two statements that might lead us to call the second, but not the first, "lawlike," although both are of universal form. Recall that it is not in virtue of their form that laws are to be distinguished from non-laws.

To begin with, the first statement seems to be an *accidental* generalization, about what in fact happens to be the case, whereas the second is a law of nature. It does not follow from the first that if someone *were* to sit on a certain bench in Boston he *would* be Irish, nor could we very well explain someone's being Irish by referring to the fact that he was sitting on that bench. But it does follow from the second that if a body *were* subject to no external forces it *would* maintain a constant velocity, and it does (intuitively) explain a body's having a constant velocity to be told that it is subject to no external forces.

Statements of the form "If *A* were (had been) the case, then *B* would be (would have been) the case," where in fact *A* is not (has not been) the case, are called *counterfactual conditionals.* The present suggestion is that lawlike statements support counterfactual conditionals, while nonlawlike statements do not. In turn, the ability to support counterfactuals (as they are called for short) is linked to the predictive, and hence explanatory, force that laws in contrast to non-laws have.

Conditional statements quite generally allow us to speak about potential (as distinct from actual) events, cases in which should *A* occur, *B* would also. There is thus a sense in which lawlike statements, insofar as they support conditionals, possess a generality that nonlawlike statements do not. The accidental generalization, "All persons sitting on a certain bench in Boston are Irish," is equivalent to the finite conjunction of statements, "Pat is sitting on a certain bench in Boston and is Irish," and so on, whereas the lawlike statement, "Any body subject to no external forces maintains a constant velocity," is unrestrictedly about all objects whatsoever. This is perhaps another way to indicate its explanatory force.

A distinction between laws and generalizations on this basis has recently been given a more than academic prominence in the controversy surrounding cigarette smoking and health. Spokesmen for the tobacco industry are inclined to say that statements expressing a correlation between cigarette smoking and, for example, lung cancer are merely accidental generalizations. A high statistical correlation should not be mistaken for a causal connection; generalizations linking cigarette smoking and lung cancer do not support conditionals to the effect that if someone were, for example, to smoke two packs of cigarettes daily for a specified period of time, the chances of his getting lung cancer would be such and such. The Public Health Service, on the other hand, tends to grant the status of laws to these same generalizations. Which is to say, at least, that they do support the appropriate conditionals. Waiving difficulties with the notion of "confirmation" for the moment, the P.H.S. might want to stake its case further on the extent to which projections made on the basis of the purported laws were in fact realized. Of course, this still would not force the tobacco industry to say that a "causal" connection had been demonstrated; other criteria of lawlikeness, they could insist, remain to be satisfied.[6]

We take it, then, that it is apparently a necessary (if not also a sufficient) criterion for being a lawlike statement that a statement of universal form support conditionals, in particular counterfactual conditionals. The usefulness of this criterion depends in part on the sureness of our grip on the notions of "support" and "counterfactual conditional."

One way of analyzing such conditionals, in terms of the so-called "material conditional" of classical logic, will not work. The material conditional— "If *P* then *Q*"—is so defined as to be true whenever "*P*" is false or "*Q*" is true. Since the antecedents of counterfactual conditionals are always unrealized, that is, "*P*" is always false, counterfactuals construed as material conditionals would always be true. But this is not acceptable, as can be seen by comparing the two counterfactuals.

1. If any body were subject to no external force, it would maintain a constant velocity.
2. If any body were subject to no external force, it would *not* maintain a constant velocity.

On the model of the material conditional, both counterfactuals are true, although their consequents are incompatible! A related way of rejecting the material conditional analysis is to point up the importance of distinguishing between conditionals that are vacuously true (true simply because their antecedents are unrealized) and those that are not. The material conditional analysis obviously does not allow us to do this.

More generally, many conditionals simply are not truth-functional. We may know the truth values of their component statements and, from this information alone, be unable to determine the truth value of the compound. For example, I may know that "Willie Mays played in the American League" is false, as is "Willie Mays hit four hundred," without knowing whether or not Mays would have hit four hundred had he played in the American League.[7]

A more promising suggestion is that a conditional is like an enthymematic argument, one premise of which is the antecedent of the conditional, the conclusion of which is the consequent. What is omitted, and what serves to connect antecedent with consequent, is simply the law (or laws) that we have taken to support it. A (vastly oversimplified) case in point: "Had the match been struck it would have lighted" is a counterfactual, the consequent of which is derivable from the antecedent with the help of certain laws about matches being struck and lighting.

The proponents of this suggestion maintain that, intuitively, there is a "connection" between maintaining a constant velocity and being acted on by no external forces, whereas there is no such "connection" between sitting on a certain bench in Boston and being Irish. It is this connection that allows for valid predictions, and hence, explanations. But the connection between antecedent and consequent in a true conditional is none other than that which a law provides. From the antecedent and the law, we can derive the consequent.

It is in this way that laws serve to support conditionals. Similarly, the *necessity* of a match's lighting when stuck is simply a function of the fact that it follows from the law as a logical consequence.

There is a circle here, of course. We have distinguished between laws and generalizations by claiming that only the former supported counterfactual conditionals, and we have analyzed such conditionals in terms of the lawlike connection that exists between their antecedent and consequent. The circle does not undermine the distinction suggested. But it does indicate that we do not understand the distinction very well unless the circle can be broken. One way in which to break the circle is to say that lawlike statements, in contrast to accidental generalizations, are *confirmed by their instances.*[8] . . .

One could also argue, as have some philosophers, that additional criteria of lawlikeness are required if laws are to play the explanatory role assigned to them. Support of counterfactual conditionals is not enough. For example, even if it were a conditional-supporting generalization that every time the sky is red in the morning it rains in the afternoon,[9] we would not explain the fact that it is raining in the afternoon by pointing to this purportedly "lawlike" statement and the fact that the sky was red this morning. Other philosophers reject this sort of distinction between explanatory laws and nonexplanatory generalizations, contending that it is rooted in naive (unexamined) causal and teleological intuitions. For them, the only distinction to be made is that between laws and accidental generalizations, by means of the counterfactual conditional criterion.

But consider these two statements:

1. All pieces of copper wire at –270° C are good conductors.
2. All unicorns are fleet of foot.

Both of these statements are unrestricted universals, and presumably both would support (insofar as they implied) the corresponding counterfactual conditionals. Take it as (nonanalytically) true that if anything were a unicorn it would be fleet of foot. Still, it is unlikely that anyone would regard the statement about unicorns as a law. Nor can the two statements be distinguished by virtue of the fact that the first but not the second has positive instances. We can easily suppose that no copper has been checked out at –270° C. The difference, rather, seems to lie in the fact that the copper-conducting statement is systematically connected with a larger theoretical framework, whereas the unicorn-fleeting statement is not. To put it in a slightly different way, what enables us to call the first but not the second statement "lawlike" is the *position* of the first in the existing body of knowledge. In particular, whether or not it has any positive instances, it will be granted law status if it *follows from* other laws and theories. That copper at –270° C is a good conductor, for instance, ostensibly is a consequence of the law that all copper is a good conductor.

On the other hand, even well-confirmed unrestricted universals will not count as laws if they are not systematically interconnected with a larger theoretical framework. What leads us to reject the red sky in the morning/ rain in the afternoon generalization as a law, or an *explanatory* law, is that it is an isolated assertion having no apparent theoretical ramifications.[10]

This point can be elaborated. It is not enough that a particular universal statement be exceptionless to qualify as a law. It must also be the case that the theoretical framework to which it is connected does not permit exceptions to it. Certainly nothing in current scientific theory precludes, for example, that anyone sitting on a certain bench in Boston is not Irish, nor that unicorns are not fleet of foot. Similarly, whether there are laws linking cigarette smoking to lung cancer depends on how the statistical generalizations correlating them relate to a larger body of scientific theory.[11] Generalizations that are not systematically connected with other laws are merely accidental, they rule out potential instances (for instance, a non-Irishman sitting on that bench in Boston) that scientific theory otherwise permits. . . .

NOTES

1. In the case of laws of nature and laws of the land, this relation seems to be very vague indeed.

2. We said earlier that certain laws are of statistical or probabilistic form. Probabilistic laws raise their own problems, but none of these affect the points to be made in this section.

3. There is a complication in the "paranoid" case. Very plausibly, we could say that suffering delusions of grandeur was a *symptom* of or criterion for paranoia and that although in virtue of this fact there was a kind of "meaning" connection between them this did not preclude "All paranoids suffer delusions of grandeur" from functioning as a law.

4. We do not mean to suggest that they are like moral rules in all repects.

5. A classic contemporary discussion of many of the points that follow can be found in Nelson Goodman's book, *Fact, Fiction, and Forecast* (Indianapolis, Indiana: The Bobbs-Merrill Company, Inc., 1965).

6. The cigarette smoking-lung cancer controversy illustrates in a very sharp way almost all the issues raised in this chapter. The Public Health Service, for example, is explicitly "inductivist" about explanation; it maintains that a high statistical correlation can, when subjected to a variety of tests, be used to assert a casual connection, that is, can be used to explain individual instances of lung cancer, and so on.

Both sides of the controversy are also quite explicitly aware that in many respects the issue is philosophical: How is the concept of cause to be analyzed? See the very interesting discussion in the Report of the Advisory Committee to the Surgeon General of the Public Health Service, *Smoking and Health* (Princeton, N.J.: Van Nostrand Reinhold Co., 1964), pp. 19-21 and *passim*.

7. The example is Robert Stalnaker's; his analysis of conditional statements will be mentioned shortly.

8. Another, extremely interesting, analysis of conditions has recently been advanced by Robert Stalnaker. See his paper, "A Theory of Conditionals," in *Studies in Logical Theory*, ed Nicholas Rescher (American Philosophical Quarterly Monograph Series, 1968). Stalnaker is concerned with the analysis of conditional statements generally, not primarily, as we have been, with counterfactuals. He rejects both of the analyses suggested above, and proposes instead an analysis in terms of possible or hypothetical states of affairs.

Stalnaker's analysis has a great deal to recommended it. It does not, as he himself notes, however, allow us to bypass the circle described in analyzing counterfactual conditionals. We may know the truth-conditions for conditional statements (that is, the conditions with respect to which they are evaluated) without knowing whether particular conditionals are true or false. And presumably those counterfactuals, at any rate, are true which are supported by laws in the way we suggested originally.

9. That is, even if this were a generalization that held without exception and had unrestricted application.

10. This point is emphasized by Ernest Nagel in the course of an extended discussion of laws and counterfactuals, in *The Structure of Science* (New York: Harcourt, Brace & World, 1961), pp. 47-78.

11. In this case, perhaps most importantly to a molecular-chemical theory.

8

Towards an Aristotelean Theory of Scientific Explanation

B. A. Brody

Let us begin by considering the following explanation of why it is that sodium normally combines with chlorine in a ratio of one-to-one[1]:

(A) (1) sodium normally combines with bromine in a ratio of one-to-one
   (2) everything that normally combines with bromine in a ratio of one-to-one normally combines with chlorine in a ratio of one-to-one
   _____
   (3) therefore, sodium normally combines with chlorine in a ratio of one-to-one.

This purported explanation meets all of the requirements laid down by Hempel's covering law model for scientific explanation ([5], pp. 248–249). After all, the law to be explained is deduced from two other general laws which are true and have empirical content. Nevertheless, this purported explanation seems to have absolutely no explanatory power. And even if one were to say, as I think it would be wrong to say, that it does have at least a little explanatory power, why is it that it is not as good an explanation of the law in question (that sodium normally combines with chlorine in a ratio of one-to-one) as the explanation of that law in terms of the atomic structure of sodium and chlorine and the theory of chemical bonding? The covering law model, as it stands, seems to offer us no answer to that question.

A defender of the covering law model would, presumably, offer the following reply: both of these explanations, each of which meets the requirements of the model, are explanations of the law in question, but the explanation in terms of atomic structure is to be preferred to the explanation in terms of the way that sodium combines with bromine because the former contains in its explanans more powerful laws than the latter. The laws about atomic structure and the theory of bonding are more powerful than the law about the ratio with which sodium combines with bromine because more phenomena can be explained by the former than by the latter.

I also find this answer highly unsatisfactory, partially because I don't see that (A) has any explanatory power at all. But that is not the real problem. The real problem is that this answer leaves something very mysterious. I can see why, on the grounds just mentioned, one would prefer to have laws like the ones about atomic structure rather than laws like the one about the ratio with which sodium and bromine combine. But why does that make explanations in terms of the latter type of laws less preferable? Or to put the question another way, why should laws that explain more explain better?

So much for my first problem for the covering-law model, a problem with its account of the way in which we explain scientific laws. I should now like to raise another problem for it, a problem with its account of the way in which we explain particular events. Consider the following three explanations:

(B) (1) If the temperature of a gas is constant, then its pressure is inversely proportional to its volume
   (2) at time t_1, the volume of the container c was v_1, and the pressure of the gas in it was p_1
   (3) the temperature of the gas in c did not change from t_1 to t_2
   (4) the pressure of the gas in container c at t_2 is $2p_1$
   _____
   (5) the volume of x at t_2 is $\frac{1}{2}v_1$.

(C) (1) if the temperature of a gas is constant, then its pressure is inversely proportional to its volume
   (2) at time t_1 the volume of the container c was v_1 and the pressure of the gas in it was p_1
   (3) the temperature of the gas in c did not change from t_1 to t_2
   (4) the volume of the gas in container c at t_2 is $\frac{1}{2}v_1$
   _____
   (5) the pressure of c at t_2 is $2p_1$.

(D) (1) if the temperature of a gas is constant, then its pressure is inversely proportional to its volume
   (2) at time t_1, the volume of the container c was v_1 and the pressure of the gas in it was p_1
   (3) the temperature of the gas in c did not change from t_1 to t_2
   (4) by t_2, I had so compressed the container by pushing on it from all sides that its volume was $\frac{1}{2}v_1$
   _____
   (5) the pressure of c at t_2 is $2p_1$.

All three of these purported explanations meet all of the requirements of Hempel's model. The explanandum, in each case, is deducible from the explanans which, in each case, contains at least one true general law with empirical content. And yet, there are important differences between the three. My intuitions are that (B) is no explanation at all (thereby providing us with a clear counter-example to Hempel's model), that (C) is a poor explanation, and that (D) is a much better one. But if your intuitions are that (B) is still an explanation, even if not a very good one, that makes no difference for now. The important point is that there is a clear difference between the explanatory power of these three explanations, and the covering law model provides us with no clue as to what it is.

These problems and counter-examples are not isolated cases. I shall give, later on in this paper after I offer my own analysis and solution of them, a recipe for constructing loads of additional problems and counter-examples. Now the existence of these troublesome cases led me to suspect that there is something fundamentally wrong with the whole covering law model and that a new approach to the understanding of scientific explanation is required. At the same time, however, I felt that this model, which fits so many cases and seems so reasonable, just couldn't be junked entirely. This left me in a serious dilemma, one that I only began to see my way out of after I realized that Aristotle, in the *Posterior Analytics,* had already seen these problems and had offered a solution to them, one that contained both elements of Hempel's model and some other elements entirely foreign to it. So let me begin my presentation of my solution to these problems by looking at some aspects of Aristotle's theory of scientific explanation.

Aristotle (*ibid.,* I, 13), wanted to draw a distinction between knowledge of the fact (knowledge that *p* is so) and knowledge of the reasoned fact (knowledge why *p* is so) and he did so by asking us to consider the following two arguments, the former of which only provides us with knowledge of the fact while the latter of which provides us with knowledge of the reasoned fact:

(E) (1) the planets do not twinkle
  (2) all objects that do not twinkle are near the earth

   (3) therefore, the planets are near the earth.

(F) (1) the planets are near the earth
  (2) all objects that are near the earth do not twinkle

   (3) therefore, the planets do not twinkle.

The interesting thing about this point, for our purposes, is that while both of these arguments fit Hempel's model,[2] only one of them, as Aristotle already saw, provides us with an explanation of its conclusion. Moreover, his account of why this is so seems just right:

> . . . of two reciprocally predictable terms the one which is not the cause may quite easily be the better known and so become the middle

term of the demonstration. . . . This syllogism, then, proves not the reasoned fact but only the fact; since they are not near because they do not twinkle. The major and middle of the proof, however, may be reversed, and then the demonstration will be of the reasoned fact . . . since its middle term is the proximate cause. (78^a 28–78^b 3)

In other words, nearness is the cause of not twinkling, and not vice versa, so the nearness of the planets to the earth explains why they do not twinkle, but their not twinkling does not explain why they are near the earth.

It is important to note that such an account is incompatible with the logical empiricists' theory of causality as constant conjunction. After all, given the truth of the premises of (E) and (F), nearness and nontwinkling are each necessary and sufficient for each other, so, on the constant conjunction account each is equally the cause of the other.[3] And even if the constant conjunction account is supplemented in any of the usual ways, nearness and nontwinkling would still equally be the cause of each other. After all, both "all near celestial objects twinkle" and "all twinkling celestial objects are near" contain purely qualitative predicates, have a potentially infinite scope, are deducible from higher-order scientific generalizations and support counterfactuals. In other words, both of these generalizations are lawlike generalizations, and not mere accidental ones, so each of the events in question is, on a sophisticated Humean account, the cause of the other. So Aristotle's account presupposes the falsity of the constant conjunction account of causality. But that is okay. After all, the very example that we are dealing with now, where nearness is clearly the cause of nontwinkling but not vice versa, shows us that the constant conjunction theory of causality (even in its normal more-sophisticated versions) is false.

Now if we apply Aristotle's account to our example with the gas, we get a satisfactory account of what is involved there. The decrease in volume (due, itself, to my pressing on the container from all sides) is the cause of the increase in pressure, but not vice versa, so the former explains the latter but not vice versa. And Aristotle's account also explains a phenomenon called to our attention by Bromberger [2], viz. that while we can deduce both the height of a flagpole from the length of the shadow it casts and the position of the sun in the sky and the length of the shadow it casts from the height of the flagpole and the position of the sun in the sky, only the latter deduction can be used in an explanation. It is easy to see why this is so; it is the sun striking at a given angle the flagpole of the given height that causes its shadow to have the length that it does, but the sun striking the flagpole when its shadow has the length of the flagpole is surely not the cause of the height of the flagpole.

Generalizing this point, we can add a new requirement for explanation: a deductive-nomological explanation of a particular event is a satisfactory explanation of the event when (besides meeting all of Hempel's requirements) its explanans contains essentially a description of the event which is the cause of the event described in the explanandum. If they do not then it may not be a satisfactory explanation. And similarly, a deductive-nomological explanation of a law is a satisfactory explanation of that law when (besides meeting all of Hempel's requirements) every event which is a case of the law to be explained is caused by an event which is a case of one (in each case, the same) of the laws contained essentially in the explanans.[4]

It might be thought that what we have said so far is sufficient to explain why it is that (A) is not an explanation and why it is that the explanation of sodium and chlorine's combining in a one-to-one ratio in terms of the atomic structure of sodium and chlorine is an explanation. After all, no event which is a case of sodium and chlorine combining in a one-to-one ratio is caused by any event which is a case of sodium and bromine combining in a one-to-one ratio. So, given our requirements, deduction (A), even though it meets all of Hempel's requirements, need not be (and indeed is not) an explanation. But every event which is a case of sodium and chlorine combining in a one-to-one ratio is caused by the sodium and chlorine in question having the atomic structure that they do (after all, if they had a different atomic structure, they would combine in a different ratio). So an explanation involving the atomic structure would meet our new requirement and would therefore be satisfactory.

The trouble with this account is that it incorrectly presupposes that it is the atomic structure of sodium and chlorine that causes them to combine in a one-to-one ratio. A whole essay would be required to show, in detail, what is wrong with this presupposition; I can, here, only briefly indicate the trouble and hope that this brief indication will be sufficient for now: a given case of sodium combining with chlorine is the same event as that sodium combining with that chlorine in a one-to-one ratio, and, like all other events, that event has only one cause.[5] It is, perhaps, that event which brings it about that the sodium and chlorine are in proximity to each other under the right conditions. That is the cause of the event in question, and not the atomic structure of the sodium and chlorine in question (which, after all, were present long before they combined). To be sure, these atomic structures help explain one aspect of the event in question, the ratio in which they combine, but that does not make them the cause of the event.[6]

To say that the atomic structure of the atoms in question is not the cause of their combining in a one-to-one ratio is *not* to say that a description of that structure is not an essential part of any causal explanation of their combining. It obviously is. But equally well, to say that a description of it is a necessary part of any causal explanation is *not* to say that it is (or is part of) the cause of their combining. There is a difference, after all, between causal explanations and causes and between parts of the former and parts of the latter. Similarly, to say that the atomic structure is not the cause of their combining is *not* to say that that event had no cause; indeed, we suggested one (the event which brought about the proximity of the atoms) and others can also be suggested (the event of the atoms acquiring certain specific electrical and quantum mechanical properties). It is only to say that the atomic structure is not the cause.

Keeping these two points in mind, we can see that all that we said before was that the perfectly satisfactory explanation, in terms of the atomic structure of the atoms, of their combining in a one-to-one ratio does not meet the condition just proposed because it contains no description of the event which caused the combining to take place. But since it obviously is a good explanation, some additional types of explanations must be allowed for.

So Aristotle's first suggestion, while quite helpful in solving some of our problems, does not solve all of them. There is, however, another important suggestion that he makes that will, I believe, solve the rest of them. Aristotle says:

> Demonstrative knowledge must rest on necessary basic truths; for the object of scientific knowledge cannot be other than it is. Now attributes attaching essentially to their subjects attach necessarily to them. . . . It follows from this that premises of the demonstrative syllogism must be connections essential in the sense explained: for all attributes must inhere essentially or else be accidental, and accidental attributes are not necessary to their subjects. (*Posterior Analytics* 74b 5-12)

There are many aspects of this passage that I do not want to discuss now. But one part of it seems to me to suggest a solution to our problem. It is the suggestion that a demonstration can be used as an explanation (can provide us with "scientific knowledge") when at least one of the explanans essential to the derivation states, that a certain class of objects has a certain property, and (although the explanans need not state this) that property is possessed by those objects essentially.

Let us, following that suggestion, now look at our two proposed explanations as to why sodium combines with chlorine in a ratio of one-to-one. In one of them, we are supposed to explain this in terms of the fact that sodium combines with bromine in a one-to-one ratio. In the other explanation, we are supposed to explain this in terms of the atomic structure of sodium and chlorine. Now in both of these cases, we can demonstrate from the fact in question (and certain additional facts) that sodium does combine with chlorine in a one-to-one ratio. But there is an important difference between these two proposed explanations. The atomic structure of some chunk of sodium or mass of chlorine is an essential property of that object. Something with a different atomic number would be (numerically) a different object. But the fact that it combines with bromine in a one-to-one ratio is not an essential property of the sodium chunk, although it may be true of every chunk of sodium. One can, after all, imagine situations[7] in which it would not combine in that ratio but in which it would still be (numerically) the same object. Therefore, one of our explanans, the one describing the atomic structure of sodium and chlorine, contains a statement that attributes to the sodium and chlorine a property which is an essential property of that sodium and chlorine (even if the statement does not say that it is an essential property), while the other of our explanans, the one describing the way in which sodium combines with bromine, does not. And it is for just this reason that the former explanans, but not the latter, explains the phenomenon in question.

Generalizing this Aristotelean point, we can set down another requirement for explanations as follows: a deductive-nomological explanation of a particular event is a satisfactory explanation of that event when (besides meeting all of Hempel's requirements) its explanans contains essentially a statement attributing to a certain class of objects a property had essentially by that class of objects (even if the statement does not say that they have it essentially) and when at least one object involved in the event described in the explanandum is a member of that class of objects. If this requirement is unfulfilled, then it may not be a satisfactory explanation. And similarly, a deductive-nomological explanation of a law is a satisfactory explanation of that law when (besides meeting all of Hempel's requirements) each event which is a case of the law which is the explanandum, involves an entity which is a member of a class (in each case, the same class) such that the explanans contain a statement attributing to that class a property which each of its members have essentially (even if the statement does not say that they have it essentially).

It is important to note that such an account is incompatible with the logical empiricist conception of theoretical statements as instruments and not as statements describing the world. For after all, many of these essential attributions are going to be theoretical statements, and they can hardly be statements attributing to a class of objects an essential property if they aren't really statements at all. But that is okay, for it just gives us one more reason for rejecting an account, more notable for the audacity of its proponents in proposing it than for its plausability or for the illumination it casts.

There are two types of objections to essential explanations that we should deal with immediately. The first really has its origin in Duhem's critique of the idea that scientific theories explain the observable world ([3], Ch. 1). Duhem argued that if we view a theory as an explanation of an observable phenomenon, we would have to suppose that the theory gives us an account of the physical reality underlying what we observe. Such claims about the true nature of reality are, however, empirically unverifiable metaphysical hypotheses, which scientists should shun, and therefore we must not view a theory as an attempt to explain what we observe. Now contemporary theories of explanation, like the deductive-nomological model, avoid this problem, by not requiring of an explanation that its explanans describe the true reality underlying the observed explanandum. But if we now claim that a deductive-nomological explanation is a satisfactory explanation when (among other possibilities) its explanans describe essential properties of some objects involved in the explanandum event, aren't we introducing these disastrous, because empirically undecidable, issues about the true nature of the reality of these objects into science? After all, the scientist will now have to decide, presumably by nonempirical means, whether the explanans do describe the essence of the objects in question.

The trouble with this objection is that it just assumes, without any arguments, that claims about the essences of objects would have to be empirically undecidable claims, claims that could be decided only upon the basis of metaphysical assumptions. This presupposition, besides being unsupported, just seems false. After all, the claim that the essential property of sodium is its atomic number (and not its atomic weight, or its color, or its melting point) can be defended empirically, partially by showing that for this property, unlike the others just mentioned, there are no obvious cases of sodium which do not have it, and partially by showing how all objects that have this property behave alike in many important respects while objects which do not have this property in common do not behave alike in these important respects. Now a lot more has to be said about the way in which we determine empirically the essence of a given object (or a given type of object), and we will return to this issue below, but enough has been said, I think, to justify the claim that the idea that scientific explanation is essential explanation does not mean that scientific explanation involves empirically undecidable claims.

It should be noted, by the way, that this idea of the discovery of essences by empirical means is not new to us. It was already involved in Aristotle's theory of *epagoge* (*op. cit.,* II, 19). I do not now want to enter into the question as to exactly what Aristotle had in mind, if he did have anything exact in mind, when he was describing that process. It is sufficient to note that he, like all other true adherents to the theory of essential explanation, saw our knowledge of essences as the result of reflection upon what we have observed and not as the result of some strange sort of metaphysical knowledge.

The second objection to essential explanations has been raised by Popper. He writes:

> The essentialist doctrine that I am contesting is solely the doctrine that science aims at ultimate explanation; that is to say, an explanation which (essentially, or, by its very nature) cannot be further explained, and which is in no need of any further explanation. Thus my criticism of essentialism does not aim at establishing the nonexistence of essences; it merely aims at showing the obscurantist character of the role played by the idea of essences in the Galilean philosophy of science. ([6], p. 105)

Popper's point really is very simple. If our explanans contain a statement describing essential properties (e.g., sodium has the following atomic structure . . .), then there is nothing more to be said by way of explaining these explanans themselves. After all, what could we say by way of answering the question "why does sodium contain the atomic structure that it does?" so the use of essential explanations leads us to unexplainable explanans, and therefore to no new insights gained in the search for explanations of these explanans, and therefore to scientific sterility. Therefore, science should reject essential explanations.

There are, I believe, two things wrong with this objection. To begin with, Popper assumes that essential explanations will involve unexplainable explanans, and this is usually only partially true. Consider, after all, our explanation of sodium's combining with chlorine in a one-to-one ratio in terms of the atomic structure of sodium and chlorine. The explanans of that explanation, besides containing statements attributing to sodium and chlorine their essences (viz. their atomic number), also contain the general principles of chemical bonding, and these are not unexplainable explanans since they are not claims about essences. In general, even essential explanations leave us with some part (usually the most interesting part) of their explanans to explain, and they do not therefore lead to sterility in future enquiry. But, in addition, even if we did have an essential explanation all of whose explanans were essential statements and therefore unexplainable explanans, what are we to do according to Popper? Should we reject the explanation? Should we keep it but believe that it is not an essential explanation? Neither of these strategies seem very plausible in those cases where we have good reasons both for supposing that the explanation is correct and for supposing that the explanans do describe the essential properties of the objects in question. It cannot after all, be a good scientific strategy to reject what we have good reasons to accept. So even if Popper's claim about their sterility for future scientific enquiry is true for some essential explanations, I cannot see that it gives us any reasons for rejecting these explanations, or for rejecting their claim to be essential explanations, when these explanations and claims are empirically well supported.

There is, of course, a certain point to Popper's objection, a point that I gladly concede. As is shown by his example from the history of gravitational theory, people may rush to treat a property as essential, without adequate empirical evidence for that claim, and then it may turn out that they were wrong. They may even have good evidence for the claim that the property is essential and still be wrong. In either case, enquiry has been blocked where it should not have been blocked. We should certainly therefore be cautious in making claims about essential properties and should, even when we make them on the basis of good evidence, realize that they may still be wrong. But these words of caution are equally applicable to all scientific claims; the havoc wreaked by false theories that lead enquiry along mistaken paths can be as bad as the havoc wreaked by false essential claims that block enquiry. And since they are only words of caution, they should not lead us to give up either theoretical explanations in general or essential explanations in particular.

Let us see where we now stand. We have, so far, rejected Hempel's requirements for an explanation on the grounds that they are not sufficient and we have suggested two alternative Aristotelean conditions such that, for the set of explanations meeting Hempel's requirements, any explanation meeting either of these requirements is an adequate explanation.[8] . . .

It only remains, therefore, to consider the one serious objection to this whole Aristotelean theory, an objection that we have already touched upon when we dealt with Duhem. Given what we mean by 'causality' and 'essence,' can we ever know that e_1 is the cause of e_2 or that P is an essential property of e_1, and if so, how can we know this?

This problem can be sharpened considerably. There is no problem, in principle, about our coming to know that events of type E_1 are constantly conjoined with events of type E_2. All that we have to do is to observe that this is so in enough varied cases. And if 'e_1 causes e_2' only means that 'e_1 is an event of type E_2,' we can easily see how we could come to know that e_1 is the cause of e_2. But if, as our Aristotelean account demands, 'e_1 causes e_2' means something more than that, can we know that it is true, and if we can, how can we know that it is true? Similarly, there is no problem, in principle, about our coming to know that objects of type O_1 have a certain property P_1 in common. All that we have to do is to observe that this is so in enough varied cases. And if 'P_1 is an essential property of o_1' only means that 'o_1 is an object of type O_1 and all objects of type O_1 have P_1,' we can easily see how we could come to know that P_1 is an essential property of o_1. But if, as our Aristotelean theory demands, 'P_1 is an essential property of o_1' means something more than that, can we know that this is true, and if we can, how can we know that this is true?

There is an important difference between these questions. If we conclude that we cannot, or do not, know the truth of statements of the form 'e_1 causes e_2' or 'P_1 is an essential property of o_1' (where these statements are meant in the strong sense required by our theory), then our theory must be rejected. After all, knowledge of the truth of statements of that form is, according to our theory, a necessary condition for knowing that we have (although not for having) adequate explanations. And we obviously do know, in at least some cases, that a given explanation is adequate. So if we cannot, or do not, know statements of the above form, our theory is false. However, if we conclude that we can, and do, know the truth of statements of the above-mentioned form, but we don't know how we know their truth, then all that we have left is a research project, viz. to find out how we know their truth; what we don't have is an objection to our theory.

This is an extremely important point. I shall show, in a moment, that we do have, and a fortiori can have, knowledge of these statements. But, to be quite frank, I have no adequate account (only the vague indications mentioned above when talking about Duhem) of how we have this knowledge. So, on the basis of this last point, I conclude that the Aristotelean theory of explanation faces a research problem about knowledge (hence the title of this paper), but no objection about knowledge.

Now for the proof that we do, and a fortiori can, have knowledge of the above-mentioned type. Our examples will, I am afraid, be familiar ones. It seems obvious that we know that

    (1) if the temperature of a gas is constant, then an increase in its pressure is invariably accompanied by an inversely proportional decrease in its volume

(2) if the temperature of a gas is constant, then a decrease in its volume is invariably accompanied by an inversely proportional increase in its pressure

(3) if the temperature of a gas is constant, then an increase in its pressure does not cause an inversely proportional decrease in its volume

(4) if the temperature of a gas is constant, then a decrease in its volume does cause an inversely proportional increase in its pressure.

Here we have causal knowledge of the type required, since the symmetry between (1) and (2) and the asymmetry between (3) and (4) show that the causal knowledge that we have when we know (3) and (4) is not mere knowledge about constant conjunctions. Similarly, it seems obvious that we know that

(1) all sodium has the property of normally combining with bromine in a one-to-one ratio

(2) all sodium has the property of having the atomic number 11

(3) the property of normally combining with bromine in a one-to-one ratio is not an essential property of sodium

(4) the property of having the atomic number 11 is an essential property of sodium.

Here we have essential knowledge of the type required, since the symmetry between (1) and (2) and the asymmetry between (3) and (4) show that the essential knowledge that we have when we know (3) and (4) is not mere knowledge about all members of a certain class having a certain property.

I conclude, therefore, that we have every good reason to accept, but none to reject, the Aristotelean theory of explanation sketched in this paper. And I also conclude that it therefore behooves us to find out how we have the type of knowledge mentioned above, the type of knowledge that lies behind our knowledge that certain explanations that we offer really are adequate explanations.

NOTES

1. I first called attention to the problems raised by this type of explanation in my [1].

2. Leaving aside the question, irrelevant for us now, about the truth of these premises, we shall throughout this discussion just assume that they are true.

3. Unless one adds the requirement that the cause must be before the effect, the normal way of drawing an asymmetry between causes and effects when each are necessary and sufficient for the other, in which case neither is the cause of the other and Aristotle's account still won't do.

4. We have made this condition sufficient, but not necessary, for reasons that will emerge below. It will also be seen there that Aristotle, who had a broader notion of cause, could have made it necessary as well.

5. To be sure, e_1 can have as causes both e_2 and e_3 (where $e_2 \neq e_3$) but only when either e_2 is the cause of e_3 or e_3 the cause of e_2. That exception is of no relevance here.

6. It might, at least, be maintained that they are still the cause of that aspect of the event. But that is just a confusion—it is events, and not their aspects, that have causes.

7. Even ones in which all currently believed scientific laws hold, but in which the initial conditions are quite different from the ones that now normally hold.

8. We have not, however, required as a necessary condition that any explanation must meet one of these two conditions. This is so, partially because of the problem of statistical explanations, but partially because of the possibility, raised by Aristotle, that there are additional types of explanations. After all, our two conditions let in explanations in terms of Aristotle's efficient and formal causes. We still have to consider, but will not in this paper, possible explanations in terms of what he would call material and final causes.

REFERENCES

[1] Brody, B. A. "Natural Kinds and Real Essences." *Journal of Philosophy* (1967).

[2] Bromberger, S. "Why Questions." *Introductory Readings in the Philosophy of Science.* Edited by B. A. Brody. Englewood Cliffs: Prentice Hall, 1969.

[3] Duhem, P. *La Théorie Physique, Son Objet et sa Structure.* Paris: Chevalier et Rivière, 1914.

[4] Eberle, R. A., Kaplan, D., and Montague, R. "Hempel and Oppenheim on Explanation." *Philosophy of Science* (1961).

[5] Hempel, C. G. *Aspects of Scientific Explanation.* New York: Free Press, 1955.

[6] Popper, K. R. *Conjectures and Refutations.* London: 1963.

9

The Truth Doesn't Explain Much

Nancy Cartwright

Introduction

Scientific theories must tell us both what is true in nature, and how we are to explain it. I shall argue that these are entirely different functions and should be kept distinct. Usually the two are conflated. The second is commonly seen as a by-product of the first. Scientific theories are thought to explain by dint of the descriptions they give of reality. Once the job of describing is done, science can shut down. That is all there is to do. To describe nature— to tell its laws, the values of its fundamental constants, its mass distributions— is *ipso facto* to lay down how we are to explain it.

This is a mistake, I shall argue; a mistake that is fostered by the covering-law model of explanation. The covering-law model supposes that all we need to know are the laws of nature—and a little logic, perhaps a little probability theory—and then we know which factors can explain which others. For example, in the simplest deductive-nomological [D-N] version,[1] the covering-law model says that one factor explains another just in case the occurrence of the second can be deduced from the occurrence of the first given the laws of nature.

But the D-N model is just an example. In the sense which is relevant to my claims here, most models of explanation offered recently in the philosophy of science are covering-law models. This includes not only Hempel's own inductive statistical model,[2] but also Patrick Suppes's probabilistic model of causation,[3] Wesley Salmon's statistical relevance model,[4] and even Bengt Hanson's contextualistic model.[5] All these accounts rely on the laws of nature, and just the laws of nature, to pick out which factors we can use in explanation.

A good deal of criticism has been aimed at Hempel's original covering-law models. Much of the criticism objects that these models let in too much.

On Hempel's account it seems we can explain Henry's failure to get pregnant by his taking birth control pills, and we can explain the storm by the falling barometer. My objection is quite the opposite. Covering-law models let in too little. With a covering-law model we can explain hardly anything, even the things of which we are most proud—like the role of DNA in the inheritance of genetic characteristics, or the formation of rainbows when sunlight is refracted through raindrops. We cannot explain these phenomena with a covering-law model, I shall argue, because we do not have laws that cover them. Covering laws are scarce.

Many phenomena which have perfectly good scientific explanations are not covered by any laws. No true laws, that is. They are at best covered by *ceteris paribus* generalizations—generalizations that hold only under special conditions, usually ideal conditions. The literal translation is "other things being equal"; but it would be more apt to read *"ceteris paribus"* as "other things being *right*."

Sometimes we act as if this does not matter. We have in the back of our minds an "understudy" picture of *ceteris paribus* laws: *ceteris paribus* laws are real laws; they can stand in when the laws we would like to see are not available and they can perform all the same functions, only not quite so well. But this will not do. *Ceteris paribus* generalizations, read literally without the *"ceteris paribus"* modifier, are false. They are not only false, but held by us to be false; and there is no ground in the covering-law picture for false laws to explain anything. On the other hand, with the modifier the *ceteris paribus* generalizations may be true, but they cover only those few cases where the conditions are right. For most cases, either we have a law that purports to cover, but cannot explain because it is acknowledged to be false, or we have a law that does not cover. Either way, it is bad for the covering-law picture.

1. *Ceteris Paribus* Laws

When I first started talking about the scarcity of covering laws, I tried to summarize my view by saying "There are no exceptionless generalizations." Then a friend asked, "How about 'All men are mortal'?" She was right. I had been focusing too much on the equations of physics. A more plausible claim would have been that there are no exceptionless quantitative laws in physics. Indeed not only are there no exceptionless laws, but in fact our best candidates are known to fail. This is something like the Popperian thesis that *every theory is born refuted*. Every theory we have proposed in physics, even at the time when it was most firmly entrenched, was known to be deficient in specific and detailed ways. I think this is also true for every precise quantitative law within a physics theory.

But this is not the point I had wanted to make. Some laws are treated, at least for the time being, as if they were exceptionless, whereas others are not, even though they remain "on the books." Snell's law (about the angle of incidence and the angle of refraction for a ray of light) is a good example of this latter kind. In the optics text I use for reference (Miles V. Klein, *Optics*),[6] it first appears on page 21, and without qualification:

Snell's Law: At an interface between dielectric media, there is (also) *a refracted ray* in the second medium, lying in the plane of incidence, making an angle θ_t with the normal, and obeying Snell's law:

$$sin\ \theta / sin\ \theta_t = n_2 / n_1$$

where v_1 and v_2 are the velocities of propagation in the two media, and $n_1 = (c/v_1)$, $n_2 = (c/v_2)$ are the indices of refraction.

It is only some 500 pages later, when the law is derived from the "full electromagnetic theory of light," that we learn that Snell's law as stated on page 21 is true only for media whose optical properties are *isotropic*. (In anisotropic media, "there will generally be *two* transmitted waves.") So what is deemed true is not really Snell's law as stated on page 21, but rather a refinement of Snell's law:

Refined Snell's Law: For any two media which are optically isotropic, at an interface between dielectrics there is a refracted ray in the second medium, lying in the plane of incidence, making an angle θ_t with the normal, such that:

$$sin\ \theta / sin\ \theta_t = n_2 / n_1$$

The Snell's law of page 21 in Klein's book is an example of a *ceteris paribus* law, a law that holds only in special circumstances—in this case when the media are both isotropic. Klein's statement on page 21 is clearly not to be taken literally. Charitably, we are inclined to put the modifier *"ceteris paribus"* in front to hedge it. But what does this *ceteris paribus* modifier do? With an eye to statistical versions of the covering law model (Hempel's I-S picture, or Salmon's statistical relevance model, or Suppes's probabilistic model of causation) we may suppose that the unrefined Snell's law is not intended to be a universal law, as literally stated, but rather some kind of statistical law: *for the most part,* at an interface between dielectric media there is *a* refracted ray. . . . But this will not do. For *most* media are optically anisotropic, and in an anisotropic medium there are *two* rays. I think there are no more satisfactory alternatives. If *ceteris paribus* laws are to be true laws, there are no statistical laws with which they can generally be identified.

2. When Laws Are Scarce

Why do we keep Snell's law on the books when we both know it to be false and have a more accurate refinement available? There are obvious pedagogic reasons. But are there serious scientific ones? I think there are, and these reasons have to do with the task of explaining. Specifying which factors are explanatorily relevant to which others is a job done by science over and above the job of laying out the laws of nature. Once the laws of nature are known, we still have to decide what kinds of factors can be cited in explanation.

One thing that *ceteris paribus* laws do is to express our explanatory commitments. They tell what kinds of explanations are permitted. We know from the refined Snell's law that in any isotropic medium, the angle of refraction can be explained by the angle of incidence, according to the equation *sin* $\theta / sin\ \theta_t = n_2/n_1$. To leave the unrefined Snell's law on the books is to signal that the same kind of explanation can be given even for some anisotropic media. The pattern of explanation derived from the ideal situation is employed even where the conditions are less then ideal; and we assume that we can understand what happens in *nearly* isotropic media by rehearsing how light rays behave in pure isotropic cases.

This assumption is a delicate one. It fits far better with the simulacrum account of explanation . . . than it does with any covering-law model. For the moment I intend only to point out that it *is* an assumption, and an assumption which (prior to the "full electromagnetic theory") goes well beyond our knowledge of the facts of nature. We *know* that in isotropic media, the angle of refraction is due to the angle of incidence under the equation *sin* $\theta / sin\ \theta_t = n_2/n_1$. We *decide* for the two refracted rays in anisotropic media in the same manner. We may have good reasons for the decision; in this case if the media are nearly isotropic, the two rays will be very close together, and close to the angle predicted by Snell's law; or we believe in continuity of physical processes. But still this decision is not forced by our knowledge of the laws of nature.

Obviously this decision could not be taken if we also had on the books a second refinement of Snell's law, implying that in any anisotropic media the angles are quite different from the those given by Snell's law. But laws are scarce, and often we have no law at all about what happens in conditions that are less than ideal.

Covering-law theorists will tell a different story about the use of *ceteris paribus* laws in explanation. From their point of view, *ceteris paribus* explanations are elliptical for genuine covering-law explanations from true laws which we do not yet know. When we use a *ceteris paribus* "law" which we know to be false, the covering-law theoriest supposes us to be making a bet about what form the true law takes. For example, to retain Snell's unqualified law would be to bet that the (at the time unknown) law for anisotropic media will entail values "close enough" to those derived from the original Snell law.

I have two difficulties with this story. The first arises from an extreme metaphysical possibility, in which I in fact believe. Covering-law theorists tend to think that nature is well-regulated; in the extreme, that there is a law to cover every case. I do not. I imagine that natural objects are much like people in societies. Their behavior is constrained by some specific laws and by a handful of general principles, but it is not determined in detail, even statistically. What happens on most occasions is dictated by no law at all. This is not a metaphysical picture that I urge. My claim is that this picture is as plausible as the alternative. God may have written just a few laws and grown tired. We do not know whether we are in a tidy universe or a untidy one. Whichever universe we are in, the ordinary commonplace activity of giving explanations ought to make sense.

The second difficulty for the ellipsis version of the covering-law account is more pedestrian. Elliptical explanations are not explanations: they are at best assurances that explanations are to be had. The law that is supposed to appear in the complete, correct D-N explanation is not a law we have in our theory, not a law that we can state, let alone test. There may be covering-law explanations in these cases. But those explanations are not our explanations; and those unknown laws cannot be our grounds for saying of a nearly isotropic medium, "$sin\ \theta_f \approx k\ (n_2/n_1)$ *because $sin\ \theta = k$.*"

What then are our grounds? I assert only what they are not: they are not the laws of nature. The laws of nature that we know at any time are not enough to tell us what kinds of explanations can be given at that time. That requires a decision; and it is just this decision that covering-law theorists make when they wager about the existence of unknown laws. We may believe in these unknown laws, but we do so on no ordinary grounds: they have not been tested, nor are they derived from a higher level theory. Our grounds for believing in them are only as good as our reasons for adopting the corresponding explanatory strategy, and no better.

3. When Laws Conflict

I have been maintaining that there are not enough covering laws to go around. Why? The view depends on the picture of science that I mentioned earlier. Science is broken into various distinct domains: hydrodynamics, genetics, laser theory, . . . We have many detailed and sophisticated theories about what happens within the various domains. But we have little theory about what happens in the intersection of domains.

Diagrammatically, we have laws like

$$ceteris\ paribus,\ (x)\ (S(x) \hookrightarrow I(x))$$

and

$$ceteris\ paribus,\ (x)\ (A(x) \hookrightarrow \neg\ I(x)).$$

For example, *(ceteris paribus)* adding salt to water decreases the cooking time of potatoes; taking the water to higher altitudes increases it. Refining, if we speak more carefully we might say instead, "Adding salt to water while keeping the altitude constant decreases the cooking time; whereas increasing the altitude while keeping the saline content fixed increases it"; or

$$(x) (S(x) \& \neg A(x) \hookrightarrow I(x))$$

and

$$(x) (A(x) \& \neg S(x) \hookrightarrow \neg I(x))$$

But neither of these tells what happens when we both add salt to the water and move to higher altitudes.

Here we think that probably there is a precise answer about what would happen, even though it is not part of our common folk wisdom. But this is not always the case. . . . Most real life cases involve some combination of causes; and general laws that describe what happens in these complex cases are not always available. Although both quantum theory and relativity are highly developed, detailed, and sophisticated, there is no satisfactory theory of relativistic quantum mechanics. . . . The general lesson is this: where theories intersect, laws are usually hard to come by.

4. When Explanations Can Be Given Anyway

So far, I have only argued that covering laws are scarce, and that *ceteris paribus* laws are no true laws. It remains to argue that, nevertheless, *ceteris paribus* laws have a fundamental explanatory role. But this is easy, for most of our explanations are explanations from *ceteris paribus* laws.

Let me illustrate with a humdrum example. Last year I planted camellias in my garden. I know that camellias like rich soil, so I planted them in composted manure. On the other hand, the manure was still warm, and I also know that camellia roots cannot take high temperatures. So I did not know what to expect. But when many of my camellias died, despite otherwise perfect care, I knew what went wrong. The camellias died because they were planted in hot soil.

This is surely the right explanation to give. Of course, I cannot be absolutely certain that this explanation is the correct one. Some other factor may have been responsible, nitrogen deficiency or some genetic defect in the plants, a factor that I did not notice or may not even have known to be relevant. But this uncertainty is not peculiar to cases of explanation. It is just the uncertainty that besets all of our judgments about matters of fact. We must allow for oversight; still, since I made a reasonable effort to eliminate other menaces to my camellias, we may have some confidence that this is the right explanation.

So we have an explanation for the death of my camellias. But it is not an explanation from any true covering law. There is no law that says that camellias just like mine, planted in soil which is both hot and rich, die. To the contrary, they do not all die. Some thrive; and probably those that do, do so *because* of the richness of the soil they are planted in. We may insist that there must be some differentiating factor which brings the case under a covering law: in soil which is rich and hot, camellias of one kind die; those of another thrive. I will not deny that there may be such a covering law, I merely repeat that our ability to give this humdrum explanation precedes our knowledge of that law. On the Day of Judgment, when all laws are known, these may suffice to explain all phenomena. But in the meantime we do give explanations; and it is the job of science to tell us what kinds of explanations are admissible.

In fact I want to urge a stronger thesis. If, as is possible, the world is not a tidy deterministic system, this job of telling how we are to explain will be a job which is still set when the descriptive task of science is complete. Imagine for example (what I suppose actually to be the case) that the facts about camellias are irreducibly statistical. Then it is possible to know all the general nomological facts about camellias which there are to know—for example, that 62 percent of all camellias in just the circumstances of my camellias die, and 38 percent survive.[7] But one would not thereby know how to explain what happened in my garden. You would still have to look to the *Sunset Garden Book* to learn that the *heat* of the soil explains the perishing, and the *richness* explains the plants that thrive.

5. Conclusion

Most scientific explanations use *ceteris paribus* laws. These laws, read literally as descriptive statements, are false, not only false but deemed false even in the the context of use. This is no surprise: we want laws that unify; but what happens may well be varied and diverse. We are lucky that we can organize phenomena at all. There is no reason to think that the principles that best organize will be true, nor that the principles that are true will organize much.

NOTES

1. See C. G. Hempel, "Scientific Explanation," in C. G. Hempel (ed.), *Aspects of Scientific Explanation* (New York: Free Press, 1965).

2. See C. G. Hempel, "Scientific Explanation," ibid.

3. See Patrick Suppes, *A Probabilistic Theory of Causality* (Amsterdam: North-Holland Publishing Co., 1970).

4. See Wesley Salmon, "Statistical Explanation," in Wesley Salmon (ed.), *Statistical Explanation and Statistical Relevance* (Pittsburgh: University of Pittsburgh Press, 1971).

5. See Bengt Hanson, "Explanations—Of What?" (mimeograph, Stanford University, 1974).

6. Miles V. Klein, *Optics* (New York: John Wiley and Sons, 1970), p. 21, italics added. θ is the angle of incidence.

7. Various writers, especially Suppes (footnote 3) and Salmon (footnote 4), have urged that knowledge of more sophisticated statistical facts will suffice to determine what factors can be used in explanation. I do not believe that this claim can be carried out. . . .

10

Historical Understanding as Re-thinking

W. H. Dray

The theory of historical understanding set forth in R. G. Collingwood's *Idea of History*[1] has produced some sharp divisions of opinion among philosophers of history. While the "nays" have usually been written off by their opponents as insensitive positivists, obsessed by a model of inquiry derived from the natural sciences, the "ayes" have been considered, in their turn, as woolly-minded idealists, unable to distinguish between the essential logical structure of an enquiry and its psychological and methodological frills. Even those who have accepted Collingwood's doctrine, however, have often found it difficult to say exactly what they think it commits them to. For *The Idea of History* is an irritating, as well as an exciting book. It is full of paradoxes and apparent contradictions, which in some cases appear to be not entirely unconnected with a certain contempt which Collingwood from time to time displayed towards his philosophical opponents (indeed, his readers do not always escape): a contempt well exemplified by his remark, at one point in response to the objections of an imaginary opponent: "I am not arguing; I am telling him" (p. 263). In many cases, no doubt, a kinder explanation might be sought; for the book was left unfinished at its author's death, and some parts of it apparently record the results of fairly raw, if vigorous and stimulating, reflection.

Since some of the papers incorporated into *The Idea of History* were published by Collingwood during his lifetime, however, it seems reasonable to regard them as especially authoritative on points in his general thesis which have been disputed. The best short summary of his theory of understanding is, in fact, to be found in one of these: a lecture entitled "Human Nature and Human History," which Collingwood delivered before the British Academy in 1936. The theory which he there elaborates, in the space of a few pages (pp. 213–15), could be reduced to the following three propositions: first, that human action, which is the proper concern of history, cannot be described *as* "action" at all, without mentioning the thought which it expresses—it has, in Collingwood's terms, a "thought-side"; second, that once the thought in question has been grasped by the historian, the action is understood in the sense appropriate to actions, so that it is unnecessary to go on to ask for the cause which produced it, or the law which it instantiates; third, that the understanding of action in terms of thought requires the re-thinking of the thought in question by the historian, so that, in essence, all history is "the re-enactment of past thought in the historian's own mind." No doubt there is much more to Collingwood's account than can be stated in such a condensed, schematic way. But the propositions stated do seem to contain the core of the theory.

In what follows, I propose to discuss each of Collingwood's three propositions in turn, clarifying it where that is possible, amending it where that seems necessary. The discussion cannot, of course, hope to deal with more than a few of the many objections which have been advanced against his theory in recent years. But it may perhaps serve to clear the ground a little for a sympathetic consideration of what he had to say.

I

That history is concerned with human actions, perhaps few would want to dispute; but that actions necessarily have what Collingwood calls a "thought-side" may not pass quite so easily without challenge. For exactly what is meant here by "thought"? And how is the relation between such thought and the action itself to be conceived?

It must be admitted that Collingwood's treatment of these questions is often puzzling. In the paper entitled "The Subject Matter of History," for example, it seems to be his view that the thought-side of an action is an activity of reflection[2]—as if, in order to act, an agent must first consider what to do, and then act in accordance with his reflection. If history is said to be concerned exclusively with human actions, its field of study, on such a view of the nature of action, must appear ridiculously narrow. Even a sympathetic commentator like W. H. Walsh has compared Collingwood unfavourably with the German philosopher, Willhelm Dilthey, in his apparent attempt to confine the historian's attention to "intellectual operations."[3] And Arnold Toynbee, in one of his latest volumes, visibly smarting under Collingwood's opinion of his own vast enterprise as a kind of "pigeon-holing," has expressed great amusement at Collingwood's supposed ignorance of the fact that politicians, whose activities he had represented as especially suitable to historical investigation, behave in precisely the "intellectually horrifying way" which seems, for him, to place a subject matter out of the reach of the historian's techniques.[4] Such naivete, Toynbee maliciously suggests, could be found only in a philosopher's "theorizing."

If the paper on subject matter contained Collingwood's only discussion of the thought-side of actions, it would be difficult to escape the conclusion that, as a philosopher, he sets up a definition of history so restrictive and arbitrary that it would rule out much of what he himself wrote as an historian. But the paper in question, which is one of the least finished ones, must be weighed carefully against what is said in other parts of *The Idea of History*. If this is done, I believe that a view of the relation between thought and action will emerge which is not open to the charge of intellectualism in any damaging sense, although it safeguards, nevertheless, the distinction which Collingwood was so anxious to maintain, between historical and scientific modes of understanding.

A hint of the rather innocuous character of Collingwood's supposed intellectualism might be gleaned from a remark he makes in discussing the weaknesses of Graeco-Roman historiography. If we look back "over our actions, or over any stretch of past history," he tells us, it becomes obvious that "to a very great extent people do not know what they are doing until they have done it, if then" (p. 42). That we may nevertheless *discover,* by careful inquiry, what they were doing—including its thought-side—is clearly implied in the British Academy Lecture already referred to, in which Collingwood argues that the historical understanding which we achieve of the actions of people remote in time from ourselves is identical in kind with that which we obtain every day of the actions of our friends and neighbours. We discover their thoughts by considering their actions. The difference between an action and a mere physical movement, according to Collingwood, is that the former is the "outward expression" of a thought.[5] We discover the thought by interpreting the action *as* an expression.

It might perhaps be argued that such an account of the relation of thought to action is quite compatible with the claim that when we recognize an action as expressing a certain thought, this is equivalent to treating it as evidence that some prior activity called "reflection" must have gone on, although, since the agent's "stream of consciousness" is not open to us, we are unable to verify this directly. But when Collingwood is found to extend his analysis to knowledge of our *own* thoughts, such an interpretation of his meaning becomes very unplausible. In "Human Nature and Human History" Collingwood begins his discussion with the claim that historical inquiry can provide us with a kind of self-knowledge which a natural science of human nature fails to afford. The conclusion which his argument eventually reaches is that *all* knowledge of the human mind is historical. "It is only by historical thinking," he declares, "that I can discover what I thought . . . five minute ago, by reflecting on an action that I then did, which surprised me when I realized what I had done" (p. 219). Elsewhere he makes the same point by distinguishing between memory knowledge of myself and autobiography—the latter being the discovery, by the techniques of the historian, of the thoughts actually expressed in my past actions, by contrast with what, at the time of acting, I (perhaps mistakenly) assumed my thoughts to be (pp. 295–96). As his equally celebrated successor in the chair of metaphysical philosophy at Oxford University, Professor Gilbert Ryle, was to put it: Self-knowledge is obtained, not by *introspection,* but by *retrospection.*[6]

Why does Collingwood insist that knowledge of even my own thoughts must come by a process of interpreting "expressions," after the fact? It is surely because he would agree with Ryle and Wittgenstein that having a certain thought is not, in essence, a matter of reciting certain propositions to oneself, or focusing certain images on one's internal cinema screen, or "going over" in any such way what one is about to do.[7] The being of a thought is in its expression; and thoughts are expressed in actions as well as in those internal monologues and private screenings which are associated with reflecting and planning. Covert activities of this sort cannot, on Collingwood's account, be regarded as thinking *by contrast with* overt ones. The fact that thought has *inward* expressions as well as outward ones does not give the former any privileged status as "the thought." If this is so, there is no reason to assume that reflection—however brief—must precede, or even accompany, an action for the latter to be properly regarded as an expression of thought, and hence as having a thought-side. For if this were Collingwood's view, he could scarcely claim that our knowledge of the thought-side of our own actions is by historical analysis, after the fact, since we have privileged access to the stream of consciousness in which the activity of reflection presumably goes on.

In claiming that *all* knowledge of mind is historical, however, Collingwood appears to have overstated his case. For if we allowed this claim, the following difficulty would arise. The doctrine, as he states it, is that if, in fact, I think a certain thought, *x,* at a certain time, *t,* I cannot know that I think *x* at *t,* but only at, say, *t* plus five minutes, when I can retrospect what I did and experienced at *t.* But if I say at *t plus 5* I can know, by historical inquiry, that at *t* I thought *x,* then I am claiming to know what I think, not only at *t,* but also at *t plus 5*; and on Collingwood's theory this is something I cannot justifiably do. To know what I think at *t plus 5,* I must make still another historical investigation at a later time, and so on ad infinitum. The regress which opens up would, of course, make it impossible to claim that I could *ever* know what I think at any time whatever. To stop the regress, it is necessary to claim that at some time or other I can know *all the time* what I think. Collingwood appears to have recognized this in the paper entitled "History as Re-enactment of Past Experience," when, having asked himself whether "a person who performs an act of knowing" knows "that he 'is performing or has performed' that act," concludes that he can know both (p. 292).

But although Collingwood apparently abandons, in the end, his claim that all knowledge of mind is historical, what he says about self-knowledge in the passage quoted from the British Academy Lecture makes it clear that he believes some to be. And if it is, it will be unplausible to contend that what we discover by interpreting "expressions" is an activity of reflection which we engaged in at some earlier time without being aware of it. The claim that Collingwood did not confine the thought-side of actions to "intellectual operations" gains additional support from what he says at many other points. In discussing, for example, the historian's investigation of the mind "of a community or an age"—a case where deliberate planning or reflecting would be out of the question—we are told once again that the problem is essentially one of the historical interpretation of "expressions" (p. 219). And elsewhere, in attacking what he calls "scissors and paste" conceptions of the use of documents, Collingwood claims that it is possible for the historian to discover not only what has been completely forgotten—that is, is nowhere recorded in any extant document—but also "what, until he discovered it, no one ever knew to have happened at all" (p. 238). Since, for Collingwood, historical facts always concern actions, and actions always have a thought-side, the conclusion would appear to follow that historians can discover *thoughts* which were unknown, not only to any contemporary eyewitness of the actions concerned, but even to the agents themselves. And it seems to me that this claim is perfectly justified.

It may be worth adding that, on the interpretation of Collingwood's meaning which I have argued for here, even thought*less* actions may express a thought, and hence be properly regarded as having a thought-side. For to act thoughtlessly is not necessarily to act to no purpose; it is to act, rather, without taking into account certain considerations which ought to have been taken into account. Similarly, impulsive actions are in no way extruded from the historian's concerns on the ground that they lack a thought-side; for although to do a thing on impulse is incompatible with doing it as a matter of policy, or in order to implement a plan, it is not necessarily to do it for no reason. W. H. Walsh has distinguished usefully, in this connection, between saying that a person acted with something *before his mind,* and saying that he had something *in mind*; and he points out that the historian is as interested in cases falling into the second category as into the first.[8] In arguing, however, that actions in the second category may also be said to express a thought, Walsh offers what he regards as an amendment required to bring Collingwood's theory to terms with historical inquiry as it now exists. What I have tried to show is that such cases are already provided for by a theory of mind and thought which there are grounds for believing that Collingwood actually held. In arguing thus, I am, of course, appealing without much scruple from Collingwood drunk to Collingwood sober; from "The Subject Matter of History" to "Human Nature and Human History," on the assumption that the latter can be considered as the more authoritative. That the criticisms of Walsh and Toynbee find justification in the contents of the former paper, I should not attempt to deny.

II

If we grant the foregoing analysis of what it is that the historian, in order to know another's thought, must set himself to discover, what are we to say of Collingwood's second proposition: that once the thought has been discovered, the action can be understood without our having also to know the law under which it falls, or the cause which brought it about? Collingwood expresses his claim in characteristically provocative fashion when he asserts that, in history, once we know *what* happened, we already know *why* it happened (p. 214). He says this, presumably, because what happened is an action, and this, on his view, includes an explanatory thought-side. But does the thought of the agent really have this explanatory force? Can it provide us by itself with a *complete* explanation of what was done?

In asking ourselves whether an action can be completely or satisfactorily explained in terms of the agent's thought, it will be helpful, at the outset, to remind ourselves of a peculiar feature of the question "Why?"—namely, that a person can go on asking it as long as he pleases. Any theory of the nature of explanation, therefore, which does not rule out in advance objections arising from this possibility, can never hope to gain acceptance by a really determined opponent. Thus, if a historian explains Caesar's crossing of the Rubicon by referring to his determination to oust Pompey from the capital, it cannot be taken as a defect of Collingwood's theory that this explanation is incomplete—if by this we mean only that we can still ask why Caesar wanted to get rid of Pompey. It is not a defect of Collingwood's theory because, if a defect at all, it would be a defect of *any* theory of what counts as an answer to the question "Why?" Explanations can be regarded as given at successive levels of inquiry; and the farther we carry the questioning process, the deeper the explanation may be said to be. What Collingwood has to say, however, can be fairly assessed only as a theory of what counts as an answer to the question "Why?" at a single level.

What we must ask, therefore, is whether a thought has full explanatory force—by contrast with great explanatory depth—even at one level of inquiry. And it will be seen at once that if we merely cited Caesar's goal or purpose in crossing the Rubicon, the "thought" in question would not achieve such explanatory completeness by itself. To achieve this we should have to fill in many other things which, in the course of his narrative, a historian would ordinarily be content to leave implicit or understood. We should have to take account of such other thoughts as, for example, Caesar's belief that Pompey was in Rome and would remain there; and before we were through, we should have collected a sizable and complex group of what might be called the considerations which moved Caesar to action. But although Collingwood would certainly admit that the original explanation, if criticized on the ground of its incompleteness, would have to be added to in some such way, he would insist that such addition need not refer beyond the action itself to laws or causes. The explanation is completed by rounding out the thought-side, not by adding something of an altogether different kind.

But what is the criterion of completeness, in this second, and relevant sense of the term? Collingwood himself speaks of the explanatory thought as what "moves" or "determines" the agent to act.[9] And I think it would do no violence to his meaning if we said that until the thought-side is rounded out to the point where we can see that it *necessitated* the action, no complete explanation will have been given. Perhaps this will appear, at first sight, to be too rigorous a demand. But upon reflection, I think we should have to agree that a set of considerations which shows only that a certain course of action was one of a number which *might* have been pursued by the agent, yet falls short of showing that he *had* to choose the one he did, would not explain his doing what he did. No doubt such considerations would explain something. They might explain, perhaps, how it was possible for the agent to have done what he did. But they could scarcely be regarded as answering the question "Why?"

Unfortunately, Collingwood was not as careful as he should have been to draw such distinctions between kinds of explanatory problems. In the passage of the British Academy Lecture already referred to, he gives as an example of an explanatory thought, Caesar's "defiance of Republican law"; and although this does indeed appear to be a thought which the crossing of the Rubicon could be said to express, it is difficult to see how it could be an answer, or even part of an answer, to the question: "Why did Caesar cross the Rubicon?" Caesar *could,* of course, have crossed it in order to defy Republican law; but if his purpose had been only to carry out a demonstration of this sort, there would have been no need for him to march on Rome. The thought elicited in this case seems to me to be much more plausibly represented as an answer to an entirely different sort of question: a question about the *significance* of Caesar's action.[10] Our concern here, however, is with "explanation why." The fact that, in Collingwood's example, "defiance of Republican law" does not appear to have been one of the considerations which "moved" Caesar to action, is therefore irrelevant to our assessment of the claim that a complete set of explanatory "thoughts" would be one which represented what was done as necessarily done.

If it is still not clear that this is what Collingwood is saying, the fault may lie in a certain lack of precision which should be noticed in the claim that once the thought-side of an action has been discovered, the conditions of understanding have been satisfied. For, strictly speaking, an action cannot be explained in terms of its own thought-side. As Collingwood originally states his theory, the thought-side of an action is something that must be included in the very *specification* of the action (p. 213). The action is not a "doing" at all, but simply a "movement," unless it is an expression of thought. The thought which is required to make it the action it is, therefore, cannot be considered as something logically distinct from it, by reference to which the action itself can be explained. The thought-side of an action might, of course, be called upon to explain the mere movement which is its own other "side": We might say, for instance, that Caesar's wanting to get to the other shore explains his physical progress across the river. But it is clear enough that in history, the problem will almost always be the explanation of actions, not mere movements; and in order to explain an action in terms of thought it will be necessary to refer beyond the action to a thought which is not itself part of the action as specified.

It would always be possible, of course, to incorporate this *further* thought into the specification of the action, thus expanding its thought-side. If we explained Caesar's crossing of the Rubicon, for example, in terms of his wanting to oust Pompey from the capital, we might say that his crossing expressed the latter thought as well as his merely wanting to get to the other shore. But in assessing the applicability of a theory of explanation or understanding, it is important to keep the questions, as well as the answers, straight; and it should be clear that if we allow such incorporation, we can no longer claim that Caesar's wanting to oust Pompey explains *the action*; for the action to be explained is now, not the crossing of the Rubicon, but the crossing of the Rubicon to oust Pompey. To insist on such logical niceties may appear unduly pedantic. Yet unless they are recognized, Collingwood's theory of explanation in terms of thought lies open to the charge—commonly made—that he believes human actions, by contrast with natural events, to be *self*-explanatory. And in spite of the misleading way in which he sometimes states the "inside-outside" theory, it is difficult to believe, in the light of his general view of historical thinking, that he intended to make any such claim.

If a complete explanation of an action is said to be achieved when a set of considerations, or "thoughts," not themselves included in the specification of the action, can be seen to have necessitated it, the question arises whether Collingwood can maintain the distinction between his own account and that of his positivist opponents. For it is a central doctrine of the positivists whom he attacks—a doctrine derived ultimately from Hume's classical discussion of causation—that necessities asserted of the real world are read into it on the basis of a belief in general laws. On such a view, the only way to vindicate my claim that, given *x*, *y* necessarily happened, is to argue: "Whenever *x* then *y*"; so that to say that the historian's explanation represents the action as necessitated by the thought which explains it, would commit the historian to the view that it does so by virtue of some law. Now Collingwood, at this point, is indeed questioning this positivist assumption quite directly: But it is important to see exactly how he is doing it. For his frequent remarks about the limited applicability of the generalizations which might be derived from a study of human activities in any historical period, and his denial that man's reason is itself subject to laws at all, may make it appear that his point is simply that human actions cannot be explained on the model of the natural sciences because they are not necessitated.[11] His point would, in fact, appear to be quite otherwise. For, as a study of "Human Nature and Human History" will confirm, his claim is rather that, whether "positive" laws of human nature are discoverable or not, they are not *required* for historical understanding (pp. 214, 223). They are not required because human actions can be understood when they are seen to have been necessitated in an entirely different way.

The issue between Collingwood and his opponents thus turns on the question: "How can an action be necessitated except in terms of natural law?" Collingwood's answer would be that it can be necessitated in the sense of its being rationally required. A set of antecedent conditions which explains a consequent event by virtue of a law of nature, shows the event to have been necessary in the sense of being "the thing to have expected, the laws of nature being what they are." The thoughts or considerations which explain an action in Collingwood's context of discussion show the action to have been necessary in the sense of being "the thing to have done, the principles of reason being what they are."[12] We could put the point by saying that the necessity which is required for the explanation of action in history, according to Collingwood, is a *rational* rather than a *natural* necessity. If something happens in spite of natural necessity, we call it a miracle. If an action is done in spite of rational necessity, we call it a stupidity, a mistake, an irrationality. It is Collingwood's claim that if, and only if, rational necessity can be shown, then we understand what the agent did. And he adds that such understanding does not require the further demonstration, by the methods of natural science, that what happened was a natural necessity as well.

The exact role which the concept of rational necessity plays in Collingwood's theory will appear more clearly when we go on to investigate the notion of "re-thinking." But a word should perhaps be added first about the concept of causation; for it may seem, once again, that Collingwood is simply flying in the face of the facts when he says that historians are not, or should not be, interested in the causes of actions. But his claim turns out, on closer examination, to be only that historians — their concept of understanding being what it is — do not need to discover *natural* causes for the actions they claim to understand. That historians commonly and legitimately use causal language, he does not attempt to deny. But he regards the historian's use of the term as a special one; for when it is said that it was his wanting to get rid of Pompey that caused Caesar to march on Rome, the word *cause* here implies a rational connection of the sort already examined, between what Caesar did and the considerations said to explain it (pp. 214-15). Collingwood himself speaks at various points of a thought not only causing an action but also determining or inducing it. But I think it is clear that he does not regard these locutions as reintroducing the concept of natural necessitation in terms of general laws of human mind or behaviour, which his general theory of historical understanding has ruled out as irrelevant.

III

We have still to examine Collingwood's third proposition: that discovering the explanatory thought requires its re-thinking in the historian's mind. From some critics, this feature of the theory has encountered the objection that such re-thinking is impossible; from others the complaint that it is unnecessary. It seems to me that neither objection is valid if Collingwood's point is taken in its proper sense. Let me therefore attempt, once again, to separate what I think is the basic doctrine from the misconceptions which may perhaps arise out of unfortunate forms of expression.

At least one of the reasons for questioning the possibility of re-thinking disappears in the light of our discussion of Collingwood's general conception of thought. For if thinking is logically distinguished from private imaginings and recitations, and if it is allowed that a person may sometimes not know what he thinks, there is no need to boggle at the notion of the historian *re*-thinking thoughts which may not have been fully articulated or explicitly recognized by the agent himself—even when those thoughts can be expressed by the historian as an argument. Since there are at least as many ways of thinking the same thought as there are ways of expressing it, there is nothing in Collingwood's theory which requires the historian to go through the same overt actions, or undergo the same private experiences, as the subject of his inquiry.[13] The fact that the original thought may not have been thought propositionally would therefore be no barrier to its being re-thought propositionally—the way we should naturally expect the historian to re-think it. It does not seem to be absolutely necessary, however, that the historian's re-thinking should take this form. He might, for example, re-think Nelson's thoughts with models of his ships on a table of naval operations, for a start—although he would, of course, have to express the thoughts propositionally when writing his monograph on "Nelson at Trafalgar."

The demand that the agent's thoughts be re-thought has also been seen to raise a different sort of problem. For, as Collingwood himself declares, "the mere re-enactment of another's thought does not make historical knowledge; we must also know that we are re-enacting it" (p. 289). How can the historian know that the thought he thinks is identical with the agent's? Collingwood unfortunately does not give this question the kind of consideration we should have liked it to get from a philosopher with his experience in historical research. Apart from a denial that historical arguments are either deductive or inductive in the ordinary sense,[14] and a lively dissection of the reasoning implicit in crime detection—illustrated by a detective yarn of his own invention (pp. 266 ff.)—we are left with little more than the rather dogmatic assurance that, in so far as there is knowledge at all, there are occasions on which the historian can be sure of his conclusions. Perhaps this contention would have seemed more acceptable if Collingwood had not, in an apparently unguarded moment, claimed that historical conclusions can, in some cases, be known as certainly as a proof in mathematics (p. 262). Since history proceeds, on his own showing, by the interpretation of evidence, not by formal deduction, the precise meaning of this curious claim is not obvious. But that a "weight of evidence" may, from time to time, justify a non-mathematical kind of certainty in history, would appear to be deniable only by someone whose skepticism embraced a good deal more than historical arguments.

If we grant that the historian *can* re-think his subject's thoughts, must we go on to agree that historical understanding *requires* this? Collingwood is most insistent that it does. "To know 'what someone is thinking' (or 'has thought')," he writes, "involves thinking it for oneself" (p. 288). And it is clear that he means this quite literally. In order to grasp the agent's thought, and see that it really does explain his action, the historian must do more than merely reproduce the agent's argument, whether implicit or explicit; he must also *draw his conclusion*. It is not enough merely to examine a report of the agent's "thought-process"; the historian must, on inspecting the thoughts, and treating them as premises of practical deliberation, actually *think that* the conclusion follows. The historian's "seeing" the connection between the agent's "considerations" and his action entails his *certification* of the connection between them—this entailment being a logical one. If the attempt to re-think, and thus to certify, the agent's thought-action complex breaks down—as Collingwood admits it has done in the case of certain early Roman emperors—then we have a dark spot, an unintelligibility, a failure to understand.[15]

Collingwood sometimes puts the point in terms of a distinction between knowing the agent's thoughts as "object" and as "act." In order to understand an action, he declares, "it is necessary to know 'what someone else is thinking,' not only in the sense of knowing the same object that he knows, but in the further sense of knowing the act by which he knows it" (p. 288). And again: "The act of thinking can be studied only as an act" (p. 293). To put the point in these terms is perhaps to be unnecessarily obscure. But to represent re-thinking as a sharing in an activity does serve to bring out the requirement that the connection between thought and action be *tested* by the historian, if he wishes to understand what was done. The doctrine may appear less formidable when Collingwood goes on to consider examples. In order to understand the Theodosian Code, we are told, the historian "must envisage the situation with which the emperor was trying to deal, and he must envisage it just as the emperor envisaged it. Then he must see for himself, just as if the emperor's situation were his own, how such a situation might be dealt with; he must see the possible alternatives, and the reasons for choosing one rather than another; and thus he must go through the process which the emperor went through in deciding on this particular course" (p. 283). To see that the emperor had reasons for doing what he did is thus to understand his doing it. And to see that he had reasons is, at the same time, to certify the reasons *as* reasons.

The explanation must thus be said to succeed to the extent to which it reveals the rationality of the agent. An action is said to be understood, on Collingwood's view, when it is seen to have been rationally necessary. Does this way of putting it impute to Collingwood a rationalism as divorced from the realities of historical inquiry as the intellectualism we have already denied? Some of Collingwood's dicta might seem to support such a conclusion; others point the other way. The strategy of Admiral Villeneuve at Trafalgar, he tells us, cannot possibly be understood; for the fact that he lost the battle shows that Villeneuve's strategy was wrong—as if an action must be rationally appropriate to the ,actual situation or be unintelligible.[16] On the other hand, in discussing Hegel's philosophy of history, Collingwood welcomes the "fertile and valuable principle" asserted there that "every historical character in every historical situation thinks and acts rationally as that person in that situation *can* think and act."[17] What was said above about the understanding of the Theodosian Code should be sufficient to show that in Collingwood's hands, such a principle attributes no absolute rationality to the agents whose actions historians claim to understand. For what renders an action "rational," in the sense of "understandable," is its being required by the situation as it was envisaged, not by the situation as it actually was. The historian's certification might thus be said to be a "hypothetical" one. Its implication is simply that *if* the situation had been as the agent envisaged it, then what he did would have been the rational thing to do.

But even if we interpret Hegel's "fertile principle" in terms of such a "hypothetical" rationality, the principle may possibly lead us astray. For it apparently suggests to Collingwood that when understanding fails, we can only attribute this failure to a breakdown of historical analysis—"It is the historian himself who stands at the bar of judgment . . ." (p. 219). Historical understanding being the sort of thing it is, it seems to me that a number of other possibilities would have to be taken into account.

We must allow, for example, for cases where the agent's reasoning about his situation is itself mistaken. For an agent may be in error, not only in the way he envisages his situation, but also in concluding that what he did was required by the situation as he envisaged it. Such an agent would have to be regarded by the historian as "irrational" in a stronger sense than the agent who, although he misconceived his situation, nevertheless acted in the way required by the situation as he conceived it. The thought of the latter agent can be re-thought by the historian, albeit only hypothetically; but the thought of the former cannot be re-thought at all. In so far as a person makes a mistake in the reasoning which represents what he did as rationally required, his action can only be explained *as* mistaken—a word whose function here is to rule out the possibility of explaining what was done in terms of reasons. Such an action could therefore not be "understood," in Collingwood's sense of the word.

We must allow also for cases where what is done was not intended by the agent: cases of accidental or inadvertent action, illustrated, for example, by a cabinet minister's subversion of his own government's position by an unwise speech made in its defence. It would appear to be cases of this kind which Collingwood has in mind when he denies that "every agent is wholly and directly responsible for everything that he does" (p. 41). It might be argued, I suppose, that in such cases, although there is doubtless an action (giving the speech) which is explicable in the ordinary way, what is specified as requiring explanation (bringing down the government) is not really the agent's *action* at all. Yet what was done *was,* in this case, something which the agent could be held responsible for; and his colleagues would not be slow to say that he *did* it. If for these reasons we called it an action, then it must be admitted that this, too, is a kind of action which could not be understood in Collingwood's sense.

Still another sort of case which Hegel's principle must allow for is that of arbitrary or capricious action: cases where an agent may have known certain things about his situation, and may have realized that a certain response was, in reason, demanded, yet deliberately acted otherwise. The possibility of such action has sometimes been denied. It has been alleged that what we do, we always do for some reason—even if it takes a psychoanalyst to discover it. I cannot undertake to argue the contrary here in any detail. But I think we might perhaps be a trifle wary of a theory of action which, on some occasion, might condemn a historical agent to the fate of Buridan's ass, who, on finding himself stationed equidistant between two equally succulent bundles of hay, followed reason and starved to death. The ass, admittedly, had every reason to eat one bundle before the other; and if he had eaten them successively, *something* could doubtless have been explained—for example, that he ate any hay at all, or even that he ate one bundle before the other. But it would clearly have been impossible, *ex hypothesi,* to explain in Collingwood's sense why he chose to eat the one he did before eating the other. I do not, of course, suggest that the historian will very often be confronted with an agent placed in the unhappy position of such a philosophical ass. But it is hard to see, if the ass's philosophy be not refuted, how Hegel's principle, even in its attenuated Collingwoodian form, can be accepted as universally valid.

NOTES

1. Oxford, 1946.
2. *Idea of History,* pp. 305–15.
3. *Introduction to Philosophy of History* (London, 1951), p. 50.
4. *A Study of History* (London, 1954), IX, 722.
5. *Idea of History,* p. 217. See also pp. 212, 214, 220.
6. *The Concept of Mind* (London, 1949), Chap. vi. Rylian language is employed in the two paragraphs following.
7. *Idea of History,* pp. 285, 301, 303.
8. *Philosophy of History,* p. 54.
9. E.g., *Idea of History,* pp. 216–17.
10. For a different solution, see Toynbee, *Study of History,* pp. 720–21. According to him, Caesar's action expresses "will," not "thought."
11. See *Idea of History,* pp. 220, 224.
12. I am discussing here the general *concept* of rational necessity. The qualifications requiring to be made when it is employed in historical understanding are introduced in Sec. III.
13. Collingwood's term "re-enactment" may appear more troublesome in this connection than "re-thinking"; but for Collingwood, thinking is an activity.
14. *Idea of History,* pp. 261–62. Mr. Alan Donagan has discussed this aspect of Collingwood's theory in an illuminating way in "The Verification of Historical Theses," *Philosophical Quarterly* (July 1956).
15. *Idea of History,* p. 310.
16. R. G. Collingwood, *An Autobiography* (Oxford, 1941), p. 70. T. M. Knox, in the "Editor's Preface" to *The Idea of History,* assumes that this is Collingwood's meaning. I think it possible that what he had in mind was rather the extent to which the evidence, upon which conclusions about Villeneuve's actual strategy during the battle would have been based, was destroyed by Nelson's victory.
17. *Idea of History,* p. 116.

STUDY QUESTIONS FOR PART 2

1. Which of these sentences is a request for an explanation of the sort Hempel is interested in? How can you distinguish that type of request from the others?

What does 'banal' mean?

Why did that piece of copper turn green?

How do you get to Dayton's department store?

Why do you still believe that Nixon did not know about the Watergate capers?

2. What is wrong with the claim that explaining is taking an event that is unfamiliar to us and showing that it is really a member of a class of events that is familiar to us?

3. According to Hempel, what does explanation consist of?

4. Give a counterexample to the claim that a *sufficient* condition for something being an explanation is that the explanandum be a deductive consequence of the explanans.

5. Discuss the issue of whether the condition above ought to be a *necessary* condition.

6. What might be wrong with the explanation given in the following dialogue?

Announcer: Why are the Bullets playing so much better this quarter?

Color man: Well, it's obvious that the momentum is on their side now.

7. Often it is claimed that all science does is tell us *how* things happen or, alternatively, that science just *describes*. Part of this position seems to be that explaining is incompatible with telling us or describing. Evaluate this view.

8. What conception of 'law' do Lambert and Britten hold? How does it differ from Hempel's?

9. What conception of 'explanation' do they hold? How does it differ from Hempel's?

10. What are counterfactual conditionals?

11. How does the notion of counterfactual conditionals help us to understand the concept of a law of nature, according to Lambert and Britten?

12. Brody's "sodium-bromine" and "temperature-pressure" examples are supposed to meet all of Hempel's requirements and yet not be explanations. Do they meet the requirements? What is counterintuitive about them?

13. Explain the difference between Aristotle's "knowledge of the fact" and "knowledge of the reasoned fact."

14. Be sure you see and can show that Aristotle's view of causation is different from the constant conjunction view. According to that latter view to say that *a* causes *b* is to say that *a* and *b* occurred and that from a description of *a* and some law, *b*, a description of *b* can be deduced.

15. What is the first new requirement Brody adds to the Hempelian conditions? Show how it accounts for our intuitions about the temperature-

pressure cases.

16. Why won't the new requirement handle the "sodium-bromine" case?

17. What is Brody's second requirement? Show how it explains what is wrong with the "sodium-bromine" example.

18. Give some examples of accidental and essential properties. Does Brody give any hints at a criterion for individuating them?

19. Evaluate Brody's "proof" that we have knowledge of Aristotelean-type causation and essential properties.

20. What is wrong with the covering-law (Hempelian) model of explanation, according to Cartwright? Do you agree? Why or why not?

21. What are *ceterus paribus* laws? What is their function, according to Cartwright? What don't (or can't) they do, according to her. Why not?

22. What does the author mean by tie title of the essay? Unpack and elaborate on that assertion. Why does she hold it? Do you agree? Why or why not?

23. This essay is contained in a book of Cartwright entitled *How the Laws of Physics Lie.* On the basis of this essay, what does she mean by the claim that they lie? How do they lie, according to her? If they lie, are they of any value? Do you agree with her answers? Why or why not?

24. On the basis of this essay, how does Cartwright answer the question "What is a scientific explanation?"

25. According to Collingwood, action, understood as necessarily having a thought-side, is the subject of historical inquiry. What does he mean by this? With what are actions in this sense contrasted?

26. When a historical agent acts, must he be aware of his thought-side? To answer this question you need to formulate a view on what it is to have a thought.

27. What, according to Collingwood, are the conditions for explaining an action? How do they differ from the Hempelian conditions? Give a nice example of a Collingwoodian explanation.

28. What does it mean to say one must fill out the thought-side until it *necessitates* the action? In Hempelian explanations, in what, if any, sense is the explanandum necessitated? Is the event described by the explanandum necessitated in any sense?

29. What does Collingwood seem to have in mind by his rethinking method for discovering the thought-side of another's action?

30. Is there anything about Collingwood's account of *historical* explanation that makes it *historical,* i.e., if it explains actions at all, why doesn't it work on the actions of one's friends as well as those of historical figures?

SELECTED BIBLIOGRAPHY

[1] Achinstein, P. *Law and Explanation.* Oxford: Clarendon Press, 1971. [Does not sever the logical from the pragmatic aspects of explanation.]

[2] Armstrong, D. *What Is a Law of Nature?* Cambridge, England: Cambridge University Press, 1983. [Non-regularity account of laws.]

[3] Brodbeck, M. *Readings in the Philosophy of the Social Sciences.* New York: Macmillan, 1968, sec. 3-5. [The best book of its kind.]

[4] Brody, B., ed. *Readings in the Philosophy of Science.* Englewood Cliffs, N. J.: Prentice-Hall, 1970, pt. 1. [Contains classic papers and critical responses.]

[5] Dray, William., ed. *Philosophical Analysis and History.* New York: Harper & Row, 1966. [Contains essays on historical explanation.]

[6] Hull, D. *Philosophy of Biological Science.* Englewood Cliffs, N. J.: Prentice-Hall, 1974, chap. 3. [Interesting treatment.]

[7] Kline, A. D., and Matheson, C. "How the Laws of Physics Don't Even Fib." In P.S.A. 1986, Vol. 1, edited by A. Fine and P. Machamen. East Lansing, Mich.: Philosophy of Science Association, 1986. [Critique of Cartwright.]

[8] Salmon W. *Scientific Explanation and the Causal Structure of the World.* Princeton: Princeton University Press, 1984. [Systematic non-Hempelian account of explanation.]

[9] Scheffler, I. *The Anatomy of Inquiry.* New York: Knopf, 1969, pt. 1. [Systematic and careful look at the Hempelian view.]

Part 3

Theory and Observation

Part 3: Theory and Observation

Introduction

I. The Problem

Our student newspaper recently reported two episodes. In one, a biology student was reported to have said, in defense of some religious view of his, that the theory of evolution was just that—a theory. His professor supposedly shouted back, "It's not a *theory!*" In another story, a mathematician used, as an example of one of man's greatest cognitive achievements, Einstein's *theory* of special relativity.

Though the student and biologist have some disagreements, they do not appear to be over what a theory is. But the mathematician seems to have a different concept of what it is to call something a theory. For the student and biologist to call something a theory is to reduce its cognitive authority. The mathematician thinks that at least one theory is without cognitive superiors. Someone (perhaps all three) is confused.

In this part our goal is to begin to form a coherent and informed view on the nature of theories. Before attempting to characterize the structure of a theory, let's consider a pair of examples. The explanans of two of the examples in Part 2, when considered along with the wider set of laws and assumptions in which they are embedded, provide splendid examples of theories.

Aristotle's explanation of the circular movements of the planets is just a part of his wider astronomical theory. His theory "tells" us much more about the universe than why planets move in circular orbits; e.g., it tells us that the stationary earth is at the center of the universe; it gives the spatial order of the planets and their relation to the stars; and it provides for predictions of the movements of the planets.

There is an evolutionary *explanation* of certain increases in the "complexity"

155

of life-forms as evidenced in the fossil record. But the wider *theory* of evolution provides explanations and predictions of a plethora of phenomena. For example, the theory allows us to explain why only certain species of moths in Birmingham, England, survived the pollution of that city brought on by industrialization. The theory provides us with insights into how we should go about creating more rust-resistant grains. The theory provides the causal mechanism for understanding why the descendants of certain mutants in a population come to dominate the population. And we could go on and on.

Our philosophical problem can be simply stated: What is a scientific theory? We shall see that the answer is considerably more complex.

II. The Structure of Theories

The topic of theories is perhaps the most difficult one in the philosophy of science. It is certainly the most difficult of those found in this anthology. Like the mind-body problem and the problem of perception, the topic of theories is really a constellation of intertwined problems. Furthermore, as in the area of explanation, there is a historically important view. Though this view is widely recognized as problematic, the reader of current literature often must have a substantial acquaintance with it. But unlike the Hempelian view on explanation, which can be presented to a student with minimal background, the standard view on theories cannot. Even elementary presentations require training in symbolic logic and the philosophy of language.

Fortunately, much about theories can be discussed without taking on all the details of the standard account. A place to begin is with a rough and tentative characterization of theories.

Structurally, theories are sets of statements, some of which state laws, others of which are singular factual or existential claims; e.g., that electrons exist and that electrons have a charge of minus one. Furthermore, theories contain some terms that refer to unobservable entities or properties. The statements of a theory are interrelated in such a way as to embody certain virtues: generality or comprehensiveness of explanatory and predictive power, ability to unify diverse phenomena and laws, depth of explanatory power. Theories explain not a particular law or phenomenon but whole ranges of each—this range is typically called the domain of the theory. Theories show how apparently diverse or unrelated phenomena and laws really are related, at least for explanatory purposes. Theories aim at a deep understanding of phenomena; i.e., theories often describe the causal mechanism behind regularities or appeal to microstructure in accounting for the macroscopic properties of objects.

We can consider in a little detail an example—the kinetic theory of matter and heat. In the mid-nineteenth century, J. P. Joule synthesized the work of Rumford, Bernoulli, and others to form the kinetic theory. This theory exercised the talents of many of the great nineteenth-century physicists.

Structurally, the theory contains (a) a set of laws—in particular, what we now call the laws of classical mechanics, the most central of which are Newton's laws of motion; (b) a set of singular existential and factual statements. We now refer to this set as the model of a gas. It includes the following claims: gases consist of molecules; the size of molecules is negligible; the number of molecules is very large; molecules are in random motion; molecular collisions are perfectly elastic. Notice that some of the terms in these statements refer to unobservable entities and properties.

It was claimed earlier that theories have certain virtues. The generality of the explanatory power of the kinetic theory is witnessed by the fact that it explains the gas laws (laws that relate to the pressure, temperature and volume of a gas), laws about the specific heats of gases, laws about the rates of diffusion of one gas in another, and so on. The theory unifies apparently diverse phenomena. It shows, for example, that the fact that an odiferous substance released, say, in the corner of a room spreads at the rate it does throughout the room and the fact that the earth has not lost its atmosphere are, from the point of view of the theory, rather similar phenomena. To use the gas-diffusion example again, the theory does, of course, explain this well-known phenomenon, but it also illuminates the underlying mechanism by which it occurs. The theory also takes common notions such as temperature and pressure and shows one what they "really" are. It gives the microstructure that "underlies" these properties.

III. Observation

Most philosophers agree that an appeal to unobservables is an important mark of scientific theories. But here the agreement ends. When one considers the details of this rather vague criterion, a plethora of issues are forced upon us. Exactly how are observables and unobservables to be distinguished? Is what is observable subject to changes in historical contingencies—the invention of a new instrument, for example? Is what is observable subject to theoretical contingencies; that is, given two theories, T and T' at time t, can an entity or property be observable relative to T and unobservable relative to T'?

Consider the following view that has three parts: (i) At any time, t, all the nonlogical terms of science (terms other than 'all', 'and', 'or', 'a', and so on) can be uniquely parsed into one of two classes: (a) those that refer to observable entities or properties, e.g., 'red', 'circular', 'cup', 'cat'; (These are called observation terms.) (b) those that refer to unobservable entites or properties, e.g., 'valence', 'charge', 'electron'. (These are called theoretical terms.) (ii) If a term is correctly classified as an observation or theoretical term it is permanently so classified. (iii) An entity or property is an observable if and only if normal observers in standard conditions can ascertain the presence of the entity or property by direct observation. Otherwise the entity or property is unobservable.

Something like the view above is embedded in the standard account of theories. Though, in fairness, it must be admitted to be an extreme and perhaps unsympathetic reconstruction of the standard view. Nevertheless, it will serve for anchoring our disucssion. We need to be asking whether the observational-theoretical distinction can be drawn in a way that illuminates scientific practice or certain philosophical goals or both.

IV. Status of Unobservables

Supposing that a satisfactory way has been found to make the observable/ unobservable distinction, another issue beckons us. Are unobservables real? Do they actually exist? This may strike one as an odd question. It is the case from a grammatical point of view that theoretical terms appear to refer and describe just as observation terms do. But as we shall see, philosophers have thought that the actual function of theoretical talk is quite different.

A question closely related to whether unobservables exist is whether theoretical statements are true. Theoretical statements are statements that contain only theoretical and logical terms, e.g., 'electrons have a charge of minus one.' Analogously, observation statements are statements that contain only observation and logical terms, e.g., 'that table is red.'

There are several distinct views on the questions we have been asking. It will be helpful to chart a taxonomy of the more important views. The chart can be generated by asking three questions: (Q1) Do unobservables exist? (Q2) Are theoretical statements true? (Q3) Are observation statements true? Do not be misled by (Q2) and (Q3). The question is not: Are all the theoretical or observational sentences of theories true or are some of them true; or do we know that some of them are true? The question is: Are they candidates for being true? They will not be candidates if there is some general philosophical reason for suspecting the truth of them as a class. The chart of views follows:

	Super-realism	Realism	Instrumentalism	Descriptivism
(Q1) Do unobserv- ables exist?	Yes	Yes	No	No
(Q2) Are theoretical statements true?	Yes	Yes	No	Yes
(Q3) Are observation statements true?	No	Yes	Yes	Yes

There are other possibilities, of course. The trinty, No, No, No, is an obvious one. This possibility has been taken seriously by some philosophers. But the arguments for it are not usually produced from a close look at science. They are often generated from a global attack on the possibility of knowledge. We could construct a more elaborate and finer-grained taxonomy. But since those above are the most discussed possibilities and since our purposes are merely to initiate the discussion, the above major possibilities and grain will do.

Realists are fond of regarding their view as common sense. Whether they are right or not it is true that the dialectic of the issue is such that it is tacitly assumed that the burden of proof rests with the anti-realist. We can say from personal experience that scientists often talk the instrumentalist's line and that a little philosophy often jars students from a realist stance. Whether a little philosophy is a dangerous thing or not you will have to decide.

We do not wish to review in detail the reasons for the four views—the readings do that. We do want to say enough about the views so that they are at least on the surface distinguishable.

Sir Arthur Eddington (1881–1944), the famous English astronomer, held the view I have dubbed super-realism. Eddington begins the presentation of his view in a now famous passage that both excites and teases the reader.

> I have settled down to the task of writing these lectures and have drawn up my chairs to my two tables. Two tables! Yes; there are duplicates of every object about me—two tables, two chairs, two pens.[1]

The first table, the table of common sense, is extended, permanent, colored, and substantial. The second table, the table of physics, is mostly emptiness. It is a vast number of electric charges speeding about.

For our purposes, what is interesting abut Eddington is that he denies that the first table exists, much less that there is a colored table there. In his words, "modern physics has by delicate test and remorseless logic assured me that my second table is the only one which is really there—whatever 'there' may be."[2]

Exactly how physics teaches us, if it does, that observation sentences are false is a very complicated matter. If you are interested in pursuing super-realism, [3] and [5] of the bibliography may help.

A descriptivist claims that we have absolutely no reason to believe that the theoretical "entities" and "properties" of a theory exist. This leads him to propose a new function for theoretical talk. Theoretical statements supposedly provide us with "shorthand formulae." These formulae prove convenient for organizing observables and making predictions about observables, but they should not be taken as referring to entities or properties over and above observables.

A simple example will help clarify the point. The caterer of a wedding might find it convenient to plan in terms of the "average wedding-goer." Such a concept will be helpful in summarizing certain data from past weddings and predicting features of the wedding to be. But the caterer does not think average wedding-goers are real or exist. After all, not only does the average wedding-goer drink 3.2 whiskey sours and eat 6 cocktail knishes, but he has 2.1 children.

In the same way that the average wedding-goers do not exist over and above John, Mildred, and so on, and their actual and dispositional behavior, electrons do not exist over and above the complex of actual and possible data they stand in for.

Notice that, for the descriptivist, theoretical statements are true. This, at the outset, might appear strange since theoretical entities do not exist. But given Stace's view, we see that theoretical statements are just very complex, though briefly stated, observation statements. Since observation statements are true, so are theoretical statements.

Though descriptivism and instrumentalism are often confused they are distinct views. The "no" answer for the instrumentalist to (Q2) may be misleading—misleading in the same way as your answering "no" if a child asked you if you ever sprained your kidney. A better answer would be to point out that kidneys are not the kinds of things that can be sprained or for that matter not sprained. Similarly, for the instrumentalist, theoretical statements are not the kinds of things that are true or false. Instrumentalists often refer to theoretical statements as rules, or inference tickets, or predictive instruments. Just as the rules of chess, e.g., the rule that pawns can only move forward, are neither true nor false but useful for certain purposes, playing an interesting game, so the theoretical sentences of science are neither true nor false but useful for certain purposes, making predictions. (Of course, " 'pawns can only move forward' is a rule of chess" is true or false.)

V. The Readings in Part 3

The essay by Rudolf Carnap is crucial in setting the context for the remaining essays. His essay is a non-technical presentation of the traditional conception of scientific theories. He discusses the observational-theoretical distinction and how the theoretical components of a theory are linked to the observational. The remaining essays in this part can be seen as criticizing the Carnapian conception of theories or elaborating the philosophical status of theories.

Hilary Putnam and N. R. Hanson both attack the observational-theoretical dichotomy. Putnam wants to show that the distinction cannot be coherently drawn. It turns out that some terms end up in the wrong bin from where they pre-analytically belong. Hanson's charge is of a different sort. He wants to show that there is no sort of observation important to science that is independent of theory. All significant observation is connected with theoretical claims.

Three of the main positions on the status of unobservables, descriptivism, instrumentation and realism, are covered by the essays of Stace, Toulmin and Maxwell respectively. Stace's argument for descriptivism relies very heavily on a strict observational-theoretical distinction. At the end of his piece he makes an extraordinary claim which deserves examination: "If the views which I have been expressing are followed out, they will lead to the conclusion that, strictly speaking, *nothing exists except sensations* (and the minds which perceive them)."

Toulmin's argument probes the meaning of existence claims. He points out that not every existence claim may be of the same piece. What we are really asking when we worry about the existence of theoretical entities might be quite different from what we are asking when we worry about the existence of dodos.

Maxwell's essay contains a statement and critique of both descriptivism and instrumentalism on the way to depending realism. Maxwell tries to show that the observational-theoretical distinction is not sharp. It is more like a continuous change than an abrupt one. Hence we ought not read ontological significance into it.

The essay by Matheson and Kline is on a different level. It looks at what motivates the sharp observation theory distinction and the prospects for realizing those motives. The paper argues that, at least to some extent, where you come down on the status of unobservables is a function of commitments to theses on the *structure* of theories.

A. D. K.

NOTES

1. A. Eddington. *The Nature of the Physical World.* New York: Cambridge University Press, 1929, p. ix.

2. Ibid. p. xii.

11

The Nature of Theories
Rudolf Carnap

I. Theories and Nonobservables

One of the most important distinctions between two types of laws in science
is the distinction between what may be called (there is no generally accepted
terminology for them) empirical laws and theoretical laws. Empirical laws
are laws that can be confirmed directly by empirical observations. The term
"observable" is often used for any phenomenon that can be directly observed,
so it can be said that empirical laws are laws about observables.

Here, a warning must be issued. Philosophers and scientists have quite
different ways of using the terms "observable" and "nonobservable." To a
philosopher, "observable" has a very narrow meaning. It applies to such
properties as "blue," "hard," "hot." These are properties directly perceived by
the senses. To the physicist, the word has a much broader meaning. It includes
any quantitative magnitude that can be measured in a relatively simple, direct
way. A philosopher would not consider a temperature of, perhaps, 80 degrees
centigrade, or a weight of 93½ pounds, an observable because there is no
direct sensory perception of such magnitudes. To a physicist, both are observables because they can be measured in an extremely simple way. The object
to be weighed is placed on a balance scale. The temperature is measured
with a thermometer. The physicist would not say that the mass of a molecule,
let alone the mass of an electron, is something observable, because here the
procedures of measurement are much more complicated and indirect. But
magnitudes that can be established by simple procedures—length with a ruler,
time with a clock, or frequency of light waves with a spectrometer—are called
observables.

A philosopher might object that the intensity of an electric current is not
really observed. Only a pointer position was observed. An ammeter was attached

162

to the circuit and it was noted that the pointer pointed to a mark labeled 5.3. Certainly the current's intensity was not observed. It was *inferred* from what was observed.

The physicist would reply that this was true enough, but the inference was not very complicated. The procedure of measurement is so simple, so well established, that it could not be doubted that the ammeter would give an accurate measurement of current intensity. Therefore, it is included among what are called observables.

There is no question here of who is using the term "observable" in a right or proper way. There is a continuum which starts with direct sensory observations and proceeds to enormously complex, indirect methods of observation. Obviously no sharp line can be drawn across this continuum; it is a matter of degree. A philosopher is sure that the sound of his wife's voice, coming from across the room, is an observable. But suppose he listens to her on the telephone. Is her voice an observable or isn't it? A physicist would certainly say that when he looks at something through an ordinary microscope, he is observing it directly. Is this also the case when he looks into an electron microscope? Does he observe the path of a particle when he sees the track it makes in a bubble chamber? In general, the physicist speaks of observables in a very wide sense compared with the narrow sense of the philosopher, but, in both cases, the line separating observable from nonobservable is highly arbitrary. It is well to keep this in mind whenever these terms are encountered in a book by a philosopher or scientist. Individual authors will draw the line where it is most convenient, depending on their points of view, and there is no reason why they should not have this privilege.

Empirical laws, in my terminology, are laws containing terms either directly observable by the senses or measurable by relatively simple techniques. Sometimes such laws are called empirical generalizations, as a reminder that they have been obtained by generalizing results found by observations and measurements. They include not only simple qualitative laws (such as, "All ravens are black") but also quantitative laws that arise from simple measurements. The laws relating pressure, volume, and temperature of gases are of this type. Ohm's law, connecting the electric potential difference, resistance, and intensity of current, is another familiar example. The scientist makes repeated measurements, finds certain regularities, and expresses them in a law. These are the empirical laws. As indicated in earlier chapters, they are used for explaining observed facts and for predicting future observable events.

There is no commonly accepted term for the second kind of laws, which I call *theoretical laws*. Sometimes they are called abstract or hypothetical laws. "Hypothetical" is perhaps not suitable because it suggests that the distinction between the two types of laws is based on the degree to which the laws are confirmed. But an empirical law, if it is a tentative hypothesis, confirmed only to a low degree, would still be an empirical law although it might be said that it was rather hypothetical. A theoretical law is not to be distinguished from an empirical law by the fact that it is not well established, but by the fact that it contains terms of a different kind. The terms of a theoretical law do not refer to observables even when the physicist's wide meaning for what can be observed is adopted. They are laws about such entities as molecules, atoms, electrons, protons, electromagnetic fields, and others that cannot be measured in simple, direct ways. . . .

It is true, as shown earlier, that the concepts "observable" and "non-observable" cannot be sharply defined because they lie on a continuum. In actual practice, however, the difference is usually great enough so there is not likely to be debate. All physicists would agree that the laws relating pressure, volume, and temperature of a gas, for example, are empirical laws. Here the amount of gas is large enough so that the magnitudes to be measured remain constant over a sufficiently large volume of space and period of time to permit direct, simple measurements which can then be generalized into laws. All physicists would agree that laws about the behavior of single molecules are theoretical. Such laws concern a microprocess about which generalizations cannot be based on simple, direct measurements.

Theoretical laws are, of course, more general than empirical laws. It is important to understand, however, that theoretical laws cannot be arrived at simply by taking the empirical laws, then generalizing a few steps further. How does a physicist arrive at an empirical law? He observes certain events in nature. He notices a certain regularity. He describes this regularity by making an inductive generalization. It might be supposed that he could now put together a group of empirical laws, observe some sort of pattern, make a wider inductive generalization, and arrive at a theoretical law. Such is not the case.

To make this clear, suppose it has been observed that a certain iron bar expands when heated. After the experiment has been repeated many times, always with the same result, the regularity is generalized by saying that this bar expands when heated. An empirical law has been stated, even though it has a narrow range and applies only to one particular iron bar. Now further tests are made of other iron objects with the ensuing discovery that every time an iron object is heated it expands. This permits a more general law to be formulated, namely that all bodies of iron expand when heated. In similar fashion, the still more general laws "All metals . . .," then "All solid bodies . . .," are developed. These are all simple generalizations, each a bit more general than the previous one, but they are all empirical laws. Why? Because in each case, the objects dealt with are observable (iron, copper, metal, solid bodies); in each case the increases in temperature and length are measurable by simple, direct techniques.

In contrast, a theoretical law relating to this process would refer to the behavior of molecules in the iron bar. In what way is the behavior of the molecules connected with the expansion of the bar when heated? You see at once that we are now speaking of nonobservables. We must introduce a theory—the atomic theory of matter—and we are quickly plunged into atomic laws involving concepts radically different from those we had before. It is true that these theoretical concepts differ from concepts of length and temperature only in the degree to which they are directly or indirectly observable, but the difference is so great that there is no debate about the radically different nature of the laws that must be formulated.

Theoretical laws are related to empirical laws in a way somewhat analogous to the way empirical laws are related to single facts. An empirical law helps to explain a fact that has been observed and to predict a fact not yet observed. In similar fashion, the theoretical law helps to explain empirical laws already formulated, and to permit the derivation of new empirical laws. Just as the single, separate facts fall into place in an orderly pattern when they are generalized in an empirical law, the single and separate empirical laws fit into the orderly pattern of a theoretical law. This raises one of the main problems in the methodology of science. How can the kind of knowledge that will justify the assertion of a theoretical law be obtained? An empirical law may be justified by making observations of single facts. But to justify a theoretical law, comparable observations cannot be made because the entities referred to in theoretical laws are nonobservables. . . .

How can theoretical laws be discovered? We cannot say: "Let's just collect more and more data, then generalize beyond the empirical laws until we reach theoretical ones." No theoretical law was ever found that way. We observe stones and trees and flowers, noting various regularities and describing them by empirical laws. But no matter how long or how carefully we observe such things, we never reach a point at which we observe a molecule. The term "molecule" never arises as a result of observations. For this reason, no amount of generalization from observations will ever produce a theory of molecular processes. Such a theory must arise in another way. It is stated not as a generalization of facts but as a hypothesis. The hypothesis is then tested in a manner analogous in certain ways to the testing of an empirical law. From the hypothesis, certain empirical laws are derived, and these empirical laws are tested in turn by observation of facts. Perhaps the empirical laws derived from the theory are already known and well confirmed. (Such laws may even have motivated the formulation of the theoretical law.) Regardless of whether the derived empirical laws are known and confirmed, or whether they are new laws confirmed by new observations, the confirmation of such derived laws provides indirect confirmation of the theoretical law.

The point to be made clear is this. A scientist does not start with one empirical law, perhaps Boyle's law for gases, and then seek a theory about molecules from which this law can be derived. The scientist tries to formulate a much more general theory from which a variety of empirical laws can be derived. The more such laws, the greater their variety and apparent lack of connection with one another, the stronger will be the theory that explains them. Some of these derived laws may have been known before, but the theory may also make it possible to derive new empirical laws which can be confirmed by new tests. If this is the case, it can be said that the theory made it possible to predict new empirical laws. The prediction is understood in a hypothetical way. If the theory holds, certain empirical laws will also hold. The predicted empirical law speaks about relations between observables, so it is now possible to make experiments to see if the empirical law holds. If the empirical law is confirmed, it provides indirect confirmation of the theory. Every confirmation of a law, empirical or theoretical, is, of course, only partial, never complete and absolute. But in the case of empirical laws, it is a more direct confirmation. The confirmation of a theoretical law is indirect, because it takes place only through the confirmation of empirical laws derived from the theory.

The supreme value of a new theory is its power to predict new empirical laws. It is true that it also has value in explaining known empirical laws, but this is a minor value. If a scientist proposes a new theoretical system, from which no new laws can be derived, then it is logically equivalent to the set of all known empirical laws. The theory may have a certain elegance, and it may simplify to some degree the set of all known laws, although it is not likely that there would be an essential simplification. On the other hand, every new theory in physics that has led to a great leap forward has been a theory from which new empirical laws could be derived. If Einstein had done no more than propose his theory of relativity as an elegant new theory that would embrace certain known laws—perhaps also simplify them to a certain degree—then his theory would not have had such a revolutionary effect.

Of course it was quite otherwise. The theory of relativity led to new empirical laws which explained for the first time such phenomena as the movement of the perihelion of Mercury, and the bending of light rays in the neighborhood of the sun. These predictions showed that relativity theory was more than just a new way of expressing the old laws. Indeed, it was a theory of great predictive power. The consequences that can be derived from Einstein's theory are far from being exhausted. These are consequences that could not have been derived from earlier theories. Usually a theory of such power does have an elegance, and a unifying effect on known laws. It is simpler than the total collection of known laws. But the great value of the theory lies in its power to suggest new laws that can be confirmed by empirical means.

II. Correspondence Rules

An important qualification must now be added to the discussion of theoretical laws and terms given in section I. The statement that empirical laws are derived from theoretical laws is an oversimplification. It is not possible to derive them directly because a theoretical law contains theoretical terms, whereas an empirical law contains only observable terms. This prevents any direct deduction of an empirical law from a theoretical one.

To understand this, imagine that we are back in the nineteenth century, preparing to state for the first time some theoretical laws about molecules in a gas. These laws are to describe the number of molecules per unit volume of the gas, the molecular velocities, and so forth. To simplify matters, we assume that all the molecules have the same velocity. (This was indeed the original assumption; later it was abandoned in favor of a certain probability distribution of velocities.) Further assumptions must be made about what happens when molecules collide. We do not know the exact shape of molecules, so let us suppose that they are tiny spheres. How do spheres collide? There are laws about colliding spheres, but they concern large bodies. Since we cannot directly observe molecules, we assume their collisions are analogous to those of large bodies; perhaps they behave like perfect billiard balls on a frictionless table. These are, of course, only assumptions; guesses suggested by analogies with known macrolaws.

But now we come up against a difficult problem. Our theoretical laws deal exclusively with the behavior of molecules, which cannot be seen. How, therefore, can we deduce from such laws a law about observable properties such as the pressure or temperature of a gas or properties of sound waves that pass through the gas? The theoretical laws contain only theoretical terms. What we seek are empirical laws containing observable terms. Obviously, such laws cannot be derived without having something else given in addition to the theoretical laws.

The something else that must be given is this: a set of rules connecting the theoretical terms with the observable terms. Scientists and philosophers of science have long recognized the need for such a set of rules, and their nature has often been discussed. An example of such a rule is: "If there is an electromagnetic oscillation of a specified frequency, then there is a visible greenish-blue color of a certain hue." Here something observable is connected with a nonobservable microprocess.

Another example is: "The temperature (measured by a thermometer and, therefore, an observable in the wider sense explained earlier) of a gas is proportional to the mean kinetic energy of its molecules." This rule connects a nonobservable in molecular theory, the kinetic energy of molecules, with an observable, the temperature of the gas. If statements of this kind did not exist, there would be no way of deriving empirical laws about observables from theoretical laws about nonobservables.

Different writers have different names for these rules. I call them "correspondence rules." P. W. Bridgman calls them operational rules. Norman R. Campbell speaks of them as the "Dictionary."[1] Since the rules connect a term in one terminology with a term in another terminology, the use of the rules is analogous to the use of a French-English dictionary. What does the French word "cheval" mean? You look it up in the dictionary and find that it means "horse." It is not really that simple when a set of rules is used for connecting nonobservables with observables; nevertheless, there is an analogy here that makes Campbell's "Dictionary" a suggestive name for the set of rules.

There is a temptation at times to think that the set of rules provides a means for defining theoretical terms, whereas just the opposite is really true. A theoretical term can never be explicitly defined on the basis of observable terms, although sometimes an observable can be defined in theoretical terms. For example, "iron" can be defined as a substance consisting of small crystalline parts, each having a certain arrangement of atoms and each atom being a configuration of particles of a certain type. In theoretical terms then, it is possible to express what is meant by the observable term "iron," but the reverse is not true.

There is no answer to the question: "Exactly what is an electron?" Later we shall come back to this question, because it is the kind that philosophers are always asking scientists. They want the physicist to tell them just what he means by "electricity," "magnetism," "gravity," "a molecule." If the physicist explains them in theoretical terms, the philosopher may be disappointed. "That is not what I meant at all," he will say. "I want you to tell me, in ordinary language, what those terms mean." Sometimes the philosopher writes a book in which he talks about the great mysteries of nature. "No one," he writes, "has been able so far, and perhaps no one ever will be able, to give us a straightforward answer to the question: 'What is electricity?' And so electricity remains forever one of the great, unfathomable mysteries of the universe."

There is no special mystery here. There is only an improperly phrased question. Definitions that cannot, in the nature of the case, be given, should not be demanded. If a child does not know what an elephant is, we can tell him it is a huge animal with big ears and a long trunk. We can show him a picture of an elephant. It serves admirably to define an elephant in observable terms that a child can understand. By analogy, there is a temptation to believe that, when a scientist introduces theoretical terms, he should also be able to define them in familiar terms. But this is not possible. There is no way a physicist can show us a picture of electricity in the way he can show his child a picture of an elephant. Even the cell of an organism, although it cannot be seen with the unaided eye, can be represented by a picture because the cell can be seen when it is viewed through a microscope. But we do not possess a picture of the electron. We cannot say how it looks or how it feels, because it cannot be seen or touched. The best we can do is to say that it is an extremely small body that behaves in a certain manner. This may seem to be analogous to our description of an elephant. We can describe an elephant as a large animal that behaves in a certain manner. Why not do the same with an electron?

The answer is that a physicist can describe the behavior of an electron only by stating theoretical laws, and these laws contain only theoretical terms. They describe the field produced by an electron, the reaction of an electron to a field, and so on. If an electron is in an electrostatic field, its velocity will accelerate in a certain way. Unfortunately, the electron's acceleration is an unobservable. It is not like the acceleration of a billiard ball, which can be studied by direct observation. There is no way that a theoretical concept can be defined in terms of observables. We must, therefore, resign ourselves to the fact that definitions of the kind that can be supplied for observable terms cannot be formulated for theoretical terms.

It is true that some authors, including Bridgman, have spoken of the rules as "operational definitions." Bridgman had a certain justification, because he used his rules in a somewhat different way, I believe, than most physicists use them. He was a great physicist and was certainly aware of his departure from the usual use of rules, but he was willing to accept certain forms of speech that are not customary, and this explains his departure. It was pointed out . . . that Bridgman preferred to say that there is not just one concept of intensity of electric current, but a dozen concepts. Each procedure by which a magnitude can be measured provides an operational definition for that magnitude. Since there are different procedures for measuring current, there are different concepts. For the sake of convenience, the physicist speaks of just one concept of current. Strictly speaking, Bridgman believed, he should recognize many different concepts, each defined by a different operational procedure of measurement.

We are faced here with a choice between two different physical languages. If the customary procedure among physicists is followed, the various concepts of current will be replaced by one concept. This means, however, that you place the concept in your theoretical laws, because the operational rules are just correspondence rules, as I call them, which connect the theoretical terms with the empirical ones. Any claim to possessing a definition—that is, an operational definition—of the theoretical concept must be given up. Bridgman could speak of having operational definitions for his theoretical terms only because he was not speaking of a general concept. He was speaking of partial concepts, each defined by a different empirical procedure.

Even in Bridgman's terminology, the question of whether his partial concepts can be adequately defined by operational rules is problematic. Reichenbach speaks often of what he calls "correlative definitions." . . . Perhaps correlation is a better term than definition for what Bridgman's rules actually do. In geometry, for instance, Reichenbach points out that the axiom system of geometry, as developed by David Hilbert, for example, is an uninterpreted axiom system. The basic concepts of point, line, and plane could just as well be called "class alpha," "class beta," and "class gamma." We must not be seduced by the sound of familiar words, such as "point" and "line," into thinking they must be taken in their ordinary meaning. In the axiom system, they are uninterpreted terms. But when geometry is applied to physics, these terms must be connected with something in the physical world. We can say, for example, that the lines of the geometry are exemplified by rays of light in a vacuum or by stretched cords. In order to connect the uninterpreted terms with observable physical phenomena, we must have rules for establishing the connection.

What we call these rules is, of course, only a terminological question; we should be cautious and not speak of them as definitions. They are not definitions in any strict sense. We cannot give a really adequate definition of the geometrical concept of "line" by referring to anything in nature. Light rays, stretched strings, and so on are only approximately straight; moreover, they are not lines, but only segments of lines. In geometry, a line is infinite in length and absolutely straight. Neither property is exhibited by any phenomenon in nature. For that reason, it is not possible to give an operational definition, in the strict sense of the word, of concepts in theoretical geometry. The same is true of all the other theoretical concepts of physics. Strictly speaking, there are no "definitions" of such concepts. I prefer not to speak of "operational definitions" or even to use Reichenbach's term "correlative definitions." In my publications (only in recent years have I written about this question), I have called them "rules of correspondence" or, more simply, "correspondence rules."

Campbell and other authors often speak of the entities in theoretical physics as mathematical entities. They mean by this that the entities are related to each other in ways that can be expressed by mathematical functions. But they are not mathematical entities of the sort that can be defined in pure mathematics. In pure mathematics, it is possible to define various kinds of numbers, the function of logarithm, the exponential function, and so forth. It is not possible, however, to define such terms as "electron" and "temperature" by pure mathematics. Physical terms can be introduced only with the help of nonlogical constants, based on observations of the actual world. Here we have an essential difference between an axiomatic system in mathematics and an axiomatic system in physics.

If we wish to give an interpretation of a term in a mathematical axiom system, we can do it by giving a definition in logic. Consider, for example, the term "number" as it is used in Peano's axiom system. We can define it in logical terms, by the Frege-Russell method, for example. In this way the concept of "number" acquires a complete, explicit definition on the basis of pure logic. There is no need to establish a connection between the number 5 and such observables as "blue" and "hot." The terms have only a logical interpretation; no connection with the actual world is needed. Sometimes an axiom system in mathematics is called a theory. Mathematicians speak of set theory, group theory, matrix theory, probability theory. Here the word "theory" is used in a purely analytic way. It denotes a deductive system that makes no reference to the actual world. We must always bear in mind that such a use of the word "theory" is entirely different from its use in reference to empirical theories such as relativity theory, quantum theory, psychoanalytical theory, and Keynesian economic theory.

A postulate system in physics cannot have, as mathematical theories have, a splendid isolation from the world. Its axiomatic terms—"electron," "field," and so on—must be interpreted by correspondence rules that connect the terms with observable phenomena. This interpretation is necessarily incomplete. Because it is always incomplete, the system is left open to make it possible to add new rules of correspondence. Indeed, this is what continually happens in the history of physics. I am not thinking now of a revolution in physics, in which an entirely new theory is developed, but of less radical changes that modify existing theories. Nineteenth-century physics provides a good example, because classical mechanics and electromagnetics had been established, and, for many decades, there was relatively little change in fundamental laws. The basic theories of physics remained unchanged. There was, however, a steady addition of new correspondence rules, because new procedures were continually being developed for measuring this or that magnitude.

Of course, physicists always face the danger that they may develop correspondence rules that will be incompatible with each other or with the theoretical laws. As long as such incompatibility does not occur, however, they are free to add new correspondence rules. The procedure is never-ending. There is always the possibility of adding new rules, thereby increasing the amount of interpretation specified for the theoretical terms; but no matter how much this is increased, the interpretation is never final. In a mathematical system, it is otherwise. There a logical interpretation of an axiomatic term *is* complete. Here we find another reason for reluctance in speaking of theoretical terms as "defined" by correspondence rules. It tends to blur the important distinction between the nature of an axiom system in pure mathematics and one in theoretical physics.

Is it not possible to interpret a theoretical term by correspondence rules so completely that no further interpretation would be possible? Perhaps the actual world is limited in its structure and laws. Eventually a point may be reached beyond which there will be no room for strengthening the interpretation of a term by new correspondence rules. Would not the rules then provide a final, explicit definition for the term? Yes, but then the term would no longer be theoretical. It would become part of the observation language. The history of physics has not yet indicated that physics will become complete; there has been only a steady addition of new correspondence rules and a continual modification in the interpretations of theoretical terms. There is no way of knowing whether this is an infinite process or whether it will eventually come to some sort of end.

It may be looked at this way. There is no prohibition in physics against making the correspondence rules for a term so strong that the term becomes explicitly defined and therefore ceases to be theoretical. Neither is there any basis for assuming that it will always be possible to add new correspondence rules. Because the history of physics has shown such a steady, unceasing modification of theoretical concepts, most physicists would advise against correspondence rules so strong that a theoretical term becomes explicitly defined. Moreover, it is a wholly unnecessary procedure. Nothing is gained by it. It may even have the adverse effect of blocking progress.

Of course, here again we must recognize that the distinction between observables and nonobservables is a matter of degree. We might give an explicit definition, by empirical procedures, to a concept such as length, because it is so easily and directly measured, and is unlikely to be modified by new observations. But it would be rash to seek such strong correspondence rules that "electron" would be explicitly defined. The concept "electron" is so far removed from simple, direct observations that it is best to keep it theoretical, open to modifications by new observations.

III. How New Empirical Laws Are Derived from Theoretical Laws

. . . The [previous] discussion concerned the ways in which correspondence rules are used for linking the nonobservable terms of a theory with the observable terms of empirical laws. This can be made clearer by a few examples of the manner in which empirical laws have actually been derived from the laws of a theory.

The first example concerns the kinetic theory of gases. Its model, or schematic picture, is one of small particles called molecules, all in constant agitation. In its original form, the theory regarded these particles as little balls, all having the same mass and, when the temperature of the gas is constant, the same constant velocity. Later it was discovered that the gas would not be in a stable state if each particle had the same velocity; it was necessary to find a certain probability distribution of velocities that would remain stable. This was called the Boltzmann-Maxwell distribution. According to this distribution, there was a certain probability that any molecule would be within a certain range on the velocity scale.

When the kinetic theory was first developed, many of the magnitudes occurring in the laws of the theory were not known. No one knew the mass of a molecule, or how many molecules a cubic centimeter of gas at a certain temperature and pressure would contain. These magnitudes were expressed by certain parameters written into the laws. After the equations were formulated, a dictionary of correspondence rules was prepared. These correspondence rules connected the theoretical terms with observable phenomena in a way that made it possible to determine indirectly the values of the parameters in the equations. This, in turn, made it possible to derive empirical laws. One correspondence rule states that the temperature of the gas corresponds to the mean kinetic energy of the molecules. Another correspondence rule connects the pressure of the gas with the impact of molecules on the confining wall of a vessel. Although this is a continuous process involving discrete molecules, the total effect can be regarded as a constant force pressing on the wall. Thus, by means of correspondence rules, the pressure that is measured macroscopically by a manometer (pressure gauge) can be expressed in terms of the statistical mechanics of molecules.

What is the density of the gas? Density is mass per unit volume, but how do we measure the mass of a molecule? Again our dictionary—a very simple dictionary—supplies the correspondence rule. The total mass M of the gas is the sum of the masses m of the molecules. M is observable (we simply weigh the gas), but m is theoretical. The dictionary of correspondence rules gives the connection between the two concepts. With the aid of this dictionary, empirical tests of various laws derived from our theory are possible. On the basis of the theory, it is possible to calculate what will happen to the pressure of the gas when its volume remains constant and its temperature is increased. We can calculate what will happen to a sound wave produced by striking the side of the vessel, and what will happen if only part of the gas is heated.

These theoretical laws are worked out in terms of various parameters that occur within the equations of the theory. The dictionary of correspondence rules enables us to express these equations as empirical laws, in which concepts are measurable, so that empirical procedures can supply values for the parameters. If the empirical laws can be confirmed, this provides indirect confirmation of the theory. Many of the empirical laws for gases were known, of course, before the kinetic theory was developed. For these laws, the theory provided an explanation. In addition, the theory led to previously unknown empirical laws.

The power of a theory to predict new empirical laws is strikingly exemplified by the theory of electromagnetism, which was developed about 1860 by two great physicists, Michael Faraday and James Clerk Maxwell. (Faraday did most of the experimental work, and Maxwell did most of the mathematical work.) The theory dealt with electric charges and how they behaved in electrical and magnetic fields. The concept of the electron—a tiny particle with an elementary electric charge—was not formulated until the very end of the century. Maxwell's famous set of differential equations, for describing electromagnetic fields, presupposed only small discrete bodies of unknown nature, capable of carrying an electric charge or a magnetic pole. What happens when a current moves along a copper wire? The theory's dictionary made this observable phenomenon correspond to the actual movement along the wire of little charged bodies. From Maxwell's theoretical model, it became possible (with the help of correspondence rules, of course) to derive many of the known laws of electricity and magnetism.

The model did much more than this. There was a certain parameter c in Maxwell's equations. According to his model, a disturbance in an electromagnetic field would be propagated by waves having the velocity c. Electrical experiments showed the value of c to be approximately 3×10^{10} centimeters per second. This was the same as the known value for the speed of light, and it seemed unlikely that it was an accident. Is it possible, physicists asked themselves, that light is simply a special case of the propagation of an electromagnetic oscillation? It was not long before Maxwell's equations were providing explanations for all sorts of optical laws, including refraction, the velocity of light in different media, and many others.

Physicists would have been pleased enough to find that Maxwell's model explained known electrical and magnetic laws; but they received a double bounty. The theory also explained optical laws! Finally, the great strength of the new model was revealed in its power to predict, to formulate empirical laws that had not been previously known.

The first instance was provided by Heinrich Hertz, the German physicist. About 1890, he began his famous experiments to see whether electromagnetic waves of low frequency could be produced and detected in the laboratory. Light is an electromagnetic oscillation and propagation of waves at very high frequency. But Maxwell's laws made it possible for such waves to have *any* frequency. Hertz's experiments resulted in his discovery of what at first were called Hertz waves. They are now called radio waves. At first, Hertz was able to transmit these waves from one oscillator to another over only a small distance—first a few centimeters, then a meter or more. Today a radio broadcasting station sends its waves many thousands of miles.

The discovery of radio waves was only the beginning of the derivation of new laws from Maxwell's theoretical model. X-rays were discovered and were thought to be particles of enormous velocity and penetrative power. Then it occurred to physicists that, like light and radio waves, these might be electromagnetic waves, but of extremely high frequency, much higher than the frequency of visible light. This also was later confirmed, and laws dealing with X-rays were derived from Maxwell's fundamental field equations. X-rays proved to be waves of a certain frequency range within the much broader frequency band of gamma rays. The X-rays used today in medicine are simply gamma rays of certain frequency. All this was largely predictable on the basis of Maxwell's model. His theoretical laws, together with the correspondence rules, led to an enormous variety of new empirical laws.

The great variety of fields in which experimental confirmation was found contributed especially to the strong overall confirmation of Maxwell's theory. The various branches of physics had originally developed for practical reasons; in most cases, the divisions were based on our different sense organs. Because the eyes perceive light and color, we call such phenomena optics; because our ears hear sounds, we call a branch of physics acoustics; and because our bodies feel heat, we have a theory of heat. We find it useful to construct simple machines based on the movements of bodies, and we call it mechanics. Other phenomena, such as electricity and magnetism, cannot be directly perceived, but their consequences can be observed.

In the history of physics, it is always a big step forward when one branch of physics can be explained by another. Acoustics, for instance, was found to be only a part of mechanics, because sound waves are simply elasticity waves in solids, liquids, and gases. We have already spoken of how the laws of gases were explained by the mechanics of moving molecules. Maxwell's theory was another great leap forward toward the unification of physics. Optics was found to be a part of electromagnetic theory. Slowly the notion grew that the whole of physics might some day be unified by one great theory. At present there is an enormous gap between electromagnetism on the one side and gravitation on the other. Einstein made several attempts to develop a unified field theory that might close this gap; more recently, Heisenberg and others have made similar attempts. So far, however, no theory has been devised that is entirely satisfactory or that provides new empirical laws capable of being confirmed.

Physics originally began as a descriptive macrophysics, containing an enormous number of empirical laws with no apparent connections. In the beginning of a science, scientists may be very proud to have discovered hundreds of laws. But, as the laws proliferate, they become unhappy with this state of affairs; they begin to search for unifying principles. In the nineteenth century, there was considerable controversy over the question of underlying principles.

Some felt that science must find such principles, because otherwise it would be no more than a description of nature, not a real explanation. Others thought that that was the wrong approach, that underlying principles belong only to metaphysics. They felt that the scientist's task is merely to describe, to find out *how* natural phenomena occur, not *why*.

Today we smile a bit about the great controversy over description versus explanation. We can see that there was something to be said for both sides, but that their way of debating the question was futile. There is no real opposition between explanation and description. Of course, if description is taken in the narrowest sense, as merely describing what a certain scientist did on a certain day with certain materials, then the opponents of mere description were quite right in asking for more, for a real explanation. But today we see that description in the broader sense, that of placing phenomena in the context of more general laws, provides the only type of explanation that can be given for phenomena. Similarly, if the proponents of explanation mean a metaphysical explanation, not grounded in empirical procedures, then their opponents were correct in insisting that science should be concerned only with description. Each side had a valid point. Both description and explanation, rightly understood, are essential aspects of science.

The first efforts at explanation, those of the Ionian natural philosophers, were certainly partly metaphysical; the world is all fire, or all water, or all change. Those early efforts at scientific explanation can be viewed in two different ways. We can say: "This is not science, but pure metaphysics. There is no possibility of confirmation, no correspondence rules for connecting the theory with observable phenomena." On the other hand, we can say: "These Ionian theories are certainly not scientific, but at least they are pictorial visions of theories. They are the first primitive beginnings of science."

It must not be forgotten that, both in the history of science and in the psychological history of a creative scientist, a theory has often first appeared as a kind of visualization, a vision that comes as an inspiration to a scientist long before he has discovered correspondence rules that may help in confirming his theory. When Democritus said that everything consists of atoms, he certainly had not the slightest confirmation for this theory. Nevertheless, it was a stroke of genius, a profound insight, because two thousand years later his vision was confirmed. We should not, therefore, reject too rashly any anticipatory vision of a theory, provided it is one that may be tested at some future time. We are on solid ground, however, if we issue the warning that no hypothesis can claim to be scientific unless there is the *possibility* that it can be tested. It does not have to be confirmed to be a hypothesis, but there must be correspndence rules that will permit, in principle, a means of confirming or disconfirming the theory. It may be enormously difficult to think of experiments that can test the theory; this is the case today with various unified field theories that have been proposed. But if such tests are possible in principle, the theory can be called a scientific one. When a theory is first proposed, we should not demand more than this.

The development of science from early philosophy was a gradual, step-by-step process. The Ionian philosophers had only the most primitive theories. In contrast, the thinking of Aristotle was much clearer and on more solid scientific ground. He made experiments, and he knew the importance of experiments, although in other respects he was an apriorist. This was the beginning of science. But it was not until the time of Galileo Galilei, about 1600, that a really great emphasis was placed on the experimental method in preference to aprioristic reasoning about nature. Even though many of Galileo's concepts had previously been stated as theoretical concepts, he was the first to place theoretical physics on a solid empirical foundation. Certainly Newton's physics (about 1670) exhibits the first comprehensive, systematic theory, containing unobservables as theoretical concepts: the universal force of gravitation, a general concept of mass, theoretical properties of light rays, and so on. His theory of gravity was one of great generality. Between any two particles, small or large, there is a force proportional to the square of the distance between them. Before Newton advanced this theory, science provided no explanation that applied to both the fall of a stone and the movements of planets around the sun.

It is very easy for us today to remark how strange it was that it never occurred to anyone before Newton that the same force might cause the apple to drop and the moon to go around the earth. In fact, this was not a thought likely to occur to anyone. It is not that the *answer* was so difficult to give; it is that nobody had asked the *question*. This is a vital point. No one had asked: "What is the relation between the force that heavenly bodies exert upon each other and terrestrial forces that cause objects to fall to the ground?" Even to speak in such terms as "terrestrial" and "heavenly" is to make a bipartition, to cut nature into two fundamentally different regions. It was Newton's great insight to break away frm this division, to assert that there is no such fundamental cleavage. There is one nature, one world. Newton's universal law of gravitation was the theoretical law that explained for the first time both the fall of an apple and Kepler's laws for the movements of planets. In Newton's day, it was a psychologically difficult, extremely daring adventure to think in such general terms.

Later, of course, by means of correspondence rules, scientists discovered how to determine the masses of astronomical bodies. Newton's theory also said that two apples, side by side on a table, attract each other. They do not move toward each other because the attracting force is extremely small and the friction on the table very large. Physicists eventually succeeded in actually measuring the gravitational forces between two bodies in the laboratory. They used a torsion balance consisting of a bar with a metal ball on each end, suspended at its center by a long wire attached to a high ceiling. (The longer and thinner the wire, the more easily the bar would turn.) Actually, the bar never came to an absolute rest but always oscillated a bit. But the mean point of the bar's oscillation could be established. After the exact position of the mean point was determined, a large pile of lead bricks was constructed near the bar. (Lead was used because of its great specific gravity. Gold had an even higher specific gravity, but gold bricks are expensive.) It was found that the mean of the oscillating bar had shifted a tiny amount to bring one of the balls on the end of the bar nearer to the lead pile. The shift was only a fraction of a millimeter, but it was enough to provide first observation of a gravitational effect between two bodies in a laboratory—an effect that had been predicted by Newton's theory of gravitation.

It had been known before Newton that apples fall to the ground and that the moon moves around the earth. Nobody before Newton could have predicted the outcome of the experiment with the torsion balance. It is a classic instance of the power of a theory to predict a new phenomenon not previously observed.

NOTE

1. See Percy W. Bridgman, *The Logic of Modern Physics* (New York: Macmillan, 1927), and Norman R. Campbell, *Physics: The Elements* (Cambridge: Cambridge University Press, 1920). Rules of correspondence are discussed by Ernest Nagel, *The Structure of Science* (New York: Harcourt, Brace & World, 1961), pp.97–105.

12

What Theories Are Not

Hilary Putnam

The announced topic for this symposium was the role of models in empirical science; however, in preparing for this symposium, I soon discovered that I had first to deal with a different topic, and this different topic is the one to which this paper actually will be devoted. The topic I mean is the role of *theories* in empirical science; and what I do in this paper is attack what may be called the "received view" on the role of theories—that theories are to be thought of as "partially interpreted calculi" in which only the "observation terms" are "directly interpreted" (the theoretical terms being only "partially interpreted," or, some people even say, "partially understood").

To begin, let us review this received view. The view divides the nonlogical vocabulary of science into two parts:

OBSERVATION TERMS	THEORETICAL TERMS
such terms as 'red', 'touches', 'stick', etc.	such terms as 'electron', 'dream', 'gene', etc.

The basis for the division appears to be as follows: the observation terms apply to what may be called publicly observable things and signify observable qualities of these things, while the theoretical terms correspond to the remaining unobservable qualities and things.

This division of terms into two classes is then allowed to generate a division of statements into two[1] classes as follows:

OBSERVATIONAL STATEMENTS	THEORETICAL STATEMENTS
statements containing only observation terms and logical vocabulary	statements containing theoretical terms

Lastly, a scientific theory is conceived of as an axiomatic system which may be thought of as initially uninterpreted, and which gains "empirical meaning" as a result of a specification of meaning *for the observation terms alone.* A kind of partial meaning is then thought of as drawn up to the theoretical terms, by osmosis, as it were.

One can think of many distinctions that are crying out to be made ('new' terms vs. 'old' terms, technical terms vs. non-technical ones, terms more-or-less peculiar to one science vs. terms common to many, for a start). My contention here is simply:

(1) The *problem* for which this dichotomy was invented ('how is it possible to interpret theoretical terms?') does not exist.

(2) A basic reason some people have given for introducing the dichotomy is false: namely, justification in science does *not* proceed "down" in the direction of observation terms. In fact, justification in science proceeds in any direction that may be handy—more observational assertions sometimes being justified with the aid of more theoretical ones, and vice versa. Moreover, as we shall see, while the notion of an *observation report* has some importance in the philosophy of science, such reports cannot be identified on the basis of the vocabulary they do or do not contain.

(3) In any case, whether the reasons for introducing the dichotomy were good ones or bad ones, the double distinction (observation terms—theoretical terms, observation statements—theoretical statements) presented above is, in fact, completely broken-backed. This I shall try to establish now.

In the first place, it should be noted that the dichotomy under discussion was intended as an explicative and not merely a stipulative one. That is, the words 'observational' and 'theoretical' are not having arbitrary new meanings bestowed upon them; rather, pre-existing uses of these words (expecially in the philosophy of science) are presumably being sharpened and made clear. And, in the second place, it should be recalled that we are dealing with a double, not just a single, distinction. That is to say, part of the contention I am criticizing is that, once the distinction between observational and theoretical *terms* has been drawn as above, the distinction between theoretical statements and observational reports or assertions (in something like the sense usual in methodological discussions) can be drawn in terms of it. What I mean when I say that the dichotomy is "completely broken-backed" is this:

(A) If an 'observation term' is one that cannot apply to an unobservable, then there are no observation terms.[2]

(B) Many terms that refer primarily to what Carnap would class as "unobservables" are not theoretical terms; and at least some theoretical terms refer primarily to observables.

(C) Observational reports can and frequently do contain theoretical terms.

(D) A scientific theory, properly so-called, may refer only to observables. (Darwin's theory of evolution, as originally put forward, is one example.)

To start with the notion of an "observation term": Carnap's formulation in *Testability and Meaning* [1] was that for a term to be an observation term not only must it correspond to an observable quality, but the determination whether the quality is present or not must be able to be made by the observer in a relatively short time, and with a high degree of confirmation. In his most recent authoritative publication [2], Carnap is rather brief. He writes, "the terms of V_0 [the 'observation vocabulary'—H.P.] are predicates designating observable properties of events or things (e.g., 'blue', 'hot', 'large', etc.) or observable relations between them (e.g., 'x is warmer than y,' 'x is contiguous to y', etc.)" [2, p. 41)]. The only other clarifying remarks I could find are the following: "The name 'observation language' may be understood in a narrower or in a wider sense; the observation language in the wider sense includes the disposition terms. In this article I take the observation language L_0 in the narrower sense" [2, p. 63]. "An observable property may be regarded as a simple special case of a testable disposition: for example, the operation for finding out whether a thing is blue or hissing or cold, consists simply in looking or listening or touching the thing, respectively. Nevertheless, *in the reconstruction of the language* [italics mine—H.P.] it seems convenient to the take some properties for which the test procedure is extremely simple (as in the examples given) as directly observable, and use them as primitives in L_0" [2, p. 63].

These paragraphs reveal that Carnap, at least, thinks of observation terms as corresponding to qualities that can be detected without the aid of instruments. But always so detected? Or can an observation term refer sometimes to an observable thing and sometimes to an unobservable? While I have not been able to find any explicit statement on this point, it seems to me that writers like Carnap must be *neglecting* the fact that *all* terms—including the 'observation terms'—have at least the possibility of applying to unobservables. Thus their problem has some times been formulated in quasi-historical terms—"How could theoretical terms have been introduced into the language?" And the usual discussion strongly suggests that the following puzzle is meant: if we imagine a time at which people could only talk about observables (had not available any theoretical terms), how did they ever manage to *start* talking about unobservables?

It is possible that I am here doing Carnap and his followers an injustice. However, polemics aside, the following points must be emphasized:

(1) Terms referring to unobservables are *invariably* explained, in the actual history of science, with the aid of already present locutions referring to unobservables. There never was a stage of language at which it was impossible to talk about unobservables. Even a three-year-old child can understand a story about "people too little to see"[3] and not a single 'theoretical term' occurs in this phrase.

(2) There is not even a single *term* of which it is true to say that it *could not* (without changing or extending its meaning) be used to refer to unobservables. 'Red', for example, was so used by Newton when he postulated that red light consists of *red corpuscles.*[4]

In short: if an 'observation term' is a term which *can*, in principle, only be used to refer to observable things, then *there are no observation terms.* If, on the other hand, it is granted that locutions consisting of just observation terms can refer to unobservables, there is no longer any reason to maintain *either* that theories and speculations about the unobservable parts of the world must contain 'theoretical (= nonobservation) terms' *or* that there is any general problem as to how one can introduce terms referring to unobservables. Those philosophers who find a difficulty in how we understand theoretical terms should find an equal difficulty in how we understand 'red' and 'smaller than'.

So much for the notion of an 'observation term'. Of course, one may recognize the point just made—that the 'observation terms' also apply, in some contexts, to unobservables—and retain the class (with a suitable warning as to how the label 'observation term' is to be understood). But can we agree that the complementary class—what should be called the 'non-observation terms'—is to be labelled 'theoretical terms'? No, for the identification of 'theoretical terms' with 'term (other than the 'disposition terms', which are given a special place in Carnap's scheme) designating an unobservable quality' is unnatural and misleading. On the one hand, it is clearly an enormous (and, I believe, insufficiently motivated) extension of common usage to classify such terms as 'angry', 'loves', and so forth, as 'theoretical terms' simply because they allegedly do not refer to public observables. A theoretical term, properly so-called, is one which comes from a scientific *theory* (and the almost untouched problem, in thirty years of writing about 'theoretical terms' is what is *really* distinctive about such terms). In this sense (and I think it the sense important for discussions of science) 'satellite' is, for example, a theoretical term (although the things it refers to are quite observable[5]) and 'dislikes' clearly is not.

Our criticisms so far might be met by re-labeling the first dichotomy (the dichotomy of terms) "observation vs. non-observation," and suitably 'hedging' the notion of 'observation.' But more serious difficulties are connected with the identification upon which the second dichotomy is based—the identification of "theoretical statements" with statements containing non-observation ('theoretical') terms, and "observation statements" with 'statements in the observational vocabulary'.

That observation statements may contain theoretical terms is easy to establish. For example, it is easy to imagine a situation in which the following sentence might occur: "We also *observed* the creation of two electron-positron pairs."

This objection is sometimes dealt with by proposing to "relativize" the observation-theoretical dichotomy to the context. (Carnap, however, rejects this way out in the article we have been citing.) This proposal to "relativize" the dichotomy does not seem to me to be very helpful. In the first place, one can easily imagine a context in which 'electron' would occur, in the same text, in *both* observational reports and in theoretical conclusions from those reports. (So that one would have distortions if one tried to put the term in either the "observational term" box or in the "theoretical term" box.) In the second place, for what philosophical problem or point does one require even the relativized dichotomy?

The usual answer is that sometimes a statement A (observational) is offered in support of a statement B (theoretical). Then, in order to explain why A is not itself questioned in the context, we need to be able to say that A is functioning, in that context, as an observation report. But this misses the point I have been making! I do not deny the need for some such notion as 'observation report'. What I deny is that the distinction between observation reports and, among other things, theoretical statements, can or should be drawn on the basis of vocabulary. In addition, a relativized dichotomy will not serve Carnap's purposes. One can hardly maintain that theoretical terms are only partially interpreted, whereas observational terms are completely interpreted, if no sharp line exists between the two classes. (Recall that Carnap takes his problem to be "reconstruction of the language," not of some isolated scientific context.) . . .

NOTES

1. Sometimes a *tripartite* division is used: observation statements, theoretical statements (containing *only* theoretical terms), and 'mixed' statements (containing both kinds of terms). This refinement is not considered here, because it avoids none of the objections presented below.

2. I neglect the possibility of trivially constructing terms that refer only to observables: namely, by conjoining "and is an observable thing" to terms that would otherwise apply to some unobservables. "Being an observable thing" is, in a sense, highly theoretical and yet applies only to observables!

3. Von Wright has suggested (in conversation) that this is an *extended* use of language (because we first learn words like "people" in connection with people we *can* see). This argument from "the way we learn to use the word" appears to be unsound however (cf.[4]).

4. Some authors (although not Carnap) explain the intelligibility of such discourse in terms of logically possible submicroscopic observers. But (a) such observers could not see single photons (or light corpuscles) even on Newton's theory; and (b) once such physically impossible (though logically possible) 'observers' are introduced, why not go further and have observers with sense organs for electric charge, or the curvature of space, etc.! Presumably because *we* can see *red*, but not *charge*. But then, this just makes the point that we *understand* 'red' even when applied outside our normal 'range', even though we learn it ostensively, without *explaining* that fact. (The explanation lies in this: that understanding any term—even "red"—involves at least two elements: internalizing the syntax of a natural language, and acquiring a background of ideas. Overemphasis on the way 'red' is *taught* has led some philosophers to misunderstand how it is *learned*.)

5. Carnap might exclude 'satellite' as an observation term, on the ground that is takes a comparatively long time to verify that something is a satellite with the naked eye, even if the satellite is close to the parent body (although this could be debated). However, 'satellite' cannot be excluded on the quite different ground that many satellites are too far away to see (which is the ground that first comes to mind) since the same is true of the huge majority of all *red* things.

REFERENCES

[1] Carnap, R. "Testability and Meaning," Pp. 47-92 in *Reading in the Philosophy of Science,* H. Feigl and M. Brodbeck, eds., New York, Appleton-Century-crofts, 1955, x + 517 pp. Reprinted from *Philosophy*

of *Science*, 3 (1936) and 4 (1937).

[2] Carnap, R. "The Methodological Character of Theoretical Concepts," Pp. 1-74 in *Minnesota Studies in the Philosophy*, I., H. Feigl *et al.*, eds., Minneapolis, University of Minnesota Press, 1956, x + 517 pp.

[3] Carnap, R. *The Foundations of Logic and Mathematics*. Vol. 4, no. 3 of the *International Encyclopedia of United Science*, Chicago, University of Chicago Press, 1939, 75 pp.

[4] Fodor, J. "Do Words Have Uses?" Submitted to *Inquiry*.

[5] Putnam, H. "Mathematics and the Existence of Abstract Entities," *Philosophical Studies*, 7 (1957), pp. 81-88.

[6] Quine, W. V. O. "The Scope and Language of Science," *British Journal for the Philosophy of Science*, 8 (1957), pp. 1-17.

13

Observation
N. R. Hanson

Were the eye not attuned to the Sun,
The sun could never be seen by it.
                    GOETHE[1]

A

Consider two microbiologists. They look at a prepared slide; when asked what they see, they may give different answers. One sees in the cell before him a cluster of foreign matter: it is an artefact, a coagulum resulting from inadequate staining techniques. This clot has not more to do with the cell, *in vivo,* than the scars left on it by the archaeologist's spade have to do with the original shape of some Grecian urn. The other biologist identifies the clot as a cell organ, a "Golgi body." As for techniques, he argues: "The standard way of detecting a cell organ is by fixing and staining. Why single out this one technique as producing artefacts, while others disclose genuine organs?"

The controversy continues.[2] It involves the whole theory of microscopical technique; nor is it an obviously experimental issue. Yet it affects what scientists say they see. Perhaps there is a sense in which two such observers do not see the same thing, do not begin from the same data, though their eyesight is normal and they are visually aware of the same object.

Imagine these two observing a Protozoon—*Amoeba.* One sees a one-celled animal, the other a non-celled animal. The first sees *Amoeba* in all its analogies with different types of single cells: liver cells, nerve cells, epithelium cells. These have a wall, nucleus, cytoplasm, etc. Within this class *Amoeba* is distinguished only by its independence. The other, however, sees *Amoeba*'s homology not with single cells, but with whole animals. Like all animals *Amoeba* ingests its food, digests and assimilates it. It excretes, reproduces and is mobile—more like a complete animal than an individual tissue cell.

This is not an experimental issue, yet it can affect experiment. What either man regards as significant questions or relevant data can be determined by whether he stresses the first or the last term in "unicellular animal."[3]

Some philosophers have a formula ready for such situations: "Of course they see the same thing. They make the same observation since they begin from the same visual data. But they interpret what they see differently. They construe the evidence in different ways."[4] The task is then to show how these data are moulded by different theories or interpretations or intellectual constructions.

Considerable philosophers have wrestled with this task. But in fact the formula they start from is too simple to allow a grasp of the nature of observation within physics. Perhaps the scientists cited above do not begin their inquiries from the same data, do not make the same observations, do not even see the same thing? Here many concepts run together. We must proceed carefully, for wherever it makes sense to say that two scientists looking at x do not see the same thing, there must always be a prior sense in which they do see the same thing. The issue is, then, "Which of these senses is most illuminating for the understanding of observational physics?"

These biological examples are too complex. Let us consider Johannes Kepler: imagine him on a hill watching the dawn. With him is Tycho Brahe. Kepler regarded the sun as fixed: it was the earth that moved. But Tycho followed Ptolemy and Aristotle in this much at least: the earth was fixed and all other celestial bodies moved around it. *Do Kepler and Tycho see the same thing in the east at dawn?*

We might think this an experimental or observational question, unlike the questions "Are there Golgi bodies?" and "Are Protozoa one-celled or non-celled?" Not so in the sixteenth and seventeenth centuries. Thus Galileo said to the Ptolemaist ". . . neither Aristotle nor you can prove that the earth is *de facto* the centre of the universe. . . ."[5] "Do Kepler and Tycho see the same thing in the east at dawn?" is perhaps not a *de facto* question either, but rather the beginning of an examination of the concepts of seeing and observation.

The resultant discussion might run:

"Yes, they do."

"No, they don't."

"Yes, they do!"

"No, they don't!" . . .

That this is possible suggests that there may be reasons for both contentions.[6] Let us consider some points in support of the affirmative answer.

The physical processes involved when Kepler and Tycho watch the dawn are worth noting. Identical photons are emitted from the sun; these traverse solar space, and our atmosphere. The two astronomers have normal vision; hence these photons pass through the cornea, aqueous humour, iris, lens and vitreous body of their eyes in the same way. Finally their retinas are affected.

Similar electro-chemical changes occur in their selenium cells. The same configuration is etched on Kepler's retina as on Tycho's. So they see the same thing.

Locke sometimes spoke of seeing in this way: a man sees the sun if his is a normally-formed retinal picture of the sun. Dr. Sir W. Russell Brain speaks of our retinal sensations as indicators and signals. Everything taking place behind the retina is, as he says, "an intellectual operation based largely on non-visual experience. . . ."[7] What we *see* are the changes in the *tunica retina*. Dr. Ida Mann regards the macula of the eye as itself "seeing details in bright light," and the rods as "seeing approaching motor-cars." Dr. Agnes Arber speaks of the eye as itself seeing.[8] Often, talk of seeing can direct attention to the retina. Normal people are distinguished from those for whom no retinal pictures can form: we may say of the former that they can see whilst the latter cannot see. Reporting when a certain red dot can be seen may supply the occulist with direct information about the condition of one's retina.[9]

This need not be pursued, however. These writers speak carelessly: seeing the sun is not seeing retinal pictures of the sun. The retinal images which Kepler and Tycho have are four in number, inverted and quite tiny.[10] Astronomers cannot be referring to these when they say they see the sun. If they are hypnotized, drugged, drunk or distracted they may not see the sun, even though their retinas register its image in exactly the same way as usual.

Seeing is an experience. A retinal reaction is only a physical state—a photochemical excitation. Physiologists have not always appreciated the differences between experiences and physical states.[11] People, not their eyes, see. Cameras, and eye-balls, are blind. Attempts to locate within the organs of sight (or within the neurological reticulum behind the eyes) some nameable called "seeing" may be dismissed. That Kepler and Tycho do, or do not, see the same thing cannot be supported by reference to the physical states of their retinas, optic nerves or visual cortices: there is more to seeing than meets the eyeball.

Naturally, Tycho and Kepler sees the same physical object. They are both visually aware of the sun. If they are put into a dark room and asked to report when they see something—anything at all—they may both report the same object at the same time. Suppose that the only object to be seen is a certain lead cylinder. Both men see the same thing: namely this object—whatever it is. It is just here, however, that the difficulty arises, for while Tycho sees a mere pipe, Kepler will see a telescope, the instrument about which Galileo has written to him.

Unless both are visually aware of the same object there can be nothing of philosophical interest in the question whether or not they see the same thing. Unless they both see the sun in this prior sense our question cannot even strike a spark.

Nonetheless, both Tycho and Kepler have a common visual experience of some sort. This experience perhaps constitutes their seeing the same thing. Indeed, this may be a seeing logically more basic than anything expressed in the pronouncement "I see the sun" (where each means something different by "sun"). If what they meant by the word "sun" were the only clue, then Tycho and Kepler could not be seeing the same thing, even though they were gazing at the same object.

If, however, we ask, not "Do they see the same thing?" but rather "What is it that they both see?," an unambiguous answer may be forthcoming. Tycho and Kepler are both aware of a brilliant yellow-white disc in a blue expanse over a green one. Such a "sense-datum" picture is single and uninverted. To be unaware of it is not to have it. Either it dominates one's visual attention completely or it does not exist.

If Tycho and Kepler are aware of anything visual, it must be of some pattern of colours. What else could it be? We do not touch or hear with our eyes, we only take in light.[12] This private pattern is the same for both observers. Surely if asked to sketch the contents of their visual fields they would both draw a kind of semicircle on a horizon-line.[13] They say they see the sun. But they do not see every side of the sun at once; so what they really see is discoid to begin with. It is but a visual aspect of the sun. In any single observation the sun is a brilliantly luminescent disc, a penny painted with radium.

So something about their visual experiences at dawn is the same for both: a brilliant yellow-white disc centred between green and blue colour patches. Sketches of what they both see could be identical—congruent. In this sense Tycho and Kepler see the same thing at dawn. The sun appears to them in the same way. The same view, or scene, is presented to them both.

In fact, we often speak in this way. Thus the account of a recent solar eclipse:[14] "Only a thin crescent remains; white light is now completely obscured; the sky appears a deep blue, almost purple, and the landscape is a monochromatic green . . . there are the flashes of light on the disc's circumference and now the brilliant crescent to the left. . . ." Newton writes in a similar way in the *Opticks*: "These Arcs at their first appearance were of a violet and blue Colour, and between them were white Arcs of Circles, which . . . became a little tinged in their inward Limbs with red and yellow. . . ."[15] Every physicist employs the language of lines, colour patches, appearances, shadows. In so far as two normal observers use this language of the same event, they begin from the same data: they are making the same observation. Differences between them must arise in the interpretations they put on these data.

Thus, to summarize, saying that Kepler and Tycho see the same thing at dawn just because their eyes are similarly affected is an elementary mistake. There is a difference between a physical state and a visual experience. Suppose, however, that it is argued as above—that they see the same thing because they have the same sense-datum experience. Disparities in their accounts arise in *ex post facto* interpretations of what is seen, not in the fundamental visual data. If this is argued, further difficulties soon obtrude.

B

Normal retinas and cameras are impressed similarly by fig. 1.[16] Our visual sense-data will be the same too. If asked to draw what we see, most of us will set out a configuration like fig. 1.

Do we all see the same thing?[17] Some will see a perspex cube viewed from below. Others will see it from above. Still others will see it as a kind of polygonally-cut gem. Some people see only criss-crossed lines in a plane. It may be seen as a block of ice, an aquarium, a wire frame for a kite—or any of a number of other things.

Do we, then, all see the same thing? If we do, how can these differences be accounted for?

Fig. 1

Here the "formula" re-enters: "These are different *interpretations* of what all observers see in common. Retinal reactions to fig. 1 are virtually identical; so too are our visual sense-data, since our drawings of what we see will have the same content. There is no place in the seeing for these differences, so they must lie in the interpretations put on what we see."

This sounds as if I do two things, not one, when I see boxes and bicycles. Do I put different interpretations on fig. 1 when I see it now as a box from below, and now as a cube from above? I am aware of no such thing. I mean no such thing when I report that the box's perspective has snapped back into the page.[18] If I do not mean this, then the concept of seeing which is natural in this connexion does not designate two diaphanous components, one optical the other interpretative. Fig. 1 is simply seen now as a box from below, now as a cube from above; one does not first soak up an optical pattern and then clamp an interpretation on it. Kepler and Tycho just see the sun. That is all. That is the way the concept of seeing works in this connexion.

"But," you say, "seeing fig. 1 first as a box from below, then as a cube from above, involves interpreting the lines differently in each case." Then for you and me to have a different interpretation of fig. 1 just *is* for us to see something different. This does not mean we see the same thing and then interpret it differently. When I suddenly exclaim "Eureka—a box from above," I do not refer simply to a different interpretation. (Again, there is a logically prior sense in which seeing fig. 1 as from above and then as from below is seeing the same thing differently, i.e. being aware of the same diagram in different ways. We can refer just to this, but we need not. In this case we do not.)

Besides, the word "interpretation" is occasionally useful. We know where it applies and where it does not. Thucydides presented the facts objectively; Herodotus put an interpretation on them. The word does not apply to everything—it has a meaning. Can interpreting always be going on when we see? Sometimes, perhaps, as when the hazy outline of an agricultural machine looms up on a foggy morning and, with effort, we finally identify it. Is this the "interpretation" which is active when bicycles and boxes are clearly seen? Is it active when the perspective of fig. 1 snaps into reverse? There was a time when

Herodotus was half-through with his interpretation of the Graeco-Persian wars. Could there be a time when one is half-through interpreting fig. 1 as a box from above, or as anything else?

"But the interpretation takes very little time—it is instantaneous." Instantaneous interpretation hails from the Limbo that produced unsensed sensibilia, unconscious inference, incorrigible statements, negative facts and *Objektive*. These are ideas which philosophers force on the world to preserve some pet epistemological or metaphysical theory.

Only in contrast to "Eureka" situations (like perspective reversals, where one cannot interpret the data) is it clear what is meant by saying that though Thucydides could have put an interpretation on history, he did not. Moreover, whether or not an historian is advancing an interpretation is an empirical question: we know what would count as evidence one way or the other. But whether we are employing an interpretation when we see fig. 1 in a certain way is not empirical. What could count as evidence? In no ordinary sense of "interpret" do I interpret fig. 1 differently when its perspective reverses for me. If there is some extraordinary sense of that word it is not clear, either in ordinary language, or in extraordinary (philosophical) language. To insist that different reactions to fig. 1 *must* lie in the interpretations put on a common visual experience is just to reiterate (without reasons) that the seeing of *x must* be the same for all observers looking at *x*.

"But 'I see the figure as a box' means: I am having a particular visual experience which I always have when I interpret the figure as a box, or when I look at a box. . . ." ". . . if I meant this, I ought to know it. I ought to be able to refer to the experience directly and not only indirectly. . . ."[19]

Ordinary accounts of the experiences appropriate to fig. 1 do not require visual grist going into an intellectual mill: theories and interpretations are "there" in the seeing from the outset. How can interpretations "be there" in the seeing? How is it possible to see an object according to an interpretation? "The question represents it as a queer fact; as if something were being forced into a form it did not really fit. But no squeezing, no forcing took place here."[20]

Consider now the reversible perspective figures which appear in textbooks on Gestalt psychology: the tea-tray, the shifting (Schröder) staircase, the tunnel. Each of these can be seen as concave, as convex, or as a flat drawing.[21] Do I really see something different each time, or do I only interpret what I see in a different way? To interpret is to think, to do something; seeing is an experiential state.[22] The different ways in which these figures are seen are not due to different thoughts lying behind the visual reactions. What could "spontaneous" mean if these reactions are not spontaneous? When the staircase "goes into reverse" it does so spontaneously. One does not think of anything special; one does not think at all. Nor does one interpret. One just sees, now a staircase as from above, now a staircase as from below.

The sun, however, is not an entity with such variable perspective. What has all this to do with suggesting that Tycho and Kepler may see different things in the east at dawn? Certainly the cases are different. But these reversible perspective figures are examples of different things being seen in the same configuration, where this difference is due neither to differing visual pictures, nor to any "interpretation" superimposed on the sensation. . . .

Fig. 2

A trained physicist could see one thing in fig 2: an X-ray tube viewed from the cathode. Would Sir Lawrence Bragg and an Eskimo baby see the same thing when looking at an X-ray tube? Yes, and no. Yes—they are visually aware of the same object. No—the *ways* in which they are visually aware are profoundly different. Seeing is not only the having of a visual experience; it is also the way in which the visual experience is had.

At school the physicist had gazed at this glass-and-metal instrument. Returning now, after years in University and research, his eye lights upon the same object once again. Does he see the same thing now as he did then? Now he sees the instrument in terms of electrical circuit theory, thermodynamic theory, the theories of metal and glass structure, thermionic emission, optical transmission, refraction, diffraction, atomic theory, quantum theory and special relativity.

Contrast the freshman's view of college with that of his ancient tutor. Compare a man's first glance at the motor of his car with a similar glance ten exasperating years later.

"Granted, one learns all these things," it may be countered, "but it all figures in the interpretation the physicist puts on what he sees. Though the layman sees exactly what the physicist sees, he cannot interpret it in the same way because he has not learned so much."

Is the physicist doing more than just seeing? No, he does nothing over and above what the layman does when he sees an X-ray tube. What are you doing over and above reading these words? Are you interpreting marks on a page? When would this ever be a natural way of speaking? Would an infant see what you see here, when you see words and sentences and he sees but marks and lines? One does nothing beyond looking and seeing when one dodges bicycles, glances at a friend, or notices a cat in the garden.

"The physicist and the layman see the same thing," it is objected, "but they do not make the same thing of it." The layman can make nothing of it. Nor is that just a figure of speech. I can make nothing of the Arab word for *cat*, though my purely visual impressions may be distinguishable from those of the Arab who can. I must learn Arabic before I can see what he sees. The layman must learn physics before he can see what the physicist sees.

If one must find a paradigm case of seeing it would be better to regard as such not the visual apprehension of colour patches but things like seeing what time it is, seeing what key a piece of music is written in, and seeing whether a wound is septic.[23]

Pierre Duhem writes:

> Enter a laboratory; approach the table crowded with an assort-
> ment of apparatus, an electric cell, silk-covered copper wire, small
> cups of mercury, spools, a mirror mounted on an iron bar; the
> experimenter is inserting into small openings the metal ends of
> ebony-headed pins; the iron oscillates, and the mirror attached to it
> throws a luminous band upon a celluloid scale; the forward-
> backward motion of this spot enables the physicist to observe the
> minute oscillations of the iron bar. But ask him what he is doing.
> Will he answer "I am studying the oscillations of an iron bar which
> carries a mirror?" No, he will say that he is measuring the electric
> resistance of the spools. If you are astonished, if you ask him what
> his words mean, what relation they have with the phenomena he has
> been observing and which you have noted at the same time as he, he
> will answer that your question requires a long explanation and that
> you should take a course in electricity.[24]

The visitor must learn some physics before he can see what the physicist sees. Only then will the context throw into relief those features of the objects before him which the physicist sees as indicating resistance.

This obtains in all seeing. Attention is rarely directed to the space between the leaves of a tree, save when a Keats brings it to our notice.[25] (Consider also what was involved in Crusoe's seeing a vacant space in the sand as a footprint.) Our attention most naturally rests on objects and events which dominate the visual field. What a blooming, buzzing, undifferentiated confusion visual life would be if we all arose tomorrow without attention capable of dwelling only on what had heretofore been overlooked.[26]

The infant and the layman can see: they are not blind. But they cannot see what the physicist sees; they are blind to what he sees.[27] We may not hear that the oboe is out of tune, though this will be painfully obvious to the trained musician. (Who, incidentally, will not hear the tones and *interpret* them as being out of tune, but will simply hear the oboe to be out of tune.[28] We simply see what time it is; the surgeon simply sees a wound to be septic; the physicist sees the X-ray tube's anode overheating.) The elements of the visitor's visual field, though identical with those of the physicist, are not organized for him as for the physicist; the same lines, colours, shapes are apprehended by both, but not in the same way. There are indefinitely many ways in which a constellation of lines, shapes, patches, may be seen. *Why* a visual pattern is seen differently is a question for psychology, but *that* it may be seen differently is important in any examination of the concepts of seeing and observation. Here, as Wittgenstein might have said, the psychological is a symbol of the logical.

You see a bird, I see an antelope; the physicist sees an X-ray tube, the child a complicated lamp bulb; the microscopist sees coelenterate mesoglea, his new student sees only a gooey, formless stuff. Tycho and Simplicius see a mobile sun, Kepler and Galileo see a static sun.[29]

It may be objected, "Everyone, whatever his state of knowledge, will see fig. 1 as a box or cube, viewed as from above or as from below." True; almost everyone, child, layman, physicist, will see the figure as box-like one way or another. But could such observations be made by people ignorant of the construction of box-like objects? No. This objection only shows that most of us — the blind, babies, and dimwits excluded — have learned enough to be able to see this figure as a three-dimensional box. This reveals something about the sense in which Simplicius and Galileo do see the same thing (which I have never denied): they both see a brilliant heavenly body. The schoolboy and the physicist both see that the X-ray tube will smash if dropped. Examining how observers see different things in *x* marks something important about their seeing the same thing when looking at *x*. If seeing different things involves having different knowledge and theories about *x,* then perhaps the sense in which they see the same thing involves their sharing knowledge and theories about *x*. Bragg and the baby share no knowledge of X-ray tubes. They see the same thing only in that if they are looking at *x* they are both having some visual experience of it. Kepler and Tycho agree on more: they see the same thing in a stronger sense. Their visual fields are organized in much the same way. Neither sees the sun about to break out in a grin, or about to crack into ice cubes. (The baby is not "set" even against these eventualities.) Most people today see the same thing at dawn in an even stronger sense: we share much knowledge of the sun. Hence Tycho and Kepler see different things, and yet they see the same thing. That these things can be said depends on their knowledge, experience, and theories.

. . . The elements of their experiences are identical; but their conceptual organization is vastly different. Can their visual fields have a different organization? Then they can see different things in the east at dawn.

It is the sense in which Tycho and Kepler do not observe the same thing which must be grasped if one is to understand disagreements within microphysics. Fundamental physics is primarily a search for intelligibility — it is philosophy of matter. Only secondarily is it a search for objects and facts (though the two endeavours are as hand and glove). Microphysicists seek new modes of conceptual organization. If that can be done the finding of new entities will follow. Gold is rarely discovered by one who has not got the lay of the land.

To say that Tycho and Kepler, Simplicius and Galileo, Hooke and Newton, Priestley and Lavoisier, Soddy and Einstein, De Broglie and Born, Heisenberg and Bohm all make the same observations but use them differently is too easy.[30] It does not explain controversy in research science. Were there no sense in which they were different observations they could not be used differently. This may perplex some: that researchers sometimes do not appreciate data in the same way is a serious matter. It is important to realize, however, that sorting out differences about data, evidence, observation, may require more than simply gesturing at observable objects. It may require a comprehensive reappraisal of one's subject matter. This may be difficult, but it should not obscure the fact that nothing less than this may do. . . .

NOTES

1.   Wär' nicht das Auge sonnenhaft,
             Die Sonne könnt' es nie erblicken;
       Goethe, *Zahme Xenien* (Werke, Weimar, 1887-1918), Bk. 3, 1805.

2. Cf. the papers by Baker and Gatonby in *Nature,* 1949-present.

3. This is not a *merely* conceptual matter, of course. Cf. Wittgenstein, *Philosophical Investigations* (Blackwell, Oxford, 1953), p. 196.

4. (1) G. Berkeley, *Essay Towards a New Theory of Vision* (in *Works,* vol. I (London, T. Nelson, 1948-56), pp. 51 ff.

(2) James Mill, *Analysis of the Phenomena of the Human Mind* (Longmans, London, 1869), vol. I, p. 97.

(3) J. Sully, *Outlines of Psychology* (Appleton, New York, 1885).

(4) William James, *The Principles of Psychology* (Holt, New York, 1890-1905), vol. II, pp. 4, 78, 80 and 81; vol. I, p. 221.

(5) A Schopenhauer, *Satz vom Grunde* (in *Sämmtliche Werke,* Leipzig, 1888), ch. IV.

(6) H. Spencer, *The Principles of Psychology* (Appleton, New York, 1897), vol. IV, chs. IX, X.

(7) E. von Hartmann, *Philosophy of the Unconscious* (K. Paul, London, 1931), B, chs. VII, VIII.

(8) W. M. Wundt, *Vorleşungen über die Menschen und Thierseele* (Voss, Hamburg, 1892), IV, XIII.

(9) H. L. F. von Helmholtz, *Handbuch der Physiologischen Optik* (Leipzig, 1867), pp. 430, 447.

(10) A. Binet, *La psychologie du raisonnement, recherches expérimentales par l'hypnotisme* (Alcan, Paris, 1886), chs. III, V.

(11) J. Grote, *Exploratio Philosophica* (Cambridge, 1900), vol. II, pp. 201 ff.

(12) B. Russell, in *Mind* (1913), p. 76. *Mysticism and Logic* (Longmans, New York, 1918), p. 209. *The Problems of Philosophy* (Holt, New York, 1912), pp. 73, 92, 179, 203.

(13) Dawes Hicks, *Arist. Soc. Sup.* vol. II (1919), pp. 176-8.

(14) G. F. Stout, *A Manual of Psychology* (Clive, London, 1907, 2nd ed.), vol. II, 1 and 2, pp. 324, 561-4.

(15) A. C. Ewing, *Fundamental Questions of Philosophy* (New York, 1951), pp. 45 ff.

(16) G. W. Cunningham, *Problems of Philosophy* (Holt, New York, 1924), pp. 96-7.

5. Galileo, *Dialogue Concerning the Two Chief World Systems* (California, 1953), "The First Day," p. 33.

6. "'Das ist doch kein Sehen!'–'Das ist doch ein Sehen!' Beide müssen sich begrifflich recht-fertigen lassen" (Wittgenstein, *Phil. Inv.* p. 203).

7. Brain, *Recent Advances in Neurology* (with Strauss) (London, 1929), p. 88. Compare Helmholtz: "The sensations are signs to our consciousness, and it is the task of our intelligence to learn to understand their meaning" (*Handbuch der Physiologischen Optik* (Leipzig, 1867), vol. III, p. 433).

See also Husserl, "Ideen zu einer Reinen Phaenomenologie," in *Jahrbuch für Philosophie*, vol. I (1913), pp. 75, 79, and Wagner's *Handwörterbuch der Physiologie*, vol. III, section I (1846), p. 183.

8. Mann, *The Science of Seeing* (London, 1949), pp. 48-9. Arber, *The Mind and the Eye* (Cambridge, 1954). Compare Müller: "In any field of vision, the retina sees only itself in its spatial extension during a state of affection. It perceives itself as . . . etc." (*Zur vergleichenden Physiologie des Gesichtesinnes des Menschen und der Thiere* (Leipzig, 1826), p. 54).

9. Kolin: "An astigmatic eye when looking at millimeter paper can accommodate to see sharply either the vertical lines or the horizontal lines" (*Physics* (New York, 1950), pp. 570 ff.).

10. Cf. Whewell, *Philosophy of Discovery* (London, 1860), "The Paradoxes of Vision."

11. Cf. e.g. J. Z. Young, *Doubt and Certainty in Science* (Oxford, 1951, The Reith Lectures), and Gray Walter's article in *Aspects of Form,* ed. by L. L. Whyte (London, 1953). Compare Newton: "Do not the Rays of Light in falling upon the bottom of the Eye excite Vibrations in the Tunica Retina? Which Vibrations, being propagated along the solid Fibres of the Nerves into the Brain, cause the Sense of seeing" (*Opticks* (London, 1769), Bk. III, part I).

12. "Rot und grün kann ich nur sehen, aber nicht hören" (Wittgenstein, *Phil. Inv.* p. 209).

13. Cf. "An appearance is the same whenever the same eye is affected in the same way" (Lambert, *Photometria* (Berlin, 1760)); "We are justified, when different perceptions offer themselves to us, to infer that the underlying real conditions are different" (Helmholtz, *Wissenschaftliche Abhandlungen* (Leipzig, 1882), vol. II, p. 656), and Hertz: "We form for ourselves images or symbols of the external objects; the manner in which we form them is such that the logically necessary *(denknotwendigen)* consequences of the images in thought are invariably the images of materially necessary (*naturnotwendigen*) consequences of the corresponding objects" (*Principles of Mechanics* (London, 1889), p. 1).

Broad and Price make depth a feature of the private visual pattern. However, Weyl (*Philosophy of Mathematics and Natural Science* (Princeton, 1949), p. 125) notes that a single eye perceives qualities spread out in a *two*-dimensional field, since the latter is dissected by any one-dimensional line running through it. But our conceptual difficulties remain even when Kepler and Tycho keep one eye closed.

Whether or not two observers are having the same visual sense-data reduces directly to the question of whether accurate pictures of the contents of their visual fields are identical, or differ in some detail. We can then discuss the publicly observable pictures which Tycho and Kepler draw of what they see, instead of those private, mysterious entities locked in their visual consciousness. The accurate picture and the sense-datum must be identical; how could they differ?

14. From the B.B.C. report, 30 June 1954.

15. Newton, *Opticks,* Bk. II, part I. The writings of Claudius Ptolemy sometimes read like a phenomenalist's textbook. Cf. e.g. *The Almagest* (Venice, 1515), VI, section II, "On the Directions in the Eclipses," "When it touches the shadow's circle from within," "When the circles touch each other from without." Cf. also VII and VIII, IX (section 4). Ptolemy continually seeks to chart and predict "the appearances"–the points of light on the celestial globe. *The Almagest* abandons any attempt to explain the machinery behind these appearances.

Cf. Pappus: "The (circle) dividing the milk-white portion which owes its colour to the sun, and the portion which has the ashen colour natural to the moon itself is indistinguishable from a great circle" (*Mathematical Collection* (Hultsch, Berlin and Leipzig, 1864), pp. 554-60).

16. This famous illusion dates from 1832, when L. A. Necker, the Swiss naturalist, wrote a letter to Sir David Brewster describing how when certain rhomboidal crystals were viewed on end the perspective could shift in the way now familiar to us. Cf. *Phil. Mag.* III, no. I (1832), 329-37, especially p. 336. It is important to the present argument to note that this observational phenomenon began life not as a psychologist's trick, but at the very frontiers of observational science.

17. Wittgenstein answers: "Denn wir sehen eben wirklich zwei verschiedene Tatsachen" (*Tractatus*, 5. 5423).

18. "Auf welche Vorgänge spiele ich an?" (Wittgenstein, *Phil. Inv.* p. 214).

19. *Ibid.* p. 194 (top).

20. *Ibid.* p. 200.

21. This is *not* due to eye movements, or to local retinal fatigue. Cf. Flugel, *Brit. J. Psychol.* VI (1913), 60; *Brit. Psychol.* V (1913), 357. Cf. Donahue and Griffiths, *Amer. J. Psychol.* (1931), and Luckiesch, *Visual Illusions and their Applications* (London, 1922). Cf. also Peirce, *Collected Papers* (Harvard, 1931), 5, 183. References to psychology should not be misunderstood; but as one's acquaintance with the psychology of perception deepens, the character of the conceptual problems one regards as significant will deepen accordingly. Cf. Wittgenstein, *Phil. Inv.* p. 206 (top). Again, p. 193: "Its causes are of interest to psychologists. We are interested in the concept and its place among the concepts of experience."

22. Wittgenstein, *Phil. Inv.* p. 212.

23. Often "What do you see?" only poses the question "Can you identify the object before you?" This is calculated more to test one's knowledge than one's eyesight.

24. Duhem, *La théorie physique* (Paris, 1914), p. 218.

25. Chinese poets felt the significance of "negative features" like the hollow of a clay vessel or the central vacancy of the hub of a wheel (cf. Waley, *Three Ways of Thought in Ancient China* (London, 1939), p. 155).

26. Infants are indiscriminate; they take in spaces, relations, objects and events as being of equal value. They still must learn to organize their visual attention. The camera-clarity of their visual reactions is not by itself sufficient to differentiate elements in their visual fields. Contrast Mr. W. H. Auden who recently said of the poet that he is "bombarded by a stream of varied sensations which would drive him mad if he took them all in. It is impossible to guess how much energy we have to spend every day in not-seeing, not-hearing, not-smelling, not-reacting."

27. "He was blind to the *expression* of a face. Would his eyesight on that account be defective?" (Wittgenstein, *Phil. Inv.* p. 210) and "Because they seeing see not; and hearing they hear not, neither do they understand" (Matt. xiii. 10–13).

28. "Es hört doch jeder nur, was er versteht" (Goethe, *Maxims* (*Werke,* Weimar, 1887–1918)).

29. Against this Professor H. H. Price has argued: "Surely it appears to both of them to be rising, to be moving upwards, across the horizon . . . they both see a moving sun: they both see a round bright body which appears to be rising." Philip Frank retorts: "Our sense observation shows only that in the morning the distance between horizon and sun is increasing, but it does not tell us whether the sun is ascending or the horizon is descending . . ." (*Modern Science and its Philosophy* (Harvard, 1949), p. 231). Precisely. For Galileo and Kepler the horizon drops; for Simplicius and Tycho the sun rises. This is the difference Price misses, and which is central to this essay.

30. This parallels the too-easy epistemological doctrine that all normal observers see the same things in *x,* but interpret them differently.

14

Science and the Physical World

W. T. Stace

So far as I know scientists still talk about electrons, protons, neutrons, and so on. We never directly perceive these, hence if we ask how we know of their existence the only possible answer seems to be that they are an inference from what we do directly perceive. What sort of an inference? Apparently a causal inference. The atomic entities in some way impinge upon the sense of the animal organism and cause that organism to perceive the familiar world of tables, chairs, and the rest.

But is it not clear that such a concept of causation, however interpreted, is invalid? The only reason we have for believing in the law of causation is that we *observe* certain regularities or sequences. We observe that, in certain conditions, A is always followed by B. We call A the cause, B the effect. And the sequence A-B becomes a causal law. It follows that all *observed* causal sequences are between sensed objects in the familiar world of perception, and that all known causal laws apply solely to the world of sense and not to anything beyond or behind it. And this in turn means that we have not got, and never could have, one jot of evidence for believing that the law of causation can be applied *outside* the realm of perception, or that that realm can have any causes (such as the supposed physical objects) which are not themselves perceived.

Put the same thing in another way. Suppose there is an observed sequence A-B-C, represented by the vertical lines in the diagram below.

The observer X sees, and can see, nothing except things in the familiar world of perception. What *right* has he, and what *reason* has he, to assert causes of A, B, and C, such as a′, b′, c′, which he can never observe, behind the perceived world? He has no *right*, because the law of causation on which he is relying has never been observed to operate outside the series of perceptions, and he can have, therefore, no evidence that it does so. And he has no *reason*

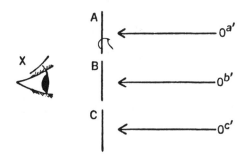

because the phenomenon C is *sufficiently* accounted for by the cause B, B by A, and so on. It is unnecessary and superfluous to introduce a *second* cause b' for B, c' for C, and so forth. To give two causes for each phenomenon, one in one world and one in another, is unnecessary, and perhaps even self-contradictory.

Is it denied, then, it will be asked, that the star causes light waves, that the waves cause retinal changes, that these cause changes in the optic nerve, which in turn causes movement in the brain cells, and so on? No, it is not denied. But the observed causes and effects are all in the world of perception. And no sequences of sense-data can possibly justify going outside that world. If you admit that we never observe anything except sensed objects and their relations, regularities, and sequences, then it is obvious that we are completely shut in by our sensations and can never get outside them. Not only causal relations, but all other observed relations, upon which *any* kind of inferences might be founded, will lead only to further sensible objects and their relations. No inference, therefore, can pass from what is sensible to what is not sensible.

The fact is that atoms are *not* inferences from sensations. No one denies, of course, that a vast amount of perfectly valid inferential reasoning takes place in the physical theory of the atom. But it will not be found to be in any strict logical sense inference from *sense-data to atoms*. An *hypothesis* is set up, and the inferential processes are concerned with the application of the hypothesis, that is, with the prediction by its aid of further possible sensations and with its own internal consistency.

That atoms are not inferences from sensations means, of course, that from the existence of sensations we cannot validly infer the existence of atoms. And this means that we cannot have any reason at all to believe that they exist. And that is why I propose to argue that they do not exist—or at any rate that no one could know it if they did, and that we have absolutely no evidence of their existence.

What status have they, then? Is it meant that they are false and worthless, merely untrue? Certainly not. No one supposes that the entries in the nautical almanac "exist" anywhere except on the pages of that book and in the brains of its compilers and readers. Yet they are "true," inasmuch as they enable us to predict certain sensations, namely, the positions and times of certain perceived objects which we call the stars. And so the formulae of the atomic theory are true in the same sense, and perform a similar function.

I suggest that they are nothing but shorthand formulae, ingeniously worked out by the human mind, to enable it to predict its experience, i.e. to predict what sensations will be given to it. By "predict" here I do not mean to refer solely to the future. To calculate that there was an eclipse of the sun visible in Asia Minor in the year 585 B.C. is, in the sense in which I am using the term, to predict.

In order to see more clearly what is meant, let us apply the same idea to another case, that of gravitation. Newton formulated a law of gravitation in terms of "forces." It was supposed that this law—which was nothing but a mathematical formula—governed the operation of these existent forces. Nowadays it is no longer believed that these forces exist at all. And yet the law can be applied just as well without them to the prediction of astronomical phenomena. It is a matter of no importance to the scientific man whether the forces exist or not. That may be said to be a purely philosophical question. And I think the philosopher should pronounce them fictions. But that would not make the law useless or untrue. If it could still be used to predict phenomena, it would be just as true as it was.

It is true that fault is now found with Newton's law, and that another law, that of Einstein, has been substituted for it. And it is sometimes supposed that the reason for this is that forces are no longer believed in. But this is not the case. Whether forces exist or not simply does not matter. What matters is the discovery that Newton's law does *not* enable us accurately to predict certain astronomical facts such as the exact position of the planet Mercury. Therefore another formula, that of Einstein, has been substituted for it which permits correct predictions. This new law, as it happens, is a formula in terms of geometry. It is pure mathematics and nothing else. It does not contain anything about forces. In its pure form it does not even contain, so I am informed, anything about "humps and hills in space-time." And it does not matter whether any such humps and hills exist. It is truer than Newton's law, not because it substitutes humps and hills for forces, but solely because it is a more accurate formula of prediction.

Not only may it be said that forces do not exist. It may with equal truth be said that "gravitation" does not exist. Gravitation is not a "thing," but a mathematical formula, which exists only in the heads of mathematicians. And as a mathematical formula cannot cause a body to fall, so gravitation cannot cause a body to fall. Ordinary language misleads us here. We speak of the law "of" gravitation, and suppose that this law "applies to" the heavenly bodies. We are thereby misled into supposing that there are *two* things, namely, the gravitation and the heavenly bodies, and that one of these things, the gravitation, causes changes in the other. In reality nothing exists except the moving bodies. And neither Newton's law nor Einstein's law is, strictly speaking, a law of gravitation. They are both laws of moving bodies, that is to say, formulae which tell us how these bodies will move.

Now, just as in the past "forces" were foisted into Newton's law (by himself, be it said), so now certain popularizers of relativity foisted "humps and hills in space-time" into Einstein's law. We hear that the reason why the planets move in curved courses is that they cannot go through these humps and hills, but have to go round them! The planets just get "shoved about," not by forces, but by the humps and hills! But these humps and hills are pure metaphors. And anyone who takes them for "existences" gets asked awkward questions as to what "curved space" is curved "in."

It is not irrelevant to our topic to consider *why* human beings invent these metaphysical monsters of forces and bumps in space-time. The reason is that they have never emancipated themselves from the absurd idea that science "explains" things. They were not content to have laws which merely told them *that* the planets will, as a matter of fact, move in such and such ways. They wanted to know "why" the planets move in those ways. So Newton replied, "Forces." "Oh," said humanity, "that explains it. We understand forces. We feel them every time someone pushes or pulls us." Thus the movements were supposed to be "explained" by entities familiar because analogous to the muscular sensations which human beings feel. The humps and hills were introduced for exactly the same reason. They seem so familiar. If there is a bump in the billiard table, the rolling billiard ball is diverted from a straight to a curved course. Just the same with the planets. "Oh, I see!" says humanity, "that's quite simple. That *explains* everything."

But scientific laws, properly formulated, never "explain" anything. They simply state, in an abbreviated and generalized form, *what happens*. No scientist, and in my opinion no philosopher, knows *why* anything happens, or can "explain" anything. Scientific laws do nothing except state the brute fact that "when *A* happens, *B* always happens too." And laws of this kind obviously enable us to predict. If certain scientists substituted humps and hills for forces, then they have just substituted one superstition for another. For my part I do not believe that *science* has done this, though some *scientists* may have. For scientists, after all, are human beings with the same craving for "explanations" as other people.

I think that atoms are in exactly the same position as forces and the humps and hills of space-time. In reality the mathematical formulae which are the scientific ways of stating the atomic theory are simply formulae for calculating what sensations will appear in given conditions. But just as the weakness of the human mind demanded that there should correspond to the formula of gravitation a real "thing" which could be called "gravitation itself" or "force," so the same weakness demands that there should be a real thing corresponding to the atomic formulae, and this real thing is called the atom. In reality the atoms no more cause sensations than gravitation causes apples to fall. The only causes of sensations are other sensations. And the relation of atoms to sensations to be felt is not the relation of cause to effect, but the relation of a mathematical formula to the facts and happenings which it enables the mathematician to calculate.

Some writers have said that the physical world has no color, no sound, no taste, no smell. It has no spatiality. Probably it has not even number. We must not suppose that it is in any way like our world, or that we can understand it by attributing to it the characters of our world. Why not carry this progress to its logical conclusion? Why not give up the idea that it has even the character of "existence" which our familiar world has? We have given up smell, color, taste. We have given up even space and shape. We have given up number. Surely, after all that, mere existence is but a little thing to give up. No? Then is it that the idea of existence conveys "a sort of halo"? I suspect so. The "existence" of atoms is but the expiring ghost of the pellet and billiard-ball atoms of our forefathers. They, of course, had size, shape, weight, hardness. These have gone. But thinkers still cling to their existence, just as their fathers clung to the existence of forces, and for the same reason. Their reason is not in the slightest that science has any use for the existent atom. But the *imagination* has. It seems somehow to explain things, to make them homely and familiar.

It will not be out of place to give one more example to show how common fictitious existences are in science, and how little it matters whether they really exist or not. This example has no strange and annoying talk of "bent spaces" about it. One of the foundations of physics is, or used to be, the law of the conservation of energy. I do not know how far, if at all, this has been affected by the theory that matter sometimes turns into energy. But that does not affect the lesson it has for us. The law states, or used to state, that the amount of energy in the universe is always constant, that energy is never either created or destroyed. This was highly convenient, but it seemed to have obvious exceptions. If you throw a stone up into the air, you are told that it exerts in its fall the same amount of energy which it took to throw it up. But suppose it does not fall. Suppose it lodges on the roof of your house and stays there. What has happened to the energy which you can nowhere perceive as being exerted? It seems to have disappeared out of the universe. No, says the scientist, it still exists as *potential* energy. Now what does this blessed word "potential" – which is thus brought in to save the situation – mean as applied to energy? It means, of course, that the energy does not exist in any of its regular "forms," heat, light, electricity, etc. But this is merely negative. What positive meaning has the term? Strictly speaking, none whatever. Either the energy exists or it does not exist. There is no realm of the "potential" half-way between existence and non-existence. And the existence of energy can only consist in its being exerted. If the energy is not being exerted, then it is not energy and does not exist. Energy can no more exist without energizing than heat can exist without being hot. The "potential" existence of the energy is, then, a fiction. The actual empirically verifiable facts are that if a certain quantity of energy e exists in the universe and then disappears out of the universe (as happens when the stone lodges on the roof), the same amount of energy e will always reappear, begin to exist again, in certain known conditions. That is the fact which the law of the conservation of energy actually expresses. And the fiction of potential energy is introduced simply because it is convenient and makes the equations easier to work. They could be worked quite well without it, but would be slightly more complicated. In either case the function of the law is the same. Its object is to apprise us that if in certain conditions we have certain perceptions (throwing up the stone), then in certain other conditions we shall get certain other perceptions (heat, light, stone hitting skull, or other such). But there will always be a temptation to hypostatize the potential energy as an "existence," and to believe that it is a "cause" which "explains" the phenomena.

If the views which I have been expressing are followed out, they will lead to the conclusion that, strictly speaking, *nothing exists except sensations* (and the minds which perceive them). The rest is mental construction or fiction. But this does not mean that the conception of a star or the conception of an electron are worthless or untrue. Their truth and value consist in their capacity for helping us to organize our experience and predict our sensations.

15

Do Sub-Microscopic Entities Exist?

Stephen Toulmin

Non-scientists are often puzzled to know whether the electrons, genes and other entities scientists talk about are to be thought of as really existing or not. Scientists themselves also have some difficulty in saying exactly where they stand on this issue. Some are inclined to insist that all these things are just as real, and exist in the same sense as tables and chairs and omnibuses. But others feel a certain embarrassment about them, and hesitate to go so far; they notice the differences between establishing the existence of electrons from a study of electrical phenomena, inferring the existence of savages from depressions in the sand, and inferring the existence of an inflamed appendix from a patient's signs and symptoms; and it may even occur to them that to talk about an electromagnet in terms of 'electrons' is a bit like talking of Pyrexia of Unknown Origin when the patient has an unaccountable temperature. Yet the theory of electrons does *explain* electrical phenomena in a way in which no mere translation into jargon, like 'pyrexia', can explain a sick man's temperature; and how, we may ask, could the electron theory work at all if, after all, electrons did not really exist?

Stated in this way, the problem is confused: let us therefore scrutinize the question itself a little more carefully. For when we compare Robinson Crusoe's discovery with the physicist's one, it is not only the sorts of discovery which are different in the two cases. To talk of existence in both cases involves quite as much of a shift, and by passing too swiftly from one use of the word to the other we may make the problem unnecessarily hard for ourselves.

Notice, therefore, what different ideas we may have in mind when we talk about things 'existing'. If we ask whether dodos exist or not, i.e., whether there are any dodos left nowadays, we are asking whether the species has survived or is extinct. But when we ask whether electrons exist or not, we certainly do not have in mind the possibility that they may have become extinct: in whatever sense we ask this question, it is not one in which 'exists' is opposed to 'does not exist any more'. Again, if we ask whether Ruritania exists, i.e., whether there is such a country as Ruritania, we are asking whether there really is such a country as Ruritania or whether it is an imaginary, and so a non-existent country. But we are not interested in asking of electrons whether they are genuine instances of a familiar sort of thing or non-existent ones: the way in which we are using the term 'exist' is not one in which it is opposed to 'are non-existent'. In each case, the word 'exist' is used to make a slightly different point, and to mark a slightly different distinction. As one moves from Man Friday to dodos, and on from them to Ruritania, and again to electrons, the change in the nature of the cases brings other changes with it: notably in the way one has to understand sentences containing the word 'exist'.

What, then, of the question, "Do electrons exist?" How is this to be understood? A more revealing analogy than dodos or Ruritania is to be found in the question, "Do contours exist?" A child who had read that the equator was 'an imaginary line drawn round the center of the earth' might be struck by the contours, parallels of latitude and the rest, which appear on maps along with the towns, mountains and rivers, and ask of them whether *they* existed. How should we reply? If he asked his question in bare words, "Do contours exist?" one could hardly answer him immediately: clearly the only answer one can give to this question is "Yes and No." They 'exist' all right, but do they *exist*? It all depends on your manner of speaking. So he might be persuaded to restate his question, asking now, "Is there really a line on the ground whose height is constant?"; and again the answer would have to be "Yes and No," for there is (so to say) a 'line', but then again not what you might call a *line.* . . . And so the cross-purposes would continue until it was made clear that the real question was: "Is there anything to show for contours—anything visible on the terrain, like the white lines on a tennis court? Or are they only cartographical devices, having no geographical counterparts?" Only then would the question be posed in anything like an unambiguous manner. The sense of 'exists' in which a child might naturally ask whether contours existed is accordingly one in which 'exists' is opposed not to 'does not exist any more' or to 'is non-existent', but to 'is only a (cartographical) fiction'.

This is very much the sense in which the term 'exists' is used of atoms, genes, electrons, fields and other theoretical entities in the physical sciences. There, too, the question "Do they exist?" has in practice the force of "Is there anything to show for them, or are they only theoretical fictions?" To a working physicist, the question "Do neutrinos exist?" acts as an invitation to 'produce a neutrino', preferably by making it *visible*. If one could do this one would indeed have something to show for the term 'neutrino', and the difficulty of doing it is what explains the peculiar difficulty of the problem. For the problem arises acutely only when we start asking about the existence of *sub-microscopic* entities, i.e., things which by all normal standards are invisible. In the nature of the case, to produce a neutrino must be a more sophisticated business than producing a dodo or a nine-foot man. Our problem is accordingly complicated by the need to decide what is to count as 'producing' a neutrino, a field or a gene. It is not obvious what sorts of thing ought to count: certain things are, however, generally regarded by scientists as acceptable—for instance, cloud-chamber pictures of α-ray tracks, electron microscope photographs or, as a second-best, audible clicks from a Geiger counter. They would regard such striking demonstrations as these as sufficiently like being shown a live dodo on the lawn to qualify as evidence of the existence of the entities concerned. And certainly, if we reject these as insufficient, it is hard to see what more we can reasonably ask for: if the term 'exists' is to have any application to such things, must not this be it?

What if no such demonstration were possible? If one could not show, visibly, that neutrinos existed, would that necessarily be the end of them? Not at all; and it is worth noticing what happens when a demonstration of the preferred type is not possible, for then the difference between talking about the existence of electrons or genes, and talking about the existence of dodos, unicorns or nine-foot men becomes all-important. If, for instance, I talk plausibly about unicorns or nine-foot men and have nothing to show for them, so that I am utterly unable to say, when challenged, under what circumstances a specimen might be, or might have been seen, the conclusion may reasonably be drawn that my nine-foot men are imaginary and my unicorns a myth. In either case, the things I am talking about may be presumed to be non-existent, i.e., are discredited and can be written off. But in the case of atoms, genes and the like, things are different: the failure to bring about or describe circumstances in which one might point and say, "There's one!" need not, as with unicorns, be taken as discrediting them.

Not all those theoretical entities which cannot be shown to exist need be held to be non-existent: there is for them a middle way. Certainly we should hesitate to assert that any theoretical entity really existed until a photograph or other demonstration had been given. But, even if we had reason to believe that no such demonstration ever could be given, it would be too much to conclude that the entity was non-existent; for this conclusion would give the impression of discrediting something that, as a fertile explanatory concept, did not necessarily deserve to be discredited. To do so would be like refusing to take any notice of contour lines because there were no visible marks corresponding to them for us to point to on the ground. The conclusion that the notion must be dropped would be justified only if, like 'phlogiston,' 'caloric fluid' and the 'ether', it had also lost all explanatory fertility. No doubt scientists would be happy if they could refer in their explanations only to entities which could be shown to exist, but at many stages in the development of science it would have been crippling to have insisted on this condition too rigorously. A scientific theory is often accepted and in circulation for a long time, and may have to advance for quite a long way, before the question of the real existence of the entities appearing in it can even be posed.

The history of science provides one particularly striking example of this. The whole of theoretical physics and chemistry in the nineteenth century was developed round the notions of atoms and molecules: both the kinetic theory of matter, whose contribution to physics was spectacular, and the theory of chemical combinations and reactions, which turned chemistry into an exact science, made use of these notions, and could hardly have been expounded except in terms of them. Yet not until 1905 was it definitively shown by Einstein that the phenomenon of Brownian motion could be regarded as a demonstration that atoms and molecules really existed. Until that time, no such demonstration had ever been recognized, and even a Nobel prize-winner like Ostwald, for whose work as a chemist the concepts 'atom' and 'molecule' must have been indispensable, could be skeptical until then about the reality of atoms. Moreover by 1905 the atomic theory had ceased to be the last word in physics: some of its foundations were being severly attacked, and the work of Niels Bohr and J. J. Thomson was beginning to alter the physicist's whole picture of the constitution of matter. So, paradoxically, one finds that the major triumphs of the atomic theory were achieved at a time when even the greatest scientist could regard the idea of atoms as hardly more than a useful fiction, and that atoms were definitely shown to exist only at a time when the classical atomic theory was beginning to lose its position as the basic picture of the constitution of matter.

Evidently, then, it is a mistake to put questions about the reality or existence of theoretical entities too much in the center of the picture. In accepting a theory scientists need not, to begin with, answer these questions either way: certainly they do not, as Kneale suggests, commit themselves thereby to a belief in the existence of all the things in terms of which the theory is expressed. To suppose this is a variant of the Man Friday fallacy. In fact, the question whether the entities spoken of in a theory exist or not is one to which we may not even be able to give a meaning until the theory has some accepted position. The situation is rather like that we encountered earlier in connection with the notion of light traveling. It may seem natural to suppose that a physicist who talks of light as traveling must make some assumptions about what it is that is traveling: on investigation, however, this turns out not to be so, for the question, what it is that is traveling, is one which cannot even be asked without going beyond the phenomena which the notion is originally used to explain. Likewise, when a scientist adopts a new theory, in which novel concepts are introduced (waves, electrons or genes), it may seem natural to suppose that he is committed to a belief in the existence of the things in terms of which his explanations are expressed. But again, the question whether genes, say, really exist takes us beyond the original phenomena explained in terms of 'genes'. To the scientist, the real existence of his theoretical entities is contrasted with their being only useful theoretical fictions: the fact of an initial explanatory success may therefore leave the question of existence open.

There is a converse to this form of the Man Friday fallacy. Having noticed that a theory may be accepted long before visual demonstrations can be produced of the existence of the entities involved, we may be tempted to conclude that such things as cloud-chamber photographs are rather overrated: in fact, that they only seem to bring us nearer to the things of which the physicist speaks as a result of mere illusion. This is a conclusion which Kneale has advanced, on the ground that physical theories do not stand or fall by the results obtained from cloud-chambers and the like rather then by the results of any other physical experiments. But this is still to confuse two different questions, which may be totally independent: the question of the acceptability of the theories and the question of the reality of the theoretical entities. To regard cloud-chamber photographs as showing us that electrons and α-particles really exist need not mean giving the cloud chamber a preferential status among our grounds for accepting current theories of atomic structure. These theories were developed and accepted before the cloud-chamber was, or indeed could have been invented. Nevertheless, it was the cloud-chamber which first showed in a really striking manner just how far nuclei, electrons, α-particles and the rest could safely be thought of as real things; that is to say, as more than explanatory fictions.

16

The Ontological Status
of Theoretical Entities

Grover Maxwell

That anyone today should seriously contend that the entities referred to by scientific theories are only convenient fictions, or that talk about such entities is translatable without remainder into talk about sense contents or everyday physical objects, or that such talk should be regarded as belonging to a mere calculating device and, thus, without cognitive content—such contentions strike me as so incongruous with the scientific and rational attitude and practice that I feel this paper *should* turn out to be a demolition of straw men. But the instrumentalist views of outstanding physicists such as Bohr and Heisenberg are too well known to be cited, and in a recent book of great competence, Professor Ernest Nagel concludes that "the opposition between [the realist and the instrumentalist] views [of theories] is a conflict over preferred modes of speech" and "the question as to which of them is the 'correct position' has only terminological interest."[1] The phoenix, it seems, will not be laid to rest.

The literature on the subject is, of course, voluminous, and a comprehensive treatment of the problem is far beyond the scope of one essay. I shall limit myself to a small number of constructive arguments (for a radically realistic interpretation of theories) and to a critical examination of some of the more crucial assumptions (sometimes tacit, sometimes explicit) that seem to have generated most of the problems in this area.[2]

The Problem

Although this essay is not comprehensive, it aspires to be fairly self-contained. Let me, therefore, give a pseudohistorical introduction to the problem with a piece of science fiction (or fictional science).

In the days before the advent of microscopes, there lived a Pasteur-like scientist whom, following the usual custom, I shall call Jones. Reflecting on the fact that certain diseases seemed to be transmitted from one person to another by means of bodily contact or by contact with articles handled previously by an afflicted person, Jones began to speculate about the mechanism of the transmission. As a "heuristic crutch," he recalled that there is an obvious *observable* mechanism for transmission of certain afflictions (such as body lice), and he postulated that all, or most, infectious diseases were spread in a similar manner but that in most cases the corresponding "bugs" were too small to be seen and, possibly, that some of them lived inside the bodies of their hosts. Jones proceeded to develop his theory and to examine its testable consequences. Some of these seemed to be of great importance for preventing the spread of disease.

After years of struggle with incredulous recalcitrance, Jones managed to get some of his preventative measures adopted. Contact with or proximity to diseased persons was avoided when possible, and articles which they handled were "disinfected" (a word coined by Jones) either by means of high temperatures or by treating them with certain toxic preparations which Jones termed "disinfectants." The results were spectacular: within ten years the death rate had declined 40 per cent. Jones and his theory received their well-deserved recognition.

However, the "crobes" (the theoretical term coined by Jones to refer to the disease-producing organisms) aroused considerable anxiety among many of the philosophers and philosophically inclined scientists of the day. The expression of this anxiety usually began something like this: "In order to account for the facts, Jones must assume that his crobes are too small to be seen. Thus the very postulates of his theory preclude their being observed; they are *unobservable in principle.*" (Recall that no one had envisaged such a thing as a microscope.) This common prefatory remark was then followed by a number of different "analyses" and "interpretations" of Jones' theory. According to one of these, the tiny organisms were merely convenient fictions—*façons de parler*—extremely useful as heuristic devices for facilitating (in the "context of discovery") the thinking of scientists but not to be taken seriously in the sphere of cognitive knowledge (in the "context of justification"). A closely related view was that Jones' theory was merely an instrument, useful for organizing observation statements and (thus) for producing desired results, and that, therefore, it made no more sense to ask what was the nature of the entities to which it referred than it did to ask what was the nature of the entities to which a hammer or any other tool referred.[3] "Yes," a philosopher might have said, "Jones' theoretical expressions are just meaningless sounds or marks on paper which, when correlated with observation sentences by appropriate syntactical rules, enable us to predict successfully and otherwise organize data in a convenient fashion." These philosophers called themselves "instrumentalists."

According to another view (which, however, soon became unfashionable), although expressions containing Jones' theoretical terms were genuine sentences, they were translatable without remainder into a set (perhaps infinite) of observation sentences. For example, 'There are crobes of disease X on this article' was said to translate into something like this: 'If a person handles this article without taking certain precautions, he will (probably) contact disease X; and if this article is first raised to a high temperature, then if a person handles it at any time afterward, before it comes into contact with another person with disease X, he will (probably) not contract disease X; and . . .'

Now virtually all who held any of the views so far noted granted, even insisted, that theories played a useful and legitimate role in the scientific enterprise. Their concern was the elimination of "pseudo problems" which might arise, say, when one began wondering about the "reality of supraempirical entities," etc. However, there was also a school of thought, founded by a psychologist named Pelter, which differed in an interesting manner from such positions as these. Its members held that while Jones' crobes might very well exist and enjoy "full-blown reality," they should not be the concern of medical research at all. They insisted that if Jones had employed the correct methodology, he would have discovered, even sooner and with much less effort, all of the observation laws related to disease contraction, transmission, etc. without introducing superfluous links (the crobes) into the causal chain.

Now, lest any reader find himself waxing impatient, let me hasten to emphasize that this crude parody is not intended to convince anyone, or even to cast serious doubt upon sophisticated varieties of any of the reductionistic positions caricatured (some of them not too severely, I would contend) above. I am well aware that there are theoretical entities and theoretical entities, some of whose conceptual and theoretical statuses differ in important respects from Jones' crobes. (I shall discuss some of these later.) Allow me, then, to bring the Jonesean prelude to our examination of observability to a hasty conclusion.

Now Jones had the good fortune to live to see the invention of the compound microscope. His crobes were "observed" in great detail, and it became possible to identify the specific kind of *microbe* (for so they began to be called) which was responsible for each different disease. Some philosophers freely admitted error and were converted to realist positions concerning theories. Others resorted to subjective idealism or to a thoroughgoing phenomenalism, of which there were two principal varieties. According to one, the one "legitimate" observation language had for its descriptive terms only those which referred to sense data. The other maintained the stronger thesis that *all* "factual" statements were *translatable* without remainder into the sense-datum language. In either case, any two non-sense data (e.g., a theoretical entity and what would ordinarily be called an "observable physical object") had virtually the same status. Others contrived means of modifying their views much less drastically. One group maintained that Jones' crobes actually never had been unobservable in principle, for, they said, the theory did not imply the impossibility of finding a means (e.g., the microscope) of observing them. A more radical contention was that the crobes were not observed at all; it was argued that what was seen by means of the microscope was just a shadow or an image rather than a corporeal organism.

The Observational-Theoretical Dichotomy

Let us turn from these fictional philosophical positions and consider some of the actual ones to which they roughly correspond. Taking the last one first, it is interesting to note the following passage from Bergmann: "But it is only fair to point out that if this . . . methodological and terminological analysis [for the thesis that there are no atoms] . . . is strictly adhered to, even stars and microscopic objects are not physical things in a literal sense, but merely by courtesy of language and pictorial imagination. This might seem awkward. But when I look through a microscope, all I see is a patch of color which creeps through the field like a shadow over a wall. And a shadow, though real, is certainly not a physical thing."[4]

I should like to point out that it is also the case that if this analysis is strictly adhered to, we cannot observe physical things through opera glasses, or even through ordinary spectacles, and one begins to wonder about the status of what we see through an ordinary windowpane. And what about distortions due to temperature gradients—however small and, thus, always present—in the ambient air? It really *does* "seem awkward" to say that when people who wear glasses describe what they see they are talking about shadows, while those who employ unaided vision talk about physical things—or that when we look through a windowpane, we can only *infer* that it is raining, while if we raise the window, we may "observe directly" that it is. The point I am making is that there is, in principle, a continuous series beginning with looking through a vacuum and containing these as members: looking through a windowpane, looking through glasses, looking through binoculars, looking through a low-power microscope, looking through a high-power microscope, etc., in the order given. The important consequence is that, so far, we are left without criteria which would enable us to draw a nonarbitrary line between "observation" and "theory." Certainly, we will often find it convenient to draw such a to-some-extent-arbitrary line; but its position will vary widely from context to context. (For example, if we are determining the resolving characteristics of a certain microscope, we would certainly draw the line beyond ordinary spectacles, probably beyond simple magnifying glasses, and possibly beyond another microscope with a lower power of resolution.) But what ontological ice does a mere methodologically convenient observational-theoretical dichotomy cut? Does an entity attain physical thinghood and/or "real existence" in one context only to lose it in another? Or, we may ask, recalling the continuity from observable to unobservable, is what is seen through spectacles a "little bit less real" or does it "exist to a slightly less extent" than what is observed by unaided vision?[5]

However, it might be argued that things seen through spectacles and binoculars look like ordinary physical objects, while those seen through microscopes and telescopes look like shadows and patches of light. I can only reply that this does not seem to me to be the case, particularly when looking at the moon, or even Saturn, through a telescope or when looking at a small, though "directly observable," physical object through a low-power microscope. Thus, again, a continuity appears.

"But," it might be objected, "theory tells us that what we see by means of a microscope is a real image, which is certainly distinct from the object on the stage." Now first of all, it should be remarked that it seems odd that one who is espousing an austere empiricism which requires a sharp observational-language/theoretical-language distinction (and one in which the former language has a privileged status) should need a theory in order to tell him what is observable. But, letting this pass, what is to prevent us from saying that we still observe the object on the stage, even though a "real image" may be involved? Otherwise, we shall be strongly tempted by phenomenalistic demons, and at this point we are considering a physical-object observation language rather than a sense-datum one. (Compare the traditional puzzles: Do I see one physical object or two when I punch my eyeball? Does one object split into two? Or do I see one object and one image? Etc.)

Another argument for the continuous transition from the observable to the unobservable (theoretical) may be adduced from theoretical considerations themselves. For example, contemporary valency theory tells us that there is a virtually continuous transition from very small molecules (such as those of hydrogen) through "medium-sized" ones (such as those of the fatty acids, polypeptides, proteins, and viruses) to extremely large ones (such as crystals of the salts, diamonds, and lumps of polymeric plastic). The molecules in the last-mentioned group are macro, "directly observable" physical objects but are, nevertheless, genuine, single molecules; on the other hand, those in the first mentioned group have the same perplexing properties as subatomic particles (de Broglie waves, Heisenberg indeterminacy, etc.). Are we to say that a large protein molecule (e.g., a virus) which can be "seen" only with an electron microscope is a little less real or exists to somewhat less an extent than does a molecule of a polymer which can be seen with an optical microscope? And does a hydrogen molecule partake of only an infinitesimal portion of existence or reality? Although there certainly *is* a continuous transition from observability to unobservability, any talk of such a continuity from full-blown existence to nonexistence is, clearly, nonsense.

Let us now consider the next to last modified position which was adopted by our fictional philosophers. According to them, it is only those entities which are *in principle* impossible to observe that present special problems. What kind of impossibility is meant here? Without going into a detailed discussion of the various types of impossibility, about which there is abundant literature with which the reader is no doubt familiar, I shall assume what usually seems to be granted by most philosophers who talk of entities which are unobservable in principle—i.e., that the theory(s) itself (coupled with a physiological theory of perception, I would add) entails that such entities are unobservable.

We should immediately note that if this analysis of the notion of unobservability (and, hence, of observability) is accepted, then its use as a means of delimiting the observation language seems to be precluded for those philosophers who regard theoretical expressions as elements of a calculating device—as meaningless strings of symbols. For suppose they wished to determine whether or not 'electron' was a theoretical term. First, they must see whether the theory entails the sentence 'Electrons are unobservable.' So far, so good, for their calculating devices are said to be able to select genuine sentences, provided they contain no theoretical terms. But what about the selected "sentence" itself? Suppose that 'electron' is an observation term. It follows that the expression is a genuine sentence and asserts that electrons are unobservable. But this entails that 'electron' is *not* an observation term. Thus if 'electron' is an observation term, then it is *not* an observation term. Therefore it is not an observation term. But then it follows that 'Electrons are unobservable' is not a genuine sentence and does not assert that electrons are unobservable, since it is a meaningless string of marks and does not assert anything whatever. Of course, it could be stipulated that when a theory "selects" a meaningless expression of the form 'Xs are unobservable,' then 'X' is to be taken as a theoretical term. But this seems rather arbitrary.

But, assuming that well-formed theoretical expressions are genuine sentences, what shall we say about unobservability in principle? I shall begin by putting my head on the block and argue that the present-day status of, say, electrons is in many ways similar to that of Jones' crobes before microscopes were invented. I am well aware of the numerous theoretical arguments for the impossibility of observing electrons. But suppose new entities are discovered which interact with electrons in such a mild manner that if an electron is, say, in an eigenstate of position, then, in certain circumstances, the interaction does not disturb it. Suppose also that a drug is discovered which vastly alters the human perceptual apparatus—perhaps even activates latent capacities so that a new sense modality emerges. Finally, suppose that in our altered state we are able to perceive (not necessarily visually) by means of these new entities in a manner roughly analogous to that by which we now see by means of photons. To make this a little more plausible, suppose that the energy eigenstates of the electrons in some of the compounds present in the relevant perceptual organ are such that even the weak interaction with the new entities alters them and also that the cross sections, relative to the new entities, of the electrons and other particles of the gases of the air are so small that the chance of any interaction here is negligible. Then we might be able to "observe directly" the position and possibly the approximate diameter and other properties of some electrons. It would follow, of course, that quantum theory would have to be altered in some respects, since the new entities do not conform to all its principles. But however improbable this may be, it does not, I maintain, involve any logical or conceptual absurdity. Furthermore, the modification necessary for the inclusion of the new entities would not necessarily change the meaning of the term 'electron.'[6]

Consider a somewhat less fantastic example, and one which does not involve any change in physical theory. Suppose a human mutant is born who is able to "observe" ultraviolet radiation, or even X rays, in the same way we "observe" visible light.

Now I think that it is extremely improbable that we will ever observe electrons directly (i.e., that it will ever be reasonable to assert that we have so observed them). But this is neither here nor there; it is not the purpose of this essay to predict the future development of scientific theories, and, hence, it is not its business to decide what actually is observable or what will become observable (in the more or less intuitive sense of 'observable' with which we are now working). After all, we are operating, here, under the assumption that it is theory, and thus science itself, which tells us what is or is not, in this sense, observable (the 'in principle' seems to have become superfluous). And this is the heart of the matter; for it follows that, at least for this sense of 'observable,' there are no a priori or philosophical criteria for separating the observable from the unobservable. By trying to show that we can talk about the *possibility* of observing electrons without committing logical or conceptual blunders, I have been trying to support the thesis that any (nonlogical) term is a possible candidate for an observation term.

There is another line which may be taken in regard to delimitation of the observation language. According to it, the proper term with which to work is not 'observable' but, rather 'observed.' There immediately comes to mind the tradition beginning with Locke and Hume (No idea without a preceding impression!), running through Logical Atomism and the Principle of Acquaintance, and ending (perhaps) in contemporary positivism. Since the numerous facets of this tradition have been extensively examined and criticized in the literature, I shall limit myself here to a few summary remarks.

Again, let us consider at this point only observation languages which contain ordinary physical-object terms (along with observation predicates, etc., of course). Now, according to this view, all descriptive terms of the observation language must refer to that which has been observed. How is this to be interpreted? Not too narrowly, presumably, otherwise each language user would have a different observation language. The name of my Aunt Mamie, of California, whom I have never seen, would not be in my observation language, nor would 'snow' be an observation term for many Floridians. One could, of course, set off the observation language by means of this awkward restriction, but then, obviously, not being the referent of an observation term would have no bearing on the ontological status of Aunt Mamie or that of snow.

Perhaps it is intended that the referents of observation terms must be members of a *kind* some of whose members have been observed or instances of a *property* some of whose instances have been observed. But there are familiar difficulties here. For example, given any entity, we can always find a kind whose only member is the entity in question; and surely expressions such as 'men over 14 feet tall' should be counted as observational even though no instances of the "property" of being a man over 14 feet tall have been observed. It would seem that this approach must soon fall back upon some notion of simples or determinables vs. determinates. But is it thereby saved? If it is held that only those terms which refer to observed simples or observed determinates are observation terms, we need only remind ourselves of such instances as Hume's notorious missing shade of blue. And if it is contended that in order to be an observation term an expression must at least refer to an observed determinable, then we can always find such a determinable which is broad enough in scope to embrace any entity whatever. But even if these difficulties can be circumvented, we see (as we knew all along) that this approach leads inevitably into phenomenalism, which is a view with which we have not been concerning ourselves.

Now it is not the purpose of this essay to give a detailed critique of phenomenalism. For the most part, I simply assume that it is untenable, at least in any of its translatability varieties.[7] However, if there are any unreconstructed phenomenalists among the readers, my purpose, insofar as they are concerned, will have been largely achieved if they will grant what I suppose most of them would stoutly maintain anyway, i.e., that theoretical entities are no worse off than so-called observable physical objects.

Nevertheless, a few considerations concerning phenomenalism and related matters may cast some light upon the observational-theoretical dichotomy and, perhaps, upon the nature of the "observation language." As a preface, allow me some overdue remarks on the latter. Although I have contended that the line between the observable and the unobservable is diffuse, that it shifts from one scientific problem to another, and that it is constantly being pushed toward the "unobservable" end of the spectrum as we develop better means of observation—better instruments—it would, nevertheless, be fatuous to minimize the importance of the observation base, for it is absolutely necessary as a confirmation base for statements which do refer to entities which are unobservable at a given time. But we should take as its basis and its unit not the "observational term" but, rather, the quickly decidable sentence. (I am indebted to Feyerabend, *loc. cit.,* for this terminology.) A quickly decidable sentence (in the technical sense employed here) may be defined as a singular, nonanalytic sentence such that a reliable, reasonably sophisticated language user can very quickly decide[8] whether to assert it or deny it when he is reporting on an occurrent situation. 'Observation term' may now be defined as a 'descriptive (nonlogical) term which may occur in a quickly decidable sentence,' and 'observation sentence' as a 'sentence whose only descriptive terms are observation terms.'

Returning to phenomenalism, let me emphasize that I am not among those philosophers who hold that there are no such things as sense contents (even sense data), nor do I believe that they play no important role in our perception of "reality." But the fact remains that the referents of most (not all) of the statements of the linguistic framework used in everyday life and in science are *not* sense contents but, rather, physical objects and other publicly observable entities. Except for pains, odors, "inner states," etc., *we do not usually observe sense contents*; and although there is good reason to believe that they play an indispensable role in observation, *we are usually not aware of them when we visually* (or tactilely) observe physical objects. For example, when I observe a distorted, obliquely reflected image in a mirror, I may seem to be seeing a baby elephant standing on its head; later I discover it is an image of Uncle Charles taking a nap with his mouth open and his hand in a peculiar position. Or, passing my neighbor's home at a high rate of speed, I observe that he is washing a car. If asked to report these observations I could quickly and easily report a baby elephant and a washing of a car; I probably would not, without subsequent observations, be able to report what colors, shapes, etc. (i.e., what sense data) were involved.

Two questions naturally arise at this point. How is it that we can (sometimes) quickly decide the truth or falsity of a pertinent observation sentence? and, What role do sense contents play in the appropriate tokening of such sentences? The heart of the matter is that these are primarily scientific-theoretical questions rather than "purely logical," "purely conceptual," or "purely epistemological." If theoretical physics, psychology, neuro-physiology, etc., were sufficiently advanced, we could give satisfactory answers to these questions, using, in all likelihood, the physical-thing language as our observation language and *treating sensations, sense contents, sense data, and "inner states" as theoretical* (yes, theoretical!) *entities.*[9]

It is interesting and important to note that, even before we give completely satisfactory answers to the two questions considered above, we can, with due effort and reflection, train ourselves to "observe directly" what were once theoretical entities — the sense contents (color sensations, etc.) — involved in our perception of physical things. As has been pointed out before, we can also come to observe other kinds of entities which were once theoretical. Those which most readily come to mind involve the use of instruments as aids to observation. Indeed, using our painfully acquired theoretical knowledge of the world, we come to see that we "directly observe" many kinds of so-called theoretical things. After listening to a dull speech while sitting on a hard bench, we begin to become poignantly aware of the presence of a considerably strong gravitational field, and as Professor Feyerabend is fond of pointing out, if we were carrying a heavy suitcase in a changing gravitational field, we could observe the changes of the $G\mu\nu$ of the metric tensor.

I conclude that our drawing of the observational-theoretical line at any given point is an accident and a function of our physiological makeup, our current state of knowledge, and the instruments we happen to have available and, therefore, that it has no ontological significance whatever. . . .

NOTES

1. E. Nagel, *The Structure of Science* (New York: Harcourt, Brace, and World, 1961), Ch. 6.

2. For the genesis and part of the content of some of the ideas expressed herein, I am indebted to a number of sources; some of the more influential are H. Feigl, "Existential Hypotheses," *Philosophy of Science,* 17: 35–62 (1950); P. K. Feyerabend, "An Attempt at a Realistic Interpretation of Experience," *Proceedings of the Aristotelian Society,* 58: 144–170 (1958); N. R. Hanson, *Patterns of Discovery* (Cambridge: Cambridge University Press, 1958); E. Nagel, *loc. cit*; Karl Popper, *The Logic of Scientific Discovery* (London: Hutchinson, 1959); M. Scriven, "Definitions, Explanations, and Theories," in *Minnesota Studies in the Philosophy of Science,* Vol. II, H. Feigl, M. Scriven, and G. Maxwell, eds. (Minneapolis: University of Minnesota Press, 1958); Wilfrid Sellars, "Empiricism and the Philosophy of Mind," in *Minnesota Studies in the Philosophy of Science,* Vol. I, H. Feigl and M. Scriven, eds. (Minneapolis: University of Minnesota Press, 1956), and "The Language of Theories," in *Current Issues in the Philosophy of Science,* H. Feigl and G. Maxwell, eds. (New York: Holt, Rinehart, and Winston, 1961).

3. I have borrowed the hammer analogy from E. Nagel, "Science and [Feigl's] Semantic Realism," *Philosophy of Science,* 17: 174–181 (1950), but it should be pointed out that Professor Nagel makes it clear that he does not necessarily subscribe to the view which he is explaining.

4. G. Bergmann, "Outline of an Empiricist Philosophy of Physics," *American Journal of Physics,* 11: 248–258; 335–342 (1943), reprinted in *Readings in the Philosophy of Science,* H. Feigl and M. Brodbeck, eds. (New York: Appleton-Century-Crofts, 1953), pp. 262–287.

5. I am not attributing to Professor Bergmann the absurd views suggested by these questions. He seems to take a sense-datum language as his observation language (the base of what he called "the empirical hierarchy"), and, in some ways, such a position is more difficult to refute than one which purports to take an "observable-physical-object" view. However, I believe that demolishing the straw men with which I am now dealing amounts to desirable preliminary "therapy." Some nonrealist interpretations of theories which embody the presupposition that the observable-theoretical distinction is sharp and ontologically crucial seem to me to entail positions which correspond to such straw men rather closely.

6. For arguments that it is possible to alter a theory without altering the meanings of its terms, see my "Meaning Postulates in Scientific Theories," in *Current Issues in the Philosophy of Science,* Feigl and Maxwell, eds.

7. The reader is no doubt familiar with the abundant literature concerned with this issue. See, for example, Sellars' "Empiricism and the Philosophy of Mind," which also contains references to other pertinent works.

8. We may say "noninferentially" decide, provided this is interpreted liberally enough to avoid starting the entire controversy about observability all over again.

9. Cf. Sellars, "Empiricism and the Philosophy of Mind." As Professor Sellars points out, this is the crux of the "other-minds" problem. Sensations and inner states (relative to an intersubjective observation language, I would add) are theoretical entities (and they "really exist") and *not* merely actual and/or possible behavior. Surely it is the unwillingness to countenance theoretical entities—the hope that every sentence is translatable not only into some observation language but into the physical-thing language—which is responsible for the "logical behaviorism" of the neo-Wittgensteinians.

17

Is There a Significant Observational-Theoretical Distinction?

Carl A. Matheson and A. David Kline

Introduction

Twentieth-century philosophy of science has been dominated by efforts to develop and criticize the two-tier conception of scientific theories.[1] Given the most optimistic prognosis the view was dead by 1970 and seriously ill for at least a decade prior to that. Nevertheless the view still has profound effects. Much of the now fashionable debates over scientific progress and realism/ anti-realism get their wind from the critique of the two-tier conception and the lack of a well developed, coherent alternative story.

At the quick of the old view is an observational-theoretical distinction. This essay will be concerned with two very important questions: (1) What led to the demise of the observational-theoretical distinction? Our concern will not be so much with detailed criticisms but rather structural defects. We want to show how the distinction did not realize the goals that motivated it. (2) How does the distinction spawn the realism/anti-realism controversy? Furthermore given its demise what is left of the controversy? More particularly, section I gives a standard way of making the distinction plus an account of what motivates it. In section II it is shown how the distinction plus the framework that motivates it leads to what we call the "old" realism issue. After the critique of the distinction in section III, we show in section IV how the "new" realism issue is born. In the final section some general remarks are made on what is left of the distinction. Does it retain any philosophical importance?

I

Defenders of the two-tier conception begin with an intuitive or pre-analytical belief that terms such as "desk" and "brown" are importantly different from "electron" and "valence." Surprisingly little effort has been spent on developing a careful criterion for making the distinction. The following by Carl Hempel is an instance of a common and very influential way of making the distinction:

> In regard to an observational term it is possible, under suitable circumstances, to decide by means of direct observation whether the term does or does not apply to a given situation. . . . Theoretical terms, on the other hand, usually purport to refer to not directly observable entities and their characteristics.[2]

What are "suitable" circumstances? How are we to understand "direct observation"? It is not plausible to think that the logical empiricists were unaware of these difficulties. Their lack of effort in sharpening the criterion can perhaps be attributed to the belief that, no matter how the distinction finally gets put, there will be the issue of how observational and theoretical terms are related. Furthermore this latter issue is more suitably investigated by the methods of the philosopher.[3]

Rather than rehearse ways of formulating the observational-theoretical distinction, we shall consider the more fruitful and fundamental issues that motivate the distinction. There are in fact three interrelated motivations. They concern issues pertaining to meaning, justification, and theory comparison.

The explanans of adequate explanations must have empirical significance. Consider the following example:

> Why has the water cooled after being placed over a flame then removed? "The water had initially been deprived of its glubbification through action of the flame (which generally has this effect); removed from the flame, it has become increasingly glubbified again and hence cooler, in accordance with the general principle that glubbification varies inversely with warmth."[4]

One suspects that the problem with the above is deeper than that some of the claims are merely false. They lack meaning or significance. This sort of case would not stump anyone but, more interestingly, violations of meaning occur in serious science.

Bishop Berkeley, an eighteenth-century divine and philosopher, had a number of worries about the physics of his day.

> In works on motion by more recent and sober thinkers of our age, not a few terms of somewhat abstract and obscure signification are used, such as *solicitation of gravity, urge, dead forces,* etc., terms which darken writings in other respects very learned, and beget

opinions at variance with truth and the common sense of men.
These terms must be examined with great care. . . .[5]

Without being so arrogant as to actually doubt the significance of some of the claims of contemporary physics or psychology, we might ask what provides for the significance of talk about charm and attenuators. More generally what provides for the meaningfulness of theoretical discourse?

Logical empiricism provides a general answer.

> It is a basic principle of contemporary empiricism that a sentence makes a cognitively significant assertion, and thus can be said to be true or false, if and only if either (1) it is analytic or contradictory—in which case it is said to have purely logical meaning or significance—or else (2) it is capable, at least potentially, of test by experiential evidence—in which case it is said to have empirical meaning or significance.[6]

Notice that the empiricist account of meaningfulness connects issues of meaning with issues of knowledge or justification. We can now see clearly what motivates a sharp observational-theoretical distinction. In contrast to what is problematic, i.e., theoretical discourse, observation reports or statements appear to be transparently meaningful in virtue of their obvious openness to testing.[7] The project for the philosopher will be to connect the observational components of a theory, by some to be specified relation, with the theoretical components in order to insure the testability and hence meaningfulness of the latter. This is precisely the project of the two-tier conception of science. It all rests on exploiting the supposed virtues of the observational domain.

Another motivation concerns providing a framework in which theory comparison is possible. If T and T^* are to be compared, we must find some implication of T, say I, for which T^* implies I or the negation of I. It must be the case that (i) I has the same meaning for proponents of T and T^*, otherwise I and its negation would not be contradictory, and (ii) the truth or falsity of I must be determinable independently of T and T^*, otherwise the testing procedure would be circular. Furthermore, we want the proponents of T and T^* to be able to come to agreement about the truth or falsity of I and hence the truth or falsity of T and T^*. A sharp observational-theoretical dichotomy would solve all these problems. The truth of observation sentences is easily determinable independently of any theory.

II

As we saw in section I, a goal of the traditional conception of theories is to specify the meaning of the theoretical in terms of the observational vocabulary. In other words, we must specify a relation, R, between the terms comprising the observational and theoretical vocabularies. The history of efforts to specify *R* is very rich. Two importantly different formulations are crucial for setting the context for the "old" realism issue.

Consider a theoretical term, *T*, e.g., "fragile." According to the *explicit definition* account of *R*, necessary and sufficient conditions should be given for the application of *T* in observation terms. Those conditions, to continue the example, may be in terms of "being sharply struck" and "breaking." More precisely consider the following definition:

Object, *O*, is fragile.
If and only if
O is sharply struck, then *O* will break

Given this account of *R*, what should we say about the reality of theoretical entities? Let us begin with the view that seems to be embedded in common sense:

> REALISM: (i) Theoretical sentences have truth values, i.,e., they are either true or false and (ii) theoretical terms can refer to un-observable properties and entities.

If we ask whether theories that require explicit definitions are to be interpreted realistically, the answer is no. But we need to be careful here. Since theoretical talk summarizes observational talk or functions as a shorthand for observational talk, theoretical sentences like the observational sentences they summarize, have a truth value. But theoretical terms do not refer to nonobservables. They in fact refer to observables or relations among observables. To use another example, we might try to define "electric current" in terms of the meter readings of a galvanometer. There is no unobservable entity or property, electric current, but rather talk of electric current is a way to simplify a good deal of talk about observables. Let us call the interpretation of theories generated from the insistence upon explicit definitions, *reductionism*. Reductionism is a species of anti-realism.

There are two fundamental difficulties with explicit definition as an account of *R*. First consider the sample definition for "fragile." On standard inter-pretations of logic the if-then or conditional sentence is true in those cases where the antecedent is false. That is, if *O* is *not* sharply struck the whole conditional is true. The disastrous consequence of this is that if *O* is not struck, *O* is fragile given our definition of fragile. Crowbars and properly cooked linguine, as long as they are not struck, will be fragile.

Secondly, if additional explicit definitions are given for "fragile" we will have to regard them, given that they provide necessary and sufficient conditions, as defining new concepts. Since this will hold for all theoretical terms and since many theoretical terms are given multiple definitions, concepts will proliferate at a dizzying rate. Put another way, a description of scientific practice does not reveal a proliferation of concepts for each observationally different way of indicating the application of a term; therefore, the explicit definition procedure does not reflect scientific practice. Even putting scientific practice aside, the methodological virtue of simplicity seems to rule out explicit definitions as a general procedure.

Given the above criticisms, an effort was made to provide an improved specification of *R*. The requirement of giving a necessary condition for the application of a given theoretical term was dropped. Consider the form of the new *partial definitions* on our old example of fragility:

If object *O* is sharply struck,
then
O breaks if and only if *O* is fragile.

Partial definitions immediately repair the defects of explicit definitions: no longer does every definition define a new concept and it is not the case that every unstruck object is fragile.

What commitment to unobserved entities does this account encourage? The commonly held view is that partial interpretation is consistent both with a realist and an instrumentalist interpretation.[8]

> METAPHYSICAL INSTRUMENTALISM: (i) Theoretical sentences do not have a truth value, (ii) theoretical terms can not refer to unobservable properties or entities, and (iii) theories are sets of rules or algorithms for making predictions.

On an instrumentalist interpretation, one should speak of theories being adequate or inadequate, more or less useful, but not true or false. Instrumentalism is a species of anti-realism.

Instrumentalism, it is thought, does not follow merely from the partial interpretation specification of *R*. Some additional argument is needed: for example, the fact that most of the theoretical concepts of science are highly idealized or that without blushing, incompatible theories are employed for the same subject. A liquid may be regarded as a set of discrete particles for one purpose and as a continuous medium for another. We are not insisting that these are good arguments. They are simple examples of considerations that have pushed people to instrumentalism.[9]

Despite the received wisdom here, we believe that partial interpretation by itself encourages instrumentalism. After all, explicit definitions are historically and perhaps logically the ideal fulfillment of the empiricist program. Once one buys into specifying the meaning of terms by test conditions, can one really pull back from demanding explicit definitions? It does not seem that just giving sufficient conditions for the application of a term is sufficient for determining the reference of the term. But if the terms have no reference, how can the sentences containing them have a truth value? They appear to be meaningless. Hence instrumentalism. Even if we granted that the meaning of a term is partially specified by a partial definition, this would allow for experimental conditions in which there is no truth of the matter as to whether the term applies or not—again, albeit a modified, instrumentalism.

There are difficulties with the partial interpretation specification of R, but to consider them would take us too far afield. The task of this section was to indicate how the "old" realism/anti-realism issue is a consequence of the specification of R. Recall that the need to specify R was a result of the strict observational-theoretical distinction. Theoretical talk, unlike its counterpart observational, is suspect. There is an opening to raise questions about the reality of the entities that seem to be mentioned by theoretical discourse.

III

We want to turn to efforts to criticize the observational-theoretical dichotomy. The most popular form of criticism has been to challenge particular ways of *drawing* the distinction. Challenges have been of two importantly different species. An example of one species is Peter Achinstein's critique of Carnap's formulation according to which observation terms designate observable properties and relations whereas theoretical terms designate unobservable properties and relations.[10] Achinstein points out that according to the ordinary use of 'observe', scientists can observe electrons passing through a cloud chamber. Let us call this species of objection one from linguistic usage. There are a number of such objections in the literature, none of which are particularly persuasive. The reason is that the logical empiricists are not trying to formulate a distinction that necessarily fits ordinary or scientific usage. They are willing to deviate from ordinary usage to achieve a reconstruction of science that is philosophically sound.

The second type of challenge takes a particular way of drawing the distinction and shows that in its own terms it does not parse the terms of science in the way the proponent of the distinction had in mind. In fairness to Achinstein there is a way to read his criticism along the second line. "Look, you haven't told me what you mean by 'observe'. All I've got to go on is the ordinary usage. On that usage electrons turn out to be observable—a result that you do not want. If you have some technical sense of 'observe' let's hear it. Then we can see if it parses terms like you want." This is clearly a more powerful objection. It takes a proponent's distinction and shows that in its own terms it does not achieve the desired goals.

There is a considerable body of literature challenging given ways of drawing the distinction.[11] The account mentioned in section I in terms of "direct observation" has been the subject of much criticism. Unfortunately, even when of the second species, these critiques fail to end the matter, for one always wonders whether with a little work the distinction could be put more successfully.

Rather than repeat specific challenges, we want to turn to two different sorts of critiques. They are aimed at undermining the motivation for the distinction. One of those motivations concerned the epistemological transparency of observational discourse. This motivation is doubly important in that the meaningfulness of discourse was thought to be parasitic upon its epistemological status. Is the observational epistemologically privileged and in what way? There is a philosophical program that made strong claims for the observational—it provides a class of sentences whose truth or falsity could be determined with certainty.

It should be immediately clear that what we would normally classify as an observational matter fails to meet the condition of certainty. According to our everyday use of the term 'observable', a barn is observable: that I see a barn counts as an observational truth. However, as Descartes and many others have shown, I *could* be wrong about any observational report. What I see could be no more than a barn facade. Worse, I could be hallucinating or dreaming. There is no certainty to be had here. We must look elsewhere for the observational basis. With the concept of a sense-datum, the basis is located inside the mind of the observer.

According to proponents of sense datum theory, a sense-datum is what one is really aware of when one makes an observation. In a sense, the man who sees real pink elephants at the animal decoration center and the drunkard who merely hallucinates them, are not seeing the same thing. The drunkard is not seeing anything in the world. He is merely falsely believing himself to do so. But in another sense, what they see is the same: both of them have the same mental images and it is that similar pair of mental images that leads to their similar utterances of "I see pink elephants." A sense-datum statement, then is just a report of that internal mental state.

The proponents of sense-datum theory go on to say that, while we can be wrong in our perceptual reports of the outside world, we simply cannot be wrong in our sense-datum reports. If I think I see pink elephants, there may be no pink elephants out there in the world, but I must have pink-elephant sense data. Supposedly, sense-datum reports are infallible. They are known with certainty. As such, they and they alone provide the proper realm of the observational.

Sense-datum reports, of course, will not provide one wing of an observational-theoretical distinction that mimics anything in common talk or scientific practice. But they do seem to help secure a class of sentences that could accomplish the philosophical purposes of empiricism. The reports claim epistemic privilege in a strong and clear way.

Unfortunately matters have not gone well for the sense-datum theory. An immediate problem concerns getting from sense-datum reports to claims about ordinary objects. We do want to talk about dogs and chairs. How is such talk related to sense-datum talk? Some relation not unlike our previous *R*, will have to be specified to bridge the gap. It has not proved to be the case that statements about ordinary objects can be captured by (translated into) sense-datum statements alone.

But there is a much less technical difficulty. Recall that the reason we are interested in sense-datum reports is that they are supposedly knowable with certainty: if I think that I am having a pink square sense-datum, then I must be having one. However, an examination of the nature of sense data might cause us to doubt this claim. For instance suppose that the sense-datum in question is the mental image. Then, the sense-datum report will be a sentence (or perhaps belief) about that image. As such, the report presupposes an *interpretation* of the datum. Suppose I have a mental image consisting of fifteen green spots, but due to an unfortunate inability to count properly, I acquire the belief that I have a fourteen-spotted sense-datum. My mistake came through my interpretation. Whenever there is an interpretation, there is a possibility of mistake.

The observational-theoretical distinction is supposed to capture an important epistemological difference. Sense-datum theory fails as an effort to show what is privileged about the observational. Interestingly there is no serious alternative to sense-datum theory as an account of what is privleged about the observational. If there is an important epistemological difference we need a convincing story about it. (See section V.)

Let us examine the final motivation for a strict observational-theoretical distinction, viz., theory comparison. If we are to compare T and T^* we must find some implications of the theories whose truth or falsity can be determined *independently* of the truth of the theories. This seems to be part of what is meant by a fair, impartial or objective test. We do not ask Nancy Reagan for an assessment of some of her husband's actions in order to test President Reagan's "theory" of the Iran arms deal. We suspect that Nancy and Ron hold the same theory and assess events in terms of it. The truth of the assessment is not independent of the theory, or so we think.

Observation is alleged to provide a theory-neutral framework for testing theories. The most penetrating critique of this idea comes from Norwood Hanson.[12] Hanson begins by asking whether the famous observational astronomer Tycho Brahe and Johannas Kepler saw the *same thing* when they looked east at dawn. (They held very different theories, the Ptolemaic and Copernican views respectively.) According to a popular account, the sensory core theory, they do see the same thing. Seeing involves (i) having a sense datum and (ii) interpreting the sense datum. So seeing an apple is having a reddish, heart shaped, pushed-in-on-the-bottom datum and interpreting it as an apple. Brahe and Kepler both see the sun in the east but they may have different interpretations—the sun rising or the earth rotating.

Hanson has a number of criticisms of the sensory core theory. He appeals to psychological evidence to question seeing as a two-stage process. In seeing one does not experience the two stages. One simply sees. Interpretation takes time. It makes sense to talk about being half done. But seeing is, at least as experienced, instantaneous.

Yet these sorts of considerations and others like them are not the quick of Hanson's objection. Hanson confronts the sensory core theory with a dilemma: If seeing the same thing comes down to having the same sense-datum, seeing in that sense is irrelevant to science. If seeing is such that it is relevant to science, it is theory-laden. But then theory-laden seeing is not the neutral observation that the proponents of the observational-theoretical distinction wanted. It is not capable of solving the issue of theory comparison as they conceive it.

Let's consider the horns of the dilemma in more detail. To be relevant to science in this context, we mean being relevant to the testing of a scientific theory. Theories, ontologically, are sets of statements. It is statements that can come into logical relationships with theories. Now Hanson can admit that Brahe and Kepler have a number of similar physiological states, e.g., they have similar patterns of retinal stimulation. But, of course, having these patterns is not seeing in any interesting sense even though they may be necessary for seeing. Physiological states strictly speaking are irrelevant to theories. Physiological states and theories are from different incomparable categories. It will not help to bring in sense-data or any other kind of entity. To get something that will bear on scientific theories it must have a propositional form.

Turning to the second horn, an example of observation or seeing relevant to science is the following: John *sees that* the paper turned blue. "That the paper turned blue" is potentially relevant to testing theories. But Hanson is quick to point out that what one can "see that" is dependent upon one's theories. What true propositions are produced in seeing depends upon what one knows. One person might see that something turned red. Another person might see that the driver in front is putting on his brakes. Walking into a physics museum a child might see that a hunk of glass and metal is in the case. You mght see that there is an old-fashioned X-ray tube in the case. The crucial point is that what we see depends on our theories. So we have no theory-neutral seeing. One might be tempted to fall back on sense-data at this point. Remember even if in some sense they are neutral, they are of no use to science until interpreted—until one brings theory to them.

We believe that Hanson's arguments destroy the sensory core theory in particular and quests for theory-neutral observation in general. In so far as the observational-theoretical distinction was motivated by finding a set of theory-independent statements, it is motivated by something that cannot be had.

A serious question remains: Given that observation is theory-laden, can theories be rationally compared? If theory-neutral observations are required, we are in trouble. Perhaps we can grant theory-ladenness and still show how theory comparison is rationally possible.

For instance, the fact that our observational terms are theory-laden does not mean that they are laden in a significant way with the higher-level theories to which we attach them. Why should it not be possible for two very different fundamental theories of the world to *share* their observational sub-theories? We might be able to think of our theories of the observable world as modules that can be transported whole from one theory to another. If two theories share the same observational sub-theory, then their observational claims can be compared. If they are not (or cannot be) united with the same observational sub-theory, then they cannot be compared. Thus, it may be that theory-comparison is possible but not guaranteed. In other words:

> (i) Because of the theory-ladenness of observation, it may be impossible *in certain cases* to compare different scientific theories on the basis of observation.

However, according to certain philosophers, the situation is much worse than (i) might indicate. According to Paul Feyerabend, the definition of a term is fixed by its role in a theory. Thus, the definition of "mass" as it occurs in Newtonian mechanics is given by *everything* that Newtonian mechanics has to say about mass. If a theory were to give "mass" even a slightly different role, then that theory would be working with a different definition of mass. For example, according to Newtonian mechanics, the mass of an object is a constant that does not depend the object's speed; however, mass is dependent on velocity in special relativity. Therefore, Feyerabend infers that "mass" differs in meaning across the two theories. It follows from this that terms related to "mass," like "force" and "energy," will differ in meaning across the two theories as well. In fact, given the all-pervasive interconnections between terms in theories, it becomes at least plausible to say that any change in a theory will lead to a change in meaning of all of that theory's terms. However, if the terms of the earlier theory do not mean the same as the terms in the later theory, then there is no sense in which the two theories agree or disagree, either observationally or not. And, if there is no sense in which they can be said to agree or disagree, then there seems to be no sense in which they can be rationally compared. Hence, if Feyerabend's theory is true, it seems that theoretical comparison is impossible.[13] Instead of (i), we are left with:

> (ii) Because of the theory-ladenness of observation, it is impossible to compare different scientific theories on the basis of observation.

Both (i) and (ii) pose problems for the philosopher of science. The very idea of science seems to depend on the idea of objectivity, the idea that we can rationally compare our scientific theories. If objectivity and rational theory choice are impossible, then the adoption of a scientific theory threatens to be no more than an arbitrary whim, reflecting no more than the prejudices of a moment, culture, or political viewpoint. The term "scientific knowledge" becomes a cruel irony and a badge of naivete for those who persist in using it. Clearly the threat is much worse given (ii) than (i). If we can never compare theories, then no rational theory choice seems possible. However, the threat is not completely dispelled by (i); the possibility of important but inadjudicable disputes remains. Regardless of whether we accept (i) or (ii), our conception of scientific progress will be challenged. And, it seems that Hanson's arguments for the theory-ladenness of observation leave us no other alternatives.

IV

Do Hanson's claims also have effects on the realism debate? The best answer is that they might. They do have one definite negative effect. With his arguments for the theory-ladenness of observation, Hanson lays to rest the idea that the observational-theoretical distinction is metaphysically or ontologically important. We had already rejected the idea that we could build an adequate theory of meaning that placed observational terms at its foundations. We had also given up the idea that observational statements provided a crucial link between truth and knowledge once we found that we could be wrong about them, too. Hanson's arguments lead us to believe that the mere existence of observational terms does not allow us to take the comparability of our scientific theories for granted. Therefore, there seems to be absolutely no motivation remaining for worrying about unobservable objects and theoretical statements in particular. If there is nothing particularly special about observable objects and observational terms, then we should not ask questions like "Do unobservables exist in the same way as observables?" and "Should we (and can we) build a theory of meaning according to which the meaning of non-observational terms is parasitic on observational ones?" We might as well ask questions like "Do gophers exist in the same sense as whales?" and "Can we interpret our cutlery talk in terms of our major kitchen appliance vocabulary?" Divisions without an underlying metaphysical motive usually don't have any metaphysical import.

It may seem that, taken together, the attacks on the observational-theoretical distinction send anti-realism into bankruptcy. Appearances can be misleading. If anything, they have caused a metaphysical boom. To see how this could be, notice that the realist's task was to make everything else as safe as observation. Since we found out that observation was not all that safe, in a sense, the realist succeeded: everything else *was* as safe as observation. But instead of securing all of our theories on the firm rock of observation, we found out that the "rock" was made of cork and was placidly floating along with us. All of the questions that we believed to apply to the nonobservational realm turned out to apply to everything. Where we used to ask about the sense in which nonobservational sentences were true, we must now ask about the nature of truth in general. Where we used to ask the ways in which unobservables could be said to exist, we must now ask about the way in which anything exists.

Hanson's arguments add some spice to these problems. Suppose that you endorse one theory and I another. Further, suppose that observational terms are theory-laden to a degree that makes rational theory comparison impossible. In such a situation we could draw one of the following morals about the nature of truth:

> RELATIVISM: There is no such thing as *the* truth. Instead, the notion of truth should be regarded as relative to one's basic theoretical standpoint. Where "Waves exist" may be true-for-you, it may not

be true-for-me; and, there is no final standpoint outside of our way
of looking at things that can transcend our theoretical prisons.

Relativism is plausible as long as we believe that truth is something that
we can find out. Once we grant this, if you and I have an irreconcilable
difference, one for which there is no objective and rational solution, then
neither of us could be either simply right or simply wrong. However, if we
reject the claim that the truth must be discoverable, we will not be forced
into relativism. Instead we might embrace something else.

SKEPTICISM: Whatever our rational practices do, there is not
much reason to think that they take us towards the truth.

Since there are rationally inadjudicable disputes between ways of thinking,
we may be locked into a way of thinking from which there is no rational
road to the truth. In a way, this position saves the notion of objective truth
only to make it useless. Because of this, the skeptic who wishes to maintain
that we do science rationally cannot base rationality on truth. For the skeptic,
the concept of truth would eventually drop out of his account of the practice
and goals of science.

It seems that even limited theory-ladenness—i.e., claim (i) of the previous
section—generates some interesting possibilities for the nature of truth and
existence. But notice how strange things would be if theory-ladenness were
complete and all-pervasive, that is, if (ii) were true rather than (i). The resulting
skepticism would be total, for there would never be any way to move rationally
from one theory to a successor theory. Furthermore, if we took the other
route, the form of relativism we would end up with would be startling:

CONVENTIONALISM: What is true is entirely a matter of stipulation. Different theories are just different decisions on how to use
theoretical terms. We can never rationally compare theories.

Conventionalism represents relativism taken to its logical limit. Where the
relativist says that there are limits to what rationality can do, the conventionalist
says that there is nothing that rationality can do. The conventionalist might
look for other mechanisms that underly theory change. Perhaps it reflects
rationally unmotivated shifts in the attitude of the population as a whole.
For instance, it has been argued that the shift to quantum mechanics should
not be understood as a rational scientific transition so much as an effect of
Weimar Germany's disaffection with a mechanistic and deterministic world
view, a view that they credited for taking Germany into the First World War.[14]
Perhaps scientific change reflects something more political than cognitive:
Michel Foucault has argued that one can best understand the birth of psychiatry
and the modern concept of insanity in terms of the state's need to control
a huge population.[15] Whatever, theoretical change neither reflects a convergence

upon universal truth nor the embodiment of a universal rationality.

The debates concerning these positions are sometimes maddening but they are always fascinating. However, we could not begin to follow them out in this paper. Instead we have just tried to show the sorts of realism debate that arise from the weakening of the observational-theoretical distinction. There is no doubt that these are very different from the relatively tame one about the status of theoretical terms. The varieties of anti-realism described above attack a much more cherished realism, the belief that there is one reality, one truth, where that truth is to be discovered by human beings, not invented by them.

V

We have seen that the observational-theoretical distinction fails to do the things that it was intended to do. It does not give us a way of explicating all scientific language. It does not provide us with a totally solid ground for all of our knowledge. And, it does not provide us with a sure way of objectively comparing all of our scientific theories. The distinction seems to be no more than a measure of our physiological limitations. The boundary of the distinction represents no more than the limits of our sensations: what is observable is what we can see or hear without the aid of instruments. What possible strength or importance could such a distinction have?

First, now that we realize what the distinction has turned out to be, it is difficult to argue that the distinction has any bearing on the question of what exists or what the concept of truth is: that our sensory limitations should delimit the class of things that exist is simply ludicrous. But, that does not mean that the distinction cannot play a very important role in our analysis of how we know things. In other words, although the distinction is almost certainly metaphysically barren, it may still retain some epistemological strength. None of the arguments that we have reviewed have attacked the position that observational statements are epistemically privileged. There are successful arguments against the position that observational statements are so privileged that they are certain. However, we can reject the certainty of observational statements without also rejecting the claim that they are somehow special.

What could this specialness amount to, given that certainty is ruled out? It would have to amount to our being more justified in our observational beliefs than in our nonobservational ones. In the final section of this paper we are going to determine whether there are good arguments for saying that observational statements are special. For the moment, let us suppose that they are, so that we can discuss the sort of anti-realism that can arise out of a purely epistemological distinction. It is a purely epistemological form of anti-realism, but it makes strong claims nevertheless:

EPISTEMOLOGICAL INSTRUMENTALISM: Although we can have justified beliefs (and know) about the observable realm, we cannot come to know about the unobservable realm.

Note the great difference between epistemological instrumentalism and the form of instrumentalism we discussed earlier. Where, according to the old instrumentalism, nonobservational terms do not refer and nonobservational statements do not say anything, the epistemological instrumentalist says that they can and do have truth values: it is just that we can never find out what those truth values are. The two forms of instrumentalism agree about the scientific role of nonobservational statements, which are held to be important only insofar as they lead to theories that are true at the observational level. It follows from this that the two forms of instrumentalism also agree on the goal of science. We do not do science in order to find the fundamental unobservable truth that will explain the world of experimental phenomena. We do science in order to control and predict the observable world. Thus, the realist that the epistemological instrumentalists take themselves to be opposing is someone who not only believes that nonobservational statements have truth values but also someone who believes both that these statements are knowable and that coming to know them constitutes a main goal of science.[16]

Again, it is not our goal to determine whether epistemological empiricism is true, but only to ascertain the relevance of the observational-nonobservational distinction for it. Although epistemological instrumentalism does not require the strongest of distinctions, it does require one for which observational statements are much more privileged than nonobservational ones. After all, epistemological instrumentalists do not merely hold that, in general, our observational beliefs are more justified than our nonobservational ones. They hold that our nonobservational beliefs are *never* justified. What feature of our observational beliefs (short of certainty) could serve as a foundation for this claim. In short, what epistemological strength does the distinction really have?

Despite the above brand of anti-realism receiving enormous attention, even its proponents have not drawn the needed distinction in a perspicuous way. We want to provide the best argument we can for a distinction that could form the basis for epistemological instrumentalism. But the distinction will be interesting in its own right if it illuminates the pre-analytical epistemological difference between the observational and the theoretical.

We could try this as a distinction: a state (i.e., the ball being red) is observable just in case there is a reliable way that could be used for finding out whether the state obtains without the use of measuring instruments. For example, if there is a red ball around us we can set up certain conditions; we can open our eyes and turn the lights on. Given those conditions, there is a reliable connection between the ball being red and our being in a certain sort of sensory state. In other words, the ball being red registers on our sensory apparatus.[17]

From this it follows that not all states are observable. However, some that are not *observable* may be *detectable:* a state (the electron having an energy of –13.6 ev) is detectable just in case we have a reliable way of finding out whether the state obtains, where this may involve the use of measuring instruments. If the electron has an energy of –13.6 ev, then we can set up our experimental apparatus so that there is a reliable connection between the electron's having that energy and our apparatus' being in a certain observable state. If the electron has a certain energy, then our experimental apparatus will show a reading of –13.6 in nice big red numbers. This reading is observable; it will register on our sensory apparatus.[18]

But, if this is the sense of observable that we are left with, then what motivation could there be for epistemological instrumentalism? It seems that observation and detection both provide us with reliable ways of finding out about the world. As such, we should conclude that if we know about observable states then we know about unobservable but detectable states as well. To answer this question we have to give a further specification of what's supposed to be reliable. Take the electron case as an example. We set up our experimental apparatus. Given the fact that our experimental apparatus is set up as a background condition, it seems that the electron will have an energy of –13.6 ev in exactly those cases where our apparatus reads –13.6. But there are other conditions that have to be met in order for our test to be foolproof. The one that we want to concentrate on is the condition that basic electron theory is true. We can't rule out the possibility of another globally different view of the world that talks about completely different sorts of entities.[19] Someone who holds that theory could describe conditions that didn't involve electrons but which, if met, would entail that the apparatus would read –13.6. Thus although the combination of electron theory and experimental set up guarantees our meter reading, our meter reading does not guarantee the existence of electrons. The fact that electrons may be detectable doesn't necessarily give us good reasons to believe in the existence of electrons.

Perhaps defenders of epistemological instrumentalism believe that the situation is different in the case of observable states. Observing that my dog has fleas does give me good reasons for believing in fleas. This raises a question: can there be different accounts of the observable world *alone* each of which by its own lights is completely observationally accurate? Epistemological instrumentalism requires that observing be immune to the underdetermination that infects detection.

We are not completely convinced that the alleged asymmetry of underdetermination exists. The issue is presently an area of active discussion.

Conclusion

Here is a summary of our results: (1) The observational-theoretical distinction does not do the jobs for which it was originally intended. It does not guarantee us a sound philosophy of language, the possibility of scientific comparison, or a body of epistemologically transparent statements. As such, even if there is a significant distinction, it will not be one that will make the metaphysical status of unobservables problematic.

(2) Given the breakdown of the unobservable as a metaphysical haven, the metaphysical problems that were originally thought to concern only unobservables and statements about them can now be seen to concern all entities and statements. Our worries are now global ones about truth and existence in general. There is no special reason to worry about the existence of theoretical objects.

(3) If there is any significance to the observational-theoretical distinction, it will be epistemological. However, no definitive arguments have been given for its significance; and if it is significant, it may still not be strong enough to support the claim that we do know about observables but not about unobservables.[20]

NOTES

1. For a detailed exposition and critique of the two-tier view see Frederick Suppe, *The Structure of Scientific Theories* (Urbana: University of Illinois Press, 1974). The essay by Carnap in the present volume is an example of the view.

2. Carl Hempel, "The Theoretician's Dilemma" in *Aspects of Scientific Explanation* (New York: Macmillan, 1965), pp. 178–79.

3. This seems to be the position of Rudolf Carnap in his paper "Testability and Meaning," *Philosophy of Science,* 3 (1936):420–71.

4. The example is from Israel Scheffler, *The Anatomy of Inquiry* (New York: Alfred A. Knopf, 1969), p. 127.

5. George Berkeley, *De Motu* in *Berkeley's Philosophical Writings,* ed. David Armstrong (New York: Macmillan, 1965), p. 251.

6. Carl Hempel, "Empiricist Criteria of Cognitive Significance: Problems and Changes," in *Aspects of Scientific Explanation,* p. 101.

7. Observational statements are statements whose non-logical terms are observation terms.

8. Frederick Suppe, *The Structure of Scientific Theories,* p. 30.

9. See Ernest Nagel, *The Structure of Science* (New York: Harcourt, Brace and World, 1961), pp. 129–140.

10. Peter Achinstein, *Concepts of Science* (Baltimore: The Johns Hopkins Press, 1968), p. 160.

11. See the essays by Putnam and Maxwell in this volume and Peter Achinstein, *Concepts of Science,* pp. 157–78.

12. See the essay by Hanson in this volume.

13. P. K. Feyerabend, "Explanation, Reduction and Empiricism" in *Scientific Explanation, Space and Time, Minnesota Studies in the Philosophy of Science,* Vol. III, ed. by H. Feigl and G. Maxwell (Minneapolis: University of Minnesota Press, 1962), pp. 28–97.

14. P. Forman, "Weimar Culture, Causality and Quantum Theory" in *Historical Studies in the Physical Sciences,* ed. by R. McCormmach (Philadelphia: University of Pennsylvania Press, 1971), pp. 1–115.

15. Michel Foucault, *The Birth of the Clinic* (New York: Vintage Books, 1975).

16. For an example of what we are calling epistemological instrumentalism see Bas C. Van Fraassen, *The Scientific Image* (Oxford: Clarendon Press, 1980).

17. This way of making the distinction is only meant to be suggestive. One needs to put what counts as the use of a measuring device in a precise way. On the present view, seeing that an electron is moving to the left by seeing a jet of smoke in a cloud chamber would

be by using a measuring device.

18. A rigorous way of making the distinction between observation and detection in an alternative vocabulary is Fred Dretske's distinction between primary and secondary seeing. Fred Dretske, *Seeing and Knowing* (Chicago: University of Chicago Press, 1969).

19. For an introductory discussion of this possibility see Rudolf Carnap, *An Introduction to the Philosophy of Science,* ed. by M. Gardner (New York: Basic Books, 1966), Chap. 15.

20. More material on the relevance of the history of the observational-theoretical debate for the evolution of types of realism can be found in Carl Matheson, *Does Scientific Realism Matter,* dissertation, Syracuse University, 1986.

STUDY QUESTIONS FOR PART 3

1. Why can not theoretical terms be explicitly defined in observation terms?
2. What is Carnap's distinction between empirical and theoretical laws?
3. What is the nature of Carnap's continuum of observation? Is it similar to the continuum of observation for which Maxwell argues?
4. Putnam claims that the observational-theoretical dichotomy was intended as an explicative not a stipulative distinction. Discuss whether he is correct.
5. Consider Carnap's way of making the observational-theoretical dichotomy. Do Putnam's efforts to show the dichotomy broken-backed (A-D) succeed?
6. Suppose one tried to defend the claim that there is a sense in which two scientists see the same thing by citing the fact that they have the same retinal images. What does Hanson find wrong with this?
7. Here is another defense of the claim above. Try to state precisely what Hanson's objections are to it. "Surely all normal observers, when looking at the same thing, see the same thing. They have the same visual sense-data. Their differences are not in what they see but in the way they interpret what they see."
8. Hanson admits that "wherever it makes sense to say that two scientists looking at X do not see the same thing, there must always be a prior sense in which they do see the same thing." Sometimes he spells out the prior sense by saying that they must be *visually aware* of the same object. Why isn't this just to grant the point of those who Hanson is arguing against?
9. Try to state some of the consequences of Hanson's view for the standard observational-theoretical distinction.
10. Recently, when driving along the Interstate, I heard a thumping sound and made a causal inference to the car having a flat tire. I was right, unfortunately. Notice that initially I did not directly perceive the flat tire but made an inference to it from something I did directly perceive. What is the difference between this example and the kind of inference scientists supposedly make to electrons, and so on? Surely my inference is innocent enough but, according to Stace, the scientist's is not. How come?
11. Stace does not believe that theoretical entities exist. But he seems to believe that theoretical statements are true. Why? What does he think it is for a statement to be true?
12. Why do scientists, according to Stace, insist on thinking that forces, electrons, and so on, exist? Try to evaluate his argument.

SELECTED BIBLIOGRAPHY

[1] Churchland, P. *Scientific Realism and the Plasticity of Mind.* Cambridge: Cambridge University Press, 1979. [Argues for a version of scientific realism and against the importance of the observational-theoretical distinction.]

[2] Dretske, F. *Seeing and Knowing.* Chicago: University of Chicago Press, 1969. [Relevant to understanding observation; intermediate level.]

[3] Eddington, A. *The Nature of the Physical World.* New York: Cambridge University Press, 1929, pp. ix-xiii, 282-289. [A super-realist.]

[4] Grandy, R., ed. *Theories and Observation in Science.* Englewood Cliffs, N.J.: Prentice-Hall, 1973. [Classical essays on the two-tier conception of scientific theories and its problems.]

[5] Gutting, G. "Philosophy of Science." In *The Synoptic Vision,* ed. by F. Delaney et al. Notre Dame, Ind.: University of Notre Dame Press, 1977, pp. 73-86. [Overview of W. Sellars's super-realism; will guide one to the Sellars literature.]

[6] Harre, R. *The Philosophies of Science.* Oxford: Oxford University Press, 1972, chap. 3. [Nice examples of theories; elementary.]

[7] Hempel, C. *Philosophy of Natural Science.* Englewood Cliffs, N.J.: Prentice-Hall, 1966, chap 6. [Basic survey of field.]

[8] Holton, G., and Roller, D. *Foundations of Modern Physical Science.* Reading, Mass.: Addison-Wesley, 1958. [An introduction to physics written by a physicist and a historian of science; only requires high school algebra; good examples of theories.]

[9] Kuhn, T. *The Structure of Scientific Revolutions.* Chicago: University of Chicago Press, 1962. [An exciting work that has received enormous attention; presents an account of theories, observation (similar to Hanson's) and theory change; views are developed by way of historical examples.]

[10] Leplin, J., ed. *Scientific Realism.* Berkeley: University of California Press, 1984. [Contemporary essays on scientific realism.]

[11] Nagel, E. *The Structure of Science.* New York: Harcourt, Brace and World, 1961, chaps. 5 and 6. [An excellent discussion of the status of unobservables.]

[12] Suppe, F. *The Structure of Theories.* Urbana, Ill.: University of Illinois Press, 1977. [Detailed description of the standard view of theories, plus a review of all the work critical of the standard view; excellent bibliography; intermediate level.]

Part 4

Confirmation and Acceptance

Part 4: Confirmation and Acceptance

Introduction

I. The Problem

In Parts 2 and 3, we addressed the structure of explanations and theories. In this part, the concern will be with how we justify our belief in a particular explanation or theory. Since hypotheses or lawlike statements are at the heart of both explanations and theories, the discussion will center on their justifications.

We are often told that scientists justify their hypotheses by comparing them to the facts or seeing how they fare in the face of the facts. There is a certain truth in this, though as with most slogans it is a misleading oversimplification. A purpose of the orienting remarks that follow is to make and motivate some of the bold distinctions to which a sensitive theory of justification must attend.

II. Confirmation

The following are examples of hypotheses:
- (a) Lead melts at 327° C.
- (b) Myelinated A-fibers transmit signals at 100 meters/second.
- (c) The price of goods is inversely proportional to the demand for the goods.
- (d) The pressure of a gas times the volume of the gas is a constant ($PV = c$ or $P_1/P_2 = V_2/V_1$).

How do scientists justify their belief (or disbelief) in (a)-(d)? Of course, they give reasons for their belief.

A place to begin in order to understand this reason-giving process is a distinction between two basic kinds of reasons: (i) epistemic reasons, (ii) practical reasons. Epistemic reasons count toward the truth or falsity of a hypothesis.

Practical reasons do not bear on truth or falsity but rather on the usefulness of believing the hypothesis.

Consider the hypothesis that your next-door neighbor is madly in love with you. That she gives you gifts and winks at you as you leave for classes is an epistemic reason for believing the hypothesis.

Suppose further that you have an incredible inferiority complex. Unless you believe that people will greet you with open arms, you simply cannot face them at all. Furthermore, suppose that you wish very much to meet your neighbor. Now these facts about your psychology and goals are reasons for believing the hypothesis, but not epistemic reasons. They do not count toward the truthfulness of the hypothesis, but they make it useful for you to believe the hypothesis.

Later in this essay, the distinction above will be put to work. But, at least at the outset, it is not unreasonable to think that scientists offer epistemic reasons for (a)-(d). But what reasons?

In example (a), intuitively 'that this piece of lead melted at 327° C' is an epistemic reason for believing (a). Typically it is called a confirming instance. A hypothesis that has the form of our (a), viz., everything that is A is B, has four types of instances: this thing is A and B, this thing is A and not B, this thing is not A and B, this thing is not A and not B. Members of the first type are confirming instances; members of the second type are disconfirming instances.

So far then, a hypothesis is justified by appeal to epistemic reasons where epistemic reasons are confirming instances of the hypothesis. Even though a certain amount of jargon has been introduced, what has been said is fairly commonsensical. In fact it seems to be what is behind the slogans that initiated the discussion. But notice that, even supposing what has been said is beyond doubt, it is vague at some crucial points.

We spelled out the meaning of 'instance' for a hypothesis of the form 'Everything that is A is B.' But what about hypotheses of other forms such as (c) or (d)? A similar account of 'instance' is needed for these and hypotheses of other forms. Though this will require a little formal sophistication there are no obvious theoretical problems in the way.

The second vague spot belies a deeper issue. Though we gave examples of *confirming* and *disconfirming* instances we did not define these notions. A careful reader might have noticed that we were conspicuously silent on how to understand 'this thing is not A and B' and 'this thing is not A and not B.'

One worry can be simply put. A hypothesis of the form 'Everything that is A is B' is logically equivalent to a hypothesis of the form 'Everything that is not B is not A.' If you think that 'this A is a B' confirms the first hypothesis, as surely you must, then by parity of reasoning 'this thing is not B and not A' ought to confirm the latter. Since the two hypotheses are logically equivalent it seems reasonable that 'This thing is not B and not A' should also confirm 'Everything that is A is B.' But then 'that this wax melts at 100° C' would confirm 'all lead melts at 327° C.'[1]

There are further paradoxes but we need not pursue any of these.[2] The purpose of our reconnaissance is to spot pockets of resistance, not necessarily to eliminate them.

Suppose we could, with a little philosophical tenacity, define confirming (disconfirming) instances. Our theory of justification is far from complete. Just as one birdie does not a good round of golf make, though it surely helps, one confirming instance does not a hypothesis justify, though it counts toward the justification. We have been discussing what philosophers call qualitative features of confirmation—that is, defining *a* confirming instance. There are also quantitative features of confirmation.

An example will illustrate these features. The eighteenth-century chemist Robert Boyle is credited with discovering the law expressed in (d). He justified the hypothesis by providing the reader with the following data. In the first column, *A*, are values for the volume of a gas. In the second column, *B*, are the corresponding experimentally determined values for the pressure.

A	B	C
48	29 2/16	29 2/16
46	30 9/16	30 6/16
44	31 15/16	31 12/16
42	33 8/16	33 1/7
40	35 5/16	35
38	37	36 15/19
36	39 5/16	38 7/8
34	41 10/16	41 2/17
32	44 3/16	43 11/16
30	47 1/16	46 3/5
28	50 5/16	50
26	54 5/16	53 10/13
24	58 13/16	58 2/8
23	61 5/16	60 18/23
22	64 1/16	63 6/11
21	67 1/16	66 4/7
20	70 11/16	70
19	74 2/16	73 11/19
18	77 14/16	77 2/3
17	82 12/16	82 4/17
16	87 14/16	87 3/8
15	93 1/16	93 1/5
14	100 7/16	99 6/7
13	107 13/16	107 7/13
12	117 9/16	116 4/8

Boyle justifies his hypothesis not by a single confirming instance but by a set of confirming instances. Furthermore, he does not give us repeated measurements corresponding to a row in the chart but measures the pressure and volume over a range of values. Column C is also significant. If one plugs in V_1 and V_2, and P_1 and computes P_2 according to (d), he will discover a difference between the computed values for P_2 and the experimentally determined values. C gives the expected values. The differences are so slight that Boyle was willing to chalk them up to human error and defects in the experimental apparatus.[3]

This example brings out clearly that certain quantitative features of confirmation are relevant to the justification of a hypothesis. As a rule of thumb—the larger the quantity, the more diverse; and the more accurate the confirming instances, the greater the justification for the hypothesis.

Though this rule is surely correct, at least as a rough rule, it does not pass without inducing philosophical perplexity. How accurately must the "confirming instances" conform to the expected data in order to be *confirming* rather than disconfirming? How many instances are required before one can reasonably assert the truth of the hypothesis?

So far we have seen that a theory of justification must contain a theory of confirmation. Furthermore, one must distinguish qualitative aspects of confirmation from the quantitative aspects. There is one final feature of confirmation that needs to be sketched.

The distinction between observational and theoretical hypotheses, putting aside the difficulties in precisely drawing the distinction, is well known. The sample lawlike statements (a)-(d) are a subclass of observation statements. One important consequence of this is that the instances of these hypotheses can be known by observation in a fairly direct way. One can simply see if this piece of lead melts at 327° C. But with theoretical hypotheses this will not be true.

Some simple examples of theoretical hypotheses follow:

(e) All electrons have a charge of minus one.

(f) The weight of the "sea of air" surrounding the earth exerts a pressure on objects within the sea.

(g) The current density for any point within a conductor equals the reciprocal of the resistance of the conductor times the applied electrical field or
$$j = \frac{1}{p} E.$$

The problem presented by theoretical hypotheses is not that they do not have instances, but rather since their instances cannot be directly known by observation one cannot in any straightforward way "compare the hypothesis to the facts."

Theoretical hypotheses are tested by deducing a test implication from the hypothesis and observing whether the test implication is true or not. If it is true, it is said to confirm the hypothesis; otherwise disconfirm. To distinguish these "instances" from the confirming and disconfirming instances let us call them confirming or disconfirming test implications.

Continuing our pneumatic examples, consider (f). Torricelli, a precursor of Boyle, deduced a number of test implications from the hypothesis. On one particularly impressive case he reasoned as follows: If (f) is true, then the pressure on objects at the top of a mountain ought to be less than on objects in the mountain's valley, since the column of air pushing on them would be less. So if (f) is true, then a barometer should read less on the top of a mountain than on the bottom. He tried this out and found a spectacular confirming test implication. The general structure of Torricelli's reasoning or the successful justification of a theoretical hypothesis can be represented by the following schema: (H = hypothesis; TI = test implication)

(s) if H then TI

TI

Therefore, H is confirmed.

The disconfirmation schema looks like this:

(t) if H then TI

not TI

Therefore, H is disconfirmed.

Just as quantitative considerations are important in justifying observational hypotheses, so are they in justifying theoretical hypotheses. The quantity and diversity and accuracy of test implications are again relevant. Torricelli strengthened his case by just such considerations.

One final point about confirmation must be made. There is a dissimilarity between (s) and (t). (S) is not a valid argument form. Hence from the premises of (s) it is fallacious to conclude that H is true. This point is marked by claiming only that H is supported or confirmed. H *could* turn out to be false, though in so far as TI is the case, one has some reason to believe that H is true.

Since schema (t) is valid, it looks like one ought to be able to conclude not just that H is disconfirmed but that H is false. Given what has been said, that would be the correct conclusion. But the assumption that (t) captures the structure of disconfirmation is an oversimplification.

The actual form of the first premise of (t), and for that matter (s), is (n) if H and A_1 and A_2 and . . . A_n, then TI.

A_1, A_2, etc. are auxiliary hypotheses—hypotheses assumed when it is claimed that H implies TI. For example, Torricelli was at least assuming that the pressure on the surface of a liquid is transferred through the liquid and that one can veridically observe the height of mercury through a glass barrier, i.e., that glass does not have some systematic distorting effects that will make it look as though the mercury has not risen when it really has. Contemporary philosophers believe that the first premise will always contain auxiliary hypotheses.

If one is more realistic about the first premise of (t), then formally the conclusion is: Therefore, H is false or A_1 is false or A_2 is false or . . . A_n is false. In other words, if we substitute (n) for the first premise of (t), then as a matter of pure logic alone one has a reason to conclude that at least one of H-A_n is false, but he has no reason to pick out a particular false statement from this set.

This point of this discussion of schema (t) is to show that just as confirmation does not prove that H is true, disconfirmation does not prove that H is false.

On the assumption that the needed auxiliary hypotheses are highly confirmed the appropriate conclusion from (t) is that *H* has been disconfirmed, not found false.

II. Acceptance

There is a difference between having reasons that count toward the truth or falsity of a hypothesis and the acceptance of a hypothesis as true or the rejection of a hypothesis as false. During the Watergate hearings, most people would admit that testimony was given that counted toward the truth of the statement, "Nixon is a liar." Yet many of these people would not accept the statement as true.

Acceptance as usually understood is a broader notion than confirmation. Part of the reason for the acceptance or rejection of a hypothesis is the extent to which it has been confirmed or disconfirmed. But many philosophers have thought that there are additional criteria for acceptance or rejection. The following are often mentioned candidates: (a) the simplicity of a hypothesis, (b) the theoretical fecundity of a hypothesis, (c) the compatibility of a hypothesis with certain moral, political, or religious views, (d) the harm incurred if one's decision to accept or reject a hypothesis is mistaken.

We have already seen some hints as to what motivates the need for additional criteria. By way of confirmation and disconfirmation one cannot *prove* that a hypothesis is true or false. Of course, quantitative features are relevant, but when has one observed enough test implications or when are the test results accurate enough? There are further problems. When evaluating a given hypothesis, various quantitative features may be at odds, for example, as the variety of test implications increases the accuracy may decrease. It is also often the case that for a given hypothesis that is to explain certain phenomena there will be alternative hypotheses that are equally well confirmed and explain the same phenomena.

We shall briefly summarize the readings momentarily, but first some general questions to keep in mind when evaluating the importance of additional criteria such as (a)-(d). (1) From the scientific point of view, should *practical reasons* have anything to do with the acceptance of a hypothesis? (2) Of the additional criteria suggested, which are epistemic and which are practical? (3) Is it really the business of the scientist as a scientist to *accept* hypotheses? (The paper by R. Rudner in Part 5 will help here.)

III. The Readings in Part 4

In the essay "Hypothesis," W. V. Quine and J. S. Ullian list six virtues of a hypothesis. It is not clear whether some of these are fancy ways of talking about confirmation or whether they are additional criteria. You will have to evaluate each one individually.

Quine and Ullian have a lengthy discussion of simplicity. Simplicity is the additional criterion most often mentioned by philosophers. Try to decide whether it is an epistemic or a practical reason for acceptance. This essay has some arguments on the matter.

Giere's essay is a careful treatment of the confirmation of theoretical hypotheses. He provides some nice examples of theories which should help make sense of this somewhat formal topic. It might prove useful to compare Giere's treatment to that mentioned briefly in the introduction to this part.

The essays by Kuhn and Frank deal with what we have called additional criteria of acceptance. Kuhn wishes to emphasize the difference between argumentation in mathematics and argumentation in science. A consequence of the differences is, according to Kuhn, that two scientists can disagree about which of two competing hypotheses to accept, after a "complete" effort at confirmation, yet both scientists have good reasons for their views. Supposing Kuhn is correct, what does it tell us about the nature of the additional criteria?

Frank insists that, historically, such factors as compatibility with religious views have been decisive in which hypothesis is accepted. Furthermore, given how he understands theoretical talk, viz., instrumentally, he does not find such factors improper, or unscientific. In fact, Frank seems to support the use of these criteria.

In Carl Hempel's essay some deep issues are raised about the philosophy of science itself. Is the philosopher describing scientific practice or giving a normative account of how science should ideally be done? Kuhn claims that in his work he is doing both. Hempel finds this joint task puzzling and is trying to see in what sense, if any, it is coherent.

A.D.K.

NOTES

1. See Hempel's "Studies in the Logic of Confirmation" in [1] of the bibliography for Part 4.

2. See Goodman's "The New Riddle of Induction" in [2] of the bibliography for Part 4.

3. For the historical and logical details of Boyle's work, see "Robert Boyle's Experiments in Pneumatics" in *Harvard Case Histories in Experimental Science,* ed. by J. Conant and L. Nash. Vol. 1. Cambridge, Mass.: Harvard University Press, 1948. pp. 1-64.

18

Hypothesis

W. V. Quine and J. S. Ullian

Some philosophers once held that whatever was true could in principle be proved from self-evident beginnings by self-evident steps. The trait of absolute demonstrability, which we attributed to the truths of logic in a narrow sense and to relatively little else, was believed by those philosophers to pervade all truth. They thought that but for our intellectual limitations we could find proofs for any truths, and so, in particular, predict the future to any desired extent. These philosophers were the rationalists. Other philosophers, a little less sanguine, had it that whatever was true could be proved by self-evident steps from two-fold beginnings: self-evident truths and observations. Philosophers of both schools, the rationalists and the somewhat less sanguine ones as well, strained toward their ideals by construing self-evidence every bit as broadly as they in conscience might, or somewhat more so.

Actually even the truths of elementary number theory are presumably not in general derivable, we noted, by self-evident steps from self-evident truths. We owe this insight to Godel's theorem, which was not known to the old-time philosophers.

What then of the truths of nature? Might these be derivable still by self-evident steps from self-evident truths together with observations? Surely not. Take the humblest generalization from observation: that giraffes are mute, that sea water tastes of salt. We infer these from our observations of giraffes and sea water because we expect instinctively that what is true of all observed samples is true of the rest. The principle involved here, far from being self-evident, does not always lead to true generalizations. It worked for the giraffes and the sea water, but it would have let us down if we had inferred from a hundred observations of swans that all swans are white.

Such generalizations already exceed what can be proved from observations and self-evident truths by self-evident steps. Yet such generalizations are still only a small part of natural science. Theories of molecules and atoms are not related to any observations in the direct way in which the generalizations about giraffes and sea water are related to observations of mute giraffes and salty sea water.

It is now recognized that deduction from self-evident truths and observation is not the sole avenue to truth nor even to reasonable belief. A dominant further factor, in solid science as in daily life, is *hypothesis*. In a word, hypothesis is guesswork; but it can be enlightened guesswork:

It is the part of scientific rigor to recognize hypothesis as hypothesis and then to make the most of it. Having accepted the fact that our observations and our self-evident truths do not together suffice to predict the future, we frame hypotheses to make up the shortage.

Calling a belief a hypothesis says nothing as to what the belief is about, how firmly it is held, or how well founded it is. Calling it a hypothesis suggests rather what sort of reason we have for adopting or entertaining it. People adopt or entertain a hypothesis because it would explain, if it were true, some things that they already believe. Its evidence is seen in its consequences. . . .

Hypothesis, where successful, is a two-way street, extending back to explain the past and forward to predict the future. What we try to do in framing hypotheses is to explain some otherwise unexplained happenings by inventing a plausible story, a plausible description or history of relevant portions of the world. What counts in favor of a hypothesis is a question not to be lightly answered. We may note five virtues that a hypothesis may enjoy in varying degrees.

Virtue I is *conservatism*. In order to explain the happenings that we are inventing it to explain, the hypothesis may have to conflict with some of our previous beliefs; but the fewer the better. Acceptance of a hypothesis is of course like acceptance of any belief in that it demands rejection of whatever conflicts with it. The less rejection of prior beliefs required, the more plausible the hypothesis—other things being equal.

Often some hypothesis is available that conflicts with no prior beliefs. Thus we may attribute a click at the door to arrival of mail through the slot. Conservatism usually prevails in such a case; one is not apt to be tempted by a hypothesis that upsets prior beliefs when there is no need to resort to one. When the virtue of conservatism deserves notice, rather, is when something happens that cannot evidently be reconciled with our prior beliefs.

There could be such a case when our friend the amateur magician tells us what card we have drawn. How did he do it? Perhaps by luck, one chance in fifty-two; but this conflicts with our reasonable belief, if all unstated, that he would not have volunteered a performance that depended on that kind of luck. Perhaps the cards were marked; but this conflicts with our belief that he had had no access to them, they being ours. Perhaps he peeked or pushed, with help of a sleight-of-hand; but this conflicts with our belief in our perceptiveness. Perhaps he resorted to telepathy or clairvoyance; but this would wreak havoc with our whole web of belief. The counsel of conservatism is the sleight-of-hand.

Conservatism is rather effortless on the whole, having inertia in its favor. But it is sound strategy too, since at each step it sacrifices as little as possible of the evidential support, whatever that may have been, that our overall system of beliefs has hitherto been enjoying. The truth may indeed be radically remote from our present system of beliefs, so that we may need a long series of conservative steps to attain what might have been attained in one rash leap. The longer the leap, however, the more serious an angular error in the direction. For a leap in the dark the likelihood of a happy landing is severely limited. Conservatism holds out the advantages of limited liability and a maximum of live options for each next move.

Virtue II, closely akin to conservatism, is *modesty.* One hypothesis is more modest than another if it is weaker in a logical sense: if it is implied by the other, without implying it. A hypothesis *A* is more modest than *A* and *B* as a joint hypothesis. Also, one hypothesis is more modest than another if it is more humdrum: that is, if the events that it assumes to have happened are of a more usual and familiar sort, hence more to be expected.

Thus suppose a man rings our telephone and ends by apologizing for dialing the wrong number. We will guess that he slipped, rather than that he was a burglar checking to see if anyone was home. It is the more modest of the two hypotheses, butterfingers being rife. We could be wrong, for crime is rife too. But still the butterfingers hypothesis scores better on modesty than the burglar hypothesis, butterfingers being rifer.

We habitually practice modesty, all unawares, when we identify recurrent objects. Unhesitatingly we recognize our car off there where we parked it, though it may have been towed away and another car of the same model may have happened to pull in at that spot. Ours is the more modest hypothesis, because staying put is a more usual and familiar phenomenon than the alternative combination.

It tends to be the counsel of modesty that the lazy world is the likely world. We are to assume as little activity as will suffice to account for appearances. This is not all there is to modesty. It does not apply to the preferred hypothesis in the telephone example, since Mr. Butterfingers is not assumed to be a less active man than one who might have plotted burglary. Modesty figured there merely in keeping the assumptions down, rather than in actually assuming inactivity. In the example of the parked car, however, the modest hypothesis does expressly assume there to be less activity than otherwise. This is a policy that guides science as well as common sense. It is even erected into an explicit principle of mechanics under the name of the law of least action.

Between modesty and conservatism there is no call to draw a sharp line. But by Virtue I we meant conservatism only in a literal sense—conservation of past beliefs. Thus there remain grades of modesty still to choose among even when Virtue I—compatibility with previous beliefs—is achieved to perfection; for both a slight hypothesis and an extravagant one might be compatible with all previous beliefs.

Modesty grades off in turn into Virtue III, *simplicity*. Where simplicity considerations become especially vivid is in drawing curves through plotted points on a graph. Consider the familiar practice of plotting measurements. Distance up the page represents altitude above sea level, for instance, and distance across represents the temperature of boiling water. We plot our measurements on the graph, one dot for each pair. However many points we plot, there remain infinitely many curves that may be drawn through them. Whatever curve we draw represents our generalization from the data, our prediction of what boiling temperatures would be found at altitudes as yet untested. And the curve we will choose to draw is the simplest curve that passes through or reasonably close to all the plotted points.

There is a premium on simplicity in any hypothesis, but the highest premium is on simplicity in the giant joint hypothesis that is science, or the particular science, as a whole. We cheerfully sacrifice simplicity of a part for greater simplicity of the whole when we see a way of doing so. Thus consider gravity. Heavy objects tend downward: here is an exceedingly simple hypothesis, or even a mere definition. However, we complicate matters by accepting rather the hypothesis that the heavy objects around us are slightly attracted also by one another, and by the neighboring mountains, and by the moon, and that all these competing forces detract slightly from the downward one. Newton propounded this more complicated hypothesis even though, aside from tidal effects of the moon, he had no means of detecting the competing forces; for it meant a great gain in the simplicity of physics as a whole. His hypothesis of universal gravitation, which has each body attracting each in proportion to mass and inversely as the square of the distance, was what enabled him to make a single neat system of celestial and terrestrial mechanics.

A modest hypothesis that was long supported both by theoretical considerations and by observation is that the trajectory of a projectile is a parabola. A contrary hypothesis is that the trajectory deviates imperceptibly from a parabola, constituting rather one end of an ellipse whose other end extends beyond the center of the earth. This hypothesis is less modest, but again it conduces to a higher simplicity: Newton's laws of motion and, again, of gravitation. The trajectories are brought into harmony with Kepler's law of the elliptical orbits of the planets.

Another famous triumph of this kind was achieved by Count Rumford and later physicists when they showed how the relation of gas pressure to temperature could be accounted for by the impact of oscillating particles, for in this way they reduced the theory of gases to the general laws of motion. Such was the kinetic theory of gases. In order to achieve it they had to add the hypothesis, by no means a modest one, that gas consists of oscillating particles or molecules; but the addition is made up for, and much more, by the gain in simplicity accruing to physics as a whole.

What is simplicity? For curves we can make good sense of it in geometrical terms. A simple curve is continuous, and among continuous curves the simplest are perhaps those whose curvature changes most gradually from point to point. When scientific laws are expressed in equations, as they so often are, we can make good sense of simplicity in terms of what mathematicians call the degree of an equation, or the order of a differential equation. This line was taken by Sir Harold Jeffreys. The lower the degree, the lower the order, and the fewer the terms, the simpler the equation. Such simplicity ratings of equations agree with the simplicity ratings of curves when the equations are plotted as in analytical geometry.

Simplicity is hard to define when we turn away from curves and equations. Sometimes in such cases it is not to be distinguished from modesty. Commonly a hypothesis *A* will count as simpler than *A* and *B* together; thus far simplicity and modesty coincide. On the other hand the simplicity gained by Newton's hypothesis of universal gravitation was not modesty, in the sense that we have assigned to that term; for the hypothesis was not logically implied by its predecessors, nor was it more humdrum in respect of the events that it assumed. Newton's hypothesis was simpler than its predecessors in that it covered in a brief unified story what had previously been covered only by two unrelated accounts. Similar remarks apply to the kinetic theory of gases.

In the notion of simplicity there is a nagging subjectivity. What makes for a brief unified story depends on the structure of our language, after all, and on our available vocabulary, which need not reflect the structure of nature. This subjectivity of simplicity is puzzling, if simplicity in hypotheses is to make for plausibility. Why should the subjectively simpler of two hypotheses stand a better chance of predicting objective events? Why should we expect nature to submit to our subjective standard of simplicity?

That would be too much to expect. Physicists and others are continually finding that they have to complicate their theories to accommodate new data. At each stage, however, when choosing a hypothesis subject to subsequent correction, it is still best to choose the simplest that is not yet excluded. This strategy recommends itself on much the same grounds as the strategies of conservatism and modesty. The longer the leap, we reflected, the more and wilder ways of going wrong. But likewise, the more complex the hypothesis, the more and wilder ways of going wrong; for how can we tell which complexities to adopt? Simplicity, like conservatism and modesty, limits liability. Conservatism can be good strategy even though one's present theory be ever so far from the truth, and simplicity can be good strategy even though the world be ever so complicated. Our steps toward the complicated truth can usually be laid out most dependably if the simplest hypothesis that is still tenable is chosen at each step. It has even been argued that this policy will lead us at least asymptotically toward a theory that is true.

There is more, however, to be said for simplicity: the simplest hypothesis often just is the likeliest, apparently, quite apart from questions of cagy strategy. Why should this be? There is a partial explanation in our ways of keeping score on predictions. The predictions based on the simpler hypotheses tend to be scored more leniently. Thus consider curves, where simplicity comparisons are so clear. If a curve is kinky and complex, and if some measurement predicted from the curve turns out to miss the mark by a distance as sizable as some of the kinks of the curve itself, we will count the prediction a failure. We will feel that so kinky a curve, if correct, would have had a kink to catch this wayward point. On the other hand, a miss of the same magnitude might be excused if the curve were smooth and simple. It might be excused as due to inaccuracy of measurement or to some unexplained local interference. This cynical doctrine of selective leniency is very plausible in the case of the curves. And we may reasonably expect a somewhat similar but less easily pictured selectivity to be at work in the interest of the simple hypotheses where curves are not concerned.

Considering how subjective our standards of simplicity are, we wondered why we should expect nature to submit to them. Our first answer was that we need not expect it; the strategy of favoring the simple at each step is good anyway. Now we have noted further that some of nature's seeming simplicity is an effect of our bookkeeping. Are we to conclude that the favoring of simplicity is entirely our doing, and that nature is neutral in the matter? Not quite. Darwin's theory of natural selection offers a causal connection between subjective simplicity and objective truth in the following way. Innate subjective standards of simplicity that make people prefer some hypotheses to others will have survival value insofar as they favor successful prediction. Those who predict best are likeliest to survive and reproduce their kind, in a state of nature anyway, and so their innate standards of simplicity are handed down. Such standards will also change in the light of experience, becoming still better adapted to the growing body of science in the course of the individual's lifetime. (But these improvements do not get handed down genetically.)

Virtue IV is *generality*. The wider the range of application of a hypothesis, the more general it is. When we find electricity conducted by a piece of copper wire, we leap to the hypothesis that all copper, not just long thin copper, conducts electricity.

The plausibility of a hypothesis depends largely on how compatible the hypothesis is with our being observers placed at random in the world. Funny coincidences often occur, but they are not the stuff that plausible hypotheses are made of. The more general the hypothesis is by which we account for our present observation, the less of a coincidence it is that our present observation should fall under it. Hence, in part, the power of Virtue IV to confer plausibility.

The possibility of testing a hypothesis by repeatable experiment presupposes that the hypothesis has at least some share of Virtue IV. For in a repetition of an experiment the test situation can never be exactly what it was for the earlier run of the experiment; and so, if both runs are to be relevant to the hypothesis, the hypothesis must be at least general enough to apply to both test situations.[1] One would of course like to have it much more general still.

Virtues I, II, and III made for plausibility. So does Virtue IV to some degree, we see, but that is not its main claim; indeed generality conflicts with modesty. But generality is desirable in that it makes a hypothesis interesting and important if true.

We lately noted a celebrated example of generality in Newton's hypothesis of universal gravitation, and another in the kinetic theory of gases. It is no accident that the same illustrations should serve for both simplicity and generality. Generality without simplicity is cold comfort. Thus take celestial mechanics with its elliptical orbits, and take also terrestrial mechanics with its parabolic trajectories, just take them in tandem as a bipartite theory of motion. If the two together cover everything covered by Newton's unified laws of motion, then generality is no ground for preferring Newton's theory to the two taken together. But Virtue II, simplicity, is. When a way is seen of gaining great generality with little loss of simplicity, or great simplicity with no loss of generality, the conservatism and modesty give way to scientific revolution.

The aftermath of the famous Michelson-Morley experiment of 1887 is a case in point. The purpose of this delicate and ingenious experiment was to measure the speed with which the earth travels through the ether. For two centuries, from Newton onward, it had been a well entrenched tenet that something called the ether pervaded all of what we think of as empty space. The great physicist Lorentz (1853–1928) had hypothesized that the ether itself was stationary. What the experiment revealed was that the method that was expected to enable measurement of the earth's speed through the ether was totally inadequate to that task. Supplementary hypotheses multiplied in an attempt to explain the failure without seriously disrupting the accepted physics. Lorentz, in an effort to save the hypothesis of stationary ether, shifted to a new and more complicated set of formulas in his mathematical physics. Einstein soon cut through all this, propounding what is called the special theory of relativity.

This was a simplification of physical theory. Not that Einstein's theory is as simple as Newton's had been; but Newton's physics had been shown untenable by the Michelson-Morley experiment. The point is that Einstein's theory is simpler than Newton's as corrected and supplemented and complicated by Lorentz and others. It was a glorious case of gaining simplicity at the sacrifice of conservatism; for the time-honored ether went by the board, and far older and more fundamental tenets went by the board too. Drastic changes were made in our conception of the very structure of space and time. . . .

Yet let the glory not blind us to Virtue I. When our estrangement from the past is excessive, the imagination boggles; genius is needed to devise the new theory, and high talent is needed to find one's way about in it. Even Einstein's revolution, moreover, had its conservative strain; Virtue I was not wholly sacrificed. The old physics of Newton's classical mechanics is, in a way, preserved after all. For the situations in which the old and the new theories would predict contrary observations are situations that we are not apt to encounter without sophisticated experiment—because of their dependence on exorbitant velocities or exorbitant distances. This is why classical mechanics held the field so long. Whenever, even having switched to Einstein's relativity theory, we dismiss those exorbitant velocities and distances for the purpose of some practical problem, promptly the discrepancy between Einstein's theory and Newton's becomes too small to matter. Looked at from this angle, Einstein's theory takes on the aspect not of a simplification but a generalization. We might say that the sphere of applicability of Newtonian mechanics in its original simplicity was shown, by the Michelson-Morley experiment and related results, to be less than universal; and then Einstein's theory comes as a generalization, presumed to hold universally. Within its newly limited sphere, Newtonian mechanics retains its old utility. What is more, the evidence of past centuries for Newtonian mechanics even carries over, within these limits, as evidence for Einstein's physics; for, as far as it goes, it fits both.

What is thus illustrated by Einstein's relativity is more modestly exemplified elsewhere, and generally aspired to: the retention, in some sense, of old theories in new ones. If the new theory can be so fashioned as to diverge from the old only in ways that are undetectable in most ordinary circumstances, then it inherits the evidence of the old theory rather than having to overcome it. Such is the force of conservatism even in the context of revolution.

Virtues I through IV may be further illustrated by considering Neptune. That Neptune is among the planets is readily checked by anyone with reference material; indeed it passes as common knowledge, and there is for most of us no need to check it. But only through extensive application of optics and geometry was it possible to determine, in the first instance, that the body we call Neptune exists, and that it revolves around the sun. This required not only much accumulated science and mathematics, but also powerful telescopes and cooperation among scientists.

In fact it happens that Neptune's existence and planethood were strongly suspected even before that planet was observed. Physical theory made possible the calculation of what the orbit of the planet Uranus should be, but Uranus' path differed measurably from its calculated course. Now the theory on which the calculations were based was, like all theories, open to revision or refutation. But here conservatism operates: one is loath to revise extensively a well-established set of beliefs, especially a set so deeply entrenched as a basic portion of physics. And one is even more loath to abandon as spurious immense numbers of observation reports made by serious scientists. Given that Uranus had been observed to be as much as two minutes of arc from its calculated position, what was sought was a discovery that would render this deviation explicable within the framework of accepted theory. Then the theory and its generality would be unimpaired, and the new complexity would be minimal.

It would have been possible in principle to speculate that some special characteristic of Uranus exempted that planet from the physical laws that are followed by other planets. If such a hypothesis had been resorted to, Neptune would not have been discovered; not then, at any rate. There was a reason, however, for not resorting to such a hypothesis. It would have been what is called an *ad hoc hypothesis,* and ad hoc hypotheses are bad air; for they are wanting in Virtues III and IV. Ad hoc hypotheses are hypotheses that purport to account for some particular observations by supposing some very special forces to be at work in the particular cases at hand, and not generalizing sufficiently beyond those cases. The vice of an ad hoc hypothesis admits of degrees. The extreme case is where the hypothesis covers only the observations it was invented to account for, so that it is totally useless in prediction. Then also it is insusceptible of confirmation, which would come of our verifying its predictions.

Another example that has something of the implausibility of an ad hoc hypothesis is the water-diviner's belief that a willow wand held above the ground can be attracted by underground water. The force alleged is too special. One feels, most decidedly, the lack of an intelligible mechanism to explain the attraction. And what counts as intelligible mechanism? A hypothesis strikes us as giving an intelligible mechanism when the hypothesis rates well in familiarity, generality, simplicity. We attain the ultimate in intelligibility of mechanism, no doubt, when we see how to explain something in terms of physical impact or the familiar and general laws of motion.

There is an especially notorious sort of hypothesis which, whether or not properly classified also as ad hoc, shares the traits of insusceptibility of confirmation and uselessness in prediction. This is the sort of hypothesis that seeks to save some other hypothesis from refutation by systematically excusing the failures of its predictions. When the Voice from Beyond is silent despite the incantations of the medium, we may be urged to suppose that "someone in the room is interfering with the communication." In an effort to save the prior hypothesis that certain incantations will summon forth the Voice, the auxiliary hypothesis that untoward thoughts can thwart audible signals is advanced. This auxiliary hypothesis is no wilder than the hypothesis that it was invoked to save, and thus an uncritical person may find the newly wrinkled theory no harder to accept than its predecessor had been. On the other hand the critical observer sees that evidence has ceased altogether to figure. Experimental failure is being milked to fatten up theory.

These reflections bring a fifth virtue to the fore: *refutability,* Virtue V. It seems faint praise of a hypothesis to call it refutable. But the point, we have now seen, is approximately this: some imaginable event, recognizable if it occurs, must suffice to refute the hypothesis. Otherwise the hypothesis predicts nothing, is confirmed by nothing, and confers upon us no earthly good beyond perhaps a mistaken peace of mind.

This is too simple a statement of the matter. Just about any hypothesis, after all, can be held unrefuted no matter what, by making enough adjustments in other beliefs—though sometimes doing so requires madness. We think loosely of a hypothesis as implying predictions when, strictly speaking, the implying is done by the hypothesis together with a supporting chorus of ill-distinguished background beliefs. It is done by the whole relevant theory taken together.

Properly viewed, therefore, Virtue V is a matter of degree, as are its four predecessors. The degree to which a hypothesis partakes of Virtue V is measured by the cost of retaining the hypothesis in the face of imaginable events. The degree is measured by how dearly we cherish the previous beliefs that would have to be sacrificed to save the hypothesis. The greater the sacrifice, the more refutable the hypothesis.

A prime example of deficiency in respect of Virtue V is astrology. Astrologers can so hedge their predictions that they are devoid of genuine content. We may be told that a person will "tend to be creative" or "tend to be outgoing," where the evasiveness of a verb and the fuzziness of adjectives serve to insulate the claim from repudiation. But even if a prediction should be regarded as a failure, astrological devotees can go on believing that the stars rule our destinies; for there is always some item of information, perhaps as to a planet's location at a long gone time, that may be alleged to have been overlooked. Conflict with other beliefs thus need not arise.

All our contemplating of special virtues of hypotheses will not, we trust, becloud the fact that the heart of the matter is observation. Virtues I through V are guides to the framing of hypotheses that, besides conforming to past observations, may plausibly be expected to conform to future ones. When they fail on the latter score, questions are reopened. Thus it was that the Michelson-Morley experiment led to modifications, however inelegant, of Newton's physics at the hands of Lorentz. When Einstein came out with a simpler way of accommodating past observations, moreover, his theory was no mere reformulation of the Newton-Lorentz system; it was yet a third theory, different in some of its predicted observations and answerable to them. Its superior simplicity brought plausibility to its distinctive consequences.

Hypotheses were to serve two purposes: to explain the past and predict the future. Roughly and elliptically speaking, the hypothesis serves these purposes by implying the past events that it was supposed to explain, and by implying future ones. More accurately speaking, as we saw, what does the implying is the whole relevant theory taken together, as newly revised by adoption of the hypothesis in question. Moreover, the predictions that are implied are mostly not just simple predictions of future observations or other events; more often they are conditional predictions. The hypothesis will imply that we will make these further observations if we look in such and such a place, or take other feasible steps. If the predictions come out right, we can win bets or gain other practical advantages. Also, when they come out right, we gain confirmatory evidence for our hypotheses. When they come out wrong, we go back and tinker with our hypotheses and try to make them better.

What we called limiting principles in Chapter IV are, when intelligible, best seen as hypotheses—some good, some bad. Similarly, of course, for scientific laws generally. And similarly for laws of geometry, set theory, and other parts of mathematics. All these laws—those of physics and those of mathematics equally—are among the component hypotheses that fit together to constitute our inclusive scientific theory of the world. The most general hypotheses tend to be the least answerable to any particular observation, since subsidiary hypotheses can commonly be juggled and adjusted to accommodate conflicts; and on this score of aloofness there is no clear boundary between theoretical physics and mathematics. Of course hypotheses in various fields of inquiry may tend to receive their confirmation from different kinds of investigation, but this should in no way conflict with our seeing them all as hypotheses.

We talk of framing hypotheses. Actually we inherit the main ones, growing up as we do in a going culture. The continuity of belief is due to the retention, at each particular time, of most beliefs. In this retentiveness science even at its most progressive is notably conservative. Virtue I looms large. A reasonable person will look upon some of his or her retained beliefs as self-evident, on others as common knowledge though not self-evident, on others as vouched for by authority in varying degree, and on others as hypotheses that have worked all right so far.

But the going culture goes on, and each of us participates in adding and dropping hypotheses. Continuity makes the changes manageable. Disruptions that are at all sizable are the work of scientists, but we all modify the fabric in our small way, as when we conclude on indirect evidence that the schools will be closed and the planes grounded or that an umbrella thought to have been forgotten by one person was really forgotten by another.

NOTE

1. We are indebted to Nell E. Scroggins for suggesting this point.

19

Justifying Scientific Theories

Ronald Giere

Scientists sometimes talk about *justifying* theories, but more often they talk about *testing* models, hypotheses, or theories. To understand how theories are justified, then, we must first understand what constitutes a *test* of a model, hypothesis, or theory. Then we must learn how the results of tests are related to the *justification* of a theory.

Since *theories* are generalized *theoretical hypotheses,* justifying a theory is justifying a theoretical hypothesis. . . . But justifying a theoretical hypothesis itself requires that *it* be the *conclusion* of an argument in which some other statements are premises. We already know that the appropriate argument in this case will be an *inductive* argument. Now we must learn about the detailed structure of these arguments. This involves discovering what kinds of statements may serve as premises. . . .

I. TESTING NEWTON'S THEORY: HALLEY'S COMET

Newton's work on mechanics was first published in 1687. Around 1695, an English astronomer, Edmond Halley, began applying Newton's ideas to the motions of comets. He was probably acting on Newton's own suggestion that comets may be like small planets with very large elliptical orbits. In any case, comets were very interesting phenomena because they had always been viewed as mysterious or even ominous. Their appearances certainly exhibited no apparent regularity. If Newton's suggestion was correct, however, the behavior of comets would exhibit a great deal of underlying regularity.

Halley began investigating a comet that he himself had observed in 1682. The observations of 1682 gave a quite precise location, relative to the sun and the background stars, of the comet's path while it was within sight. However, since only a small part of the total orbit could be observed, it was not possible to determine how big it was and thus how long it would take for the comet to return. Indeed, it was impossible to determine whether the orbit was an ellipse, as Newton suggested, or a parabola. Newton's theory allowed the possibility of a parabolic orbit, but such an orbit would mean that the comet would come by only once and then leave the solar system forever. If, however, the orbit was elliptical, as Newton suggested, the comet should have traveled that same path many times before.

Halley began digging into the records of observations for previous comets. He found 24 cases, going back roughly 150 years, for which the observations were precise enough to compare with the observations of 1682. For two of these, one in 1606-1607 and one in 1530-1531, the recorded orbits were very close to that of the 1682 comet. The 1606 comet had in fact been observed by Kepler himself. Halley argued that it was extremely unlikely that three *different* comets should have such similar orbits, and concluded that these were three appearances of the *same* comet in an elliptical orbit with a period of roughly 76 years. He speculated, but could not prove, that the slight discrepancies in the three orbits were due to gravitational influences from the planets, particularly Jupiter.

But Halley didn't stop here. Using the data from all three cases, together with the hypothesis that he was dealing with a Newtonian system (or approximately Newtonian, since the observed orbits were not perfectly identical), Halley calculated the time of the next return. He boldly predicted that the comet should be seen again sometime in December, 1758. Figure 1 will help you to keep in mind the relevant details of this example. It is obviously not drawn to scale.

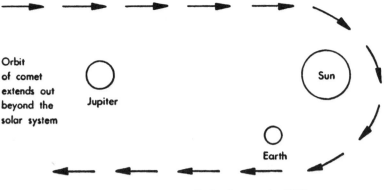

Figure 1. Halley's comet

Halley published his work on comets in 1705. It was well received by Newton and the growing band of English Newtonians. It did little, however, to convince the French, who continued in the older theoretical tradition of Descartes. Halley himself died, a respected scientist, in 1743, fifteen years before the predicted return of the comet. By this time even the French were coming around to the Newtonian way of thinking. And Halley's prediction was remembered. In 1756 the French Academy of Science offered a prize for the best calculation of the return of the comet. The comet reappeared, as predicted, on Christmas Day, 1758, and was offically named "Halley's comet." This date provides a convenient point to mark the final triumph of the Newtonian theoretical tradition over the Cartesian.

Intuitively it seems quite clear that the success of Halley's *prediction* did provide substantial *justification* for Newton's *theory*. Why is this so? What made this a *good test* of Newton's theory? How does the experimental verification of Halley's prediction provide an *argument* that justifies the theory?

II. The Basic Elements of a Test

The preceding section is fairly typical of reports describing the justification of theoretical hypotheses. Such reports do not generally distinguish the *experiment* itself, the *result* of the experiment, and the *justification* of the hypothesis. These things must be distinguished, however, if we are to develop a general account that can be applied to a variety of cases. Because it is simpler and more typical, we will take Halley's second test, the predicted return of the comet in 1758, as our standard example. Later we will return to consider the first test, that based on earlier observations of the comet.

Experiments, Results, and Justification

Before we examine the details, it will be helpful to see some of the basic distinctions set out in a preliminary way. This will give you some idea of how the various pieces are supposed to fit together so that you can better appreciate the details as they are presented.

The basic idea behind any *experiment* is to arrange things so that in the end you will get the information you need to argue either that the hypothesis is true or that it is false. You ought to be able to tell at the beginning, *before* the experiment is actually performed, whether or not things have been so arranged. It was clear in 1705 that the predicted return of the comet in 1758 constituted a good test of Halley's hypothesis.

When the experiment terminates, something will have happened, or failed to happen. This is the *result* of the experiment. You cannot know what this is, of course, until the experiment is over. In Halley's case the results were not in until 1758, fifteen years after Halley himself had died. In this example the experiment was simple. Just wait until 1758 and look to see whether the comet reappears. The result of this experiment, of course, was that it did reappear. But it might *not* have. "The comet will reappear in 1758," is a contingent statement.

Now, to *justify* either the hypothesis or its negation, one constructs an *argument*. The premises of this argument will be statements that relate both to the experiment and to its results. Indeed, in our account, such arguments will have only two premises, one describing the experiment and one describing its results. The conclusion of the argument will be either the hypothesis or its negation.

The Basic Elements

The Hypothesis. The most important element in a test is the *hypothesis* whose truth or falsity is at issue. The whole point of designing an experiment is to be able to come up with a justification either for the hypothesis or for its negation.

In Halley's case, the theoretical hypothesis at issue is that the comet and the sun together form a particular type of Newtonian Particle System, one in which a small mass (the comet) is in elliptical orbit around a large mass (the sun). Or, in light of the possible effects of Jupiter, the hypothesis is that they are *approximately* a Newtonian system of this type. Of course Halley was not only concerned with this one comet. He was concerned to show that all comets are Newtonian systems. Halley was also concerned with what is often called Newton's *celestial mechanics*—the *theory* that all celestial objects, including the Earth, form a Newtonian Particle System. We will later consider the status of these broader hypotheses.

The Prediction. The word "prediction" can be used to refer either to the possible *event* whose occurrence is predicted or to the *statement* that describes this possible event. It will generally be clear from the context which reference is intended.

In an experimental test of some hypothesis, the *prediction* always describes the occurrence of a possible state of some real system under investigation. To assert the prediction, then, is to say that the state will occur at the indicated time. This is clearly a contingent statement—that is, a statement that might be true or might be false. In our example, the prediction was that the comet would again be visible from the earth in December 1758. It turned out to be true.

Typically, as in Halley's second test, the prediction describes some possible *future* state of the system under study. That is why we use the word "prediction." However, it is not necessary for the prediction to describe a state of the system that lies in the future relative to the experiment. In Halley's first test, the "predicted" events were the *past* appearances of the comet. Similarly, in archaeology or evolutionary biology one studies systems that operated long ago. All the events in the history of these systems are in the past relative to the present investigation. In such investigations, then, the "prediction" would still describe some state of those systems, but a state that occurred long ago. The important thing, as you will soon learn, is whether the investigators knew about the predicted event and whether this knowledge played any part in the construction of the theory.

Initial Conditions. The term "initial conditions" may also be used to refer either to the *occurrence* of a state of the system or to a *statement* describing this occurrence. Typically, the initial conditions describe the occurrence of some state at the beginning of the experiment—thus the term "initial" conditions. In Halley's second test, the initial conditions described the positions and velocities of the comet that were recorded prior to 1705. Halley used this information in his calculation of the shape of the orbit and of the time of the comet's next return. In general, as illustrated by Halley's first test, it is not necessary that the initial conditions describe some state that occurred *before* the event described by the prediction. But they must describe some *other* state.

This brief rundown of the basic elements of a test leaves many important questions unanswered. Most of these questions, however, will be covered in the following discussion of the way these elements fit together in a *good* test of a scientific theory. . . .

III. What Makes a Good Test?

We will now see how the elements of a test fit together to make a *good* test, that is, a test that provides the basis for a *justification* either of the hypothesis or of its negation. A test of a theoretical hypothesis is obviously a very complicated thing. It is nevertheless possible to isolate several general features of tests that are sufficient to determine the justified conclusion.

The Prediction Is Deducible

Halley began with the *theoretical hypothesis* that the comet and the sun together are (approximately) a Newtonian system of a particular type. Using Newton's theoretical model, together with the observed *initial conditions* (the partial orbits observed during previous appearances of the comet), he calculated, that is, *deduced,* the *prediction* that the comet would again be visible at the end of 1758. The first general feature of a *good test* of a theoretical hypothesis, then, is:

> The prediction is logically deducible from the hypothesis together
> with the initial conditions.

Note that whether a test has this feature is not a contingent matter of fact. It is a purely *logical* issue. It is equivalent to the question whether the *argument* from the hypothesis and the initial conditions to the prediction is *deductively valid.* . . . So this feature of a good test can be ascertained without assuming that the hypothesis is true and without knowing whether the prediction will be true or not. In general, being told that the prediction was calculated mathematically is sufficient for you to conclude that the prediction is deducible.

That there must be *some* connections between the hypothesis and the prediction is obvious, because otherwise there would be no reason to regard the prediction as part of a test of the hypothesis. What we have found is that *one* connection is a *deductive* connection. This is a logical connection that goes *from* the hypothesis (plus initial conditions) *to* the prediction. The relationships in this first characteristic of a good test are pictured in Figure 2.

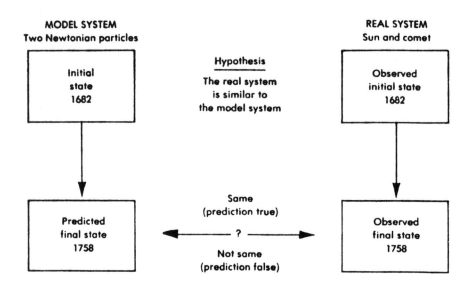

Figure 2. Theoretical hypothesis, initial condition, and prediction.

It is important to realize why the *initial conditions* must be inlcuded among the premises of the deduction. A theoretical hypothesis asserts only that some system has a specified *general structure*. It therefore tells you all the kinds of things that the system is *capable* of doing. But it does not tell you what the system is *in fact* doing at any particular moment. Thus it is impossible to deduce from the hypothesis alone any prediction that specified the actual state of the system at some definite time. The initial conditions, however, pin down the state of the system at some particular time. If the system is deterministic, as Newtonian systems are, that is sufficient to pin it down for all time.

The Prediction Is Improbable

To have a good test of a theoretical hypothesis, it is not enough that the prediction be implied. This is *necessary,* but *not sufficient.* To take a simple example, consider the different, and quite vague, prediction that some comet with some orbit or other would be observed after 1705. Now, this vague prediction also follows logically from Halley's hypothesis and observed data. Indeed, it follows logically from Halley's actual prediction that his comet would return in 1758. And as a matter of fact, a number of comets were observed between 1705 and Halley's death in 1743. Yet neither Halley nor anyone else ever claimed that these events justified his hypothesis. Why not? What was special about the prediction Halley made?

The trouble with the vague prediction of observing some comet or other after 1705 is that anyone with a basic knowledge of seventeenth-century astronomy could have made that prediction without knowing anything about Newton—and been quite confident of being correct. Good-sized comets had been appearing at least once every five years, on the average. Indeed, Halley himself had observed comets in both 1680 and 1681. Thus, given such frequent appearances by various comets, one wouldn't have needed Newton's ideas at all in order to make the vague prediction. In fact, then, even if the comet and sun were nothing at all like a simple two-particle Newtonian system, the prediction that some comet would be observed after 1705 was known to be highly likely to be true.

Halley's actual prediction was quite different. He predicted the appearance of a comet in a definite thirty-day period 53 years in the future (relative to when the prediction was published in 1705). Moreover, he did not predict any old comet. He predicted a comet with a precisely specified orbit. Anyone in 1705, knowledgeable about astronomy but ignorant of Newton's work, would have to have concluded that the appearance of a comet in December 1758 with that precisely specified orbit was *highly unlikely.* But not impossible! Nothing known in 1705 ruled out the *possibility* that such a comet would be observed. But everything known at the time (apart from Newton's hypotheses) counted against the prediction coming true. Without Newton's model, anyone would have to have regarded the success of Halley's prediction as a cosmic coincidence.

Whether the prediction is unlikely to be true is also in principle a *logical* matter that can be judged when the experiment is proposed without knowing whether the hypothesis or prediction are true. It is a matter of considering everything (other than the hypothesis at issue) then known to be relevant to the truth or falsity of the prediction, and determining whether this knowledge makes the truth of the prediction likely or not. In *principle* this could be a matter of deducing the improbability of the prediction from all current knowledge. In *practice* we must rely on scientists' informal judgments. Indeed, in Halley's time, probability theory was in its infancy. No one could have even pretended to calculate a definite probability for the appearance of a comet with the prescribed orbit. But any knowledgeable person could judge quite correctly that, leaving Newton's ideas aside, the prediction was not likely to come true.

The second general feature of a good test, then, can be summarized as follows:

Relative to everything else known at the time (excluding the hypothesis being tested), it must be improbable that the prediction will turn out to be true.

*   *   *

The Prediction Is Verifiable

There is one important aspect of tests that we have thus far simply assumed. Before proceeding, we should make this assumption explicit.

It must be possible, at the appropriate time, to verify whether the prediction is in fact true or false.

This is required because the truth or falsity of the prediction is going to provide part of the *justification* for our conclusion concerning the hypothesis. Thus it must be something we can justify *independently* of the truth or falsity of the hypothesis. Since a prediction is generally a description of the state of some system at a specified time, the predicted state must be one that can be observed or otherwise reliably detected.

As an illustration of the importance of this requirement, imagine that Halley had calculated the time and place at which the comet would be *farthest* from the Earth. He could have deduced such a prediction and it would have been very unlikely, apart from Newton's theory, that there should be a comet at that exact time and place. And this event would have happened well within Halley's lifetime so he could have been around to collect the glory. But no one had any way of telling whether this prediction was fulfilled or not. The comet is so small and the place so far away that even the best telescopes of the day could not have located it. The return to our solar system, however, was something which almost anyone could see with their naked eyes.

There is no necessity, of course, that the truth of the prediction be so directly observable as the return of Halley's comet. In modern science, the predictions that justify current hypotheses are often quite complex and require millions of dollars worth of equipment to verify. That doesn't matter. All that matters is that it can be done. . . .

IV. Justifying Theoretical Hypotheses

Good *experimental design* lies at the heart of good scientific research. An experiment is the scientists' way of asking Nature a question. The question has the form: Is this theoretical hypothesis true or false? Nature answers by exhibiting the prediction as true or false. If the prediction is true, the scientist, justifiably, concludes that the hypothesis is true. If the prediction is false, the hypothesis is refuted.

We will now look more closely at this form of reasoning, beginning with a general overview and then moving on to consider the *arguments* involved.

A Simple Inductive Rule

In justifying theoretical hypotheses, scientists follow a *simple inductive rule.*

> If the prediction is successful, the hypothesis is justified.
> If the prediction fails, the hypothesis is refuted.

The rule assumes, of course, that the experiment was well designed, which means that our conditions for a *good test* are satisfied. Figure 3 will help you at least to begin to see why this rule is a good rule.

Since the hypothesis is a contingent statement, either it is (approximately) *true* or it is *not* (approximately) *true.* Similarly, the prediction is a contingent statement that was chosen partly because it could be verified as true or false. Thus there are only two possible outcomes of the experiment: either the prediction is true or it is false. Applying the simple inductive rule, then, leads to one of two possible conclusions: the hypothesis is *justified* or it is *refuted.*

There are *four* possibilities shown in Figure 3. The hypothesis might be (approximately) true and end up either justified or refuted. Likewise, it might be false (not approximately true) and end up either justified or refuted. However, if the experiment satisfies the requirements for a *good test,* then two of these possibilities will be very likely and the other two very unlikely.

	If hypothesis approximately true	If hypothesis NOT approximately true
Hypothesis justified	Likely	Unlikely
Hypothesis refuted	Unlikely	Likely

Figure 3. Likelihood of results using the simple inductive rule.

Suppose first that the hypothesis is (approximately) *true*. Then, so long as the initial conditions are true, the prediction should also be true. Following the simple inductive rule, we shall conclude that the hypothesis is justified—which is what we should conclude. That is, we will justifiably claim that the hypothesis is (approximately) true when in fact it is. Of course, it is possible that something goes wrong somewhere along the line and that we end up concluding that the hypothesis is false when it is in fact true. But that should be highly unlikely.

Now suppose that the hypothesis is *false* (not approximately true). The prediction has been chosen so that it would be very unlikely to come out true unless the hypothesis is (approximately) true. That was one of our requirements for a good test. So in this case the prediction is likely to fail. Applying the simple inductive rule, we conclude that the hypothesis is refuted, that is, false (or not approximately true). This is what we should conclude. It is possible, of course, that the prediction succeeds even though the hypothesis is not even approximately true. It was possible, for example, that some other comet should have appeared in December 1758. It is even possible that the same comet, tossed about by other forces far outside the solar system, nevertheless, by accident, appeared as predicted. In these cases we would conclude, mistakenly, that the hypothesis is (approximately) true. Given everything known when the prediction was made, however, this would be an unlikely circumstance.

The simple inductive rule, then, satisfies our earlier definition of good *inductive* reasoning. It does not guarantee a true conclusion, but it does make it very likely that the conclusion reached is in fact true. What we have yet to see is the reasoning behind the rule set out explicitly in argument form with premises and conclusion. That comes next.

The Premises

We will begin by setting out the *general form* of the arguments for and against theoretical hypotheses. Then we will wrap up the Halley case, which is an example of an argument *for* a hypothesis. For a look at an argument *against* a theoretical hypothesis we shall need a new example.

As you might have guessed, arguments for or against theoretical hypotheses have the general form of *conditional arguments*. Their first premise will be a *conditional statement*. The second premise will include the *result* of the experiment, that is, either the prediction or its negation. And the conclusion will be either the hypothesis or its negation. So our main task is to formulate the conditional first premises of these arguments.

If the experiment is a *good test* of the hypothesis, then the prediction can be deduced from the hypothesis together with appropriate initial conditions. This means that the following *argument* form is *valid*:

H. IC. Thus, P.

where "H" stands for the Hypothesis, "IC" for the Initial Conditions, and "P" for the Prediction. This means. . . that the following *conditional statement* is a tautology:

Condition 1: If (H and IC), then P.

Since Condition 1 is justified by the corresponding deduction, it might be called the *deductibility condition* (or deducibility requirement). Being a tautology, this statement needs no further justification. It must be true.

Our second major requirement for a *good test* was that the prediction be something known to be *improbable* when the test is designed. In order to capture this requirement in a conditional statement, we must explicitly take account of the knowledge used to justify the claim that the prediction is indeed improbable. Such knowledge is often quite diverse. Let us therefore abbreviate all this knowledge by the letter "B," for *background* knowledge. The required conditional statement, then, may be written as:

Condition 2: If (Not H and IC and B), then very probably Not P.

This might be called the *improbability* condition (or improbability requirement).

If Condition 2 is true, its truth is in principle also a matter of logic. That is, in principle we can suppose that the statement "very probably Not P" can be deduced from the conjunction (Not H and IC and B). That such judgments are generally made informally, not by explicit calculation, does not change the logical status of the conditional statement.

This way of representing the second condition for a good test requires that theoretical hypotheses *not* be taken as asserting that the model *exactly* fits the real system. If we were to interpret H as asserting an exact fit, then it would not longer follow from (Not H and IC and B) that P is improbable. To see why this is so we need only imagine a model of mechanical motion that differs only slightly from Newton's. For example, instead of having the gravitational force vary inversely as the second power of the distance, it might be said to vary inversely as the 2.00001 power. This modified model provides us with a version of Not H, where H represents the exact Newtonian hypothesis. However, if we were to use this version of Not H, it would no longer follow that Not P is probable. Indeed, the difference between the two models is so slight that P would be very probable. Thus the "Not H" in Condition 2 must be read as saying that H is *not* even *approximately* true. This rules out all models that are sufficiently similar in structure to the chosen model that they would make P a likely outcome. So whether the prediction is judged likely or not then depends primarily on the rest of our knowledge at the time. Does everything else that is known imply that the prediction is improbable?

If Not H means that H is *not* approximately true, then H must mean that H *is* approximately true. Since no prediction is ever made with perfect accuracy, if only because there is always some uncertainty in the initial conditions, the degree of approximation in H need only be assumed to introduce less variation than the initial conditions. Then P, including its range of variation, follows deductively as required for Condition 1 to be justified. Recall that Halley's prediction was only accurate to within one month.

Assuming that the truth or falsity of the prediction can be verified at the appropriate time, Conditions 1 and 2 provide an alternate, if somewhat abstract, way of characterizing a *good test* of a theoretical hypothesis.

> A test of a theoretical Hypothesis is a good test if and only if both Condition 1 and Condition 2 are true.

Alternatively, we are *justified* in regarding the test as a good test if and only if we are *justified* in claiming that both conditions are true. The virtue of defining a good test this way is that these same conditions will be the conditional premises for any *argument* used to justify or refute the hypothesis.

Refuting Argument

The theoretical hypothesis cannot be justified or refuted until the result of the experiment is in—that is, until the truth or falsity of the prediction has been determined. Once this is known, the appropriate argument can be constructed. Since the argument that would refute a hypothesis is simpler than one that would justify it, we will begin with refuting arguments.

Suppose, then, that the specified hypothesis, H, has been subjected to a good test. This means that both Condition 1 and Condition 2 have been justified. Now suppose it turns out that the *prediction* is *false*. That is, Not P is true. We now have all the ingredients to construct an argument justifying the conclusion Not H. We will set out this argument in full detail. You should work through it carefully, step by step, at least once, to convince yourself that it is indeed a valid argument. Later on we will use a condensed, short form, of the argument.

The argument proceeds as follows:

First Premise:	If (H and IC), then P.
Second Premise:	Not P.
Preliminary Conclusion:	Not (H and IC).
Preliminary Conclusion:	Not H or Not IC.
Additional Premise:	IC.
Final Conclusion:	Not H.

Every step in this argument is deductively valid. The first premise is just Condition 1. The second premise is the result of the experiment; that is, the prediction failed. By the valid step of *denying the consequent* we reach the first preliminary conclusion. This conclusion is the denial of a conjunction, which we know leads validly to the next preliminary conclusion, a disjunction of the negations of the original component statements. . . . Finally, we must explicitly assert the Initial Conditions if we are to reach the conclusion that H is false. The final step is a valid *disjunctive syllogism*. Since every premise has been justified in advance, and every step in the argument is deductively valid, the conclusion is justified.

Once you understand the details of the above argument, it is much easier to collapse it into two premises and the conclusion as follows:

If (H and IC), then P.
Not P and IC.
Thus, Not H.

Justifying Argument

As before, we assume that some theoretical hypothesis, H, has been subjected to a *good test*. This time, however, the *prediction* comes true. In this case the argument justifying the hypothesis has the following form:

First Premise: If (Not H and IC and B), then very probably Not P.
Second Premise: P.
Preliminary Conclusion: Not (Not H and IC and B).
Preliminary Conclusion: H or Not IC or Not B.
Additional Premise: IC and B.
Conclusion: H.

Here again, we will go through this argument in detail before collapsing it into a shorter form.

The first premise is merely Condition 2. The second is the result of the test. The argument from these two premises to the first preliminary conclusion is an *inductive* argument. This is the *only* inductive step in the argument. The second preliminary conclusion is reached by *denying the conjunction,* a valid deductive inference. Only the step, "Not Not H, Thus H," has been left out. Finally, the initial conditions and the background knowledge are explicitly acknowledged as premises. This leads to the conclusion by a valid *disjunctive syllogism.*

Now we can collapse the argument into two premises and the conclusion:

If (Not H and IC and B), then very probably Not P.
P and IC and B.
Thus (inductively), H.

We will always use this "short form" in later discussions.

At this point, one warning is in order. You should recognize that the inductive step in the above argument looks a lot like *denying the consequent,* which is a valid argument. You might therefore be tempted to think that *any* argument of this form is a good inductive argument—a kind of inductive version of denying the consequent. Unfortunately, things are not so simple. Not all arguments of this form are good inductive arguments. What makes this one good is the assumption that we started out with a *good test* of H. This means that it is also true that H and IC imply P. Only with this additional assumption is it correct that the truth of the premises makes it very probable that the conclusion is also true.

*   *   *

V. Celestial Mechanics and the Phlogiston Theory

The previous section was pretty abstract. Let us now put some flesh on these abstractions by examining two examples.

Justifying a Theory: Celestial Mechanics

It is about time we wrapped up the Halley episode. The *elements* of the test are:

> H: The comet/sun system is (approximately) a Newtonian
>   Particle System.
> IC: The previously observed orbits of the comet.
> P: The return of the comet in December 1758.

The prediction is easily verifiable when the time comes. The prediction was calculated (deduced) from the hypothesis and the initial conditions. And all prior information, B, indicated that, apart from Newton's hypothesis, the appearance of such a comet, as predicted, would be very improbable. So the test was a *good test* of the hypothesis.

The prediction turned out to be *true.* Applying the *simple inductive rule,* we conclude, with ample justification, that H is true. In order to exhibit the *argument* that shows in detail how the conclusion is justified, we formulate *Condition 2* and add the required additional premises. The argument, then, is,

> If (Not H and IC and B), then very probably Not P.
> P and IC and B.
> Thus (inductively), H.

That is, the sun/comet system is (at least to a good approximation) a Newtonian Particle System of the type in question.

There is only one further part of the story to complete. In 1758 the conclusion everyone drew was much broader than Halley's hypothesis. In the first place, they appear to have concluded not only that Halley's comet is a Newtonian system, but that *all comets* are Newtonian systems. The justification for this conclusion might seem to be fairly weak since it amounts to generalizing on a *single* case. Yet they were by that time pretty well justified in regarding comets as being fundamentally alike. So any fundamental characteristic true of one is likely to be true of all. And its motions in space and time are surely a fundamental property. But the details of this type of reasoning are not easy to set out.

In the second place, Halley's success was taken to justify Newton's *theory* of *celestial mechanics*. This is the generalization that all celestial bodies fit Newtonian models. Here again the justification for this broad generlization is better than it might at first appear. By 1758 it was well established that the moon and planets obey Newtonian laws. Apart from the distant stars, comets were the only observable celestial motions not yet explicitly tested. By showing that comets are also Newtonian systems, Halley completed the generalization over known types of celestial bodies. Moreover, comets were correctly judged to be the most difficult case for Newtonian models because they exhibited the least apparent regularity of any celestial objects. If even comets are Newtonian systems, what celestial objects could not be?

Finally, Halley's success helped solidify the by then already strong Newtonian *theoretical tradition*. It would be 150 years before anyone seriously questioned the applicability of Newtonian models to celestial motions.

Why Independent Tests Are Desirable

Halley's prediction of the comet's return in 1758 was the basis for the *second* of two tests of the hypothesis that the 1682 comet is in an elliptical Newtonian orbit around the sun. The first test utilized the prediction that previous records of comets would show evidence of the same comet at earlier times. This test is complicated by the fact that it requires assumptions about the record-keeping system of earlier astronomers. To deduce the existence of appropriate records requires that there be record keepers. Halley was lucky that the period of his comet was short enough for it to have been observed by people such as Kepler. Moreover, the records kept have to be precise enough to distinguish comets with different orbits. To the extent that the records are imprecise, the probability of mistaking some other comet for the predicted comet increases. Halley's confidence in the precision of the more recent observations was sufficiently great for him to claim that it would be "next to a miracle" if the comets of 1530-1531, 1606-1607, and 1682 were three different comets with similar orbits. So he, at least, thought that his first prediction was deducible, improbable, and verifiable.

If Halley thought the first test was so good, what is the value of the second test? It makes the justification for the hypothesis even stronger. Roughly speaking, the more *improbable* the prediction relative to previous background knowledge, the stronger the justification if the prediction is successful. But that two improbable predictions should be successful is even more improbable than that either one by itself should be successful. This judgment requires no technical knowledge of probability theory. Being dealt a hand with four aces in an evening of bridge is improbable. Being dealt two such hands in a single evening is twice as improbable. So, even leaving aside the fact that the observations in 1682 and 1758 were more precise than previously, four matching orbits by four different comets would be more improbable than three. So the justification for the hypothesis had to be better in 1758 than it had been in 1705.

In general, then, the more independent tests, the stronger the justification for the hypothesis. But here, as everywhere, one soon reaches a point of diminishing returns. The appearance of Halley's comet in 1985–1986 adds little to the justification of Halley's original hypothesis.

Refuting a Theory: Phlogiston

To call a test of some hypothesis a *good test* does not mean that it ended up providing justification for the hypothesis being tested. It is not necessarily good from the standpoint of someone who wants to justify the hypothesis. A test is good in the more neutral sense that it is designed to provide *an* answer. The answer may be that the hypothesis is justified. But it may also be the reverse. The hypothesis may be refuted. It all depends on whether the prediction was true or not. That a test is a good test also does not mean that the prediction came out true. It only means that there was a clear prediction whose truth or falsity became known at the end of the experiment.

In Halley's case, of course, the prediction came true and the hypothesis was justified. In science, as in everyday life, one tends to remember only the winners. And history is the same. The losers tend to be forgotten. Some losers, however, are remembered, if only because they had a period of considerable success before their downfall. A famous loser is the phlogiston theory.

Fire, like motion and heredity, has always fascinated people. In the Western world, recorded speculation about the nature of fire also goes back to the Greeks. To them we owe both the myth of Prometheus and the view that the world is made up of a few separate "elements": earth, air, fire, and water. All four are present in the process of combustion. The common-sense view of combustion is that something is driven out of the burning object, leaving only ashes behind.

By the eighteenth century, this "something" had a well-established name, *phlogiston*—the fire stuff. Assuming that combustible material contains phlogiston explains most of the obvious facts about combustion. Heating drives off the phlogiston into the air; cooling makes it less volatile; smothering holds it in. The well-known fact that a burning candle placed in an enclosed container soon goes out was explained by saying that the enclosed air gets saturated with phlogiston so that the phlogiston remaining in the wax has nowhere to go.

Phlogiston accounts not only for combustion but also for the very important process of smelting. This is the process by which crude ores are turned into more refined metals. Generally this is done by carefully heating the ores, together with a measured amount of charcoal, to a controlled temperature. It was claimed that the charcoal contains an excess of phlogiston which, at moderately high temperatures, leaves the charcoal and combines with the ore to form the metal. This hypothesis was substantiated by the fact that further heating at higher temperatures returns the metal to its original state. The phlogiston is driven out of the metal by the higher temperature. Even rusting was explained as the result of the phlogiston slowly escaping from the metal.

These claims may be taken as the "laws" that define *phlogiston models.* Such models lay behind many hypotheses about systems undergoing combustion, rusting, or the process of smelting. The *phlogiston theory* was the general hypothesis that this sort of model fits most cases of combustion, smelting, rusting, and so on. In what follows we shall concentrate on combustion.

Combustion is very difficult to study. Most things we commonly burn are made of many different substances and give off many different gasses when burned. Moreover, combustion generally is rapid and violent. Progress in such studies required finding some simple, well-controlled subjects for experimentation. (Remember Mendel's pea plants.) In the 1770s, chemists developed a number of techniques for performing such experiments. The leaders were Joseph Priestley in England and Antoine Lavoisier in France. Priestly supported the phlogiston theory; Lavoisier led the revolution that overthrew it.

In the 1770s, utilizing techniques first developed by Priestley, Lavoisier performed a number of careful experiments with mercury. In one of these experiments he floated a precisely measured amount of mercury on a liquid and covered it with a glass jar, thus enclosing a known amount of air (see figure 4). The mercury was then heated using the rays of the sun focused by a powerful magnifying glass (a burning glass). In such circumstances, as Lavoisier well knew, a red powder, or ash, forms on the surface of the mercury. Some of the mercury undergoes a controlled burning.

Applying the phlogiston model to this experiment, one would expect two things. First, the resulting mercury plus red ash should weigh *less* than the original sample of mercury alone. This is because some phlogiston must be driven off, leaving the ash behind. And the volume of air inside the jar should *increase* since it now contains the phlogiston that was driven out of the mercury. This means that the level of the liquid inside the jar would drop to make room for the additional "air."

Figure 4. Lavoisier's experiment

Regarding this experiment as a test of the *phlogiston theory,* the elements of the test are these:

H: The experimental setup roughly fits a phlogiston model of combustion.

IC: The various facts describing the experiment are as outlined above.

P: The remaining mercury and red powder together weigh *less* than the original sample of mercury alone. And the level of the liquid inside the jar should go *down.*

Now, does this experiment constitute a *good test* of the hypothesis? There seems little reason whether the prediction *logically* follows from the hypothesis and initial conditions. This follows if anything does. So Condition 1 is satisfied. But is the prediction all that improbable given everything else known at the time? In other words, is Condition 2 justified? This is not so clear. The predicted results are, after all, the common-sense results. The phlogiston model is the common-sense model. Let's withhold judgment on Condition 2 and proceed with the story.

When Lavoisier completed the experiment, the water level had gone *up,* not down, and the mercury/ash combination weighed *more* than the original mercury alone. The prediction was *false.* Applying the simple inductive rule we conclude immediately that the hypothesis is false.

To construct the *argument* justifying our conclusion, we combine Condition 1 with the result of the experiment as follows:

If (H and IC), then P.
Not P and IC.
Thus, Not H.

And this argument is deductively valid.

So in the end the fact that Condition 2 was questionable did not matter. We didn't need it. Of course, if things had gone the other way, then Lavoisier would not have been in a strong position to argue that H is true. But then again, Lavoisier was not out to justify the phlogiston hypothesis. He was trying to refute it.

If the *phlogiston theory* includes the general hypothesis that *all* combusion-like processes fit phlogiston models, then Lavoisier's experiment refuted the theory as well. But no defender of the phlogiston theory interpreted it so broadly. What in fact happened is that members of the *theoretical tradition* based on phlogiston models *modified* their models to accommodate Lavoisier's results. This is a scientifically sound strategy for dealing with unwelcome facts. But the strategy does not pay off unless these new models yield justifiable hypotheses. Merely coming up with a revised model that fits the known results is not enough. Justification requires full-fledged tests that satisfy Condition 2 as well as Condition 1. Phlogiston theorists were not able to do this successfully.

Some of the revised phlogiston models attributed a *negative mass* to phlogiston. This put phlogiston chemists at odds with Newtonian physicists, for whom all particles have *positive* mass. Some models postulated that phlogiston is lighter than air and thus exhibits a buoyancy effect—like the bladder in a fish or the hot air balloons that were then popular in France. Other models specified that the escaping phlogiston is replaced by water vapor, which has greater mass and greater volume than phlogiston. This accounts both for the increased mass of the mercury sample and the decreased volume of the air. But none of these models were justified in applications to further experiments. They kept on being refuted. By 1789 the phlogiston tradition was effectively dead, even though Priestley himself defended it in a text published as late as 1796. By that time Lavoisier was also dead, a victim of "the terror" that followed the French Revolution. But the theoretical tradition he founded continues. We know it as oxygen chemistry.

This example illustrates an important new (for us) feature of the scientific enterprise. It is easier to refute hypotheses than to justify them. To *refute* a hypothesis all you need is a single logical consequence that is false. To *justify* a hypothesis you need a logical consequence that is initially improbable but nevertheless turns out to be true. That is a much more difficult trick.

By the same token, trying to justify hypotheses is a much riskier business than trying to refute them. To justify a hypothesis you must find a prediction that all previous knowledge indicates is likely to be false. Thus, if the hypothesis in question is indeed false, this is very likely to be discovered in the very process of conducting an experiment that would justify the hypothesis.

It is sometimes thought that any objectivity there is in science is due to scientists being objective people. Some claim that this means being dispassionate regarding the truth or falsity of one's hypotheses. Others have even held that scientists should actively try to refute their own hypotheses! But this is a mistake. The objectivity of *science,* imperfect as it is, is not a function of the objectivity of *scientists.* It is a function of the "logical" rules of the game. These are embodied in the specification of a good test, and thus in Conditions 1 and 2. So there is no reason why scientists should not try to justify their hypotheses and be very disappointed if they are refuted. The rules of the game ensure that the harder one tries to get a good justification, the greater the risk of refutation—unless the hypothesis is indeed on the right track.

20

Objectivity, Value Judgment, and Theory Choice

Thomas Kuhn

In the penultimate chapter of a controversial book first published fifteen years ago, I considered the ways scientists are brought to abandon one time-honored theory or paradigm in favor of another. Such decision problems, I wrote, "cannot be resolved by proof." To discuss their mechanism is, therefore, to talk "about techniques of persuasion, or about argument and counterargument in a situation in which there can be no proof." Under these circumstances, I continued, "lifelong resistance [to a new theory] . . . is not a violation of scientific standards. . . . Though the historian can always find men—Priestley, for instance—who were unreasonable to resist for as long as they did, he will not find a point at which resistance becomes illogical or unscientific."[1] Statements of that sort obviously raise the question of why, in the absence of binding criteria for scientific choice, both the number of solved scientific problems and the precision of individual problem solutions should increase so markedly with the passage of time. Confronting that issue, I sketched in my closing chapter a number of characteristics that scientists share by virtue of the training which licenses their membership in one or another community of specialists. In the absence of criteria able to dictate the choice of each individual, I argued, we do well to trust the collective judgment of scientists trained in this way. "What better criterion could there be," I asked rhetorically, "than the decision of the scientific group?"[2]

A number of philosophers have greeted remarks like these in a way that continues to surprise me. My views, it is said, make of theory choice "a matter of mob psychology."[3] Kuhn believes, I am told, that "the decision of a scientific group to adopt a new paradigm cannot be based on good reasons of any kind, factual or otherwise."[4] The debates surrounding such choices must, my critics claim, be for me "mere persuasive displays without deliberative substance."[5] Reports of this sort manifest total misunderstanding, and I have occassionally said as much in papers directed primarily to other ends. But those passing protestations have had negligible effect, and the misunderstandings continue to be important. I conclude that it is past time for me to describe, at greater length and with greater precision, what has been on my mind when I have uttered statements like the ones with which I just began. If I have been reluctant to do so in the past, that is largely because I have preferred to devote attention to areas in which my views diverge more sharply from those currently received than they do with respect to theory choice.

What, I ask to begin with, are the characteristics of a good scientific theory? Among a number of quite usual answers I select five, not because they are exhaustive, but because they are individually important and collectively sufficiently varied to indicate what is at stake. First, a theory should be accurate: within its domain, that is, consequences deducible from a theory should be in demonstrated agreement with the results of existing experiments and observations. Second, a theory should be consistent, not only internally or with itself, but also with other currently accepted theories applicable to related aspects of nature. Third, it should have broad scope: in particular, a theory's consequences should extend far beyond the particular observations, laws, or subtheories it was initially designed to explain. Fourth, and closely related, it should be simple, bringing order to phenomena that in its absence would be individually isolated and, as a set, confused. Fifth—a somewhat less standard item, but one of special importance to actual scientific decisions—a theory should be fruitful of new research findings: it should, that is, disclose new phenomena or previously unnoted relationships among those already known.[6] These five characteristics—accuracy, consistency, scope, simplicity, and fruitfulness—are all standard criteria for evaluating the adequacy of a theory. If they had not been, I would have devoted far more space to them in my book, for I agree entirely with the traditional view that they play a vital role when scientists must choose between an established theory and an upstart competitor. Together with others of much the same sort, they provide *the* shared basis for theory choice.

Nevertheless, two sorts of difficulties are regularly encountered by the men who must use these criteria in choosing, say, between Ptolemy's astronomical theory and Copernicus's, between the oxygen and phlogiston theories of combustion, or between Newtonian mechanics and the quantum theory. Individually the criteria are imprecise: individuals may legitimately differ about their application to concrete cases. In addition, when deployed together, they repeatedly prove to conflict with one another; accuracy may, for example, dictate the choice of one theory, scope the choice of its competitor. Since these difficulties, especially the first, are also relatively familiar, I shall devote little time to their elaboration. Though my argument does demand that I illustrate them briefly, my views will begin to depart from those long current only after I have done so.

Begin with accuracy, which for present purposes I take to include not only quantitative agreement but qualitative as well. Ultimately it proves the most nearly decisive of all the criteria, partly because it is less equivocal than the others but especially because predictive and explanatory powers, which depend on it, are characteristics that scientists are particularly unwilling to give up. Unfortunately, however, theories cannot always be discriminated in terms of accuracy. Copernicus's system, for example, was not more accurate than Ptolemy's until drastically revised by Kepler more than sixty years after Copernicus's death. If Kepler or someone else had not found other reasons to choose heliocentric astronomy, those improvements in accuracy would never have been made, and Copernicus's work might have been forgotten. More typically, of course, accuracy does permit discriminations, but not the sort that lead regularly to unequivocal choice. The oxygen theory, for example, was universally acknowledged to account for observed weight relations in chemical reactions, something the phlogiston theory had previously scarcely attempted to do. But the phlogiston theory, unlike its rival, could account for the metals' being much more alike than the ores from which they were formed. One theory thus matched experience better in one area, the other in another. To choose between them on the basis of accuracy, a scientist would need to decide the area in which accuracy was more significant. About the matter chemists could and did differ without violating any of the criteria outlined above, or any others yet to be suggested.

However important it may be, therefore, accuracy by itself is seldom or never a sufficient criterion for theory choice. Other criteria must function as well, but they do not eliminate problems. To illustrate I select just two— consistency and simplicity—asking how they functioned in the choice between the heliocentric and geocentric systems. As astronomical theories both Ptolemy's and Copernicus's were internally consistent, but their relation to related theories in other fields was very different. The stationary central earth was an essential ingredient of received physical theory, a tight-knit body of doctrine which explained, among other things, how stones fall, how water pumps function, and why the clouds move slowly across the skies. Heliocentric astronomy, which required the earth's motion, was inconsistent with the existing scientific explanation of these and other terrestrial phenomena. The consistency criterion, by itself, therefore, spoke unequivocally for the geocentric tradition.

Simplicity, however, favored Copernicus, but only when evaluated in a quite special way. If, on the one hand, the two systems were compared in terms of the actual computational labor required to predict the position of a planet at a particular time, then they proved substantially equivalent. Such computations were what astronomers did, and Copernicus's system offered them no labor-saving techniques; in that sense it was not simpler then Ptolemy's. If, on the other hand, one asked about the amount of mathematical apparatus required to explain, not the detailed quantitative features—limited elongation, retrograde motion, and the like—then, as every schoolchild knows, Copernicus required only one circle per planet, Ptolemy two. In that sense the Copernican theory was the simpler, a fact vitally important to the choices made by both Kepler and Galileo and thus essential to the ultimate triumph of Copernicanism. But that sense of simplicity was not the only one available, nor even the one most natural to professional astronomers, men whose task was the actual computation of planetary position.

Because time is short and I have multiplied examples elsewhere, I shall here simply assert that these difficulties in applying standard criteria of choice are typical and that they arise no less forcefully in twentieth-century situations than in the earlier and better-known examples I have just sketched. When scientists must choose between competing theories, two men fully committed to the same list of criteria for choice may nevertheless reach different conclusions. Perhaps they interpret simplicity differently or have different convictions about the range of fields within which the consistency criterion must be met. Or perhaps they agree about these matters but differ about the relative weights to be accorded to these or to other criteria when several are deployed together. With respect to divergences of this sort, no set of choice criteria yet proposed is of any use. One can explain, as the historian characteristically does, why particular men made particular choices at particular times. But for that purpose one must go beyond the list of shared criteria to characteristics of the individuals who make the choice. One must, that is, deal with characteristics which vary from one scientist to another without thereby in the least jeopardizing their adherence to the canons that make science scientific. Though such canons do exist and should be discoverable (doubtless the criteria of choice with which I began are among them), they are not by themselves sufficient to determine the decisions of individual scientists. For that purpose the shared canons must be fleshed out in ways that differ from one individual to another.

Some of the differences I have in mind result from the individual's previous experience as a scientist. In what part of the field was he at work when confronted by the need to choose? How long had he worked there; how successful had he been; and how much of his work depended on concepts and techniques challenged by the new theory? Other factors relevant to choice lie outside the sciences. Kepler's early election of Copernicanism was due in part to his immersion in the Neoplatonic and Hermetic movements of his day; German Romanticism predisposed those it affected toward both recognition and acceptance of energy conservation; nineteenth-century British social thought had a similar influence on the availability and acceptability of Darwin's concept of the struggle for existence. Still other significant differences are functions of personality. Some scientists place more premium than others on originality and are correspondingly more willing to take risks; some scientists prefer comprehensive, unified theories to precise and detailed problem solutions of apparently narrower scope. Differentiating factors like these are described by my critics as subjective and are contrasted with the shared or objective criteria from which I began. Though I shall later question that use of terms, let me for the moment accept it. My point is, then, that every individual choice between competing theories depends on a mixture of objective and subjective factors, or of shared and individual criteria. Since the latter have not ordinarily figured in the philosophy of science, my emphasis upon them has made my belief in the former hard for my critics to see.

What I have said so far is primarily simply descriptive of what goes on in the sciences at times of theory choice. As description, furthermore, it has not been challenged by my critics, who reject instead my claim that these facts of scientific life have philosophic import. Taking up that issue, I shall begin to isolate some, though I think not vast, differences of opinion. Let me begin by asking how philosophers of science can for so long have neglected the subjective elements which, they freely grant, enter regularly into the actual theory choices made by individual scientists? Why have these elements seemed to them an index only of human weakness, not at all of the nature of scientific knowledge?

One answer to that question is, of course, that few philosophers, if any, have claimed to possess either a complete or an entirely well-articulated list of criteria. For some time, therefore, they could reasonably expect that further research would eliminate residual imperfections and produce an algorithm able to dictate rational, unanimous choice. Pending that achievement, scientists would have no alternative but to supply subjectively what the best current list of objective criteria still lacked. That some of them might still do so even with a perfected list at hand would then be an index only of the inevitable imperfection of human nature.

That sort of answer may still prove to be correct, but I think no philosopher still expects that it will. The search for algorithmic decision procedures has continued for some time and produced both powerful and illuminating results. But those results all pre-suppose that individual criteria of choice can be unambiguously stated and also that, if more than one proves relevant, an appropriate weight function is at hand for their joint application. Unfortunately, where the choice at issue is between scientific theories, little progress has been made toward the first of these desiderata and none toward the second. Most philosophers of science would, therefore, I think, now regard the sort of algorithm which has traditionally been sought as a not quite attainable ideal. I entirely agree and shall henceforth take that much for granted.

Even an ideal, however, if it is to remain credible, requires some demonstrated relevance to the situations in which it is supposed to apply. Claiming that such demonstration requires no recourse to subjective factors, my critics seem to appeal, implicitly or explicitly, to the well-known distinction between the contexts of discovery and of justification.[7] They concede, that is, that the subjective factors I invoke play a significant role in the discovery or invention of new theories, but they also insist that that inevitably intuitive process lies outside of the bounds of philosophy of science and is irrelevant to the question of scientific objectivity. Objectivity enters science, they continue, through the processes by which theories are tested, justified, or judged. Those processes do not, or at least need not, involve subjective factors at all. They can be governed by a set of (objective) criteria shared by the entire group competent to judge.

I have already argued that that position does not fit observations of scientific life and shall now assume that that much has been conceded. What is now at issue is a different point: whether or not this invocation of the distinction between contexts of discovery and of justification provides even a plausible and useful idealization. I think it does not and can best make my point by suggesting first a likely source of its apparent cogency. I suspect that my critics have been misled by science pedagogy or what I have elsewhere called textbook science. In science teaching, theories are presented together with exemplary applications, and those applications may be viewed as evidence. But that is not their primary pedagogic function (science students are distressingly willing to receive the word from professors and texts). Doubtless *some* of them were *part* of the evidence at the time actual decisions were being made, but they represent only a fraction of the considerations relevant to the decision process. The context of pedagogy differs almost as much from the context of justification as it does from that of discovery.

Full documentation of that point would require longer argument than is appropriate here, but two aspects of the way in which philosophers ordinarily demonstrate the relevance of choice criteria are worth noting. Like the science textbooks on which they are often modelled, books and articles on the philosophy of science refer again and again to the famous crucial experiments: Foucault's pendulum, which demonstrates the motion of the earth; Cavendish's demonstration of gravitational attraction; or Fizeau's measurement of the relative speed of sound in water and air. These experiments are paradigms of good reason for scientific choice; they illustrate the most effective of all the sorts of argument which could be available to a scientist uncertain which of two theories to follow; they are vehicles for the transmission of criteria of choice. But they also have another characteristc in common. By the time they were performed no scientist still needed to be convinced of the validity of the theory their outcome is now used to demonstrate. Those decisions had long since been made on the basis of significantly more equivocal evidence. The exemplary crucial experiments to which philosophers again and again refer would have been historically relevent to theory choice only if they had yielded unexpected results. Their use as illustrations provides needed economy to science pedagogy, but they scarcely illuminate the character of the choices that scientists are called upon to make.

Standard philosophical illustrations of scientific choice have another troublesome characteristic. The only arguments discussed are, as I have previously indicated, the ones favorable to the theory that, in fact, ultimately triumphed. Oxygen, we read, could explain weight relations, phlogiston could not; but nothing is said about the phlogiston theory's power or about the oxygen theory's limitations. Comparisons of Ptolemy's theory with Copernicus's proceed in the same way. Perhaps these examples should not be given since they contrast a developed theory with one still in its infancy. But philosophers regularly use them nonetheless. If the only result of their doing so were to simplify the decision situation, one could not object. Even historians do not claim to deal with the full factual complexity of the situations they describe. But these simplifications emasculate by making choice totally unproblematic. They eliminate, that is, one essential element of the decision situations that scientists must resolve if their field is to move ahead. In those situations there are always at least some good reasons for each possible choice. Considerations relevant to the context of discovery are then relevant to justification as well; scientists who share the concerns and sensibilities of the individual who discovers a new theory are ipso facto likely to appear disproportionately frequently among that theory's first supporters. That is why it has been difficult to construct algorithms for theory choice, and also why such difficulties have seemed so thoroughly worth resolving. Choices that present problems are the ones philosophers of science need to understand. Philosophically interesting decision procedures must function where, in their absence, the decision might still be in doubt.

That much I have said before, if only briefly. Recently, however, I have recognized another, subtler source for the apparent plausibility of my critics' position. To present it, I shall briefly describe a hypothetical dialogue with one of them. Both of us agree that each scientist chooses between competing theories by deploying some Bayesian algorithm which permits him to compute a value for $p(T,E)$, i.e., for the probability of a theory T on the evidence E available both to him and to the other members of his professional group at a particular period of time. "Evidence," furthermore, we both interpret broadly to include such considerations as simplicity and fruitfulness. My critic asserts, however, that there is only one such value of p, that corresponding to objective choice, and he believes that all rational members of the group must arrive at it. I assert, on the other hand, for reasons previously given, that the factors he calls objective are insufficient to determine in full any algorithm at all. For the sake of the discussion I have conceded that each individual has an algorithm and that all their algorithms have much in common. Nevertheless, I continue to hold that the algorithms of individuals are all ultimately different by virtue of the subjective considerations with which each must complete the objective criteria before any computations can be done. If my hypothetical critic is liberal, he may now grant that these subjective differences do play a role in determining the hypothetical algorithm on which each individual relies during the early stages of the competition between rival theories. But he is also likely to claim that, as evidence increases with the passage of time, the algorithms of different individuals converge to the algorithm of objective choice with which his presentation began. For him the increasing unanimity of individual choices is evidence for their increasing objectivity and thus for the elimination of subjective elements from the decision process.

So much for the dialogue, which I have, of course, contrived to disclose the non sequitur underlying an apparently plausible position. What converges as the evidence changes over time need only be the values of p that individuals compute from their individual algorithms. Conceivably those algorithms themselves also become more alike with time, but the ultimate unanimity of theory choice provides no evidence whatsoever that they do so. If subjective factors are required to account for the decisions that initially divide the profession, they may still be present later when the profession agrees. Though I shall not here argue the point, consideration of the occasions on which a scientific community divides suggests that they actually do so.

My argument has so far been directed to two points. It first provided evidence that the choices scientists make between competing theories depend not only on shared criteria—those my critics call objective—but also on idiosyncratic factors dependent on individual biography and personality. The latter are, in my critics' vocabulary, subjective, and the second part of my argument has attempted to bar some likely ways of denying their philosophic import. Let me now shift to a more positive approach, returning briefly to the list of shared criteria—accuracy, simplicity, and the like—with which I began. The considerable effectiveness of such criteria does not, I now wish to suggest, depend on their being sufficiently articulated to dictate the choice of each individual who subscribes to them. Indeed, if they were articulated to that extent, a behavior mechanism fundamental to scientific advance would cease to function. What the tradition sees as eliminable imperfections in its rules of choice I take to be in part responses to the essential nature of science.

As so often, I begin with the obvious. Criteria that influence decisions without specifying what those decisions must be are familiar in many aspects of human life. Ordinarily, however, they are called, not criteria or rules, but maxims, norms, or values. Consider maxims first. The individual who invokes them when choice is urgent usually finds them frustratingly vague and often also in conflict one with another. Contrast "He who hesitates is lost" with "Look before you leap," or compare "Many hands make light work" with "Too many cooks spoil the broth." Individually maxims dictate different choices, collectively none at all. Yet no one suggests that supplying children with contradictory tags like these is irrelevant to their education. Opposing maxims alter the nature of the decision to be made, highlight the essential issues it presents, and point to those remaining aspects of the decision for which each individual must take responsibility himself. Once invoked, maxims like these alter the nature of the decision process and can thus change its outcome.

Values and norms provide even clearer examples of effective guidance in the presence of conflict and equivocation. Improving the quality of life is a value, and a car in every garage once followed from it as a norm. But quality of life has other aspects, and the old norm has become problematic. Or again, freedom of speech is a value, but so is preservation of life and property. In application, the two often conflict, so that judicial soul-searching, which still continues, has been required to prohibit such behavior as inciting to riot or shouting fire in a crowded theater. Difficulties like these are an appropriate source for frustration, but they rarely result in charges that values have no function or in calls for their abandonment. That response is barred to most of us by an acute consciousness that there are societies with other values and that these value differences result in other ways of life, other decisions about what may and what may not be done.

I am suggesting, of course, that the criteria of choice with which I began function not as rules, which determine choice, but as values, which influence it. Two men deeply committed to the same values may nevertheless, in particular situations, make different choices as, in fact, they do. But that difference in outcome ought not to suggest that the values scientists share are less than critically important either to their decisions or to the development of the enterprise in which they participate. Values like accuracy, consistency, and scope may prove ambiguous in application, both individually and collectively; they may, that is, be an insufficient basis for a *shared* algorithm of choice. But they do specify a great deal: what each scientist must consider in reaching a decision, what he may and may not consider relevant, and what he can legitimately be required to report as the basis for the choice he has made. Change the list, for example by adding social utility as a criterion, and some particular choices will be different, more like those one expects from a engineer. Subtract accuracy of fit to nature from the list, and the enterprise that results may not resemble science at all, but perhaps philosophy instead. Different creative disciplines are characterized, among other things, by different sets of shared values. If philosophy and engineering lie too close to the sciences, think of literature of the plastic arts. Milton's failure to set *Paradise Lost* in a Copernican universe does not indicate that he agreed with Ptolemy but that he had things other than science to do.

Recognizing that criteria of choice can function as values when incomplete as rules has, I think, a number of striking advantages. First, as I have already argued at length, it accounts in detail for aspects of scientific behavior which the tradition has seen as anomalous or even irrational. More important, it allows the standard criteria to function fully in the earliest stages of theory choice, the period when they are most needed but when, on the traditional view, they function badly or not at all. Copernicus was responding to them during the years required to convert heliocentric astronomy from a global conceptual scheme to mathematical machinery for predicting planetary position. Such predictions were what astronomers valued; in their absence, Copernicus would scarely have been heard, something which had happened to the idea of a moving earth before. That his own version convinced very few is less important than his acknowledgment of the basis on which judgments would have to be reached if heliocentricism were to survive. Though idiosyncrasy must be invoked to explain why Kepler and Galileo were early converts to Copernicus's system, the gaps filled by their efforts to perfect it were specified by shared values alone.

That point has a corollary which may be more important still. Most newly suggested theories do not survive. Usually the difficulties that evoked them are accounted for by more traditional means. Even when this does not occur, much work, both theoretical and experimental, is ordinarily required before the new theory can display sufficient accuracy and scope to generate widespread conviction. In short, before the group accepts it, a new theory has been tested over time by the research of a number of men, some working within it, others within its traditional rival. Such a mode of development, however, *requires* a decision process which permits rational men to disagree, and such disagreement would be barred by the shared algorithm which philosophers have generally sought. If it were at hand, all conforming scientists would make the same decision at the same time. With standards for acceptance set too low, they would move from one attractive global viewpoint to another, never giving traditional theory an opportunity to supply equivalent attractions. With standards set higher, no one satisfying the criterion of rationality would be inclined to try out the new theory, to articulate it in ways which showed its fruitfulness or displayed its accuracy and scope. I doubt that science would survive the change. What from one viewpoint may seem the looseness and imperfection of choice criteria conceived as rules may, when the same criteria are seen as values, appear an indispensable means of spreading the risk which the introduction of support of novelty always entails.

Even those who have followed me this far will want to know how a value-based enterprise of the sort I have described can develop as a science does, repeatedly producing powerful new techniques for prediction and control. To that question, unfortunately, I have no answer at all, but that is only another way of saying that I make no claim to have solved the problem of induction. If science did progress by virtue of some shared and binding algorithm of choice, I would be equally at a loss to explain its success. The lacuna is one I feel acutely, but its presence does not differentiate my position from the tradition.

It is, after all, no accident that my list of the values guiding scientific choice is, as nearly as makes any difference, identical with the tradition's list of rules dictating choice. Given any concrete situation to which the philosopher's rules could be applied, my values would function like his rules, producing the same choice. Any justification of induction, any explanation of why the rules worked, would apply equally to my values. Now consider a situation in which choice by shared rules proves impossible, not because the rules are wrong but because they are, as rules, intrinsically incomplete. Individuals must then still choose and be guided by the rules (now values) when they do so. For that purpose, however, each must first flesh out the rules, and each will do so in a somewhat different way even though the decision dictated by the variously completed rules may prove unanimous. If I now assume, in addition, that the group is large enough so that individual differences distribute on some normal curve, then any argument that justifies the philosopher's choice by rule should be immediately adaptable to my choice by value. A group too small, or a distribution excessively skewed by external historical pressures, would, of course, prevent the argument's transfer.[8] But those are just the circumstances under which scientific progress is itself problematic. The transfer is not then to be expected.

I shall be glad if these references to a normal distribution of individual differences and to the problem of induction make by position appear very close to more traditional views. With respect to theory choice, I have never thought my departures large and have been correspondingly startled by such charges as "mob psychology," quoted at the start. It is worth noting, however, that the positions are not quite identical, and for that purpose an analogy may be helpful. Many properties of liquids and gases can be accounted for on the kinetic theory by supposing that all molecules travel at the same speed. Among such properties are the regularities known as Boyle's and Charles's law. Other characteristics, most obviously evaporation, cannot be explained in so simple a way. To deal with them one must assume that molecular speeds differ, that they are distributed at random, governed by the laws of chance. What I have been suggesting here is that theory choice, too, can be explained only in part by a theory which attributes the same properties to all the scientists who must do the choosing. Essential aspects of the process generally known as verification will be understood only by recourse to the features with respect to which men may differ while still remaining scientists. The tradition takes it for granted that such features are vital to the process of discovery, which it at once and for that reason rules out of philosophical bounds. That they may have significant functions also in the philosophically central problem of justifying theory choice is what philosophers of science have to date categorically denied.

What remains to be said can be grouped in a somewhat miscellaneous epilogue. For the sake of clarity and to avoid writing a book, I have throughout this paper utilized some traditional concepts and locutions about the viability of which I have elsewhere expressed serious doubts. For those who know the work in which I have done so, I close by indicating three aspects of what I have said which would better represent my views if cast in other terms, simultaneously indicating the main directions in which such recasting should proceed. The areas I have in mind are: value invariance, subjectivity, and partial communication. If my views of scientific development are novel—a matter about which there is legitimate room for doubt—it is in areas such as these, rather than theory choice, that my main departures from tradition should be sought.

Throughtout this paper I have implicitly assumed that, whatever their initial source, the criteria or values deployed in theory choice are fixed once and for all, unaffected by their participation in transitions from one theory to another. Roughly speaking, but only very roughly, I take that to be the case. If the list of relevant values is kept short (I have mentioned five, not all independent) and if their specification is left vague, then such values as accuracy, scope, and fruitfulness are permanent attributes of science. But little knowledge of history is required to suggest that both the application of these values and, more obviously, the relative weights attached to them have varied markedly with time and also with field of application. Furthermore, many of these variations in value have been associated with particular changes in scientific theory. Though the experience of scientists provides no philosophical justification for the values they deploy (such justification would solve the problem of induction), those values are in part learned from that experience, and they evolve with it.

The whole subject needs more study (historians have usually taken scientific values, though not scientific methods, for granted), but a few remarks will illustrate the sort of variations I have in mind. Accuracy, as a value, has with time increasingly denoted quantitative or numerical agreement, sometimes at the expense of qualitative. Before early modern times, however, accuracy in that sense was a criterion only for astronomy, the science of the celestial region. Elsewhere it was neither expected nor sought. During the seventeenth century, however, the criterion of numerical agreement was extended to mechanics, during the late eighteenth and early nineteenth centuries to chemistry and such other subjects as electricity and heat, and in this century to many parts of biology. Or think of utility, an item of value not on my initial list. It too has figured significantly in scientific development, but far more strongly and steadily for chemists than for, say, mathematicians and physicists. Or consider scope. It is still an important scientific value, but important scientific advances have repeatedly been achieved at its expense, and the weight attributed to it at times of choice has diminished correspondingly.

What may seem particularly troublesome about changes like these is, of course, that they ordinarily occur in the aftermath of a theory change. One of the objections to Lavoisier's new chemistry was the roadblocks with which it confronted the achievement of what had previously been one of chemistry's traditional goals; the explanation of qualities, such as color and texture, as well as of their changes. With the acceptance of Lavoisier's theory such explanations ceased for some time to be a value for chemists; the ability to explain qualitative variation was no longer a criterion relevant to the evaluation of chemical theory. Clearly, if such value changes had occurred as rapidly or been as complete as the theory changes to which they related, then theory choice would be value choice, and neither could provide justification for the other. But, historically, value change is ordinarily a belated and largely unconscious concomitant of theory choice, and the former's magnitude is regularly smaller than the latter's. For the functions I have here ascribed to values, such relative stability provides a sufficient basis. The existence of a feedback loop through which theory change affects the values which led to that change does not make the decision process circular in any damaging sense.

About a second respect in which my resort to tradition may be misleading, I must be far more tentative. It demands the skills of an ordinary language philosopher, which I do not possess. Still, no very acute ear for language is required to generate discomfort with the ways in which the terms "objectivity" and, more especially, "subjectivity" have functioned in this paper. Let me briefly suggest the respects in which I believe language has gone astray. "Subjective" is a term with several established uses: in one of these it is opposed to "objective," in another to "judgmental." When my critics describe the idiosyncratic features to which I appeal as subjective, they resort, erroneously I think, to the second of these senses. When they complain that I deprive science of objectivity, they conflate that second sense of subjective with the first.

A standard application of the term "subjective" is to matters of taste, and my critics appear to suppose that that is what I have made of theory choice.

But they are missing a distinction standard since Kant when they do so. Like sensation reports, which are also subjective in the sense now at issue, matters of taste are undiscussable. Suppose that, leaving a movie theater with a friend after seeing a western, I exclaim: "How I liked that terrible potboiler!" My friend, if he disliked the film, may tell me I have low tastes, a matter about which, in these circumstances, I would readily agree. But, short of saying that I lied, he cannot disagree with my report that I liked the film or try to persuade me that what I said about my reaction was wrong. What is discussable in my remark is not my characterization of my internal state, my exemplification of taste, but rather my *judgment* that the film was a potboiler. Should my friend disagree on that point, we may argue most of the night, each comparing the film with good or great ones we have seen, each revealing, implicitly or explicitly, something about how he *judges* cinematic merit, about his aesthetic. Though one of us may, before retiring, have persuaded the other, he need not have done so to demonstrate that our difference is one of judgment, not taste.

Evaluations or choices of theory have, I think exactly this character. Not that scientists never say merely, I like such and such a theory, or I do not. After 1926 Einstein said little more than that about his opposition to the quantum theory. But scientists may always be asked to explain their choices, to exhibit the bases for their judgments. Such judgments are eminently discussable, and the man who refuses to discuss his own cannot expect to be taken seriously. Though there are, very occasionally, leaders of scientific taste, their existence tends to prove the rule. Einstein was one of the few, and his increasing isolation from the scientific community in later life shows how very limited a role taste alone can play in theory choice. Bohr, unlike Einstein, did discuss the bases for his judgment, and he carried the day. If my critics introduce the term "subjective" in a sense that opposes it to judgmental—thus suggesting that I make theory choice undiscussable, a matter of taste—they have seriously mistaken my position.

Turn now to the sense in which "subjectivity" is opposed to "objectivity," and note first that it raises issues quite separate from those just discussed. Whether my taste is low or refined, my report that I liked the film is objective unless I have lied. To my judgment that the film was a potboiler, however, the objective-subjective distinction does not apply at all, at least not obviously and directly. When my critics say I deprive theory choice of objectivity, they must, therefore, have recourse to some very different sense of subjective, presumably the one in which bias and personal likes or dislikes function instead of, or in the face of, the actual facts. But that sense of subjective does not fit the process I have been describing any better than the first. Where factors dependent on individual biography or personality must be introduced to make values applicable, no standards of factuality or actuality are being set aside. Conceivably my discussion of theory choice indicates some limitations of objectivity, but not by isolating elements properly called subjective. Nor am I even quite content with the notion that what I have been displaying are limitations. Objectivity ought to be analyzable in terms of criteria like accuracy and consistency. If these criteria do not supply all the guidance that we have customarily expected of them, then it may be the meaning rather than the limits of objectivity that my argument shows.

Turn, in conclusion, to a third respect, or set of respects, in which this paper needs to be recast. I have assumed throughout that the discussions surrounding theory choice are unproblematic, that the facts appealed to in such discussions are independent of theory, and that the discussions' outcome is appropriately called a choice. Elsewhere I have challenged all three of these assumptions, arguing that communication between proponents of different theories is inevitably partial, that what each takes to be facts depends in part on the theory he exposes, and that an individual's transfer of allegiance from theory to theory is often better described as conversion than as choice. Though all these theses are problematic as well as controversial, my commitment to them is undiminished. I shall not now defend them, but must at least attempt to indicate how what I have said here can be adjusted to conform with these more central aspects of my view of scientific development.

For that purpose I resort to an analogy I have developed in other places. Proponents of different theories are, I have claimed, like native speakers of different languages. Communication between them goes on by translation, and it raises all translation's familiar difficulties. That analogy is, of course, incomplete, for the vocabulary of the two theories may be identical, and most words function in the same ways in both. But some words in the basic as well as in the theoretical vocabularies of the two theories—words like "star" and "planet," "mixture" and "compound," or "force" and "matter"—do function differently. Those differences are unexpected and will be discovered and localized, if at all, only by repeated experience of communication breakdown. Without pursuing the matter further, I simply assert the existence of significant limits to what the proponents of different theories can communicate to one another. The same limits make it difficult or, more likely, impossible for an individual to hold both theories in mind together and compare them point by point with each other and with nature. That sort of comparison is, however, the process on which the appropriateness of any word like "choice" depends.

Nevertheless, despite the incompleteness of their communication, proponents of different theories can exhibit to each other, not always easily, the concrete technical results achievable by those who practice within each theory. Little or no translation is required to apply at least some value criteria to those results. (Accuracy and fruitfulness are most immediately applicable, perhaps followed by scope. Consistency and simplicity are far more problematic.) However incomprehensible the new theory may be to the proponents of tradition, the exhibit of impressive concrete results will persuade at least a few of them that they must discover how such results are achieved. For that purpose they must learn to translate, perhaps by treating already published papers as a Rosetta stone or, often more effective, by visiting the innovator, talking with him, watching him and his students at work. Those exposures may not result in the adoption of the theory; some advocates of the tradition may return home and attempt to adjust the old theory to produce equivalent results. But others, if the new theory is to survive, will find that at some point in the language-learning process they have ceased to translate and begun instead to speak the language like a native. No process quite like choice has occurred, but they are practicing the new theory nonetheless. Furthermore, the factors that have led them to risk the conversion they have undergone are just the ones this paper has underscored in discussing a somewhat different process, one which, following the philosophical tradition, it has labelled theory choice.

NOTES

1. *The Structure of Scientific Revolutions,* 2d ed. (Chicago, 1970), pp. 148, 151-52, 159. All the passages from which these fragments are taken appeared in the same form in the first edition, published in 1962.

2. Ibid., p. 170.

3. Imre Lakatos, "Falsification and the Methodology of Scientific Research Programmes," in I. Lakatos and A. Musgrave. eds., *Criticism and the Growth of Knowledge* (Cambridge, 1970), pp. 91–195. The quoted phrase, which appears on p. 178, is italicized in the original.

4. Dudley Shapere. "Meaning and Scientific Change," in R. G. Colodny. ed., *Mind and Cosmos: Essays in Contemporary Science and Philosophy,* University of Pittsburgh Series in the Philosophy of Science, vol. 3 (Pittsburgh, 1966), pp. 41-85. The quotation will be found on p. 67.

5. Israel Scheffler, *Science and Subjectivity* (Indianapolis, 1967), p. 81.

6. The last criterion, fruitfulness, deserves more emphasis than it has yet received. A scientist choosing between two theories ordinarily knows that his decision will have a bearing on his subsequent research career. Of course he is especially attracted by a theory that promises the concrete successes for which scientists are ordinarily rewarded.

7. The least equivocal example of this position is probably the one developed in Scheffler, *Science and Subjectivity,* chap. 4.

8. If the group is small, it is more likely that random fluctuations will result in its members' sharing an atypical set of values and therefore making choices different from those that would be made by a larger and more representative group. External environment—intellectual, ideological, or economic—must systematically affect the value system of much larger groups, and the consequences can include difficulties in introducing the scientific enterprise to societies with inimical values or perhaps even the end of that enterprise within societies where it had once flourished. In this area, however, great caution is required. Changes in the environment where science is practiced can also have fruitful effects on research. Historians often resort, for example, to differences between national environments to explain why particular innovations were initiated and at first disproportionately pursued in particular countries, e.g., Darwinism in Britain, energy conservation in Germany. At present we know substantially nothing about the minimum requisites of the social milieux within which a science-like enterprise might flourish.

21

Scientific Rationality:
Analytic vs. Pragmatic Perspectives
Carl G. Hempel

I. Introduction

Of all the current topics of inquiry in the philosophy of science, none has provoked a more intensive and fruitful discussion than the conflicting conceptions of science and its methodology that have been developed by analytic empiricists on one hand and by historically and sociologically oriented thinkers on the other.

By analytic empiricism, I understand here a body of ideas that has its roots in the logical empiricism of the Vienna Circle and the Berlin group, as well as in the work of kindred thinkers, such as Popper, Braithwaite, and Nagel. Among the protagonists of the more recent historic-sociological approach, I have in mind particularly Thomas Kuhn, Paul Feyerabend, and the late R. N. Hanson.

The considerations I propose to put before you concern two fundamental problems that have been at the center of the controversy between the two schools: namely

(1) *The problem of the rationality of science:* in what sense, on what grounds, and to what extent can scientific inquiry be qualified as a rational enterprise?

and

(2) *The problem of cognitive status of the methodology and philosophy of science:* are the principles set forth by these disciplines intended to

provide norms for rational scientific inquiry, or are they meant to give an explanatory account of scientific research as a human activity?

Let me broadly and somewhat schematically, sketch the background for this discussion. Analytic empiricism views the philosophy of science as a discipline which by "logical analysis" and "rational reconstruction" seeks to "explicate" the meanings of scientific terms and sentences and to exhibit the logical structure and the rationale of scientific theorizing. The philosophy of science is regarded as concerned exclusively with the logical and systematic aspects of sound scientific theorizing and of the knowledge claims it yields. On this view, the psychological, sociological, and historical facets of science as a human enterprise are irrelevant to the philosophy of science, much as the genetic and psychological aspects of human reasoning are held to be irrelevant for pure logic, which is concerned only with questions of the deductive validity of inferences, logical truth and falsity, consistency, provability, definability, and the like. The principles of logical theory clearly do not, and are not meant to, give a descriptive account of "how we think," of how human beings actually reason; but in so far as they provide criteria of logical validity and truth, they can be employed normatively, as standards for the critical appraisal of particular inferences and logical claims.

In view of analytic empiricism, the methodology of science similarly has the task of explicating standards for rational modes of formulating, appraising, and changing scientific knowledge claims; such explications may then serve as norms for the guidance of inquiry and for the critical appraisal of particular research procedures and theoretical claims: the logical empiricists' rejection of neo-vitalism as a pseudo-theory and Popper's exclusion of psychoanalysis from the realm of scientific theories illustrate this point.

The historic-sociological school, on the other hand, rejects the idea of methodological principles arrived at, as it seems, by purely philosophical analysis; it insists that an adequate methodology must be based on a close study of the practice of scientific inquiry and must be capable of explaining certain characteristics of past and present research and theory change in science.

The contrasting views of the two schools have been thrown into sharp relief in their debate over the extent to which and the grounds on which it is possible to formulate and justify methodological principles for a rational choice between competing scientific theories.

According to analytic empiricism, such methodological principles have the character to generate criteria for rational theory choice; they might determine, for example, which of two competing theories possesses the higher rational credibility or acceptablity in consideration of all the pertinent information available at the time. In fact, analytic attempts at explicating the notions of confirmation and of inductive probability and at formulating "rules of acceptance" for scientific hypotheses were efforts in just that direction.

Kuhn, in whose account of scientific revolutions the problem of choice between conflicting paradigmatic theories plays a central role, regards the search for such analytic criteria as basically misguided and as doomed to failure. He does acknowledge that there are certain considerations, noted also in the earlier philosophy of science, which influence the decisions scientists make in the context of theory choice; he speaks of them as professionally shared preferences or values. Among them are a preference for theories of quantitative form whose predictions show a close fit with experimental or observational findings; for theories of wide scope; for theories that correctly predict novel phenomena; and some others. All these characteristics, he says, provide "good reasons for theory choice."[1]

But Kuhn rightly notes that those desiderata do not remotely suffice to determine a unique choice between competing theories, and he further insists that there are no methodological criteria which have that power and which would command the assent of the scientific community: there are no generally binding rules that compel the choice between theories on the basis of logic and experiment alone.[2] Theory choice is emphatically presented as the result of group decisions which are not determined by rules of rational procedure of the sort analytic empiricism would envision.

Yet despite this naturalistic emphasis, Kuhn views science as a rational enterprise. Thus, he says: "scientific behavior, taken as a whole, is the best example we have of rationality" and "if history or any other empirical discipline leads us to believe that the development of science depends essentially on behavior that we have previously thought to be irrational, then we should conclude not that science is irrational, but that our notion of rationality needs adjustment here and there."[3] Thus, Kuhn regards his account of science as both empirical and normative. In response to the question, raised by Feyerabend, whether his pronouncements are to be read as descriptive or as prescriptive, he has said quite explicitly: "they should be read in both ways at once."[4]

II. The Janus-head of Rational Explanation and the Idea of an E-N Methodology

But surely, the principles of a given methodology cannot literally be both explanatory and normative. For in the former case, they would form an empirical theory, supported by pertinent evidence, which would serve to explain certain significant aspects of the research behavior of scientists; whereas in the latter case, they would express conditions of rationality for scientific inquiry.

Yet the conception of a methodology, or some methodological principles, having this double aspect can be given a plausible construal, as is suggested by the following consideration: An explanation of a particular case of theory-choice or paradigm-change is clearly an explanation of a human decision. Now, human decisions and actions are typically explained by reference to the agent's motivating reasons; and in the formulation and even in the philo-sophical analysis of such accounts two distinct senses of accounting are not infrequently confounded or fused, namely, accounting for a decision in the sense of explaining it and accounting for a decision in the sense of justifying it. This is illustrated by formulations of the following type:

> Agent A intended to attain goal G and had a set B of beliefs about the circumstances in which he had to act—particularly about alternative means available to him for attaining his goal. But given A's goal and his beliefs, the appropriate or rational thing for him to do was X. That is why A decided on course of action X.

But surely, an account of this kind cannot explain why A did in fact choose X. For the norm it invokes about the proper thing to do under the specified circumstances has no explanatory force at all. Even if the norm be granted, it is entirely possible that A may have been aware of, or not committed to, the standard of appropriateness or rationality it expresses, and that he might, therefore, in fact not have chosen X. The argument invoking the normative principle offers no explanation of A's choice; but it does offer a *justification* for it by showing that what A chose to do was appropriate in the sense of the cited norm.

A corresponding *explanation* requires, instead of that norm, a psychological hypothesis to the effect that A had adopted the norm and thus had acquired a disposition to act in accordance with it. Let us note in passing that whereas a justificatory account will be acceptable only if the norm in question is acknowledged as sound, the acceptability of the corresponding explanatory account is subject to no such condition. If indeed A was disposed to act in accordance with the cited norm, then this fact can be invoked to explain A's decision, no matter whether the norm is deemed to be sound.

The tendency to fuse explanation with justification in accounting for human decisions is thus closely linked to the fact that when a decision is explained by attributing to the agent certain motivating considerations, then these considerations, if suitably spelled out, can be evaluated in their own right as to their "rationality"; and such evaluation may indeed afford a justification of the given decision. An account which does possess this double aspect of explanation and justification might be called an *ideal rational account.*

There are some kinds of human decision which seem, in fairly close approximation, to admit of such a two-faced account. Consider, for example, the case of an engineer in charge of quality control who has to decide, on the basis of sample tests, whether a given batch of hormone tablets or of ball bearings manufactured by his firm is to be released for sale or rather to be reprocessed or destroyed because of excessive flaws. His decisions may well be explainable, and indeed predictable, on the basis of the sample findings, by the assumption that he has acquired the disposition to follow such and such specific decision criteria; while on the other hand, the criteria—or some more general decision-theoretical principles from which they can be derived—provide a justification for his particular decisions.

These considerations suggest a plausible construal (I am inclined to think:

the only plausible construal) of the idea that certain principles in the method-ology of science can play both an explanatory and a normative role. Such a two-faced, Janus-head methodological theory would have to present certain aspects of scientific research, such as theory testing and theory choice, as activities aimed at certain scientific goals, and carried out in accordance with specified rules which can be justified by showing that the modes of procedure they prescribe are rational means of pursuing the given goals.

In order to fulfill both its explanatory and its justificatory function, such a methodological theory for science or for some segment of it would have to specify certain goals of inquiry for the given field and certain procedural norms or rules for the pursuit of those goals; and it would then have to make two quite different claims:

(i) an explanatory claim, briefly to the effect that the practitioners of the science in question share a commitment, and thus a general disposition, to pursue the specified goals in accordance with the specified rules; and that, as a consequence, certain professional decisions made by the scientists can be explained by reference to those commitments;

(ii) a justificatory claim to the effect that the specified procedural rules determine approporiate, or "rational," ways of pursuing the given goals. (How the notion of rationality might be construed here is a question that will be considered shortly.)

I shall refer to a methodological theory of the kind here adumbrated as an explanatory-normative methodology, or as an *E-N methodology* for short. This is clearly an idealized notion: it is not to be expected that an *E-N methodology* can be formulated which would afford a satisfactory explanation even for the major turns in the development of science. Thus, for example, Lakatos, whose conception of a methodological theory has a certain affinity to that of an *E-N methodology,* emphasizes that for an explanation of actual occurrences in the history of science, "external" factors must often be invoked in addition to "internal," methodological, considerations.[5]

III. On the Notion of Scientific Rationality

Let me now turn to the idea of rationality of scientific inquiry, which has been the subject of extensive controversy in the recent philosophy of science.

I think it interesting, but also somewhat disturbing, that Popper, Lakatos, Kuhn, Feyerabend, and others have made diverse pronouncements concerning the rationality or irrationality of science or of certain modes of inquiry without, however, as far as I am aware, giving a reasonably explicit characterization of the concept of rationality which they have in mind and which they seek to illuminate or to disparage in their methodological investigations. Thus we find Lakatos bringing the charge of irrationalism against Kuhn's account of scientific theorizing, whereas Kuhn, as noted earlier, claims that his account takes scientific research behavior, as a whole, to be the best example we have of rationality.

What is to be understood here by "rationality," and what kinds of consideration could be properly adduced in a critical appraisal of attributions of rationality to science as a whole or to certain modes of inquiry? I have no satisfactory general answers to these questions, but I would like to put before you some tentative reflections on the subject.

First, a mode of procedure or a rule calling for that procedure surely can be called rational or irrational only relative to the goals the procedure is meant to attain. In so far as a methodological theory does propose rules or norms, these norms have to be regarded as instrumental norms: their appropriateness must be judged by reference to the objectives of the inquiry to which they pertain or, more ambitiously, by reference to the goals of pure scientific research in general.

Any attempt to give a characterization of "the goals of science" faces serious difficulties. But I hope you will permit me to begin with an avowedly oversimplified construal of those objectives; for even this schematic conception can serve quite well as a background against which to formulate some reflections concerning rationality which should be relevant also to more complex construals of the goals of scientific inquiry.

Let us assume, then, that science aims at establishing a sequence of increasingly comprehensive and accurate systems of empirical knowledge. Each such system might be thought of as represented by a set K of sentences which has been adopted, and is bound to be modified, in accordance with certain procedural rules.

Given this goal, there are certain methodological norms which can be qualified as requirements of rational procedure on the ground that—speaking somewhat charitably—they are necessary conditions for anyone of the changing systems K which science might accept at some time or another.

Among these necessary conditions are the requirement of intersubjective testability and the requirement of actual test with satisfactory outcome. Another such condition would require that any of the classes K be deductively closed, since the logical consequences of sentences accepted as presumably true must be presumed to be true as well. Another necessary condition would be that of logical consistency; and there may well be some others.

The goal-dependence of these conditions of rationality is clear. If, for example, it should be our goal to form a set of beliefs about the world that is emotionally reassuring or esthetically satisfying, then different procedural principles would qualify as rational. To further the attainment of our objectives, we might do well not to acknowledge all the logical consequences of accepted sentences and not to judge proposed beliefs in the light of all the relevant evidence obtainable—or better yet, perhaps, simply to forego empirical testing altogether.

In his plea for methodological anarchy, Feyerabend raises the question whether instead of "science as we know it today (the science of critical rationalism that has been freed from all inductive elements)," we would not prefer a science that is "more anarchistic and more subjective."[6] One might surely prefer the pursuit of the goals suggested by Feyerabend, and one might be convinced, as he seems to be, that it would be better for humanity to abandon "science as we know it"; but this does not change the fact that the modes of procedure appropriate for the pursuit of Feyerabend's objectives are not rational for science as it is commonly understood, and certainly not for the pursuit of the goals of science envisaged in our simple construal.

The modest norms of scientific rationality we have noted so far reflect necessary conditions for the attainment of the objectives of science. Could there be procedural norms reflecting sufficient conditions? Surely not; for such norms would, in effect, afford a solution to the problem of induction.

Let us look next at the familiar features—also mentioned by Kuhn—which scientists agree in regarding as desirable characteristics of scientific theories, and which therefore provide some basis for choosing between competing theories: closeness of quantitative fit between theoretical predictions and scientific data, large scope, prediction of novel effects, and some others. It seems to me that most of these desiderata are best regarded as providing a fuller characterization of the goals of scientific theorizing rather than as instrumental norms aimed at enhancing the prospects of achieving those goals. (Simplicity might similarly be regarded as a feature characterizing the goals of scientific theorizing; but alternatively, it might be viewed as an instrumental norm on the ground of the belief that the simpler theory is more likely to be true.)

But regardless of what role is assigned to the desiderata, it is clear, as Kuhn has stressed, that even if they are generally acknowledged by (belong to the "shared values" of) a scientific community, different scientists may, and do, understand them in somewhat different ways and may therefore differ in their judgments as to which of two theories satisfies a particular desideratum more fully. Moreover, scientists may differ in the priorities or relative weights they assign to the various desiderata. In sum, commitment to those norms does not ensure a uniform decision as to which of two theories outranks the other, by way of satisfying the entire set of desiderata.

Now, these last considerations are psychological and sociological and cannot, of course, prove it impossible to formulate precise general criteria of theory choice embodying those desiderata; but the difficulties encountered by analytic efforts to explicate such notions as the simplicity of theories or the degree of variety of the empirical phenomena covered by a theory (and thus, perhaps, its scope) do not augur well for the attainability of those analytic objectives. Indeed, Ernest Nagel argued long ago, on essentially the grounds just surveyed, that efforts to construct a general criterion of this kind were futile.[7]

IV. On the Relevance of Decision Theory to Problems of Theory Choice

The preceding considerations also cast serious doubt on the promise of another idea that might suggest itself here, namely, an appeal to mathematical decision theory as a possible source of rational standards for a choice between competing theories, or knowledge systems, or paradigms.

Decision theory does provide objective criteria for choosing between alternative hypotheses; but these criteria presuppose that in addition to the hypotheses in question, a precise comparative or quantitative specification is given of the advantages that would result from adopting a given hypothesis if it is true, and the disadvantages that would result from adopting it if it should be false; and similarly, a specification of advantages or disadvantages connected with the rejection of a hypothesis which may in fact be true or false. "Utilities" and "disutilities" of the requisite kind can plausibly be specified in certain cases where the adoption of a hypothesis amounts to its application for some particular practical purpose, as in the case of industrial quality control. For theory choice is pure science, the requisite utilities or disutilities would have to express the gain or loss that would come from the adoption or the rejection of a true theory or a false one, in the light of the objectives of scientific research. But among those objectives are the desiderata considered a moment ago; and as far as these defy precise explication, decision theory is inapplicable.

Considerations of the kind outlined in the preceding section concerning the widely acknowledged desiderata for scientific theories led Kuhn to the claim that there are no generally binding rules of scientific procedure which unambiguously determine theory choice in the light of logic and experience alone. Kuhn therefore presented theory choice as the result of group decisions made by the scientists in the field, which are not fully governed by general rules, and which have to be accounted for in terms of the common training of the members of the group. This characterization was received by some critics with the charge of irrationalism and of appeal to mob psychology—a charge that may have seemed to be substantiated by Kuhn's comparison of theory change in science to a religious conversion experience involving a leap of faith. This may have seemed to license the adoption of any theory one might have faith in. But the requirements of testability, predictivity, evidential fit, and large scope, which Kuhn acknowledges, would suffice, despite their vagueness, to rule out, say, astrology or chiromancy, and in a competition with currently accepted theories.

And as for Kuhn's invocation, in the context of theory choice, of group decisions not governed by general rules of procedure, it may be of interest to note that in the first decade of this century, Pierre Duhem expressed quite a similar view. He argued, on purely logical grounds, that the outcome of a scientific experiment cannot refute a theoretical assumption in isolation, but only a comprehensive set of assumptions. If the experimental findings conflict with predictions deducible from the set, then some change has to be made in the total theory; but no objective logical criteria determine uniquely what changes should be made. That decision, Duhem says, must be left to "the good sense" of the scientists in the field.[8] Here, then, normative methodology leaves off, and only socio-psychological considerations are invoked, with perhaps a vaguely explanatory intent.

As for the charge of irrationalism that has been brought against Kuhn's account, I have to say that I cannot point to any justifiable canons of rational inquiry that Kuhn could be accused of having denied or slighted.

V. Rationality and Incommensurability

I want to take issue, however, with one argument, offered especially by Feyerabend, for the thesis that there can be no general criteria of choice between competing comprehensive theories. The argument is based on the idea that such theories do not share a single statement, that they are "completely disjointed, or incommensurable"; he cites classical and relativistic physics as an example.[9] I have strong doubts about this idea, largely because the notion of incommensurability is not made sufficiently clear. Feyerabend seems to hold that in the transition from one paradigm to another, all the terms taken over from the old theory into the new one come to function in a new set of theoretical principles and therefore change their meanings,—that this is the case even for the terms used to describe instrument readings and observational findings, and that therefore there is no possibility at all of comparing the two theories or the bodies of evidence relevant to them. In fact, Feyerabend concludes, concerning the possible bases of theory choice: "What remains are esthetic judgments, judgments of taste, and our subjective wishes."[10] Kuhn, too, has placed considerable emphasis on the incommensurability of paradigms, but he has not drawn quite such extreme and subjective conclusions.

Now, the transition from one paradigm to another clearly does bring with it considerable changes in the *use* of the terms taken over into the new theory: the paradigms differ in many of the sentences containing those terms. But why should a change of this kind be taken to signal a change in the meanings of the terms concerned rather than a change in the claims made about the entities they refer to? To illustrate: In *The Structure of Scientific Revolutions,* Kuhn remarks that the transition from the Ptolemaic to the Copernican System effected a change in the meanings of such terms as 'planet', 'earth', and 'motion'.[11] But on what grounds can it be claimed that the change in the statements containing those terms reflects a change in the meanings of the words rather than a change in what is assumed or asserted about the earth, the planets, and their motions?

In the absence of a more explicit account of meaning change for theoretical terms, claims of incommensurability cannot, I think, establish the impossibility of formulating criteria for a comparative evaluation of competing paradigms. It seems clear, for example, that the results of parallax measurements constitute evidence that is relevant to the Copernican as well as to the Ptolemaic theory, and that they thus form some basis for a comparison between the two.

VI. On the "Timelessness" of Methodological Norms

The methodological efforts of logical empiricism were not very much concerned with problems of theory change in science; but they did yield theories of confirmation and of probability for scientific hypotheses, which propounded explicit and precise standards for the comparison or appraisal of hypotheses in regard to the evidential support conferred upon them by the available empirical data. Carnap referred to his quantitative theory of confirmation as "inductive logic"; as the term suggests, the principles aimed at by theories of inductive support were thought of as being analogous to the principles of valid deductive inference formulated by deductive logic. At least implicitly, I think, it was assumed that methodological principles for appraising the rational credibility of hypotheses would have to hold *a priori* as it were, independently of any empirical matters, and immutably at all times—all this in analogy to the standard conception of the timelessness and immutable validity of the principles of deductive logic.

But it seems to me open to question whether this conception can be reasonably applied to all methodological principles of rational theory choice. For what kinds of theory can be reasonably entertained, or be regarded as worth serious consideration, will depend on the general view of the world—especially of its deep and pervasive features—that prevails at the time.

Thus, for example, Maxwell held that space and time coordinates should enter into scientific laws and theories, not absolutely or explicitly, but only in the form of differences; his reason being that the mere spatio-temporal location of an event could exert no causal influence on the course taken by that event: what occurs, under given physical conditions, at one spatio-temporal location will under the same physical conditions, equally happen at any other spatio-temporal location. Maxwell regarded this principle as providing a more precise expression of the idea that "the same causes will always produce the same effects."[12] Actually, we might note, his condition is satisfied not only by strictly causal or deterministic laws, but also by the probabilistic laws of contemporary science. It may be said to impose a constraint on rational theory choice, reflecting the assumption that in our world spatio-temporal locations have no "nomic efficacy," whether of a causal or of a probabilistic kind. But it is conceivable that that assumption may eventually come to be abandoned in the light of new scientific findings: and in this case, the methodological norm would have to be abandoned as well.

Similarly, 150 years ago, a theory propounding quantization of energy or perhaps even of space and time, or postulating the creation of electrons from empty space, would presumably not have been regarded as a rationally open theoretical option.

And Carnap himself, the leading figure among logical analysts, provided in his theory of inductive probability for a "continuum of inductive methods," each characterized by a real-number value of a parameter lambda, with the explicit understanding that the value of that parameter, and thereby the principles of the inductive methodology, could be changed in consideration of certain very general features of the empirical knowledge available at a given time.

That the standards of choice among the hypotheses or theories should depend on such general assumptions about the causal structure or about the basic articulation and the degree of orderliness of the world seems quite plausible and reasonable: but then, the conception of timelessness for all standards of rational theory choice must be abandoned. On this point, I find myself in agreement even with Feyerabend, though, as indicated earlier, I cannot follow him the rest of the way to anarchy.

VII. The Conception of Rationality in Kuhn's Perspective on Science

I have argued that to the extent that a methodological theory of science is to provide standards of rationality for scientific inquiry as well as a basis for explaining certain aspects of the actual research behavior of scientists, the theory must have the character of an *E-N* methodology: its norms must express goal-dependent, instrumental, conditions of rationality; and its explanatory potential must lie in its ability to "rationalize" significant aspects of scientific research, i.e., to explain them by the assumption that the scientists in question are disposed to act in accordance with the specified norms.

Consider from this point of view Kuhn's remark, cited earlier, that his methodological pronouncements should be read as prescriptive and as descriptive at once.

Let us look first at their prescriptive import, which Kuhn characterizes schematically as follows: "The structure of my argument is simple and, I think, unexceptionable: scientists behave in the following ways; those modes of behavior have (here theory enters) the following essential functions; in the absence of an alternate mode *that would serve similar functions,* scientists should behave essentially as they do if their concern is to improve scientific knowledge."[13] This statement does seem to reflect an instrumental conception of the rationality of scientific behavior, the "essential function" of such behavior being the improvement of scientific knowledge. But surely, a methodological theory can yield prescriptions for scientific inquiry only in so far as it formulates explicit rules or norms for the conduct of inquiry: and it seems very questionable to me whether a theory in Kuhn's style and spirit can provide the requisite rules or norms.

I referred earlier to Kuhn's remark that scientific behavior is the best example we have of rationality, and that we had better change our standards of rationality if science seems to violate them. But any given piece of behavior can be described in many different ways; yet it can be qualified as rational or as irrational, if at all, then only under certain particular kinds of description, which represent it as a rule-following activity conforming to certain explicitly specified rules, in the pursuit of specified goals.

To put the point somewhat differently: Kuhn's remark that "scientists should behave essentially as they do if their concern is to improve scientific knowledge" leaves open the question: in what respects? What aspects, what characteristics of the actual behavior of scientists are the ones that matter, the ones to be emulated in a rational pursuit of the improvement of scientific knowledge? And in what sense, and on what grounds, can those characteristics be held to serve the function of improving scientific knowledge?

Kuhn's construal of the explanatory import of his ideas for actual cases of theory choice seems to me open to similar questions. Kuhn describes that import as follows: "take a *group* of the ablest available people with the most appropriate motivation; train them in some science and in the special ties relevant to the choice at hand; imbue them with the value system, the ideology, current in their discipline (and to a great extent in other scientific fields as well); and, finally, *let them make their choice*. If that technique does not account for scientific development as we know it, then no other will."[14]

But, literally speaking, a technique for training or programming people does not constitute an explanation of any part of their subsequent behavior. For that, we need an empirical theory which yields explicit specifications of those beliefs, values, ideological principles, etc. whose acceptance will account for the theory choices in question. The claim that persons who are motivated and trained in the ways in which scientists are will make the choices actually encountered in science fails to specify just what aspects of the behavior of scientists are relevant to the explanation of theory choice; and in so far as those aspects are not made explicit, no explanatory claim can be made for the methodological theory.

VIII. Conclusion

The conception of science as the exemplar of the rational pursuit of knowledge was emphatically held also by logical empiricism, which frequently supported and revised its explications of scientific concepts and procedures by appeal to scientific usage. One familiar example of this process is the gradual expansion of the ways in which Carnap explicated scientific modes of introducing new terms: from explicit definition to the use of reduction sentences and chains of such sentences on to the global specification of a set of theoretical concepts by means of theoretical postulates and correspondence rules: ever closer attention to the modes and needs of scientific theorizing led here to a far-reaching liberalization of what were regarded as essential conditions for the introduction of "meaningful" new terms. In this sense, the rational reconstructions formulated by logical empiricists did have a descriptive facet. But it must be acknowledged that the analytic empiricist concern with clarity and rigor and with systematic comprehensiveness and formal simplicity encouraged the formulation of some technically very impressive explicatory systems which are rather far removed from the objectives and modes of thinking that prompt scientific investigations; those systems, accordingly, possess only very limited explanatory potential.

Reconsideration and reorientation are thus clearly needed, and the critical and constructive ideas of the historic-pragmatic school have opened highly illuminating and promising new perspectives on issues of central concern to the methodology of science. But in so far as a proposed methodological theory of science is to afford an account of scientific inquiry as a rational pursuit, it will have to specify certain goals of scientific inquiry as well as some methodological principles observed in their pursuit; finally, it will have to exhibit the instrumental rationality of the principles in relation to the goals. Only to the extent that this can be done does the conception of science as the exemplar of rationality appear to be viable.

NOTES

1. See Kuhn (1970a), pp. 155ff.: (1970b), pp. 261f.
2. Kuhn (1971), pp. 144–145.
3. Kuhn (1971), p. 144.
4. Kuhn (1970b), p. 237.
5. See, for example, Lakatos (1971), pp. 105–108.
6. Feyerabend (1970), p. 76.
7. Nagel (1939), Chapter 11, sec. 8.
8. Cf. Duhem (1962), Part II, chapter VI, section 10.
9. Feyerabend (1970), p. 280.
10. Feyerabend (1970), p. 90.
11. Kuhn (1970a), pp. 128, 149–150.
12. Maxwell (1887), pp. 31–32.
13. Kuhn (1970b), p. 237 (italics in original).
14. Kuhn (1970b), pp. 237–238 (italics in original).

REFERENCES

Duhem, P. (1962). *The Aim and Structure of Physical Theory* (New York: Atheneum. (French original first published in 1906).

Feyerabend, P. (1970). "Against Method: Outline of an Anarchistic Theory of Knowledge," in Radner, M. and Winokur, S., eds., *Minnesota Studies in the Philosophy of Science,* vol. IV, pp. 17–130.

Kuhn, T. S. (1970a). *The Structure of Scientific Revolutions,* Second edition, (Chicago University Press).

———. (1970b). "Reflections on My Critics," in Lakatos, I. and Musgrave, A., ed., *Criticism and the Growth of Knowledge* (Cambridge University Press), pp. 231–278.

———. (1971). "Notes on Lakatos," in Cohen, R. S. and Buck, R. C., eds., *P.S.A. 1970, Boston Studies in the Philosophy of Science,* vol. VIII, pp. 137–146.

Lakatos, I. (1971), "History of Science and Its Rational Reconstruction," in Cohen, R. S. and Buck, R. C., eds., *P.S.A. 1970, Boston Studies in the Philosophy of Science,* vol. VIII, pp. 91–136.

Maxwell, J. C. (1878). *Matter and Motion* (New York: D. Van Nostrand).

Nagel, E. (1939). *Principles of the Theory of Probability* (University of Chicago Press).

Popper, K. R. (1959). *The Logic of Scientific Discovery* (London: Hutchinson).

22

The Variety of Reasons
for the Acceptance of Scientific Theories
Philipp G. Frank

Among scientists it is taken for granted that a theory "should be" accepted if and only if it is "true"; to be true means in this context to be in agreement with the observable facts that can be logically derived from the theory. Every influence of moral, religious, or political considerations upon the acceptance of a theory is regarded as "illegitimate" by the so-called "community of scientists." This view certainly has had a highly salutary effect upon the evolution of science as a human activity. It tells the truth—but not the whole truth. It has never happened that all the conclusions drawn from a theory have agreed with the observable facts. The scientific community has accepted theories only when a vast number of facts has been derived from few and simple principles. A familiar example is the derivation of the immensely complex motions of celestial bodies from the simple Newtonian formula of gravitation, or the large variety of electromagnetic phenomena from Maxwell's field equations.

If we restrict our attention to the two criterions that are called "agreement with observations" and "simplicity," we remain completely within the domain of activities that are cultivated and approved by the community of scientists. But, if we have to choose a certain theory for acceptance, we do not know what respective weight should be attributed to these two criterions. There is obviously no theory that agrees with *all* observations and no theory that has "perfect" simplicity. Therefore, in every individual case, one has to make a choice of a theory by a compromise between both criterions. However, when we try to specify the degree of "simplicity" in different theories, we soon notice that attempts of this kind lead us far beyond the limits of physical science. Everybody would agree that a linear function is simpler than a function of the second or higher degree; everybody would also admit that a circle is simpler than an ellipse. For this reason, physics is filled with laws that express proportionality, such as Hooke's law in elasticity or Ohm's law in electro-dynamics. In all these cases, there is no doubt that a nonlinear relationship would describe the facts in a more accurate way, but one tries to get along with a linear law as much as possible.

There was a time when, in physics, laws that could be expressed without using differential calculus were preferred, and in the long struggle between the corpus-cular and the wave theories of light, the argument was rife that the corpuscular theory was mathematically simpler, while the wave theory required the solution of boundary problems of partial differential equations, a highly complex mat-ter. We note that even a purely mathematical estimation of simplicity depends upon the state of culture of a certain period. People who have grown up in a mathematical atmosphere—that is, saturated with ideas about invariants—will find that Einstein's theory of gravitation is of incredible beauty and simplicity; but to people for whom ordinary calculus is the center of interest, Einstein's theory will be of immense complexity, and this low degree of simplicity will not be compensated by a great number of observed facts.

However, the situation becomes much more complex, if we mean by *simplicity* not only simplicity of the mathematical scheme but also simplicity of the whole discourse by which the theory is formulated. We may start from the most familiar instance, the decision between the Copernican (heliocentric) and the Ptolemaic (geocentric) theories. Both parties, the Roman Church and the followers of Copernicus, agreed that Copernicus' system, from the purely mathematical angle, was simpler than Ptolemy's. In the first one, the orbits of planets were plotted as a system of concentric circles with the sun as center, whereas in the geocentric system, the planetary orbits were sequences of loops. The observed facts covered by these systems were approximately the same ones. The criterions of acceptance that are applied in the community of scien-tists today are, according to the usual way of speaking, in agreement with observed facts and mathematical simplicity. According to them, the Coper-nican system had to be accepted unhesitatingly. Since this acceptance did not happen before a long period of doubt, we see clearly that the criterions "agree-ment with observed facts" and "mathematical simplicity" were not the only criterions that were considered as reasons for the acceptance of a theory.

As a matter of fact, there were three types of reasons against the acceptance of the Copernican theory that remained unchallenged at the time when all "scientific" reasons were in favor of that theory. First, there was the incompatibility of the Copernican system with the traditional interpretation of the Bible. Second, there was the disagreement between the Copernican system and the prevailing philosophy of that period, the philosophy of Aristotle as it was interpreted by the Catholic schoolmen. Third, there was the objection that the mobility of the earth, as a real physical fact, is incompatible with the common-sense interpretation of nature. Let us consider these three types of reasons more closely. In the Book of Joshua this leader prays to God to stop the sun in its motion in order to prolong the day and to enable the people of Israel to win a decisive victory. God indeed "stopped the sun." If interpreted verbally, according to the usage of words in our daily language, this means that the sun is moving, in flagrant contradiction with the Copernican theory. One could, of course, give a more sophisticated interpretation and say that "God stopped the sun" means that he stopped it in its motion relative to the earth. This is no longer contradictory to the Copernican system. But now the question arises: Should we adopt a simple mathematical description and a complicated, rather "unnatural" interpretation of the Bible or a more complicated mathematical description (motion in loops) and a simple "natural" interpretation of the biblical text? The decision certainly cannot be achieved by any argument taken from physical science.

If one believes that all questions raised by science must be solved by the "methods" of this special science, one must say: Every astronomer who lived in the period between Copernicus and Galileo was "free" to accept either the Copernican or the Ptolemaic doctrine; he could make an "arbitrary" decision. However, the situation is quite different if one takes into consideration that physical science is only a part of science in general. Building up astronomical theories is a particular act of human behavior. If we consider human behavior in general, we look at physical science as a part of a much more general endeavor that embraces also psychology and sociology. It is called by some authors "behavioristics." From this more general angle, the effect of a simplification in the mathematical formula and the simplification in biblical interpretation are quite comparable with each other. There is meaning in asking by which act the happiness of human individuals and groups is more favorably influenced. This means that, from the viewpoint of a general science of human behavior, the decision between the Copernican and Ptolemaic systems was never a matter of arbitrary decision.

The compatibility of a physical theory with a certain interpretation of the Bible is a special case of a much more general criterion: the compatibility of a physical theory with theories that have been advanced to account for observable phenomena outside the domain of a physical science. The most important reason for the acceptance of a theory beyond the "scientific criterions" in the narrower sense (agreement with observation and simplicity of the mathematical pattern) is the fitness of a theory to be generalized, to be the basis of a new theory that does not logically follow from the original one, and to allow prediction of more observable facts. This property is often called the "dynamical" character or the "fertility" of a theory. In this sense, the Copernican theory is much superior to the geocentric one. Newtonian laws of motion have a simple form only if the sun is taken as a system of reference and not the earth. But the decision in favor of the Copernican theory on this basis could be made only when Newton's laws came into existence. This act requires, however, creative imagination or, to speak more flippantly, a happy guessing that leads far beyond the Copernican and Ptolemaic systems.

However, long before the "dynamical" character of the Copernican system was recognized, the objection was raised that the system was incompatible with "the general laws of motion" that could be derived from principles regarded as "immediately intelligible" or, in other words, "self-evident" without physical experiment or observations. From such "self-evident" principles there followed, for example, the physical law that only celestial bodies (like sun or moon) moved "naturally" in circular orbits, while terrestrial bodies (like our earth) moved naturally along straight lines as a falling stone does. Copernicus' theory of a "motion of the earth in a circular orbit" was, therefore, incompatible with "self-evident" laws of nature.

Medieval scientists were faced with the alternatives: Should they accept the Copernican theory with its simple mathematical formulas and drop the self-evident laws of motion, or should they accept the complicated mathematics of the Ptolemaic system along with the intelligible and self-evident general laws of motion. Acceptance of Copernicus' theory would imply dropping the laws of motion that had been regarded as self-evident and looking for radically new laws. This would also mean dropping the contention that a physical law can be derived from "intelligible" principles. Again, from the viewpoint of physical science, this decision cannot be made. Although an arbitrary decision may seem to be required, if one looks at the situation from the viewpoint of human behavior it is clear that the decision, by which the derivation of physical laws from self-evident principles is abandoned, would alter the situation of man in the world fundamentally. For example, an important argument for the existence of spiritual beings would lose its validity. Thus, social science had to decide whether the life of man would become happier or unhappier by the acceptance of the Copernican system.

The objections to this system, on the basis of self-evident principles, have also been formulated in a way that looks quite different but may eventually, when the chips are down, not be so very different. Francis Bacon, the most conspicuous adversary of Aristotelianism in the period of Galileo, fought the acceptance of the Copernican theory on the basis of common-sense experience. He took it for granted that the principles of science should be as analogous as possible to the experience of our daily life. Then, the principles could be presented in the language that has been shaped for the purpose of describing, in the most convenient way, the experience of our daily existence—the language that everyone has learned as a child and that is called "common-sense language." From this daily experience, we have learned that the behavior of the sun and the planets is very different from that of the earth. While the earth does not emit any light, the sun and the planets are brilliant; while every earthly object that becomes separated from the main body will tend to fall back toward the center and stop there, the celestial objects undergo circular motion eternally around the center.

To separate the sun from the company of the planets and put the earth among these brilliant and mobile creatures, as Copernicus suggested, would have been not only unnatural but a serious violation of the rule to keep the principles of science as close to common sense as possible. We see by this example that one of the reasons for the acceptance of a theory has frequently been the compatibility of this theory with daily life experience or, in other words, the possibility of expressing the theory in common-sense language. Here is, of course, the source of another conflict between the "scientific" reasons for the acceptance of a theory and other requirements that are not "scientific" in the narrower sense. Francis Bacon rejected the Copernican system because it was not compatible with common sense.

In the eighteenth and nineteenth centuries, Newton's mechanics not only had become compatible with common sense but had even been identified with common-sense judgment. As a result, in twentieth century physics, the theory of relativity and the quantum theory were regarded by many as incompatible with common sense. These theories were regarded as "absurd" or, at least, "unnatural." Lenard in Germany, Bouasse in France, O'Rahilly in Ireland, and Timiryaseff in Russia rejected the theory of relativity, as Francis Bacon had rejected the Copernican system. Looking at the historical record, we notice that the requirement of compatibility with common sense and the rejection of "unnatural theories" have been advocated with a highly emotional undertone, and it is reasonable to raise the question: What was the source of heat in those fights against new and absurd theories? Surveying these battles, we easily find one common feature, the apprehension that a disagreement with common sense may deprive scientific theories of their value as incentives for a desirable human behavior. In other words, by becoming incompatible with common sense, scientific theories lose their fitness to support desirable attitudes in the domain of ethics, politics, and religion.

Examples are abundant from all periods of theory-building. According to an old theory that was prevalent in ancient Greece and was accepted by such men as Plato and Aristotle, the sun, planets, and other celestial bodies were made of a material that was completely different from the material of which our earth consists. The great gap between the celestial and the terrestrial bodies was regarded as required by our common-sense experience. There were men—for example, the followers of Epicurus—who rejected this view and assumed that all bodies in the universe, earth and stars, consist of the same material. Nevertheless, many educators and political leaders were afraid that denial of the exceptional status of the celestial bodies in physical science would make it more difficult to teach the belief in the existence of spiritual beings as distinct from material bodies; and since it was their general conviction that the belief in spiritual beings is a powerful instrument to bring about a desirable conduct among citizens, a physical theory that supported this belief seemed to be highly desirable.

Plato, in his famous book *Laws,* suggested that people in his ideal state who taught the "materialistic" doctrine about the constitution of sun and stars should be jailed. He even suggested that people who knew about teachers of that theory and did not report them to the authorities should also be jailed. We learn from this ancient example how scientific theories have served as instruments of indoctrination. Obviously, fitness to support a desirable conduct of citizens or, briefly, to support moral behavior, has served through the ages as a reason for acceptance of a theory. When the "scientific criterions" did not uniquely determine a theory, its fitness to support moral or political indoctrination became an important factor for its acceptance. It is important to learn that the interpretation of a scientific theory as a support of moral rules is not a rare case but has played a role in all periods of history.

This role probably can be traced back to a fact that is well known to modern students of anthropology and sociology. The conduct of man has always been shaped according to the example of an ideal society; on the other hand, this ideal has been represented by the "behavior" of the universe, which is, in turn, determined by the laws of nature, in particular, by the physical laws. In this sense, the physical laws have always been interpreted as examples for the conduct of man or, briefly speaking, as moral laws. Ralph Waldo Emerson wrote in his essay *Nature* that "the laws of physics are also the laws of ethics." He used as an example the law of the lever, according to which "the smallest weight may be made to lift the greatest, the difference of weight being compensated by time."

We see the connection of the laws of desirable human conduct with the physical laws of the universe when we glance at the Book of Genesis. The first chapter presents a physical theory about the creation of the world. But the story of the creation serves also as an example for the moral behavior of men; for instance, because the creation took 7 days, we all feel obliged to rest on each seventh day. Perhaps the history of the Great Flood is even more instructive. When the Flood abated, God established a Covenant with the human race: "Never again shall all flesh be cut off by the waters of a flood; neither shall there any more be a flood to destroy the earth." As a sign of the Covenant the rainbow appeared: "When I bring clouds over the earth and the bow is seen in the clouds, I will remember the Covenant which is between me and you, and the waters shall never again become a flood to destroy all flesh." If we read the biblical text carefully, we understand that what God actually pledged was to maintain, without exception, the validity of the physical laws or, in other words, of the causal law. God pledged: "While the earth remains, seedtime and harvest, cold and heat, summer and winter, day and night shall not cease."

All the physical laws, including the law of causality, were given to mankind as a reward for moral behavior and can be canceled if mankind does not behave well. So even the belief in the validity of causal laws in the physical world has supported the belief in God as the supreme moral authority who would punish every departure from moral behavior by abolishing causality. We have seen that Epicurean physics and Copernican astronomy were rejected on moral grounds. We know that Newton's physics was accepted as supporting the belief in a God who was an extremely able engineer and who created the world as a machine that performed its motions according to its plans. Even the generalization of Newtonian science that was advanced by 18th century materialism claimed to serve as a support for the moral behavior of man. In his famous book *Man a Machine,* which has often been called an "infamous book," La Mettrie stresses the point that by regarding men, animals, and planets as beings of the same kind, man is taught to regard them all as his brothers and to treat them kindly.

It would be a great mistake to believe that this situation has changed in the nineteenth and twentieth centuries. A great many authors have rejected the biological theory that organisms have arisen from inanimate matter (spontaneous generation), because such a theory would weaken the belief in the dignity of man and in the existence of a soul and would, therefore, be harmful to moral conduct. In twentieth century physics, we have observed that Einstein's theory of relativity has been interpreted as advocating an "idealistic" philosophy, which, in turn, would be useful as a support of moral conduct. Similarly, the quantum theory is interpreted as supporting a weakening of mechanical determinism and, along with it, the introduction of "indeterminism" into physics. In turn, a great many educators, theologians, and politicians have enthusiastically acclaimed this "new physics" as providing a strong argument for the acceptance of "indeterminism" as a basic principle of science.

The special mechanism by which social powers bring about a tendency to accept or reject a certain theory depends upon the structure of the society within which the scientist operates. It may vary from a mild influence on the scientist by friendly reviews in political or educational dailies to promotion of his book as a best seller, to ostracism as an author and as a person, to loss of his job, or, under some social circumstances, even to imprisonment, torture, and execution. The honest scientist who works hard in his laboratory or computation-room would obviously be inclined to say that all this is nonsense—that his energy should be directed toward finding out whether, say, a certain theory is "true" and that he "should not" pay any attention to the fitness of a theory to serve as an instrument in the fight for educational or political goals. This is certainly the way in which the situation presents itself to most active scientists. However, scientists are also human beings and are definitely inclined toward some moral, religious, or political creed. Those who deny emphatically that there is any connection between scientific theories and religious or political creeds believe in these creeds on the basis of indoctrination that has been provided by organizations such as churches or political parties. This attitude leads to the conception of a "double truth" that is not only logically confusing but morally dangerous. It can lead to the practice of serving God on Sunday and the devil on weekdays.

The conviction that science is independent of all moral and political influences arises when we regard science either as a collection of facts or as a picture of objective reality. But today, everyone who has attentively studied the logic of science will know that science actually is an instrument that serves the purpose of connecting present events with future events and deliberately utilizes this knowledge to shape future physical events as they are desired. This instrument consists of a system of propositions—principles—and the operational definitions of their terms. These propositions certainly cannot be derived from the facts of our experience and are not uniquely determined by these facts. Rather they are hypotheses from which the facts can be logically derived. If the principles or hypotheses are not determined by the physical facts, by what are they determined? We have learned by now that, besides the agreement with observed facts, there are other reasons for the acceptance of a theory: simplicity, agreement with common sense, fitness for supporting a desirable human conduct, and so forth. All these factors participate in the making of a scientific theory. We remember, however, that according to the opinion of the majority of active scientists, these extrascientific factors "should not" have any influence on the acceptance of a scientific theory. But who has claimed and who can claim that they "should not"?

This firm conviction of the scientists comes from the philosophy that they have absorbed since their early childhood. The theories that are built up by "scientific" methods, in the narrower sense, are "pictures" of physical reality. Presumably they tell us the "truth" about the world. If a theory built up exclusively on the ground of its agreement with observable facts tells the "truth" about the world, it would be nonsense to assume seriously that a scientific theory can be influenced by moral or political reasons. However, we learned that "agreement with observed facts" does not single out one individual theory. We never have one theory that is in full agreement but several theories that are in partial agreement, and we have to determine the final theory by a compromise. The final theory has to be in fair agreement with observations and also has to be sufficiently simple to be usable. If we consider this point, it is obvious that such a theory cannot be "the truth." In modern science, a theory is regarded as an instrument that serves toward some definite purpose. It has to be helpful in predicting future observable facts on the basis of facts that have been observed in the past and the present. It should also be helpful in the construction of machines and devices that can save us time and labor. A scientific theory is, in a sense, a tool that produces other tools according to a practical scheme.

In the same way that we enjoy the beauty and elegance of an airplane, we also enjoy the "elegance" of the theory that makes the construction of the plane possible. In speaking about any actual machine, it is meaningless to ask whether the machine is "true" in the sense of its being "perfect." We can ask only whether it is "good" or sufficiently "perfect" for a certain purpose. If we require speed as our purpose, the "perfect" airplane will differ from one that is "perfect" for the purpose of endurance. The result will be different again if we choose safety, or fun, or convenience for reading and sleeping as our purpose. It is impossible to design an airplane that fulfills all these purposes in a maximal way. We have to make some compromises. But then, there is the question: Which is more important, speed or safety, or fun or endurance? These questions cannot be answered by any agreement taken from physical science. From the viewpoint of "science proper" the purpose is arbitrary, and science can teach us only how to construct a plane that will achieve a specified speed with a specified degree of safety. There will be a debate, according to moral, political, and even religious lines, by which it will be determined how to produce the compromise. The policymaking authorities are, from the logical viewpoint, "free" to make their choice of which type of plane should be put into production. However, if we look at the situation from the viewpoint of a unified science that includes both physical and social science, we shall understand how the compromise between speed and safety, between fun and endurance is determined by the social conditions that produce the conditioned reflexes of the policymakers. The conditioning may be achieved, for example, by letters written to congressmen. As a matter of fact, the building of a scientific theory is not essentially different from the building of an airplane.

If we look for an answer to the question of whether a certain theory, say the Copernican system or the theory of relativity, is perfect or true, we have to ask the preliminary questions: What purpose is the theory to serve? Is it only the purely technical purpose of predicting observable facts? Or is it to obtain a simple and elegant theory that allows us to derive a great many facts from simple principles? We choose the theory according to our purpose. For some groups, the main purpose of a theory may be to serve as a support in teaching a desirable way of life or to discourage an undesirable way of life. Then, we would prefer theories that give a rather clumsy picture of observed facts, provided that we can get from the theory a broad view of the universe in which man plays the role that we desire to give him. If we wish to speak in a more brief and general way, we may distinguish just two purposes of a theory: the usage for the construction of devices (technological purpose) and the usage for guiding human conduct (sociological purpose).

The actual acceptance of theories by man has always been a compromise between the technological and the sociological usage of science. Human conduct has been influenced directly by the latter, by supporting specific religious or political creeds, while the technological influence has been rather indirect. Technological changes have to produce social changes that manifest themselves in changing human conduct. Everybody knows of the Industrial Revolution of the nineteenth century and the accompanying changes in human life from a rural into an urban pattern. Probably the rise of atomic power will produce analogous changes in man's way of life.

The conflict between the technological and the sociological aims of science is the central factor in the history of science as a human enterprise. If thoroughly investigated, it will throw light upon a factor that some thinkers, Marxist as well as religious thinkers, regard as responsible for the social crisis of our time: the backwardness of social progress compared with technological progress. To cure this illness of our time, an English bishop recommended, some years ago, the establishment of a "truce" in the advancement in technology, in order to give social progress some time to keep up with technological advancement. We have seen examples of this conflict in Plato's indictment of astrophysical theories that could be used as a support of "materialism." We note the same purpose in the fight against the Copernican system and, in our own century, against the Darwinian theory of evolution, against Mendel's laws of heredity, and so forth.

A great many scientists and educators believe that such a conflict no longer exists in our time, because now it is completely resolved by "the scientific method," which theory is the only valid one. This opinion is certainly wrong if we consider theories of high generality. In twentieth century physics, we note clearly that a formulation of the general principles of subatomic physics (quantum theory) is accepted or rejected according to whether we believe that introduction of "indeterminism" into physics gives comfort to desirable ethical postulates or not. Some educators and politicians have been firmly convinced that the belief in "free will" is necessary for ethics and that "free will" is not compatible with Newtonian physics but is compatible with quantum physics. The situation in biology is similar. If we consider the attitude of biologists toward the question whether living organisms have developed from inanimate matter, we shall find that the conflict between the technological and the sociological purposes of theories is in full bloom. Some prominent biologists say that the existence of "spontaneous generation" is highly probable, while others of equal prominence claim that it is highly improbable. If we investigate the reasons for these conflicting attitudes, we shall easily discover that, for one group of scientists, a theory that claims the origin of man not merely from the "apes" but also from "dead matter" undermines their belief in the dignity of man, which is the indispensable basis for all human morality. We should note in turn that, for another group, desirable human behavior is based on the belief that there is a unity in nature that embraces all things.

In truth, many scientists would say that scientific theories "should" be based only on purely scientific grounds. But, exactly speaking, what does the word *should* mean in this context? With all the preceding arguments it can mean only: If we consider exclusively the technological purpose of scientific theories, we could exclude all criterions such as agreement with common sense or fitness for supporting desirable conduct. But even if we have firmly decided to do away with all "nonsense," there still remains the criterion of "simplicity," which is necessary for technological purposes and also contains, as we learned previously, a certain sociological judgment. Here, restriction to the purely technological purpose does not actually lead unambiguously to a scientific theory. The only way to include theory-building in the general science of human behavior is to refrain from ordering around scientists by telling them what they "should" do and to find how each special purpose can be achieved by a theory. Only in this way can science as a human activity be "scientifically" understood and the gap between the scientific and the humanistic aspect be bridged.

STUDY QUESTIONS FOR PART 4

1. How do Quine and Ullian dash the hope of absolute demonstrability in science?

2. What do Quine and Ullian mean by 'hypothesis'?

3. Answer the critic who says that the so-called virtue of conservatism is just an expression of the reactionary attitude of the powerful scientists in the scientific institutions.

4. Do conservatism and modesty amount to more than features of quantitative confirmation?

5. How do Quine and Ullian define simplicity? Do they think considerations of simplicity provide epistemic or practical reasons? What is their argument?

6. Explain how modesty and generality conflict? How do Ouine and Ullian reconcile them?

7. What are *ad hoc* hypotheses and what is wrong with them?

8. Why must hypotheses be refutable?

9. How can refutability and conservatism both be virtues of a hypothesis?

10. Explain, using an example other than Giere's, why the second general feature of a test is required.

11. In the statement of the second general feature of a test, why not omit the phrase "known at the time"?

12. Suppose that one or more of the initial conditions used in testing a hypothesis are false. How will this effect Giere's refuting and justifying arguments?

13. How does Kuhn account for the fact that different scientists using the same criteria choose different theories?

14. What is the distinction between the context of discovery and the context of justification? How have Kuhn's critics tried to use the distinction against him? What is Kuhn's response and is he correct?

15. What for Kuhn is the philosophical significance of thinking of criteria for theory choice as values rather than rules that determine choice?

16. Has Kuhn made theory choice "subjective"?

17. What is the difference between understanding principles as norms of rational scientific inquiry as opposed to an explanatory account of scientific practice?

18. What is an ideal rational account? How does it solve the tension between normative and explanatory accounts?

19. Hempel claims that proposed methodological norms must be regarded as *instrumental* norms. What does he mean by this and what argument does he offer for it?

20. What is Feyerabend's argument for the claim that there can be no general criteria for theory comparison? What is Hempel's response?

21. How does Frank show that with the Copernican system other reasons than agreement with observed facts and simplicity were used in determining its acceptance? What were some of the additional criteria?

316 Study Questions for Part 4

22. Is it unreasonable or unscientific to put much weight on Frank's additional criteria? Discuss.

23. Why is it important that scientific theories agree with common sense?

24. According to Frank, what view on the status of unobservables and theoretical statements fits best with the recognition of the importance of "additional criteria"? Evaluate his view.

SELECTED BIBLIOGRAPHY

[1] Brody, B., ed. *Readings in the Philosophy of Science,* Englewood Cliffs, N.J.: Prentice-Hall, 1970, part 3. [Contains essay as on confirmation and acceptance.]

[2] Goodman, N. *Fact, Fiction, and Forecast.* New York: Bobbs-Merrill, 1965, part 3. [Presents a serious paradox for a theory of confirmation.]

[3] Gutting, G., ed. *Paradigms and Revolutions.* Notre Dame: University of Notre Dame Press, 1980. [Extends and criticizes Kuhn's ideas.]

[4] Hacking, I., ed. *Scientific Revolutions.* Oxford: Oxford University Press, 1981. [Essay representative of post logical empiricism philosophy of science.]

[5] Kuhn, T. *The Structure of Scientific Revolutions.* Chicago: University of Chicago Press, 1962. [A wealth of material on acceptance.]

[6] Laudan, L. *Progress and Its Problems.* Berkeley: University of California Press, 1977. [A theory of scientific change.]

[7] Popper, K. *Conjectures and Refutations.* New York: Harper & Row, 1963. [Contains many relevant essays; see especially 10.]

[8] Scheffler, I. *The Anatomy of Inquiry.* New York: Knopf, 1969, part 3. [Tight discussion of confirmation.]

[9] ———. *Science and Subjectivity.* New York: Bobbs-Merrill, 1967. [Tries to blunt what he sees as the relativistic consequences of Kuhn's view.]

Part 5

Science and Values

Part 5: Science and Values

Introduction

I. The Problems

Problems about the role of value judgments within *science* and ethical disputes about *the uses of* science (e.g., in technology and social policy) are commonplace. Recent discussion of genetic engineering, behavior control, safety in nuclear power plants, human experimentation (e.g., deception and manipulation in research), medical ethics, and the IQ controversy are only the most dramatic instances of such problems. The basic problems are by no means new: just think of the controversy between Galileo and the Catholic Church about the nature of the solar system, or controversies between Darwin and his critics over the question of evolution.

However, underlying the many disputes covered by the phrase "science and values," there are several fundamental and persisting issues. Among the most obvious are these:

1. Can (is/should) science be "value free" or "neutral"? What do "value free" and "value neutral" mean in such contexts? What kinds of values are at issue? (This raises the question "What is value?" which must be bypassed here.) For instance, not all values are *moral* values, so that science may be *morally* neutral even though not *value* neutral in some other (or in a wider) sense. As we shall see, it is open to question whether science is or can be even morally neutral, much less value neutral.

2. If science *is* value free (in either the extended or the narrower sense of morally neutral: unless otherwise specified I shall mean the former whenever "value free" is used) what implications does this have for our conception of science, knowledge, and values, and for our views about the nature and aims of science and the social uses of science and technology? If science is *not* value free, what does *this* imply about the foregoing?

3. What are the best or most defensible concepts or theories about knowledge, values (moral or nonmoral), science, and the best ways of conceptualizing their interconnections (or the lack thereof)? Here we must eventually deal with the concepts of rationality, objectivity, subjectivity, pure and applied science, and so on. (See Part 1 of this volume.) And we must eventually decide what sorts of views will or will not be plausible candidates for helping us understand science, values, and their connections. For instance, will any theory according to which science and values are, and should be, totally unrelated be acceptable to us? This is a question that is discussed later on in this introduction.

It should come as no surprise that these and other issues have been given a variety of answers, and have generated a number of complex and often conflicting theories about science, values, and their interrelations. There is no point in attempting to even list, much less discuss, all or even many of these views in an introductory essay. Instead, some historical and philosophical backdrop for the selections in Part 5 will be provided. The emphasis will be on those developments which get to the very heart of the issues, and which bear most directly on the readings.

It will prove instructive to begin with the question of *why* there is, or even should be, any problems about the relationships between science and values at all. This question is by no means rhetorical, but rather gets to the nub of the issue, which involves the relationship between science (and, more generally, knowledge) and values which finds expression in modern science and philosophy. It is here, after all, that we must look for the ideas that continue to dominate our culture's general outlooks on these questions.

II. Why Is There a Problem About "Science and Values"?

The problems briefly outlined above come into existence with the advent of modern philosophy and science, especially the scientific revolution of the seventeenth century. In order to appreciate why, and how, this happens, it will be helpful to briefly sketch the views of the ancient Greeks—the molders of Western culture—on the issues of knowledge and values (or, at any rate, on the Greek approximations to these issues as they have since come to be understood). Then we can go on to sketch the development of the modern problems as they arise at the beginning of "modern history," which shall be dated here from the seventeenth century.

For the ancient Greeks, there are no distinctions between (a) science or knowledge and "values" or "the good" or between (b) science and philosophy or between (c) the objective and the subjective (as these concepts are understood within modern science and philosophy) or between (d) a "factual" or "descriptive" account of the world (e.g., in terms of the structural properties of things and the laws which govern them) and a "normative" or "evaluative" or (even) a "moral" interpretation of the world, as embodying a certain order, pattern, beauty, purpose, and even "goodness." (What is natural is also good in this view.) The most influential, and most forceful, presentation of the Greek view of the cosmos is articulated by Plato in his *Republic* (bks. iv–vii). For Plato, "objective" reality is characterized in terms of the idea or form of "the good." Reality is a unified, patterned, or ordered whole. In order to understand experience, we have to arrive at a knowledge of the laws and structures governing everything, as well as the order, patterning, or "purpose" which pervades all experience and which unifies it in a coherent and "meaningful" fashion. Such knowledge, which Plato calls "Dialectic," is not to be equated with what is today called "knowledge," since our term 'knowledge' is often used as a synonym for 'science' or 'scientific knowledge'. On Plato's view, the aims and methods of the empirical sciences are designed to give us at best only a limited insight into reality; more specifically, an insight into a certain kind of experience, a certain level of reality (the level of objects of experience like trees, rocks, and so on). They must be complemented by an insight into the more basic principles and patterns which govern everything. What for Plato is the "most real" is also the most abstract and the least accessible to ordinary experience. (Modern theoretical science, e.g., atomic theory, quantum physics, genetics, and chemistry, embody this Platonic ideal to some extent.) An "objective account" of things is not complete until everything is ordered into a unified picture; which involves the idea that purpose and norms (i.e., ordering principles) are not eliminable from such an account. It also involves the idea that science cannot give us either a complete account of everything, or an adequate account of even the objects of its legitimate concern, since these objects must be ultimately understood in terms of the principles which govern everything, including themselves and their place in the whole scheme.

One of the chief features of modern science and modern philosophy is the attempt to deny or else to truncate this platonic vision of the universe, and of the nature of knowledge and the good. In what follows, a brief sketch of these developments will be given.

III. Origin and Nature of the Problem

The issues concerning the relationship between science and values, including the role of values *in* science (the issue of value-neutrality) comes into modern Western history with the advent of the so-called mechanical picture of the world (especially classical Newtonian science), and the scientific revolution, most especially the epistemological and methodological revolution in science and philosophy inspired by its main architect, René Descartes (1596–1650).

According to this view, we must make a sharp distinction between what is objective and what is subjective in order to acquire reliable (i.e., "objective") knowledge of the world (including knowledge of human beings) by the use of reliable ("rational") methods of inquiry. Since, according to the mechanical world picture, nature is a vast machine governed by quantitative laws and rela-tionships (nature is written in the language of mathematics), the objective features of the world turn out to be those features—matter, motion, and physical magnitudes—which constitute the nuts and bolts of the machine, together with the laws governing it. Only such features of experience are truly objective. Thus a rational methodology for inquiring about the machine's working—i.e., for acquiring knowledge—must take into account only those features which can be quantified, i.e., written in nature's language. The very essence of the world is given by the objective properties just mentioned, together with the mechanical laws which govern them. (These essential features of the world are dubbed "primary qualities" by Galileo and Locke.) Everything else, e.g., colors, values, interpretations, purpose, and theories, are not "objective" and thus do not belong in an objective account of the world, unless they can be "reduced" to objective terms, or explained away as illusory phenomena by such an account. (Later thinkers expanded the province of science to include those "subjective" items—called "secondary qualities"—that had an autonomous status for Descartes (e.g., mental phenomena and values) so that these came to be "reduced" to objective features or explained away entirely, as in modern behaviorism and materialism.)

In sum, objectivity means both: (a) objective in the sense of being about what is objective, and (b) objective in the sense of arriving at objective truths by methods which themselves take no account of anything "subjective," i.e., which are unbiased. (The search for mechanical "fool-proof" methods, e.g., computer algorithms, cost benefit decisions, is the ultimate outcome of this ideal of rational, objective method.)

IV. Initial Objections to "Objectivism"

This view already has insuperable difficulties: at least *we* can now see this (which is not to make the anachronistic claim that its classical proponents were flawed for not seeing it: it is just as easy to be a "Monday-morning quarter-back" in history as in football).

First of all, to paraphrase Woody Allen (*Love and Death*): Objectivity is subjective, and subjectivity is objective; at least the latter point is certainly true: the fact that I am (say) in pain is no less objective a fact about me than the fact that I weigh 160 pounds.

Second, the view being considered is, paradoxically, rooted in the notion that "objective knowledge" is a "rational reconstruction" of the private, i.e., "subjective," experiences of a collection of knowers (viz., out of those subjec-tive experiences which represent the essence of the world). Modern epistemology is rooted in this conundrum.

Third, as M. Polanyi [6] and others show, if we merely wanted objective truths, we (as a species) would devote virtually all of our intellectual energy to studying interstellar dust, and only a fraction of a microsecond studying ourselves (or anything else, for that matter) since, objectively speaking, human beings are of no cosmic significance in the objective order of things! Obviously no one would take this requirement on objectivity seriously (this concept of objectivity is theological – God sees the world objectively as an outside omniscient observer). What we are seeking are truths which are interesting, which are useful and valuable to us. In a word, knowledge, truth, and objectivity are (or are rooted in) values and human purposes.

Fourth, not only do knowledge, objectivity, and truth – and thus methodology – turn out to be, or at least be grounded in, values; on some views they are, or are grounded in, moral ideals. In any event, the search for knowledge expresses a value; and thus distinctions between reliable and unreliable knowledge claims, between good and bad methods, and so on, are partly normative judgments. (See the articles by Rescher and Scriven; also [5].)

(The question as to whether knowledge is an *intrinsic* value, as it is for those, such as Plato and Aristotle, for whom the life of contemplation is the highest good or *"summum bonum,"* or whether it is an *instrumental* value (Bacon's maxim that knowledge is power), as well as the issue whether such values are (ultimately) moral values, will be taken up in the introduction to Part 6. At this point it may be worth citing the words of N. I. Bukharin, who says: "The idea of the self-sufficient character of science . . . is naive; it confuses the *subjective passions* of the professional scientist . . . with the *objective social role* of this kind of activity, as an activity of vast practical importance.")

V. Some Implications of "Objectivism"

Despite these "obvious" difficulties, the fact remains that the distinction between objectivity and subjectivity, as regards claims governing methodology and the content of an objective world picture, dominate modern science, philosophy, and Western culture from Descartes and Galileo up to the present. The ideas of value neutrality, the uses of cost-benefit analyses to arrive at "rational" decisions in politics, science, and technology, the attempt to use knowledge for social and political ends (e.g., behavior control techniques), and so on, are just sophisticated outgrowths of this cluster of ideas. So, too, is the idea that scientific method affords the only rational methods for solving problems, so that value judgments are either not rational, or else are concerned merely with problems about calculating efficiency, or about decision-making under conditions of uncertainty. Both proponents and opponents of the classical picture of the world and the attendant ideas of objectivity and rationality (e.g., behaviorists, on the one hand, and so-called "neo-romantics" and existentialists, on the other) share this conception that values are essentially subjective and irrational if they are anything more than predictions or calculations about means to an end.

But it is becoming glaringly obvious that these assumptions are connected with an inadequate conception of *both* science *and* values, and of the

324 Introduction to Part 5

interrelationships between the two areas. (See especially the Scriven article in this part.)

As Gerwirth [5] points out, no one is reluctant to distinguish between "good" and "bad" science, or between science and nonscience or pseudoscience (e.g., astronomy vs. astrology). (See Part 1.) Yet on the view being discussed we are not supposed to be able to distinguish between good and bad moralities, or between acceptable vs. unacceptable value judgments. But this combination of "normative" science and "positive" ethics is internally incoherent and grossly inadequate.

VI. Some Corollaries of "Objectivism"

Two clusters of ideas conspire to produce this result. (i) Many advocates of the view being discussed either attempt to turn ethics into a science, or to explain value judgments scientifically (e.g., in terms of conditioning or historical or economic determinism). The latter kind of strategy usually leads to some form of ethical nihilism or extreme ethical relativism: All we can do is explain the origins of ethical behavior in terms of some objective scientific theory. On this view the point or content (i.e., the "autonomy") of value judgments is either lost or obscured. But this strategy explains why, for an advocate of this approach, "positive ethics" is the inevitable result. Moreover, it is just because "normative science" shows that objectivism is the only correct scientific approach that "positive ethics" turns out to be compatible, indeed, required by, objectivism. (ii) The idea of value neutrality, especially as this idea shows up in the social and policy sciences, is greatly influenced by views which attempt to reconcile "objective" science and "subjective" morality, by drawing theoretical limits to science, in order to save morality and human freedom. On this view, (a) science and morality cannot conflict (they are "complementary") since (b) they have nothing to do with each other: they govern different spheres of experience (these relate to the differences between "man as object" and as actor). But the price to be paid for this move is just the idea that science is, and must be, value neutral and that value judgments are merely subjective and irrational acts of the will.

Connected with this view is the idea that rational justification is essentially (hypothetico) deductive. The ultimate principles of a system, whether a moral system, a scientific theory, or a formal system, such as geometry, or the "brute facts" or "data" are beyond rational dispute. They must either be arbitrarily stipulated and accepted or be taken as self-evident, and then used to define what a rational proof or justification is *within* the system. The "ultimates" must be accepted as given. Relativism is the view that there are different, equally rational or acceptable (incompatible) ultimates. When one reaches these ultimates, be it a body of "hard facts," or axioms or moral principles, one has reached bedrock. One can then either accept or reject them. If the former, one can then show that the principles which follow from them are rational. In the latter case, one is free to adopt different "ultimates." At the same time, finding rational principles, or making rational decisions within the system, becomes a matter of, say, finding the best means of optimizing the ultimate principles or ends postulated by the system.

As P. Diesing [3] puts it:

> Such a conception of rationality limits its scope rather severely. The criterion of efficiency is applicable to means and not to ends. . . . Thus ultimate ends, the basic aims of life, cannot be selected or evaluated by rational procedures; they must be dealt with by arbitrary preference, or intuition, or by cultural and biological determinism. And yet it seems unfortunate to have rational procedures available for the relatively less important decisions of life and to have none for dealing with the most important decisions. Nor is this all. Several rather common types of activity can only with great difficulty be assimilated to the category of efficient action and be evaluated by standards of efficiency. ([3], p. 1)

Ultimately, this theory of justification is part and parcel of the idea that science is value free, that value judgments are really objective judgments about the best means of optimizing goals which cannot be rationally assessed, and of the view that value judgments can and must be explained objectively (e.g., by deterministic explanations) or else are merely arbitrary fiats of individuals or cultures (which view amounts to nihilism or relativism). This is the most dramatic way in which the theory of objectivity we are discussing is already pregnant with modern nihilism; for this view already structures our view of values as either just objective items of a social system or an individual's behavioral repertoire or else as just "subjective" reactions to the objective facts, which do not belong in an objective scientific picture of the world.

It turns out, as shall be seen in the part on science and culture, that *both* of these approaches to values amount to a kind of relativism, which often embodies a very conservative ideology, i.e., supports the idea that existing views of morality cannot be challenged, and thus that value judgments are really judgments about the best means to those ends and values which are in existence. (This is why cost-benefit analyses embody the view that the optimization of a given end is the only standard for making value judgments.) It thus turns out, on the "C–B" view, that the idea of value neutrality really amounts to the idea that value judgments (to the degree that they are rational and objective) are just judgments of efficiency concerning the best means to a given end. The ends (e.g., purposes) are determined scientifically, and this means (ultimately) they are either given or explained by some deterministic theory as being inevitable, ultimate facts. In any event, objectivism certainly is not "value-free."

VII. The Readings in Part 5

In his essay Rudner argues that the need for scientists to decide when and if the available evidence is strong enough or good enough to warrant the acceptance of a hypothesis is a normative or evaluative activity; hence, science is essentially value-laden.

Hempel discusses a number of basic relations between science and values. "Categorical" value judgments—e.g., "X is good/right or bad/wrong," are not part of science or provable/disprovable by science. Science can help us make "hypothetical" value judgments, however. Thus, "if we want X, then we should do A" can be assessed by science, since scientific knowledge can help us predict the outcome of decisions, find the most efficient means to our ends, etc. Science can also explain how and why individuals and groups have the values they do.

McMullin looks at the issues discussed by Rudner and Hempel in a broad historical and analytic framework. His views about the normative nature of science and values are broader and more radical than either Rudner's or Hempel's, although he seems to be less radical in his views about science, values, and theory choice than Kuhn.

R. H.

23

The Scientist *Qua* Scientist
Makes Value Judgments

Richard Rudner

The question of the relationship of the making of value judgments in a typically ethical sense to the methods and procedures of science has been discussed in the literature at least to that point which e. e. cummings somewhere refers to as "The Mystical Moment of Dullness." Nevertheless, albeit with some trepidation, I feel that something more may fruitfully be said on the subject.

In particular the problem has once more been raised in an interesting and poignant fashion by recently published discussions between Carnap[1] and Quine[2] on the question of the ontological commitments which one may make in the choosing of language systems.

I shall refer to this discussion in more detail in the sequel; for the present, however, let us briefly examine the current status of what is somewhat loosely called the "fact-value dichotomy."

I have not found the arguments which are usually offered, by those who believe that scientists do essentially make value judgments, satisfactory. On the other hand the rebuttals of some of those with opposing viewpoints seem to have had at least a *prima facie* cogency although they too may in the final analysis prove to have been subtly perverse.

Those who contend that scientists do essentially make value judgments generally support their contentions by either

(a) pointing to the fact that our having a science at all somehow "involves" a value judgment, or
(b) by pointing out that in order to select, say among alternative problems, the scientist must make a value judgment; or (perhaps most frequently)
(c) by pointing to the fact that the scientist cannot escape his quite human self—he is a "mass of predilections," and these predilections must inevitably influence all of his activities not excepting his scientific ones.

To such arguments, a great many empirically oriented philosophers and scientists have responded that the value judgments involved in our decisions to have a science, or to select problem (a) for attention rather than problem (b) are, *of course,* extra-scientific. If (they say) it is necessary to make a decision to have a science before we can have one, then this decision is literally pre-scientific and the act has thereby certainly not been shown to be any part of the *procedures* of science. Similarly the decision to focus attention on one problem rather than another is extra-problematic and forms no part of the procedures involved in dealing with the problem *decided* upon. Since it is *these* procedures which constitute the method of science, value judgments, so they respond, have not been shown to be involved in the scientific method as such. Again, with respect to the inevitable presence of our predilections in the laboratory, most empirically oriented philosophers and scientists agree that this is "unfortunately" the case; but, they hasten to add, if science is to progress toward objectivity the influence of our personal feelings or biases on experimental results must be minimized. We must try not to let our personal idiosyncrasies affect our scientific work. The perfect scientist—the scientist *qua* scientist does not allow this kind of value judgment to influence his work. However much he may find doing so unavoidable *qua* father, *qua* lover, *qua* member of society, *qua* grouch, *when* he does so he is not behaving *qua* scientist.

As I indicated at the outset, the arguments of neither of the protagonists in this issue appear quite satisfactory to me. The empiricists' rebuttals, telling prima facie as they may against the specific arguments that evoke them, nonetheless do not appear ultimately to stand up, but perhaps even more importantly, *the original arguments* seem utterly too frail.

I believe that a much stronger case may be made for the contention that value judgments are essentially involved in the procedures of science. And what I now propose to show is that scientists as scientists *do* make value judgments.

Now I take it that no analysis of what constitutes the method of science would be satisfactory unless it comprised some assertion to the effect that the scientist as scientist accepts or rejects hypotheses.

But if this is so then clearly the scientist as scientist does make value judgments. For, since no scientific hypothesis is ever completely verified, in accepting a hypothesis the scientist must make the decision that the evidence is *sufficiently* strong or that the probability is *sufficiently* high to warrant the acceptance of the hypothesis. Obviously our decision regarding the evidence and respecting how strong is "strong enough," is going to be a function of the *importance,* in the typically ethical sense, of making a mistake in accepting or rejecting the hypothesis. Thus, to take a crude but easily manageable example, if the hypothesis under consideration were to the effect that a toxic ingredient of a drug was not present in lethal quantity, we would require a relatively high degree of confirmation or confidence before accepting the hypothesis—for the consequences of making a mistake here are exceedingly grave by our moral standards. On the other hand, if, say, our hypothesis stated that, on the basis of a sample, a certain lot of machine stamped belt buckles was not defective, the degree of confidence we should require would be relatively not so high. *How sure we need to be before we accept a hypothesis will depend on how serious a mistake would be.*

The examples I have chosen are from scientific inferences in industrial quality control. But the point is clearly quite general in application. It would be interesting and instructive, for example, to know just how high a degree of probability the Manhattan Project scientists demanded for the hypothesis that no uncontrollable pervasive chain reaction would occur, before they proceeded with the first atomic bomb detonation or first activated the Chicago pile above a critical level. It would be equally interesting and instructive to know why they decided that *that* probability value (if one was decided upon) was high enough rather than one which was higher; and perhaps most interesting of all to learn whether the problem in this form was brought to consciousness at all.

In general then, before we can accept any hypothesis, the value decision must be made in the light of the seriousness of a mistake, that the probability is *high enough* or that, the evidence is *strong enough,* to warrant its acceptance.

Before going further, it will perhaps be well to clear up two points which might otherwise prove troublesome below. First I have obviously used the term "probability" up to this point in a quite loose and pre-analytic sense. But my point can be given a more rigorous formulation in terms of a description of the process of making statistical inference and of the acceptance or rejection of hypotheses in statistics. As is well known, the acceptance or rejection of such a hypothesis presupposes that a certain level of significance or level of confidence or critical region be selected.[3]

It is with respect at least to the *necessary* selection of a confidence level or interval that the necessary value judgment in the inquiry occurs. For, "the size of the critical region (one selects) is related to *the risk one wants to accept* in testing a statistical hypothesis."[3*, p. 435]

And clearly how great a risk one is willing to take of being wrong in accepting or rejecting the hypothesis will depend upon how seriously in the typically ethical sense one views the consequences of making a mistake.

I believe, of course, that an adequate rational reconstruction of the procedures of science would show that every scientific inference is properly constructable as a statistical inference (i.e., as an inference from a set of characteristics of a sample of a population to a set of characteristics of the total population) and that such an inference would be scientifically in control only in so far as it is statistically in control. But it is not necessary to argue this point, for even if one believes that what is involved in some scientific inferences is not statistical probability but rather a concept like strength of evidence or degree of confirmation, one would still be concerned with making the decision that the evidence was *strong enough* or the degree of confirmation *high enough* to warrant acceptance of the hypothesis. Now, many empiricists who reflect on the foregoing considerations agree that acceptances or rejections of hypotheses do essentially involve value judgments, but they are nonetheless loathe to accept the conclusion. And one objection which has been raised against this line of argument by those of them who are suspicious of the intrusion of value questions into the "objective realm of science," is that actually the scientist's task is only to *determine* the degree of confirmation or the strength of the evidence which *exists* for a hypothesis. In short, they object that while it may be a function of the scientist *qua member of society* to decide whether a degree of probability associated with the hypothesis is high enough to warrant its acceptance, *still* the task of the scientist *qua* scientist is *just the determination* of the degree of probability or the strength of the evidence for a hypothesis and not the acceptance or rejection of that hypothesis.

But a little reflection will show that the plausibility of this objection is merely apparent. For the determination that the degree of confirmation is say, *p,* or that the strength of evidence is such and such, which is on this view being held to be the indispensable task of the scientist *qua* scientist, is clearly nothing more than *the acceptance by the scientist of the hypothesis that the degree of confidence is p or that the strength of the evidence is such and such*; and as these men have conceded, acceptance of hypotheses does require value decisions. The second point which it may be well to consider before finally turning our attention to the Quine-Carnap discussion has to do with the nature of the suggestions which have thus far been made in this essay. In this connection, it is important to point out that the preceding remarks do *not* have as their import that an empirical description of every present day scientist ostensibly going about his business would include the statement that he made a value judgment at such and such a juncture. This is no doubt the case; but it is a hypothesis which can only be confirmed by a discipline which cannot be said to have gotten extremely far along as yet; namely, the Sociology and Psychology of Science, whether such an empirical description is warranted, cannot be settled from the armchair.

My remarks have, rather, amounted to this: Any adequate analysis or (if I may use the term) rational reconstruction of the method of science must comprise the statement that the scientist *qua* scientist accepts or rejects hypotheses; and further that an analysis of that statement would reveal it to entail that the scientist *qua* scientist makes value judgments.

I think that it is in the light of the foregoing arguments, the substance of which has, in one form or another, been alluded to in past years by a number of inquirers (notably C. W. Churchman, R. L. Ackoff, and A. Wald), that the Quine-Carnap discussion takes on heightened interest. For, if I understand that discussion and its outcome correctly, although it apparently begins a good distance away from any consideration of the fact-value dichotomy, and although all the way through it both men touch on the matter in a way which indicates that they believe that questions concerning the dichotomy are, if anything, merely tangential to their main issue, yet it eventuates with Quine by an independent argument apparently in agreement with at least the conclusion here reached and also apparently having forced Carnap to that conclusion. (Carnap, however, is expected to reply to Quine's article and I may be too sanguine here.)

The issue of ontological commitment between Carnap and Quine has been one of relatively long standing. In this recent article,[1] Carnap maintains that we are concerned with two kinds of questions of existence relative to a given language system. One is what *kinds* of entities it would be permissible to speak about as existing when that language system is used, i.e., what kind of *framework* for speaking of entities should our system comprise. This, according to Carnap, is an *external* question. It is the *practical* question of what sort of linguistic system we want to choose. Such questions as "Are there abstract entities?" or "Are there physical entities?" thus are held to belong to the category of external questions. On the other hand, having made the decision regarding which linguistic framework to adopt, we can then raise questions like "Are there any black swans?" "What are the factors of 544?" etc. Such questions are *internal* questions.

For our present purposes, the important thing about all of this is that while for Carnap *internal* questions are theoretical ones, i.e., ones whose answers have cognitive content, external questions are not theoretical at all. They are *practical questions*—they concern our decisions to employ one language structure or another. They are of the kind that face us when for example we have to decide whether we ought to have a Democratic or a Republican administration for the next four years. In short, though neither Carnap nor Quine employ the epithet, they are *value questions.*

Now if this dichotomy of existence questions is accepted Carnap can still deny the essential involvement of the making of value judgments in the procedures of science by insisting that concern with *external* questions, admittedly necessary and admittedly axiological, is nevertheless in some sense a pre-scientific concern. But most interestingly, what Quine then proceeds to do is to show that the dichotomy, as Carnap holds it, is untenable. This is not the appropriate place to repeat Quine's arguments which are brilliantly presented in the article referred to. They are in line with the views he has expressed in his "Two Dogmas of Empiricism" essay and especially with his introduction to his recent book, *Methods of Logic.* Nonetheless the final paragraph of the Quine article I'm presently considering sums up his conclusions neatly:

> Within natural science there is a continuum of gradations, from the statements which report observations to those which reflect basic features say of quantum theory or the theory of relativity. The view which I end up with, in the paper last cited, is that statements of ontology or even of mathematics and logic form a continuation of this continuum, a continuation which is perhaps yet more remote from observation than are the central principles of quantum theory or relativity. The differences here are in my view differences only in degree and not in kind. Science is a unified structure, and in principle it is the structure as a whole, and not its component statements one by one, that experience confirms or shows to be imperfect. Carnap maintains that ontological questions, and likewise questions of logical or mathematical principle, are questions not of fact but of

choosing a convenient conceptual scheme or framework for science; and with this I agree only if the same be conceded for every scientific hypothesis. (n. 2, pp. 71–72.)

In the light of all this I think that the statement that *Scientists qua Scientists* make value judgments is also a consequence of Quine's position.

Now, if the major point I have here undertaken to establish is correct, then clearly we are confronted with a first order crisis in science and methodology. The positive horror which most scientists and philosophers of science have of the intrusion of value considerations into science is wholly understandable. Memories of the (now diminished but a certain extent still continuing) conflict between science and, e.g., the dominant religions over the intrusion of religious value considerations into the domain of scientific inquiry, are strong in many reflective scientists. The traditional search for objectivity exemplifies science's pursuit of one of its most precious ideals. But for the scientist to close his eyes to the fact that scientific method *intrinsically* requires the making of value decisions, for him to push out of his consciousness the fact that he does make them, can in no way bring him closer to the ideal of objectivity. To refuse to pay attention to the value decisions which *must* be made, to make them intuitively, unconsciously, haphazardly, is to leave an essential aspect of scientific method scientifically out of control.

What seems called for (and here no more than the sketchiest indications of the problem can be given) is nothing less than a radical reworking of the ideal of scientific objectivity. The slightly juvenile conception of the coldblooded, emotionless, impersonal, passive scientist mirroring the world perfectly in the highly polished lenses of his steel rimmed glasses—this stereotype—is no longer, if it ever was, adequate.

What is being proposed here is that objectivity for science lies at least in becoming precise about what value judgments are being and might have been made in a given inquiry—and even, to put it in its most challenging form, what value decisions ought to be made; in short that a science of ethics is a necessary requirement if science's progress toward objectivity is to be continuous.

Of course the establishment of such a science of ethics is a task of stupendous magnitude and it will probably not even be well launched for many generations. But a first step is surely comprised of the reflective self awareness of the scientist in making the value judgments he must make.

NOTES

1. R. Carnap, "Empiricism, Semantics, and Ontology," *Revue Internationale de Philosophie,* XI, 1950, pp. 20–40.

2. W. V. Quine, "On Carnap's Views on Ontology," *Philosophical Studies,* II, No. 5, 1951.

3. "In practice three levels are commonly used: 1 per cent, 5 per cent and 0.3 of one per cent. There is nothing sacred about these three values; *they have become established in practice without*

any rigid theoretical justification." (my italics) (subnote 3*, p. 435). To establish significance at the 5 per cent level means that one is willing to take the risk of accepting a hypothesis as true when one will be thus making a mistake, one time in twenty. Or in other words, that one will be wrong (over the long run) once every twenty times if one employed an .05 level of significance. See also (subnote 3† Chap. v) for such statements as "which of these two errors is most *important* to avoid (it being necessary to make such a decision in order to accept or reject the given hypothesis) is a *subjective matter* . . ." (my italics) (subnote 3†, p. 262).

* A. C. Rosander, *Elementary Principles of Statistics* (New York: D. Van Nostrand Co., 1951).
† J. Neyman, *First Course in Probability and Statistics* (New York: Henry Holt & Co., 1950).

24

Science and Human Values

Carl G. Hempel

1. The Problem

Our age is often called an age of science and of scientific technology, and with good reason: the advances made during the past few centuries by the natural sciences, and more recently by the psychological and sociological disciplines, have enormously broadened our knowledge and deepened our understanding of the world we live in and of our fellow men; and the practical application of scientific insights is giving us an ever increasing measure of control over the forces of nature and the minds of men. As a result, we have grown quite accustomed, not only to the idea of a physico-chemical and biological technology based on the results of the natural sciences, but also to the concept, and indeed the practice, of a psychological and sociological technology that utilizes the theories and methods developed by behavioral research.

This growth of scientific knowledge and its applications has vastly reduced the threat of some of man's oldest and most formidable scourges, among them famine and pestilence; it has raised man's material level of living, and it has put within his reach the realization of visions which even a few decades ago would have appeared utterly fantastic, such as the active exploration of interplanetary space.

But in achieving these results, scientific technology has given rise to a host of new and profoundly disturbing problems: The control of nuclear fission has brought us not only the comforting prospect of a vast new reservoir of energy, but also the constant threat of the atom bomb and of grave damage, to the present and to future generations, from the radioactive by-products of the fission process, even in its peaceful uses. And the very progress in biological and medical knowledge and technology which has so strikingly reduced infant mortality and increased man's life expectancy in large areas of our globe has significantly contributed to the threat of the "population explosion," the rapid growth of the earth's population which we are facing today, and which, again, is a matter of grave concern to all those who have the welfare of future generations at heart.

Clearly, the advances of scientific technology on which we pride ourselves, and which have left their characteristic imprint on every aspect of this "age of science," have brought in their train many new and grave problems which urgently demand a solution. It is only natural that, in his desire to cope with these new issues, man should turn to science and scientific technology for further help. But a moment's reflection shows that the problems that need to be dealt with are not straightforward technological questions but intricate complexes of technological and moral issues. Take the case of the population explosion, for example, To be sure, it does pose specific technological problems. One of these is the task of satisfying at least the basic material needs of a rapidly growing population by means of limited resources; another is the question of means by which population growth itself may be kept under control. Yet these technical questions do not exhaust the problem. For after all, even now we have at our disposal various ways of counteracting population growth; but some of these, notably contraceptive methods, have been and continue to be the subject of intense controversy on moral and religious grounds, which shows that an adequate solution of the problem at hand requires, not only knowledge of technical means of control, but also standards for evaluating the alternative means at our disposal; and this second requirement clearly raises moral issues.

There is no need to extend the list of illustrations: any means of technical control that science makes available to us may be employed in many different ways, and a decision as to what use to make of it involves us in questions of moral valuation. And here arises a fundamental problem to which I would now like to turn: Can such valuational questions be answered by means of the objective methods of empirical science, which have been so successful in giving us reliable, and often practically applicable, knowledge of our world? Can those methods serve to establish objective criteria of right and wrong and thus to provide valid moral norms for the proper conduct of our individual and social affairs?

2. Scientific Testing

Let us approach this question by considering first, if only in brief and sketchy outline, the way in which objective scientific knowledge is arrived at. We may leave aside here the question of *ways of discovery*; i.e., the problem of how a new scientific idea arises, how a novel hypothesis or theory is first conceived; for our purposes it will suffice to consider the scientific *ways of validation*; i.e., the manner in which empirical science goes about examining a proposed new hypothesis and determines whether it is to be accepted or rejected. I will use the word 'hypothesis' here to refer quite broadly to any statements or set of statements in empirical science, no matter whether it deals with some particular event or purports to set forth a general law or perhaps a more or less complex theory.

As is well known, empirical science decides upon the acceptability of a proposed hypothesis by means of suitable tests. Sometimes such a test may involve nothing more than what might be called direct observation of pertinent facts. This procedure may be used, for example, in testing such statements as 'It is raining outside,' 'All the marbles in this urn are blue,' 'The needle of this ammeter will stop at the scale point marked 6,' and so forth. Here a few direct observations will usually suffice to decide whether the hypothesis at hand is to be accepted as true or to be rejected as false.

But most of the important hypotheses in empirical science cannot be tested in this simple manner. Direct observation does not suffice to decide, for example, whether to accept or to reject the hyoptheses that the earth is a sphere, that hereditary characteristics are transmitted by genes, that all Indo-European languages developed from one common ancestral language, that light is an electromagnetic wave process, and so forth. With hypotheses such as these, science resorts to indirect methods of test and validation. While these methods vary greatly in procedural detail, they all have the same basic structure and rationale. First, from the hypothesis under test, suitable other statements are inferred which describe certain directly observable phenomena that should be found to occur under specifiable circumstances if the hypothesis is true; then those inferred statements are tested directly; i.e., by checking whether the specified phenomena do in fact occur; finally, the proposed hypothesis is accepted or rejected in the light of the outcome of these tests. For example, the hypothesis that the earth is spherical in shape is not directly testable by observation, but it permits us to infer that a ship moving away from the observer should appear to be gradually dropping below the horizon; that circumnavigation of the earth should be possible by following a straight course; that high-altitude photographs should show the curving of the earth's surface; that certain geodetic and astronomical measurements should yield such and such results; and so forth. Inferred statements such as these can be tested more or less directly; and as an increasing number and variety of them are actually borne out, the hypothesis becomes increasingly confirmed. Eventually, a hypothesis may be so well confirmed by the available evidence that it is accepted as having been established beyond reasonable doubt. Yet no scientific hypothesis is ever proved completely and definitively; there is always at least the theoretical possibility that new evidence will be discovered which conflicts with some of the observational statements inferred from the hypothesis, and which thus leads to its rejection. The history of science records many instances in which a once accepted hypothesis was subsequently abandoned in the light of adverse evidence.

3. Instrumental Judgments of Value

We now turn to the question whether this method of test and validation may be used to establish moral judgments of value, and particularly judgments to the effect that a specified course of action is good or right or proper, or that it is better than certain alternative courses of action, or that we ought—or ought not—to act in certain specified ways.

By way of illustration, consider the view that it is good to raise children permissively and bad to bring them up in a restrictive manner. It might seem that, at least in principle, this view could be scientifically confirmed by appropriate empirical investigations. Suppose, for example, that careful research had established (1) that restrictive upbringing tends to generate resentment and aggression against parents and other persons exercising educational authority, and that this leads to guilt and anxiety and an eventual stunting of the child's initiative and creative potentialities; whereas (2) permissive upbringing avoids these consequences, makes for happier interpersonal relations, encourages resourcefulness and self-reliance, and enables the child to develop and enjoy his potentialities. These statements, especially when suitably amplified, come within the purview of scientific investigation; and though our knowledge in the matter is in fact quite limited, let us assume, for the sake of the argument, that they had actually been strongly confirmed by careful tests. Would not scientific research then have objectively shown that it is indeed better to raise children in a permissive rather than in a restrictive manner?

A moment's reflection shows that this is not so. What would have been established is rather a conditional statement; namely, that *if* our children are to become happy, emotionally secure, creative individuals rather than guilt-ridden and troubled souls *then* it is better to raise them in a permissive than in a restrictive fashion. A statement like this represents a *relative, or instrumental, judgment of value.* Generally, a relative judgment of value states that a certain kind of action, M, is good (or that it is better than a given alternative M_1) *if* a specified goal G is to be attained; or more accurately, that M is good, or appropriate, for the attainment of goal G. But to say that is tantamount to asserting either that, in the circumstances at hand, course of action M will definitely (or probably) lead to the attainment of G, or that failure to embark on course of action M will definitely (or probably) lead to the nonattainment of G. In other words, the instrumental value judgment asserts either that M is a (definitely or probably) sufficient means for attaining the end or goal G, or that it is a (definitely or probably) necessary means for attaining it. Thus, a relative, or instrumental, judgment of value can be reformulated as a statement which expresses a universal or a probabilistic kind of means-ends relationship, and which contains no terms of moral discourse—such as 'good,' 'better,' 'ought to'—at all. And a statement of this kind surely is an empirical assertion capable of scientific test.

4. Categorical Judgments of Value

Unfortunately, this does not completely solve our problem; for after a relative judgment of value referring to a certain goal G has been tested and, let us assume, well confirmed, we are still left with the question of whether the goal G ought to be pursued, or whether it would be better to aim at some alternative goal instead. Empirical science can establish the conditional statement, for example, that if we wish to deliver an incurably ill person from intolerable suffering, then a large dose of morphine affords a means of doing so; but it may also indicate ways of prolonging the patient's life, if also his suffering. This leaves us with the question whether it is right to give the goal of avoiding hopeless human suffering precedence over that of preserving human life. And this question calls, not for a relative but for an *absolute, or categorical, judgment of value* to the effect that a certain state of affairs (which may have been proposed as a goal or end) is good, or that it is better than some specified alternative. Are such categorical value judgments capable of empirical test and confirmation?

Consider, for example, the sentence 'Killing is evil'. It expresses a categorical judgment of value which, by implication, would also categorically qualify euthanasia as evil. Evidently, the sentence does not express an assertion that can be directly tested by observation; it does not purport to describe a directly observable fact. Can it be indirectly tested, then, by inferring from it statements to the effect that under specified test conditions such and such observable phenomena will occur? Again, the answer is clearly in the negative. Indeed, the sentence 'Killing is evil' does not have the function of expressing an assertion that can be qualified as true or false; rather, it serves to express a standard for moral appraisal or a norm for conduct. A categorical judgment of value may have other functions as well; for example, it may serve to convey the utterer's approval or disapproval of a certain kind of action, or his commitment to the standards of conduct expressed by the value judgment. Descriptive empirical import, however, is absent; in this respect a sentence such as 'Killing is evil' differs strongly from, say, 'Killing is condemned as evil by many religions', which expresses a factual assertion capable of empirical test.

Categorical judgments of value, then, are not amenable to scientific test and confirmation or disconfirmation; for they do not express assertions but rather standards or norms for conduct. It was Max Weber, I believe, who expressed essentially the same idea by remarking that science is like a map: it can tell us how to get to a given place, but it cannot tell us where to go. Gunnar Myrdal, in his book *An American Dilemma* (p. 1052), stresses in a similar vein that "factual or theoretical studies alone cannot logically lead to a practical recommendation. A practical or valuational conclusion can be derived only when there is at least one valuation among the premises."

Nevertheless, there have been many attempts to base systems of moral standards on the findings of empirical science; and it would be of interest to examine in some detail the reasoning which underlies those procedures. In the present context, however, there is room for only a few brief remarks on this subject.

It might seem promising, for example, to derive judgments of value from the results of an objective study of human needs. But no cogent derivation of this sort is possible. For this procedure would presuppose that it is right, or good, to satisfy human needs—and this presupposition is itself a categorical judgment of value: it would play the role of a valuational premise in the sense of Myrdal's statement. Furthermore, since there are a great many different, and partly conflicting, needs of individuals and of groups, we would require not just the general maxim that human needs ought to be satisfied, but a detailed set of rules as to the preferential order and degree in which different needs are to be met, and how conflicting claims are to be settled; thus, the valuational premise required for this undertaking would actually have to be a complex system of norms; hence, a derivation of valuational standards simply from a factual study of needs is out of the question.

Several systems of ethics have claimed the theory of evolution as their basis; but they are in serious conflict with each other even in regard to their most fundamental tenets. Some of the major variants are illuminatingly surveyed in a chapter of G. G. Simpson's book, *The Meaning of Evolution*. One type, which Simpson calls a "tooth-and-claw ethics," glorifies a struggle for existence that should lead to a survival of the fittest. A second urges the harmonious adjustment of groups or individuals to one another so as to enhance the probability of their survival, while still other systems hold up as an ultimate standard the increased aggregation of organic units into higher levels of organization, sometimes with the implication that the welfare of the state is to be placed above that of the individuals belonging to it. It is obvious that these conflicting principles could not have been validly inferred from the theory of evolution—unless indeed that theory were self-contradictory, which does not seem very likely.

But if science cannot provide us with categorical judgments of value, what then can serve as a source of unconditional valuations? This question may either be understood in a pragmatic sense, as concerned with the sources from which human beings do in fact obtain their basic values. Or it may be understood as concerned with a systematic aspect of valuation; namely, the question where a proper system of basic values is to be found on which all other valuations may then be grounded.

The pragmatic question comes within the purview of empirical science. Without entering into details, we may say here that a person's values—both those he professes to espouse and those he actually conforms to—are largely absorbed from the society in which he lives, and especially from certain influential subgroups to which he belongs, such as his family, his schoolmates, his associates on the job, his church, clubs, unions, and other groups. Indeed his values may vary from case to case depending on which of these groups dominates the situation in which he happens to find himself. In general, then, a person's basic valuations are no more the result of careful scrutiny and critical appraisal of possible alternatives than is his religious affiliation. Conformity to the standards of 'certain groups plays a very important role here, and only rarely are basic values seriously questioned. Indeed, in many situations, we decide and act unreflectively in an even stronger sense; namely, without any attempt to base our decisions on some set of explicit, consciously adopted, moral standards.

Now, it might be held that this answer to the pragmatic version of our question reflects a regrettable human inclination to intellectual and moral inertia; but that the really important side of our question is the systematic one: If we do want to justify our decisions, we need moral standards of conduct of the unconditional type—but how can such standards be established? If science cannot provide categorical value judgments, are there any other sources from which they might be obtained? Could we not, for example, validate a system of categorical judgments of value by pointing out that it represents the moral standards held up by the Bible, or by the Koran, or by some inspiring thinker or social leader? Clearly, this procedure must fail, for the factual information here adduced could serve to validate the value judgments in question only if we were to use, in addition, a valuational presupposition to the effect that the moral directives stemming from the source invoked *ought* to be complied with. Thus, if the process of justifying a given decision or a moral judgment is ever to be completed, certain judgments of value have to be accepted without any further justification, just as the proof of a theorem in geometry requires that some propositions be accepted as postulates, without proof. The quest for a justification of *all* our valuations overlooks this basic characteristic of the logic of validation and of justification. The value judgments accepted without further justification in a given context need not, however, be accepted once and for all, with a commitment never to question them again. This point will be elaborated further in the final section of this essay.

As will hardly be necessary to stress, in concluding the present phase of our discussion, the ideas set forth in the preceding pages do not imply or advocate moral anarchy; in particular, they do not imply that any system of values is just as good, or just as valid, as any other, or that everyone should adopt the moral principles that best suit his convenience. For all such maxims have the character of categorical value judgments and cannot, therefore, be implied by the preceding considerations, which are purely descriptive of certain logical, psychological, and social aspects of moral valuation.

5. Rational Choice: Empirical and Valuational Components

To gain further insight into the relevance of scientific inquiry for categorical valuation let us ask what help we might receive, in dealing with a moral problem, from science in an ideal state such as that represented by Laplace's conception of a superior scientific intelligence, sometimes referred to as

Laplace's demon. This fiction was used by Laplace, early in the nineteenth century, to give a vivid characterization of the idea of universal causal determinism. The demon is conceived as a perfect observer, capable of ascertaining with infinite speed and accuracy all that goes on in the universe at a given moment; he is also an ideal theoretician who knows all the laws of nature and has combined them into one universal formula; and finally, he is a perfect mathematician who, by means of that universal formula, is able to infer, from the observed state of the universe at the given moment, the total state of the universe at any other moment; thus past and future are present before his eyes. Surely, it is difficult to imagine that science could ever achieve a higher degree of perfection!

Let us assume, then, that, faced with a moral decision, we are able to call upon the Laplacean demon as a consultant. What help might we get from him? Suppose that we have to choose one of several alternative courses of action open to us, and that we want to know which of these we *ought* to follow. The demon would then be able to tell us, for any contemplated choice, what its consequences would be for the future course of the universe, down to the most minute detail, however remote in space and time. But, having done this for each of the alternative courses of action under consideration, the demon would have completed his task: he would have given us all the information that an ideal science might provide under the circumstances. And yet he would not have resolved our moral problem, for this requires a decision as to which of the several alternative sets of consequences mapped out by the demon as attainable to us is the best; which of them we ought to bring about. And the burden of this decision would still fall upon our shoulders: it is we who would have to commit ourselves to an unconditional judgment of value by singling out one of the sets of consequences as superior to its alternatives. Even Laplace's demon, or the ideal science he stands for, cannot relieve us of this responsibility.

In drawing this picture of the Laplacean demon as a consultant in decision-making, I have cheated a little; for if the world were as strictly deterministic as Laplace's fiction assumes, then the demon would know in advance what choice we were going to make, and he might disabuse us of the idea that there were several courses of action open to us. However that may be, contemporary physical theory has cast considerable doubt on the classical conception of the universe as a strictly deterministic system: the fundamental laws of nature are now assumed to have a statistical or probabilistic rather than a strictly universal, deterministic, character.

But whatever may be the form and the scope of the laws that hold in our universe, we will obviously never attain a perfect state of knowledge concerning them; confronted with a choice, we never have more than a very incomplete knowledge of the laws of nature and of the state of the world at the time when we must act. Our decisions must therefore always be made on the basis of incomplete information, a state which enables us to anticipate the consequences of alternative choices at best with probability. Science can render an indispensable service by providing us with increasingly extensive and reliable information relevant to our purpose; but again it remains for us to *evaluate* the various probable sets of consequences of the alternative choices under consideration. And this requires the adoption of pertinent valuational standards which are not objectively determined by the empirical facts.

This basic point is reflected also in the contemporary mathematical theories of decision-making. One of the objectives of these theories is the formulation of decision rules which will determine an optimal choice in situations where several courses of action are available. For the formulation of decision rules, these theories require that at least two conditions be met: (1) Factual information must be provided specifying the available courses of action and indicating for each of these its different possible outcomes—plus, if feasible, the probabilities of their occurrence; (2) there must be a specification of the values—often prosaically referred to as utilities—that are attached to the different possible outcomes. Only when these factual and valuational specifications have been provided does it make sense to ask which of the available choices is the best, considering the values attaching to their possible results.

In mathematical decision theory, several criteria of optimal choice have been proposed. In case the probabilities for the different outcomes of each action are given, one standard criterion qualifies a choice as optimal if the probabilistically expectable utility of its outcome is at least as great as that of any alternative choice. Other rules, such as the maximin and the maximax principles, provide criteria that are applicable even when the probabilities of the outcomes are not available. But interestingly, the various criteria conflict with each other in the sense that, for one and the same situation, they will often select different choices as optimal.

The policies expressed by the conflicting criteria may be regarded as reflecting different attitudes towards the world, different degrees of optimism or pessimism, of venturesomeness or caution. It may be said therefore that the analysis offered by current mathematical models indicates two points at which decision-making calls not solely for factual information, but for categorical valuation, namely, in the assignment of utilities to the different possible outcomes and in the adoption of one among many competing decision rules or criteria of optimal choice. . . .

6. Valuational "Presuppositions" of Science

The preceding three sections have been concerned mainly with the question whether, or to what extent, valuation and decision presuppose scientific investigation and scientific knowledge. This problem has a counterpart which deserves some attention in a discussion of science and valuation; namely, the question whether scientific knowledge and method presuppose valuation.

The word 'presuppose' may be understood in a number of different senses which require separate consideration here. First of all, when a person decides to devote himself to scientific work rather than to some other career, and again, when a scientist chooses some particular topic of investigation, these choices will presumably be determined to a large extent by his preferences, i.e., by how highly he values scientific research in comparison with the alternatives open to him, and by the importance he attaches to the problems he proposes to investigate. In this explanatory, quasi-causal sense the scientific *activities* of human beings may certainly be said to presuppose valuations.

Much more intriguing problems arise, however, when we ask whether judgments of value are presupposed by the body of scientific *knowledge,* which might be represented by a system of statements accepted in accordance with the rules of scientific inquiry. Here presupposing has to be understood in a systematic-logical sense. One such sense is invoked when we say, for example, that the statement 'Henry's brother-in-law is an engineer' presupposes that Henry has a wife or a sister: in this sense, a statement presupposes whatever can be logically inferred from it. But, as we noted earlier, no set of scientific statements logically implies an unconditional judgment of value; hence, scientific knowledge does not, in this sense, presuppose valuation.

There is another logical sense of presupposing, however. We might say, for example, that in Euclidean geometry the angle-sum theorem for triangles presupposes the postulate of the parallels in the sense that that postulate is an essential part of the basic assumptions from which the theorem is deduced. Now, the hypotheses and theories of empirical science are not normally validated by deduction from supporting evidence (though it may happen that a scientific statement, such as a prediction, is established by deduction from a previously ascertained, more inclusive set of statements); rather, as was mentioned in section 2, they are usually accepted on the basis of evidence that lends them only partial, or "inductive," support. But in any event it might be asked whether the statements representing scientific knowledge presuppose valuation in the sense that the grounds on which they are accepted include, sometimes or always, certain unconditional judgments of value. Again the answer is in the negative. The grounds on which scientific hypotheses are accepted or rejected are provided by empirical evidence, which may include observational findings as well as previously established laws and theories, but surely no value judgments. Suppose for example that, in support of the hypothesis that a radiation belt of a specified kind surrounds the earth, a scientist were to adduce, first, certain observational data, obtained perhaps by rocket-borne instruments; second, certain previously accepted theories invoked in the interpretation of those data; and finally, certain judgments of value, such as 'it is good to ascertain the truth'. Clearly, the judgments of value would then be dismissed as lacking all logical relevance to the proposed hypothesis since they can contribute neither to its support nor to its disconfirmation.

But the question whether science presupposes valuation in a logical sense can be raised, and recently has been raised, in yet another way, referring more specifically to valuational presuppositions of scientific *method*. In the preceding considerations, scientific knowledge was represented by a system of statements which are sufficiently supported by available evidence to be accepted in accordance with the principles of scientific test and validation. We noted that as a rule the observational evidence on which a scientific hypothesis is accepted is far from sufficient to establish that hypothesis conclusively. For example, Galileo's law refers not only to past instances of free fall near the earth, but also to all future ones; and the latter surely are not covered by our present evidence. Hence, Galileo's law, and similarly any other law in empirical science, is accepted on the basis of incomplete evidence. Such acceptance carries with it the "inductive risk" that the presumptive law may not hold in full generality, and that future evidence may lead scientists to modify or abandon it.

A precise statement of this conception of scientific knowledge would require, among other things, the formulation of rules of two kinds: First, *rules of confirmation,* which would specify what kind of evidence is confirmatory, what kind disconfirmatory for a given hypothesis. Perhaps they would also determine a numerical *degree* of evidential support (or confirmation, or inductive probability) which a given body of evidence could be said to confer upon a proposed hypothesis. Secondly, there would have to be *rules of acceptance*: these would specify how strong the evidential support for a given hypothesis has to be if the hypothesis is to be accepted into the system of scientific knowledge; or, more generally, under what conditions a proposed hypothesis is to be accepted, under what conditions it is to be rejected by science on the basis of a given body of evidence.

Recent studies of inductive inference and statistical testing have devoted a great deal of effort to the formulation of adequate rules of either kind. In particular, rules of acceptance have been treated in many of these investigations as special instances of decision rules of the sort mentioned in the preceding section. The decisions in question are here either to accept or to reject a proposed hypothesis on the basis of given evidence. As was noted earlier, the formulation of "adequate" decision rules requires, in any case, the antecedent specification of valuations that can then serve as standards of adequacy. The requisite valuations, as will be recalled, concern the different possible outcomes of the choices which the decision rules are to govern. Now, when a scientific rule of acceptance is applied to a specified hypothesis on the basis of a given body of evidence, the possible "outcomes" of the resulting decision may be divided into four major types: (1) the hypothesis is accepted (as presumably true) in accordance with the rule and is in fact true; (2) the hypothesis is rejected (as presumably false) in accordance with the rule and is in fact false; (3) the hypothesis is accepted in accordance with the rule, but is in fact false; (4) the hypothesis is rejected in accordance with the rule, but is in fact true. The former two cases are what science aims to achieve; the possibility of the latter two represents the inductive risk that any acceptance rule must involve. And the problem of formulating adequate rules of acceptance and rejection has no clear meaning unless standards of adequacy have been provided by assigning definite values or disvalues to those different possible "outcomes" of acceptance or rejection. It is in this sense that the method of establishing scientific hypotheses "presupposes" valuation: the justification of the rules of acceptance and rejection requires reference to value judgments.

In the cases where the hypothesis under test, if accepted, is to be made the basis of a specific course of action, the possible outcomes may lead to success or failure of the intended practical application; in these cases, the values and disvalues at stake may well be expressible in terms of monetary gains or losses; and for situations of this sort, the theory of decision functions has developed various decision rules for use in practical contexts such as industrial quality control. But when it comes to decision rules for the acceptance of hypotheses in pure scientific research, where no practical applications are contemplated, the question of how to assign values to the four types of outcome mentioned earlier becomes considerably more problematic. But in a general way, it seems clear that the standards governing the inductive procedures of pure science reflect the objective of obtaining a certain goal, which might be described somewhat vaguely as the attainment of an increasingly reliable, extensive, and theoretically systematized body of information about the world. Note that if we were concerned, instead, to form a system of beliefs or a world view that is emotionally reassuring or esthetically satisfying to us, then it would not be reasonable at all to insist, as science does, on a close accord between the beliefs we accept and our empirical evidence; and the standards of objective testability and confirmation by publicly ascertainable evidence would have to be replaced by acceptance standards of an entirely different kind. The standards of procedure must in each case be formed in consideration of the goals to be attained; their justification must be relative to those goals and must, in this sense, presuppose them.

7. Concluding Comparisons

If, as has been argued in section 4, science cannot provide a validation of categorical value judgments, can scientific method and knowledge play any role at all in clarifying and resolving problems of moral valuation and decision? The answer is emphatically in the affirmative. I will try to show this in a brief survey of the principal contributions science has to offer in this context.

First of all, science can provide factual information required for the resolution of moral issues. Such information will always be needed, for no matter what system of moral values we may espouse—whether it be egoistic or altruistic, hedonistic or utilitarian, or of any other kind—surely the specific course of action it enjoins us to follow in a given situation will depend upon the facts about that situation; and it is scientific knowledge and investigation that must provide the factual information which is needed for the application of our moral standards.

More specifically, factual information is needed, for example, to ascertain (a) whether a contemplated objective can be attained in a given situation; (b) if it can be attained, by what alternative means and with what probabilities; (c) what side effects and ulterior consequences the choice of a given means may have apart from probably yielding the desired end; (d) whether several proposed ends are jointly realizable, or whether they are incompatible in the sense that the realization of some of them will definitely or probably prevent the realization of others.

By thus giving us information which is indispensable as a factual basis for rational and responsible decision, scientific research may well motivate us to change some of our valuations. If we were to discover, for example, that a certain kind of goal which we had so far valued very highly could be attained only at the price of seriously undesirable side effects and ulterior consequences, we might well come to place a less high value upon that goal. Thus, more extensive scientific information may lead to a change in our basic valuations—not by "disconfirming" them, of course, but rather by motivating a change in our total appraisal of the issues in question.

Secondly, and in a quite different manner, science can illuminate certain problems of valuation by an objective psychological and sociological study of the factors that affect the values espoused by an individual or a group; of the ways in which such valuational commitments change; and perhaps of the manner in which the espousal of a given value system may contribute to the emotional security of an individual or the functional stability of a group.

Psychological, anthropological, and sociological studies of valuational behavior cannot, of course, "validate" any system of moral standards. But their results can psychologically effect changes in our outlook on moral issues by broadening our horizons, by making us aware of alternatives not envisaged, or not embraced, by our own group, and by thus providing some safeguard against moral dogmatism or parochialism.

Finally, a comparison with certain fundamental aspects of scientific knowledge may help to illuminate some further questions concerning valuation.

If we grant that scientific hypotheses and theories are always open to revision in the light of new empirical evidence, are we not obliged to assume that there is another class of scientific statements which cannot be open to doubt and reconsideration, namely, the observational statements describing experiential findings that serve to test scientific theories? Those simple, straightforward reports of what has been directly observed in the laboratory or in scientific field work, for example—must they not be regarded as immune from any conceivable revision, as irrevocable once they have been established by direct observation? Reports on directly observed phenomena have indeed often been considered as an unshakable bedrock foundation for all scientific hypotheses and theories. Yet this conception is untenable; even here, we find no definitive, unquestionable certainty.

For, first of all, accounts of what has been directly observed are subject to error that may spring from various physiological and psychological sources. Indeed, it is often possible to check on the accuracy of a given observation report by comparing it with the reports made by other observers, or with relevant data obtained by some indirect procedure, such as a motion picture taken of the finish of a horse race; and such comparison may lead to the rejection of what had previously been considered as a correct description of a directly observed phenomenon. We even have theories that enable us to explain and anticipate some types of observational error, and in such cases, there is no hesitation to question and to reject certain statements that purport simply to record what has been directly observed.

Sometimes relatively isolated experimental findings may conflict with a theory that is strongly supported by a large number and variety of other data; in this case, it may well happen that part of the conflicting data, rather than the theory, is refused admission into the system of accepted scientific statements—even if no satisfactory explanation of the presumptive error of observation is available. In such cases it is not the isolated observational finding which decides whether the theory is to remain in good standing, but it is the previously well-substantiated theory which determines whether a purported observation report is to be regarded as describing an actual empirical occurrence. For example, a report that during a spiritualistic séance, a piece of furniture freely floated above the floor would normally be rejected because of its conflict with extremely well-confirmed physical principles, even in the absence of some specific explanation of the report, say, in terms of deliberate fraud by the medium, or of high suggestibility on the part of the observer. Similarly, the experimental findings reported by the physicist Ehrenhaft, which were claimed to refute the principle that all electric charges are integral multiples of the charge of the electron, did not lead to the overthrow, nor even to a slight modification, of that principle, which is an integral part of a theory with extremely strong and diversified experimental support. Needless to say, such rejection of alleged observation reports by reason of their conflict with well-established theories requires considerable caution; otherwise, a theory, once accepted, could be used to reject all adverse evidence that might subsequently be found—a dogmatic procedure entirely irreconcilable with the objectives and the spirit of scientific inquiry.

Even reports on directly observed phenomena, then, are not irrevocable; they provide no bedrock foundation for the entire system of scientific knowledge. But this by no means precludes the possibility of testing scientific theories by reference to data obtained through direct observation. As we noted, the results obtained by such direct checking cannot be considered as absolutely unquestionable and irrevocable; they are themselves amenable to further tests which may be carried out if there is reason for doubt. But obviously if we are ever to form any beliefs about the world, if we are ever to accept or to reject, even provisionally, some hypothesis or theory, then we must stop the testing process somewhere; we must accept some evidential statements as sufficiently trustworthy not to require further investigation for the time being. And on the basis of such evidence, we can then decide what credence to give to the hypothesis under test, and whether to accept or to reject it.

This aspect of scientific investigation seems to me to have a parallel in the case of sound valuation and rational decision. In order to make a rational choice between several courses of action, we have to consider, first of all, what consequences each of the different alternative choices is likely to have. This affords a basis for certain relative judgments of value that are relevant to our problem. If *this* set of results is to be attained, this course of action ought to be chosen; if *that other* set of results is to be realized, we should choose such and such another course; and so forth. But in order to arrive at a decision, we still have to decide upon the relative values of the alternative sets of consequences attainable to us; and this, as was noted earlier, calls for the acceptance of an unconditional judgment of value, which will then determine our choice. But such acceptance need not be regarded as definitive and irrevocable, as forever binding for all our future decisions: an unconditional judgment of value, once accepted, still remains open to reconsideration and to change. Suppose, for example, that we have to choose, as voters or as members of a city administration, between several alternative social policies, some of which are designed to improve certain material conditions of living, whereas others aim at satisfying cultural needs of various kinds. If we are to arrive at a decision at all, we will have to commit ourselves to assigning a higher value to one or the other of those objectives. But while the judgment thus accepted serves as an unconditional and basic judgment of value for the decision at hand, we are not for that reason committed to it forever—we may well reconsider our standards and reverse our judgment later on; and though this cannot undo the earlier decision, it will lead to different decisions in the future. Thus, if we are to arrive at a decision concerning a moral issue, we have to accept some unconditional judgments of value; but these need not be regarded as ultimate in the absolute sense of being forever binding for all our decisions, any more than the evidence statements relied on in the test of a scientific hypothesis need to be regarded as forever irrevocable. All that is needed in either context are *relative* ultimates, as it were: a set of judgments—moral or descriptive—which are accepted at the time as not in need of further scrutiny. These relative ultimates permit us to keep an open mind in regard to the possibility of making changes in our heretofore unquestioned commitments and beliefs; and surely the experience of the past suggests that if we are to meet the challenge of the present and the future, we will more than ever need undogmatic, critical, and open minds.

25

Values in Science

Ernan McMullin

Thirty years ago, Richard Rudner argued in a brief essay in *Philosophy of Science* that the making of value-judgments is an essential part of the work of science. He fully realized how repugnant such a claim would be to the positivist orthodoxy of the day, so repugnant indeed that its acceptance (he prophesied) would bring about a "first-order crisis in science and methodology" (1953, p. 6). Carnap, in particular, has been emphatic in excluding values from any role in science proper. His theory of meaning had led him to conclude that "the objective validity of a value . . . cannot be asserted in a meaningful statement at all" (1932/1959, p. 77). The contrast between science, the paradigm of meaning, and all forms of value-judgment could scarcely have been more sharply drawn: "it is altogether impossible to make a statement that expresses a value-judgment." No wonder, then, that Rudner's thesis seemed so shocking.

Thirty years later, the claim that science is value-laden might no longer even seem controversial, among philosophers of science, at least, who have become accustomed to seeing the pillars of positivism fall, one by one. One might even characterize the recent deep shifts in theory of science as consequences (many of them, at least) of the growing realization of the part played by value-judgment in scientific work. If this way of describing the Kuhnian "revolution" seems unfamiliar, it is no doubt due in part to the uneasiness that the ambiguity of the terms 'value' and 'value-judgment' still engenders. There are other ways of describing what has happened since the 1950's on philosophy of science that do not require so much preliminary ground-clearing.

Nevertheless, I shall try to show that the watershed between "classic" philosophy of science (by this meaning, not just logical positivism but the logicist tradition in theory of science stretching back through Immanuel Kant and René Descartes to Aristotle) and the "new" philosophy of science can best be understood by analyzing the change in our perception of the role played by values in science. I shall begin with some general remarks about the nature of value, go on to explore some of the historical sources for the claim that judgment in science is value-laden, and conclude by reflecting on the implications of this claim for traditional views of the objectivity of scientific knowledge-claims. I will not address the problem of the social sciences, where these issues take on an added complexity. They are, as we shall soon see, already complicated enough in the context of natural sciences.

I. The Anatomy of Value

'Value' is one of those weasel words that slip in and out of the nets of the philosopher. We shall have to try to catch it first, or else what we have to say about the role of values in science may be of small use. It is not much over a hundred years since the German philosopher, Hermann Lotze, tried to construct a single theory of value which would unite the varied value-aspects of human experience under a single discipline. The venture was, of course, not really new since Plato had attempted a similar project long before, using the cognate term 'good' instead of 'value'. Aristotle's response to Plato's positing of the Good as a common element answering to one idea was to point to the great diversity of ways in which the term 'good' might be used. In effect, our response to Lotze's project of a general axiology would likewise be to question the usefulness of trying to find a single notion of value that would apply to all contexts equally well.

Let us begin with the sense of 'value' that the founders of value-theory seem to have preferred. They took it to correspond to such features of human experience as attraction, emotion, and feeling. They wanted to secure an experiential basis for value in order to give the realm of value an empirical status just as valid as that of the (scientific) realm of fact. The reality of *emotive* value (as it may be called) lies in the feelings of the subject, not primarily in a characteristic of the object. Value-differences amount, then, to differences of attitude or of emotional response in specific subjects.

If one takes 'value' in this sense, value-decision becomes a matter of clarifying emotional responses. To speak of value-*judgment* here (as indeed is often done) is on the whole misleading since 'judgment' could suggest a cognitive act, a weighing-up. When the value of something is determined by one's attitude to it, the declaration of this value is a matter of value-*clarification* rather than of judgment, strictly speaking. It was primarily from this sense of value that the popular positivist distinction between differences of belief and differences of attitude took its origin, though C. L. Stevenson (who, when specifying his own notion of attitude, recalls R. B. Perry's definition of "interest" as a psychological disposition to be for or against something) allows that value-differences may have components both of attitude *and* belief (1949, p. 591).

It seems plausible to hold that emotive values are alien to the work of natural science. There is no reason to think that human emotionality is a trustworthy guide to the structures of the natural world. Indeed, there is every reason, historically speaking, to view emotive values, as Francis Bacon did, as potentially distortive "Idols," projecting in anthropomorphic fashion the pattern of human wants, desires, and emotions on a world where they have no place. When "ideology" is understood as a systematization of such values, it automatically becomes a threat to the integrity of science. The notion of value which is implicit in much recent social history of science, as well as in many analyses of the science-ideology relationship, is clearly that of emotive value.

A second kind of "value" is more important for your quest. A property or set of properties may count as a value in an entity of a particular kind because it is desirable for an entity of that kind. (The same property in a different entity might *not* count as a value.) The property can be a desirable one for various sorts of reasons. Speed is a desirable trait in wild antelope because it aids survival. Sound heart action is desirable in an organism with a circulatory system because of the functional needs of the organism. A retentive memory is desirable for a lawyer because of the nature of the lawyer's task. Sharpness is desirable in a knife because of the way in which it functions as a utensil. Efficiency is desirable in a business firm if the firm is to accomplish the ordinary ends of business. . . .

Let us focus on what these examples have in common. (In another context, we might be more concerned about their differences.) In each case, the desirable property is an objective characteristic of the entity. We can thus call it a *characteristic* value. In some cases, it is relative to a pattern of human ends; in others, it is not. In some cases, a characteristic value is a means to an end served by the entity possessing it; in others, it is not. In all cases, it serves to make its possessor function better as an entity of that kind.

Assessment of characteristic values can take on two quite different forms. One can judge the extent to which a particular entity realizes the value. We may be said to *evaluate* when we judge the speediness of a particular antelope or the heart-beat of a particular patient. On the other hand, we may be asked to judge whether or not (or to what extent) this characteristic really *is* a value for this kind of entity. How much do we *value* the characteristic? Here we are dealing, not with particulars, but with the more abstract relation of characteristic and entity under a particular description. Why *ought* one value speed in an antelope, rather than strength, say? How important *is* a retentive memory to a lawyer?

The logical positivists stressed the distinction between these two types of value-judgment, what I have called evaluation and valuing.[1] Valuing they took to be subjective and thus foreign to science. Evaluation, however, may be permissible because it expresses an estimate of the degree to which some commonly recognized (and more or less clearly defined) type of action, object, or institution is embodied in a given instance" (Nagel 1961, p. 492).[2] Notice the presupposition here: clear definition of the characteristic is required in order that there be a standard against which an estimate may be made. It was already a large concession to allow a role for mere estimation (as against measurement proper) in science; no further concession would be allowed.

Value-judgment, in the sense of evaluation could thus fall on the side of the factual, and the old dichotomy between fact and value could still be maintained. Value-judgment in the sense either of valuing or of evaluating, where the characteristic value is *not* sharply defined, was still to be rigorously excluded from science. Such value-judgment (so the argument went) is necessarily subjective; it involves a decision which is not rule-guided, and therefore has an element of the arbitrary. It intrudes individual human norms into what should ideally (if it were to be properly scientific) be an impersonal mapping of propositions onto the world.

What was offensive about value-judgment, then, was *not* its concern with characteristic values. Indeed, when such values are *measured* (when, for example, human blood-pressure is measured as a means to determining any departure from "normality"), the results are obviously "scientific" in the most conservative sense. Not every judgment in regard to characteristic value counts therefore as a "value-judgment," as this term has come to be used. Such a judgment must not only be concerned with value, but must function, not as measurement does, but in a non-mechanical, individual way. Since it is a matter of experience and skill, individual differences in judgment can thus in the normal course be expected.

It is clear, therefore, where the tension arises between value-judgment and not only the positivist view of science but the entire classical theory of science back to Aristotle. Max Weber spoke for that long tradition when, in his effort to eliminate value-judgment from social science, he opposed any form of assessment which could not immediately be enforced on all. The objectivity of science (he insisted) requires public norms accessible to all, and interpreted by all in the same way (Weber 1917).

What I want to argue here is that value-judgment, in just the sense that Weber deplored, *does* play a central role in science. Both evaluation *and* value are involved. The attempt to construe all forms of scientific reasoning as forms of deductive or inductive inference fails. The sense of my claim that science is value-laden is that there are certain characteristic *epistemic* values which are integral to the entire process of assessment in science. Since my topic is "values in science," there are, however, some other construals of this title that ought to be briefly addressed first, in order to be laid aside.

II. Other Construals

One value, namely truth itself, has always been recognized as permeating science. In the classic account, it was in fact the goal of the entire enterprise. Unlike other values, it was deemed to have nothing of the personal about it. On the contrary, it connoted an objective relation of proposition and world and thus was constitutive of the very category of fact itself. But this was not thought to weaken the maxim that science should be value-free, because the values that were thus being enjoined from intrusion into the work of science were the particular ones that would tend to compromise the objectivity of the effort and not the transcendental one which defined the tradition of science itself.

There has been much debate in recent philosophy of science about the sense in which truth can still be taken to be constitutive of science. The correspondence view of truth as a matching of language and mind-independent reality has been assailed by Ludwig Wittgenstein and many other more recent critics like Hilary Putnam and Richard Rorty. More to the point here, it seems clear that when a scientist "accepts" a theory, even a long-held theory, he is not claiming that it is *true*. The predicate in terms of which theory is valued is not truth, as the earlier account held it to be. We speak of a theory as being "well-supported," rationally acceptable," or the like. To speak of it as *true* would suggest that a later anomaly that would force a revision or even abandonment of the theory can in principle be excluded. The recent history of science would make both scientists and philosophers wary of any such presumption, except perhaps in cases of very limited theories or ones which are vaguely stated.

It can, however, be argued that truth is still a sort of horizon-concept or ideal of the scientific enterprise, even though we may not be able to assert truth in a definitive manner of any component of science along the way. There are many variations of this view, one which was clearly articulated a century ago by C. S. Peirce. I do not intend to discuss this issue further here (though I will return to it obliquely in my conclusion), because to argue that truth is at least in some sense a characteristic value admissible in science is hardly novel, and does not constitute the point of division with classic logicist theories of science that I am seeking to identify.

Nor am I concerned here with *ethical* values. Weber and the positivists of the last century and this one recognized that the work of science makes ethical demands on its practitioners, demands of honesty, openness, and integrity. Science is a communal work. It cannot succeed unless results are honestly reported, unless every reasonable precaution be taken to avoid experimental error, unless evidence running counter to one's own view is fairly handled, and so on. These are severe demands, and scientists do not always live up to them. Outright fraud, as we have been made uncomfortably aware in recent years, does occur. But so far as we can tell, it is rare and does not threaten the integrity of the research enterprise generally. In any event, there never has been any disagreement about the value-ladenness of science where moral values of this kind are concerned. If I am to make a claim about a change in regard to the recognition of the proper presence in science of value-judgment, it cannot be in regard to those moral values which have always been seen as essential to the success of communal inquiry.[3]

In support of his claim that "value-judgments are essentially involved in the procedures of science," Rudner argued that the acceptance of a scientific hypothesis:

> is going to be a function of the importance, in the typically ethical
> sense, of making a mistake in accepting or rejecting the hypothesis.
> Thus, to take a crude but easily manageable example, if the hypothesis
> under consideration were to the effect that a toxic ingredient of
> a drug was not present in lethal quantity, we would require a rela-
> tively high degree of confirmation or confidence before accepting
> the hypothesis, for the consequences of making a mistake here are
> exceedingly grave by our moral standards. (1953, p. 2)

This notion of hypothesis "acceptance" is dangerously ambiguous. Rudner takes it to mean: "approve as a basis for a specific kind of action." But acceptance in this sense is not part of theoretical science, strictly speaking. When a physicist "accepts" a particular theory, this can mean that he believes it to be the best-supported of the alternatives available or that he sees it as offering the most fruitful research-program for the immediate future. These are *epistemic* assessments; they attach no values to the theoretical alternatives other than those of likelihood or probable fertility. On the other hand, if theory is being applied to practical ends, and the theoretical alternatives carry with them outcomes of different value to the agents concerned, we have the typical decision-theoretic grid involving not only likelihood estimates but also "utilities" of one sort or another. Such utilities are irrelevant to theoretical science proper and the scientist is not called upon to make value-judgments in their regard as part of his scientific work. The values of life and death involved in a decision to use or not to use a possibly toxic drug in a case where it alone seems to offer a chance of recovery are not relevant to the much more limited question as to whether or not the drug *would* be toxic for this patient.

The utilities typically associated with the application of science to human ends in medicine, engineering and the like, cannot, therefore, be cited as a reason for holding natural science itself to be value-laden. The conclusion that Rudner draws from his analysis of hypothesis-"acceptance" is that "a science of ethics is a necessary requirement if science's progress toward objectivity is to be continuous." But scientists are (happily!) not called on to "accept" hypotheses in the sense he is presupposing,[4] and so his conclusion does not go through.[5] If we are to hold that the work of science is value-laden, it ought to be for another reason.

My argument for the effective presence of "values in science" does not, then, refer to the constitutive role in science of the value or truth; nor does it refer to the ethical values required for the success of science as a communal activity, or to the values implicit in decision-making in applied science. Rather, it is directed to showing that the appraisal of theory is in important respects closer in structure to value-judgment than it is to the rule-governed inference that the classic tradition in philosophy of science took for granted.

Not surprisingly, the recognition of this crucial epistemological shift has been slow and painful. Already there are intimations of it among the more perceptive nineteenth-century philosophers of science. William Whewell, for example, describes a process very like value-judgment in his influential account of the "consilience of inductions," though he draws back from the threatening subjectivism of this line of thought, asserting that consilience will amount to "demonstration" in the long run (Laudan 1981). The logical positivists, as already noted, resolutely turned the theory of science back into the older logicist channels once more. Yet as they (and their critics) tried to characterize the strategies of science in closer detail, doubts began to grow. To these earlier anticipations of our theme, I now briefly turn.

III. Anticipations

The prevailing inductivism of the nineteenth century made it seem as though science ultimately consisted of *laws,* that is, statements of empirical regularities. These laws were arrived at by generalization from the facts of observation; the facts themselves were regarded as an unproblematic starting-point for the process of induction. It was, of course, realized that the laws were open to revision as measuring apparatus was improved, as the ranges of the variables were extended, as new relevant factors were discovered. There was no *logic,* strictly speaking, which would lead from a finite set of observation-statements to a universally valid law of nature.

Human decision had to enter in, therefore, by way of curve-fitting, extrapolation, and estimates of relevance. Such decision was not arbitrary; there were skills and techniques to be learnt which would aid the scientist in drawing the best generalizations from the data available. Was this not a matter of value-judgment rather than of a common logic of formal rules? We would say so today. But the point was not so evident then, or perhaps it would be more accurate to say that it seemed of little importance.

The reason was that the laws were taken to be true to a degree of approximation that could be improved indefinitely. Thus the influence of these decisional aspects, where the individual skills of curve-fitting, extrapolation, and estimation of relevance, entered into the process of formulating a law, would be progressively lessened, as the law came closer and closer to being an exact description of the real, that is, as the law gradually attained the status of fact. Thus, even though value-judgment did enter, in a number of ways, into the process of inductive generalization, its presence could in practice be ignored. It was, after all, no more than an accessory activity, of little significance to the ultimate deliverances of science, namely, the exact statements of the laws of nature.

The logical positivists still adhered to this nomothetic ideal. But from the beginning, they encountered difficulties as soon as they tried to spell out how an inductive method might work. The story is a familiar one. I am going to focus on only two episodes in it, one involving Karl Popper and the other Rudolf Carnap, in order to show how "value-uneasiness" was already in evidence among philosophers of science fifty years ago, though in neither of these episodes was it altogether satisfactorily characterized.

As we all know, Popper rejected the nomothetic ideal of science that the logical positivists took over from the nineteenth century. For him, science is a set of conjectures rather than a set of laws. The testing of conjectures is thus the central element in scientific method and it can work only by falsification, when a basic statement conflicts with a conjectured explanation, leading to the rejection of the conjecture. The entire logical weight of this operation is carried by the "basic statements," that is, reports of observable events at particular locations in space and time.

But now a difficulty arises. Could not the basic statements themselves be falsified? They could not consistently be held immune to the test-challenge that Popper saw as the criterion of demarcation between science and non-science. But if the basic statements themselves are open to challenge, how is the whole procedure of falsification of conjecture to work? It sounds as if a destructive regress cannot be avoided.

Popper's answer is to say that:

> Every test of a theory, whether resulting in its corroboration or falsification, must stop at some basic statement or other which we decide to accept. . . . Considered from a logical point of view, the situation is never such that it compels us to stop at this particular basic statement rather than at that. . . . For any basic statement can again in its turn be subjected to tests, using as a touchstone any of the basic statements which can be deduced from it, with the help of some theory, either the one under test or another. This process has no natural end. Thus if the test is to lead anywhere, nothing remains but to stop at some point or other and say we are satisfied for the time being. (1934/1959, p. 104)

Thus the designation of a statement as a "basic" one is not definitive, and hence falsification is not quite the decisive logical step Popper would have liked it to be. He continues: "Basic statements are accepted as the result of a decision or convention; and to that extent they are conventions" (p. 106). His choice of the term 'convention' here is a surprising one since it carries the overtone of arbitrariness, of *arbitrary* choice and not just choice. But Popper is explicit in excluding this suggestion. He criticizes Otto Neurath, in fact, who (he says) made a "notable advance" by recognizing that protocol statements are not irrevocable, but then failed to specify a method by which they might be evaluated. Such a move, he goes on,

> leads nowhere if it is not followed by another step; we need a set of rules to limit the arbitrariness of 'deleting' (or else 'accepting') a protocol sentence. Neurath fails to give any such rules and thus unwittingly throws empiricism overboard. For without such rules, empirical statements are no longer distinguished from any other sort of statements. (p. 97)

For Popper, the need for such a line of demarcation takes precedence over any other demand. So if there are to be decisions regarding the basic statements, these must (he says) be "reached in accordance with a procedure governed by rules" (p. 106). If there are *rules,* however, to guide the decision, it sounds as though a definite answer might be obtained by the application of these rules in any given case. And so the properly *decisional* element would be minimal, and value-judgment (as we have defined it) would not enter in.

But, in fact, we discover that the word, 'rule', here (like the word, 'convention') is not to be taken literally. When Popper specifies how these "rules" would operate, all he has to say is that we can arrive at:

> a procedure according to which we stop only at a kind of statement
> that is especially easy to test. For it means that we are stopping
> at statements about whose acceptance or rejection the various
> investigators are likely to reach agreement. (p. 104)

So that ease in testing is to guide the investigator in deciding which statements to designate as basic. But this clearly operates here as a *value* rather than as a *rule.* There could be differences in judgment as to the extent to which the value was realized in a given case. Popper himself says of his "rules" that though they are "based on certain fundamental principles" which aim at the discovery of objective truth, "they sometimes leave room not only for subjective convictions but even for subjective bias" (p. 110).

Thus what we have here is value-judgment, not the application of rule, strictly speaking. There is no *rule* as to where to stop the testing process. If some investigators prolong it further than others do, we would not be inclined to describe this as either "following" or "breaking" a rule. But we *would* call it the pursuing of a particular goal or value.

Popper's use of the term 'convention' to describe the element of value-judgment in the designation of basic statements has proved misleading to later commentators, even though he explicitly rejected classical conventionalism, mainly because it was unable, in his view, to generate a proper criterion of demarcation between science and non-science (McMullin 1978a, section 7). Imre Lakatos, for example, described Popper's view as a form of "revolutionary conventionalism" because of its explicit admission of the role of decisional elements in the scientific process. This led him to characterize his own MSRP as a way of "rationalizing classical conventionalism," rational because the criteria for distinguishing between "hard core" and "protective belt" can be partially specified, as can the criteria of theory-choice, but "conventional" because the process is not one of a mechanical application of rule, involving, as it does, individual judgment (1970, p. 134). Joseph Agassi likewise proposed that the most accurate label for Popper's theory of science is 'modified conventionalism' (Agassi 1974, p. 693) to which suggestion Popper rather testily responded "I am not a conventionalist, whether modified or not" (Popper 1974, p. 1117).

Much of the confusion prompted by Popper's use of the term 'convention' might have been avoided if he had used the notion of value-judgment instead. It has precisely the flexibility that he needed in order to distance himself, as he wished to do, from both positivism and conventionalism, from positivism because of his insistence upon the decisional elements in the selection of basic statements and from conventionalism because he believed that the values guiding judgment in this case are grounded in the "autonomous aim" of science, which is the pursuit of objective knowledge (Popper 1974, p. 1117).

Though the admission of value-judgment into science had moved Popper away from his rationalist moorings, it is significant that he never extended the range of value-judgment to theory-choice, which today to us would seem the much more likely locus. Even though he allows that "the choice of any theory is an act, a practical matter" (1935/1959, p. 109), his opposition to verification made him wary of allowing that theories might ever be "accepted." To the extent that they are, it is a provisional affair, he reminds us. But this sort of provisional acceptance is still, in his view, *decisively* influenced by the success of the theory in avoiding falsification (McMullin 1978a, p. 224). Rationalism is thus preserved at this level by the assumption of a more or less decisive method of choosing between theories at any given stage of development.

This is the assumption that Carnap helped, somewhat unwittingly perhaps, to undermine. In 1950, he drew his famous distinction between "internal" questions, which can be answered within a given linguistic framework and "external" questions, which bear on the acceptability of the framework itself (1950, p. 214). The point of the distinction was to clarify the debate about the existence of such abstract entities as classes or numbers to which Carnap assimilated the question of theoretical entities like electrons. To ask about the existence of such entities *within* a given linguistic framework is perfectly legitimate, he said, and an answer can be given along logical or empirical lines. But to ask about the *reality* of such a system of entities taken as a whole is to pose a metaphysical question to which only a pseudo-answer can be given. The question can, however, be framed in a different way and then it becomes perfectly legitimate. We can ask whether the linguistic framework itself is an appropriate one for our purposes, whatever they may be. This is the form in which external questions *should* be put in order to avoid idle philosopher's questions about the existence of numbers or electrons.

Once the question is put in this way, he goes on, it is seen to be a practical, not a theoretical matter. The decision to accept a particular framework:

> although itself not of a cognitive nature, will nevertheless usually be influenced by theoretical knowledge, just like any other deliberate decision concerning the acceptance of linguistic or other rules. The purposes for which the language is intended to be used, for instance, the purpose of communicating factual knowledge, will determine which factors are relevant for the decision. (1950, p. 208)

And he goes on to enumerate some of the factors that might influence a pragmatic decision of this sort: he mentions the "efficiency, fruitfulness and simplicity" of the language, relative to the purposes for which it is intended. These are *values,* of course, and so what he is talking about here (though he does not explicitly say so) is value-judgment.

In this essay, Carnap is worrying mainly about the challenge of the nominalists to such entities as classes, properties, and numbers. He wants to answer this challenge, not be asserting the existence of these entities directly—this would violate his deepest empiricist convictions—but by appealing to the practical utility of everyday language where terms corresponding to these entities play an indispensable role. And so he counters Occam's razor with a plea for "tolerance in permitting linguistic forms" (1950, p. 220). As long as the language is efficient as an instrument, he says, it would be foolish, indeed harmful, to impoverish it on abstract nominalist grounds.

But Carnap conceded much more than he may have realized by this manoeuvre. By equating the general semantical problem of abstract entities with the problem of theoretical entities in science, he implied that pragmatic "external" criteria are the appropriate ones for deciding on the acceptability of the linguistic frameworks of science, that is, of scientific theories. For the first time, he is implicitly admitting that the tight "internal" logicist criteria which he had labored so long to impose on the problems of confirmation and explanation are inappropriate when it is the very language of science itself, that is, the theory, that is in question.

It is the *theory* that leads us to speak of electrons; to assess this usage, we have to evaluate as a single unit the *theory* in which this concept occurs and by means of which it is defined. If more than one "linguistic framework" for theory is being defended in some domain, the decision as to which is the better one has to be resolved, not by inductive logic, but by these so-called "external" criteria.

The term, 'external', was obviously an unhappy choice, as things would turn out. The questions Carnap dubs "external" would be external to science only if theory-decision is external to science. They were external to his logicist conception of how science ought to be carried on, of course. Only if science can be regarded as a "given" formal system can be enterprise of the logician get under way. The question of whether a particular theory *should* be "given" or whether another might not accomplish the theoretical ends of science better, cannot be properly (i.e., "internally") posed in the original positivist scheme of things.

Once Carnap *allowed* it to be posed, however "externally," it would not be long until theory-evaluation would be clearly recognized as the most "internal" of all scientific issues, defining as it does scientific rationality and scientific progress. After we have discarded his term 'external', we still retain his insight that the structure of decision in regard to the acceptability of a theoretical language is not one of logical rule but of value-judgment.

IV. Theory-choice as Value-judgment

This gets us up only to 1950, which seems like *very* long ago in philosophy of science. Yet the shape of things to come is already clear to us, even though it was by no means clear then. The watershed between classic theory of science and our as yet unnamed post-logicist age has been variously defined since then. But for our purposes here, it can best be laid out in four propositions, three of them familiar, the other (P3) a little less so.

P1: The goal of science is theoretical knowledge.

P2: The theories of science are underdetermined by the empirical evidence.

P3: The assessment of theories involves value-judgment in an essential way.

P4: Observation in science is theory-dependent.

P1 tells us that the basic explanatory form in science is theory, not law, and thus that retroduction, not induction, is the main form of scientific validation. Theories by their very nature are hypothetical and tentative; they remain open to revision or even to rejection. P2 reminds us that there is no direct logical link, of the sort that classical theories of science expected, between evidence and theory. Since one is not compelled, as one would be in a logical or mathematical demonstration, one has to rely on oblique modes of assessment. And P3 tells us that these take the form of value-judgments.

P4 serves to emphasize that a thesis in regard to theory-appraisal has broader scope. To the extent that scientific observation is theory-dependent, it is also indirectly value-impregnated. This last point is not stressed any further in what follows, but it is well that it should be kept in mind lest it be thought that only *one* element in science, theory-choice, is affected by the shift described here, and that the traditional logicist/empiricist picture might be sustained at all other points.

So much for the schema. It can be found, more or less in the form in which I have sketched it here, in the work of Kuhn, specifically in his 1973 essay "Objectivity, Value-judgment, and Theory Choice" (1977). He asks there what are the characteristic values of a good scientific theory and lists, as a start, five that would be pretty well agreed upon. I will rework his list just a little, and add some comments.

Predictive accuracy is the desideratum that scientists would usually list first. But one has to be wary about the emphasis given it. As Lakatos and Feyerabend in particular have emphasized, scientists must often tolerate a certain degree of inaccuracy, especially in the early stages of theory-development. Nearly every theory is "born refuted"; there will inevitably be anomalies it cannot handle. There will be idealizatons that have to be worked out in order to test the theory in complex concrete contexts. Were this demand to be enforced in a mechanical manner, the results for science could be disastrous. Nevertheless, a high degree of predictive accuracy is in the long run something a theory *must* have if it is to be acceptable.

A second criterion is *internal coherence.* The theory should hang together properly; there should be no logical inconsistencies, no unexplained coincidences. One recalls the primary motivating factor for many astronomers in abandoning Ptolemy in favor of Copernicus. There were too many features of the Ptolemaic orbits, particularly the incorporation in each of a one-year cycle and the handling of retrograde motions, that seemed to leave coincidence unexplained and thus, though predictively accurate, to appear as *ad hoc.*

A third is *external consistency:* consistency with other theories and with the general background of expectation. When steady-state cosmology was proposed as an alternative to the Big Bang hypothesis in the late 1940's, the criticism it first had to face was that it flatly violated the principle of conservation of energy, which long ago attained the status almost of an *a priori* in mechanics. Even if Fred Hoyle had managed to make his model satisfy the other demands laid on it, such as the demand that it yield testable predictions in advance and not just after the fact, it would always have had a negative rating on the score of external consistency.

A fourth feature that scientists value is *unifying power,* the ability to bring together hitherto disparate areas of inquiry. The standard illustration is James Maxwell's electromagnetic theory. A more limited, but quite striking, example would be the plate-tectonic model in geology. Over the past twenty years, it has successfully explained virtually all major features of the earth's surface. What has impressed geologists sufficiently to persuade most (not all) of them to overcome the scruples that derive, for example, from the lack of a mechanism to account for the plate-movements themselves, is not just its predictive accuracy but the way in which it has brought together previously unrelated domains of geology under a single explanatory roof.

A further, and quite crucial, criterion is *fertility.* This is rather a complex affair (McMullin 1976). The theory proves able to make novel predictions that were not part of the set of original explananda. More important, the theory proves to have the imaginative resources, functioning here rather as a metaphor might in literature, to enable anomalies to be overcome and new and powerful extensions to be made. Here it is the *long-term* proven ability of the theory or research program to generate fruitful additions and modifications that has to be taken into account.

One other, and more problematic, candidate as a theory-criterion is *simplicity.* It was a favorite among the logical positivists because it could be construed pragmatically as a matter of convenience or of aesthetic taste, and seemed like an optional extra which the scientist could decide to set aside, without affecting the properly epistemic character of the theory under evaluation (Hempel 1966, pp. 40-45). Efforts to express a criterion of "simplicity" in purely formal terms continue to be made, but have not been especially successful.

One could easily find other desiderata. And it would be important to supply some detailed case-histories in order to illustrate the operation of the ones I have just listed. But my concern here is rather to underline that these criteria clearly operate as *values* do, so that theory choice is basically a matter of value-judgment. Kuhn puts it this way:

> The criteria of [theory] choice function not as rules, which determine choice, but as values which influence it. Two men deeply committed to the same values may nevertheless, in particular situations, make different choices, as in fact they do. (1977, p 331)

They correspond to the two types of value-judgement discussed above in section 1. First, different scientists may *evaluate* the fertility, say, of a particular theory differently. Since there is no algorithm for an assessment of this sort, it will depend on the individual scientist's training and experience. Though there is likely to be a very large measure of agreement, nonetheless the skills of evaluation here are in part personal ones, relating to the community consensus in complex ways.

Second, scientists may not attach the same relative weights to different characteristic values of theory, that is they may not *value* the characteristics in the same way, when, for example, consistency is to be weighed over against predictive accuracy. It is above all because theory has more than one criterion to satisfy, and because the "valuings" given these criteria by different scientists may greatly differ, that disagreement in regard to the merits of rival theories can on occasion be so intractable.

It would be easy to illustrate this by calling on the recent history of science. A single example will have to suffice. The notorious disagreement between Niels Bohr and Albert Einstein in regard to the acceptability of the quantum theory of matter did not bear on matters of predictive accuracy. Einstein regarded the new theory as lacking both in coherence and in consistency with the rest of physics. He also thought it failing in simplicity, the value that he tended to put first. Bohr admitted the lack of consistency with classical physics, but played down its importance. The predictive successes of the new theory obviously counted much more heavily with him than they did with Einstein. The differences between their assessments were not solely due to differences in the values they employed in theory-appraisal. Disagreement in substantive metaphysical belief about the nature of the world also played a part. But there can be no doubt from the abundant testimony of the two physicists themselves that they had very different views as to what constituted a "good" theory.

The fact that theory-appraisal is a sophisticated form of value-judgment explains one of the most obvious features of science, a feature that could only appear as a mystery in the positivist scheme of things. Controversy, far from being rare and wrong-headed, is a persistent and pervasive presence in science at all levels. Yet if the classical logicist view of science had been right, controversy would be easily resolvable. One would simply employ an algorithm, a "method," to decide which of the contending theories is best confirmed by the evidence available. At any given moment, there would then be a "best" theory, to which scientists properly versed in their craft ought to adhere.

But, of course, not only is this *not* the case, but it would be a disaster if it *were* to be the case (McMullin 1983). The clash of theories, Popper has convinced us, is needed in order that weak spots may be probed and potentialities fully developed. Popper's own theory of science made it difficult to see how such a pluralism of theories could be maintained. But once theory-appraisal is recognized to be a complex form of value-judgment, the persistence of competing theories immediately follows as a consequence.

Thomas Kuhn characteristically sees the importance of value-difference not so much in the clash of theories—such controversy is presumably not typical of his "normal science"—as in the period of incipient revolution when a new paradigm is struggling to be born:

> Before the group accepts it, a new theory has been tested over time by the research of a number of men, some working within it, others within its traditional rival. Such a mode of development, however, *requires* a decision process which permits rational men to disagree, and such disagreement would be barred by the shared algorithm which philosophers generally have sought. If it were at hand, all conforming scientists would make the same decision at the same time. . . . I doubt that science would survive the change. What from one point of view may seem the looseness and imperfection of choice criteria conceived as rules may, when the same criteria be seen as values, appear an indispensable means of spreading the risk which the introduction or support of novelty always entails. (1961, p. 220)

It almost seems as though the value-ladenness of theory-decision is specially designed to ensure the continuance of controversy and to protect endangered but potentially important new theoretical departures. A Hegelian might see in this, perhaps, the cunning of Reason in bringing about a desirable result in a humanly unpremeditated way. But, of course, these are just the fortunate consequences of the nature of theory-decision itself. It is not as though theories could be appraised in a different more rule-guided way. One is forced to recognize that the value-ladenness described above derives from the problematic and epistemologically complex way in which theory relates to the world. It is *only* through theory that the world is scientifically understood. There is no alternative mode of access which would allow the degree of "fit" between theory and world to be independently assessed, and the values appropriate to a good theory to be definitively established. And so there is no way to exchange the frustrating demands of value-judgment for the satisfying simplicities of logical rule.

V. Epistemic Values

Even though we cannot *definitively* establish the values appropriate to the assessment of theory, we saw just a moment ago that we can provide a tentative list of criteria that have gradually been shaped over the experience of many centuries, the values that are implicit in contemporary scientific practice. Such characteristic values I will call *epistemic,* because they are presumed to promote the truth-like character of science, its character as the most secure knowledge available to us of the world we seek to understand. An epistemic value is one we have reason to believe will, if pursued, help toward the attainment of such knowledge. I have concentrated here on the values that one expects a good *theory* to embody. But there are, of course, many other epistemic values, like that of reproducibility in an experiment or accuracy in a measurement.

When I say that science is value-laden, I would not want it to be thought that these values derive from theory-appraisal only. Value-judgment permeates the work of science as a whole, from the decision to allow a particular experimental result to count as "basic" or "accepted" (the decisional element that Popper stressed), to the decision not to seek an alternative to a theory which so far has proved satisfactory. Such values as these may be pragmatic rather than epistemic; they may derive from the finiteness of the time or resources available to the experimenter, for example. And sometimes the borderline between the epistemic and the pragmatic may be hard to draw, since (as Pierre Duhem and Karl Popper among others have made clear) it is essential to the process of science that pragmatic decisions be made, on the temporary suspension of further testing for example.

Of course, it is not pragmatic values that pose the main challenge to the epistemic integrity of the appraisal process. If values are needed in order to close the gap between underdetermined theory and the evidence brought in its support, presumably all sorts of values can slip in: political, moral, social, and religious. The list is as long as the list of possible human goals. I shall lump these values together under the single blanket term, 'non-epistemic'. The decision as to whether a value is epistemic or non-epistemic in a particular context can sometimes be a difficult one. But the grounds on which it should be made are easy to specify in the abstract. When no sufficient case can be made for saying that the imposition of a particular value on the process of theory choice is likely to improve the *epistemic* status of the theory, that is, the conformity between theory and world, this value is held to be non-epistemic in the context in question. This decision is itself, of course, a value-judgment and there is an obvious danger of a vicious regress at this point. I hope it can be headed off, and will return to this task in a moment.

But first, one sort of factor that plays a role in theory-assessment can be hard to situate. Externalist historians of science have been accustomed to grouping under the elastic term 'value' not only social and personal goals but also various elements of world-view, metaphysical, theological, and the like. Thus, for example, when Newton's theology or Bohr's metaphysics affected the choice each made of "best" theory in mechanics, such historians have commonly described this as an influence of "values" upon science (see, for example, Graham 1981).

Since I have been arguing so strongly here for the value-ladenness of science, it might seem that I should welcome this practice. But it is rooted, I think, in a sort of residual positivism that is often quite alien to the deepest convictions of the historians themselves who indulge in it (McMullin 1982). They would be the first to object to the label 'externalist', but here they are assuming that a philosophical world-view is of its nature so "external" to science that it must be flagged as a "value," and consequently dealt with quite differently from the point of view of explanation.

Let me try to clarify the source of my opposition to this practice. A philosophical system can in certain contexts serve as a value, as a touchstone of decision. So for that matter can a scientific theory. But this does not convert it into a "value" in the sense in which social historians sometimes interpret this term, namely as something for which socio-psychological explanation is all-sufficient. The effect of calling metaphysics a "value" can be to shift it from the category of *belief* to be explained in terms of reasons adduced, in the way that science is ordinarily taken, to the category of *goal* to be explained, in terms of character, upbringing, community pressures, and the rest.

What I am arguing for is the potentially *epistemic* status that philosophical or theological world-view can have in science. From the standpoint of today, it would be inadmissible to use theological argumentation in mechanics. Yet Isaac Newton in effect did so on occasion. In describing this, it is important to note that theology functioned for him as an *epistemic* factor, as a set of reasons that *Newton* thought were truth-bearing (McMullin 1978b, p. 55). It did *not* primarily operate as a value if by 'value' one were to mean a socio-psychological causal factor, superimposed upon scientific argument from the outside, to be understood basically as a reflection of underlying social or psychological structures.

Now, of course, the historian may find that someone's use of theological or philosophical considerations *did,* on a given occasion, reflect such structures. But this has to be historically *proven.* The question must not be begged by using the term 'value' as externalist historians have too often done. Incidentally, the pervasive presence of nonstandard epistemic factors in the history of science is the main reason, to my mind, why the one-time popular internal-external dichotomy fails. Sociologists of science in the "strong program" tradition are more consistent in this respect. They *do* take metaphysics and theology to be a reflection of socio-pychological structure, but of course, they regard science itself in the same epistemically unsympathetic light. My point here has simply been that it is objectionable to single out nonstandard forms of argument in science by an epistemically pejorative use of the term 'value' (McMullin 1983).

VI. The Place of Act in a World of Values

That being said, let me return to the question that must by now be uppermost in the reader's mind. What is left of the vaunted objectivity of science, the element of the factual, in all this welter of value-judgment? Once the camel's nose is inside, the tent rapidly becomes uncomfortable. Is there any reasoned way to stop short of a relativism that would see in science no more than the product of a contingent social consensus, bearing testimony to the historical particularity of culture and personality much more than to an objective truth about the world? I think there is, but I can at this stage only provide an outline of the argument needed. It requires two separate steps.

Step one is to examine the epistemic values employed in theory-appraisal, the values that lie at the heart of the claim that theory assessment in science is essentially value-laden, and to ask how they in turn are to be validated, and how in particular, circularity is to be avoided in doing so. First, let me recall how the skills of epistemic value-judgment are *learnt*. Apprentice scientists learn them not from a method book but from watching others exercise them. They learn what to expect in a "good" theory. They note what kinds of considerations carry weight, and why they do so. They get a feel for the relative weight given the different kinds of considerations, and may quickly come to realize that there are divergences here in practice. Their own value-judgments will gradually become more assured, and will be tested against the practice of their colleagues as well as against historical precedent (Polanyi 1958; Kuhn 1962).[6]

What is the epistemic worth of the consensus from which these skills derive? Kuhn is worried about the validity of invoking history as warrant in this case:

> Though the experience of scientists provides no philosophical justification for the values they deploy (such justification would solve the problem of induction), those values are in part learned from that experience and they evolve with it. (1977, p. 335)

This is to take the Hume-Popper challenge to induction far too seriously (unless, of course, 'justification' were to be taken to mean definitive proof). The characteristic values guiding theory-choice are firmly rooted in the complex learning experience which is the history of science; this is their primary justification, and it is an adequate one.

We have gradually learnt from this experience that human beings have the ability to create those constructs we call "theories" which can provide a high degree of accuracy in predicting what will happen, as well as accounting for what has happened, in the world around us. It has been discovered, further, that these theories can embody other values too, such values as coherence and fertility, and that an insistence on these other values is likely to enhance the chances over the long run of the attainment of the first goal, that of empirical accuracy.

It was not always clear that these basic values *could* be pursued simultaneously.[7] In medieval astronomy, it seemd as though one had to choose between predictive accuracy and explanatory coherence, the Ptolemaic epicycles exemplifying one and Aristotelian cosmology the other. Since the two systems were clearly incompatible, philosophers like Aquinas reluctantly concluded that there were two sorts of astronomical science, one (the "mathematical") which simply "saved the appearances," and the other (the "physical") whose goal it was to explain the *truth* of things (Duhem, 1908/1969, chapter 3). Galileo's greatest accomplishment, perhaps, was to demonstrate the possibility of a single science in which the values of both the physical and the mathematico-predictive traditions could be simultaneously realized (Machamer 1978).

There was nothing *necessary* about this historical outcome. The world might well have turned out to be one in which our mental constructions would *not* have been able to combine these two ideals. What became clear in the course of the seventeenth century was that they *can* be very successfully combined, and that other plausible values can be worked in as well. When I say "plausible" here, I am suggesting that there is a second convergent mode of validation for these values of theory-appraisal (for "valuings" in the sense defined in section 1).

We can endeavor to *account for* their desirability in terms of a higher-order epistemological account of scientific knowing. This is to carry retroduction to the next level upwards. It is asking the philosopher to provide a theory in terms of which such values as fertility would be shown to be appropriate demands to lay on scientific theory. The philosopher's ability to provide just such a theory (and it is not difficult to do this) in turn then testifies to the reliability to taking these criteria to be proper values for theory-appraisal in the first place. This is only the outline of an argument, and much more remains to be filled in. But perhaps I have said enough to indicate how one could go about showing that the characteristic values scientists have come to expect a theory to embody are a testimony to the *objectivity* of the theory, as well as of the involvement of the subjectivity of the scientist in the effort to attain that objectivity.

There is a further argument I would use in support of this conclusion, but it is based on a premise that is not shared by all. That is the thesis of scientific realism. I think that there are good reasons to accept a cautious and carefully-restricted form of scientific realism, prior to posing the further question of the objective basis of the values we use in theory-appraisal (McMullin 1983). The version of realism I have in mind would suggest that in many parts of science, like geology and cell-biology, we have good reasons to believe that the models postulated by our current theories gives us a reliable, though still incomplete, insight into the structures of the physical world.

Thus, for example, we would suppose that the success of certain sorts of theoretical model would give us strong reason to believe that the core of the earth *is* composed of iron, or that stars *are* glowing masses of gas. We have no direct testimony regarding either of these beliefs, of course. To claim that the world *does* resemble our theoretical models in these cases, is to claim that the method of retroduction of which they are based, and which rests finally on the values of theory-appraisal I have already discussed, is in fact (at least in certain sorts of cases) reliable in what it claims.[8] Obviously, the realist thesis will not hold, or will hold only in attenuated form, where theory is still extremely underdetermined (as in current elementary-particle theory) or where the ontological implications of the theory are themselves by no means clear (as in classical mechanics).

And so, to conclude step one, there is reason to trust in the values used commonly in current science for theory-appraisal as something much more than the contingent consensus of a peculiar social sub-group.

But a further step is needed, because these values do not of themselves *determine* theory-choice, a point I have stressed from the beginning. And so other values *can* and *do* enter in, the sorts of value that sociologists of science have so successfully been drawing to our attention of late, as they scrutinize particular episodes in the history of science. I am thinking of such values as the personal ambition of the scientist, the welfare of the social class to which he or she belongs, and so on. Has the camel not, then, poked its wet nose in beside us once again?

It has, of course, but perhaps we can find a way to push it out—or almost out—one final time. The process of science is one long series of test and tentative imaginative extensions. When a particular theory seems to have triumphed, when Louis Pasteur has overcome Felix Pouchet, to cite one nineteenth-century illustration that has recently come in for a lot of attention from social historians of science (Farley and Geison 1976), it is not as though the view that has pevailed is allowed to reign in peace. Other scientists attempt to duplicate experimental claims; theoreticians try to extend the theories involved in new and untried ways; various tests are devised for the more vulnerable theoretical moves involved, and so on. This is not just part of the mythology of science. It really *does* happen, and is easy to document.

To the extent that non-epistemic values and other non-epistemic factors have been instrumental in the original theory-decision (and sociologists of science have rendered a great service by revealing how much more pervasive these factors are than one might have expected), they are gradually sifted by the continued application of the sort of value-judgment we have been describing here. The non-epistemic, by very definition, will not in the long run survive this process. The process is designed to limit the effects not only of fraud and carelessness, but also of ideology, understood in its perjorative sense as distortive intrusion into the slow process of shaping our thought to the world.

NOTES

1. The terminology of "evaluation" and "valuing" is used by Kovesi (1967) in a somewhat different way. He supposes value-judgment to apply to things via their discriptions. Thus,

we "evaluate" particulars insofar as they "fall under a certain description" (p. 151). Whereas we "value" things "insofar as they are such and such." We would "evaluate" a particular lawyer *as* a lawyer (being given a description of the qualities that make up a lawyer), whereas we would "value" lawyers for what they are, as indispensable to the conduct of complex communities or however we might wish to describe their "value" in some broader context. (His aim is to contrast "evaluation" with moral judgement.) My focus is on specific characteristic values, on the Y-ness of X's, where his is on entity-descriptions, on X-ness itself as a subject for evaluation or valuing. The advantage of the former is that it makes the basis of the value-judgment specific. It focuses evaluation on the characteristic which can be present to a greater or lesser degree. And it provides a *context* for valuing which Kovesi's notion appears to lack, thus risking confusion with emotive value. Finally, Kovesi's emphasis on description could mislead, since the characteristic value need not be *described,* strictly speaking. Indeed, as we shall see below, the frequent inability to give explicit descriptions of characteristic values is an essential feature of evaluation as it occurs in science. The emphasis on X-ness (which does need describing) rather than on the Y-ness of X's (where the Y may be only summarily indicated) is the root of the difference. I am indebted to Carl Hempel and David Solomon for discussions of the topics of this section.

2. Nagel used the terms 'characterize' and 'appraise' instead of our 'evaluate' and 'value'. The example he gives of "characterizing" is the evaluation of the degree of anemia a particular animal suffers from against a standard of "normality" in the red blood-corpuscle count. (See "The Value-Oriented Bias of Social Inquiry," Nagel 1961, pp. 485-502.)

3. Some philosophers assimilate epistemic values to moral values, so that for them the values implicit in theory-appraisal are broadly moral ones. Putnam, for example, takes adherence to these values on the part of scientists to be "part of our idea of human cognitive flourishing, and in hence part of our idea of total human flourishing, of Eudaimonia" (1981, p. 134). The analysis of characteristic value given in section 1, and even more the discussion of the warrant for epistemic value in section 6 below, would lead me to question this assimilation of the epistemic to the moral under the very vague notion of "flourishing." To pursue this further would, however, require further analysis of the nature of moral knowledge.

4. A point already made by Richard Jeffrey (1956) in a response to the Rudner article.

5. In fairness, it should be added that Rudner drew attention in the same paper to the value-implications of the new directions that Carnap and Quine were just beginning to chart. But these consequences were obscured by his emphasis on the ethical aspects of theory-acceptance. He evidently supposed that all of these considerations would converge, but in fact, they did not, and could not.

6. Polanyi and Kuhn relate such skills as that of theory-assessment (and pattern-recognition, which is ultimately theory-dependent) in rather different ways to the learning experience of the apprentice scientist. I would lean more to Kuhn's analysis in this case, but in the context of my argument here, it is sufficient to note the affinity between these two authors rather than to press their differences.

7. Kunn attaches a higher degree of fixity to the epistemic values of theory-choice then I would. He takes the five he describes to be "permanent attributes of science," provided the specification be left vague (1977, p. 335).

8. This is where I would diverge from Putnam (1981), who otherwise defends a view of the role of value-judgment in science similar to the one outlined here. In the spirit of Kant, he wants to find a middle way between objectivism and subjectivism, between what he regards as the extremes of "metaphysical realism" and "cultural relativism." The former he defines as being based on "the notion of a transcendental match between our representation and the world" which he briskly characterizes as "nonsense" (1981, p. 134). Blocked from taking the epistemic values to be the means of gradually achieving such a correspondence, he is thus forced to make them in some sense ultimates. "Truth is not the bottom line; truth itself gets its life from our criteria of rational acceptability" (p. 130). What he wants to stress, he says, is "the dependence of the empirical world on our criteria of rational acceptability"

370 Values in Science

(p. 134). Instead of merely holding that "our knowledge of the world presupposes values" (the thesis that I am arguing for in this essay), he is led then to "the more radical claim that what *counts* as the real world depends upon our values" (p. 137).

But such a position leaves him (in my view) with no vantage-point from which it would be possible to correct, or gradually adjust, the epistemic values themselves. They constitute for him "part of our conception of human flourishing" (p. xi). But there can be many such comceptions; against Aristotle (whom he takes to defend a single ideal of human flourishing), he argues for a "diversity" of ways in which such flourishing might properly he construed (p. 148). But how then can he *also* reject some such ways as "wrong, as infantile, as sick. as one sided" (p. 198)? What grounds are available in his system for such a rejection? He says that "we revise our very criteria of rational acceptability "in the light of our theoretical picture of the empirical world" (p. 134), but gives no hint as how this is to be done in practice. He cities "coherence" as a sort of super-criterion which appears to be necessary to *any* ideal of human flourishing (p. 132). But what if someone were to *reject* such a criterion? Putnam says such a person is "sick." But are there *arguments* he could use to warrant this diagnosis?

I do not think that in the end this "middle way" works. The tilt to idealism is obvious. But it would take a more elaborate analysis to show this. (This footnote and footnote 3 were added in proof. Had I seen Putnam's book before I wrote this text, I would have attempted a fuller discussion of it.)

REFERENCES

Agassi, Joseph. (1974). "Modified Conventionalism Is More Comprehensive than Modified Essentialism." In Schilpp (1974), pp. 693–696.

Carnap, Rudolf. (1932). "Überwindung der Metaphysik durch logische Analyse der Sprache." *Erkenntnis* 2:219–241. (Reprinted as "The Elimination of Metaphysics Through Logical Analysis of Language." (trans.) Arthur Pap. In *Logical Positivism*. Edited by A. J. Ayer. Glencoe, Ill.: Free Press, 1959, pp. 60–81.)

———. (1950). "Empiricism, Semantics and Ontology." *Revue internationale de philosophie* 4: 20–40. (As reprinted in *Meaning and Necessity*. 2nd ed. Chicago: University of Chicago Press, 1956, pp. 205–221.)

Duhem, Pierre. (1908). Εψ́ζειν τά φαι νόμεvα: *Essai sur la notion de théorie physique de Platon a Galilée*. Paris: A. Hermann. (Reprinted as *To Save the Phenomena: An Essay on the Idea of Physical Theory from Plato to Galileo*. (trans.) E. Doland and C. Maschler. Chicago: University of Chicago Press, 1969.)

Farley, John and Geison, Gerald. (1976). "Science, Politics, and Spontaneous Generation in 19th Century France: The Pasteur-Pouchet Debate." *Bulletin of the History of Medicine* 48: 161–198.

Graham, Loren. (1981). *Between Science and Values*. New York: Columbia.

Hempel, Carl G. (1966). *Philosophy of Natural Science*. Englewood Cliffs, N.J.: Prentice-Hall.

Jeffrey, Richard. (1956). "Valuation and Acceptance of Scientific Hypotheses." *Philosophy of Science* 23: 237–246.

Kovesi, Julius (1967). *Moral Notions*. London: Routledge and Kegan Paul.

Kuhn, Thomas. (1961). "The Function of Measurement in Modern Physical Science." *Isis* 52: 161–190. (As reprinted in Kuhn, Thomas. *The Essential Tension*. Chicago: University of Chicago Press, 1977, pp. 178–224.)

———. (1962). *The Structure of Scientific Revolutions*. Chicago: University of Chicago Press.

————. (1977). "Objectivity, Value Judgment, and Theory Choice." In *The Essential Tension*. Chicago: University of Chicago Press, pp. 320–339.

Lakatos, Imre. (1970). "Falsification and the Methodology of Scientific Research Programmes." In *Criticism and the Growth of Knowledge*. Edited by I. Lakatos and A. Musgrave. Cambridge: Cambridge University Press, pp. 91–195.

Laudan, Larry. (1981). "William Whewell on the Consilience of Inductions." In *Science and Hypothesis. (University of Western Ontario Series in Philosophy of Science,* Volume 19.) Dordrecht: Reidel, pp. 163–180.

Machamer, Peter. (1978). "Galileo and the Causes." In *New Perspectives on Galileo. (University of Western Ontario Series in Philosophy of Science,* Volume 14.) Edited by R. Butts and J. Pitt. Dordrecht: Reidel, pp. 161–180.

McMullin, Ernan. (1976). "The Fertility of Theory and the Unit for Appraisal in Science." In *Essays in Honor of Imre Lakatos. (Boston Studies in the Philosophy of Science,* Volume 39.) Edited by P. Feyerabend et al. Dordrecht: Reidel, pp. 395–432.

————. (1978a). "Philosophy of Science and its Rational Reconstructions." In *Progress and Rationality in Science. (Boston Studies in the Philosophy of Science,* Volume 58.) Edited by G. Radnitzky and G. Andersson. Dordrecht: Reidel, pp. 221–252.

————. (1978b). *Newton on Matter and Activity.* Notre Dame, Ind.: University of Notre Dame Press.

————. (1982). "The Role of 'Values' in Understanding Science." *Hastings Center Report* 12((6): 38–40.

————. (1983). "Scientific Controversy and its Termination." In *Scientific Controversies.* Edited by A. Kaplan and H. T. Engelhardt. Cambridge University Press.

————. (1985). "The Case for Scientific Realism." In *Scientific Realism.* Edited by J. Leplin. Los Angeles: University of California Press.

Nagel, Ernest. (1961). *The Structure of Science.* New York: Harcourt, Brace.

Polyani, Michael. (1958). *Personal Knowledge.* London: Routledge and Kegan Paul.

Popper, Karl. (1934). *Logik der Forschung.* Vienna: Springer. (Reprinted as *The Logic of Scientific Discovery.* London: Hutchinson, 1959.)

————. (1974). "Replies to My Criticism." In Schilpp (1974), pp. 961–1197.

Putnam, Hilary. (1981). *Reason, Truth and History.* Cambridge: Cambridge University Press.

Rudner, Richard. (1953). "The Scientist *qua* Scientist Makes Value-judgments." *Philosophy of Science* 20: 1–6.

Schilpp, Paul A. (ed.). (1974). *The Philosophy of Karl Popper. (The Library of Living Philosophers,* Volume 14, Book II.) LaSalle, Ill.: Open Court.

Stevenson, Charles. (1949). "The Nature of Ethical Disagreement." In *Readings in Philosophical Analysis.* Edited by H. Feigl and W. Sellars. New York: Appleton-Century-Crofts, pp. 587–593.

Weber, Max. (1917). "Der Sinn der 'Wertfreiheit' der soziologischen und ökonomischen Wissenschraften." *Logos* 7: 40–88. (Reprinted as "The Meaning of 'Ethical Neutrality' in Sociology and Economics." In *The Methodology of the Social Sciences.* (trans.) E. A. Shils and H. A. Finch. Glencoe, Ill: The Free Press, 1949, pp. 1–47.)

STUDY QUESTIONS FOR PART 5

1. Why must scientists make value judgments in order for science to be possible, according to Rudner?

2. What objections to his thesis does Rudner consider? How does he respond to them?

3. How does the debate between Carnap and Quine relate to Rudner's thesis?

4. Do Rudner and Kuhn share any similar views about the relations between science and values?

5. Why does Hempel think that "categorical" value judgments cannot be part of, or supported by, science?

6. How can science legitimately contribute to disputes about values, according to Hempel?

7. Does Hempel's paper contain any criticisms of Rudner's thesis? If so, how convincing are they?

8. In what ways does McMullin agree with Rudner, and in what ways does he disagree?

9. Does McMullin share Hempel's views about the relations between science and values? If not, how does he disagree?

10. To what extent does McMullin support the views of Popper and Kuhn?

11. Compare McMullin, Kuhn, Feyerabend, Rudner and Hempel on "epistemic values" and theory choice.

12. Why does McMullin call the last section of his paper "The place of fact in a world of value"?

13. In his play "The Doctor's Dilemma," G. B. Shaw said "No man is allowed to put his mother in the stove because he desires to know how long an adult woman will survive the temperature of 500 degrees, no matter how important or interesting that particular addition to the store of human knowledge may be." What does this remark have to do with the issues of Part 5 of this volume?

SELECTED BIBLIOGRAPHY

[1] Baumrin, B. and Freedman B., ed. *Moral Responsibility and the Professions.* New York: Haven, 1983. [Section III: "Ethics and The Sciences" contains good essays.]

[2] Bronowski, J. *Science and Human Values.* New York: Harper, 1965. [Discusses interrelations between knowledge and values.]

[3] Caws, P. *Science and the Theory of Value.* New York: Random House, 1967. [A "naturalistic" account of science and values, in the tradition of American Pragmatism.]

[4] Diesing, P. *Reason in Society.* Urbana: University of Illinois Press, 1962. (Cost-benefit models in economics, sociology, political science, law and management science.)

[5] Edel, A. *Ethical Judgement.* New York: Free Press, 1955. [Relations between various sciences on the issue of moral relativism.]

[6] Engelhardt, H. T. and Callahan, D., ed. *Morals, Science and Society.* New York: Hastings Center, 1978. [A recent collection of essays.]

[7] ———. *Science, Ethics and Medicine.* New York: The Hastings Center, 1976. [Essays deal with issues relevant to the topics of Part 5.]

[8] Gewirth, A. " 'Positive' Ethics and 'Normative' Science. Rerinted in Thompson, J. and Dworkin G. ed. *Ethics.* New York: Harper, 1968, 27-47. [A critique of the positivist's view of science and morality.]

[9] Haan, N.; Bellah, R.; et al., ed. *Social Science and Moral Inquiry.* New York: Columbia University Press, 1983. [Advanced discussions on relations between morality and human sciences.]

[10] Harding, S. *The Science Question in Feminism.* Ithaca, N.Y.: Cornell University Press, 1986. [Discusses issues about sex biases in scientific research and methods.]

[11] Milgram, S. *Obedience to Authority.* New York: Harper, 1974. [A famous experiment illustrating the conflict between science and morality.]

[12] Polanyi, M. *Personal Knowledge.* New York: Harper, 1958. [Science as a moral enterprise; truth as a moral ideal.]

[13] Rapp, F. *Analytical Philosophy of Technology.* Boston: Reidel, 1981. [Useful survey of competing analyses of Science and Technology.]

[14] Ravetz, J. *Scientific Knowledge and Its Social Problems.* New York: Oxford, 1971. [Interesting approach to the relations between science, values and society in terms of the idea of crafts.]

[15] Riley G. ed. *Values, Objectivity and the Social Sciences.* Reading, Mass: Addison Wesley, 1974. [Classic and recent essays.]

[16] Singer, P. *The Expanding Circle: Ethics and Sociobiology.* New York: Farrar, Strauss, Giroux 1981. [Discusses the biological approach to values.]

[17] Skinner, B. F. *Beyond Freedom and Dignity.* New York: Knopf, 1971. [A program for the redesign of culture through behavioral engineering.]

Part 6

Science and Culture

Part 6: Science and Culture

Introduction

I. Science, Purpose and Morality

Since the general topic of science and culture takes in far too many issues to be even mentioned in an introduction, it will be necessary to limit this discussion to one or two central issues, so as to make the readings intelligible. The most obvious place to begin is with some of the issues that were mentioned, but not discussed, in the introduction to Part 5.

The first issue concerns the notion of purpose or order in the universe. As was mentioned earlier, for the Greeks it is impossible to eliminate any reference to purpose, ordering, patterning, beauty or the good in trying to understand the cosmos and our place in it, since what is natural is good. To be sure, these are not ("subjective") *human* purposes or goods, although knowing the universe is needed to know what is good for humans, and what is a human purpose or "function." But the point remains: The mechanical picture of objectivism begins by eliminating purpose from science, because the world is seen as devoid of it. Later developments, e.g., in the social sciences, try to eliminate or "reduce" human purposes and values, or else treat these as merely subjective labels which we tack on to an objective world. Hence, critics of science and its effect on our culture (see Roszak) take modern science to portray the world, and human life, as devoid of purpose or meaning. Such views often appeal to the platonic vision as an alternative to this picture, which, they claim, gives rise to the idea that life is meaningless, and reflects the extent to which modern life is dehumanizing, alienating, and immoral or amoral.

The second issue concerns the relationship between science and morality, especially the relationship between the uses (and abuses) of science and our moral beliefs and principles. As we have said, some authors hold the view that knowledge, truth, and inquiry—and thus science itself—either express or are motivated by moral ideals, such as honesty, fairness, and truthfulness. This dimension of science is addressed by Rescher in Part 5, and will not be pursued further. It is to the moral issues concerning the uses of science and technology that we shall now turn.

A convenient point of departure into this important and complex topic is furnished by our earlier discussion of the "objectivist" accounts of value. This account, which is basically nihilistic, takes two forms: (A) Value judgments express arbitrary personal acts of the will or commitments, which are irrational and subjective, or social commitments with the same status; or (B) Value judgments are a species of scientific statement which explain or describe personal and social behavior (e.g., in terms of some variant of deterministic laws in history, psychology, sociology, economics, and so forth). The only real (nonexplanatory) function of "objective," "rational" value judgments is to predict or calculate the best means of achieving a given end or purpose. Such ends are, on either (A) or (B), to be taken as given, and certainly as beyond rational dispute. In either case, morality leads to a kind of relativism, or else to the idea that (at least) *ultimate* values cannot be challenged or even discussed in any rational manner.

Nihilism about values thus dovetails with the idea that the universe, and thus life itself, is meaningless or devoid of purpose. At least this is the way these two ideas are connected for critics of modern "scientism" and "objectivism." ("Scientism," which is being used here as a rough equivalent to "objectivism," is often defined as the view that science and its methods provide universal standards for rationality and objectivity, as well as universally valid beliefs about the world.) The "bottom line," so to speak, of this outlook, is that "'tis not contrary to reason to prefer the destruction of the world to the scratching of my little finger," which is the eighteenth-century philosopher David Hume's claim about the relation between the ultimate "facts" about human nature and the role of reason in morality.

What does this claim really mean? One thing it seems to lead to is the idea that if our ultimate values and purposes cannot be rationally discussed or evaluated, but must be taken as either conceptual axioms or conventions or as biological, psychological, historical, or personal "ultimates," "reason" only plays an "instrumental role" in life. This amounts to the idea that value judgments only tell us *how* to maximize our goals; they cannot help us to decide which goals to pursue—and which goals not to pursue. As a result, the criteria of morality and those of efficiency or expediency become merged. Coupled with the scientific attempt to reduce or eliminate human purposes to some kind of "objective" variables—e.g., economic or psychological—we are faced with a picture of values and purposes in which the ultimate values and purposes of a person or a group must be accepted as brute facts or ultimate postulates. Thus, many scientists and philosophers interpret the ultimates as facts about human psychology (all human actions are motivated by the desire for pleasure or the avoidance of pain), or else as facts about the value of a culture's survival. Given these assumptions, value judgments become the search for "objective" evidence about what will produce a maximum of pleasure (or a net balance of pleasure over pain) for a given individual or a society. Or ethics becomes the search for principles which tell us how to predict what the rational means are for promoting the survival of a culture. In short, "practical success" or efficiency, measured by standards that purport to be scientifically justified, becomes the hallmark of the adequacy and, indeed, the very meaning of values. Utilitarianism, cost-benefit models of decision-making, and so on, operate upon the assumptions embedded in this view. The only alternative to it (i.e., to (B) above) is supposed to be (A): the idea that value judgments are totally irrational acts of subjective preference, which can no more be rationally assessed than can one's preferences for chocolate ice cream or red convertibles.

II. The Cultural Impact of "Scientism" and "Objectivism"

Two vivid expressions of the connections between these issues about values and the larger themes raised by the label "science and culture" find expression in the writings of Orwell (*1984*) and the psychoanalyst Erich Fromm. Fromm says this:

> [Technological civilization] is programmed by two principles that direct the efforts and thoughts of everyone working in it: The first principle is the maxim that something *ought* to be done because it is technically possible to do it. If it is possible to build nuclear weapons they must be built even if they might destroy us all. . . . This principle means the negation of all values which the humanist tradition has developed. This tradition says that something should be done because it is needed for man, for his growth, joy, reason, because it is beautiful, good, true. Once the principle is accepted that something ought to be done because it is technically possible to do it, all other values are dethroned, and technological development becomes the foundation of ethics.

The second principle is that of maximal efficiency and output. (See [9], p. 15.) According to this view, the understanding of values and the cost-benefit model of rational decision-making are but manifestations of a turning away from the humanist tradition — roughly speaking, the tradition embodied in the Platonic ideals outlined in the introduction to Part 5, and carried through into the religious, philosophical, and common-sense tradition of Western culture. The scientific world picture, as outlined in the introduction to Part 5, leads to a situation in which the only "objective" variables are those which can be treated scientifically, which means only those variables which can be controlled and manipulated. Coupled with the understanding of value judgments that is attendant upon this idea of objectivity, Western culture comes to be dominated by the "technological imperative" (of Fromm's first maxim).

According to critics, science was originally rooted in certain practical, moral, and purposive contexts. Seen in its larger context, scientific knowledge was valued instrumentally, as a means for realizing the practical and moral ideals of civilization. Later, in "modern" (Western) history, science lost its roots in such concerns and began to develop values and techniques which proceeded in a cultural vacuum. Once this was done, this account continues, the progress of science came to be measured by standards that actually undermined the social utility of knowledge, because science and its values came to be seen as ends in themselves, rather than as means to human goals such as happiness and well-being.

To be more specific, two assumptions influenced this change: the assumption that knowledge is power (pragmatism) and the assumption that reality can be defined in terms of what can be measured and controlled by human beings (this assumption is shared by objectivism *and* its critics). When science was still a practical instrument for social and moral progress, these two assumptions could be used as standards for the use of knowledge. The more we learned, the more power we had to bring about the ends which science was designed to fulfill. However, suppose we imagine that science becomes isolated from the social and moral concerns which were to guide its developments. Then these two assumptions are no longer merely instrumentally valuable as means to ends; but they become ends in themselves, i.e., knowledge, power, and the ability to control nature become ends in themselves. Once the social and policy sciences develop, the extension of these values amounts to the idea that it is intrinsically valuable to be able to control human behavior. Coupled with the assumption that all there is to things is what can be measured and controlled, the uses of the social sciences and technology come to be guided by the maxims Fromm discusses. The result is that science and technology come to control our lives, instead of functioning as means to human ends. This is alienation in a nutshell.

For instance, on the assumption that scientific knowledge should be seen in a larger social framework, the ability to build more sophisticated weapons would have to be justified in terms of whether such activities further what Fromm calls "humanistic values." But on the assumption that the ability to produce technological improvements is an end in itself, i.e., worthwhile for its own sake, the very ability to build such weapons becomes a justification for doing so. Taken together with certain other assumptions, e.g., that science and technology are either morally neutral or a substitute for morality, or that values and ends cannot be rationally evaluated, or that the expedient and the right are the same, we come full circle to Fromm's initial remarks.

Another avenue to the same point is furnished by the following remarks of Orwell, which relate to the way in which science and technology have become ideologies for a totalitarian society in *1984*. According to Orwell:

Science and technology were developing at a prodigious speed, and it seemed natural to assume that they would go on developing. This failed to happen . . . partly because scientific and technological progress depended on the empirical habit of thought, which could not survive in a strictly regimented society. . . . The search for new weapons continues unceasingly, and is one of the very few remaining activities in which the inventive or speculative type of mind can find any outlet. In Oceania at the present day, Science, in the old sense, has almost ceased to exist. In Newspeak there is no word for "science." The empirical method of thought, on which all the scientific achievements of the past were founded, is opposed to the most fundamental principles of Ingsoc. And even technological progress only happens when its products can in some way be used for the diminution of human liberty . . . in matters of vital importance— meaning, in effect, war and police espionage—the empirical approach is still encouraged, or at least tolerated. The two aims of the party are to conquer the whole surface of the earth and to extinguish once and for all the possibility of independent thought. There are, therefore, two great problems which the party is concerned to solve. One is how to discover, against his will, what another human being is thinking, and the other is how to kill several hundred million people in a few seconds without giving warning beforehand. In so far as scientific research still continues, this is its subject matter. The scientist of today is either a mixture of psychologist and inquisitor, studying with extraordinary minuteness the meaning of facial expressions, etc. and testing the truth-producing effects of drugs, shock therapy, hypnosis and physical torture; or he is a chemist, physicist or biologist concerned only with such branches of his special subject which are relevant to the taking of life. . . .

Here, in quite a striking passage, is the logical outcome of Fromm's maxims. What has gone wrong? To belabor the obvious, let me mention some of the factors that perverted science and technology. For seeing that they have been perverted will, we think, sustain the view that there is nothing instrinsically or inevitably dehumanizing, manipulative, or alienating in them.

1. The empirical habit of thought is stifled; i.e., free scientific inquiry, diversity of opinions, lack of authoritarianism, and the need for independent evidence are lost. Science is an ideological tool which must serve as a means to preordained goals.

2. The loss of free thinking—which is considered both useless and dangerous—turns science into a purely practical concern. But there are no standards to tell whether "what works" is good or bad. Rather, the standards for utility are the survival of the society and the perpetuation of its goal, no matter how morally objectionable.

3. Scientific research is not, although it might be claimed to be, morally neutral; and the search for truth, together with democratic procedures for

finding it, are absent in science and the rest of society. (This is a classic illustration of how the open society and free scientific inquiry stand or fall together.)

4. What is real is a function of what is manipulable; indeed, one of the doctrines in *1984* is that reality is what is in the mind of the party; i.e., subjective idealism, coupled with the lack of any independent evidence, or independent thought, conspire to keep people in ignorance, and thus in slavery. (Idealism is actually the product of objectivism's view that reality is defined by what can be manipulated and controlled.)

5. Morality and truth are defined in terms of what some authoritarian fiat defines as "moral" or "true." That is, an extreme form of relativism, coupled with an equally radical variant of idealism, lead to the absence of both knowledge and morality. Whatever is expedient for the stated aims of the party become true and moral.

6. Science and technology are no longer paths to utopia, nor even important in the practical affairs of life for everyone, but are the property of dictators and their lackeys.

To summarize: Science and technology, according to these interpretations, have come to be dominated by ideals of rationality, values, and objectivity that are rooted in the conceptions of knowledge as power and of reality as a system of manipulable variables. When dislodged from the humanist tradition, or when attached to a social and political system guided by an ideology of domination, the technological maxim takes on a life of its own; i.e., it becomes a self-sustaining and self-certifying criterion of rational choice and action—an intrinsic value is placed upon control, technique, and efficiency, or at any rate technological or instrumental rationality comes to dominate all thinking, in which case we effectively get the same result.

Other factors operating in our culture play a role in these developments: e.g., (a) the loss of "purpose" or "meaning," (b) the nihilistic account of morality embedded in both the objectivist and subjectivist variants on nihilism (i.e., (A) and (B) above), (c) the social division of labor and responsibility [(c) often leads to the use of evasions to avoid responsibility and ignore the misuses of science and technology and the emphasis on expediency and efficiency that are so pervasive in our society]. The prevalence of these factors provide additional support for Fromm's remark that the "technological maxim" underlies our conscious and unconscious behavior to an extent we often are unwilling or unable to recognize.

III. The Readings in Part 6

Baier discusses the question whether there is any sense to the view that life and the cosmos have any meaning, once we abandon the religious view of the universe. He argues that we must give up the idea that life has any "objective" meaning or purpose. However, we can give our lives meaning, i.e., find meaning in life, in terms of our individual and collective projects and values (which are not, for Baier, as subjective as they are for Weber). Moreover, contrary to religious objections to science, the only explanations we require in order to understand our universe are those provided by the scientific outlook and its achievements.

Hollinger argues that the views of Weber bring together two apparently conflicting strands in Western thought about science, knowledge and values. But these views are really identical in crucial respects, as is seen by discussing the impact of a number of discussions that occur after Weber. In a final section, Habermas' criticisms of the traditions that culminate in Weber's views are summarized, and his own attempt to reconstruct the ideas of knowledge, values, objectivity, and rationality are outlined.

In his paper, Feigl considers, and tries to reject, a number of standard objections to the use of science to deal with social problems, and to the view that science is in conflict with humanistic values. He argues that science, and its applications to social problems, enhances rather than undermines the values of humanism.

R.H.

26

The Meaning of Life

Kurt Baier

Tolstoy, in his autobiographical work, "A Confession," reports how, when he was fifty and at the height of his literary success, he came to be obsessed by the fear that life was meaningless.

"At first I experienced moments of perplexity and arrest of life, as though I did not know what to do or how to live; and I felt lost and became dejected. But this passed, and I went on living as before. Then these moments of perplexity began to recur oftener and oftener, and always in the same form. They were always expressed by the questions: What is it for? What does it lead to? At first it seemed to me that these were aimless and irrelevant questions. I thought that it was all well known, and that if I should ever wish to deal with the solution it would not cost me much effort; just at present I had no time for it, but when I wanted to, I should be able to find the answer. The questions however began to repeat themselves frequently, and to demand replies more and more insistently, and like drops of ink always falling on one place they ran together into one black blot."[1]

A Christian living in the Middle Ages would not have felt any serious doubts about Tolstoy's questions. To him it would have seemed quite certain that life had a meaning and quite clear what it was. The medieval Christian world picture assigned to man a highly significant, indeed the central part in the grand scheme of things. The universe was made for the express purpose of providing a stage on which to enact a drama starring Man in the title role.

To be exact, the world was created by God in the year 4004 B.C. Man was the last and the crown of this creation, made in the likeness of God, placed in the Garden of Eden on earth, the fixed centre of the universe, round which revolved the nine heavens of the sun, the moon, the planets and the fixed stars, producing as they revolved in their orbits the heavenly harmony of the spheres.

And this gigantic universe was created for the enjoyment of man, who was originally put in control of it. Pain and death were unknown in paradise. But this state of bliss was not to last. Adam and Eve ate of the forbidden tree of knowledge, and life on this earth turned into a death-march through a vale of tears. Then, with the birth of Jesus, new hope came into the world. After He had died on the cross, it became at least possible to wash away with the purifying water of baptism some of the effects of Original Sin and to achieve salvation. That is to say, on condition of obedience to the law of God, man could now enter heaven and regain the state of everlasting, deathless bliss, from which he had been excluded because of the sin of Adam and Eve.

To the medieval Christian the meaning of human life was therefore perfectly clear. The stretch on earth is only a short interlude, a temporary incarceration of the soul in the prison of the body, a brief trial and test, fated to end in death, the release from pain and suffering. What really matters, is the life after the death of the body. One's existence acquires meaning not by gaining what this life can offer but by saving one's immortal soul from death and eternal torture, by gaining eternal life and everlasting bliss.

The scientific world picture which has found ever more general acceptance from the beginning of the modern era onwards is in profound conflict with all this. At first, the Christian conception of the world was discovered to be erroneous in various important details. The Copernican theory showed up the earth as merely one of several planets revolving round the sun, and the sun itself was later seen to be merely one of many fixed stars each of which is itself the nucleus of a solar system similar to our own. Man, instead of occupying the centre of creation, proved to be merely the inhabitant of a celestial body no different from millions of others. Furthermore, geological investigations revealed that the universe was not created a few thousand years ago, but was probably millions of years old.

Disagreements over details of the world picture, however, are only superficial aspects of a much deeper conflict. The appropriateness of the whole Christian outlook is at issue. For Christianity, the world must be regarded as the "creation" of a kind of Superman, a person possessing all the human excellences to an infinite degree and none of the human weaknesses, Who has made man in His image, a feeble, mortal, foolish copy of Himself. In creating the universe, God acts as a sort of playwright-cum-legislator-cum-judge-cum-executioner. In the capacity of playwright, He creates the historical world process, including man. He erects the stage and writes, in outline, the plot. He creates the *dramatis personae* and watches over them with the eye partly of a father, partly of the law. While on stage, the actors are free to extemporise, but if they infringe the divine commandments, they are later dealt with by their creator in His capacity of judge and executioner.

Within such a framework, the Christian attitudes towards the world are natural and sound: it is natural and sound to think that all is arranged for the best even if appearances belie it; to resign oneself cheerfully to one's lot; to be filled with awe and veneration in regard to anything and everything that happens; to want to fall on one's knees and worship and praise the Lord. These are wholly fitting attitudes within the framework of the world view just outlined. And this world view must have seemed wholly sound and acceptable because it offered the best explanation which was then available of all the observed phenomena of nature.

As the natural sciences developed, however, more and more things in the universe came to be explained without the assumption of a supernatural creator. Science, moreover, could explain them better, that is, more accurately and more reliably. The Christian hypothesis of a supernatural maker, whatever other needs it was capable of satisfying, was at any rate no longer indispensable for the purpose of explaining the existence or occurrence of anything. In fact, scientific explanations do not seem to leave any room for this hypothesis. The scientific approach demands that we look for a natural explanation of anything and everything. The scientific way of looking at and explaining things has yielded an immensely greater measure of understanding of, and control over, the universe than any other way. And when one looks at the world in this scientific way, there seems to be no room for a personal relationship between human beings and a supernatural perfect being ruling and guiding men. Hence many scientists and educated men have come to feel that the Christian attitudes towards the world and human existence are inappropriate. They have become convinced that the universe and human existence in it are without a purpose and therefore devoid of meaning.[2]

1. The Explanation of the Universe

Such beliefs are disheartening and unplausible. It is natural to keep looking for the error that must have crept into our arguments. And if an error has crept in, then it is most likely to have crept in with science. For before the rise of science, people did not entertain such melancholy beliefs, while the scientific world picture seems literally to force them on us.

There is one argument which seems to offer the desired way out. It runs somewhat as follows. Science and religion are not really in conflict. They are, on the contrary, mutually complementary, each doing an entirely different job. Science gives provisional, if precise, explanations of small parts of the universe, religion gives final and over-all, if comparatively vague, explanations of the universe as a whole. The objectionable conclusion, that human existence is devoid of meaning, follows only if we use scientific explanations where they do not apply, namely, where total explanations of the whole universe are concerned.[3]

After all, the argument continues, the scientific world picture is the inevitable outcome of rigid adherence to scientific method and explanation, but scientific, that is, causal explanations for their very nature are incapable of producing real illumination. They can at best tell us *how* things are or have come about, but never *why*. They are incapable of making the universe intelligible, comprehensible, meaningful to us. They represent the universe as meaningless, not because it *is* meaningless, but because scientific explanations are not designed to yield answers to investigations into the why and wherefore, into the meaning, purpose, or point of things. Scientific explanations (this argument continues) began, harmlessly enough, as partial and provisional explanations of the movement of material bodies, in particular the planets, within the general framework of the medieval world picture. Newton thought of the universe as a clock made, originally wound up, and occasionally set right by God. His laws of motion only revealed the ways in which the heavenly machinery worked. Explaining the movement of the planets by these laws was analogous to explaining the machinery of a watch. Such explanations showed *how* the thing worked, but not *what it was for or why* it existed. Just as the explanation of how a watch works can help our understanding of the watch only if, in addition, we assume that there is a watchmaker who has designed it for a purpose, made it, and wound it up, so the Newtonian explanation of the solar system helps our understanding of it only on the similar assumption that there is some divine artificer who has designed and made this heavenly clockwork for some purpose, has wound it up, and perhaps even occasionally sets it right, when it is out or order.

Socrates, in the Phaedo complained that only explanations of a thing showing the good or purpose for which it existed could offer a *real* explanation of it. He rejected the kind of explanation we now call "causal" as no more than mentioning "that without which a cause could not be a cause," that is, as merely a necessary condition, but not the *real* cause, the real explanation.[4] In other words, Socrates held that *all* things can be explained in two different ways: either by mentioning merely a necessary condition, or by giving the *real* cause. The former is not an elucidation of the explicandum, not really a help in understanding it, in grasping its "why" and "wherefore."

This Socratic view, however, is wrong. It is not the case that there are two kinds of explanation for everything, one partial, preliminary, and not really clarifying, the other full, final, and illuminating. The truth is that these two kinds of explanation are equally explanatory, equally illuminating, and equally full and final, but that they are appropriate for different kinds of explicanda.

When in an uninhabited forest we find what looks like houses, paved streets, temples, cooking utensils, and the like, it is no great risk to say that these things are the ruins of a deserted city, that is to say, of something man-made. In such a case, the appropriate explanation is teleological, that is, in terms of the purposes of the builders of that city. On the other hand, when a comet approaches the earth, it is similarly a safe bet that, unlike the city in the forest, it was not manufactured by intelligent creatures and that, therefore, a teleological explanation would be out of place, whereas a causal one is suitable.

It is easy to see that in some cases causal, and in others teleological explanations are appropriate. A small satellite circling the earth may or may not have been made by man. We may never know which is the true explanation, but either hypothesis is equally explanatory. It would be wrong to say that only a teleological explanation can *really* explain it. Either explanation would yield complete clarity although, of course, only one can be true. Teleological explanation is only one of several that are possible.

It may indeed be strictly correct to say that the question "*Why* is there a satellite circling the earth?" can only be answered by a teleological explanation. It may be true that "Why?"-questions can really be used properly only in order to elicit *someone's reasons for* doing something. If this is so, it would explain our dissatisfaction with causal answers to "Why?"-questions. But even if it is so, it does not show that "Why is the satellite there?" *must be answered by a teleological explanation.* It shows only that either it must be so answered or it must not be asked. The question "Why have you stopped beating your wife?" can be answered only by a teleological explanation, but if you have never beaten her, it is an improper question. Similarly, if the satellite is not man-made, "Why is there a satellite?" is improper since it implies an origin it did not have. Natural science can indeed only tell us *how* things in nature have come about and not *why,* but this is so not because something else can tell us the *why* and *wherefore,* but because there is none.

There is, however, another point which has not yet been answered. The objection just stated was that causal explanations did not even set out to answer the crucial question. We ask the question "Why?" but science returns an answer to the question "How?" It might now be conceded that this is no ground for a complaint, but perhaps it will instead be said that causal explanations do not give complete or full answers even to that latter question. In causal explanations, it will be objected, the existence of one thing is explained by reference to its cause, but this involves asking for the cause of that cause, and so on, ad infinitum. There is no resting place which is not as much in need of explanation as what has already been explained. Nothing at all is ever fully and completely explained by this sort of explanation.

Leibniz has made this point very persuasively. "Let us suppose a book of the elements of geometry to have been eternal, one copy always having been taken down from an earlier one; it is evident that, even though a reason can be given for the present book out of a past one, nevertheless, out of any number of books, taken in order, going backwards, we shall never come upon *a full* reason; though we might well always wonder why there should have been such books from all time—why there were books at all, and why they were written in this manner. What is true of books is true also of the different states of the world; for what follows is in some way copied from what precedes. . . . And so, however far you go back to earlier states, you will never find in those states *a full reason* why there should be any world rather than none, and why it should be such as it is."[5]

However, a moment's reflection will show that if any type of explanation is merely preliminary and provisional, it is teleological explanation, since it presupposes a background which itself stands in need of explanation. If I account for the existence of the man-made satellite by saying that it was made by some scientists for a certain purpose, then such an explanation can clarify the existence of the satellite only if I assume that there existed materials out of which the satellite was made, and scientists who made it for some purpose. It therefore does not matter what type of explanation we give, whether causal or teleological: either type, any type of explanation, will imply the existence of something by reference to which the explicandum can be explained. And this in turn must be accounted for in the same way, and so on for ever.

But is not God a necessary being? Do we not escape the infinite regress as soon as we reach God? It is often maintained that, unlike ordinary intelligent beings, God is eternal and necessary hence His existence, unlike theirs, is not in need of explanation. For what is it that creates the vicious regress just mentioned? It is that, if we accept the principle of sufficient reason (that there must be an explanation for the existence of anything and everything the existence of which is not logically necessary, but merely contingent[6]), the existence of all the things referred to in any explanation requires itself to be explained. If, however, God is a logically necessary being, then His existence requires no explanation. Hence the vicious regress comes to an end with God.

Now, it need not be denied that God is a necessary being in some sense of that expression. In one of these senses, I, for instance, am a necessary being: it is impossible that I should not exist, because it is self-refuting to say "I do not exist." The same is true of the English language and of the universe. It is self-refuting to say "There is no such thing as the English language" because this sentence is in the English language, or "There is no such thing as the universe" because whatever there is, *is* the universe. It is impossible that these things should not in fact exist since it is impossible that we should be mistaken in thinking that they exist. For what possible occurrence could even throw doubt on our being right on these matters, let alone show that we are wrong? I, the English language, and the universe, are necessary beings, simply in the sense in which all is necessarily true which has been *proved* to be true. The occurrence of utterances such as "I exist," "The English language exists" and "the universe exists" is in itself sufficient proof of their truth. These remarks are therefore necessarily true, hence the things asserted to exist are necessary things.

But this sort of necessity will not satisfy the principle of sufficient reason, because it is only hypothetical or consequential necessity.[7] *Given that* someone says "I exist," then it is logically impossible that *he* should not exist. Given the evidence we have, the English language and the universe most certainly do exist. But there is no necessity about the evidence. On the principle of sufficient reason, we must explain the existence of the evidence, for its existence is not logically necessary.

In other words, the only sense of "necessary being" capable of terminating the vicious regress is "logically necessary being," but it is no longer seriously in dispute that the notion of a logically necessary being is self-contradictory.[8] Whatever can be conceived of as existing can equally be conceived of as not existing.

However, even if per impossibile, there were such a thing as a logically necessary being, we could still not make out a case for the superiority of teleological over causal explanation. The existence of the universe cannot be explained in accordance with the familiar model of manufacture by a crafts-man. For that model presupposes the existence of materials out of which the product is fashioned. God, on the other hand, must create the materials as well. Moreover, although we have a simple model of "creation out of nothing," for composers create tunes out of nothing, yet there is a great differ-ence between creating *something to be sung,* and making the sounds which are a singing of it, or producing the piano on which to play it. Let us, however, waive all these objections and admit, for argument's sake, that creation out of nothing is conceivable. Surely, even so, no one can claim that it is the kind of explanation which yields the clearest and fullest understanding. Surely, to round off scientific explanations of the origin of the universe with creation out of nothing, does not add anything to our *understanding.* There may be merit of some sort in this way of speaking, but whatever it is, it is not greater clarity or explanatory power.[9]

What then, does all this amount to? Merely to the claim that scientific explanations are no worse than any other. All that has been shown is that all explanations suffer from the same defect: all involve a vicious infinite regress. In other words, no type of human explanation can help us to unravel the ultimate, unanswerable mystery. Christian ways of looking at things may not be able to render the world any more lucid than science can, but at least they do not pretend that there are no impenetrable mysteries. On the contrary, they point out untiringly that the claims of science to be able to elucidate everything are hollow. They remind us that science is not merely limited to the exploration of a tiny corner of the universe but that, however far our probing instruments may eventually reach, we can never even approach the answers to the last ques-tions: "Why is there a world at all rather than nothing?" and "Why is the world such as it is and not different?" Here our finite human intellect bumps against its own boundary walls.

Is it true that scientific explanations involve an infinite vicious regress? Are scientific explanations really only provisional and incomplete? The crucial point will be this. Do *all* contingent truths call for explanation? Is the principle of sufficient reason sound? Can scientific explanations never come to a definite end? It will be seen that with a clear grasp of the nature and purpose of explanation we can answer these questions.[10]

Explaining something to someone is making him understand it. This involves bringing together in his mind two things, a model which is accepted as already simple and clear, and that which is to be explained, the explicandum, which is not so. Understanding the explicandum is seeing that it belongs to a range of things which could legitimately have been expected by anyone familiar with the model and with certain facts.

There are, however, two fundamentally different positions which a person may occupy relative to some explicandum. He may not be familiar with any model capable of leading him to expect the phenomenon to be explained. Most of us, for instance, are in that position in relation to the phenomena occurring in a good séance. With regard to other things people will differ. Someone who can play chess, already understands chess, already has such a model. Someone who has never seen a game of chess has not. He sees the moves on the board but he cannot understand, cannot follow, cannot make sense of what is happening. Explaining the game to him is giving him an explanation, is making him understand. He can understand or follow chess moves only if he can see them as conforming to a model of a chess game. In order to acquire such a model, he will, of course, need to know the constitutive rules of chess, that is, the permissible moves. But that is not all. He must know that a normal game of chess is a competition (not all games are) between two people, each trying to win, and he must know what it is to win at chess: to manoeuvre the opponent's king into a position of check-mate. Finally, he must acquire some knowledge of what is and what is not conducive to winning: the tactical rules or canons of the game.

A person who has been given such an explanation and who has mastered it—which may take quite a long time—has now reached understanding, in the sense of the ability to follow each move. A person cannot in that sense understand merely one single move of chess and no other. If he does not understand any other moves, we must say that he has not yet mastered the explanation, that he does not really understand the single move either. If he has mastered the explanation, then he understands all those moves which he can see as being in accordance with the model of the game inculcated in him during the explanation.

However, even though a person who has mastered such an explanation will understand many, perhaps most, moves of any game of chess he cares to watch, he will not necessarily understand them all, as some moves of a player may not be in accordance with his model of the game. White, let us say, at his fifteenth move, exposes his queen to capture by Black's knight. Though in accordance with the constitutive rules of the game, this move is nevertheless perplexing and calls for explanation, because it is not conducive to the achievement by White of what must be assumed to be his aim: to win the game. The queen is a much more valuable piece than the knight against which he is offering to exchange.

An onlooker who has mastered chess may fail to understand this move, be perplexed by it, and wish for an explanation. Of course he may fail to be perplexed, for if he is a very inexperienced player he may not *see* the disadvantageousness of the move. But there is such a need whether anyone sees it or not. The move *calls for* explanation because to anyone who knows the game it must appear to be incompatible with the model which we have learnt during the explanation of the game, and by reference to which we all explain and understand normal games.

However, the required explanation of White's 15th move is of a very different kind. What is needed now is not the acquisition of an explanatory model, but the removal of the real or apparent incompatibility between the player's move and the model of explanation he has already acquired. In such a case the perplexity can be removed only on the assumption that the incompatibility between the model and the game is merely apparent. As our model includes a presumed aim of both players, there are the following three possibilities: (a) White has made a mistake: he has overlooked the threat to his queen. In that case, the explanation is that White thought his move conducive to his end, but it was not. (b) Black has made a mistake: White set a trap for him. In that case, the explanation is that Black thought White's move was not conducive to White's end, but it was. (c) White is not pursuing the end which any chess player may be presumed to pursue: he is not trying to win his game. In that case, the explanation is that White has made a move which he knows is not conducive to the end of winning his game because, let us say, he wishes to please Black who is his boss.

Let us now set out the differences and similarities between the two types of understanding involved in these two kinds of explanation. I shall call the first kind "model"-understanding and explaining, respectively, because both involve the use of a model by reference to which understanding and explaining is effected. The second kind I shall call "unvexing," because the need for this type of explanation and understanding arises only when there is a perplexity arising out of the incompatibility of the model and the facts to be explained.

The first point is that unvexing presupposes model-understanding, but not vice versa. A person can neither have nor fail to have unvexing-understanding of White's fifteenth move at chess, if he does not already have model-understanding of chess. Obviously, if I don't know how to play chess, I shall fail to have model-understanding of White's fifteenth move. But I can neither fail to have nor, of course, can I have unvexing-understanding of it, for I cannot be perplexed by it. I merely fail to have model-understanding of this move as, indeed, of any other move of chess. On the other hand, I may well have model-understanding of chess without having unvexing understanding of every move. That is to say, I may well know how to play chess without understanding White's fifteenth move. A person cannot fail to have unvexing-understanding of the move unless he is vexed or perplexed by it, hence he cannot even fail to have unvexing-understanding unless he already has model-understanding. It is not true that one either understands or fails to understand. On certain occasions, one neither understands nor fails to understand.

The second point is that there are certain things which cannot call for unvexing-explanations. No one can for instance call for an unvexing-explanation of White's first move, which is Pawn to King's Four. For no one can be perplexed or vexed by this move. Either a person knows how to play chess or he does not. If he does, then he must understand this move, for if he does not understand it, he has not yet mastered the game. And if he does not know how to play chess, then he cannot yet have, or fail to have, unvexing-understanding, he cannot therefore need an unvexing-explanation. Intellectual problems do not arise out of ignorance, but out of insufficient knowledge. An ignoramus is puzzled by very little. Once a student can see problems, he is already well into the subject.

The third point is that model-understanding implies being able, without further thought, to have model-understanding of a good many other things, unvexing-understanding does not. A person who knows chess and therefore has model-understanding of it, must understand a good many chess moves, in fact all except those that call for unvexing-explanations. If he claims that he can understand White's first move, but no others, then he is either lying or deceiving himself or he really does not understand any move. On the other hand, a person who, after an unvexing-explanation, understands White's fifteenth move, need not be able, without further explanation, to understand Black's or any other further move which calls for unvexing-explanation.

What is true of explaining deliberate and highly stylized human behaviour such as playing a game of chess is also true of explaining natural phenomena. For what is characteristic of natural phenomena, that they recur in essentially the same way, that they are, so to speak, repeatable, is also true of chess games, as it is not of games of tennis or cricket. There is only one important difference: man himself has invented and laid down the rules of chess, as he has not invented or laid down the "rules or laws governing the behaviour of things." This difference between chess and phenomena is important, for it adds another way to the three already mentioned,[11] in which a perplexity can be removed by an unvexing-explanation, namely, by abandoning the original explanatory model. This is, of course, not possible in the case of games of chess, because the model for chess is not a "construction" on the basis of the already existing phenomena of chess, but an invention. The person who first thought up the model of chess could not have been mistaken. The person who first thought of a model explaining some phenomenon could have been mistaken.

Consider an example. We may think that the following phenomena belong together: the horizon seems to recede however far we walk towards it; we seem to be able to see further the higher the mountain we climb; the sun and moon seem every day to fall into the sea on one side but to come back from behind the mountains on the other side without being any the worse for it. We may explain these phenomena by two alternative models: (a) that the earth is a large disc; (b) that it is a large sphere. However, to a believer in the first theory there arises the following perplexity: how is it that when we travel long enough towards the horizon in any one direction, we do eventually come back to our starting point without ever coming to the edge of the earth? We may at first attempt to "save" the model by saying that there is only an apparent contradiction. We may say either that the model does not require us to come to an edge, for it may be possible only to walk round and round on the flat surface. Or we may say that the person must have walked over the edge without noticing it, or perhaps that the travellers are all lying. Alternatively, the fact that our model is "constructed" and not invented or laid down enables us to say, what we could not do in the case of chess, that the model is inadequate or unsuitable. We can choose another model which fits all the facts, for instance, that the earth is round. Of course, then we have to give an unvexing-explanation for why it *looks* flat, but we are able to do that.

We now can return to our original question, "Are scientific explanations true and full explanations or do they involve an infinite regress, leaving them for ever incomplete?"

Our distinction between model- and unvexing-explanations will help here. It is obvious that only those things which are perplexing *call for* and *can be given* unvexing-explanations. We have already seen that in disposing of one perplexity, we do not necessarily raise another. On the contrary, unvexing-explanations truly and completely explain what they set out to explain, namely, how something is possible which, on our explanatory model, seemed to be impossible. There can therefore be no infinite regress here. Unvexing-explanations are real and complete explanations.

Can there be an infinite regress, then, in the case of model-explanations? Take the following example. European children are puzzled by the fact that their antipodean counterparts do not drop into empty space. This perplexity can be removed by substituting for their explanatory model another one. The European children imagine that throughout space there is an all-pervasive force operating in the same direction as the force that pulls them to the ground. We must, in our revised model, substitute for this force another acting everywhere in the direction of the centre of the earth. Having thus removed their perplexity by giving them an adequate model, we can, however, go on to ask *why* there should be such a force as the force of gravity, why bodies should "naturally," in the absence of forces acting on them, behave in the way stated in Newton's laws. And we might be able to give such an explanation. We might for instance construct a model of space which would exhibit as derivable from it what in Newton's theory are "brute facts." Here we would have a case of the brute facts of one theory being explained within the framework of another, more general theory. And it is a sound methodological principle that we should continue to look for more and more general theories.

Note two points, however. The first is that we must distinguish, as we have seen, between *the possibility* and *the necessity* of giving an explanation. Particular occurrences can be explained by being exhibited as instances of regularities, and regularities can be explained by being exhibited as instances of more general regularities. Such explanations make things clearer. They organize the material before us. They introduce order where previously there was disorder. But absence of this sort of explanation (model-explanation) does not leave us with a puzzle or perplexity, an intellectual restlessness or cramp. The unexplained things are not unintelligible, incomprehensible, or irrational. Some things, on the other hand, call for, require, demand an explanation. As long as we are without such an explanation, we are perplexed, puzzled, intellectually perturbed. We need an unvexing-explanation.

Now, it must be admitted that we may be able to construct a more general theory, from which, let us say, Newton's theory can be derived. This would further clarify the phenomena of motion and would be intellectually satisfying. But failure to do so would not leave us with an intellectual cramp. The facts stated in Newton's theory do not require, or stand in need of, unvexing-explanations. They could do so only if we already had another theory or model with which Newton's theory was incompatible. They could not do so, by themselves, prior to the establishment of such another model.

The second point is that there is an objective limit to which such explanations tend, and beyond which they are pointless. There is a very good reason for wishing to explain a less general by a more general theory. Usually, such a unification goes hand in hand with greater precision in measuring the phenomena which both theories explain. Moreover, the more general theory, because of its greater generality, can explain a wider range of phenomena, including not only phenomena already explained by some other theories but also newly discovered phenomena, which the less general theory cannot explain. Now, the ideal limit to which such expansions of theories tend is an all-embracing theory which unifies all theories and explains all phenomena. Of course, such a limit can never be reached, since new phenomena are constantly discovered. Nevertheless, theories may be tending towards it. It will be remembered that the contention made against scientific theories was that there is no such limit because they involve an infinite regress. On that view, which I reject, there is no conceivable point at which scientific theories could be said to have explained the whole universe. On the view I am defending, there is such a limit, and it is the limit towards which scientific theories are actually tending. I claim that the nearer we come to this limit, the closer we are to a full and complete explanation of everything. For if we were to reach the limit, then though we could, of course, be left with a model which is itself unexplained and could be yet further explained by derivation from another model, there would be no need for, and no point in, such a further explanation. There would be no need for it, because any clearly defined model permitting us to expect the phenomena it is designed to explain offers full and complete explanations of these phenomena, however narrow the range. And while, at lower levels of generality, there is a good reason for providing more general models, since they further simplify, systematize, and organize the phenomena, this, which is the only reason for building more general theories, no longer applies once we reach the ideal limit of an all-embracing explanation.

It might be said that there is another reason for using different models: that they might enable us to discover new phenomena. Theories are not only instruments of explanation, but also of discovery. With this I agree, but it is irrelevant to my point: that *the needs of explanation* do not require us to go on for ever deriving one explanatory model from another.

It must be admitted, then, that in the case of model-explanations there is a regress, but it is neither vicious nor infinite. It is not vicious because, in order to explain a group of explicanda, a model-explanation *need* not itself be derived from another more general one. It gives a perfectly full and consistent explanation by itself. And the regress is not infinite, for there is a natural limit, an all-embracing model, which can explain all phenomena, beyond which it would be pointless to derive model-explanations from yet others.

What about our most serious question, "Why is there anything at all?" Sometimes, when we think about how one thing has developed out of another and that one out of a third, and so on back throughout all time, we are driven to ask the same question about the universe as a whole. We want to add up all things and refer to them by the name, "the world," and we want to know why the world exists and why there is not nothing instead. In such moments, the world seems to us a kind of bubble floating on an ocean of nothingness. Why should such flotsam be adrift in empty space? Surely, its emergence from the hyaline billows of nothingness is more mysterious even than Aphrodite's emergence from the sea. Wittgenstein expressed in these words the mystification we all feel: "Not *how* the world is, is the mystical, but *that* it is. The contemplation of the world *sub specie aeterni* is the contemplation of it as a limited whole. The feeling of the world as a limited whole is the mystical feeling."[12]

Professor J. J. C. Smart expresses his own mystification in these moving words:

"That anything should exist at all does seem to me a matter for the deepest awe. But whether other people feel this sort of awe, and whether they or I ought to is another question. I think we ought to. If so, the question arises: If 'Why should anything exist at all?' cannot be interpreted after the manner of the cosmological argument, that is, as an absurd request for the non-sensical postulation of a logically necessary being, what sort of question is it? What sort of question is this question 'Why should anything exist at all?' All I can say is that I do not yet know."[13]

It is undeniable that the magnitude and perhaps the very existence of the universe is awe-inspiring. It is probably true that it gives many people "the mystical feeling." It is also undeniable that our awe, our mystical feeling, aroused by contemplating the vastness of the world, is justified, in the same sense in which our fear is justified when we realize we are in danger. There is no more appropriate object for our awe or for the mystical feeling than the magnitude and perhaps the existence of the universe, just as there is no more appropriate object for our fear than a situation of personal peril. However, it does not follow from this that it is a good thing to cultivate, or indulge in, awe or mystical feelings, any more than it is necessarily a good thing to cultivate, or indulge in, fear in the presence of danger.

In any case, whether or not we ought to have or are justified in having a mystical feeling or a feeling of awe when contemplating the universe, having such a feeling is not the same as asking a meaningful question, although having it may well *incline us* to utter certain forms of words. Our question "Why is there anything at all?" may be no more than the expression of our feeling of awe or mystification, and not a meaningful question at all. Just as the feeling of fear may naturally but illegitimately give rise to the question "What sin have I committed?," so the feeling of awe or mystification may naturally but illegitimately lead to the question "Why is there anything at all?" What we have to discover, then, is whether this question makes sense or is meaningless.

Yes, of course, it will be said, it makes perfectly good sense. There is an undeniable fact and it calls for explanation. The fact is that the universe exists.

In the light of our experience, there can be no possible doubt that something or other exists, and the claim that the universe exists commits us to no more than that. And surely this calls for explanation, because the universe must have originated somehow. Everything has an origin and the universe is no exception. Since the universe is the totality of things, it must have originated out of nothing. If it had originated out of something, even something as small as one single hydrogen atom, what has so originated could not be the whole universe, but only the universe minus the atom. And then the atom itself would call for explanation, for it too must have had an origin, and it must be *an origin out of nothing.* And how can anything originate out of nothing? Surely that calls for explanation.

However, let us be quite clear what is to be explained. There are two facts here, not one. The first is that the universe exists, which is undeniable. The second is that the universe must have originated out of nothing, and that is not undeniable. It is true that, *if it has originated at all,* then it must have originated out of nothing, or else it is not the universe that has originated. But need it have originated? Could it not have existed for ever?[14] It might be argued that nothing exists for ever, that everything has originated out of something else. That may well be true, but it is perfectly compatible with the fact that the universe is everlasting. We may well be able to trace the origin of any thing to the time when, by some transformation, it has developed out of some other thing, and yet it may be the case that no thing has its origin in nothing, and the universe has existed for ever. For even if every *thing* has a beginning and an end, the total of mass and energy may well remain constant.

Moreover, the hypothesis that the universe originated out of nothing is, empirically speaking, completely empty. Suppose, for argument's sake, that the annihilation of an object without remainder is conceivable. It would still not be possible for any hypothetical observer to ascertain whether space was empty or not. Let us suppose that *within the range of observation of our observer* one object after another is annihilated without remainder and that only one is left. Our observer could not then tell whether in remote parts of the universe, beyond his range of observation, objects are coming into being or passing out of existence. What, moreover, are we to say of the observer himself? Is he to count for nothing? Must we not postulate him away as well, if the universe is to have arisen out of nothing?

Let us, however, ignore all these difficulties and assume that the universe really has originated out of nothing. Even that does not prove that the universe has not existed for ever. If the universe can conceivably develop out of nothing, then it can conceivably vanish without remainder. And it can arise out of nothing again, and subside into nothingness once more, and so on ad infinitum. Of course, "again" and "once more" are not quite the right words. The concept of time hardly applies to such universes. It does not make sense to ask whether one of them is earlier or later than, or perhaps simultaneous with, the other because we cannot ask whether they occupy the same or different spaces. Being separated from one another by "nothing," they are not separated from one another by "anything." We cannot therefore make any statement about their mutual spatio-temporal relations. It is impossible to distinguish between one long continuous universe and two universes separated by nothing. How, for instance, can we tell whether the universe including ourselves is not frequently annihilated and "again" reconstituted just as it was?

Let us now waive these difficulties as well. Let us suppose for a moment that we understand what is meant by saying that the universe originated out of nothing and that this has happened only once. Let us accept this as a fact. Does this fact call for explanation?

It does not call for an unvexing-explanation. That would be called for only if there were a perplexity due to the incompatibility of an accepted model with some fact. In our case, the fact to be explained is the origination of the universe out of nothing, hence there could not be such a perplexity, for we need not employ a model incompatible with this. If we had a model incompatible with our "fact," then that would be the wrong model and we would simply have to substitute another for it. The model we employ to explain the origin of the universe out of nothing could not be based on the similar origins of other things for, of course, there is nothing else with a similar origin.

All the same, it seems very surprising that something should have come out of nothing. It is contrary to the principle that every thing has an origin, that is, has developed out of something else. It must be admitted that there is this incompatibility. However, it does not arise because a well-established model does not square with an undeniable fact; it arises because a well-established model does not square with *an assumption* of which it is hard even to make sense and for which there is no evidence whatsoever. In fact, the only reason we have for making this assumption is a simple logical howler: that because every thing has an origin, the universe must have an origin, too, except, that, being the universe, it must have originated out of nothing. This is a howler, because it conceives of the universe as a big thing, whereas in fact it is the totality of things, that is, not a thing. That every thing has an origin does not entail that the totality of things has an origin. On the contrary, it strongly suggests that it has not. For to say that every thing has an origin implies that any given thing must have developed out of something else which in turn, being a thing, must have developed out of something else, and so forth. If we assume that every thing has an origin, we need not, indeed it is hard to see how we can, assume that the totality of things has an origin as well. There is therefore no perplexity, because we need not and should not assume that the universe has originated out of nothing.

If, however, in spite of all that has been said just now, someone still wishes to assume, contrary to all reason, that the universe has originated out of nothing, there would still be no perplexity, for then he would simply have to give up the principle which is incompatible with this assumption, namely, that no thing can originate out of nothing. After all, this principle *could* allow for exceptions. We have no proof that it does not. Again, there is no perplexity, because no incompatibility between our assumption and an inescapable principle.

But it might be asked, do we not need a model-explanation of our supposed fact? The answer is No. We do not need such an explanation, for there could not possibly be a model for this origin other than this origin itself. We cannot say that origination out of nothing is like birth, or emergence, or evolution, or anything else we know for it is not like anything we know. In all these cases, there is *something* out of which the new thing has originated.

To sum up. The question, "Why is there anything at all?" looks like a perfectly sensible question modelled on "Why does *this* exist?" or "How has *this* originated?" It looks like a question about the origin of a thing. However, it is not such a question, for the universe is not a thing, but the totality of things. There is therefore no reason to assume that the universe has an origin. The very assumption that it has is fraught with contradictions and absurdities. If, nevertheless, it were true that the universe has originated out of nothing, then this would not call either for an unvexing or a model-explanation. It would not call for the latter, because there could be no model of it taken from another part of our experience, since there is nothing analogous in our experience to origination out of nothing. It would not call for the former, because there can be no perplexity due to the incompatibility of a well-established model and an undeniable fact, since there is no undeniable fact and no well-established model. If, on the other hand, as is more probable, the universe has not originated at all, but is eternal, then the question why or how it has originated simply does not arise. There can then be no question about why anything at all exists, for it could not mean how or why the universe had originated, since ex hypothesi it has no origin. And what else could it mean?

Lastly, we must bear in mind that the hypothesis that the universe was made by God out of nothing only brings us back to the question who made God or how God originated. And if we do not find it repugnant to say that God is eternal, we cannot find it repugnant to say that the universe is eternal. The only difference is that we know for certain that the universe exists, while we have the greatest difficulty in even making sense of the claim that God exists.

To sum up. According to the argument examined, we must reject the scientific world picture because it is the outcome of scientific types of explanation which do not really and fully explain the world around us, but only tell us *how* things have come about, not *why*, and can give no answer to the ultimate question, why there is anything at all rather than nothing. Against this, I have argued that scientific explanations are real and full, just like the explanations of everyday life and of the traditional religions. They differ from those latter only in that they are more precise and more easily disprovable by the observation of facts.

My main points dealt with the question why scientific explanations were thought to be merely provisional and partial. The first main reason is the misunderstanding of the difference between teleological and causal explanations. It is first, and rightly, maintained that teleological explanations are answers to "Why?"-questions, while causal explanations are answers to "How?"-questions. It is further, and wrongly, maintained that, in order to obtain real and full explanations of anything, one must answer both "Why?" and "How?" questions. In other words, it is thought that all matters can and must be explained by both teleological and causal types of explanation. Causal explanations, it is believed, are merely provisional and partial, waiting to be completed by teleological explanations. Until a teleological explanation has been given, so the story goes, we have not *really* understood the explicandum. However, I have shown that both types are equally real and full explanations. The difference between them is merely that they are appropriate to different types of explicanda.

It should, moreover, be borne in mind that teleological explanations are not, in any sense, unscientific. They are rightly rejected in the natural sciences, not however because they are unscientific, but because no intelligences or purposes are found to be involved there. On the other hand, teleological explanations are very much in place in psychology, for we find intelligence and purpose involved in a good deal of human behaviour. It is not only not unscientific to give teleological explanations of deliberate human behaviour, but it would be quite unscientific to exclude them.

The second reason why scientific explanations are thought to be merely provisional and partial, is that they are believed to involve a vicious infinite regress. Two misconceptions have led to this important error. The first is the general misunderstanding of the nature of explanation, and in particular the failure to distinguish between the two types which I have called model- and unvexing-explanations, respectively. If one does not draw this distinction, it is natural to conclude that scientific explanations lead to a vicious infinite regress. For while it is true of those perplexing matters which are elucidated by unvexing-explanations that they are incomprehensible and cry out for explanation, it is not true that after an unvexing-explanation has been given, this itself is again capable, let alone in need of, a yet further explanation of the same kind. Conversely, while it is true that model-explanations of regularities can themselves be further explained by more general model-explanations, it is not true that, in the absence of such more general explanations, the less general are incomplete, hang in the air, so to speak, leaving the explicandum incomprehensible and crying out for explanation. The distinction between the two types of explanation shows us that an explicandum is either perplexing and incomprehensible, in which case an explanation of it *is necessary* for clarification and, when given, *complete,* or it is a regularity capable of being subsumed under a model, in which case a further explanation *is possible* and often profitable, but *not necessary* for clarification.

The second misconception responsible for the belief in a vicious infinite regress is the misrepresentation of scientific explanation *as essentially causal.* It has generally been held that, in a scientific explanation, the explicandum is the effect of some event, the cause, temporally prior to the explicandum. Combined with the principle of sufficient reason, (the principle that anything is in need of explanation which might conceivably have been different from what it is), this error generates the nightmare of determinism. Since any event might have been different from what it was, acceptance of this principle has the consequence that *every* event must have a reason or explanation. But if the reason is itself an event *prior in time,* then every reason must have a reason preceding it, and so the infinite regress of explanation is necessarily tied to the time scale stretching infinitely back into the endless past. It is, however, obvious from our account that science is not primarily concerned with the forging of such causal chains. The primary object of the natural sciences is not historical at all. Natural science claims to reveal, not the beginnings of things, but their underlying reality. It does not dig up the past, it digs down into the structure of things existing here and now. Some scientists do allow themselves to speculate, and rather precariously at that, about origins. But their hard work is done on the structure of what exists now. In particular those explanations which are themselves further explained are not explanations linking event to event in a gapless chain reaching back to creation day, but generalisations of theories tending towards a unified theory.

2. The Purpose of Man's Existence

Our conclusion in the previous section has been that science is in principle able to give complete and real explanations of every occurrence and thing in the universe. This has two important corollaries: (i) Acceptance of the scientific world picture cannot be *one's reason for* the belief that the universe is unintelligible and therefore meaningless, though coming to accept it, after having been taught the Christian world picture, may well have been, in the case of many individuals, *the only or the main cause* of their belief that the universe and human existence are meaningless. (ii) It is not in accordance with reason to reject this pessimistic belief on the grounds that scientific explanations are only provisional and incomplete and must be supplemented by religious ones.

In fact, it might be argued that the more clearly we understand the explanations given by science, the more we are driven to the conclusion that human life has no purpose and therefore no meaning. The science of astronomy teaches us that our earth was not specially created about 6,000 years ago, but evolved out of hot nebulae which previously had whirled aimlessly through space for countless ages. As they cooled, the sun and the planets formed. On one of these planets at a certain time the circumstances were propitious and life developed. But conditions will not remain favourable to life. When our solar system grows old, the sun will cool, our planet will be covered with ice, and all living creatures will eventually perish. Another theory has it that the sun will explode and that the heat generated will be so great that all organic life on earth will be destroyed. That is the comparatively short history and prospect of life on earth. Altogether it amounts to very little when compared with the endless history of the inanimate universe.

Biology teaches us that the species man was not specially created but is merely, in a long chain of evolutionary changes of forms of life, the last link, made in the likeness not of God but of nothing so much as an ape. The rest of the universe, whether animate or inanimate, instead of serving the ends of man, is at best indifferent, at worst savagely hostile. Evolution to whose operation the emergence of man is due is a ceaseless battle among members of different species, one species being gobbled up by another, only the fittest surviving. Far from being the gentlest and most highly moral, man is simply the creature best fitted to survive, the most efficient if not the most rapacious and insatiable killer. And in this unplanned, fortuitous, monstrous, savage world man is madly trying to snatch a few brief moments of joy, in the short intervals during which he is free from pain, sickness, persecution, war or famine until, finally, his life is snuffed out in death. Science has helped us to know and understand this world, but what purpose or meaning can it find in it?

Complaints such as these do not mean quite the same to everybody, but one thing, I think, they mean to most people: science shows life to be meaningless, because life is without purpose. The medieval world picture provided life with a purpose, hence medieval Christians could believe that life had a meaning. The scientific account of the world takes away life's purpose and with it its meaning.

There are, however, two quite different senses of "purpose." Which one is meant? Has science deprived human life of purpose in both senses? And if not, is it a harmless sense, in which human existence has been robbed of purpose? Could human existence still have meaning if it did not have a purpose in that sense?

What are the two senses? In the first and basic sense, purpose is normally attributed only to persons or their behaviour as in "Did you have a purpose in leaving the ignition on?" In the second sense, purpose is normally attributed only to things, as in "What is the purpose of that gadget you installed in the workshop?" The two uses are intimately connected. We cannot attribute a purpose to a thing without implying that someone did something, in the doing of which he had some purpose, namely, to bring about the thing with the purpose. Of course, *his* purpose is not identical with *its* purpose. In hiring labourers and engineers and buying materials and a site for a factory and the like, the entrepreneur's purpose, let us say, is to manufacture cars, but the purpose of cars is to serve as a means of transportation.

There are many things that a man may do, such as buying and selling, hiring labourers, ploughing, felling trees, and the like, which it is foolish, pointless, silly, perhaps crazy, to do if one has no purpose in doing them. A man who does these things without a purpose is engaging in inane, futile pursuits. Lives crammed full with such activities devoid of purpose are pointless, futile, worthless. Such lives may indeed be dismissed as meaningless. But it should also be perfectly clear that acceptance of the scientific world picture does not force us to regard our lives as being without a purpose in this sense. Science has not only not robbed us of any purpose which we had before, but it has furnished us with enormously greater power to achieve these purposes. Instead of praying for rain or a good harvest or offspring, we now use ice pellets, artificial manure, or artificial insemination.

By contrast, having or not having a purpose, in the other sense, is value neutral. We do not think more or less highly of a thing for having or not having a purpose. "Having a purpose," in this sense, confers no kudos, "being purposeless" carries no stigma. A row of trees growing near a farm may or may not have a purpose: it may or may not be a windbreak, may or may not have been planted or deliberately left standing there in order to prevent the wind from sweeping across the fields. We do not in any way disparage the trees if we say they have no purpose, but have just grown that way. They are as beautiful, made of as good wood, as valuable, as if they had a purpose. And, of course, they break the wind just as well. The same is true of living creatures. We do not disparage a dog when we say that it has no purpose, is not a sheep dog or a watch dog or a rabbiting dog, but just a dog that hangs around the house and is fed by us.

Man is in a different category, however. To attribute to a human being a purpose in that sense is not neutral, let alone complimentary: it is offensive. It is degrading for a man to be regarded as merely serving a purpose. If, at a garden party, I ask a man in livery, "What is your purpose?" I am insulting him. I might as well have asked, "What are you *for*?" Such questions reduce him to the level of a gadget, a domestic animal, or perhaps a slave. I imply that *we* allot to *him* the tasks, the goals, the aims which he is to pursue; that *his* wishes and desires and aspirations and purposes are to count for little or nothing. We are treating him, in Kant's phrase, merely as a means to our ends, not as an end in himself.

The Christian and the scientific world pictures do indeed differ fundamentally on this point. The latter robs man of a purpose in this sense. It sees him as a being with no purpose allotted to him by anyone but himself. It robs him of any goal, purpose, or destiny appointed for him by any outside agency. The Christian world picture, on the other hand, sees man as a creature, a divine artefact, something halfway between a robot (manufactured) and an animal (alive), a homunculus, or perhaps Frankenstein, made in God's laboratory, with a purpose or task assigned him by his Maker.

However, lack of purpose in this sense does not in any way detract from the meaningfulness of life. I suspect that many who reject the scientific outlook because it involves the loss of purpose of life, and therefore meaning, are guilty of a confusion between the two senses of "purpose" just distinguished. They confusedly think that if the scientific world picture is true, then their lives must be futile because that picture implies that man has no purpose given him from without. But this is muddled thinking, for, as has already been shown, pointlessness is implied only by purposelessness in the other sense, which is not at all implied by the scientific picture of the world. These people mistakenly conclude that there can be no purpose *in* life because there is no purpose *of* life; that *men* cannot themselves adopt and achieve purposes because *man,* unlike a robot or a watchdog, is not a creature with a purpose.[15]

However, not all people taking this view are guilty of the above confusion. Some really hanker after a purpose of life in this sense. To some people the greatest attraction of the medieval world picture is the belief in an omnipotent, omniscient, and all-good Father, the view of themselves as His children who worship Him, of their proper attitude to what befalls them as submission, humility, resignation in His will, and what is often described as the "creaturely feeling."[16] All these are attitudes and feelings appropriate to a being that stands to another in the same sort of relation, though of course on a higher plane, in which a helpless child stands to his progenitor. Many regard the scientific picture of the world as cold, unsympathetic, unhomely, frightening, because it does not provide for any appropriate object of this creaturely attitude. There is nothing and no one in the world, as science depicts it, in which we can have faith or trust, on whose guidance we can rely, to whom we can turn for consolation, whom we can worship or submit to—except other human beings. This may be felt as a keen disappointment, because it shows that the meaning of life cannot lie in submission to His will, in acceptance of whatever may come, and in worship. But it does not imply that life can have *no* meaning. It merely implies that it must have a different meaning from that which it was thought to have. Just as it is a great shock for a child to find that he must stand on his own feet, that his father and mother no longer provide for him, so a person who has lost his faith in God must reconcile himself to the idea that he has to stand on his own feet, alone in the world except for whatever friends he may succeed in making.

But is not this to miss the point of the Christian teaching? Surely, Christianity can tell us the meaning of life because it tells us the grand and noble end for which God has created the universe and man. No human life, however pointless it may seem, is meaningless because in being part of God's plan, every life is assured of significance.

This point is well taken. It brings to light a distinction of some importance: we call a person's life meaningful not only if it is worthwhile, but also if he has helped in the realization of some plan or purpose transcending his own concerns. A person who knows he must soon die a painful death can give significance to the remainder of his doomed life by, say, allowing certain experiments to be performed on him which will be useful in the fight against cancer. In a similar way, only on a much more elevated plane, every man, however humble or plagued by suffering, is guaranteed significance by the knowledge that he is participating in God's purpose.

What, then, on the Christian view, is the grand and noble end for which God has created the world and man in it? We can immediately dismiss that still popular opinion that the smallness of our intellect prevents us from stating meaningfully God's design in all its imposing grandeur.[17] This view cannot possibly be a satisfactory answer to our question about the purpose of life. It is, rather, a confession of the impossibility of giving one. If anyone thinks that this "answer" can remove the sting from the impression of meaninglessness and insignificance in our lives, he cannot have been stung very hard.

If, then, we turn to those who are willing to state God's purpose in so many words, we encounter two insuperable difficulties. The first is to find a purpose grand and noble enough to explain and justify the great amount of undeserved suffering in this world. We are inevitably filled by a sense of pathos when we read statements such as this: ". . . history is the scene of a divine purpose, in which the whole of history is included, and Jesus of Nazareth is the centre of that purpose, both as revelation and as achievement, as the fulfilment of all that was past, and the promise of all that was to come . . . If God is God, and if He made all these things, why did He do it? . . . God created a universe, bounded by the categories of time, space, matter, and causality, because He desired to enjoy for ever the society of a fellowship of finite and redeemed spirits which have made to His love the response of free and voluntary love and service."[18] Surely this cannot be right? Could a God be called omniscient, omnipotent, *and* all-good who, for the sake of satisfying his desire to be loved and served, imposes (or has to impose) on his creatures the amount of undeserved suffering we find in the world?

There is, however, a much more serious difficulty still: God's purpose in making the universe must be stated in terms of a dramatic story many of whose key incidents symbolize religious conceptions and practices which we no longer find morally acceptable: the imposition of a taboo on the fruits of a certain tree, the sin and guilt incurred by Adam and Eve by violating the taboo, the wrath of God,[19] the curse of Adam and Eve and all their progeny, the expulsion from Paradise, the Atonement by Christ's bloody sacrifice on the cross which makes available by way of the sacraments God's Grace by which alone men can be saved (thereby, incidentally, establishing the valuable power of priests to forgive sins and thus alone make possible a man's entry to heaven[20]) Judgment Day on which the sheep are separated from the goats and the latter condemned to eternal torment in hell-fire.

Obviously it is much more difficult to formulate a purpose for creating the universe and man that will justify the enormous amount of undeserved suffering which we find around us, if that story has to be fitted in as well. For now we have to explain not only why an omnipotent, omniscient, and all-good God should create such a universe and such a man, but also why, foreseeing every move of the feeble, weak-willed, ignorant, and covetous creature to be created, He should nevertheless have created him and, having done so, should be incensed and outraged by man's sin, and why He should deem it necessary to sacrifice His own son on the cross to atone for this sin which was, after all, only a disobedience of one of his commands, and why this atonement and consequent redemption could not have been followed by man's return to Paradise—particularly of those innocent children who had not yet sinned—and why, on Judgment Day, this merciful God should condemn some to eternal torment.[21] It is not surprising that in the face of these and other difficulties, we find, again and again, a return to the first view: that God's purpose cannot meaningfully be stated.

It will perhaps be objected that no Christian today believes in the dramatic history of the world as I have presented it. But this is not so. It is the official doctrine of the Roman Catholic, the Greek Orthodox, and a large section of the Anglican Church.[22] Nor does Protestantism substantially alter this picture. In fact, by insisting on "Justification by Faith Alone" and by rejecting the ritualistic, magical character of the medieval Catholic interpretation of certain elements in the Christian religion, such as indulgences, the sacraments, and prayer, while at the same time insisting on the necessity of grace, Protestantism undermined the moral element in medieval Christianity expressed in the Catholics' emphasis on personal merit.[23] Protestantism, by harking back to St. Augustine, who clearly realized the incompatibility of grace and personal merit,[24] opened the way for Calvin's doctrine of Predestination (the intellectual parent of that form of rigid determinism which is usually blamed on science) and Salvation or Condemnation from all eternity.[25] Since Roman Catholics, Lutherans, Calvinists, Presbyterians and Baptists officially subscribe to the views just outlined, one can justifiably claim that the overwhelming majority of professing Christians hold or ought to hold them.

It might still be objected that the best and most modern views are wholly different. I have not the necessary knowledge to pronounce on the accuracy of this claim. It may well be true that the best and most modern views are such as Professor Braithwaite's who maintains that Christianity is, roughly speaking, "morality plus stories," where the stories are intended merely to make the strict moral teaching both more easily understandable and more palatable.[26] Or it may be that one or the other of the modern views on the nature and importance of the dramatic story told in the sacred Scriptures is the best. My reply is that, even if it is true, it does not prove what I wish to disprove, that one can extract a sensible answer to our question, "What is the meaning of life?" from the kind of story subscribed to by the overwhelming majority of Christians, who would, moreover, reject any such modernist interpretation at least as indignantly as the scientific account. Moreover, though such views can perhaps avoid some of the worst absurdities of the traditional story, they are hardly in a much better position to state the purpose for which God has created the universe and man in it, because they cannot overcome the difficulty of finding a purpose grand and noble enough to justify the enormous amount of undeserved suffering in the world.

Let us, however, for argument's sake, waive all these objections. There remains one fundamental hurdle which no form of Christianity can overcome: the fact that it demands of man a morally repugnant attitude towards the universe. It is now very widely held[27] that the basic element of the Christian religion is an attitude of worship towards a being supremely worthy of being worshipped and that it is religious feelings and experiences which apprise their owner of such a being and which inspire in him the knowledge or the feeling of complete dependence, awe, worship, mystery, and self-abasement. There is, in other words, a bi-polarity (the famous "I-Thou relationship") in which the object, "the wholly-other," is exalted whereas the subject is abased to the limit. Rudolf Otto has called this the "creature-feeling"[28] and he quotes as an expression of it, Abraham's words when venturing to plead for the men of Sodom: "Behold now, I have taken upon me to speak unto the Lord, which am but dust and ashes" (Gen. XVIII.27). Christianity thus demands of men an attitude inconsistent with one of the presuppositions of morality: that man is not wholly dependent on something else, that man has free will, that man is in principle capable of responsibility. We have seen that the concept of grace is the Christian attempt to reconcile the claim of total dependence and the claim of individual responsibility (partial independence), and it is obvious that such attempts must fail. We may dismiss certain doctrines, such as the doctrine of original sin or the doctrine of eternal hellfire or the doctrine that there can be no salvation outside the Church as extravagant and peripheral, but we cannot reject the doctrine of total dependence without rejecting the characteristically Christian attitude as such.

3. The Meaning of Life

Perhaps some of you will have felt that I have been shirking the real problem. To many people the crux of the matter seems as follows. How can there be any meaning in our life if it ends in death? What meaning can there be in it that our inevitable death does not destroy? How can our existence be meaningful if there is no after-life in which perfect justice is meted out? How can life have any meaning if all it holds out to us are a few miserable earthly pleasures and even these to be enjoyed only rarely and for such a piteously short time?

I believe this is the point which exercises most people most deeply. Kirilov, in Dostoevsky's novel, *The Possessed,* claims, just before committing suicide, that as soon as we realize that there is no God, we cannot live any longer, we must put an end to our lives. One of the reasons which he gives is that when we discover that there is no paradise, we have nothing to live for.

". . . there was a day on earth, and in the middle of the earth were three crosses. One on the cross had such faith that He said to another, 'To-day thou shalt be with me in paradise.' The day came to an end, both died, and they went, but they found neither paradise nor resurrection. The saying did not come true. Listen: that man was the highest of all on earth . . . There has never been any one like Him before or since, and never will be . . . And if that is so, if the laws of Nature did not spare even *Him,* and made even him live in the midst of lies and die for a lie, then the whole planet is a lie and is based on a lie and a stupid mockery. So the very laws of the planet are a lie and a farce of the devil. What, then, is there to live for?"[29] And Tolstoy, too, was nearly driven to suicide when he came to doubt the existence of God and an after-life.[30] And this is true of many.

What, then, is it that inclines us to think that if life is to have a meaning, there would be an after-life? It is this. The Christian world view contains the following three propositions. The first is that since the Fall, God's curse of Adam and Eve, and the expulsion from Paradise, life on earth for mankind has not been worth while, but a vale of tears, one long chain of misery, suffering, unhappiness, and injustice. The second is that a perfect after-life is awaiting us after the death of the body. The third is that we can enter this perfect life only on certain conditions, among which is also the condition of enduring our earthly existence to its bitter end. In this way, our earthly existence which, in itself, would not (at least for many people if not all) be worth living, acquires meaning and significance: only if we endure it, can we gain admission to the realm of the blessed.

It might be doubted whether this view is still held today. However, there can be no doubt that even today we all imbibe a good deal of this view with our earliest education. In sermons, the contrast between the perfect life of the blessed and our life of sorrow and drudgery is frequently driven home and we hear it again and again that Christianity has a message of hope and consolation for all those "who are weary and heavy laden."[31]

It is not surprising, then, that when the implications of the scientific world picture begin to sink in, when we come to have doubts about the existence of God and another life, we are bitterly disappointed. For if there is no afterlife, then all we are left is our earthly life which we have come to regard as a necessary evil, the painful fee of admission to the land of eternal bliss. But if there is no eternal bliss to come and if this hell on earth is all, why hang on till the horrible end?

Our disappointment therefore arises out of these two propositions, that the earthly life is not worth living, and that there is another perfect life of eternal happiness and joy which we may enter upon if we satisfy certain conditions. We can regard our lives as meaningful, if we believe both. We cannot regard them as meaningful if we believe merely the first and not the second. It seems to me inevitable that people who are taught something of the history of science, will have serious doubts about the second. If they cannot overcome these, as many will be unable to do, then they must either accept the sad view that their life is meaningless or they must abandon the first proposition: that this earthly life is not worth living. They must find the meaning of their life in this earthly existence. But is this possible?

A moment's examination will show us that the Christian evaluation of our earthly life as worthless, which we accept in our moments of pessimism and dissatisfaction, is not one that we normally accept. Consider only the question of murder and suicide. On the Christian view, other things being equal, the most kindly thing to do would be for every one of us to kill as many of our friends and dear ones as still have the misfortune to be alive, and then to commit suicide without delay, for every moment spent in this life is wasted. On the Christian view, God has not made it that easy for us. He has forbidden us to hasten others or ourselves into the next life. Our bodies are his private property and must be allowed to wear themselves out in the way decided by Him, however painful and horrible that may be. We are, as it were, driving a burning car. There is only one way out, to jump clear and let it hurtle to destruction. But the owner of the car has forbidden it on pain of eternal tortures worse than burning. And so we do better to burn to death inside.

On this view, murder is a less serious wrong than suicide. For murder can always be confessed and repented and therefore forgiven, suicide cannot—unless we allow the ingenious way out chosen by the heroine of Graham Greene's play, The Living Room, who swallows a slow but deadly poison and, while awaiting its taking effect, repents having taken it. Murder, on the other hand, is not so serious because, in the first place, it need not rob the victim of anything but the last lap of his march in the vale of tears, and, in the second place, it can always be forgiven. Hamlet, it will be remembered, refrains from killing his uncle during the latter's prayers because, as a true Christian, he believes that killing his uncle at that point, when the latter has purified his soul by repentance, would merely be doing him a good turn, for murder at such a time would simply despatch him to undeserved and everlasting happiness.

These views strike us as odd, to say the least. They are the logical consequence of the official medieval evaluation of this our earthly existence. If this life is not worth living, then taking it is not robbing the person concerned of much. The only thing wrong with it is the damage to God's property, which is the same both in the case of murder and suicide. We do not take this view at all. Our view, on the contrary, is that murder is the most serious wrong because it consists in taking away from some one else against his will his most precious possession, his life. For this reason, when a person suffering from an incurable disease asks to be killed, the mercy killing of such a person is regarded as a much less serious crime than murder because, in such a case, the killer is not robbing the other of a good against his will. Suicide is not regarded as a real crime at all, for we take the view that a person can do with his own possessions what he likes.

However, from the fact that these are our normal opinions, we can infer nothing about their truth. After all, we could easily be mistaken. Whether life is or is not worthwhile, is a value judgment. Perhaps all this is merely a matter of opinion or taste. Perhaps no objective answer can be given. Fortunately, we need not enter deeply into these difficult and controversial questions. It is quite easy to show that the medieval evaluation of earthly life is based on a misguided procedure.

Let us remind ourselves briefly of how we arrive at our value judgments. When we determine the merits of students, meals, tennis players, bulls, or bathing belles, we do so on the basis of some criteria and some standard or norm. Criteria and standards notoriously vary from field to field and even from case to case. But that does not mean that we have *no* idea about what are the appropriate criteria or standards to use. It would not be fitting to apply the criteria for judging bulls to the judgment of students or bathing belles. They score on quite different points. And even where the same criteria are appropriate as in the judgment of students enrolled in different schools and universities, the standards will vary from one institution to another. Pupils who would only just pass in one, would perhaps obtain honours in another. The higher the standard applied, the lower the marks, that is, the merit conceded to the candidate.

The same procedure is applicable also in the evaluation of a life. We examine it on the basis of certain criteria and standards. The medieval Christian view uses the criteria of the ordinary man: a life is judged by what the person concerned can get out of it: the balance of happiness over unhappiness, pleasure over pain, bliss over suffering. Our earthly life is judged not worth while because it contains much unhappiness, pain, and suffering, little happiness, pleasure, and bliss. The next life is judged worth while because it provides eternal bliss and no suffering.

Armed with these criteria, we can compare the life of this man and that, and judge which is more worth while, which has a greater balance of bliss over suffering. But criteria alone enable us merely to make comparative judgments of value, not absolute ones. We can say which is more and which is less worth while, but we cannot say which is worth while and which is not. In order to determine the latter, we must introduce a standard. But what standard ought we to choose?

Ordinarily, the standard we employ is the average of the kind. We call a man and a tree tall if they are well above the average of their kind. We do not say that Jones is a short man because he is shorter than a tree. We do not judge a boy a bad student because his answer to a question in the Leaving Examination is much worse than that given in reply to the same question by a young man sitting for his finals for the Bachelor's degree.

The same principles must apply to judging lives. When we ask whether a given life was or was not worth while, then we must take into consideration the range of worthwhileness which ordinary lives normally cover. Our end poles of the scale must be the best possible and the worst possible life that one finds. A good and worthwhile life is one that is well above average. A bad one is one well below.

The Christian evaluation of earthly lives is misguided because it adopts a quite unjustifiably high standard. Christianity singles out the major shortcomings of our earthly existence: there is not enough happiness; there is too much suffering; the good and bad points are quite unequally and unfairly distributed; the underprivileged and underendowed do not get adequate compensation; it lasts only a short time. It then quite accurately depicts the perfect or ideal life as that which does not have any of these shortcomings. Its next step is to promise the believer that he will be able to enjoy this perfect life later on. And then it adopts as its standard of judgment the perfect life, dismissing as inadequate anything that falls short of it. Having dismissed earthly life as miserable, it further damns it by characterizing most of the pleasures of which earthly existence allows as bestial, gross, vile, and sinful, or alternatively as not really pleasurable.

This procedure is as illegitimate as if I were to refuse to call anything tall unless it is infinitely tall, or anything beautiful unless it is perfectly flawless, or any one strong unless he is omnipotent. Even if it were true that there is available to us an after-life which is flawless and perfect, it would still not be legitimate to judge earthly lives by this standard. We do not fail every candidate who is not an Einstein. And if we do not believe in an after-life, we must of course use ordinary earthly standards.

I have so far only spoken of the worthwhileness, only of what a person can get out of a life. There are other kinds of appraisal. Clearly, we evaluate people's lives not merely from the point of view of what they yield to the persons that lead them, but also from that of other men on whom these lives have impinged. We judge a life more significant if the person has contributed to the happiness of others, whether directly by what he did for others, or by the plans, discoveries, inventions, and work he performed. Many lives that hold little in the way of pleasure or happiness for its owner are highly significant and valuable, deserve admiration and respect on account of the contributions made.

It is now quite clear that death is simply irrelevant. If life can be worthwhile at all, then it can be so even though it be short. And if it is not worthwhile at all, then an eternity of it is simply a nightmare. It may be sad that we have to leave this beautiful world, but it is so only if and because it is beautiful. And it is no less beautiful for coming to an end. I rather suspect that an eternity of it might make us less appreciative, and in the end it would be tedious.

It will perhaps be objected now that I have not really demonstrated that life has a meaning, but merely that it can be worthwhile or have value. It must be admitted that there is a perfectly natural interpretation of the question, "What is the meaning of life?" on which my view actually proves that life has no meaning. I mean the interpretation discussed in section 2 of this lecture, where I attempted to show that, if we accept the explanations of natural science, we cannot believe that living organisms have appeared on earth in accordance with the deliberate plan of some intelligent being. Hence, on this view, life cannot be said to have a purpose, in the sense in which man-made things have a purpose. Hence it cannot be said to have a meaning or significance in that sense.

However, this conclusion is innocuous. People are disconcerted by the thought that *life as such* has no meaning in that sense only because they very naturally think it entails that no individual life can have meaning either. They naturally assume that *this* life or *that* can have meaning only if *life as such* has meaning. But it should by now be clear that your life and mine may or may not have meaning (in one sense) even if life as such has none (in the other). Of course, it follows from this that your life may have meaning while mine has not. The Christian view guarantees a meaning (in one sense) to every life, the scientific view does not (in any sense). By relating the question of the meaning-fulness of life to the particular circumstances of an individual's existence, the scientific view leaves it an open question whether an individual's life has meaning or not. It is, however, clear that the latter is the important sense of "having a meaning." Christians, too, must feel that their life is wasted and meaningless if they have not achieved salvation. To know that even such lost lives have a meaning in another sense is no consolation to them. What matters is not that life should have a guaranteed meaning, whatever happens here or here-after, but that, by luck (Grace) or the right temperament and attitude (Faith) or a judicious life (Works) a person should make the most of his life.

"But here lies the rub," it will be said. "Surely, it makes all the difference whether there is an after-life. This is where morality comes in." It would be a mistake to believe that. Morality is not the meting out of punishment and reward. To be moral is to refrain from doing to others what, if they followed reason, they would not do to themselves, and to do for others what, if they followed reason, they would want to have done. It is, roughly speaking, to recognize that others, too, have a right to a worthwhile life. Being moral does not make one's own life worthwhile, it helps others to make theirs so.

Conclusion

I have tried to establish three points: (i) that scientific explanations render their explicanda as intelligible as pre-scientific explanations; they differ from the latter only in that, having testable implications and being more precisely formulated, their truth or falsity can be determined with a high degree of probability; (ii) that science does not rob human life of purpose, in the only sense that matters, but, on the contrary, renders many more of our purposes capable of realization; (iii) that common sense, the Christian world view, and the scientific approach agree on the criteria but differ on the standard to be employed in the evaluation of human lives; judging human lives by the standards of perfection, as Christians do, is unjustified; if we abandon this excessively high standard and replace it by an everyday one, we have no longer any reason for dismissing earthly existence as not worthwhile.

On the basis of these three points I have attempted to explain why so many people come to the conclusion that human existence is meaningless and to show that this conclusion is false. In my opinion, this pessimism rests on a combination of two beliefs, both partly true and partly false: the belief that the meaningfulness of life depends on the satisfaction of at least three conditions, and the belief that this universe satisfies none of them. The conditions are, first, that the universe is intelligible, second, that life has a purpose, and third, that all men's hopes and desires can ultimately be satisfied. It seemed to medieval Christians and it seems to many Christians today that Christianity offers a picture of the world which can meet these conditions. To many Christians and non-Christians alike it seems that the scientific world picture is incompatible with that of Christianity, therefore with the view that these three conditions are met, therefore with the view that life has a meaning. Hence they feel that they are confronted by the dilemma of accepting either a world picture incompatible with the discoveries of science or the view that life is meaningless.

I have attempted to show that the dilemma is unreal because life can be meaningful even if not all of these conditions are met. My main conclusion, therefore, is that acceptance of the scientific world picture provides no reason for saying that life is meaningless, but on the contrary every reason for saying that there are many lives which are meaningful and significant. My subsidiary conclusion is that one of the reasons frequently offered for retaining the Christian world picture, namely, that its acceptance gives us a guarantee of a meaning for human existence, is unsound. We can see that our lives can have a meaning even if we abandon it and adopt the scientific world picture instead. I have, moreover, mentioned several reasons for rejecting the Christian world picture: (i) the biblical explanations of the details of our universe are often simply false; (ii) the so-called explanations of the whole universe are incomprehensible or absurd; (iii) Christianity's low evaluation of earthly existence (which is the main cause of the belief in the meaninglessness of life) rests on the use of an unjustifiably high standard of judgment.

NOTES

1. Count Leo Tolstoy, "A Confession," reprinted in *A Confession, The Gospel in Brief, and What I Believe,* No. 229, The World's Classics (London: Geoffrey Cumberlege, 1940).

2. See e.g. Edwyn Bevan, *Christianity,* pp. 211–227. See also H. J. Paton, *The Modern Predicament* (London: George Allen and Unwin Ltd., 1955) pp. 103–116, 374.

3. See for instance, L. E. Elliott-Binns, *The Development of English Theology in the Later Nineteenth Century* (London: Longmans, Green & Co., 1952) pp. 30–33.

4. See "Phaedo" (*Five Dialogues* by Plato, Everyman's Library No. 456) para. 99, p. 189.

5. "On the Ultimate Origination of Things" (*The Philosophical Writings of Leibniz,* Everyman's Library No. 905) p. 32.

6. See "Monadology" (*The Philosophical Writings of Leibniz,* Everyman's Library No. 905) para. 32–38, pp. 8–10.

7. To borrrow the useful term coined by Professor D. A. T. Gasking of Melbourne University.

8. See e.g., J. J. C. Smart, "The Existence of God," reprinted in *New Essays in Philosophical Theology,* ed. by A. Flew and A. MacIntyre (London: S.C.M. Press, 1957) pp. 35–39.

9. That creation out of nothing is not a clarificatory notion becomes obvious when we learn that "in the philosophical sense" it does not imply creation at a particular time. The universe could be regarded as a creation out of nothing even if it had no beginning. See e.g. E. Gilson, *The Christian Philosophy of St. Thomas Aquinas* (London: Victor Gollancz Ltd. 1957) pp. 147–155 and E. L. Mascall, *Via Media* (London: Longmans, Green & Co., 1956) pp. 28 ff.

10. In what follows I have drawn heavily on the work of Ryle and Toulmin. See for instance G. Ryle, *The Concept of Mind* (London: Hutchinson's University Library, 1949) pp. 56–60 &c. and his article, "If, So, and Because," in *Philosophical Analysis* by Max Black, and S. E. Toulmin, *Introduction to the Philosophy of Science* (London: Hutchinson's University Library, 1953).

11. See above, p. 10, points (a)–(c).

12. L. Wittgenstein, *Tractatus Logico-*Philosophicus (London: Routledge & Kegan Paul Ltd., 1922), Sect. 6.44–6.45.

13. Op. cit. p. 46. See also Rudolf Otto, *The Idea of the Holy* (London: Geoffrey Cumberlege, 1952) esp. pp. 9–29.

14. Contemporary theologians would admit that it cannot be proved that the universe must have had a beginning. They would admit that we know it only through revelation. (See footnote No. 9.) I take it more or less for granted that Kant's attempted proof of the Thesis in his First Antinomy of Reason [Immanuel Kant's *Critique of Pure Reason,* trans. by Norman Kemp Smith (London: Macmillan and Co. Ltd., 1950) pp. 396–402] is invalid. It rests on a premise which is false: that the completion of the infinite series of succession of states, which must have preceded the present state if the world has had no beginning, is logically impossible. We can persuade ourselves to think that this infinite series is logically impossible if we insist that it is a series which must, literally, be *completed.* For the verb "to complete," as normally used, implies an activity which, in turn, implies

an agent who must have *begun* the activity at some time. If an infinite series is a whole that must be *completed* then, indeed, the world must have had a beginning. But that is precisely the question at issue. If we say, as Kant does at first, "that an eternity has elapsed," we do not feel the same impossibility. It is only when we take seriously the words "synthesis" and "completion," both of which suggest or imply "work" or "activity" and therefore "beginning," that it seems necessary that an infinity of successive states cannot have elapsed. [See also R. Crawshay-Williams, *Methods and Criteria of Reasoning* (London: Routledge & Kegan Paul, 1957) App. iv.]

15. See e.g. "Is Life Worth Living?" B.B.C. Talk by the Rev. John Sutherland Bonnell in *Asking Them Questions,* Third Series, ed. by R. S. Wright (London: Geoffrey Cumberlege, 1950).

16. See e.g. Rudolf Otto, *The Idea of the Holy,* pp. 9–11. See also C. A. Campbell, *On Selfhood and Godhood* (London: George Allen & Unwin Ltd., 1957) p. 246, and H. J. Paton, *The Modern Predicament,* pp. 69–71.

17. For a discussion of this issue, see the eighteenth century controversy between Deists and Theists, for instance, in Sir Leslie Stephen's *History of English Thought in the Eighteenth Century* (London: Smith, Elder & Co., 1902) pp. 112–119 and pp. 134–163. See also the attacks by Toland and Tindal on "the mysterious" in *Christianity not Mysterious* and *Christianity as Old as the Creation, or the Gospel a Republication of the Religion of Nature,* resp., parts of which are reprinted in Henry Bettenson's *Doctrines of the Christian Church,* pp. 426–431. For modern views maintaining that mysteriousness is an essential element in religion, see Rudolf Otto, *The Idea of the Holy,* esp. pp. 25–40, and most recently M. B. Foster, *Mystery and Philosophy* (London: S.C.M. Press, 1957) esp. Chs. IV. and VI. For the view that statements about God must be nonsensical or absurd, see e.g. H. J. Paton, op. cit. pp. 119–120, 367–369. See also "Theology and Falsification" in *New Essays in Philosophical Theology,* ed. by A. Flew and A. MacIntyre (London: S.C.M. Press, 1955) pp. 96–131; also N. McPherson, "Religion as the Inexpressible," ibid, esp. pp. 137–143.

18. Stephen Neill, *Christian Faith To-day* (London: Penguin Books, 1955) pp. 240–241.

19. It is difficult to feel the magnitude of this first sin unless one takes seriously the words, "Behold, the man has eaten of the fruit of the tree of knowledge of good and evil, and is become as one of us; and now, may he not put forth his hand, and take also of the tree of life, and eat, and live for ever?" Genesis iii, 22.

20. See in this connection the pastoral letter of 2nd February, 1905, by Johannes Katschtaler, Prince Bishop of Salzburg on the honour due to priests, contained in *Quellen zur Geschichte des Papsttums,* by Mirbt pp. 497–9, translated and reprinted in *The Protestant Tradition,* by J. S. Whale (Cambridge: University Press, 1955) pp. 259–262.

21. How impossible it is to make sense of this story has been demonstrated beyond any doubt by Tolstoy in his famous "Conclusion of A Criticism of Dogmatic Theology," reprinted in *A Confession, The Gospel in Brief, and What I Believe.*

22. See "The Nicene Creed," "The Tridentine Profession of Faith," "The Syllabus of Errors," reprinted in *Documents of the Christian Church,* pp. 34, 373 and 380 resp.

23. See e.g. J. S. Whale, *The Protestant Tradition,* Ch. IV., esp. pp. 48–56.

24. See ibid., pp. 61 ff.

25. See "The Confession of Augsburg" esp. Articles II., IV., XVIII., XIX., XX.; "Christianae Religionis Institutio," "The Westminster Confession of Faith," esp. Articles III., VI., IX., X., XI., XVI., XVII.; "The Baptist Confession of Faith," esp. Articles III., XXI., XXIII., reprinted in *Documents of the Christian Church,* pp. 294 ff., 298 ff., 344 ff., 349 ff.

26. See e.g. his *An Empiricist's View of the Nature of Religious Belief* (Eddington Memorial Lecture).

27. See e.g. the two series of Gifford Lectures most recently published: *The Modern Predicament* by H. J. Paton (London: George Allen & Unwin Ltd., 1955) pp. 69 ff. and *On Selfhood and Godhood* by C. A. Campbell (London: George Allen & Unwin Ltd., 1957) pp. 231–250.

28. Rudolf Otto, *The Idea of the Holy,* p. 9.

29. Fyodor Dostoyevsky, *The Devils* (London: The Penguin Classics, 1953) pp. 613–614.

30. Leo Tolstoy, *A Confession, The Gospel in Brief, and What I Believe,* The World's Classics, p. 24.

31. See for instance J. S. Whale, *Christian Doctrine,* pp. 171, 176–178, &c. See also Stephen Neill, *Christian Faith To-day,* p. 241.

27

From Weber to Habermas

Robert Hollinger

I. The Dialectics of Objectivism

In many respects, all the issues about science and values discussed in Part 5 represent the logical culmination of the dialectic of Objectivism that begins with Descartes and Galileo. It will be helpful to briefly summarize this view (which is spelled out in more detail elsewhere in this book).[1] According to Objectivism, the world, which is the subject of scientific investigation, is governed by laws and processes that are quite independent of human beliefs, values, desires, and interpretations. Knowledge must mirror or correspond to the objective world; and our methods must also be objective, i.e., unbiased and nonpersonal, so as to guarantee this result. But this requires that science and our methods must purge themselves of anything subjective, i.e., any biases, psychological factors, values, etc., that would prevent our methods from resulting in objective knowledge. On this view, claims not capable of being described in the language of science, and any method that is not totally person free, and interest neutral, must be discarded. Hence, value judgments must either (A) be capable of being expressed in the language of science or else (B) are merely subjective expressions of preferences, and not truth claims, and thus belong outside of science.

The first of these attitudes towards value judgments, i.e., (A), attempts to turn ethical and political questions into scientific or technological problems, especially within modern utilitarian and cost-benefit terms. Value judgments are divided into two types: "categorical" and "instrumental." A categorical value judgment is of the form "X is good/bad" or "X is right/wrong." Some categorical value judgments are said to be "ultimate" or "basic," i.e., since they don't derive from any other values or from any facts. Instrumental value judgments are judgments about what is the best means of achieving some categorical (including basic) values. Categorical values are often called "intrinsic" values, because they are valued for themselves; e.g., health, pleasure, happiness. Instrumental values are usually sought because they help us realize other valued things, especially intrinsic values. Thus, if health is an intrinsic value, going to the doctor is an instrumental one, relative to the value we place on health. Health, and some intrinsic values, may also be instrumentally valued with respect to other values. And some instrumental values may, in some situations, be regarded as instrinsic values. Those who talk about ultimate values often believe that some values are only intrinsic and that all other values are really instrumental to the realization of our ultimate values.

Thesis (A) can now be expressed as follows. All ultimate values must be expressible in the language of science. But since the language of science is a description of the Objective world, all ultimate value judgments are descriptions of some aspect of the objective world. E.g., the "naturalistic" view of values, according to which "good" means "whatever human beings ultimately value," implies that it is just a fact about human beings that if pleasure is our ultimate value, good just is pleasure. We cannot raise the question whether it is right or wrong, good or bad, that somebody values X because it gives him/her pleasure. Ultimate values cannot be proved right or wrong, good or bad. We can only prove that people do have them. More generally, no categorical value judgment can be proven or disproven as right or wrong, good or bad, by science. Instrumental values, which tell us how to maximize our categorical (and thus our ultimate) values, can be shown by science to either effectively maximize our categorical values or not. Utilitarianism and modern cost-benefit analysis are the expressions of these assumptions. Given any ultimate value (or categorical value judgment) X, all we need to do is to discover which means or instrumental value will get us X in the most cost efficient way. (See Hempel's in Part 5.) So ethics becomes a branch of applied science: we need to predict how to realize our ultimate and other categorical values in the most rational ways open to us. This is sometimes called the thesis of technological or instrumental rationality. (See Introduction to Part 6.)

The second way of dealing with values, i.e., (B), is the idea that all value judgments, perhaps even scientific knowledge itself, to the extent that it relies on value judgments, are either arbitrary, nonrational, or irrational. They are the result of sociological, cultural, and psychological factors that can explain the prevalence of certain ideas and values, but cannot justify them on "rational" grounds. Thus, many versions of Marxism, which take knowledge and value claims to be "ideological," and writings in the "Sociology of Knowledge," explain our scientific beliefs and moral values in cultural, economic, and historical terms, while presupposing thereby that questions about their truth and rationality are out of the question. On some versions of (B), basic values are just matters of taste, and therefore cannot be rationally discussed or shown to be right or wrong, good or bad. The basic argument in either case is that only science contains statements that can be true or false, and thus objective.

Ethics does not contain such statements, and cannot be reformulated in the language of science. Therefore ethics does not express or deal with knowledge.

It seems as if (A) and (B) are in some ways different and even incompatible views. But some writers believe that in at least one crucial respect they amount to the same thing. The claim that these two approaches to values amount to the same thing was first articulated by Edmund Husserl (1859-1938), the founder of Phenomenology. In Kuhn's language, the claim is that (A) and (B) are variants of a single paradigm. The underlying assumptions of this paradigm: (1) Everything is divided into the "objective" and the "subjective." (2) Only scientific Knowledge is objective. (3) Ultimate value judgments are either scientific or subjective. (4) Ultimate values, whether they are taken to reflect basic facts about human nature, personal decisions, or a culture's dominant values, cannot be rationally debated, or proven right or wrong, good or bad. Husserl believed that both (A) and (B) are embodied in the logic of Objectivism. On this view, (A) an (B) lead to the view that there are no moral absolutes; that there is no rational way of assessing the great variety of ultimate value judgments; the unreflective acceptance of certain values; the growing inability of society to reach rational agreement about ethical issues. In short, they lead to wholesale acceptance of whatever ultimate values in fact exist, even if they rest upon prejudice.

But we should be able to be reflective about our basic moral judgments, discuss them, criticize them, and correct them in rational ways. We should also aspire to some sort of universal moral consensus or agreement. But (A) and (B), according to Husserl, do not let us do so. This is the force of his claim that they must accept basic values as "given."

All "naturalistic" attempts to reduce human values and mental life to the law of the natural and physical sciences actually presuppose, for Husserl, an allegiance to certain values, e.g., science is the best way of enhancing human life, that ultimate values cannot be proven right, or even questioned, within the framework of modern science. Such a judgment of ultimate value must be accepted without being provable. But in denying the possibility of rationally defending ultimate values, modern science simultaneously rests upon a set of values: those embedded in the dominant views about knowledge and values mentioned above under (A) and (B). Husserl claimed that this picture thus rested on a contradiction. Moreover, by being unable and unwilling to question its own methods and assumptions, modern science is unable to raise, let alone address, questions about its own significance. The value of modern science as the best way of enhancing human life is thus (on his view) an assumption. Yet the scientific views about knowledge and values have become the dominant views of our culture. But what if these views are just unfounded prejudices, asks Husserl? In particular, what if the view that only the modern sciences tell us what's real, true, or valuable is unjustified and unjustifiable? What would we be left with? Nothing, according to Husserl. That is, our culture would be pervaded by nihilism, the claim that everything is meaningless and without value, which is just what Husserl believed had happened to Western culture.

Husserl believed that the cultural and political implications of both of these versions of nihilism are very dangerous. Husserl wanted to be able to get behind the unexamined prejudices that underlie both of these views, to show that modern science and human values equally are rooted in the practical activities of human beings, which could eventually be shown to rest upon universal and rational criteria. He hoped that we could eventually undermine both objectivism and the various ramifications of it, discussed under (A) and (B) above.

II. Weber

Max Weber's (1864-1920) views about knowledge, reality, and values manage to combine themes from both (A) and (B). Our world is a meaningless, infinite flux. In order to understand it, we have to adopt some point of view, which is determined by our personal interests and values, or by those of our culture. This is the thesis of "value relevance." Our values and interests, which are subjective, give us an angle of vision on a narrow range of data, which can then be explained scientifically, i.e., objectively. For example, if we decide to find out why there are more suicides in the United States during the Christmas season than at other times of the year, our interests and values determine what we'll study. We can still get some objective answers to the questions we pose, if we use scientific method in an unbiased way. But our quest for knowledge is always severely restricted, since the world, and therefore any chunk of it we may want to study, is tremendously complex, and since there are any number of equally valid, but equally arbitrary, points of view we can adopt. For instance, we can study nature in many ways and for many reasons, and from many points of view. Each point of view is limited: it lets us understand only very small bits of nature. We can never, according to Weber, explain everything within the framework of any one point of view or theory. The world is too complex and we are too ignorant to even hope for a unified account of everything. This is even more true of any attempt to study human history or society. We can, for example, study Western culture from an unlimited number of perspectives. Moreover, Weber believed that we cannot expect to piece all of them together to get a unified and coherent history of our culture. So there is a sense in which Weber does undermine the idea of objective knowledge, if this is construed as the search for a unified scientific world picture (as Objectivism aspires to be).

In addition, value judgments are subjective for Weber, because they cannot be proven by science. Thus, the sciences must be value free or value neutral. Categorical value judgments are subjective. Science can tell us what the consequences of subjectively based decisions are, so that we can be aware of the consequences of our actions. This is what Weber calls "the ethics of responsibility." Modern societies must be governed by this model: public (and private) actions and policies are a combination of arbitrary preferences and cost-effective means for achieving them.

Let us consider the political implications of this view. In modern liberal democracies there exists a plurality of interests, points of view, values, and goals. (One need only reflect upon the abortion controversy.) How can democratic societies prevent chaos, and institute public policies? Weber's answer is roughly this: The values and goals of our political leaders are no more rational than those of anybody else. But leaders must be strong enough to convince legislators and bureaucrats to accept their goals and policies. They must, at the same time, exercise the ethics of responsibility by consulting scientific experts, who will advise them of the consequences, and thus the wisdom, of their values and decisions. (For Weber, scientists cannot make political decisions, because the sciences must be value-free, and because value judgments are subjective.) Responsible political leaders will also have some convictions, but will balance these moral ideals with an assessment of the consequences of acting upon them. Considering only consequences is dangerous, because it can lead to expediency at the cost of noble ideals. Attention to ideals regardless of the consequences leads to fanaticism, which is (at least) equally dangerous in a political leader.

Weber's views about science, values, and politics dominate the world today. Political and moral issues become technological problems, and political goals and values are the result of a so-called consensus of all the interests involved, or else are taken to be "obvious," "rational," or even scientifically proven (given the use of the utilitarian idea that it is rational to maximize benefits over costs). All value judgments are equally valid, all points of view must have their say, we must be tolerant of all points of view and use cost-benefit analysis, together with the democratic political process, to arrive at "rational," value-neutral, "scientific" solutions to our problems. Since the values of individuals and a culture must be accepted as "givens," yet are all equally subjective, politics takes the form of a power struggle among the various values and interests, with the "right" solution being determined by whoever has the most power or persuasive force and a cost-benefit argument that their interests will benefit the greatest number of people.

What are the practical implications of all this? On some views, modern life oscillates between two ideals: the view that all social and personal problems require some combination of scientific knowledge, technological expertise and cost-benefit analysis; and the idea that politics is a continual power struggle among competing values and interests. On either alternative (in practice they are often combined), some fear, democracy is in danger (either by a growing technological form of public decision making, or by virtue of an increasing lack of basic consensus). Thus, many people seem to believe that our judgment (say) not to help starving people in another country can be justified in cost-benefit terms (promoting their survival will make things worse, given the world population problem and the scarcity of world resources) or else the judgment whether to help or not becomes almost a matter of taste or individual preference.

If these fears are well founded, we may well ask what has gone wrong. How can we explain how modern science, together with liberal, humane values, result in this state of affairs?

III. Between Weber and Habermas

There have been a number of answers to this question, beginning perhaps with the analysis of Western culture that one finds in Friedrich Nietzsche (1844-1900), Karl Marx (1818-1883), as well as Weber himself. Nietzsche claimed that our culture is dominated by nihilism, and that the modern scientific outlook is rooted in the belief in God and in an absolute, objective perspective on the universe. But this illusion is actually rooted in certain values and interests, which Nietzsche believed are unhealthy, because they are symptomatic of a hatred for life, of diversity and change (and ultimately a fear of death). The belief in moral absolutes is part of this same cluster of values. Nietzsche believed that individuals should learn to affirm life and create their own values. He also felt society needs strong creative leaders, who would be artists and philosophers, and not scientists or technicians. They would create a set of cultural ideal and values, and society would not be democratic, but guided by this elite class of creative people. Life requires the dominance of healthy artistic illusions, on Nietzsche's view, since only art affirms life.

While Marx did believe in objective truth, he also believed it was necessary to see that all knowledge is rooted in human interests. It is only the interest that the downtrodden have in unmasking the ideological distortions of dominant views of knowledge, truth, and values—which served the economic interests of the ruling class—that make objective knowledge possible, because this was the only universal interest. (Hence, objective knowledge is not interest free; it is rooted in universal human interests.) So for Marx most of our beliefs and values are not true, but ideological underpinnings of the existing social order. We need to analyze and unmask the economic sources of these forms of "false consciousness" until we achieve a socialist society, where the gap between appearance and reality will be overcome, thereby making it possible to dispense with many forms of theory, in favor of a science that would give a free people the information they need to carry on their cooperative life activities.

Weber, who was strongly influenced by Marx and Nietzsche, was quite pessimistic about the dominance of technological rationality and the subjectivity of values in the modern world. But he was also very fatalistic about the possibilities of overcoming "the iron cage" in which these two factors put us. More recently, Martin Heidegger (1889-1976) has claimed that modern science is a manifestion of the will to power, our drive to dominate and control the world. Modern science is essentially technological. Moreover, Heidegger (influenced by Husserl, whom he worked under) argues against the objectivist idea that science gives us a privileged access to truth, knowledge, rational methods, and values. This is a prejudice, according to Heidegger, and is really a manifestation of nihilism. Another group of recent authors, notably Michel Foucault (1927-1984) and Jacques Derrida (b. 1930) combine insights from Nietzsche, Marx, Freud, and Heidegger to argue that Western science is essentially rooted in the will to power, which leads to dominating political practices. Many Marxists, e.g., Herbert Marcuse (1898-1979) had already combined these insights in the thirties to show that the ideal of dominating nature inevitably leads to the domination of human beings, through the development of the human sciences and the transformation of ethics and politics into branches of technology, dominated by capitalism and the model of cost-benefit analysis that is controlled by "experts."[2]

The upshot of all these analyses was a growing cultural pessimism, a move-ment away from science and humanistic—liberal ideals, an emphasis on rebellion and on art as a source of liberation; in short, a distrust of the entire Enlighten-ment. All of these writers believed that the Enlightenment project of enhancing human life through the application of more and more scientific knowledge to society had in fact resulted in just the reverse of enlightenment and liberation. Moreover, knowledge itself—especially modern natural and human science—was rooted in power relations, capitalism, the will to power, and not (arguably) in value-free objective methods and results. Hence, they believed that the Enlightenment had to fail, and thus must be completely rejected. It is one of Habermas's goals to show that this analysis is a mistake, even though he agrees that the liberating potential of the Enlightenment has not yet been fully realized.

IV. Habermas

In the remainder of this paper I want to consider the views of Jurgen Habermas (b. 1929), a contemporary German philosopher and social theorist, because he not only provides a systematic interpretretation and criticism of Weber, but also develops an important alternative picture of science, culture, and values that provides a more positive assessment of science than do the views of Nietzsche, Heidegger, Foucault, and Derrida. To some extent he agrees with their criticisms of modern society, but thinks it is too one-sided and overly pessimistic. Since Habermas's views are very complex, I shall summarize his main thoughts in a very brief and general way.[3]

In his earlier writings[4] Habermas develops the following criticism of Weber: Weber's views combine "scientism" and "decisionism." "Scientism" is the doctrine that only the results and methods of the physical and natural sciences are valid and rational. There is only one type of knowledge and one rational method. All other disciplines and practices must either be assimilated to the doctrines of the natural and physical sciences and their methods (of prediction, control, and technological rationality) or else be dismissed as irrational and not knowledge. "Decisionism" is the view that since "categorical" value judg-ments can be neither reduced to scientific knowledge nor proved by science, and therefore not by scientific method, they are the expressions of personal and arbitrary decisions. Scientism and decisionism are two sides of the same coin, according to Habermas.

Habermas believes that Weber's views, which are representative of most of Western thinking since the time of Galileo, are an expression of how scientism and decisionism are related. What Habermas does, in effect, is to provide an alternative conception of knowledge and values that undermines these two views, while also providing an argument that the pessimism of Weber and others confuses the fact that the Enlightenment project has not been realized with the false claim that it cannot be realized and must be abandoned in favor of an aesthetic model of culture, politics, and human existence.

In his book, *Knowledge and Human Interests,*[5] Habermas, who shares the idea that knowledge is rooted in universal human interests, and is not interest-free, isolates three perennial human interests. (These are historically necessary features of human life; Habermas does not try to defend the Platonic vision outlined in the Introduction to Part 5.) These are the "technical," the "practical," and "the emancipatory" interests. The "technical" interest relates to the human need to control nature for survival. "Labor" is the form of activity that fulfills this need. Modern science and cost-benefit rationality best serve this interest by allowing us to predict and control nature in rational ways. The practical interest is the interest in human communication, interaction, and a common life. This interest in "interaction" requires us to understand human behavior by adopting something like the methods advocated by W. H. Dray in his essay in Part 2 of the present volume. The human sciences cannot model themselves on the physical and natural sciences, but must find ways of understanding and interpreting human communication and interaction. They must be "hermeneutical" or "interpretive" (more like a dialogue than an experiment) and must allow us to enhance our capacity for human communication. Public life must also revitalize these ideals, which involves abandoning the notion that ethics and policies are branches of technology, and that only the experts in society have the right to participate in public debate and decision-making.[6] Finally, the emancipatory interest is the idea that knowledge should enhance our freedom and improve human life by emancipating us from oppressive forces: material, political, psychological, and ideological. "Critical theory" is that type of knowledge which best furthers this goal. In particular, it makes it possible to reflect about our basic values and beliefs, and to debate them rationally. (More about this later.)

Ideally, all three interests, and each type of knowledge—natural science, human science, critical theory—should do their proper job and work in harmony with each other. But when scientism and decisionism dominate, this does not happen. Instead, practical and emacipatory interests are reduced to the technical interest, i.e., all problems become technological problems. And all forms of knowledge are reduced to the knowledge of nature that we get from the physical and natural sciences. For Habermas, it is only the abuse of the physical and natural sciences and their technological model of rationality that causes our social problems. If left to their proper business, they would be most helpful and not dangerous. So Habermas does not want to reject or even criticize science or technical rationality, but only put them in their place, and foster the development of the other two human interests and their type of knowledge.

He therefore thinks that attempts to substitute an aesthetic for a "rational" model of life and culture—or the attempt to reject the technical interest or reduce it to the practical—which, on his view, Marcuse, Heidegger, Nietzsche, Foucault, and Derrida advocate, is just as wrong as the attempt to reduce the practical sphere to the technical domain.

One direct outgrowth of Habermas's alternative to scientism/decisionism is an attempt to revitalize the classic conception of politics.[7] The Greeks, especially Aristotle, distinguished between "technical" and "practical" questions, and believed there were three types of knowledge: theoretical, practical and productive. Theoretical knowledge, e.g., science, had no relevance to ethical and political life, which was the realm of practical knowledge and included public discussion by citizens and common deliberation about goals. Politics is not a branch of technology, but involves genuine democracy. Productive knowledge, e.g., ship building, is governed by "techne," i.e., instrumental reason, that accepts goals, and (unlike politics) does not deliberate about them. For the Greeks, these are separate activities and forms of knowledge. Political consensus arrived at by dialogue is rational. It is only by requiring that political consensus be based on scientific or technological methods that decisionism can gain a foothold, according to Habermas. We tend to confuse the practical and the technical; we conceive of politics, human interaction, and liberation as resulting from the application of theoretical knowledge—cost-benefit analysis to the "applied" sphere. This is a dangerous mistake, according to Habermas.

To sum up, the dominant attitudes about science, values, and culture that Weber's views represent is the result of the illegitimate dominance of one type of knowledge, one human value or interest, and one type of decision procedure, on modern society. By articulating the practical and emancipatory interests/values, and indicating how they are best fulfilled by practical knowledge and critical theory, Habermas claims to have undermined scientism/decisionism, preserved what is worthwhile about science and technology, refuted the idea that politics is a branch of technology, and provided a vision of democracy as based upon rational dialogue rather than cost-benefit analysis.

In his more recent writings, Habermas recasts his earlier views.[8] He also tries to show that Weber and cultural pessimists such as Marcuse, Nietzsche, and Heidegger, confuse the fact that science and technological rationality have been abused and misused (which he agrees with) from the claim that science and technology are inherently dangerous and must lead to all the ills of modern society. The Enlightenment still has a liberating potential.

This potential is for a society based upon the beneficial dimensions of science and technology, as well as the ideal of genuine democracy through citizen participation in dialogue and shared rational consensus. Politics is neither a branch of technology nor a tug of war between competing arbitrary values, but a rational dialogue that is rooted in the classic notions of deliberation and practical knowledge. A genuine dialogue can only take place when the material and ideological obstacles to human communication and cooperation are eliminated. In an ideal situation, whenever an ultimate or categorical moral or political value or issue arose, people would consider only the relevant arguments and evidence for and against, in terms of aiming at what can give rise to a rational, open consensus. Everybody would have an equal opportunity to participate in the dialogue, which should culminate in an agreement that is free, rational, and in the general interest.

Habermas now talks about the two main components of modern society: the "Systems Sphere" of science, technology, corporate capitalism, and bureaucracy, and the "Cultural Sphere"—the realm of public and private life, morality, culture, and human interaction. The systems sphere has "colonized" the cultural sphere (the "lifeworld"). We must learn how to harmonize and integrate developments in the systems sphere and the lifeworld in order to achieve a world in which our knowledge can be used for truly liberating purposes in the cultural sphere as well as the systems sphere. We must, in other words, learn to integrate science and technology with our best political and moral ideals, which are continuously evolving. Habermas develops a model of human evolution as a collective learning device, and postulates the idea of selective evolution to explain the disparity between our growing scientific and technological knowledge and our relative lack of progress in the social and political spheres. We have not yet evolved to the point where we have in place genuinely democratic ways of achieving rational consensus, owing to the dominance of the technological and subjectivist views of values and politics. This is his answer to Weber. So our present task involves a theory of the evolution of society—and the differential development of our scientific knowledge and moral ideals—which allows us to measure the disparity between developments in the systems sphere and the lifeworld, while providing a model for their integration and for moral/political progress.

Habermas accepts the idea that moral progress involves the ability to take a universal and impartial view about moral and political issues. A dialogue about basic moral issues permits people to reflect about basic values, including their own, by subjecting them to criticism and correction. Only basic values that can be accepted by all partners to an open, rational discussion are acceptable. On this view, basic values can be rationally discussed, corrected, and move toward more universal acceptance, provided the political factors necessary to promote genuine dialogue exist.

NOTES

1. A good deal of my discussion, especially in this section, summarizes the material in the Introductions to Parts 5 and 6 in this volume.

2. See here, William Leiss, *The Domination of Nature*. Boston: Beacon, 1972.

3. See here, Thomas McCarthy, *The Critical Theory of Jurgen Habermas*. Cambridge, Mass.: MIT Press, 1978.

4. Jurgen Habermas, *Knowledge and Human Interests*. Boston: Beacon, 1971. *Toward a Rational Society*. Boston: Beacon, 1970. *Theory and Practice*. Boston: Beacon, 1973.

5. See especially *Knowledge and Human Interests*.

6. See especially *Toward a Rational Society*.

7. See especially *Theory and Practice*. Cf. McCarthy, *op. cit.* ch. 1.

8. See especially Jurgen Habermas. *Theory of Communicative Action* Vol. 1. Boston: Beacon, 1984, vol. 2, 1987. Jurgen Habermas *Communication and the Evolution of Society*. Boston: Beacon, 1979.

28

The Scientific Outlook:
Naturalism and Humanism

Herbert Feigl

The main purpose of this essay is to dispel certain confusions and misunder-standings which still prevent the much-needed constructive synthesis and mutual supplementation of the scientific and humanistic elements in general education. It is my contention that the philosophical foundations of both science and the humanities are widely misconceived; and that the frequently held claim of their basic incompatibilities arises out of philosophical prejudices which, owing to cultural lag, have unfortunately not as yet been completely relegated to oblivion. Science is still identified with an absurd mechanistic reductionism, but this is the caricature of science drawn by representatives of the humanities who are largely ignorant of the nature of modern science and also of the more recent scientific outlook in philosophy. The defenders of the humanities often enough increase the existing tension by holding an equally distorted view of the philosophical basis of the humanities.

The errors committed may well be characterized respectively as *reductive* and *seductive* fallacies. It is claimed that science either ignores (perhaps by its very method cannot help ignoring) or else explains away the most essential human values. Science is here charged with the reductive fallacy. Usually the same group of thinkers maintains also that there are aspects of the human mind, manifest especially in the domains of morality, religion, and the arts, which contain an irreducible spiritual element and for that reason will never be capable of explanation by the scientific method, no matter how far it advances. I call this fallacy seductive because it is usually committed by those who indulge in what William James called "tenderminded," that is, wishful and sentimental, thinking.

The impasse between seductive thesis and reductive antithesis can be overcome only by a constructive synthesis that retains and develops whatever valid suggestions or emphases we may discover underneath the grandiose verbiage of the first and the harsh austerities of the second. Neither a philosophy of the "Something More" nor a philosophy of the "Nothing But" will do for our time. Only an approach that is resolutely guided by the question "What is what?" will avoid reading mysteries into the facts, as well as refrain from impoverishing them by reduction to something less than experience attests them to be. Such a philosophical outlook, if not yet fully achieved, is fortunately very much in the making.

Especially in the melting pot of American thought, we find that the valuable elements of naturalism and humanism are gradually united in a new integration: the pragmatism of Peirce, James, Dewey, Mead, Otto, Kallen, and Hook; the naturalistic realism of Perry, Holt, R. W. Sellars, Drake, and Santayana; the scientific empiricism of Bridgman, Hull, Tolman, Lundberg, N. Weiner, P. Frank, C. Morris, Northrop, Carnap, Reichenbach, Nagel, and others; the liberal ("American Humanist") wing of Unitarianism. All these trends of thought and many others converge in a broad movement that one may well be tempted to regard as the twentieth-century sequel to the Enlightenment of the eighteenth century.

The humanism held in common to a very large extent in the scientifically oriented philosophies is too well known to require an elaborate restatement. Suffice it to say that such human values as freedom and responsibility, rights and obligations, creative and appreciative capacities, are here disengaged from the theological and metaphysical ideologies that have traditionally pervaded their conception. Increasingly adequate and nonreductive analyses have been propounded in the last five or six decades. This reconstruction in philosophy has been and still is in the making. Under the impact of modern science philosophy is abandoning some of its earlier grandiose and overambitious claims in favor of a humbler and more useful function: the clarification of the foundations of knowledge and valuation. I shall now attempt to apply what seem to me to be the most important insights and suggestions of these currents of thought to the issues of general education.

Clearly, nothing is more urgent for education today than a social philosophy that will be appropriate and workable in an age of science. Among the various prominent philosophies of education I mention first two currents which may be styled traditionalistic and which have on the whole either ignored the facts of the age of science or have tried (unsuccessfully, I think) to dispute and combat them: Neo-Thomism and Literary Humanism. Reliance on theological or metaphysical presuppositions makes these views incompatible with the modern scientific outlook. More definitely products of the modern scientific attitude are two other schools of thought: Dialectical Materialism, the official philosophy of Soviet Russia, but also fashionable in certain English scientific groups; and, scarcely worthy of being called a philosophy, the attitude of Vocationalism, quite prevalent in American education. The common element of these two views is their exclusive interest in the practical, technological applications of the natural and the social sciences. This, as well as other short-comings, makes both points of view appear objectionable or at least badly in need of correction or supplementation. A much more acceptable position is that of Scientific Humanism. This view, at least in general outlook, is related to what is known as Progressivism or Reconstructionism in American education: a synnthesis of the scientific attitude with an active interest in the whole scale of human values. Education in both the sciences *and* the humanities is the urgent need of our time. But how can these two aims properly be combined? The question reveals an uneasy feeling as to the compatibility of science and humanism.

Misunderstandings of the nature of science are primarily responsible for the appearance of incompatibility here. A proper historical and analytical perspective of the development of the scientific outlook and its distinctive traits as compared with prescientific and nonscientific attitudes helps to show that mankind achieves intellectual adulthood only with the scientific way of thinking.

Our age is still replete with remnants of and regressions to such prescientific thought patterns as magic, animism, mythology, theology, and metaphysics. The outstanding characteristics of modern scientific method are mostly absent or at best only adumbrated in those less mature phases of intellectual growth.

Criteria of the Scientific Method

What, then, are the basic characteristics of the scientific method? The often alleged difficulties of an adequate definition of science seem to me mainly a matter of terminology. We must first distinguished between pure mathematics as an exclusively formal-conceptual discipline, and the factual (or empirical, that is, the natural and the social-cultural) sciences. The certainty, complete exactitude, and necessity of pure mathematics depends precisely on its detachment from empirical fact. Mathematics as applied in the factual sciences merely lends its forms and deductive structures to the contents furnished by experience. But no matter how predominant mathematics may be in the formulations and derivations of empirical facts, factual knowledge cannot attain either the absolute precision or necessity of pure mathematics. The knowledge claimed in the natural and the social sciences is a matter of successive approximations and of increasing degrees of confirmation. Warranted assertibility or probability is all that we can conceivably secure in the sciences that deal with the facts of experience. It is empirical science, thus conceived as an unending quest (its truth-claims to be held only "until further notice"), which is under consideration here. Science in this sense differs only in degree from the knowledge accumulated throughout the ages by sound and common sense.

The aims of science are description, explanation, and prediction. The first aim is basic and indispensable, the second and third (closely related to each other) arise as the most desirable fruits of scientific labors whenever inquiry rises beyond the mere fact-gathering stage. History, often and nowadays quite fashionably declared an art, is scientific to the extent that it ascertains its facts concerning past events by a meticulous scrutiny of present evidence. Casual interpretation of these facts (in history, but similarly also in psychology, sociology, cultural anthropology, and economics) is usually much more difficult than, but in principle not logically different from, causal interpretation (that is, explanation) in the natural sciences. The aims of the pure (empirical) sciences are then essentially the same throughout the whole field. What the scientists are seeking are descriptions, explanations, and predictions which are as adequate and accurate as possible in the given context of research.

The quest for scientific knowledge is therefore regulated by certain standards or criteria which may best be formulated in the form of ideals to be approximated, but perhaps never fully attained. The most important of these regulative ideals are:

1. *Intersubjective Testability.* This is only a more adequate formulation of what is generally meant of by the "objectivity" of science. What is here involved is not only the freedom from personal or cultural bias or partiality, but—even more fundamentally—the requirement that the knowledge claims of science be in principle capable of test (confirmation or disconfirmation, at the least indirectly and to some degree) on the part of any person properly equipped with intelligence and the technical devices of observation or experimentation. The term *intersubjective* stresses the social nature of the scientific enterprise. If there be any "truths" that are accessible only to privileged individuals, such as mystics or visionaries—that is, knowledge-claims which by their very nature cannot independently be checked by anyone else—then such "truths" are not of the kind that we seek in the sciences. The criterion of intersubjective testability thus delimits the scientific from the nonscientific activities of man.

Religious ecstasy, the elations of love, the inspiration of the artist, yes, even the flash of insight on the part of a scientific genius are not in themselves scientific activities. All these processes may eventually become subject matter for scientific study. But in themselves they do not validate knowledge-claims. They may, as in the case of the scientific intuition (or empathy in the psychological-cultural field) be instrumental in the generation of knowledge claims. But it is these knowledge-claims which have to be, first, formulated in an intersubjectively intelligible (or communicable) manner, and, second, subjected to the appropriate kind of tests in order to ascertain their validity. Beliefs transcending all possible tests by observation, self-observation, experiment, measurement, or statistical analysis are recognized as theological or metaphysical and therefore devoid of the type of meaning that we all associate with the knowledge-claims of common sense or factual science. From the point of view of the scientific outlook in philosophy it may be suggested that the sort of significance with which the in-principle-unconfirmable assertions of transcendent theology and metaphysics impress so many people is largely emotive. The pictorial, emotional, and motivational appeals of language, no matter how indispensable or valuable in the contexts of practical life, art, education, persuasion, and propaganda, must, however, not be confused with the cognitive meanings (purely formal-and/or factual-empirical) that are of the essence of science. Each type of significance has its function, and in most uses of language both are conbined or even fused. The only point stressed here is that they must not be *con*fused, that is, mistaken for one another, if we wish to be clear as to what we are about.

2. *Reliability, or a Sufficient Degree of Confirmation.* This second criterion of scientific knowledge enables us to distinguish what is generally called "mere opinion" (or worse still, "superstition") from knowledge (well-substantiated belief). It may be considered as the delimitation of the scientific from the unscientific knowledge-claims. Clearly, in contrast to the first criterion, we face here a distinction of degree. There is no sharp line of demarcation between the well-confirmed laws, theories, or hypotheses of science, and the only poorly substantiated hunches and ideas-on-trial which may ultimately either be included in the corpus of scientific knowledge or else rejected as unconfirmed. Truth-claims which we repudiate as "superstition," and, quite generally, as judgments based upon hasty generalization or weak analogy (if they fulfill the criterion of testability), differ from what we accept as "scientific truth" in the extremely low degree of probability to which they are supported by the available evidence. Astrology or alchemy, for example, are not factually meaningless, but they are considered false to fact in that all available evidence speaks overwhelmingly against them. Modern techniques of experimentation and of statistical analysis are the most powerful tools we have in the discernment between chance and law and hence the best means of enhancing the reliability of knowledge.

3. *Definiteness and Precision.* This obvious standard of scientific method requires that the concepts used in the formulation of scientific knowledge-claims be as definitely delimited as possible. On the level of the qualitative-classificatory sciences this amounts to the attempt to reduce all border-zone vagueness to a minimum. On the level of quantitative science the exactitude of the concepts is enormously enhanced through the application of the techniques of measurement. The mensurational devices usually also increase the degree of objectivity. This is especially clear when they are contrasted with purely impressionistic ways of estimating magnitudes. Of course, there is no point in sharpening precision to a higher degree than the problem in hand requires. (You need no razor to cut butter.)

4. *Coherence or Systematic Structure.* This is what T. H. Huxley had in mind when he defined science as "organized common-sense." Not a mere collection of miscellaneous items of information, but a well-connected account of the facts is what we seek in science. On the descriptive level this results, for example, in systems of classification or division, in diagrams, statistical charts, and the like. On the explanatory levels of science sets of laws, or

theoretical assumptions, are utilized. Explanation in science consists in the hypothetico-deductive procedure. The laws, theories, or hypotheses form the premises from which we derive logically, or logico-mathematically, the observed or observable facts. These facts, often belonging to heterogeneous domains, thus become integrated into a coherent, unifying structure. (Theological and metaphysical systems have, frequently enough, ambitiously tried to imitate this feature of science; but even if they succeeded in proceeding *more geometrico,* the important difference from science remains: they either lack testability or else reliability in the senses specified in our previous points.)

5. *Comprehensiveness or Scope of Knowledge.* This final point in our enumeration of criteria of science also characterizes scientific knowledge as different in degree (often enormously) from common-sense knowledge. Not only through bold and sweeping hypotheses, but especially through the ingenious devices by means of which they are tested, science acquires a reach far beyond the limits of our unaided senses. With telescopes, microscopes, spectroscopes, Geiger Counters, lie detectors, and the thousands of other contrivances of modern science we manage to amplify our senses and thus open up avenues of at least indirect access to the worlds of the very distant, the very large, the extremely small, or the disguised and concealed. The resulting increase in the completeness of our knowledge is, of course, popularly the most impressive feature of science. It must be kept in mind, however, that the scope thus achieved is a product of hard labor, and not to be confused with the sham completeness metaphysicians procure for their world pictures by verbal magic. Instead of presenting a finished account of the world, the genuine scientist keeps his unifying hypotheses open to revision and is always ready to modify or abandon them if evidence should render them doubtful. This self-corrective aspect of science has rightly been stressed as its most important characteristic and must always be kept in mind when we refer to the comprehensiveness or the unification achieved by the scientific account of the universe. It is a sign of one's maturity to be able to live with an unfinished world view.

The foregoing outline of the criteria of science has been set down in a somewhat dogmatic tone. But this was done only for the sake of brevity.[1] The spirit behind it is that of a humble account of what, I think, an impartial and elaborate study of the history of thought from magic to science would reveal. In any case, these criteria seem unquestionably the guiding ideals of present-day empirical science. They may therefore be used in a definition of science as we understand this term today. It seems rather useless to speculate about just what this term, by a change of meaning, might come to connote in the future.

It should be remembered that the criteria listed characterize the *pure* factual (empirical) sciences. The aims of the *applied* sciences—the technologies, medicine, social and economic planning, and others—are practical control, production, guidance, therapy, reform, and so forth. Responsible activity in the application of science clearly presupposes information which is fairly well substantiated by the methods of the pure sciences. (These remarks intend to draw merely a logically important distinction. The obvious practical inter-penetration and important mutual fertilization of the pure and the applied disciplines is of course not denied here.)

Critique of Misconceptions

Having indicated at least in broad outline the nature of scientific method we may now turn to the critique of some of the misconceptions to which it is all too commonly exposed. In what follows, a dozen typical charges against science are stated and answered consecutively.[2]

Science arises exclusively out of practical and social needs and has its only value in serving them in turn. (Dialectical Materialism and Vocationalism).

While this is important it does not tell the whole story. Science has always also been the pursuit of knowledge, the satisfaction of a deep-rooted curiosity. It should be recognized as one of the cultural values along with art, literature, and music. Better teaching of the sciences and their history can redress the imbalance. Fuller utilization of results and suggestions from the history and the philosophy of science would give the student a deeper appreciation of the evolution of scientific knowledge and of the scientific point of view. Through proper instruction, the student could be led to rediscover some of the important results of science. The intellectual gratification that comes with a grasp of the order of nature, with the understanding of its processes by means of laws and theories, is one of the most powerful incentives in the pursuit of pure knowledge.

Science cannot furnish a secure basis for human affairs since it is unstable. It changes its views continually. (Traditionalism)

While there is constant evolution, and occasionally a revolution, in the scientific outlook, the charge is a superficial (usually journalistic) exaggeration. The typical progress of science reveals that later views often contain much of the earlier views (to the extent that these have stood the test of repeated examination). The more radical or revolutionary changes usually amount to a revision of the conceptual frame of a scientific discipline. The criticism often also presupposes other sources of certainty which will simply not bear critical scrutiny. The quest for absolute certainty is an immature, if not infantile, trait of thinking. The best knowledge we have can be established only by the method of trial and error. It is of the essence of science to make such knowledge as reliable as is humanly and technically possible.

Science rests on uncritical or uncriticized presuppositions. It validates its outlook by its own standards. It therefore begs the question as regards alternative approaches for settling problems of knowledge and action.

Science has been clarifying and revising its basic assumptions throughout its development. Particularly since the beginning of the modern age and still more intensively since the beginning of our century, an increasing awareness of, and critical attitude toward, the fundamental presuppositions has been most fruitfully applied in the repudiation of dogmatic prejudices and in the articulation of the conceptual frame of scientific method. It can be shown (through logical analysis) that the procedure of science is the only one we are *certain* will yield the results (reliable knowledge, that is, valid explanation and predictions) *if* such results can at all be achieved. Any alleged rival method—theology, metaphysics, mysticism, intuition, dialectics—if it made any contributions at all could not be examined and appraised on any basis other than the usual inductive criteria of science. Generally, it seems that these alleged alternatives do not even aim primarily at knowledge but, like the arts, at the enrichment of experience. They may therefore more properly be said to be *non*-scientific, rather than *un*scientific.

Science distorts the facts of reality. In its Procrustean manner it introduces discontinuities where there is continuity (and vice versa). The abstractions and idealizations used in science can never do justice to the richness and complexities of experience.

Since the task of science is to discover reliable and precise knowledge of what happens under what conditions, it always tries to approximate the facts as closely as the problem on hand requires and permits. Both continuity and discontinuity can be formulated mathematically and be given an adequate formulation only with the help of modern mathematics.

Science can deal only with the measurable and therefore tends to "explain away" that which it cannot measure.

While measurement is eminently desirable in order to enhance the precision and objectivity of knowledge, it is not indispensable in many branches of science or, at least, on their more qualitative levels of analysis. Science does not explain away the qualities of experience. It aims at, and often succeeds in, making these qualities more predictable.

Science never explains, it merely describes the phenomena of experience. The reality beyond the appearances is also beyond the reach of science.

This is partly a terminological issue and partly a result of the (traditional but most misleading and useless) metaphysical distinction between appearance and reality. In the sense in which the word *explaining* is used in common life, science *does* explain facts—it deduces them from laws or theoretical assumptions. Questions which are in principle incapable of being answered by the scientific method turn out, on closer analysis, not to be questions of knowledge. They are expressions of emotional tensions or of the wish for soothing (or exciting) experience.

Science and the scientific attitude are incompatible with religion and the religious attitude.

If by religion one refers to an explanation of the universe and a derivation of moral norms from theological premises, then indeed there is logical incompatibility with the results, methods, and general outlook of science. But if religion means an attitude of sincere devotion to human values, such as justice, peace, relief from suffering, there is not only no conflict between religion and science but rather a need for mutual supplementation.

Science is responsible for the evils and maladjustments of our civilization. It is creating ever more powerful weapons of destruction. The employment of scientific techniques in the machine age has contributed to the misery, physical and mental, of the multitudes. Moreover, the biological facts of evolution imply the negation of all morality: the law the jungle.

These are particularly superficial charges. It is the social-political-economic structure of a society that is responsible for these various evils. Scientific knowledge itself is socially and morally neutral. But the manner in which it is applied, whether for the benefit or to the detriment of humanity, depends entirely on ourselves. Scientists are becoming increasingly aware that they, even more than the average citizen, have to work for enlightenment toward the proper use of knowledge. The facts and theories of evolution have been construed in many ways as regards their implications for ethics. Julian Huxley reads them very differently from the way his grandfather Thomas Henry did.[3] It should be easy to see that the forces active on the level of human civilization and intelligent communal life are not completely reducible to those involved in the ruthless struggle for survival.

The ethical neutrality of scientific truth and the ivory tower situation of the pure researcher is apt to generate an attitude of indifference toward the pressing problems of humanity.

Only maladjusted individuals are unable to combine the detachment necessary for the pursuit of truth with an ardent interest in the improvement of the condition of humanity.

Scientific method, while eminently successful in the explanation, prediction, and control of physical phenomena, is distinctly less successful in regard to the facts of organic life and almost altogether hopeless in the mental and social realm. The methods of the physical sciences are essentially mechanistic (if not materialistic) and therefore reductionistic; they cannot do justice to the complex organismic, teleological, and emergent features of life and mind.

"Scientism" as a slogan of criticism and reproach is very fashionable these days. It is true that some scientists and especially some of the popularizers of science have indulged in reductive fallacies of various sorts. But the true scientific spirit as exemplified in some of the foremost researchers is free from that impatience and simple-mindedness that tries to finish the unfinished business of science by hasty speculation. Admittedly, there are tremendous problems yet to be solved. On the other hand what method is there but the method of science to solve them? Explanations of the mechanistic type (in *one* sense of the term) have been abandoned even in physics. But mechanistic explanation in the wider sense of a search for law (deterministic or statistical) is still the indispensable procedure of all sciences that have gone beyond the purely classificatory level. Organic wholeness, teleology, and emergence can be understood, if at all, only by causal analysis on the unusual empirical basis. Purposiveness and freedom of choice, far from being incompatible with causality, presuppose causal order.

The methods of science can never replace the intuitive insight or empathic understanding of the practical psychologist, psychiatrist, cultural anthropologist, or historian. This claim is made particularly wherever the object of knowledge is the individual, the unique and unrepeatable.

It is only through the scientific method that the validity and reliability of the intuitive approach can be gauged. There is, on this ground, some doubt as to its more exaggerated claims. However, there is nothing in the principles of scientific method that would deny the occasional, or even frequent, efficacy of intuitive judgments based, as they must be, on a rich (but often not articulated) background of experience in the given field. Aside from the mere artistic contemplation of the unique and individual, knowledge, in the proper sense of the word, always means the subsumption of the specific case under general concepts or laws. This holds in the social sciences just as much as in the natural sciences.

Science cannot determine values. Since scientific knowledge can (at best) find out only what is the case, it can, by its very nature, never tell what ought to be.

This final challenge often comes from theology or metaphysics. It usually maintains that questions of aims, goals, and ideals cannot be settled by the methods of science but rather require recourse either to divine revelation, the voice of conscience, or some metaphysical a priori truths. The answer to this in a scientific age would seem to be that a mature mankind should be able to determine its own value standards on the basis of its needs, wants, and the facts of the social condition of man. But it is true that science cannot dictate value standards. It can, as in social psychology, ascertain the actual evaluations of groups and individuals, study their compatibilities and incompatibilities, and recommend (that is *applied* science!) ways and means of harmonizing conflicting evaluations. True enough, in many of the urgent issues that confront us, we do not possess enough scientific knowledge to warrant a course of action. This means that we have to act, as so often in life, on the highest probabilities available even if these probabilities be low in themselves. But such estimates of probabilities will still be made most reliable by the scientific method. Common life experience and wisdom, when freed from its adherence to prescientific thought patterns, is not fundamentally different from scientific knowledge. In both we find the procedure of self-correction, so essentially needed if knowledge is to be a guide for action. There is an important common element in mature thinking (as we find it in science) and mature social action (as we find it in democracy): progress arises out of the peaceful competition of ideas as they are put to intersubjective test. Cooperative planning on the basis of the best and fullest knowledge available is the only path left to an awakened humanity that has embarked on the adventure of science and civilization.

The scientific view of the world that we have characterized and defended against criticisms from various quarters may with historical and terminological justice be called Naturalism.[4] It differs from mechanistic materialism (too often a mere straw man put up by theologians or idealistic metaphysicians) in that it steers clear of reductive fallacies. If uninformed persons insist on viewing science as essentially materialistic and the humanities as essentially idealistic (not to say spiritualistic) the hopes of fruitful collaboration of both fields in education are slim indeed. But science, properly interpreted, is not dependent on any sort of metaphysics. It merely attempts to cover a maximum of facts by a minimum of laws. On the other side, a mature humanism requires no longer a theological or metaphysical frame either. Human nature and human history become progressively understood in the light of advancing science. It is therefore no longer justifiable to speak of science *versus* the humanities. Naturalism *and* humanism should be our maxim in philosophy and in education. A Scientific Humanism emerges as a philosophy holding considerable promise for mankind—*if* mankind will at all succeed in growing up.

NOTES

1. A thorough discussion of the logical, epistemological, methodological, and historical issues connected with the criteria would require a whole book, not just another essay.

2. These charges are not straw men. In more than twenty years of reading, listening, teaching, and argument I have encountered them again and again in Europe and just as frequently in this country. If space permitted and time were less valuable, I could quote many well-known writers in connection with each charge.

3. Compare Julian Huxley, *Touchstone for Ethics* (Harper, 1947); but see also C. D. Broad, "Review of Julian S. Huxley's Evolutionary Ethics," *Mind* 53 (1944), reprinted in H. Feigl and W. Wellars, *Readings in Philosophical Analysis* (Appleton-Century-Crofts, 1949).

4. It should scarely need mentioning that this meaning of naturalism has only a distant and tenuous relation to the other meaning in which it is applied to a certain type of literature.

STUDY QUESTIONS FOR PART 6

1. How does Baier deal with the question of whether science can provide us with the kinds of explanations and justification of life that religion does?

2. Does Baier accept Weber's analysis of values or culture?

3. How might Baier defend himself against Feyerabend's charge (in Part 1) that science *is* a religion?

4. How does Baier's view about values compare with Hempel's?

5. What kinds of arguments would support the view that science and technology are inherently immoral, dehumanizing, and politically dangerous?

6. What is Habermas's basic criticism of Weber?

7. Does Habermas's own account of science, values, and culture contain any difficulties?

8. Does Habermas satisfactorily deal with the issues about science and values?

9. Is it naive to think that critical scientists and citizens might control the abuses of science and technology?

10. Is Habermas's attempt to democratize technological society plausible?

11. Why do so many critics of science and technology use the phrase "playing God" in their criticisms? Is this just a metaphor?

12. What are the educational applications of the views of Feigl and Habermas?

13. How does Feigl respond to the claims about science made by Heidegger, Nietzsche, and others (as discussed in Hollinger's essay)?

14. What does Feigl have to say about the conflict between science and religion? Does he disagree with Baier on this issue?

15. How does "Scientific Humanism" allow us to overcome the conflicts between science and values in our culture?

16. Do you think Feigl would have any objections to Habermas, or vice versa?

SELECTED BIBLIOGRAPHY

[1] Adorno, T. ed. *The Positivist Dispute in German Sociology.* New York: Harper, 1969. [Advanced readings on Positivism vs. Critical Theory.]

[2] Albert, H. *Treatise on Critical Reason.* Princeton: Princeton University Press, 1985. [Defends Popper against Weber and Habermas.]

[3] Alford, C. F. *Science and the Revenge of Nature.* Tampa: University Presses of Florida, 1985. [Discusses the Habermas-Marcuse debate about science, technology, and culture.]

[4] Barbour, I. *Issues in Science and Religion.* New York: Harper, 1971. [Complex relations between science, religion and methodology.]

[5] Barnes, B. *Interests and the Growth of Knowledge.* Boston: Routledge, 1977. [Sociology of science.]

[6] Bernstein, R. *Beyond Objectivism and Relativism.* Philadelphia: University

438

of Pennsylvania Press, 1984. [Lucid survey of recent work that moves beyond Positivism and Romanticism.]

[7] ———. *The Reconstruction of Social and Political Theory*. Philadelphia: University of Pennsylvania Press, 1978. [Good survey of recent developments in social sciences.]

[8] Brown, J. R. ed. *Scientific Rationality: The Sociological Turn*. Boston: Reidel, 1984. [Advanced essays on Barnes and sociology of science.]

[9] Brubaker, R. *The Limits of Rationality*. Boston: Allen and Unwin, 1984. [Weber's views about science, values and politics.]

[10] Feyerabend, P. *Science in A Free Society*. New York: Schocken (New Left Books), 1978. [Defends a democratic conception of society against the idea that scientists are experts.]

[11] Geraets, T. ed. *Rationality Today*. Ottawa: University of Ottawa Press, 1979. [Essays and discussions on science, culture and theories of rationality.]

[12] Geuss, R. *The Idea of A Critical Theory*. New York: Cambridge University Press, 1981. [The best discussion of Critical Theory.]

[13] Giddens, A. *Capitalism and Social Theory*. New York: Cambridge Press, 1971. [Science, values and culture in Marx, Weber and Durkheim.]

[14] Heidegger, M. *The Question Concerning Technology and other Essays*. New York: Harper, 1978. [Difficult but important analysis of science and culture.]

[15] Held, D. *Introduction to Critical Theory*. Berkeley: University of California Press, 1980. [A detailed history and analysis of Critical Theory.]

[16] Leiss, W. *The Domination of Nature*. Boston: Beacon, 1972. [Critical Theory's analysis of science as domination of nature and human life.]

[17] Matson, F. *The Broken Image*. New York: Doubleday, 1965. [Historical impact of conceptions of nature and science on psychology and the social sciences.]

[18] Mitcham, C., and Mackey, R. eds. *Philosophy and Technology*. New York: Free Press, 1972. [Useful essays on pure and applied science, religion, technology, and culture.]

[19] Putnam, H. *Reason, Truth and History*. New York: Cambridge University Press, 1981. [An important discussion of science, rationality, and culture.]

[20] Rorty, R. *Consequences of Pragmatism*. Minneapolis: University of Minnesota Press, 1981. [Important essays in which Rorty spells out his views on science, morality, and culture in more detail.]

[21] ———. *Philosophy and the Mirror of Nature*. Princeton: Princeton University Press, 1979. [Must reading.]

[22] Weber, M. *From Max Weber*. (ed. Gerth, H., and Mills, C. .) New York: Oxford University Press, 1946. [Contains some of Weber's most important writings.]

[23] ———. *The Methodology of the Social Sciences*. New York: Free Press, 1949. [Weber's main discussions of science, values, and culture. Advanced.]

[24] Whitehead, A. N. *Science and The Modern World*. New York: Macmillan,

94438

1925. [A classic discussion of the rise of modern science and its impact on religion.]

[25] Ziman, J. *The Force of Knowledge*. New York: Cambridge University Press, 1978. [Argues against blanket generalizations about science, technology, and culture.]